ALLENFAR

An Ever-Life Story

Headset-1: The CPT Incident
Headset-2: TIME TRUST
Headset-3: Stardust

A novel by

ANDREW SARKADY

Book design by Andrew Sarkady
Cover design by Andrew Sarkady
www.sarjartworks.com

Cataloging-in-Publication Data is on file with the Library of Congress

ISBN 978-0-578-64080-8

Published by Andrew Sarkady

ACKNOWLEDGMENTS

It is with the utmost sincerity and affection that I thank my close loved ones and family members for supporting me. Thanks to my brother, Mike, for the fun banter over the years. Those sessions helped me to refine my thoughts. Thanks to my sister, Cook, for her constant positive attitude and encouragement.

To all my children and grandchildren, thank you for giving my life meaning and hope, and, in the end, for a reason to write.

And Hi, Mom and Dad. Thank You for my life! I know you are watching.

Finally, thank you, Karen, for your counsel, suggestions, and loving patience throughout rewrites and editing.

WHAT READERS SAY

"This story is Epic...a rocket ride. For those who like *soft sci-fi*, fantasy, conspiracy, or even the great mystery of life, this certainly delivers! This is a story that reinforces love, commitment, technology, and theology. It's a suspense-filled adventure for all ages. You will think and fantasize. It is a richly painted masterpiece. As an artist so creates his paintings with color and form, Sarkady has created a rich story with words as form. Ever-Life is alive, and it draws you in." Michael Dennis, Chicago Book Review

"Sarkady invites the reader on a curious journey through his futuristic world, in which he crafts a captivating story of technology, discovery, and power. Be prepared to be engaged...." Jennifer Dessert, Editors Book Review

"This is a wonderful story and a global thriller, like no other I've read. It's a Pandora's Box filled with hope and questions..." Andrea Rittenhouse, New Jersey Review

"ALLENFAR is the best book I've read in years! To me, it was a cozy Sunday reading. And I loved the its puzzles and sub plots. I could picture everything like it was a movie, adventure, science fiction, time travel...lots of fun and very thought-provoking! I liked the way the love story weaves in, too. It has something for everyone." Karen Maitzen, Tampa Florida Reviewer

"I was very intrigued by the characters and held captive by the storyline..." Lynn Ward, Arizona Book Review

PREFACE

Many authors write books to tell a story they imagine. That's fiction today. But, what if someone writes a true story that hasn't happened yet?

My adventure began when I was transported into the future, to the Ever-Life subterranean colonies, from three different ages on my born timeline. I know no other way to explain what happened, except to say it was immediate and painless but very frightening. Upon my arrival there, I was kept confined, and scientists insisted it was impossible to transport to the future; so, what I did went against everything they understood about physics. However, they did explain that time travel was possible to visit the past. Eventually, as I came  to understand the way time travel works, all the events I recount here did happen in their past. So, I rationalized that it's all a matter of perspective.

At Ever-Life, they have what are called *headsets* and *vaults*. Both are quite remarkable devices and are used together. There are four models of headsets, that I know of, all made of an organic metal, about which I am still educating myself. To use a headset, the wearer must insert a vault into a slit behind the set's earpiece. Most vaults look like old video discs, except each is only around ¼ diameter, in size, of a person's fingernail. Vaults function like old cell-phone memory-cards, yet vaults have unlimited storage. Ever-Life's vast number of vaults contain records of knowledge gathered over millennia, stored as data, up to the minute. How that happens is one of the mysteries, I have yet to understand. Interestingly, once information is stored in a vault, it cannot be erased or altered in any way. Information can only be added. After the wearer inserts a vault, the headset links the information to the wearer's brain chemistry; and, when the headset is activated, the wearer's brain uploads all the information into his or her permanent memory.

This manuscript includes three vault records from the Ever-Life library:

Headset #1: Vault 0001, The CPT Incident.

Headset #2: Vault 0002, TIME TRUST.

Headset #3: Vault 0378, Stardust.

An Ever-Life specialist gave me the first two headset sessions during the first days I arrived there. Although I received many headsets in total, the third one contained herein, I received almost a year later. These three headsets are connected and not meant as stand-alone reads. Together they tell the story of several characters and me, each of whom became involved in one another's lives, because of a remarkable discovery and the threat posed to it, by the actions of a power-hungry billionaire, Marion Brock. Out of those interactions, I met Allenfar.

In June of the year 2999, Dr. Jack Sheldon, Head of Research, at the Brock/Swanson Medical Complex, was taken to the emergency room of Andrews hospital. Sometime before that, Jack had discovered something that would change the world, an incredible medical secret, CPT, Chemical Personality Transfer, which he had prepared to introduce to the public the week of his car accident. However, at the same time, worldwide entrepreneur and billionaire partner of the Complex, Marion Brock, plotted and stopped at nothing, even murder, to steal Jack's secret. However, unknown to Brock or anyone on Earth's surface, miles below the medical complex, there was the futuristic health-base, Ever-Life. And its leaders wanted Jack's secret too.

Ever-Life specialists told me they thought that as a result of the conflict between Ever-Life and the Brock Empire, a catastrophic time-event occurred, and that's what triggered my transporting to the future. However, I was to learn differently with the help of my friend, Allenfar.

CHAPTER 1: RISEN

THE BRIGHT LIGHT OF THE ROOM shocked me. I was shaking and rubbing my eyes, trying to focus. Everything about the room seemed sterile because I noticed the faint fragrance of an antiseptic treatment. We were two men sitting across from each other on small chairs at what appeared to be a square metal card-table. The man in front of me was wearing a white glowing doctor's coat and a transparent medical mask.

"My name is Thomas Wheeler," he said. "No one is going to hurt you. Do you feel alright?"

I was disoriented, and my clothes were soaked from my body sweat. I had no idea where I was. "Can you give me something for the shaking?"

Wheeler gestured to the man, at the door, who handed him what they called a syringe, but it didn't have a needle, and it looked like a baby's balloon ear-cleaner. He took my hand, turned it palm up, placed the device against my wrist, and then he squeezed the balloon part. I felt nothing, but within 30-seconds, I stopped shaking.

Wheeler said, "You should be fine now."

After a minute or so, I was able to calm down and compose myself. Wheeler reached for a small gold box on the far corner of the table. He stuck the tip of his index finger into the box and scooped out a sort of putty-like pink substance. "This will help you," he said. "You don't have to worry, but I am going to put this in your right ear. You will feel no pain, just a slit tickle."

I pulled back at first, staring at his finger. Then, I relaxed enough for him to stick the glob in the entrance of my ear canal. After a few seconds, the soft putty grew and extended itself out over my right ear and around the back of my head. It hardened almost immediately and looked like shiny metal, quite similar to the swat-team devices I used to see police wear. Meanwhile, Wheeler had taken a tiny disc, out of the box, which looked like a small button, about one quarter size of my fingernail, and inserted it into the device, just behind my earlobe.

"Don't be alarmed," Wheeler said. "We are going to start by giving you information that may help both you and us determine why this has all happened. We think 'this particular place' is the best starting point."

"I don't understand. I have no idea what you're doing."

Wheeler pushed me gently back on the chair, and it changed into a lounge as he did so. My legs lifted, and my head felt a soft pillow as I reclined.

"Just relax," Wheeler said with a smile. "Close your eyes, and let it happen."

As I felt security straps enfold my upper body and legs, the headset began to play. Suddenly, I saw images in my mind and heard words as if I were watching a motion picture...

THE EXPLOSION ROCKED HOMES WITHIN a half mile radius. A roadster had slowed down as it approached the four-way stop between Landon Way and State highway 41. But, the car had no time to swerve away from a jack-knifing semi-trailer-truck speeding toward it at 80 mph. On impact, the roadster exploded, killing the one lone driver. A black cloud from the gasoline fire rose at least 2000 ft and continued to burn for some ten minutes. Then, the dust cleared, and by the time paramedics arrived, the sky filled with stars again.

"Hey! Ben! Over here," yelled Frank.

"What is it?" Ben walked quickly to Frank.

"It looks like a burned right arm."

They each covered their mouth and nose at the stench of burning flesh. Frank looked around as his eyes filled with tears from the odor. "Where's the rest of him?"

Carl shouted from the car itself, about 30 yards away, "Hey guys! Over here."

As the two joined Carl, they saw a male body burning without a right arm. Carl used an extinguisher to put out the fire, and they all stared at the protruding body, head-first, extending out of the driver's front window. The remains were utterly unrecognizable, and part of him looked as if it had been through a meat grinder.

"Christ, he must have died instantly," Ben said. "What a mess."

"It's a Porsche Grand," said Carl, "but no plates. He never had a chance. Look, the sticker on the window, DRS, Brock/Swanson. Holy crap! I bet he's from the medical complex."

"What about the semi?" asked Frank. "What does that driver look like?"

"I checked everywhere," Carl replied, "no driver, no registration or paperwork, no sign of anyone. And nothing is inside the truck's long trailer. I'm sure this thing should not have even been on a country road like this. Look at the wheel marks over there, no breaking skidmarks. To me that indicates the truck didn't try to stop. It jack-knifed right into the car."

"WTF!" Ben said.

Frank looked at Carl and said with urgency, "We have to get the body to Andrews Hospital."

Then, all three heard a familiar voice behind them. "Just hold on boys. I want a look; and the team here has to go through the sight before you remove anything."

It was Detective Inspector Jake Burns, Arden City Police. Jake had been known for his unorthodox style, but he always got his man. "You say there was no driver in the truck?"

Carl scratched his head and replied, "Nope, no one."

Jake walked to the semi and climbed into what was left of the driver's cab. He checked the glove compartment, nothing in it. Then, he studied the inside; and, finally, he focused on the starter. "Holy crap! It's remote. And an automatic guiding system. Someone controlled this baby from somewhere else."

Jake stepped down out of the truck and faced the three men. "So the truck came from that way?"

"Yes, we think so," answered Frank. "It had to be going over 80. Your men can confirm by checking the truck's computer records. Look, Jake, as far as we know, this guy's clothes, wallet, and everything else were burned. Not to mention, look at him. We only have that sticker to go by."

Jake leaned down and read it. "It says DRS, Brock/Swanson."

"The only way we can identify him is by his med-chip," said Frank. "The coroner is the only one who can check that. Until we get him to Andrews at the medical complex, we know nothing."

"Well," Jake said, "there's more to this than meets the eye. I'm sure this is a homicide. Why would the truck be anywhere around here in the first place? The semi-cab is empty. At 80 mph, this was a bullet aimed to hit something."

Carl looked inquisitive and asked, "Maybe it's one of those new-fangled automatic drives? You know, controlled from a different location."

"My thinking exactly," Jake replied. "But why Canadian plates? And look at the writing on the cab. 'Cumberland, Alaska.' This baby's a long way from home. Why not use a local truck? And the speed limit is 35 here. The truck didn't even slow down. Look, no tire marks. It smashed into that little buggy at full speed. This is a 4-way stop. You three call Andrews and transport the body. Go ahead and find out who he is. And the other question is, why in the world doesn't this little roadster have plates?"

At 10:35 pm, the paramedics took off to Andrews Hospital. Frank radioed into the ER-1 dispatcher. "This is bus 119 en route to you from the crash site at Landon and State Route 41. We have a deceased male, dismembered, burned and unrecognizable. He has a chip, and the sticker on his car says DRS, Brock/Swanson."

"Hold on," said the dispatcher, who covered his microphone and then turned to the nurse on call. "Get Bellos, Stat!"

Within 30 seconds, the dispatcher transferred the call to the private line of the Chief of Hospital, Mathew J. Bellos. "Bellos here, say again?"

"Sir, we are en route. One male body, severed left arm and foot, broken bones, deceased, repeat, a dead male body burned 100%, 3rd degree and worse. He has a chip. Police want ID, stat!"

Bellos replied, "Deliver to rear Surgical Entrance C. Have all body parts put on an extra wide gurney and brought to me in lab-C. Understand?"

Frank replied, "Yes, sir, estimated arrival time, 10:50 pm."

When the ambulance backed up to the Emergency Entrance, Carl and Ben situated the body parts on a gurney as instructed and covered them up with a sheet. Ben pushed the stretcher out of the vehicle, down the hallway and through the double door entrance to lab-C. Two male nurses greeted and thanked the paramedics, and then they took charge of the gurney. It was less than a minute before Dr. Mathew Bellos came through the double-doors at the other end of the room, dressed in complete surgical garb. He looked at the body and said to the nurses, "You may leave now, thank you. I'll take it from here."

As the two nurses walked out of the lab entrance, three other female nurses walked into the lab to assist Bellos. He removed the cover sheet off the gurney. Even his years as chief of hospital didn't prepare him for what he saw. The head was bashed; one eye was melted down his cheek; the left arm was severed from the sholder and lay across the bottom of his legs, one of which was also severed just below the upper thigh. The body of Jack Sheldon looked like it'd literally been through a meat grinder.

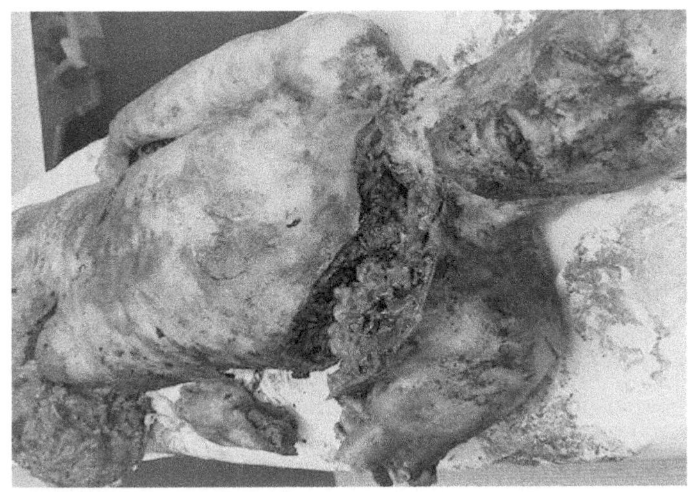

Dr. Bellos carefully cut a small incision behind Jack's right ear and removed the ID-chip. He slid it into a tracker-box by the bed and turned to the closest nurse. "Have Ron Sandry call Jack Sheldon's wife, Rachel, and have her come to ER-1." Then, he said, "Let's do this. Ready?"

They nodded yes, and thus began an intense unscheduled surgical procedure. Thank God for the medical advances of the day. It was only with robotic interface and new nano-probes technology that they were able to complete the procedure within a 2-hour period. Afterword, the nurses covered the corpse and delivered it to Focus-Ward, floor three, room 309.

Focus-Ward nurse, Angela Esposito, sat in her office, almost mesmerized, leaning on her elbow, staring at two things: the holographic medical display monitor for room 309, and the small blue vial sitting on her desk that Dr. Bellos gave her. She could not stop thinking about the events of the night, while, next to her, three green lines beeped across the flat screen monitor from left to right indicating no vital signs-no heartbeat, no brainwaves, not even hair or nail growth indicators, which record after death.

The tag on the body in 309 read: Dr. Jack Sheldon, Chief of Research, Brock/Swanson Medical Complex; but he was unrecognizable when Angie hooked up the IVs, the EKG and the EEG sensors almost an hour ago. At 2 am, Angie typed her security code into the computer and put on a sterile gown. Then, she put the blue vial into her pocket and recorded the holo-monitor's final readings on Jack Sheldon's patient chart. She turned, picked up a food tray and walked briskly to room 309. As Angie opened the room door, she jerked back in horror. Her eyes popped wide open, and she gasped, dropped the tray and grabbed her mouth. Dr. Jack Sheldon was sitting upright, pulling off the adhesive tabs, intravenous hookups and bandages, as if they were annoying insects. Angie barely regained her composure as Jack sniffed the air, oblivious to the hospital surroundings. He shook his head and looked down at himself. "Jesus! What is this? And what's that rotten smell!"

As he blinked and squinted, his eyes focused, and he did a side-to-side scan around the room. Then, he looked directly at the nurse and blurted out, "Who are you? Where the hell am I?"

In that instant, Angie reacted with raw emotion, not as a trained nurse. Terrified, she turned, threw open the door and ran out of the room shaking and repeating, "Holy shit! You're supposed to be dead! You're supposed to be dead!"

Angie Esposito was the security nurse, in charge of a particular experimental area called Focus Ward, on the third floor of Andrews Hospital. The hospital was one of 15 buildings housed on the highly secure 1600-acre campus of the Brock/Swanson Medical Complex. The Complex, located in Arden City, was some 75 miles south of Albuquerque, New Mexico, in a desert landscape west of White Sands.

Andrews itself was unique. Unlike any other building, it towered some twenty floors above ground in the southwest corner of the campus, and it had an elaborate underground construction, which extended ten floors below ground level.

Like all staff, Angie Esposito went through a comprehensive training and security clearance. She was a petite 5-ft 2-inch black haired beauty, a sharp quick thinker, loyal, dedicated, and over-experienced for her age. She completed her undergraduate studies at the Chicago, Il. Medical Center, graduating with highest honors. She had a good friend and mentor in Dr. Mathew Bellos. He took her under his wing 16 years ago, after her mother died. Bellos supported her financially and coached her through her residency, medical master's degree, as well as funded her through several private international tours. He brought her to Andrews specifically for this most trusted position on Focus Ward. Angie performed many secure tasks for Dr. B. over the years, but she could not have prepared herself, in any way, for what she just saw, a man rise from the dead.

By the time the 32-year-old nurse reached the bathroom, she was gasping for air, thinking, *this just isn't me; get a hold of yourself girl!* Angie sat on the floor cheek to bowl, motionless. After several minutes, she felt sufficiently in control to race down the stairs to the nurse's lounge on the second floor and get help. Everything started when she received the priority email earlier that evening:

Time: 10:45 p.m., U.S.A. Mountain Time
Andrews Hospital

To: Angela Esposito>3rd Floor Focus Ward

From: M. J. Bellos, Chief of Hospital>001-001
Subject: Immediate Security Priority 01-Response Required 001-Code AO-25646

I authorize you to check immediately the security attachments describing Focus Ward Protocol 060, for specific instructions regarding the emergency arrival of an expired body, resulting from an auto accident. At approx. 1 am., Patient 004 will be delivered to Focus Ward, Room 309. You are to monitor all vital signs and chart a matrix for review by 'me only.' At precisely 2 am, you are to personally deliver a food tray to Room 309 and inject vial 134 from Focus security station box 1120 [password, 2fy947t] into the subject's right carotid artery. Memorize and delete this mailing.

Mathew J. Bellos
Chief of Hospital, Brock/Swanson Labs
Security 01-Code AO-25642

When the door to the second-floor nurses' lounge flew open and slammed against the wall, it was apparent to the small group near the coffee machine that something was very wrong. Every head turned in shock to see a terrified young tearful face crying in broken English, "Help me, for God's sake!"

Barb Sawyer, the floor supervisor, moved quickly to the girl. Angie shook, babbled and pointed to upstairs. She pushed Barb away and ran to the opposite side of the room, panting, "He was dead, he was dead! Shit!"

Suddenly faint, Angie slid down the wall to her knees, and two nurses ran to her, Barb Sawyer, 45-years old, with five years of experience at Andrews, and Ralph Walker, 34-years old, Princeton graduate, who started at the hospital only a year ago. They carefully turned and laid Angie on her back; and Barb placed a small pillow behind her head. Ralph caressed her forehead and tried to comfort her. "Hey! Easy, Angie. It's me, Ralphy. You'll be alright."

Barb looked around at the group and then spoke to the young nurse in a whisper. "Angie, tell us what happened. You're safe now."

"I don't know. Dr. Jack was in pieces. They reattached his limbs in surgery. I still don't know why they bothered. The only bones not broken were in his hands."

Angie looked up at Barb and tried to talk coherently, "I got the email. His remains came to Focus Ward with no vital signs. He was a dead lump. I took the tray in. He just sat up. My God! He was alive." Angie squeezed Barb's wrist and said, "It can't be him. They must have switched bodies." She began to hyperventilate. "But, why? How could they do that? I had sensors hooked up all over him. Honestly, he was dead."

Barb motioned toward the cooler. "Give me water here. All of you may leave. We have this. Give us some breathing space, will you? Ralph, get Dr. Bellos for me, please? We need him here stat!

CHAPTER 2: RACHEL

DOCTOR JACK'S WIFE, RACHEL SHELDON, held her head in her hands, as she slumped in a cold hard ER-1 room chair at Andrews. She tried to gain her composure, but her nerves were out of control. It seemed like everything was happening so fast but taking so long. Images of their lives popped in and out of her head.

Hours earlier, she had arrived home after a full day working at the Complex and stole a few moments, laying in her favorite lounge on the screened porch, waiting for the garage door to open signaling Jack's arrival. As she dozed, she reminisced about the beautiful life they had built together and how it all began.

They met in Maryland where Rachel Tomas was working her first real job in microbiology, as a new team member under Jack. He was a young Director of Government Operations, responsible for developing new vaccines for unpopular illnesses, referred to as 'Orphan Diseases.' Their first meeting would have never happened, except, on that night, during a routine procedure, in front of five other experts; Jack's overwhelming presence caused her to make a mistake so obvious that he had to write her up. Ten write-up's and they fired you. Write-up's were posted daily at the central station for all to see.

The next day, Rachel was devastated to see her name was first on the list. She went to see Jack, hoping to corner him, after his presentation lecture on Brain Function and Control-Through Chemistry. She sat swelling with anger outside of the lecture hall. As the doors opened, she pushed and shoved her way through the exiting crowd. When she found Jack, they argued in front of everyone for a good 15 minutes. The rest was mad microbiological love. They became the most famous success team known at the agency, having discovered a record number of medical cures. They married the next January, and Rachel gave birth to her only son, Brian, in November, of that year. Brian graduated from Georgetown University Law with honors and became an apprentice to Marion Brock, billionaire, and co-founder of the Brock/Swanson Research Complex.

During the Complex's construction, Jack and Rachel built their dream home on 70 acres, conveniently located 10 miles from Andrews. Their beautiful swimming pool and botanic garden were centered within a U-shaped stone, four-bedroom ranch, where they managed 15-20 horses at a time. They had three working ranch hands and a full-time housekeeper. In the basement of the house, they furnished an entirely independent private medical laboratory, with state-of-the-art equipment, so that Jack could continue home research. Over the years, they and their research teams were credited with a stunning 30 medical breakthroughs, pioneered and patented with their longtime partner, Dr. Mathew Bellos.

Rachel was an attractive 44-year-old woman. She had medium blonde hair sprinkled with just a tad gray here and there. When she smiled, the creases around her eyes spoke of many happy times. She was 5-ft 2-inches tall and had a strikingly beautiful figure.

Jack had a buff-like appearance, even at the age of 46, standing six feet tall. His olive complexion fooled most into thinking he was Italian, rather than French. He had a magnetic demeanor and the looks to match. His full head of hair was graying at the temples, and there was no mistaking that smile or intense look, when he was concentrating or guiding his team. Years ago, Jack's young talents brought him the highest achievements tenured at Johns Hopkins School of Medicine. His career soared after receiving awards in genetic analysis during those government contract years.

Eventually, his expertise brought him to Brock /Swanson as the Head of Research. He and Rachel were the quintessential couple, and they had all the amenities befitting their exceptional expertise.

She was never to forget that horrific night, starting when Rachel awoke in her lounge at home from her cell phone ringing.

"Hello?"

"Mrs. Sheldon?"

"Yes?

"This is Ron Sandry, at Andrews Hospital. I'm sorry to call at this hour, especially to tell you this."

"What's wrong?"

"It's Mr. Sheldon, ma'am. He was in a car accident. It's bad, Mrs. Sheldon. You had better come. I don't know what to say. Dr. Bellos told me to call you. He is with your husband now. That's all I know."

Rachel felt her heart and mind race. "How bad?" Her hand shook; she almost dropped the phone. "Is he alive? I'm on my way. Where should I go?"

"Doctor said you should go to ground floor ER-1. He will be there as soon as he can. I'm sorry I can't tell you any more than that."

Now, at 2:30 a.m., Rachel paced back and forth in the private room at Andrews ER-1. Three different doctors spoke to her in the last two hours, but neither gave her a definitive prognosis. Jack had been in isolation surgery for what seemed an eternity. Rachel tried to think objectively, pondering, *"How do I accept the possibility of Jack's death? Even if he lives, life will be so different. He may be disabled. What would Jack want me to do? Matt, I need Matt! Where the hell are you?"*

She didn't want to fathom any of this. Still, somehow, she had ingrained within her the Pollyanna notion that all would be okay. She pushed the nurse's call button again, but there was no reply, and no one came.

CHAPTER 3:   THE NURSES' LOUNGE

BEFORE RALPH WALKER COULD PAGE HIM, Dr. Mathew Bellos walked into the nurses' lounge. Bellos was 52 years old, 6-ft tall and 185 pounds. He was average to describe but impressive at first sight. He was a complicated man, well-educated, extraordinarily talented and creative, with a background to envy. One of his ancestors worked with Jonas Salk, helping to research the Polio vaccine.   Most of all, Bellos was a visionary and persuasive.

After his parents died in New Mexico, young Bellos moved to Washington, DC and earned Master's-Degrees in both genetic analysis and organic chemistry. Two years later, he received a Ph.D. in political philosophy. The Washington elite welcomed his expertise and commanding presence. His published work, Viruses to Recover Life, was a best-seller and made Bellos famous worldwide. Now, at Brock/Swanson, Mathew Bellos reigned as Chief of Andrews Hospital. The buck stopped with him. Over recent years, he mentored and hired many of the hospital staff.

Tonight, during the early morning hours, news spread quickly throughout the Complex about Dr. Jack Sheldon's arrival. Overall, in the hospital's hierarchy, the entire staff thought of Jack, Rachel, and Bellos as 'the big three.' However, only a very select few knew Sheldon's injuries were fatal.

The moment Bellos entered the nurses' lounge, he went to Angie. Her face changed when she saw him, and she reached up. "Dr. Bellos, I'm so glad you're here. Listen to me. I was in Focus 309. I did everything you instructed in the e-mail. He was . . ."

Bellos placed his forefinger to his lips and smiled. "Shush; it's okay." He embraced and lifted her. She noticed that he applied significant pressure to her upper arms, guiding her out of the lounge toward a security guard in the hall. Bellos spoke firmly but quietly to the guard, "Bob, please take Ms. Angie here to my office. Stay with her until I get there. Give her anything she'd like. If she is hungry, order something from the kitchen. Let her relax."

Then, Bellos turned to Angie and reached in his pocket. "Angie, take one of these. It'll calm your nerves; doctor's orders. I will be there as soon as I can...And Bob, give her privacy. Wait outside."

Angie looked confused but took the pill. As Bob led Angie away, Barb Sawyer stepped in front of Dr. Bellos and whispered to him, trying to recount the story's bits and pieces, but Bellos interrupted, "Barb, Angie is in trauma. I need to examine her myself. Focus Ward is my special responsibility. I need to get her through this as quietly as possible. Are you with me here? I will handle this."

"Yes, of course, sir," Barb said.

Bellos turned to walk away, and then he stopped, turned back, and put his hand affectionately on Barb's shoulder. "Barb. Please, work with me here. Use that talent of yours to calm those people in there. Let them know this is a security situation. Nothing goes beyond this room, alright?"

Sawyer was a professional, loyal trooper, yet always the skeptic. She blinked and nodded, "Yes, of course. Right."

Bellos studied Barb's face as though he had an epiphany. "You've been here what, five years? You have an excellent record, Barb. You know more than most about everything here, don't you?"

"I like to think I'm up to date," she said.

"Well, until we sort this out, I am reassigning you. You are the only other person I trust who has the qualifications and experience to oversee Focus Ward. Report to me at 4 pm sharp this afternoon, to my 10th-floor office. Meantime check your computer and read all the 'redirect security protocols' involved. We will discuss your specific duties and access codes at that time. Please be prepared to perform on a 24/7 basis."

It was close to 3 am when Bellos sped off to the elevator. Barb Sawyer stood in shock at the door, watching Angie and the guard disappear down the hallway.

CHAPTER 4:   TOTAL RECALL

AS DR. BELLOS ENTERED the elevator and pushed ER-1, he couldn't help thinking about his history with Rachel and Jack. The three first met while they all worked at VIRAID—Viral Infection Research and Internal Development. At that time, it was a sub-contractor to the North American Medical Research Foundation. Jack and Rachel's team were researching a new military concept. The basic premise was that testosterone and adrenaline cause over-aggression, which is the standard basis for military behavior. The team's objective was to suppress these two hormones from being secreted into the body, by deploying a preventive gaseous contagion, deliverable during combat. One deposit of the gas covered 100 square yards. Rachel and Jack isolated and defined formulas, which, if proven correct, would prevent the human body from secreting these hormones within seconds. If the deployment was successful, the target troops could not fight. No fighting, no war. That effort was the foundation upon which Jack would later define his *chemical personality controllers.*

During that same time, Dr. Bellos' team was researching dormant viruses and their reactions to various stimuli. A virus can lay dormant for thousands of years, but if properly stimulated, it can become active, alive in every way. His research team succeeded in re-activating several viruses and some very rare bacteria. Eventually, Bellos expected to create a practical use for his findings, like protecting transported donor organs and limbs without the need for refrigeration. Later, Bellos would hypothesize that death itself was an illness, and the cure lay in the viral world.

Regardless, that day of their first meeting Dr B, Jack and Rachel attended a three-day VIRAID convention, and Mathew Bellos was the keynote speaker. What he said profoundly moved them, so, they finagled a meeting with him and they all quickly realized they had much in common, so the three bonded. They became unmatchable research team leaders.

Bellos' mind drifted as he rode in the hospital elevator. He thought about how it all seemed so convoluted now. Jack's CPT discovery changed everything. Recently, Bellos had become too embroiled with it all. He thought back to his life-changing morning on May 12, three years ago.

That morning, before work, Bellos was enjoying coffee and a croissant at Gus' Coffee Cafe in Arden, New Mexico, before driving to Andrews. He noticed a man sit down at the table next to him. Although dressed in jeans and a starched jean shirt, to Bellos the man was trying to look Southwestern. At first glance, the man reminded Bellos of the pseudo-FBI types back in DC. The man made no eye contact; however, after five minutes or so, he got up and dropped an issue of the local Arden Gazette onto Dr. B's table. Bellos looked at the man with confusion, as the man nodded and then quickly walked away. Bellos noticed part of a Post-it note wedged in the newspaper, which read:

Mathew Bellos,

You have been chosen for a high purpose. We want you as our ally in the struggle to preserve and better humanity. It is urgent you phone me @ . . .

Bridger

There was a small iconic signature stamped at the bottom, which looked like an old Christian fish symbol with a dollar sign before it. Dr. B. couldn't get the brief encounter and note off his mind all day.

That evening, in the privacy of his office study, Bellos made the phone call that would change his priorities completely.

A voice answered, "Hello, Bridger here."

Bellos froze for a second. "Yes, I am Dr. Mathew Bellos. Ah, one of your people approached me this morning and asked me to call this number."

"Oh, yes, Dr. Bellos, that wasn't one of my people, that was me. I am Tom Bridger. I apologize for the cloak and dagger. We can never be sure of our response rate from first encounters. When you learn about our organization, you'll understand."

Bellos was hardly interested. "I called because the cryptic method you used haunted me, but frankly, I'm not interested in solicitations of any kind, thank you."

Bridger was quick to reply. "Dr. Bellos, we are on the verge of making one of the most important announcements in the history of medicine; perhaps even the most important announcement in all history. But we need you. I am not exaggerating in any way."

Bellos was annoyed. "I don't have any idea what you are talking about."

"Doctor, why did you become a medical researcher? Why do you fight disease? What is your goal in medicine? Please, I cannot discuss this over the phone. I assure you; I am sincere. We must meet. It will not just change your life; you will fulfill your destiny."

Bellos said, "This is a ridiculous conversation. I am not going to commit myself to some drama that sounds like a scam to me. Goodbye!"

As Bellos pulled the phone away from his ear, he heard Bridger speak loudly, "Doctor, both your father and great-grandfather were one of us. We are your family."

Bellos pushed the phone back against his ear and heard, "Doctor, please, I know your history. We must meet. Doctor Bellos, are you there?"

"Yes, I am here."

"Good! I can't say any more. Anyone could be listening. You know that. Believe me; I am not a fake. Will you meet me at the same café, tomorrow morning, say at 7:15? It is most urgent."

"Hmm, if this is so damn important and secret, why the café? Why so out in the open?"

"Because we know it's secure. We own it, and the surrounding five stores on each side of the street. We don't own the airways, however, or the phone lines."

"Oh." Leery of it all and with a slight grin, Dr. B. hung up the phone and sat back bewildered.

The next morning, Bellos walked back to the café. He loved his morning coffee and pastries and reminiscing about the history of Gus's. It was like stepping back in time to a long since gone motif of the ancient Native Americans. Usually, there was a line stretching out the door to buy morning sweets and hot drinks; but that morning, as Bellos approached, there was only one single person sitting at an outside table. He stood up and extended his hand, "Good morning, doctor."

"Good morning," Bellos replied.

Bridger gestured, "Please, have a seat." He waved at the waitress, pointing out that his companion had arrived. "I hope you don't mind; I ordered you an espresso and donut."

"Thank you. Now tell me why I'm here?"

"I am a recruiter, so to speak. I represent an organization, which has existed for a very long time, millennia, by your records. Please, excuse me if I seem uneasy. You see, what I'm about to say will sound strange, to say the least." Bridger smiled and took a deep breath before explaining, "We have been involved in, and continue to influence most modern countries' medical and political systems. Medical advancement is our purpose, our goal; and doing political deeds is one vehicle we use to fund ourselves. The civilized world all over the globe has prospered using our medical discoveries. Anyway, you'll learn as you go."

"Learn? Learn what?"

Bellos sat looking annoyed as Bridger continued, "The thing is; only within the last 800 years have things become so fascinating and futuristic. We are without a doubt the richest, most advanced research organization on the planet. I am authorized to tell you that we are on the verge of announcing the greatest of discoveries. It will be the answer to why we all got into medicine."

Bellos' eyes widened, and he said cynically, "Really, I got into medical research to combat disease and improve the human condition. What question or answer are you talking about?"

Bridger just smirked and said, "We have followed your career and those of your close colleagues for some time. We need your help, and you need us. This is the end of a ten-thousand-year-old journey and the beginning of a new era for all humankind. Doctor, this is not some Hollywood nonsense or CIA secret plot to overthrow a government."

"Well, it sounds like wild science fiction bullshit to me."

"Perhaps, but it isn't." Bridger reached into his coat pocket, took an envelope out and handed it to Bellos. "Here, this is for you. There is a letter of instruction in there. We crossed out some words, for security purposes, but you will get the gist. There is also an airplane ticket. Only one person has the authorization to explain more, and he awaits your arrival."

Bellos unfolded the papers and looked through them.

Bridger touched Bellos' arm. "My instructions are to ask that you read the first page now and the rest after you get on the plane."

Bellos shook his head in disbelief, as he pulled a wad of money from the envelope. "And this?" He asked.

"Oh yes, and there is also $200,000; a bit of petty cash for you. You keep that, whether you go or not. If your answer is no, give me the paperwork back. That's it, doc. Now or never, no more talk until you reach the destination."

Bellos looked at Bridger and rolled his eyes. "Jesus, this is insane."

Twelve hours later that same day, Mathew Bellos reached the front stairs of the United States Capitol building in Washington, D.C. He spent some time sitting on the concrete stairs, overlooking the downtown campus, and reflecting on his past there. The streets were unusually quiet for that time of day.

Nevertheless, as instructed, he stood by the curb at 7:30 p.m., waiting for a silver stretch limousine to pick him up. Bellos scrutinized every vehicle that passed by. After a half-hour, he stood facing the street when he felt a hand on the back of his shoulder and heard a soft baritone voice, "Good evening, doctor. Thank you for being so punctual."

As Bellos turned around, he saw a tall, distinguished, white-haired man, dressed in a tailored suit, and looked approximately 60 y/o in age. Bellos extended his hand. "Good evening, I am Mathew Bellos."

"Yes, I know, I am Gordon Swanson. I must apologize for all the mystery, but our history, our purpose, and success are beyond security as you understand it. I promise I will explain everything."

A sleek looking silver limousine pulled up to the curb. The driver got out and opened the back door, as Swanson gestured politely to Bellos. "Please, doctor; come? We will talk." Bellos stepped into the vehicle and was struck by how futuristic it was inside. The cabin was fit for a king. Bellos had never seen any vehicle like this, so he tried to study everything inside. Swanson only uttered two words, "Master secured."

As Bellos listened to clicks and flinched at the blinking lights, the two side door windows became 3D monitors and pivot around in front of the passenger. Then they retracted back to windows. There was also a mid-floor projector which could receive and send any holographic communication. It displayed a video tab at the bottom running up to date news in unfamiliar languages.

"I activated security protocols; that's all," Swanson remarked.

Then, an automatic drink dispenser rose out from the dashboard and presented two perfect gin martinis.

"Here, Mathew, you will want this."

The driver made a U-turn and sped off. Bellos couldn't help but start. "Look, Mr. Swanson . . ."

"It's just Swanson."

"...Yes, well, your Mr. Bridger told me a few things that certainly would interest anyone. He was very persuasive. And the money; well, thank you. But I have many questions."

Swanson turned from looking out the window at the night sky. "I'm here to answer your questions and determine if you are indeed suitable for our organization, our society." He then took a set of pages stapled together out of the seat's back pocket in front of him and handed them to Bellos. "You may read these at your leisure and ask any question you like after you study it all."

The first page read:

Ever-Life Subterranean Posts: The following describes the Ever-Life's populated subterranean regions-Posts, worldwide. There are many transport stations within each Post. Some Carrier stations are within one mile below Earth's surface, but densely populated colonies are a minimum of five miles below the surface.

Post 1: Includes upper East Asian Continent, Mongolia, and the China Basin, stretching east and south through the Himalayas, Tibet, India and Pakistan, population: 600,000. There are 250 primary Transport Stations throughout the region.

Post 2: Europe, the Netherlands, England, and Northern Africa, population: 300,000. There are 320 primary Transport Stations within the region

Post 3: North American Continent-Canada and the United States and across Alaska including the Bering straits, population: 700,000. There are 230 primary Transport Stations throughout the region.

Post 4: The Middle East, Turkey and the Baltic, north including Russia and west bounded by Afghanistan and Kazakhstan, population: 400,000. There are 140 primary Transport Stations in the region.

Post 5: Australia and the Pacific Seas including Japanese Isles and east including South America, population: 500,000. There are 170 primary Transport Stations throughout the region.

Post 6: Mid and Southern Africa and Madagascar, population: 300,000. There are 100 primary Transport Stations within the region.

Post 7: South Pole, North Pole, Atlantic Sea and all major planet fresh waterways, population: 200,000. There are 150 primary Transport Stations throughout the region.

Post 8: The most remote Post of the colonies was 2800 miles below Earth's surface, closest to the Earth's core and directly below the Post station at the Judah Villa in Jerusalem, population: 25,000. There are 25 primary Transport Stations in that location.

"You see, Mathew, we have monitored you and two of your colleagues for quite some time. We know you have what we want, and we are confident we can provide you with all that you need."

"What exactly does that mean? Your man Bridger said the same thing. I have no idea what you are talking about."

Swanson turned to view the Washington Monument. "Did you know, doctor, it's been said that at the time of its construction, this city was designed to impress and outshine all other cities in the world? That is one reason we finally settled a key Post underground here."

Bellos was anything but impressed. "Yes, the city is beautiful, basic American history. Wait, what did you say about underground?"

Swanson said, "You could say we have been 10,000 years in the making. Did Bridger tell you how old we are?"

"Not really."

"Our organization has outlasted most cultures on the planet. We research and develop medical breakthroughs to preserve and improve humanity. Our new campus is nearly complete now in the southwestern United States. It's quite close to where you grew up, and we are starting to recruit the major players. Our culture is a bit unfamiliar to your kind. It's not a democracy. You would probably consider it a sort of monarchy. By that I mean we have only one absolute authority, one person, who is responsible for all matters and everyone."

"We call that a dictatorship."

"Far from it, actually; having authority and responsibility is entirely different from exerting power over people; indeed an argument for another day. Regardless, today our leader happens to be a man. And there have been women too, famous women who have been great leaders. And it is amazing how many people, who live on Earth's surface, are serving us, dutifully working double lives."

"What?"

"They research for countries all over the globe and submit timely reports to us about potential discoveries on the surface. It is through their loyalty and commitment that we have been so successful in exchanging our detailed findings."

"Sounds like they are committing treason. We're not at war. It sounds absurd. All of us with half a brain know standard ethics and morals, not to mention signing non-disclosure pledges."

"I suppose," said Swanson. "Ah yes, non-disclosure commitments, those are the documents that grant government and corporate dictatorships power over people. Your corporations are insecure institutions surviving by competing. They all require control to assure a profit. That, my friend, is management by fear."

"What?"

"Unlike corporation dictatorships, we neither hold creativity captive nor do we blackmail our employees. We are completely secure. Let us say, for example, a corporate researcher discovers something quite stunning. By signing a non-disclosure agreement, one is bound legally not to share the information. Whatever it is, could remain hidden, unknown for years, even decades. Eventually, at some time in the future, your global communication media would find out and announce it. Then, suddenly, it's news out of the closet. Within days, at most weeks, it becomes a standard across the globe, right? That's when we all benefit, right? On the contrary, think of what we do as shortening the whole timeline. We do not cheat or steal profits. We expedite discoveries to the public; and, of course, after we confirm that the surface is ready for our input, then we share in the wealth by selling our advancements regarding the subject. As it turns out, we help grow corporate and government profits faster. You will understand as you go."

Bellos did a double take. "Wait a minute. Let me understand this. So, you are recruiting for your new facility on a new campus? Why would I consider such a thing? And what do you mean when you say you built here underground during the 1800s? Look, I hope you did not spend this $200,000 and your valuable time to give me a history or economic lesson."

"Mathew, I brought you here for many lessons and to show you something that will change you. Our society is at a turning point in deciding whether to . . ." Swanson paused, nodded his head, and then looked Bellos, straight in his eye. "...You see, Mathew, one of your colleagues, is in the process of refining a medical hypothesis, it's revolutionary to all humanity. If proven correct, and if the wrong people get a hold of it; well, frankly chaos may result. For the first time in our history, we must decide whether to assist him, actually both you and him, or stop you. If we do help, it means our getting involved with the surface world much more than we have ever done. That would be quite contrary to our charter and usual involvement with the surface, and you are a big part of it."

"Surface? I would be a big part of what?"

Swanson ignored the questions for the moment and continued to focus. "You have contributed, you see. I know you don't understand your part in this yet; but, your viral research over the years has components that, when put together with your colleague's data, the potential medical wonders for the future are unmistakable. Although your two brilliant scientific minds have worked separately, you both have stumbled onto what we discovered, refined, and kept silent for well over 3,500 years, by your timeline. We certainly didn't expect this from any surface researcher. I neither exaggerate nor mock you in any way. If nothing else, the $200,000 petty cash was to impress upon you that what I tell you is not to be taken lightly."

"My timeline? What do you mean by that?" Bellos scratched his head. "Why are you afraid of this 'discovery' you speak of?"

"Because it could threaten the balance of life on the planet, my boy. I wish I could give you all the knowledge right now; but, please, do try to have more ear than mouth."

Bellos rolled his eyes, and then he swallowed the martini in one gulp. "What is this secret that you and Bridger speak of anyway?"

"Well, as you said, first things first. It seems the more I say, the more irritated you become. I wish to educate you, not sour you. Patience, doctor, patience," Swanson smirked. "Perhaps you'd like another martini?"

"No. Thank you."

"Frankly, when I think about it from your point of view, it is very spooky and cryptic. I will give you that. I wouldn't want to listen to me either, but it is worth it. It is well worth it."

The limo rounded Madison Street and turned into an alley. Swanson took out his key fob and pushed a button. "Mr. Mike, are we ready?"

"Yes, sir, we are here."

Suddenly, Bellos felt the front of the car nose-dive, as if they were on a rollercoaster. Bellos felt his stomach in his throat. "Whoa! What is that?"

The car circled down and around to the right, twisting and turning into a strangely lighted tunnel and accelerating in speed.

"It's alright, doctor." Swanson held tightly onto the door handle himself. "We have buildings below just about a mile or so away now. There are ramps like this throughout the city. All of them wind around like the tentacles of an octopus, eventually leading back to its head. You are going to love it.

"Our new campus will be on the surface in Arden, New Mexico. It will be much more in the open, completely different, of course; but then, security will be of a different type altogether. Ah, progress, I love it. Relax, doctor, only a few more minutes. Everything is ready for you."

Bellos was confused and aggravated. "I don't even know this place, and you're already describing a new one. What do you mean, ready for me? What a headache. I don't get this one bit, not one bit."

Gordon Swanson grinned as the car sped through a strangely lighted one-lane tunnel. After a few minutes, the tunnel opened to a broad brightly lighted area several miles in diameter. Bellos stared in wonder at the beautiful wildflowers and the unfamiliar trees that filled the fields all around the perimeter. "How is this possible? Where is the light coming from? There's no sunlight. This is a cave. Isn't it?"

In the distance, Bellos could see what looked like a sizeable carved rock structure cut out from the surrounding mountain. "What is that? It's glowing too."

"That is our destination."

Finally, the car stopped. The two men exited the limo, and Bellos squinted trying to see all the detail of the magnificent entrance. It looked like a combination of ancient Egyptian and medieval architecture. Swanson gestured, and they walked up several stairs beneath a curved sculpted stone canopy. Its underside displayed frescos worthy of Michelangelo. Bellos strained his neck studying it all. "Are we at the Venetian in Las Vegas?"

"Not quite. Come. Beautiful, isn't it? And this is just a side entrance. Wait until you see the main foyer."

Everything seemed bathed in a strange light. However, Bellos could see no source, no lamps of any kind. They walked some 20 yards in and stood at the bottom of another staircase. Bellos noticed an etching in the rock above a double doorway at the top. It resembled the outline of a huge fish.

"Mr. Swanson, what does that mean? Bridger stamped a similar fish outline on a note to me when we first met."

"Eye-catching, isn't it? Tweaked your interest, did it?"

"Yes."

"It is part of an old character alphabet that existed for who knows how long. As you know, in any language, words or phrases connote several meanings. I like to think of that etching as *thesauretical*."

"What language is that?" Bellos asked. "It looks to be like an old Christian fish with a U.S. dollar sign in its mouth."

Swanson squinted, cocking his head to one side. "Yes, it does. Very perceptive. Think back. Hundreds of years ago when cell phones first became the rage, 'Texting' was not even a word in the English language. Over the years, certain words, icons, or expressions become acceptable colloquialisms. Even down here that happens. Regardless, translated into English that symbol means, 'Money comes from God'." Swanson raised his eyebrows with a grin. "We do have Christians here too. Of course, that image may come to mean something very different to you, as time goes by."

Bellos shook his head in complete frustration as the two stepped up the dark maroon paisley-carpeted staircase. At the top, a strangely dressed guard greeted them. He stood in front of two teal metal lacquered 15-foot by 11-foot double doors. Bellos stared at his strange outfit. "Is he from the Vatican?"

"No," Swanson giggled, "although the Vatican's Swiss Guard uniforms did have similar puffy pantaloons look. Except, of course, we, on the other hand, keep up with our latest state of the art weaponry. You won't see his kind of sidearm anywhere on the surface. It fires a single burst of air, which will knock you out up to 50 yards away."

"Air?"

"Yes, it's technical."

They both entered through the doorway, the guard shut the doors behind them, and Swanson continued. "This way, doctor. It's late, and we

have a full schedule. I hope you slept on the plane. After we talk, you must
be processed, tested and remember quite a lot."

"You're going to test me?"

"Not the way you think, my friend."

They walked down what looked like a long winding library corridor.
Bellos stopped and marveled at the medical reference books on the shelves;
some printed in many different languages. At one point, he took a book and
studied it. He couldn't believe his eyes.

"*Polio Diaries* by Jonas Salk. How did you get this? The pages are
original penmanship. Salk died back in 1995, right?"

"Correct, centuries ago; that was a gift to us, resulting from an
unfortunate political negotiation, I'm sorry to say. This way. Shall we
continue?"

Swanson gestured to the other end of the room. Bellos put the book back
on the shelf, and they walked to another set of doors.

"Come in, doctor. Welcome to my endless hallway. I am rather
embarrassed that I am a bit nervous, which isn't my style. People here will
tell you; I never seem worried."

"Imagine that," Bellos chimed.

"Yes, well, this way. I should also tell you that involvement with us is for
life, doctor. Welcome to Ever-Life."

Bellos looked around. "Catchy phrase."

"Every life here benefits from the omniscience of the whole. However,
like anything else, none of it works without trust, you know. I like to think
we are one reason humanity is at the top of the food chain, Hah!"

"And that means what?" Bellos asked.

"In the final analysis, it is the genetics of it all that brought us to you. It
is you, Mathew." Swanson paused and looked Bellos straight in the eye.
"What I said before is certainly true. Your colleague is going to discover
something profound; but he will want us as much as I need you."

"Sir, you talk in riddles."

"You see, doctor, I am not just recruiting you for our new facility. The
fact is, I am Great Grand Master, Gordon G. Swanson. In our vernacular, the
population refers to me as 'GGM.' I run this place, lead it, if you will. I
represent all the lives here in the colonies. And now, I need your skills to
help me decode your friend's latest discovery. I realize this is a lot to take in.
I am recruiting you to replace me. Together, during your training, we will
decide which aspects of Ever-Life should be made public to the surface
population."

"What?" Bellos was confused to say the least. "Great Grand Master? Are you Masons?"

Swanson lifted one eyebrow. "No. Although several of their terms may have originated from us, neither 'great nor grandmaster' came from them. And, just for the record, I think you may be asking 'what?' quite a lot. Come to think of it, so did I."

"This is a mistake," said Bellos, rolling his eyes and shaking his head no.

"No, doctor, it is not!" Swanson squeezed Bellos' shoulder. "It's no mistake. I need you. We all need you. Come, I will try to explain as much as I can within what time we have."

They began walking again. "Now pay attention. I'll start with some of our basics. Here, in our world, we measure a lifetime in genetic terms, rather than in time cycle terms, as you do. That is to say; we estimate age and general health as it relates to individual DNA or gene structure, depending . . ."

"I know how important good health is," Bellos replied. "I am a doctor."

"Well, we certainly use concepts of physics, time, economics and politics; but we have concentrated our social strategies with different frames of reference. You see, we isolated, defined, and started applying the human genome to diagnose illness several thousand years ago.

Bellos looked distracted from everything he saw. "This is a crazy dream."

"Hardly, please pay attention. On the surface, you measure everything as it relates to rotations of the Earth around the Sun. You use what you call textbooks in schools, based on historical data, Newton, Darwin, Einstein, Hawking. So many people up there you worship, not just within religions but also because some have attended so many years of schooling. The point is that you are just now beginning real medical research, in-depth miniaturization, and the use of genetics."

"I hate to disappoint you," Bellos interrupted, "but we all know Newton, Einstein, and Darwin. I studied modern man's boom in discovery. It began pushing limits with the space race, back in the 1960s, ages ago. That alone started generating tremendous strides in miniaturization. Our people continued for centuries making significant discoveries, transplants, artificial limbs, skin grafts, venom vaccines. New research has been endless."

"Yes, that's right. Do not think I am belittling your accomplishments or culture. Quite the contrary, I just wanted you to know that we were where you are now, millennia ago. Imagine this. Within Ever-Life, our children learn and understand courses of study like analytics, quantum theory, organic chemistry, and genetic analysis at the primary school level. We did try to introduce our knowledge to surface Earth thousands of years ago, but it proved deadly to our ambassadors. You called them witches and burned them. The mind can be a dreadful enemy, Mathew."

"So, the $200,000 was payment for listening to this fantasy?"

"No, my point is, down here we do not see the sun. We use other frames of reference as time controls and guideposts to improve learning and progress."

"What are you talking about?"

"We are a health-based society. Sometimes we borrow things from the surface, and then we give discoveries back to them, as payment, as medical science advancements, you see. However, we are at a point now where I will need your help specifically. I am going to assist you for starters and show you exactly what I mean. We will answer all your questions. And make no mistake; you will flood me with them."

"Ha, you haven't answered one yet. I have no idea what all this is about. What about you, your health? You're replacing yourself? Why? Is there something wrong with you?"

Swanson sighed. "Yes, hmm, unfortunately in my case, I do have a genetic issue. I have a flaw that developed later in my life. It is an 'orphan's genetic disease.' I must address it. However, I must do so with and through you. Your family does not have genetic flaws. In fact, you are quite gifted genetically. My condition has no cure, yet."

Then a small smile appeared on Swanson's lips. "Given our way of measuring time down here and the progress of my condition, I must choose my successor, and that's that. There is no committee, no vote. I am the sole authority. Our laws state that my successor may be of any background, but there are specific genetic rules. Our researchers have studied the genetic codes of all the candidates within the entire global community, both on the surface and down here. Of all the people on the planet, you are the only one who can fill this position."

"Pardon me?" Bellos scratched his head and frowned. "That sounds like crap. You're going to have to do better than bring me in some strange cave and flood me with all your nonsense. I can't believe anyone would fall for this. If I knew how to leave, I would. But frankly, I have no idea how to get out of here."

"Mathew, please, your reaction is quite understandable. Just come with me a little further. I have something to show you that will clarify your confusion."

Bellos was noticeably bothered, but he agreed. They walked down another winding corridor that reminded Bellos of a church cathedral. He was in awe and stopped to study several oil paintings, sculptures, and mosaics that lined the walls. "Are these all originals? Who the hell are you guys?"

Swanson continued to walk and talk. "Leonardo donated that one to us. Beautiful, isn't it? And Look over there. That's an Islamic mosaic from the Second Crusade. It took 3-decades and heavy convincing to get it here from the Holy-land. One thing we are not, doctor, is fake. Everything in any of our facilities across the globe is authentic, not Hollywood made."

"Hmm, you sound like Bridger," Bellos chuckled.

Swanson continued. "Bridger? Hah! Well, he's been noted as quoting me. Don't get me wrong. I love movies, especially the ones from Hollywood's golden age. We watch them throughout our colonies. I envy that talent, the classics, superheroes, and their cowboys."

Swanson paused and seemed to go into a brief trance remembering. "God, do you remember that musical dancer, Fred Astaire? I just loved watching him. No one like him since. And there were movies about a librarian. What was his name? It was so long ago. I remember in one of his adventures, he fell in love with a vampire. I just love those creatures. Years ago, Bridger said I looked like a vampire. Sometimes I think I should have had his blood sucked dry. Anyway, you have to love what Hollywood 'was' in those days."

Swanson slowed and gestured to the right. "Finally, here we are."

They stopped in front of a beautiful double door, ornately carved and with gold leaf surrounding Ever-Life characters and designs. Swanson pulled a gold fob out and waved it in front of the door lock. Then, with both hands, he turned the golden knob and pulled. "I hate this door."

Slowly, the heavy door opened, leading into a stark white sterile room that looked surprisingly like one on Focus Ward back at Andrews Hospital.

With that image and the ding of the elevator, Mathew Bellos was shocked back to the reality of the present day and the ER-1, where Rachel Sheldon waited for the word she dreaded about Jack.

CHAPTER 5:   BELLOS AND RACHEL

IT WAS 3 A.M. WHEN BELLOS EXITED the elevator. Rachel Sheldon lingered in a dream-state on the hospital bed in a private room of the ER-1. She had so many thoughts about Jack; their last cup of coffee together; his lousy joke that made her force a giggle; and such a satisfying evening of loving intimacy. Jack left them both laughing.

Rachel heard the door squeak. She opened her eyes, and Mathew Bellos entered the room.

"Matt, thank God." She rose and embraced him like a brother.

"Rachel, I'm so sorry for the long delay. We've been working on Jack since he arrived."

"So, tell me for God's sake!"

Bellos led her to the bed. "Rachel, he was in a horrible car accident. I can give you details, but the point is; Rachel, he died."

Bellos drew her to him as she broke down. "No! God, no! He must be alright. I know it! You told me they were doing everything possible. I know this place, damn it!" Rachel grabbed his hospital coat lapels. "There's no way he died."

Bellos took her wrists gently. "He didn't suffer, Rach, but he died. There was no indication he regained consciousness. He didn't feel a thing. I am so sorry, honey."

"I want to see him!" Rachel turned pale white in disbelief. "I have to, damn it! I have to know he is really gone. Please Matt?"

Then she fell limp in his arms, shaking and sobbing. Bellos sat her on the bed and tried to comfort her. He received several beeps on his cell phone; however, he only took one call. After a time, Rachel gathered herself and listened to Bellos.

"Rach, please stay here, for a while at least. I want to monitor you; then, I will take you home myself. We can talk about everything in detail when you are up to it. Please? You have a lot to take in. Here, take this, it's just a mild sedative, doctor's orders. I want you to rest here, just a little while. I have to go, but I will be back shortly. If you need anything, call me. Do you have a phone?"

She took her's out. "Oh shit, it's dead."

"Here, take this." He gave her Angie's. "I'm only a click away."

Rachel nodded and took the pill. Bellos turned, exited the room and walked down the hall to the private elevator. He pushed three to Focus

Ward, and the elevator began to move up. After only a second, looking at his reflection in the bezel, he wiped his red eyes and pushed the red stop button.

CHAPTER 6:   THE BIG TOUR

THE ELEVATOR STOPPED AGAIN, and in a flash, Mathew Bellos recalled every detail of that first time he met Great Grand Master Gordon Swanson. With a hint of a smile, he thought, *what a first night that was. My heavens, sir, that hallway! I did believe that it was some movie's endless vampire castle. Those doorways, wow, so impressive. Hell, I am still impressed. Alice, your 'looking glass' was nothing.*

Bellos could see it all so clearly in his mind's eye. He had so many questions then. *"What a virgin I was. That was truly a night to remember."*

It all began when Swanson opened the massive doors in that hallway. Bellos stepped into a white pristine chamber. At first, the room brightness made it difficult for Dr. B. to focus. He wasn't sure where the walls began and the ceiling or floor started. But, after a moment, everything became easy on his eyes. The room was 25-feet wide, by 30-feet long, by 15-feet high, and oval-shaped. A large beveled glass fireplace was at the far end. Two white Santa Claus patterned high-back Victorian chairs faced each other, one on each side of a blazing fire.

Directly facing the fire was a cream-colored leather couch. On each side of the sofa sat ornately carved, white wooden lacquered end tables, each with a glowing 15-inch obelisk lamp on it. Across from the couch, above the fireplace was that iconic fish, etched out of a beautiful purple and white geode stone, measuring at least six feet long by two feet high. Each wall had window clusters, five feet long by three feet tall; but rather than being completely transparent, each pane had a vivid scene of celestial constellations meticulously cut in stained glass. The oddest thing was that each window looked like the light was shining into the room from outside. However, Bellos had no idea how, since the room was miles below the surface, and he could see no evidence of a source outside the room. Even more curious, he studied the light glowing from the obelisks on the tables. There was no bulb or filament, yet each lamp radiated a full spectrum of light without causing discomfort or eye damage. "But that's impossible," Bellos whispered to himself. He turned and marveled at the ornately carved wall-to-wall bookshelves and the exquisite drop leaf tables against the walls at each end of the room. All the books were the same size, bound in an iridescent pearl white leather-like material. Each had embossed on their binding and front cover a set of three different letters in gold leaf. While

Bellos concentrated, he hadn't noticed there were three men and a woman sitting on the furniture behind him, who stood up smiling to greet him. Each person held what looked like a wine glass filled with a sparkling white liquid that was neither milk nor champagne. Bellos smiled and continued studying the room, as Swanson introduced him.

"Good evening, everyone. I trust you all have been enjoying yourselves so far . . ."

Each person looked at the other and spoke in unison, "Yes, thank you."

Swanson placed his hand on Dr. B.'s shoulder and said, "I am proud to introduce all of you to someone I hope you will get to know quite well. This is Dr. Mathew Bellos. Dr. Bellos, this is Professor Jonathan Witt, Lionel Benton, and Dr. Andrew Pine."

Bellos bowed with a polite smile. "How do you do?"

Then, he quickly focused on the woman to the left of Dr. Pine, ignoring Swanson's voice. Bellos could not believe his eyes. As he started to move toward her, Swanson gently grabbed his arm and interrupted. "I think you two know one another; if I'm not mistaken? Dr. Bellos, you remember Ms. Carla Esposito, do you not?"

Their eyes fixed on each other. Swanson smiled politely and said, "Before you get too carried away, come this way Mathew..."

Before either Bellos or Carla could reach out and touch one another, Swanson pulled Bellos to the right. "...Mathew, may I present the last in this evening's introductions?"

A man entered the room and walked towards them. Bellos was even more shocked, if that was possible. "Dad . . . DAD?"

"Sonny?"

Richard Bellos and his wife died ten years ago, according to surface records. At that moment, Dr. B. felt emotions he never knew he had. "Dad, it's you! This is impossible. Is it really you? How?"

"Yes, son! It is me. It's a miracle!"

They grabbed one another, embraced, and Richard gestured toward Swanson. "Our friend here did it. I have no idea how or why, but I'm so happy. Son, you are so, so grown up. You have a touch of grey."

After a few minutes, suddenly, it was as if strobe lights started blinking all around them. Bellos looked at the other people in the room. Each began to pulsate and flicker. Bellos and Richard froze as they watched Carla and the other three men wiggle, blur, and vanish. Bellos did a double take, and then he looked at his father. They both looked at Swanson in complete amazement. "Mr. Swanson," Richard said. "What just happened? We were all just talking together. I only left to use the bathroom. They were as real as you or me. Professor Witt poured the drinks."

Swanson gestured most kindly. "Have a seat, gentlemen. I am sorry about Carla, Mathew. There is much both of you must learn. Our ways take time to understand. Unfortunately, you must learn quickly. I want you to remember three important facts from this." Swanson looked at Richard. "One is that we can give a person rebirth. Two is that you, Mathew, have a destiny with your daughter. Both you and your father are real; but, unfortunately, the others I introduced to you here are but solid holograms. We consider them very much alive; but, in fact, they are programmed transport models. You might think of them as artificially intelligent and humanized."

Bellos reacted, "Whatever they are, they looked very real."

"Yes," Swanson nodded. "We will come back to that. Regardless, today is an extraordinary day for you two. Richard, there is an excellent reason you both are reunited. Let's take a breath and celebrate that. Mathew, I told you I had many things to show you. Your father is the first. Trust me. There is nothing to fear at all. I am going to give you two a chance to catch up a bit. Press the red button on that table twice when you are ready. The first push will take you off privacy, and I will answer the second."

Bellos was speechless. He looked at his dad in utter amazement and asked, "Wait, what is the third thing? You said there were three facts you wanted us to remember."

"Oh, yes," Swanson winked, "the third is, we can also make people disappear."

With those words, GGM, Gordon Swanson, turned and left the room. Mathew and Richard Bellos sat and talked for about 20-minutes before considering the call button.

Richard held his head for a moment as if remembering something. "Son, I can't shake the feeling I know this place somehow. I just know it. As strange as this may sound, I sense there is nothing we should fear. Everything here feels so right. Weird, isn't it?"

Bellos said, comforting him, "They told me you worked for them."

Richard sat back on the couch. "Maybe I did. The more I study, the more I remember. I need to think and organize my thoughts."

"Dad, just try and take it all in one step at a time. I agree we should find out as much as we can."

"Well then, I guess we better get started." Richard reached over and pushed the button on the coffee table twice. It squeaked, and within a minute, Swanson reappeared and said, "Yes, you do need to take it slow, Dr. Richard. That is what we used to call you. I trust you two had a good but much too brief visit. Here, Dr. R., drink this. It's medicinal."

Swanson handed him a wine glass.

"It certainly doesn't taste medicinal. It's delicious."

"Would you two care to take a short tour with me? I think you will find things here more than interesting."

Mathew stood and replied, "Yes, of course. That's why you brought me here, right?"

"Well, as I told you, you are here because I am recruiting you to be my replacement. As a matter of fact, I am recruiting you both. Richard, try to relax. It will all come back to you. You just need time and a little help. Please, follow me."

The three walked out the far back side of the room, through a glass door and onto an outside half hallway with a guardrail. As they all stared over the railing, the newcomers were shocked and amazed at

what they saw. It was a vertical chasm about a half-mile in diameter, extending too far down to see the bottom. There were round transparent aluminum glass-like walking tubes that had no visible support. They twisted and crisscrossed over and under one another every 300 feet or so down the chasm. And what we would define as transparent skyscrapers butted out from the circumference of the abyss on 25 to 30-degree angles.

"Jesus, I won't forget this," said Bellos.

Then they looked up and squinted, straining to focus on the tiny hole at the top of the chasm. Swanson pulled what looked like the old 3D movie glasses out of his pocket and handed them to Bellos. "These should help."

The cavern was at least several miles high from where the three stood. The top itself looked like a huge round beveled glass window, similar in design to the ones on the walls in the room they'd just left. The patterns reflected gorgeous colors and what looked like fishlike creatures.

"Oh, my heavens!" Bellos uttered. Then, he tapped his dad's shoulder, gave him the glasses and said, "Look at that. How is it possible? There is no round glass structure anywhere in D.C. up there, and the light shining through the glass cannot be coming from the sun. My watch says 9 pm, east coast time."

"Frankly, I have no idea," said Richard. "My question is, look all around us. It's like daylight down here. Where is all this light coming from? Look at the rock walls. None of this can be sunlight."

They looked across the chasm and watching the Ever-Life population go about their daily duties took their breath away.

Bellos counted 30 tier levels downward that he could see. "Mr. Swanson, we don't see any lights or wires? How is all this possible?"

Swanson turned to walk again. "Yes, it's quite something, isn't it? Let's walk."

They followed him holding onto the railing, and after some 50 feet, Swanson stopped and turned to them. "I know you have many questions; so, I'll start by saying that all of this, everything you see and much more, started many thousands of years ago, when the 'first ones,' as we call them, discovered the underground, in what you know today as northeastern Mongolia. They found new and different life forms deep below. All this, what you are looking at, the light itself, are life they discovered first. They are very different life forms. They start out as you see, microscopic newborns. They are alive and far too many to count. They live in a variety of sizes and shapes. I suppose, at this stage of their life, they could be far distant cousins to deep-sea creatures that self-generate light in the dark, miles below the ocean's surface. However, I have to say, these are far more interesting. The strange fact is that biologically, they all feed off darkness itself and whatever else toxic that the earth's core expels. They don't require sunlight; they would die in it. But that is not all they do. They also filter our air. They metabolize in almost the opposite way of plant life on the surface. One by-product of their feces is light; quite mind-blowing, actually; and remarkably, there is no odor at all. In fact, their light sterilizes everything. Figure that one out, Mathew. So, we live in an environment that cleans itself and filters our air for us. This whole place is germ-free."

Bellos replied, "So, wait, the light kills them, and then they die, no?

"No, this is not sunlight. The creatures' light is made up of different photonic and particle components. But measuring the light has revealed these little creatures reflect the complete spectrum of sunlight without any damaging rays. Nevertheless, it all happens in much less than a flicker, a millisecond. It is dark. They eat, metabolize and live, reproduce, give off the light and die. Their offspring grow and duplicate the process so fast the human eye doesn't see the flickers. Our science engineers tell me it is just very technical, but I see it as very simple. Scientists get far too detailed, don't you agree? While the whole process happens as pulses, it is so fast that we see it as a steady light. Their ability to propagate is utterly fantastic. None of us has ever been able to calculate their numbers. While very few, proportionately, evolve beyond this stage, some do develop into much more complex brilliant beings. Now, come. Let's continue."

Bellos was intense with interest. "What do you mean, brilliant beings? I could spend a lifetime studying these alone." He grabbed Swanson's shoulder. "Look, I'm sorry. We are so grateful, but, the 'first ones,' who were the 'first ones'?"

Swanson stopped again, turned, and extended his arm over the chasm. "This world is unlike the one on surface Earth. There are countless levels and much life here reaching miles below. Eons ago, somewhere in Northeast Mongolia, where the cold was mother and father of all life, there lived a simple people, a tribe starving. Their leaders decided that if they didn't find food, they would die. So, they broke camp and walked to the mountain tops where they hunted large goats and rams. Unfortunately, there was a horrible earthquake. The earth opened, and everyone fell deep underground. Eventually, over time, those mountains became flatlands without evidence of the original quake. Anyway, roughly half of the tribe survived the fall. They were the 'first ones.' In the beginning, as they explored the cave structures underground, water was easy to find. It melted off the mountains and drained into the caverns. However, the deeper they went, they discovered many wonders including beautiful clean underground rivers, which were abundant with strange life. The light that you see all around you is just one of many discoveries they made. There was no way back up to the surface, so they pressed onward. They had to create and develop from the unknown that mystery and opportunity offered, much like your old pioneers moving west in the USA's 1800s. Things were so different in many ways. The deeper and darker they went, the more stable the light and environment became. They found enormous caverns of incredible beauty. These organisms not only lighted the caves but also generated a mean temperature of 65 degrees, and the little buggers purified the air. The people endured, prevailed, and began to prosper. Over time, they bypassed much of what the surface cultures went through. They survived without much of the petty stresses of the surface world. The food was plentiful down here, unlike on earth's surface, where humanity had to be on-guard when hunting life-giving essentials; and, up there, humanity became aggressive, migrating to conquer real estate, build social hierarchies, industrialize, politicize, stress, stress, stress. Down here in our world, the human mind matured quicker, bypassing man's tendency on the surface to make war. Don't get me wrong. I don't mean your ancestors were all bad. Your culture discovered so much from conflict. As you pointed out, Mathew; look at your race to space. Why, out of that alone came so many things, miniaturizations, medical applications, vaccines, Nanite research, and the electronics explosion. But you always had a fear of total annihilation. And your history records tell us that even that threat just generated political gain, especially in the 1950s through the 1990s to sidestep a Soviet war. War has been the most profitable venture of surface humanity. Otherwise, you would have never discovered the many facets of the atom, itself. And let us admit it, out of your wars grew your knowledge of physics' incredible quantum theory. No, it has not been all bad, just considerably slower and murky at times. Of course, you did have to propagate to replace all those you killed in wars; all that knowledge from all those people you destroyed in each being. Who knows how many Einstein's are gone now, not to mention the constant effort to re-teach the children what the last generation learned? Quite a waste of time when you think about it, no?"

Bellos and Richard remained speechless. Swanson smiled and patted Richard's back. "Richard; do try and remember. The truth is, Mathew, we have never made war down here; nor have we had any conflict between us like humans have on the surface. We bypassed all that like your freeways avoid the congestion of inner-city traffic. The fact is we answered many of the questions which you are only now starting to research. We learned to respect life much sooner. We found the issues of hunger, utility, ethics, morals, and curiosity itself are all matters of healthcare, improving the human condition. With good health comes progress in all aspects of life. Today, your people and mine may start to come together. You see, we have been working for a very long time on 'eternal life.' These microscopic life forms, over millennia, have been a basis for our discovering many new and wondrous things; things you must learn. Sorry, I can be a bit long-winded at times." Swanson studied the doctor's expression. "Then again, consider this. By the time we did start going to the surface, we had realized how much better off we were down here. We preferred our way of life. We invited very few of you from surface-earth to partake in our culture, but they couldn't adjust, and we sent them back up there. Conversely, as I said; over the centuries, those of us who did choose to venture up there, well, it was a one-way trip."

Bellos raised an eyebrow in question, as Swanson spoke sternly to him. "That's right; your society killed them, doctor. They killed every single person in history who ever let it be known they had our secrets of life to share with you."

Then, the GGM backed off and took a breath. "Anyway, over centuries, we developed a recruiting system, which involved selecting only people on the surface with the right genetic make-up. Today, there has to be a damn good genetic reason we approach anyone on the surface. Of course, you will fill in many gaps as time passes; but, way back then, there were very few ways up to the surface, and that in itself was motivation enough to prosper down here? Come through here. Follow me."

Bellos hung on every word. "Wait a minute. Are you saying no one from here has ever stayed topside and lived? Come on. And what you are describing is a bit too Shangri-La-ish, utopian. I don't believe it."

Swanson smiled. "Oh, yes, *Shangri-La*; I read that book a very long time ago, and I saw the movie, starring Ronald Coleman, I believe. But that took place in the Himalayas. I can tell you this. Way before you started assassinating our ambassadors, before humans up there recorded time, there were dinosaurs, and then the Ice Age. The weather alone kept us down here. However, here is the big thing, doctors. We discovered that once you give people light, oxygen and food, basic needs, they seem to sense their self-worth sooner. They do not get lazy, as your pompous ass western media purport. Every person here naturally develops his or her talents and skills, which are what have driven our culture to surpass the surface in so many ways. We are far from utopian. We are just efficient." Swanson sighed and took a breath. "Another thing, up there you grew up with time cycles as your frame of reference for all behavior. We do not have anything like that. You have sunlight-day and moonlight-night, both repeating and repeating. Face it; you have 'habituated' your lives into cyclic behaviors. You only allow yourselves to produce or achieve what 'they' tell you. And do not get me started on who *they* are up there. Let us agree that that's your culture."

Bellos looked like he was going to argue, so Swanson gestured him to stop. "And yes, we know the cycles of work that you live by have become necessary for you. As I said, we do not see sunlight. It is relative, I suppose, but topside is certainly different from down here. I do not judge. Live and let live, I say. You know, war and let war. Besides, even today, no one floods the Mongolian tundra with tourism. So, our people kept on with life and living; and, just when you don't expect it, life gives you wonder. These life forms have been below here long before anything was on the surface. They evolved, too. Today, they are much more than the basis for our light, food, oxygen, and transportation; a lot more. We owe them so much."

"Transportation?" Richard looked as if he remembered something.

"Yes," Swanson said. "That's right. Remember? Our transportation is based on magnetic energy. Frankly, down here a lot is. As some of these microscopic creatures grow, their metabolism changes and they can utilize the earth's internal magnetic forces to move at any speed they want."

Richard interrupted, "Wait. It is a bit fuzzy, but I do remember something. The adult creatures; they are called Carriers, right? They travel fast, deep within the earth across the globe, right?"

"Hmm?" Bellos raised an eyebrow. "Dad, you mean like the Asian speed trains all across the Far East?"

Swanson looked at them both with a grin and said, "Not exactly, my boy; our Carriers are much faster and far more maneuverable than a train or plane. I assure you, there are certainly no train rails of any kind down here. Now it is true that, like in some surface vehicles, we use petroleum-based materials for many applications, just not for transportation. We refine oil differently down here. Any by-products end up as food for these creatures, rather than toxic waste. Look you two; you are the only new ones I have brought here in a very long time. You two will know what very few here know, and that is for an excellent reason."

"Oh, and what is that?" asked Bellos.

"Whatever I've told you is true, gentlemen, and there is a lot more. We are not just a small group of outcasts or a sect of some sort. Our culture and its Posts are now global, not just isolated below certain cities. We are a subterranean world-wide society. You are surface inhabitants, and we are sub-surface inhabitants."

Bellos looked puzzled again. "Global? You mean you live under all of us?"

Swanson replied, "Yes, we are a planetary society, but subterranean. We even have settlements miles below the great oceans. Think about that. The barometric pressures alone should keep you wondering. Regardless, our transport system is far too travel-friendly and efficient for you or anyone from above to comprehend."

"Well, you are right about that, because I have no idea what you mean. It's all a bit difficult to remember or follow," said Bellos.

"Doctor, I don't expect you to understand everything I say right now, but I do expect you to remember most of it. If your cultures up there knew we were down here and how extensive we inhabit the planet, they would panic. That is the nature of your upbringing, fear of the unknown. You are all afraid of someone or something taking what you think belongs to you. Too many of you view cooperation as more of a concept or goal, rather than a way of life. Little by little, we help change that."

"You know, Mr. Swanson, I'm beginning to think you may have some anger management issues," Bellos said with a smirk.

Swanson grinned and replied, "Yes, well, perhaps to a degree; but, unfortunately, we have to postpone this part of our conversation. We three are on a timetable. You, me, your father, we are not like most others here. We have been chosen, cryptic term, I know, but frankly, I'm done with the seminar for now. Please, follow me."

"What does all that mean, for God's sake?" Bellos asked.

Swanson moved to his left, reaching for the glass door. "It means I brought you here for one purpose, doctors, and I have told you what that is already. Now, let us begin."

Swanson opened the glass door and led the two into what Bellos thought was a huge, pristine warehouse. In one direction were enclosed modular rooms, one next to the other like show booths in a large convention hall. In another direction, there was a medical clean room manufacturing operation. Bellos tried to focus on what looked like a giant laboratory with futuristic medical equipment. Levitating above some tables were functioning organs and stunning colorful holograms, torsos, legs, even full moving human bodies. The entire area was beautifully carpeted, tastefully decorated, and, of course, the lighting was the same as throughout the cavern.

"Mr. Swanson," Bellos said, "exactly how big is this place anyway?"

"Actually, inner earth offers a much larger inhabitable terrain than that on the surface," Swanson giggled. "Sorry; my mind wandered. This area is roughly 50,000 square feet, I think."

Bellos looked impressed. "In either case, though, what's the population? How many people are here?"

"Mathew, you are way ahead of yourself. Please focus. Try to pay attention to what I present; and, do try to stay calm. We all have much to discuss. Save it for later. Remember, first things first. Agreed? Good."

As they walked awestruck through the broad area, a man and a woman approached and greeted the GGM.

"Good morning, GGM; and good morning to you, sirs."

Both doctors wore white fabric lab coats, which just did not look right to Bellos. "Dad, there is something about their coats."

"Yes, I do believe they are glowing?" Richard said.

Swanson interrupted, "Dr. Bellos, Dr. Richard, this is Dr. LuAnne Rather and Dr. Andrew Pine, whom you met earlier."

"Hello again, sir," Richard smiled and shook his hand. "I hope you are a real person now."

"I'm leaving you two here for a bit," Swanson said. "You are in good hands. When you finish, you can push the fob, I gave you. I will return to pick you up. Please, be as attentive as you can." He smiled and walked out the door at the far end of the area.

"Well, we should get started. You may call me LuAnne, or Dr. LuAnne if you like."

Dr. Andrew fidgeted a bit and said, "W-welcome to 'Eh-Ever-Life' one-Lab-202; um. W-we are 'care holders' and 'group examiners'; um. W-we are going t-to; um."

"Oh, for God's sake, Andy," LuAnne interrupted. "You two must be buzzing with questions by now. If we let you ask, we wouldn't accomplish a thing today, and it is critical that you two give us a few minutes; so, if it's alright with you?"

Bellos and Richard shrugged.

"Alright then; to start with, Andy and I are 'care holders' of this lab section. We manage and perform special advanced medical procedures within the worldwide Ever-Life umbrella. Please follow me."

"Ever-Life umbrella?" questioned Richard.

Dr. LuAnne smiled. "Yes, in fact, in the entire world, you are the first patients today. Don't be shocked. The program is quite reliable and always evolving. It started close to 10,000 years ago. Hmm, how do I put this?"

Bellos interrupted as they walked, "Can you tell me something, doctor?"

"If I can, certainly."

"Well, Mr. Swanson said you all were global. Does everyone speak English?"

"Yes, as a matter of fact; as far as I know, we all speak pretty much every used language on the planet surface. It is fundamental. We are all able to share and learn knowledge between us. Master Swanson could give you details on that, though."

"But, how do you learn it all?"

Dr. Andrew looked at Bellos and grinned. "You will see."

"Come this way," Dr. LuAnne said. "Please, try not to let your mind wander too much. Over there, that area, that is OGD—Organ, Growth and Donate."

"Can we go over there?" asked Richard. "It looks familiar."

LuAnne gently urged them onward. "Later, if time permits, yes, of course. This Ever-Life facility consists of about 50,000 square feet of atomic, viral, cellular and final function organic growth. We research, evaluate, apply all manner of genetic biochemistry and microbiology to improve and extend life. We have records of all known life, some dating back approximately 500-million years. I know that must sound fantastic, but we utilize our data banks of genetic indexing to interpolate history of both plants and animals. We can grow almost anything organic or fungi. Over there, we seed cells of a recipient, and then we produce partial or complete organs. Then, we implant. Quite basic here."

"Well," Bellos bragged, "on the surface, we have researched and successfully grown various body parts. Some have been used in cosmetic surgery, kidney, liver and some heart applications. And we can attach limbs given certain circumstances."

"Yes, we know, doctor. Down here, that kind of thing has been standard for a long time. We can supply the needs of any person or animal. We even use insect and fungus DNA, when appropriate. Genetics and miniaturization have been the foundation of all our work for millennia."

Bellos could not be quiet. "You mean you transplant organs at will?"

"Yes of course; we do most micro, cell or tissue transplants or transfers daily, hourly. We have eliminated most genetic mistakes, diseases, and indeed most common ailments, as well as organ failures."

Bellos took a deep breath and shook his head looking at everything. "Incredible, just amazing, what is the lifespan here? How do you perform heart transplants? What are all those holograms? Can I just ask you about your coats? Are they glowing?"

"Our coats?" LuAnne laughed. "Why, yes; no, not really. I suppose, to you they glow. Here everything does really. We do not see the glow anymore. Do you, Andy?"

"Um, nope."

"You see, our coats are white too; so, I'm sure that enhances the effect. Anyway, I am sure you have hundreds of questions, but try to let me finish. We also grow organs within a body, human or otherwise; but it is more than that. You see, we can even grow whole bodies; again, based on compatible genetics, of course. Here, genetics is everything. Growing organs isn't that difficult once you have gone through our iterations."

"My God!" Richard said. "How is that possible? Is that what I am?"

The two men listened to Dr. Lu in wonder. "Our GGM has briefed us about you two; so, we are authorized to say the following: We do grow bodies, but they are not cloning as you would describe medically. We produce both males and females; however, unlike cloning efforts on the surface, ours have a complete DNA sequence. Although we can also alter the DNA, in certain structural chains, we cannot duplicate a person's memory. Therefore, we must accelerate the 'newborn's' learning process. That is what we are going to do here with your father. He is your dad, complete in every detail physically; but he has memory voids, and . . ." She looked at Richard. "...I'm afraid, as far as we know, you always will. So, one of the things we do here is to endeavor to fill some of those voids. That is why you are here today. Will you help us, son of Dr. Richard Bellos? It's completely painless, I assure you."

Mathew looked at the doctors and his father. "Why, yes. I'll do anything. But how will my dad get all the other memories he needs?"

"Follow me," Luanne said. "In here, I'll show you."

"Mathew," said his father, "I do keep having memory flashes of being part of all this; but they are fragments. It is so strange. Some things I see, I definitely remember, but others are cloudy and vague. Things come and go."

"That is a good start," LuAnne said. "Dr. Bellos, you sit here, and Dr. Richard, you here, facing your son. Here are headsets for you. Just place them on comfortably."

Bellos examined his device. "Our worlds aren't that different. I have a pair like this at home."

"Not like these, believe me. I have prepared them for just this effort. Now relax, you two. Listen, you are not in an experimental surface hospital. What happens here is not an experiment at all. It's a medical procedure and a painless one at that. So, are we ready?"

The two took a deep breath, and Dr. LuAnne touched their shoulders. "I realize this may appear futuristic to you both, but it's simple, principally. You, Dr. Bellos, have many memories of your father. These headsets will allow your mind to talk to your dad's mind, and he will remember what you say. That's it. He will have filled in many memories he wants but does not have right now. Does that make any sense to you?"

Bellos nodded and asked, "What if we learn something neither of us wants the other to know? Is Dad going to know everything I know and vice versa?"

"No. Think of it as a computer program. There are limits. We are building your father's memories. He already knows about you. It is remarkable programming, how and what information transfers. The ability to do this depends on brain DNA; again, genetics."

Richard and Bellos looked at each other, and then Bellos said, "What about his memories of this place, and the rest of his life?"

Dr. Lu clarified. "Memory has to be transferred in stages, doctor. This is only your first session. Richard, you will be back several times."

Dr. LuAnne stood between them. With her arms outstretched, she looked like the letter 'T.' Then, the two men felt her fingers lightly tap their headsets. "Okay, that's it, gentlemen. You can give me the headsets back." She giggled. "I told you, you wouldn't feel anything."

"I don't understand," Bellos said.

"Doctors," Dr. Andrew offered. "Can you feel a thought? And remember, light isn't the fastest thing; thought is."

"Not when I have a headache," Bellos chuckled.

"So, now what? What's different about me, then?" Richard asked.

"I don't know. You should remember something you didn't before. That's all we have for you two today," Dr. Lu said. "I hope we didn't frighten you."

They all heard a buzz from Dr. LuAnne's waist. "Oops, that's me. I have to answer it. You two should page the GGM now. You see that doorway over there?" She pointed opposite from the way they entered. "Yes, there. That's 'Knofer' reception for this Ever-Life section. The GGM will meet you there."

"*Knofer*?" said Bellos. "What's that?"

"It's just a term we use a lot here, 'Knofer' [know-fer]. Thank you, gentlemen. I am afraid we must part for the time being. Goodbye for now."

Bellos and Richard turned and walked to the doorway filled with amazement. Bellos pushed the fob in his pocket and, by the time they reached reception, GGM Gordon Swanson walked in.

"Hello, lads. I trust you had a fascinating visit. Do you have any questions?" He rolled his eyes and snickered as he opened the exit door. Bellos and his dad both started talking at the same time. Swanson raised his arms, as though he was stopping traffic. "Alright, one at a time, please! I know it is all a bit overwhelming. Let us get a bite to eat; and, Richard needs a drink. We'll go across the center scope there, to the food station and talk."

"I don't know where to begin," Bellos said. "Okay, first, about those gadgets there on your belt. So many people are talking into them. They project holograms too. What is a Knofer?"

"Hah! Well, you pick up quickly, Mathew. Here, look at this."

Swanson handed him the small object. "Knofer is a universal term, implying knowledge. But mostly, it refers to what you are holding."

"It reminds me of old cell phones on the surface."

"Well, I suppose you could say it is a ten-thousandth generation cell-phone."

Bellos scrutinized it carefully. It was a dull, silver gray color; oval, with an inner transparent body that swiveled on a blind axis. One end curved up a tad if one laid it on a table.

"Very comfortable to the touch; it's almost weightless, isn't it?"

There were no numbers or buttons anywhere on it; just a few small unrecognizable characters and what looked like a tiny red lens, not quite at one end.

"I give up," said Bellos, turning it over. "How does it work?"

They stopped just long enough for Swanson to take the Knofer, place it in front of his mouth, and say, "GGM-001."

After it had ticked, Swanson handed it back to Bellos.

"Would you like to know something? About something? Anything? Go ahead, ask. Speak into it, there."

"You are kidding?"

"You can ask it any question. That one has a record of most relevant knowledge."

"Relevant knowledge, what does that mean?"

Swanson clarified. "It means you can use a Knofer as a communicator, or as a library. It gives you access to all knowledge, or you can use it as a 3D projector of any image. We dictate or create a task for it to perform; here, let me have it."

Swanson spoke into it, "By authority of GGM-001-21839, this Knofer transfers to Dr. Mathew J. Bellos. There; now it is yours. Hold it up. Look at the red dot and say your name."

Bellos did.

"There. It is done. By my authorization and you looking into it, you have transferred all facts that you know into your Knofer. Now, you own that one. You need it anyway. The security is quite reliable. I see no reason to dally with some things. Now let's eat. This way. Oh, and all Knofers are defensive weapon capable; in your case, not activated yet."

Bellos scratched his head. "What? But what is it made of? Does it only respond to voice commands? How do I work it? I see now why you said I'd be asking 'what' a lot. And what are you going to use now? Where's yours?"

"Mine is right here." Swanson pulled out two more from his pocket and gave one to Richard as well.

"As I told you two, we are on a schedule. You both have a briefing about all Knofers in one hour. Don't forget to ask all your questions then. Come on; we need food."

It was years ago when that all took place, and now Bellos snapped out of it in the Andrews elevator. "Well, break's over."

He pushed three again, and the elevator started up to Focus Ward.

CHAPTER 7: ANGIE'S DISCOVERY

ANGIE ESPOSITO AND THE GUARD walked out of the elevator to Dr. Mathew Bellos' office on the 10th floor of Andrews Hospital. They stopped just outside his door, and Angela mimicked a cough, spitting the rest of the tranquilizer pill that Dr. B. gave her onto her sleeve. She looked at the guard and wiped her mouth.

"So, this is it, right? Should I be honored or am I in real trouble here?"

"You are just fine," the guard said.

Once inside, the two stood looking down two steps into an oval-shaped living room approximately 30-feet by 20-feet.

The guard smiled at Angie and turned to leave. "I will be right outside, Miss, if you need me. Dr. Bellos said you might order anything you like from the kitchen. Just use the wall-phone over there."

"Thank you." Angie smiled as he closed the door behind him. She turned and studied the remarkable room. The floor was clean dark teak wood, partially covered with a large Persian rug. During the years she had worked at Andrews, she never went into Bellos' office, although she did visit his home outside the Complex on occasion. She noticed the walls were a color-coordinated subdued beige, with just a hint of gold specks that sparkled. The big couch in the living room had a striking combination of gold and white patterns and mahogany wood feet, carved meticulously with unrecognizable characters. The other chairs and tables were striking as well with the same very articulate wood carving patterns. They seemed to tell a story reminding Angie of ancient Egyptian hieroglyphics. Masterful oil paintings were hanging on the walls, and bookshelves lined the two hallways that extended out from the main room. Angie stepped down from the foyer turning and studying everything. The walls curved around the floor, with a chandelier in the middle of the ceiling, which extended as if it were floating in the center of a dome Oculus, made of beveled and stained glass. Where the ceiling met the walls, there were strategically placed lamps that shined into the room and illuminated the glass designs of the four seasons. For a moment, she felt as if there was a touch of the church in Bellos' heart. Captivated by everything, she studied the oil paintings, remembering her college classes in art history and the trips abroad she had taken at Dr. B.'s expense.

"Manet? This painting is an original by Edouard Manet, and this is Renoir, and this one's a Matisse. They're spectacular! This is not just an office, is it, doc? How did you get all this stuff? And security cameras in every corner; not much privacy."

Between the two hallways and the front foyer, there was an unmistakable floor to ceiling glass bookcase shaped in the gothic art of the Middle Ages. Angie examined the books on the shelves. "Jesus, these are priceless medical reference books."

She opened a cabinet door and thumbed through several books.

"English, French, Latin, Greek, even Hebrew; and that's Aramaic, I think, maybe Chinese? I should have gotten my college textbooks here. And these look like Egyptian or South American Indian symbols. Who can read this stuff?"

One of the back bindings on the top shelf caught her eye. It seemed to glow.

"What the heck is that?"

There were only three letters on its binding, *J.A.S.* She found a step stool in the corner, and, even standing on her tiptoes, Angie barely could reach under the book to cause it to fall on the floor. The book had a beautiful pearl white leather binding with shiny, large gold embossed lettering on the front cover. It simply read *John Avuar Sheldon*. She picked it up, took it to the couch, and opened it to the front page.

"It feels brand new. I wonder what 'DP-111249' means?"

Just then, she heard the front door lock click. She had just enough time to shove the book behind her. The guard opened the door and asked, "Are you okay, Miss? I heard a thump. I thought you might have fallen."

"Yes, I'm fine; thanks. I tripped and hit the table, looking around at all of this. I'm sorry."

"Please, be careful. Can I do anything for you?"

"Um, yes, as a matter of fact. I need several things from my purse."

"I'm sorry, Miss. I cannot leave. I can call someone to get it for you."

"That would be great. Can you get in touch with Nurse Ralph Walker? He is staff on floor two. If you would ask him to go to my nurse locker 203? He knows where it is. Ask him to bring me my large gray bag."

"Yes, Miss."

He smiled and shut the door. Angie picked up the book again, stood up and walked back into the hallway to find a private spot to read. She did not turn on lights, trying to keep out of the security cameras vision. She intended only to glance into each room, as she passed by; but the first one was the doctor's bedroom, and she couldn't resist going in. Behind the large bed, there was an enormous bay window overlooking the hospital's atrium.

His suite was huge and had an adjacent bath with a sunken tub and power rain shower. Thoughts raced through her mind. *"What beautiful carvings in the bedposts. They're the same as the ones in the living room...the same as on all the furniture."*

Then, she noticed a small book on the nightstand. The cover read, **Language of the Carriers.** She opened it and saw characters like the carvings on the other furniture. Under one of the pictures it read, 'Carriers shall travel beyond the stars.' "My God! What is all this?"

Also, on the table and above the lamp on the wall were several photographs of Angie. *"That's me; that's me in middle school, and that's my medical school graduation. Dr. B, you were there, but why are these pictures here like this?"*

Puzzled and anxious, she put the small book back down on the table and walked out and into the next room and found a completely furnished research laboratory. She commented, "This has more equipment than most of the research sections in the Complex."

Directly across the hall from the lab was a computer room, containing three levitating paper-thin monitors and four L-shaped computers sitting on a wrap-around wooden desk. And likewise, the monitors and furniture had the same strange beautiful hieroglyphics. One item that stood out on the desk was a solid gold paperweight resembling a giant goldfish or Koi standing upright on its tail. The statue had a strange word etched on its base, *Allenfar.*

Each of the computer monitors displayed video and an audio tape tracing across the bottom of the screen. Each tape showed a different international time zone and displayed a different language. Two tapes were running characters that looked like all the hieroglyphics.

Angie walked out and further down the hall. In a second bathroom, there was just enough moonlight to sit on the commode, open the big white book and read. There was no copyright or publisher on the first pages. Page 5 began:

"The following is a duplication [DP] record of subject J.A.S. instructed by Ever-Life examiners 10362 and 10365, Lab-202, Level-red-16, this day-3635996.46."

After ten pages, Angie began to skim, but by page 50, she whispered to herself, "My God, maybe that **was** Jack Sheldon in 309."

As her eyes wandered, she saw a security camera in the ceiling's corner behind the sink. Dr. B., you watch yourself in the bathroom?" She rolled her eyes and whispered, "This can't be happening! I know what I saw and heard tonight on Focus Ward. Shit, what should I do? I have to tell someone. The person in 309 did look like Jack Sheldon, one of the big three, Bellos, Jack, and Rachel.

She had an idea. "Rachel! Dr. Jack's wife; she is a doctor too. She must know something. I have to see her."

Angie went out to the oval room. She put the book back on the shelf, got a glass of water and sat on the couch, pondering. "I need Ralphy. I know I can trust him. I know he will help. If not, then what?"

She looked up and fixed on a door in the front foyer that she hadn't noticed before. It was an elevator. Curiously, she walked over, pushed a button next to it on the wall, and the door slid open. "Why, Dr. B., you have a private elevator. According to this panel, there are 26- floors in the hospital. Everyone knows there are only 16. And what is Red-6?"

She pushed number one on the panel, but nothing happened. She pushed all the numbers repeatedly, nothing. "Damn! Maybe Ralphy can fiddle with this thing. He is good with electrical stuff."

Angie walked out and retook the white book. "The hell with it."

She said to herself. "What are they going to do to me anyway? Dr. B. told the guard to give me anything I want."

So, she took a breath and began reading from page one.

CHAPTER 8:   RACHEL AND JACK

ONLY THOSE WHO HAVE LOST TRUE LOVE can begin to imagine the emotions that flooded Rachel Sheldon. She awoke in ER-1 shaking, not knowing how much time had passed, with an overwhelming sense that she must get home. After calling and paging Bellos several times, she decided to drive the 10 miles to their ranch, but she wasn't prepared for the uncontrollable body shakes and tears that flooded her. Add to that, she was still under the effects of the sedative Bellos gave her, so, to say the least, it was a stressful drive home. When she finally arrived, she sat in the driveway; sweating, staring at nothing, thinking; *I rushed home to what?*

She made it to the couch in their living room, sank into the cushions and closed her eyes. Then, as if something unreal propelled her, she exploded off the sofa and ran through the house searching and gathering photos of family history. With her arms full and carrying three old albums, she dumped it all on the living room coffee table and sat to catch her breath. Then she made piles and tearfully studied each photo. "That's Jack and me in our downstairs lab. What are you doing, silly? This other one was from the banquet when we got the second check for the new funding from Marion. What a night; a lot of money, Jack. We never did finish the details of all that." She squinted and looked again. "My God, who is that in the background? It can't be! That has to be a mistake."

She put the one picture aside and began rearranging others. She found three more. "I must be going mad."

She left the rest in piles and studied the four carefully. Two were from Jack's cell phone; one was from Rachel's; and one was from Marion Brock's camera. She ran to the bedroom and got their old family computer pad. It seemed hours for the damn thing to start. It only took her five minutes to screen, upload and enhance the four photos. There was no question. "Oh, my God, it is Jack . . . You are there, and there, in the same photo twice. Why didn't I notice this before? You appear twice in each of these. It has to be a double exposure."

Rachel Sheldon had four undergraduate degrees, two master's degrees, and she received her Ph.D. in microbiological processing. On this day, at this time, in this intensity, she needed to bring every intellectual wherewithal she possessed to make any sense of this. Rachel took a deep breath and began again, slowly trying to reconstruct this odd puzzle; and it looked like there was a nightmare of impossibilities. She picked up the computer and studied each of the pictures with a magnifying glass.

"Jack, what's happened? Jesus, this can't be right, for God's sake!" She stood up, paced the room, and then it came to her. "Shit! Jack, your research."

She ran to the downstairs lab and muddled through his desk and files. She found his manuscript. "It has new pages, a lot of new pages . . . Christ!"

As she opened the book, she thought back to when he first told her about it.

Jack had first created his theory decades ago. However, it was not until March of the first year they met that Jack felt something he never had before; so, he began to share his work with her. He trusted her with all of it.

Way back then, she had stopped by Jack's lab to find him puttering with a microscope and writing feverishly. She bubbled with excitement and began to banter.

"Hi, honey. It's 7:30 p.m. I thought you would have hit me up for dinner by now.

"Hi! I was going to. Just give me a minute."

"Whatcha doing?" She said with a flirty smirk. "Something I can help you with, doctor; hmm?"

Jack smiled, looked up and squinted. "Yes, you can tell me what you think. But and I mean this, only if you are willing to be serious. Then, I promise dinner and whatever you want."

"Hmm, sounds like I'll pull out the chaps and hat for you, baby. Woohoo, cowboy!"

They grinned at each other, and then Rachel changed her tone.

"Fine, what is it?"

"Something I've had on my mind and toying with since I was very young. It is the reason I got into medicine. We all have our pet projects, and this is mine. I would like you to know about it and see what you think."

"Okay; but why the mystery?"

"I'm just possessive about it and haven't shared this with anyone."

"In that case, I am flattered darling'."

"Okay, well, you know how we all talked in college about the Universe and life. You remember those days?"

"Yes, of course, I do. My first real love was Ben Verona. He was so macho and smart, philosophically speaking. He knew all the theories of the time about the Universe. Oh my, but, Ben Verona. Just his name, I mean, no, sorry."

Jack giggled. "Alright, just listen to me. When I'm done, then you can do what you do." He could not help rolling his eyes. "I've been playing with my pet on a regular basis all these years, you know.

"Very funny."

"My fundamental notion has always been that the unique human personality is a single chemical cocktail. It's the sum-total of impulses acquired from our senses and our genetics. As we grow, we may or may not recall certain additional memories; but whether we do or not, our mind records each memory permanently. Nothing is ever lost; hence our individuality, our unique quality. Memories make us who we are."

Rachel cocked her head and winked. "Impressive, if I wanted psychobabble. What's your point?"

"To extend life," Jack said.

"Ha, that's what we all want as doctors, my love."

"If you expect me to explain, be serious."

"Fine," Rachel said, "our personality is one great chemical cocktail, go on."

"Unique, honey, not great, unique cocktail; and I am trying to summarize. Didn't you ever wonder why several people can look at the same event and when they recall it, no two individuals remember it the same way? That's why courtroom dramas need more than one witness, understand?"

Rachel rolled her eyes and quipped, "Uh-uh, really annoying so far."

"Anyway, our memories make up our personality. And that is stored as a chemical cocktail in our brain. Most of us think our mind is an unlimited hard drive, inputting from our senses as a computer does with its programs. But, it's not just our senses that contribute to our unique personality. Our mind also records all genetic information stored in our cells. The brain remembers how each cell functions and then it instructs and directs those needs, so everything runs smoothly, correctly. The brain must remember and process what the trillions of cells send to it every millisecond. Understand?"

"Yes DEAR, I UNDERSTAND! I thought you were summarizing. Huh, you sound like details in a textbook. We are both doctors, Jack. I don't think people care much about this unless they're sick."

"Just follow me. Cells communicate by sending synaptic impulses from one to the other. Their electrical impulses transmit through our chemistry. We remember, unconsciously, what each cell reports, upgrading that memory with every new sensation, taste, touch, etc."

"Oh sure, Jack, most everyone assumes that; and if they don't, why would they want to?"

"You miss the point," Jack said.

Sorry. So, you're saying I'm a glass containing one hell of a mixed drink," Rachel giggled.

"Yes, sort of; but where is it, and what is the drink? Are you a screwdriver or a Bloody Mary? They taste very different. Listen, Rach, I think I can define which drink you are and then extract the mix. I have found a way to move the cocktail to a different glass, or at least take it out and then put it back in, assuming one's genetics allow it."

"Okay, Dr. Bartender Frankenstein, ooh... Jack, honey, are you serious about this? I mean . . ."

"Listen to me; the brain is a mechanism that does nothing more than send and receive electrical or chemical impulses. Whether it is a body function, choice behavior or thought, every action requires a synaptic signal. That signal is an instruction, directed to and then by our memory; and, our memory is continually updating. It's a library of knowledge stored in the physical brain as a chemical cocktail. As we add learning, the mixture changes, yes; but it is always there in the same place. The challenge is to define the mix and, if we can, we can extract it, move it."

"Jack, sweetie, let's say I play along. How do you define the mix?"

"Well, first, fundamentally by reading and studying the electrical and chemical signals, the synaptic exchanges. I had to create a synaptic alphabet. Frankly, I started with something like the old Morse code, and then it evolved from neurology to physics, and back to chemistry. Anyway, I did create the new language. Finally, I translated that synaptic language into the right chemistry."

"Morse code was used in the 1800s," Rachel reacted. "A very long time ago. They were telegraph taps—dots and dashes, SOS. I don't follow you yet. But, let's say you did this. Where exactly is the language stored? And even if you found it—our personality, how do you obtain it and extract it? How do you know you got it all and not just a portion? For Christ's sake, Jack, honey, come on."

Jack had been trying to explain in the simplest of terms, but it was not going well. So, while he listened to Rachel's critique, he walked to his desk, pulled out a 2-inch thick manuscript from the bottom drawer and handed it to her. Rachel raised her eyebrows and opened it to the first page.

***"CPT–Chemical Personality Transfer**. You wrote this?"*

"Yep, you know me, babe. My presentations are not stage-worthy all the time, so just read it. That is my journal and findings, the complete text of the hypothesis, equations, final formulas, and results. It's everything. I believe that it speaks to all your microbiologic questions. Just read a little and then tell me what you think."

Rachel opened it to the middle and read a page. After a minute, she looked at Jack, flipped to the front of the book again, and sat down at his desk. After five minutes of reading and concentrating, she said, "Honey, can you get me some coffee and a donut, please? Then, get lost for a while, okay?"

Jack smiled and did as instructed. He went back to his microscope and writing at his lab table. Rachel was mesmerized from what she read, and after a half hour or so, Jack mumbled to himself, "I haven't heard her say nothing this long since I met her."

Finally, she called to him, "You found where it is? Jack, okay, you write here, '...Any bodily function, whether cellular or thought, requires an impulse—a synaptic signal, to and from the brain. The mind instantaneously sends a directive to the hypothalamus, our brain factory that makes peptides...' Okay, then you say, 'These peptides are manufactured as cells or thoughts demand...' Okay, reading on, 'Then, they are instantly sent to direct or instruct function or behavior. At the same time, our mind imprints that directive and the resulting behavior in a library of the brain, for reference.'"

Rachel stopped and briefly looked at Jack. "Here. Yes, here it is. 'The library is constantly in a state of flux from learning. It updates and stores the directive memory *in the same place*. In fact, our behaviors and memories make up our primary personality in total. Although ever-evolving, it is that record—a library of repetitive impulses' . . . And then you say . . ."

"Jeez," Jack interrupted, "it sounds exactly like what I told you in the first place, hmm."

Rachel continued. "To quote you, Jack, 'I have located the primary personality vial to be 3.33 by 1.25 centimeters and positioned .134 millimeters around the hypothalamus, partially covering the hippocampus gland, tangent to the Pons.'

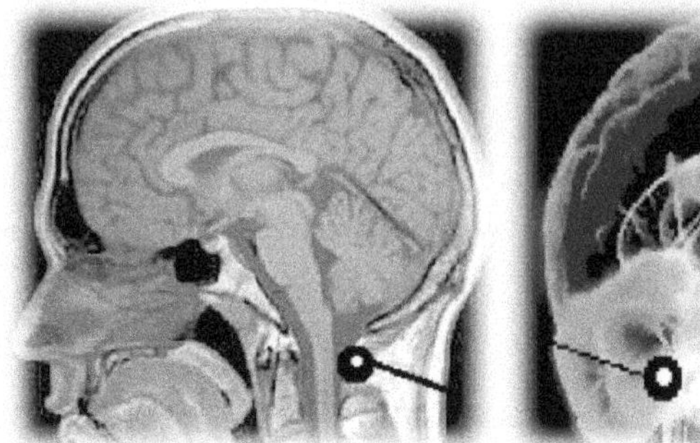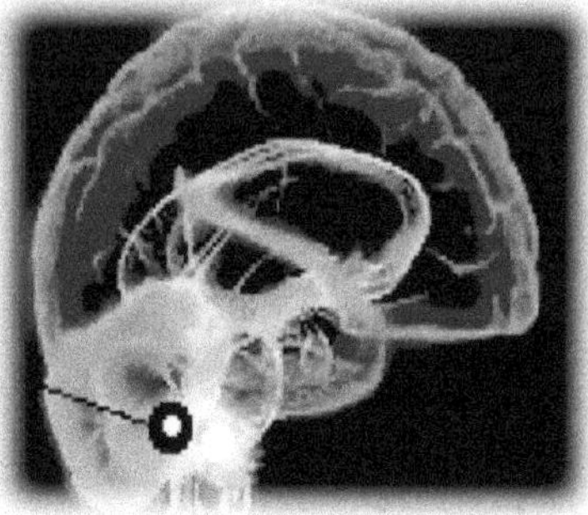

"Too techy for Ya?" Jack asked with a grin.

Rachel just ignored Jack's sarcasm and continued. "You further say, 'It's such an integral part of the cerebral cortex and cerebellum, it can't be defined until at least one hour after death.' Jack, you sound like Descartes in old college philosophy. Are you trying to define the soul, physically?"

"I suppose you could take it that way; but there are no physical limits to the personality, only to the chemistry. I am not a philosopher talking about singular self-awareness. Don't be confused, babe. Chemistry is tangible; but how big is an idea, remember? It is the link between quantum physics and microbiology that enables us to define this chemistry. Honey, it is 9:30 pm. Don't you think it's time for a good meal?"

Rachel sat with her head still in the book and replied, "So what? You started this. It's Friday, and we can do whatever I want, you said."

She waved him off aloofly and read feverishly. After a while, she blurted out, "Jack, look at me! I can't believe this. Your equations and calculations, the physics and biology are solid. Are you serious? The implications are staggering. Even the results you have so far mean that if you are right, we could define, isolate, and contain a person's personality chemistry. If we do that, and, considering recent medical breakthroughs, am I right? We could transfer a terminally ill person into a healthy body."

"Exactly. Or back into his own body." Jack grinned and walked across the room, around the desk and sat on it, facing her. "That's why I love you so, babe. You are way ahead of me sometimes. Of course, it is a bit more complicated; but it only took you two hours to get what it took me years to understand, and you haven't read it all. Look at you."

Rachel looked up at Jack with love, so excited. "I see most of the proofs are good and reliable. Others could use some work; but, yes, I think . . . Huh, I agree."

Jack nudged her, and their eyes locked. "I love you, Rachel. I did from the first minute, the first argument. I can't picture doing this, or anything else in my life without you, honey."

With those words and a tear, Jack reached down and opened the top drawer of his desk. There, glistening was a radiant 1.5-carat diamond ring. Jack took the ring out, and he held her left hand gently. As he moved off the desk to her side, he knelt, positioning himself slightly between her legs.

"Rachel Anne Tomas, will you marry me? I love you so. Please be mine through all the good, bad, happy and hard times?"

Rachel's eyes filled with tears as Jack put the ring on her finger.

"Who knows, Rach, maybe together we can make everyone else's time here better too?"

"Oh my, Jack, oh yes, my love, my only."

Jack brought her close; and, as he rose, they embraced and kissed, holding each other in a oneness that would last beyond their understanding at that moment.

That was years ago. Back in their home study, Rachel shook her head and snapped back to reality, remembering the horrific night. She looked at Jack's manuscript and flipped through it thinking, *this is so much thicker.*

She turned to the new pages in the back. "Holy shit! Jack, we never discussed any of this. There have to be some results here, some proof."

Then it hit her. "I have to see Jack. And my God, what about Brian. I haven't talked to our son about anything."

Rachel picked up her cell phone and dialed Brian. The call automatically forwarded to the Brock Building in Bethesda, Maryland. Marion Brock had one rule above all others, *Speak person to person.* Except for his private home, there were no long tedious message services anywhere throughout his multi-billion-dollar empire. Instead, a secretary always answered every incoming number 24/7. "Good morning, Brock building, may I help you?"

"Yes, my name is Rachel Sheldon. I am Brian Sheldon's mother. I am trying to reach him. It is a family emergency. I must speak to him right away."

"Just a moment, Mrs. Sheldon . . ."

Rachel sat exhausted.

"Hello, Mrs. Sheldon. Thank you for waiting. Mr. Brian Sheldon is out of town on a security matter with Mr. Brock. I will contact Mr. Brock and have your son call you as soon as possible. Can you give me time to do that? I will call you back if that's okay with you?"

"That's fine. I appreciate it."

Rachel hung up the phone.

CHAPTER 9: BROCK'S VISIT

BACK IN FOCUS WARD, ROOM 309, after Nurse Angie's exit, Jack Sheldon sat aching, confused, and unwashed. He had massive memory loss, and, in many ways, he was a grown child. Moving slowly off the gurney, he shuffled to the bathroom shaking and sat on the commode looking at the shower stall before him. It hurt relieving himself, but he noticed the ugly scar on his upper right thigh, from a chainsaw accident years ago, was completely gone. He felt physically rejuvenated somehow but confused, with brief seconds of complete disorientation. He got up and slowly stepped into the shower examining the dried blood all over his body. There were no scars, sutures, cuts or bruises anywhere. When he twisted the shower knob to turn on the water, the knob screeched. The normal ear wouldn't have noticed the noise, but to Jack, the squeaking was deafening, stinging, so high-pitched and unbearable, he lost his balance. He grabbed his head in pain, and the rush of water magnified his sense that someone was stabbing into his ears with ice picks. It only lasted a few seconds, but he almost fell over. Thank God for his quick reaction to grab the handicap guardrail. He kept his balance, came to his senses, and began washing off the stench and blood.

"My mind, what the hell happened? Rachel? We were home; I left; I was going to night shift—special duty . . . No, it was a meeting with Bruke. No. It was Brock and Brian; BRIAN, my son. Oh, my God! Brian." Then he clenched his ears again and cried, "The pain, the pain, Christ! I can't think. What the hell is that?"

Jack grabbed the towel, stuffed the ends over his ears, and crouched in the corner, unable to move. The sound was coming from the corridor outside his room. Strange, too, because Room 309 was lead-lined and locked to prevent any security breach.

"Voices!" Jack screamed! "So loud; am I going mad?"

In fact, it was a single voice. Nurse Barb Sawyer was merely whispering to herself as she entered the ward from far down the hallway. "Angie, what were you talking about? There has got to be a reasonable explanation?"

After Bellos had ordered her reassignment, Barb decided to visit Focus Ward and see if anything Angie said made sense. She was roughly 50 feet away and around a corner from Jack's room when she saw two men come out of Angie's office and walk toward her. Both were wearing tailored suits, so she shifted to automatic manners. The older of the two looked in his mid-50s, and he commanded a second look from any woman. The other was a much younger college-age looking man. "Good evening, Barb. I am Marion Brock. This is Brian Sheldon, Jack Sheldon's son. I hope we haven't arrived at too inconvenient a time?"

"Hello," Barb said

"I trust you recognize my name. I remembered you from the award ceremony two years ago. I would never forget a pretty smart lady like you."

"How do you do, Mr. Brock. You have quite a memory. You shocked me, being here like this. Can I help you?"

With a slight smile, Brock replied, "Well, we have been monitoring Brian's dad from another location; and, suddenly, all the readings went dead. So, we came directly here to try to check with the ward nurse. No one has been here since we arrived. The vital monitors read nothing. Naturally, I am concerned, not to mention Brian. We have been in that office unable to communicate with any hospital staff. They keep quite good security up here. Neither the landline phones nor wireless is working. We found out the hard way all the entrances, exits and room doors are locked. How can we find out exactly what is going on; and we would like to see Dr. Sheldon."

"I see. I am a bit confused about how you were monitoring the doctor, but first, let me say how sorry I am that this has happened to you both. You must be quite frustrated. I will help in any way I can. You see, the nurse who normally is here has taken ill. I have been assigned to the ward now; but I will not have authority for the floor until redirect, scheduled for 4 p.m. this afternoon. Until then, I can let you out and show you to Dr. Bellos' office, if that would help. I'm sure he can explain the entire matter."

"I appreciate that; I do. Maybe it would be best if, as your boss, so to speak, we have a little chat before going to see anyone. Have you ever seen one of these?"

Brock handed her a badge she had seen only once before at Andrews from Dr. Bellos and said, "That is my authorization for the entire Complex. Just to be clear and to let you know you are free to talk about anything without fear of reprisal in any way, alright?"

She turned the badge over and examined both sides.

"Please verify it before reacting," Brock added. "That is security protocol."

The three walked back into Angie's office. Barb plugged the badge through the clearance verifier and typed her code into the computer. The monitor brought up a picture of Marion Brock and his complete security clearance. With relief and a sigh, she sat back and looked at the two men. "It has been a night, one I will never forget, sir."

Brock stood up and placed his hand on her shoulder. "I can imagine. Now, can you tell us, what is Dr. Sheldon's condition?"

"I don't know. I was coming up here to check. I assumed the room doors would be open. I, like you, have never been in here. No one knows the actual security measures up here, no one except the ward nurse and Dr. Bellos. I am supposed to be indoctrinated this afternoon. So far, I know the underlying protocol to get in, but that is all. By the way, how did you two get through security?"

"Well, not to make too light of it; but I showed my badge, the guard punched six numbers on the keypad, and the door opened. Do you have access from this computer to the ER or the medical records from earlier this evening?"

"Only if I enter the proper codes, which I won't have until, as I said, redirect at 4 p.m. All medical information is stored immediately in a separate, secure hard drive, which can only be accessed by code. We retain patient records differently than anything else in the Complex."

"Hmm," Brock took a deep breath. "Please, then we should start with what happened tonight, as you know it."

Meanwhile, Jack Sheldon crouched in the shower, painfully listening, wet, and mystified. He repeatedly shouted, "Anyone who's out there . . . Stop it! Please!?"

To him, the conversation became unbearable noise, too much input too soon, and he blacked out.

Brock and Brian continued quizzing Barb, and before she uttered more than two sentences, Brock interrupted her again. "Barb, is there a comfortable waiting room on this floor?"

"Why yes, at the opposite end of the hallway, where I came in."

Brock turned to Brian. "I need a few moments with Barb here, alone. Would you mind waiting for me? I won't be long. Please try to be patient, son. We will get to the bottom of this. I just need to speak to Barb about some highly secure hospital matters. You understand?"

Brian frowned, but he did not say anything. He just turned around and walked out the door to the waiting room.

Brock gestured to Barb. "Please, continue, and feel free that the buck stops here. You have nothing to fear."

Brian Sheldon took advantage of his alone time and walked one slow step at a time, approaching each room door on his way to the lounge. He quietly turned each doorknob he passed. Every single one was locked. He had an overwhelming sense that his father needed him, and he wasn't going to give up. "My God," he said to himself, "the doors; there are no numbers. Where is Room 309? Where's Dad?"

In Angie's office, Barb Sawyer resumed her story, as Brock listened intently and then he questioned, "Barb, do you know what time the car accident happened, exactly?"

"The records indicate a time between 10:15 and 10:30 p.m. I think."

"Okay, do you know the members of the surgical team who worked on Dr. Sheldon?"

She thought a moment. "Dr. Bellos, I'm sure; then there is our Chief of Surgery—a new hire, and an anesthesiologist, along with two nurses and one backup doctor."

"Do you know where they all are now?"

"No, it's been a busy night."

Brock appeared perplexed somehow. He paced, pensively whispering to himself, "Holy crap, Jack . . . Again? I am going to find you."

Then he sat down and listened to Barb finish. She didn't take long, and for Brock, it all fit. He pretended to focus on what she was saying.

"I know the whole thing sounds bizarre, sir, which is why I came here to find, I don't know what; something to verify what the nurse said."

"Barb, you were able to get in here. Can we get out?"

"Yes, I have the passcode, but protocol says I may not disclose it for any reason to anyone. And all passcodes register immediately with the guard station for final clearance."

Brock smiled. "Of course, and I would never request you breach protocol. But I'd like you to go now and take Brian with you. It's only natural that he tried to see his father. I am sure you won't have an issue with the guard."

"But what about you? Hospital security says you can't be here. I don't know if you can get out, once I go. The guard already knows you are here. If you don't have the correct security code to leave . . ."

"I'll be okay. The important thing right now is to get you and Brian safely off this ward. Something is going on, and whatever it is, it started here. Until we all know for sure it's not contagious; I want you two out of harm's way."

"Yes, I didn't think of that."

Brock got up and gently reached for Sawyer's shoulders. "Barb, after you get out, take Brian to my flat. It's in the Fargo building on the southwest corner of the campus, just until we know what we are dealing with."

"But, sir, I can't possibly do that. I have to prepare for my redirect meeting at four."

"Hmm, yes, of course, you must." Brock stepped beside Barb, out the office door, and gestured her to follow him.

They walked fast down the hall and into the waiting room where young Sheldon sat nervously.

"Hello, Brian, that wasn't too long, was it? Um, I know this is all very difficult for you. But I need you to listen and trust me. Things are going on that I must get to the bottom of, right now. That means you need to follow my instructions, alright?"

At first, Brian seemed oblivious and inattentive.

"Brian, are you with me here?" Brock shook him slightly.

"Am I with you? My father is somewhere on this floor, and I'm going to find him, damn it! No! I am not with you."

"Brian, listen to me. Your father has been working in secret with me for months. You are my private attaché, right now. My policy is never to discuss security affairs with new employees. I couldn't tell you. I can't explain it all to you here right now. We simply don't have time. Will you just trust me, son?"

Brian was livid, but composed himself and said, "Okay, fine; but hear me, Mr. Brock, I don't give two shits if you are my boss or have billions, or if you are God himself. I will find my dad; you got it?"

"Yes, of course, son, I do. Now listen and remember. Here, this is a key to the Fargo building's main entrance. It's on the southwest corner of the campus. This key is my front door key, and this is the security remote. Push 145 to remove the security lock and then 541 to engage it, understand? I need you to go to my flat and wait for my call. Will you do that? BRIAN?"

"Yes. I've got it. Fine, I guess."

Brock turned to Barb. "Young lady, will you trust me with one more thing?"

"Yes?" She looked at him with hopeful affection.

"Good, after you get out of the meeting with Dr. Bellos, call me on 111-145, can you remember that?"

"Yes, of course."

Brock looked at them both and said, "Now, let's go."

He walked them to the ward door and studied carefully, as Barb pushed six keys on the exit keypad. The door clicked, and Barb opened it. She and Brian walked through and down the corridor to the elevator. As the ward door closed behind them, Brian turned around and saw Brock walking back to Angie's office.

When Brock got there, he sat down in front of Angie's computer. Only this time, Barb had not logged off, so, he had access to everything except the patient records and the room door locks. Brock typed in his security protocol, and two additional windows appeared on-screen; a phone face instant messenger and his control module, to communicate with his personal worldwide network. He called his secretary, who informed him of all incoming messages, including Rachel Sheldon's call to Brian. Then, he called and talked with his Chief of Staff, Rash InVoy. InVoy was Brock's top security advisor. He was a small framed man of East Indian descent and, although he stood only 5'3", his rigid, military-like facial expression commanded respect. His résumé was impressive, to say the least: Advisor to Russia's President; three years as Special Counsel to the President of the United States; leader of various covert mercenary operations within Eastern Europe and Asia war zones during the terrorist wars. And surprisingly, he spent four years as Special Envoy to his Eminence Pope James X.

Brock hired InVoy four years ago to manage his worldwide communications and his security network.

"Rash, good morning; or is it afternoon there?"

"It's almost noon, sir; good morning."

"I need an update on security matter CPT"

"Yes, sir, Clone-Six was eliminated earlier this evening, as instructed. Primary-One should be there with you. Have you recovered vials?"

"Not yet; there has been a glitch with the girl. Primary-One is here, but I haven't found him. What is the shelf life of a vial? How long do we have?"

"We don't know, exactly, but the techs say perhaps a day or two if that."

"Where are the other vials?"

"Sir, I beg your pardon, but this line is not secure. Our computer has identified a virus and tracking mode. I strongly advise you cease communication immediately and leave where you are. Do you copy?"

"Yes, damn!" Brock disconnected the protocol and shut down the computer. "Damn, damn you, Jack!"

He got up, walked down the hallway to the exit door and pushed 122607 on the keypad, duplicating Barb's input. The door unlocked and he walked out to the elevator. When he reached the first floor, the doors opened and a security guard, dressed in what looked like military garb, blocked his exit.

"Sir, excuse me."

Brock waved what he thought was his free pass-badge in front of the guard; but the guard just said, "I'm sorry, sir; please come with me. There has been a breach on floor three. We must follow procedure. I know you understand."

"Just a minute! Do you know who I am, boy? Look at that badge. I am not going anywhere but out. Step aside!"

Brock tried to walk around the guard; but, with one quick, smooth grip, the guard took Brock by his arm and yanked him to the wall.

"I'm sorry, sir; if you don't cooperate, you will be detained by force. Please walk in front of me toward the blinking light."

"Alright, fine; no need for violence."

Brock brushed himself off, and the guard escorted him down the corridor to a small elevator. They entered, and the sergeant pushed red-6 on the panel. Brock was anything but cooperative.

"Where the hell are we going? It feels like we're going down to the left. That's impossible?"

The guard stood silent, fully armed with an exotic weapon Brock had never seen.

"What kind of special ops are you, anyway? Do you realize you work for me? I am Marion Brock! My name is on the marquee. I built this place. Jesus! Are you deaf, you dipshit?"

Brock turned red-faced and looked like he was going to explode.

CHAPTER 10: TAKEN

NURSE RALPH WALKER MET ANGELA ESPOSITO in Chicago, during their undergraduate years. Ralph was visiting his father, who was City Council member for the 5th district, over a Christmas break. The two students had quite a mutual attraction for one another then, almost ten years ago. Now at Andrews, they renewed their old friendship without the romance.

The guard outside Bellos' office did what he promised Angie and paged Ralph Walker. No response recorded on his talker; but, within 10 minutes of the page, Ralph appeared at the office door.

"Hello, I'm Ralph Walker," he said to the guard. "I heard your page."

"Mr. Walker, yes, thank you; but I thought you would call me back. Ms. Angie asked me if I would relay a request to you."

"Of course, I'll do anything. But, honestly, I came to see Angie."

"I'm not sure that's possible. Dr. Bellos was very specific about instructions."

"I see." Ralph looked worried and then said, "Please, consider this. I would only be a few minutes, and, confidentially, you know, she and I are more than just friends. No one knows it, but we are engaged to be married, secretly, of course. So, keep that between us, will you? I need to be with her. She needs me, you know?"

"Hold on just a minute." The guard turned and walked several steps away. He cupped his talker closely, in front of his mouth, and spoke. A minute later, he returned to Ralph. "Mr. Walker, I can give you 10 minutes."

The guard opened the door, and Ralph walked in. There was Angie, reading on the couch. When their eyes met, Angie jumped up and ran into his open arms.

"Ralphy; I'm so happy to see you. How did you get in here?

"I had to use the 'we are engaged' story. Frankly, it's the first time it ever worked. Jesus, what is going on, anyway?"

"We have no time. Look here, next to this door. It's an elevator. I can't get it to work. You must believe me. We have to get out of here and get to Dr. Sheldon."

"What? Why?"

"I mean Rachel Sheldon, Dr. Sheldon's wife. I don't even know where they live . . . So much to do, please, Ralphy? You have to trust me on this. I swear on our past. I swear."

"Sure, of course. Elevator, eh . . ."

They walked in, and Ralph studied everything.

"Look at the panel, Ralph. It has 16 floors. Am I crazy? The hospital only has 10. And these are the same hieroglyphics I found throughout this apartment. I think they must be a language. Can you get this thing moving?"

"Language? Well its nothing I've seen or studied. I don't know. It looks very strange. And, there are no screw holes anywhere, and all the material has a give to it. Feel it."

"You're right," Angie said, "It's warm, soft; sort of like, like skin."

"Yeah, how the hell was it built? Everything in this place is unfamiliar when you examine it. Look around out there, see if you can find a crowbar, something to pry this panel off."

Angie ran out into all the rooms searching for anything to help. She found a metal back scratcher, which had a sharp fork-like edge, and brought it to Ralph.

"Well, that didn't work. I just don't see any way to pry this bezel off. What the heck is this stuff?"

"What about the wall panels?"

They both examined the corners, ceiling, and floor.

"Angie, I'm beginning to understand why this is in plain sight. Nothing in here is ordinary or familiar. Nothing is screwed down or snapped in, and there are no wires anywhere. I can't even make out what the material is. So, what are we looking at, kiddo?"

As they stood wondering, the front door of Bellos' office opened, and the guard peeked in. "Hello? Ms. Angie? Nurse Walker? Hello?"

At the same time, the elevator door quickly slid shut, trapping the couple inside.

"Holy shit; now what?" Angie asked in a panic. "Look at the door, Ralph."

The elevator then illuminated. The walls seemed to glow, and they jumped again when the elevator door became a one-way transparent window. They could see out, but no one could see in or hear them.

"What the hell is going on?" Ralph stammered.

The couple watched in disbelief as the guard walked down Bellos' foyer stairs into his oval living-room. He searched everywhere shouting, "Ms. Angie? Mr. Walker?"

Angie and Ralph pounded on the elevator door. "Hey guard! Over here, in here!". But he couldn't hear or see the two nurses at all. They watched the guard reach for his radio talker and call Bellos. When Bellos answered, the guard rushed his words, "Dr. Bellos, I'm in your office. I don't know how, sir, but they are not here. They are gone."

"You are sure?"

"Yes, sir."

Bellos just shook his head. "I'll take care of it. You may get back to your regular duties."

When the call came into Bellos' radio talker from the guard, he was still in ER-1 comforting Rachel Sheldon. "Excuse me, Rach; I have to take this."

As he turned away, he talked to the guard at his apartment and hung up. Then he quickly took his Knofer out and whispered into it the strange language of the Carriers. It was the language of the hieroglyphics on the furniture throughout his suite. *"Kshieldun Klevilun; Exhish Tuneel forktune; Childene un, Klevelsesh-Unitem Bellos Echvator'; Exish-Enubill tuke Tuneel-forktune!"* [Translation: Shield one, level one; exit 14 with my child to level red six immediately!]

Then he quietly slipped his Knofer back into his hip holster and returned to consoling Rachel about Jack's death.

At that same moment, Angie and Ralph were still baffled in the elevator. She inadvertently touched the elevator panel, leaning so her body weight forced her right hand to palm over the numbers on the bezel. The elevator moved, and she flinched. "Ralph, do you feel that?"

"Yes. Look out the door. We are going down. Shit!"

The elevator made absolutely no sound of any kind. They barely saw the guard exit the room, as the bottom of the front door closed behind him. Both of them leaned back against the wall and watched.

"I hope this is what you wanted, Luv?"

Suddenly, the entire elevator changed and became transparent. Unbelievably, Angie and Ralph could see outside the hospital. It was as though they were floating down, moving suspended in space.

"Angie, what the hell is going on? Isn't that the parking lot?"

"I think so . . ."

They stood transfixed.

"Ralph, look, up at the stars; oh my God, so beautiful."

The ride took several minutes; and, when they stopped, the inside of the elevator changed to an opaque white. After a few more seconds, a door slid open from the opposite side of the elevator. They stepped out into a lighted rock cave; the door closed behind them; and the elevator disappeared, becoming part of the tunnel wall, undetectable.

Ralph studied the tunnel. "Cute trick; now, where are we? What are we into, kiddo?"

"I think it is a tunnel, Ralph. Look at that, though. Is the rock glowing?"

They looked at each other and then started to walk, holding hands tightly. Ralph began jogging and pulling Angie in the only direction before them. After 100 yards or so, the tunnel became dark. They could see an opening ahead, and they walked out into the moonlight.

"Jesus, Luv, look at that sky. By the way, this is not the hospital parking lot."

"This is wrong, Ralph. It's just desert."

Always prepared, Ralph pulled out his trusty key chain with a flashlight and compass.

"Okay, according to this, we go that way. We should see the hospital in no time. Angie, are you with me here?"

"Yes, I guess. Tonight is undoubtedly the strangest night of my life."

They began jogging. After several minutes, Ralph checked his compass.

"Ralph, look, street lights. Where the heck are we? Let's try flagging down a car, maybe get to a police station."

Two, three, four vehicles passed, but no one stopped.

"Well, babe, it's 3:30 in the morning. Even if there is another car, nobody is going to pick up hitchhikers at this time of night."

"Really, Mr. Smarty, I remember college."

After about 15 more minutes of walking and seeing nothing, Angie saw headlights and did a few sexy poses in front of the car. "Look, Ralph! Look! They are slowing down."

Angie started jumping and hugging Ralph. "They are slowing, Ralphy. We're saved!"

A dark blue van slowed and stopped right beside the two.

It all happened so fast; Ralph had no time to react. There was a total of three men and a woman inside. Two men with hoods jumped out very quickly. They forced the two nurses apart. While one man pushed Ralph to the ground, another grabbed Angie's arms and turned her into the van's doorway. The third man, behind her, placed a black hood over her head. The first two then grabbed her on each side and swung her into the van. The last man slid the door shut and the van sped off. It was a total of 10 seconds, and they were gone, leaving Ralph lying on the roadside in disbelief. He looked up to see dust and the van a quarter mile away.

"You bastards! You bastards! WTF?"

He was alone, with only the streetlights and nothing but sand in sight. As Ralph started walking in the direction the van disappeared, he could hear a cell phone ringing. He followed its sound, found the phone on the ground, and pushed the round blinking button.

"Hello, hello; who is this? Please don't hang up."

"I'm not going to hang up," the voice said. "Just walk a mile in the opposite direction, back to the Complex. Good luck. If I were you, I would get back to the hospital as soon as I could. You don't want to miss any of this, do you?"

The phone went dead, and Ralph stood with his mouth open.

"What the hell is going on?"

CHAPTER 11:   MONEY TALKS

MARION BROCK WAS MORE than a successful billionaire philanthropist, although that would be enough for most. He had all the characteristics of a man of stature and power, not to mention six mansions in four countries and extensive contacts in top financial circles. He was not a self-made man. Instead, he inherited billions and many family businesses, all of which made up the global Brock Empire. The Brock name was known as the 'billionaire's billionaire' for generations. However, to his credit, he also held several lobbyist positions in Washington, D.C., managing that effort with a staff of Ivy League lawyers and future state and federal judicial candidates. As part of his investment portfolio, years ago, he diversified into medical related and high-tech markets; and he was the single credit carrier and financier committed to the completion of the Brock/Swanson Complex in Arden, New Mexico.

It was Gordon Swanson, who initially introduced Brock to Mathew Bellos and Jack Sheldon at one of the Complex's fundraisers. After Bellos had given his stunning presentation, 'The Cure for the Common Cold,' Brock negotiated with Swanson and the board of directors that he alone would pay to finish the campus in the American southwest. Impressively, he wrote a single check for the last 15 percent of all construction costs; and he committed to paying for updating the newest computer software and hardware annually. In return, the Complex would provide him with a personal 3000-square foot, three-bedroom suite on the sixth floor of the Fargo building, which lay in the remote area of the campus' 1600-acre landscape. Also, his name would appear first on the Complex's advertising marquees. His only other proviso was that he never be directly involved with the personnel working on the campus. They would know him by his name only. Any communication from them would have to be in writing and only come from Dr. Mathew Bellos, Chief of Hospital, or Dr. Jack Sheldon, Chief of Research. Frankly, Brock just liked Jack. He was brilliant alright; however, his financial partner, Gordon Swanson, never trusted him. Swanson knew the family's history. Part of Brock had become a famous venture capitalist, and he thought of Swanson as an old school monarchical type—un-American conservative. Swanson, so it appeared, could accomplish most anything without money. Brock could never find any information, or more importantly, dirt on Swanson. Conversely, Swanson knew every move

Brock made, primarily because he had developed such a skilled network of connections within most of Brock's global conglomerates. Nevertheless, Brock had billions and an insatiable hunger for power and greed. Their partnership was a sour mix. The name Brock/Swanson was the only voluntary sharing they did. Brock always considered Swanson a minor player, an irritating buzzing fly. Swanson saw Brock's involvement with the Complex as another way to monitor his activities.

After the new Arden, Arizona campus had been completed, Dr. Jack Sheldon continued to work on his pet theory, CPT . However, with a child and years behind them, Rachel Sheldon relinquished the urgent demands of her career at the Complex, and she moved naturally into motherhood and managing the couple's domestic affairs. The ranch's needs, finances, and raising Brian were more than enough to fill her day. As the years passed, she distanced herself from Jack's proofs. Eventually, she rarely visited the Complex at all, only occasionally attending select annual functions.

It was early last January when Jack first put it all together. He was studying one Saturday afternoon in their home laboratory and, quite unexpectedly, he surprised himself. Like an artist feverishly painting one subject and in a mistake of the brush, he realized something more beautiful than he could have ever pictured intentionally. At 4:55 p.m. on January 12; the secret was his alone. "My God, this will change everything." Jack sat staring at his notes. At last it was not just a theory; not just words. Unlike the others, this was the one proof he would act out and make a reality.

$$\oint {}_{1}^{n}Y \sum_{\propto}^{\sim} \lim_{n \to \infty} \left(7 + \frac{\pounds}{n}\right)^{n} xe^{-x^{2}} \triangleq$$

"I've got to tell Rachel..." He paced back and forth. "...No, on second thought, not until I make it real, no doubts."

He seemed to walk incessantly; then, he calmed and sat back down, talking to himself, "I have to extract and inject into the same DNA. I can't get around that. So, it has to be me. Okay, I'll need two major pieces of equipment, and I need money."

After much pondering, he wrote the proposal requisition and submitted it for budget approval the next day. Dr. Bellos received the request and studied it for three full nights. It vaguely reminded him of his hypothesis that viral-based life could 'cure' death. He approached Jack the following evening after hours in Research Lab 23, Facility Four.

"Hey, you, how are you? I need to talk to you about your requisition 81114. It's a lot of money."

"Yes, it is. I thought you might be curious."

"More than curious. You and I have known each other a long time. This kind of money must be approved by the full board, and they don't meet for months. I can get us a meeting with one of the big guys to discuss it if you're game."

"Of course, who?"

"Gordon Swanson, himself; I've arranged for you, me and him to dine Saturday night."

Jack got up and hugged Matt. "My friend, this is a long time coming for me. I owe you one."

"Have you told Rachel anything?"

"Nope, I want to surprise her when everything's right."

"So be it. We have reservations at Café Cher, 8 p.m., sharp. I'll meet you in the lobby."

That Saturday night, Jack and Matt stood together in the foyer of Santa Fe's only French restaurant.

"Well, my friend, are you ready for this?" Bellos asked.

Jack replied, "I know you can't know this, Matt. I've been theorizing, hypothesizing, formulating, and testing for over two decades about this. Honestly, I'm not sure I'm ready. But I know one thing."

"What's that?"

"I know that I have to see this through, no matter how it ends. I am going to see this through."

Bellos put his hand on Jack's shoulder. "I can't know what you know here, buddy. We never talked about it, but I can support you, and I do."

They both happened to look toward the entryway, as the revolving front door swiveled, and the tall unmistakable frame of Gordon Swanson walked in. He saw the two immediately, walked over and smiled. "Good evening, Mathew."

"Good evening, sir. You know Jack Sheldon, Chief of Research at the Complex?"

Swanson extended his hand. "Yes, hi, Jack. Too bad we only see each other during special occasions. I've always wanted to get to know you better."

"Thank you. I'm speechless."

"I trust that will not be the case tonight. Come, let's sit, eat and talk. I'm most interested in hearing what you have to say."

The maître d' led the three to a small cozy room with only one table and began serving them like kings. Gordon Swanson took the lead and got right to the point.

"So, Jack, you and the Complex's research team have made quite a name for us all in the quest to improve the human condition. I am here because your recent request is intriguing, but it is void in some respects. I want to understand the specific objectives of the equipment you need; sort of fill in the blanks, if you don't mind?"

"Jack," said Matt, "the descriptions of what you need are exact and precise, detailed and reasonable. On the other hand, your justifications are, in many respects, let's say, not as accurate as we'd like. We think we know why you are asking for the equipment, but you don't spell it out. You are talking about reanimating a life, aren't you? I'm not misreading your implications, am I? You can't keep this secret to those you trust enough to ask for this kind of backing."

Then Bellos sat back and wiped his mouth with a napkin. All three were silent until Jack spoke.

"I don't mean to be selfish here. I know this is the biggest discovery of my life; and, perhaps it will change everyone's perspective in general. It's just that I alone have to take this to the next step, without anyone else in harm's way. Let there be no misunderstanding; you are correct. I have completed the written proofs. The formulations and equations say it all. But I must be the guinea pig, no one else. I will let you read it all; and, if you agree, we go. I get the equipment. I don't know how to say it any plainer."

"Dr. Sheldon," Swanson sipped his champagne, "how soon can you give me the manuscript to study? The sooner I finish it, the sooner I can answer your proposal."

"Sir, with all respect," Jack seemed uneasy. "If anyone has to read my paper, I would prefer that only Matt here does it, if that's acceptable to you. After that, he can meet with you, or we can meet again. I would like to move as fast as possible, but with caution and security."

"That's fine with me. I trust Mathew here implicitly." Swanson smiled as he looked at Mathew and said, "Well it's settled then." He extended his hand to Jack to seal the deal. "At last; now tell me something, Jack, you have written in some journals about 'thought' and 'the process of thinking.' Tell me, in your opinion, exactly what is thought? Try and make it a simple answer for this old man, if you would, please?"

"Well, I suppose the best short answer I can give is, 'Thought is the organization and expression of our senses.'"

"Interesting take. I'm a bit of a scholarly type myself. I don't know if Mathew told you," Swanson chuckled. "Did you know that the word 'organization' has its root from the Greek word 'Organon,' as does our English derivative 'organ'?"

"No, I didn't."

"Do you believe our thoughts are really 'organs'?"

Jack paused a moment.

"Why, yes; I do."

"In that case, we should be able to transplant them, just like we do a kidney or liver, right?"

Jack looked speechless, as Swanson continued, "Well, I suppose every time we speak, we transmit a thought to someone else, don't we, Ha? I guess in that respect; we do transplant them; I mean; that is, if anyone remembers what we say, right?" Swanson winked. "By God, you are right, my boy; ha."

The evening went very well after that, and later, the three were outside the restaurant laughing and talking like old friends.

"Well, you two," said Swanson, "how long before one of you calls me?"

As they shook hands, Bellos said, "I'd like to read the manuscript right away."

"I'm certainly agreeable to giving it to Matt, tonight," said Jack.

"Really? Let's do it. You want me to follow you, or come with you, or what?"

Then, a white stretch limo pulled up to the curb. The driver got out and smiled at Swanson. "Hello, sir."

"Good evening, Mr. Mike. Mike, these are Drs. Jack Sheldon and Mathew Bellos. Gentlemen, this is my driver, Mr. Michael Warren. How long have you been with me now, Mike?"

"Sometimes it seems like forever, sir."

"Hmm, well, thanks for that, Mike, and thank you both. It was a most informative and enjoyable evening. The food wasn't too bad either? I'll wait, with great anticipation to hear from you, Mathew."

Swanson saluted them as he got into the limo. Mike looked at Bellos and, with a wink; he got into the driver's seat. The limo made a U-turn and sped off. The two doctors stood waiting for the valet.

"Matt; let's do this. I need to start the ball rolling. We can go to my house. I'm sorry, Rachel is gone for the night. She would love to see you. Anyway, I'll give you a copy of the manuscript."

Bellos replied, "I'll follow you then."

The two got into their cars and drove to Jack's home, about 30 minutes away. Jack led Matt to his basement lab. Bellos sat down in one of the recliners, while Jack opened his desk, took out the book and handed it to Matt.

"You want me to start now, or go home?" Bellos asked.

"If you want to read, I'll make some coffee and leave you alone. You may have some questions." Jack smiled, went upstairs, and Bellos read the first ten pages. Then he turned to the final pages, just as Jack returned with coffee and cake.

"Jack, can you give me a summary before I get into your micro-tech lingo. You don't explain this Chemical Personality Transfer in the requisition. Just give me the substance. I'll read the proofs in private."

"Okay; fair enough. Well, I've isolated what and where our personality/memory are located in the brain. I've defined them chemically. They are really one and the same but manifest in different ways. You follow?"

Bellos squinted. "Not sure."

"You and I both know we learn everything through sensation and genetics, right? We become aware of whatever; then we think or behave accordingly. In any case, we remember it voluntarily or involuntarily. Matt, everything we know, everything we are, is eventually stored in one location."

"Am I supposed to differentiate between the brain and the mind, Jack?"

"Elementary, of course. The brain is the physical beast, and the mind is who we are . . ."

"Sorry," Bellos laughed, "it's just that I do remember some things about being a doctor."

Jack nodded respectfully. "Anyway, if I may continue? Personality/memory is a chemical cocktail. Our mind instructs all tasks required or chosen, and it eventually stores everything in a library of thought, in one location, for historical reference, a library of conscious and unconscious permanent records. You said summarize, right?"

"Go on . . ."

"Every action or thought triggers synaptic impulses within and between cells. I found the 'link' between those signals and the chemicals we produce. At the same time the signals fire, a record of that firing imprints in your library, as a chemical. Our library is our personality, you see. Matt, I have proven that we can withdraw the library. It coagulates after death. By extracting it and reintroducing it into the deceased, the patient will reanimate. So, I called my proof CPT–Chemical Personality Transfer." Jack inhaled. "Well, that's most of it really."

Bellos' eyes bulged. "Most of it? Jesus, come on Jack; what's the rest? Why do I know you're hiding something?"

Jack stood facing Bellos and then paced the room. "Yes, well something unbelievable happens when the mixture is extracted, before it's re-injected."

"Oh, for God's sake, Jack..."

"Matt, please? Just listen carefully. The 'mixture' of the extraction reacts with the catalyst bath in the syringe, and the result is miraculous. The resulting change redistributes and reorients the patient's genetic makeup issuing new combinations, new instructions. When the new mix is reinjected, its unique chemical composition stimulates each cell to correct all flaws. The CPT bath triggers anabolic growth once again within the genes. Telomeres grow longer. We produce more healthy cells than those that die off. I would not just live again. I would become healthier than I was before I expired. There must be genetic compatibility, of course, which is why it has to be me. But the potential is staggering. Matt, eventually we could store people in small vials and reanimate them when there is a genetic match."

Bellos' cheeks swelled, and he let out a slow blow. "Boy, Jack, I can only think of a thousand questions. You have proven this?"

"Yes."

"How?"

"Mathematics, physics, chemistry, microbiology; it is all there in the manuscript."

"What about in a lab?"

"Come on; it's not like we can test rats or animals about personality."

"I know, but it seems to me that first, you need a human host."

"Yes, and I need the equipment I've requisitioned, a controlled environment, and a genetic duplicate."

"And just how do we get your body?" Bellos chuckled. "It seems to be in use at the moment."

"It has to be me, Matt, my body. There is only one unless you know something I don't." Jack smiled. "You are correct; so, I have to die; you have to extract the cocktail, re-inject me and bring me back." Jack hesitated.

"But there is a catch."

"Christ . . . I can't imagine, 'a catch?'"

"The window of completion begins after one hour of death and before 72-hours, I think. That is part of my new calculations. After that, the library is far too diluted. Death takes it."

"Listen to yourself, Jack. What are you saying? 'The brain isn't dead until 72 hours after the heart stops?' What you are proposing is crazy. Besides, why not invest in a cloning model? We have connections through affiliates."

"No, a male clone's DNA is incomplete. You know that. The brain would reject the serum in the first place. Ironic, come to think of it, isn't it? I mean 72 hours is exactly three days. My discovery will change religions."

"What? Jack, stop it!" Bellos shook his shoulders. "When and from where, exactly, do you withdraw the serum? What are the guideposts directing the operation? Where is this 'library'?"

"Read my proof, damn it! I wrote it all down...sorry, I'm kind of sensitive about all this. "Jack took a breath and sat across from Bellos. "As the body begins to deteriorate, the mind protects itself. The memory cortex changes; and, in defense of dying, it thickens the memory table, enabling a focused extraction; cool, huh? However, strange as it may seem, the removal must take place after at least one hour of death."

"And this is explained and proven here in your manuscript?"

"Yes."

"All this must happen very fast, Jack. Nobody knows when they are going to die, you know."

"Thanks for reminding me, but it's not when you die that this relates to, it's after death and before 72 hours are up."

"Hmm . . ."

"And one more thing. Matt, I am not prepared to share the formula for the catalyst bath unless I am the guinea pig. If the extraction isn't embedded in the accurate catalytic compound, it will die within moments. The bath is what stimulates the CPT to activate after reinjection."

"How long can the serum live in the right catalyst?"

"I've calculated five days, so far."

"Okay; how in God's name are you going to know who is doing what when you are the one dead? Have you thought of that?"

"Yes, I have. I need a partner whom I trust. Someone who keeps the catalyst, extracts the serum, measures the proper dose, revives me, and stores the rest.

"You mean to save the rest of the serum- the catalyst mix?"

"Right, yes; placed with the right catalyst; there should be enough for six to seven injections. After the first extraction, each 3/4-inch filled vial could be studied to try to extend the CPT mix. Matt, if successful, we could not just re-animate me; but, maybe, we could change our view of death altogether."

"Jack, I'm still trying to figure out where this coagulation is, exactly; and, for the record, I am not going to be a party to killing you."

"Well, there you have it. Details are in the pages. I need the equipment."

"It's all in here, right?"

"Yep. Will Swanson buy it?"

"There is only one way, my friend. I'll read this in detail, believe me; but you must let him read it too. I know he is more than capable of understanding it. I trust him. Besides, you have no choice, as I see it."

Jack walked to the door, closed his eyes, sighed and turned. "Fine, I don't believe I'm saying this. Set it up. I have to know right away."

Bellos took the copy and put his hand on Jack's shoulder. "I'll talk to you tomorrow."

Bellos left, and Jack fell asleep examining the original copy of his manuscript.

While he drove, Bellos took his Knofer out and put on a headset. He placed the manuscript over the Knofer and spoke into it, "Copy and transmit to Bellos GGM-TBN 010."

The Knofer inputted all information from the document and transferred it via headset into Bellos' mind. He then pulled over to the side of the road, called Swanson and sent the manuscript to him via Knofer. Swanson performed a similar procedure, and then he spoke to Bellos.

"Mathew, I don't see how we can help Jack right now. You know this is what I've been waiting for relative to my own health, but not this way. We cannot be a party to killing anyone intentionally. Besides, it will take time for Ever-Life to digest and prove the details of the manuscript. You must go back and tell your friend that I said 'no' regarding his proposal. Tell him we may be able to help in the near future, but we need to work with him systematically before committing. I am sorry, Mathew. I know how serious this is. But the potential abuse and chaos this could create are just as staggering as the possible medical advances it could bring. No one will be able to control this yet."

"I know, sir; but he wants to start now and get concrete results within five months. Jack has been working on this for 25 years, and he can taste the end. I know how he feels. I too have many questions; but would you consider our being a blind financier, at least monitor him somehow?"

"We have very few options. Don't forget, Jack must die, Mathew. I don't see how we can be involved in any way without drawing too much attention from the wrong people. Right now, this is a losing proposition. Patience is the key."

"I'll let him know in the morning."

CHAPTER 12: NEEDLES

AS THE DARK BLUE VAN SPED along the night desert road, Angie Esposito laid tied up and gagged under several heavy canvas tarps. Her muffled screams and kicking annoyed the kidnappers. Finally, a cell phone ringing broke the irritating sounds of the girl.

"Damn! Give me that phone! Hello?!"

The voice at the other end of the phone said, "Marty, have you got the girl?"

"Yes, sir."

"And she is not harmed in any way?"

"No, sir, she's a bit uncomfortable. She's a fighter. That's for sure. Now what?"

"You have to pull over and park the van; and please sedate her."

Marty tapped the driver, gestured to pull over, and the van stopped. Another kidnapper pulled a syringe out and stuck it in Angie's thigh, pushing fluid into her. They waited. A few seconds later, the voice on the phone said, "What's happening, Marty?"

"She's quiet and limp."

"Thank God! Now; please, gentlemen, the second syringe; and be careful; this is the big one."

Marty gave the phone to the man holding Angie. Then, he gently removed the hood from her head, undid her blouse and pulled the collar down from her neck. Marty followed his instructions and measured carefully. As he stuck the long needle slowly 1.25-inches into the side of her neck, he shook his head and murmured, "Its times like these; I wish I never became a paramedic."

Very carefully, Marty pulled the syringe puck back, extracting liquid. "Jesus," he whispered, "it's not red."

He took the needle off and kept the filled vial from view. Then, he picked up the phone and heard, "Are you done?"

"Yes, sir, but..."

"Marty, put the vial in the case. Complete the task. Are you there?"

"Yes, sir. Are there any changes in instructions?"

"No but be very careful. Make sure she is completely alright. Do you understand?"

"Yes. You don't need to worry."

Marty hung up the phone and laid Angie comfortably on a pillow in the back of the van. Then he climbed into the front passenger seat, and the van continued on its way.

CHAPTER 13: ANGIE AND RACHEL

RACHEL SHELDON LISTENED IN DISBELIEF to the call on her cell phone, while she sat in the downstairs lab of her house. It was Brian, while he waited for Brock to finish with Barb Sawyer. Rachel was impatient and reactive. "What the hell are you saying, Brian? What are his vital signs? How can you be so sure?"

"Mom, listen, I hear footsteps. I have to go. I will call you as soon as I can. I don't know what else to say right now. Just wait; I'll get back to you."

The phone went dead, and Rachel stood up in an adrenaline rush, pacing the room. Then, it hit her. "My God, Jack . . ."

She raced and grabbed his manuscript again and began to read it feverishly. She got a pencil and paper and started doing calculations in the book margins. The doorbell ringing interrupted her concentration. "Who can that be? It's four o'clock in the morning."

The bell rang again and again; so, she put the book down, rushed upstairs and looked through the small door porthole. But she could see nothing, so she carefully opened the door. There, at her feet, lay the unconscious body of a girl face down. Rachel quickly knelt and turned her over. It was Angela Esposito. Rachel held her head up and felt her pulse. She seemed okay but unconscious. She gently slapped her face and rubbed her hands. "Miss, Miss; hello. Are you okay? Wake up, honey."

Suddenly, Angie coughed and opened her eyes. "Oh, my! Where am I?"

"You are with me now, sweetheart. You'll be okay. Can you move?"

"Yes, I think so..." Angie looked closely. "... It's you?"

"Me? Yes, I am. Can you get up? Let's get you inside."

"...Yes; no; I mean it is you, Mrs. Sheldon, Dr. Sheldon. You are Dr. Rachel Sheldon."

"Yes, I am." Rachel looked puzzled. "Come on, stand up. That's it; try to walk with me."

They limped slowly together into the living room.

"Mrs. Sheldon, I am, I am Angie, from Focus Ward at Andrews Hospital. I need to talk to you."

The two just made it to the couch, when Angie fainted again. Rachel gave her a cold wet towel and a sip of water as she regained consciousness.

"There now; take it slow. Let's just be really careful here and relax, okay?"

Angie coughed and looked around. "Oh, my head; I can't believe I found you. How did I get here?"

"The doorbell rang. I answered, and there you were at my feet." Rachel smiled, stroked her hair, and Angie forced herself to sit up.

"Please, Mrs. Sheldon. I have to talk to you."

"Alright. You can call me Rachel."

"I am afraid something horrible is happening at the hospital, or at least something stranger than I have ever known."

"What is it?"

"As I said, I am the nurse in charge of third-floor Focus Ward at Andrews. Tonight, your husband, Dr. Sheldon, was admitted as a victim of a car accident."

"I know, baby." Rachel's eyes flooded. "I was there. I just got home a while ago. He died."

"No, Mrs. Sheldon; that's just it." Angie grabbed Rachel's shoulder. "I saw him. I saw him alive."

Rachel shocked back, stood up, and said, "Brian; his phone call; then she looked at the girl. I just talked to my son. He spoke of the third floor and Jack being alive."

"Mrs. Sheldon, I'm not a fool or a weirdo. I have been working at Andrews for three years, always on Focus Ward. The surgical team operated on your husband for hours. They reattached his arm and leg, but his heart had stopped. He was clinically dead for over an hour. I monitored him; there was no brain or heart activity. Then, I took a food tray into his room. He sat up. He just sat up." Angie took a deep breath. "I had to see you. Somehow, I thought you would believe me; please?"

Just then, Angie remembered; and, reaching into her pocket, she pulled out the two-inch long blue test tube vial. "Look at this, Mrs. Sheldon. I was supposed to inject it into his neck, but I freaked out and ran. I swear, Mrs. Sheldon, he was as alive as we are."

"What is that?"

"I remember; I got the original email around 10:30 p.m., from Dr. B. himself. It said I should inject Dr. Sheldon at precisely 2 a.m. with 'this' into his right carotid artery."

Angie handed the vial to Rachel. "After that, they took me away and locked me in Dr. Bellos' office. I found a book there. I read part of it, but I don't believe it. It said that Dr. Sheldon was alive, because of something called 'Ever-Life.'"

Rachel's eyes swelled as she stared at the vial. "Oh, my God!" She took Angie's shoulders and squeezed. "Can you walk?"

"I think so."

"Come with me."

Rachel led her downstairs to the lab, grabbed Jack's manuscript and showed it to Angie.

"Did the book look like this?"

"Why no; the book I saw was bigger. It had a white leather cover with three gold letters on it, J.A.S. Inside, it described Jack Avuar Sheldon as being 'duplicated.' There were a lot of technical definitions and medical procedures regarding DNA. He was approved for something called *Transtosis*. Yes, that's the word, I think. What does it mean?

"I have no idea. Angie, something is going on." Rachel sat down for a moment and thought out loud. "Angie, that book couldn't have been written tonight. What is the last thing you remember? You didn't just appear at my door. Can you tell me?"

"Yes, I think so." She recounted her evening to Rachel.

"Angie, we need to get back into the hospital. Can you get us into Focus Ward?"

"Yes, sure."

"I know I'm asking a lot, but you are in this, honey. Otherwise, why kidnap you and then leave you at my door?"

"Yes, alright; besides, I have to find Ralphy. The last thing I remember, he was thrown onto the street curb by thugs. I know I am right about this, Mrs. Sheldon; I know it."

"We will go to Matt's office. You carry this manuscript. We have to find the other book you speak of. Wait, on second thought, I have to see Jack first. The morgue, we will go there first. I know the department head. Come on; and Angie, whatever happens, don't lose this vial; and don't tell anybody you've got it, okay?"

"Okay; but, Mrs. Sheldon, Dr. Bellos wrote the email in the first place. He already must know I have it."

Rachel looked at her and paused. "You are right. Let's go. I have a lot of questions for Dr. Bellos.

CHAPTER 14: BELLOS AND JACK

DR. JACK SHELDON AWOKE NAKED in the corner of Room 309's bathroom shower. He slowly stood up soaked but with no pain and thought, "Okay, no bruises, no sores; Christ, I feel fine. Now I have to get myself together. What the hell has happened to me?"

He put on the terry cloth robe hanging behind the door and walked back into the bedchamber; when the room's door lock clicked, and he heard the knob twist. In walked Mathew Bellos.

"Matt, is that you?"

"Jack?" They smiled and embraced. "How are you feeling? God, it's good to see you up and about. Come, sit."

"Jesus, Matt, I had blood everywhere. I've been lying down, sitting...Christ! I fell in the shower and just woke up crouched in the corner. For God's sake, what the hell is going on?"

"I have a lot to tell you, but we don't have time right now. Here, I brought you some clothes. Get dressed. We must leave. Your body is still reacting from everything. Obviously, you have no idea what happened to you; so, just trust me."

"Now what?" Jack started to dress, but almost fell from being lightheaded.

"Here; take a sip of this," Bellos handed him a glass.

"What is it, white champagne? Not bad; guess I'm out of shape."

"Come on. You'll be okay, follow me. Try to be as quiet and quick as you can. There are people, who, if they are not here yet, they will be. They want you, and I don't mean in a good way."

The two walked out of Room 309 and down the hall into Angie's office. Bellos opened the closet door, and Jack quipped, "Matt, do we need our coats?"

Bellos turned with a sarcastic smile, and then he reached behind the hospital gowns, tapped a part of the molding and whispered strange words, *"yuroptenjen;* GGM-TBN 010."

The wall slid to one side, revealing an elevator, much like the one in Bellos' office. They stepped in, and Bellos continued speaking strange words that meant: "Master secure, initiate directive-197."

The wall closed behind them, and both men felt a slight tug down and to the right.

"What the hell was that?" Jack blurted. "Since when does the hospital have secret passages? And when did you learn Chinese, that Wong Tong, Wang Chang shit? Jesus!"

They both looked at each other and Bellos chuckled, "I'm glad you haven't lost your sense of humor."

"Thanks, that tells me nothing."

Bellos said, "The fact is, my friend, to quote your favorite science fiction, 'We are going where you have never gone before.'"

"Like that's exactly what I was thinking."

"Well," Bellos shrugged, "I have to get you far away and safe, fast. We are getting on a plane here at the Complex."

"Matt, I feel funny all of a sudden."

"Hold on, here we are."

The elevator door didn't open. It appeared to disappear, to reveal a small flight hanger and a small one-engine propeller plane, waiting for the two to climb aboard.

Jack surveyed the hanger. "Christ, Matt, this looks like it was constructed back in the 1960s? And where did you get the model airplane. Does it fly? What is this place?"

"We're flying low and slow to avoid detection. Come on up the stairs; watch your head. Just sit anywhere and put the seatbelt on, will you?"

"I feel so sleepy." Jack was disoriented again. Matt's words were of no comfort.

"You need a shot. You might as well give in to it for now. I have to see the pilot. I'll be back."

In a few minutes, even considering the roar of the engine, Jack drifted to sleep. It felt like only seconds, but it was 20 minutes in all until the plane bounced on a different landing strip and Jack woke up. To protect Jack, Bellos tried to give the impression that they were leaving the state. He filed the flight plan's destination to Las Vegas, but actually he had the plane take off from the Andrews Airfield, fly in circles, and land on a dirt road in an unfamiliar remote area on another side of the campus. Bellos tapped Jack's shoulder. "Jack, you up? We are here."

"How could I not be with that smooth landing? Where are we?"

"Let's go." Bellos led the way. The two deplaned, and the pilot immediately took off again.

Jack scratched his head. "This still looks like a desert, except of course for the massive concrete door over there. Oh, my head."

They walked toward a bright light shining at them on the door, about 50 yards away. A special ops guard in full combat regalia greeted Bellos with a smile and salute.

"Evening, sir. This way . . ."

"Well, this can't be Brazil," Jack joked. "I don't see any bikinis."

They stood before a large 20-foot square concrete door, and Jack said, "Oh, great, something else ridiculous; it looks like some old 1950s bomb shelter?"

"Don't be a smart ass," Bellos replied, "Actually, it is, or was." Bellos gestured to the guard, and the door slid open.

"Matt, I need to sit down, sorry. It's like I've had the crap beaten out of me."

Bellos held Jack's arm and guided him through the door into the first room on the right. "Here, sit and drink."

"Is this the same stuff you gave me before? What is it; and where are we?"

"Just relax. You are going through some very radical changes."

"Really; Ya think? I was in the hospital, you know."

"Just drink it. Look, Jack, I know you are upset. I said I would explain, and I will. But you have to be patient with yourself, the situation, and with me. What we are dealing with is life-threatening. It's all very sensitive. The most important thing right now is that you take it slow, just for a while."

"Upset? I am way beyond upset. It's all so frustrating, and where the hell is Rachel? I have such a headache. Christ, I am a doctor, and I can't even think. I feel like I have superpowers one second, and the next; it's like I'm going to vomit my insides out from the pain."

"Side effects, Jack, side effects. They should pass; and, if they don't, this is the one place on Earth you want to be."

"And, where is this?" Jack replied. "I see four walls, a table and chair."

Bellos put his hand on Jack's shoulder, smiled and said, "Listen; you are having massive memory issues; and I don't want to repeat myself more than three times, okay? Do you feel up to eating something?"

"Yes, the only food I've seen is what that nurse dropped on the floor."

"Then you remember the nurse?"

"Not really, maybe; I don't know."

Bellos sighed, leaned into him and examined Jack's eyes. "For now, I don't expect much. The only thing I am asking you for is patience. Are you feeling any better?"

"Yeah, right this minute, I am. The dizziness comes and goes. What's in that drink?"

"Good. Come on then, follow me. This way."

They walked out and down a hall to another door. Bellos pulled out his Knofer, waved it over the icon above the lock, and the door clicked open. Jack walked into another room. "So Matt, you've brought me from one closet into another?"

There was one lounge chair and table in front of a small round stone fireplace. A video image of a world map displayed on the wall, and what looked like a silver refrigerator stood in the corner.

"Jack, please sit. We call this room a Unit. This one's young, I mean small. It's one of many here. If I had to describe the whole area; it's sort of like a beehive. You haven't seen this part of the Complex, yet. There is nothing to fear at all, but it is highly secure."

"Obviously, if you've kept it from me."

Bellos made an annoyed look. "The important thing is that you are safer here than if you stayed in the hospital, and you get much better service. We have a lot to cover in a very short time."

"Okay, what's next?"

"I need you to get comfortable. Here; drink more wine, eat something, and maybe nap a bit."

"And how do I get food and the drink?"

"Well, see that red button? Just push it and order whatever you want. After you order, go around the corner, and you will see a small 'lift door.' Open it. Whatever you ordered will be there. Use the remote on the table there. It will enable you to monitor hospital activities on the screen above the fireplace. You can catch up a little. We have no way for you to communicate with the outside, though, sorry. As for the drink, there's more is in the refrigerator over there ready for you. Jack, this isolation is necessary for your health, just for a short time to guarantee your safety. Try to keep calm, will you? Just don't forget to drink the wine."

Jack repeated, "In case you haven't noticed, I keep asking you, what is that stuff?"

"It's an ancient and rare healing elixir. I couldn't explain it if I wanted to, but it makes you feel a lot better, doesn't it? Drink all you want."

"You are just trying to get me drunk my first day back."

"Unfortunately, buddy, the drink's effects are only temporary; and it has no alcohol in it, sorry."

Jack swallowed every drop, sat back and felt the warmth spread throughout his body.

"You must listen," Bellos said. "There are things at work here you never foresaw."

"I don't understand." Jack looked annoyed. "Quit being so damn cryptic and just spit it out, will you?"

"Do you remember CPT?"

Jack looked puzzled at first, but suddenly felt refreshed and alert. "Yes, I think so, Chemical Personality Transfer."

"Right, what else? Come on."

"It's the transfer of our personality, our memory, from a dead person to a live host . . . yes, I remember."

"Where did it come from?"

Jack strained. "From me?"

"Yes, you, and what happened, Jack?"

"Jesus, what did happen? Did I screw up?"

Bellos smiled. "No, you did quite the opposite. You succeeded; you did it; you are the proof; well your serum is."

"What are you saying?"

"I'm saying that you took all the findings and research, you combined them into one fantastic hypothesis, your manuscript, and you proved it correct. You found the formula, the chemical cocktail for yourself. Jack, you were dead, and now you are not."

"Dead?"

"You were in a car accident. It was awful; yes, dead. I had to perform a procedure we call Transtosis. I will explain details later. The point is I had no time. I had to do it right away. I didn't wait an hour as you instruct in your CPT, so I wasn't sure it would take. And I had to combine a little from each of the procedures we know too. But you seem fine so far. Now other things are in play, and I have to keep you going with that elixir until we get the vial."

"What vial? Christ! My brain keeps fading."

"Let's just say, you found the cocktail and how to extract and inject, but you weren't prepared for the corrective action required by your body. You were a wreck when we admitted you, bones broken, an arm and leg severed . . ."

"So, how did I survive?"

"Well, we gave you Fix-its to repair all body parts and functions."

"Fix-its? What the hell are you talking about?"

"You can't understand everything right now. Your mind is still repairing itself. There is a lot more to hear. Right now, the drink needs time to work. Here; have another; doctor's orders, and I want you to put on this headset. Listen to the program; relax as much as you can. Drink all of the wine, little by little. Order some food."

Jack gestured with his hands raised. "Fine, good speech, I do remember something else, too. I had help."

"We knew something like this would happen. Please, eat and drink; it's critical. Listen to the headset. You will feel better."

"Who is 'we,' Matt? Who knew this would happen, the hospital staff?"

"Jack, some nasty people want CPT and all the pre-catalyst vials. How much did you make? If they get it, they will try to duplicate it. Look, my point is that you may not even remember what we have said here unless you do as I say."

"I remember five vials; I think. I'm well enough to talk. Tell me, where am I?"

"Why do you have to know everything immediately? Right now, your wife and my daughter are in grave danger, and you have to get better ASAP to help me keep them safe."

"What? You mean Rachel. And what do you mean, 'and your daughter?'"

"Yes, my little girl. She is in this up to her eyeballs, and she doesn't even know it yet. Jack, she is the key. We have to protect her. I can't explain it alright now, but it has to do with my analysis of your formula and how it relates to others. Listen; do you remember Marion Brock?"

"He was co-investor of Brock/Swanson."

"Right. Well, Brock invested in you and your experiment to prove out CPT because of Gordon Swanson . . ."

"Gordon Swanson? Yes, I remember that bastard. He turned me down."

"Yes, and for a good reason; he didn't want to murder you."

"Are you saying someone murdered me?"

"Yes, and there was also your bad timing; your jackass impatience almost lost you your life. Now it's threatening us all. Getting Brock involved opened the door to profiteering and sabotage on a global scale."

"Wait a minute. Who is Swanson to judge and decide the future of CPT? I don't believe that."

"Well, that's why we are here. Apparently, you don't think anything bad about Brock. You don't realize the forces in play in all this. I can assure you; Gordon is one of the good guys." Bellos smiled. "And so are we. What you need to know is that we have to move fast. That means you have to heal quickly. The drink will work, but it needs a little time, and you need to listen to this headset."

"Fine, I do need to eat though, and I am so tired again all of a sudden."

Bellos patted Jack's shoulder. "It'll come and go for a while. Relax; I will be back to pick you up. Jack, you have discovered a miracle, but others have turned it into some cat and mouse game for the usual power and money. We are going to make it right."

CHAPTER 15: WHY ME?

AS MARION BROCK DESCENDED with an armed guard in the Andrews hospital elevator, he reached into one of his pant pocket and pressed the emergency button on his phone. It sent a signal to his Chief of Staff, Rash InVoy. InVoy was at his East European office in Istanbul, Turkey, reprimanding his staff leader when the message came through.

"Archer, ARCHER! Get in here."

"Yes, sir."

"I want a team at Andrews Hospital, in Arden, New Mexico, within a half hour, ready to complete stage four; and we need to get Mr. Brock out."

"Yes, sir."

"Who have we got there?"

"We have four men prepped at the Complex, in Brock's building. I can have them in the hospital within 20 minutes."

"Do it!"

Back in the Andrews elevator, Marion Brock looked like a man about to burst, thinking to himself and murmuring to the guard. "Do you know what I've done for that son of a bitch, Jack? I should have fired him six months ago. He is the one who came to *me* after his precious friends deserted him. Christ! That irresistible letter started it all:

Dear Marion,

Thank you for your recent support regarding our latest acquisition of the Dunn's programming software. It will allow us to control and read the viral stimuli variations within the quarantined floors.
Additionally, if you would consent, I would like to meet with you on a private personal matter. It is of great importance to me, to us, I believe.

Sincerely,
Jack Sheldon
Chief of Research and Development
Brock/Swanson Labs

"Jack was the first bastard employed at the Complex to see my home. Bet you didn't know that. For years, I kept faithful to my code. But smooth-talking Jack, he was right about every issue he ever wrote about to me. I remember thinking, 'What could this letter mean?' The big three, Shit! Visionaries of tomorrow, they sucked me dry, with researching the common cold, Alzheimer's, Down syndrome, and now this. Look at me, shit!"

Brock was raging red, staring at the guard. "Within two years of knowing me, they were negotiating on their own with the Pentagon, Israel and China, funding new money, making new theories. They all needed me in the first place to finish this Complex. I was there for them, no one else. My help allowed them to become famous, and that son-of-a-bitch, Jack, he changed everything. How could I resist making that first farking phone call?"

Marion remembered every word:

"Hello, Jack?"

"Yes . . . Marion?"

"Yes, yes; how are you?"

"Fine, thanks for calling."

"Well, I know I'm somewhat of a recluse. It seems we only see each other when I'm awarding you monies at some conference. Jack, I got your note. Yes, I would love to meet. When would you like to come over?"

"Fantastic! Great! I'd like to see you at your earliest convenience; if possible, today or tomorrow?"

"That's fine. As a matter of fact, I am home now. It's 4:30 p.m. If you would like to come over, I'd be glad to see you."

"I'm at home, too. I can be there at say 6 p.m.; how's that?"

"Good, I'll see you then."

So, at 6 p.m. sharp, Jack arrived and pushed the security buzzer to the penthouse entrance, outside the Fargo building. A guard answered. Jack said his name, the door opened, and he took the elevator to the penthouse, and his knock-on Brock's door began it all.

"Hello, Jack," Marion said with a smile. "Come on in."

"Thank you for seeing me on such short notice." Jack shook his hand.

"It's fine. Can I get you a drink?"

"Sure, thanks."

"Something special, I think; champagne."

Brock opened one of his many bottles and filled two tall crystal glasses.

"Here. Now, sit. Tell me, what can I do for you?"

They had a sip; and then, Jack told Brock everything about CPT and the meeting with Swanson.

"Jack, I am rarely at a loss, but this is beyond my understanding. As for me, I can offer my money and resources. What do you need?"

"Here's a list. I need this particular equipment." He handed Brock the proposal that he gave to Bellos.

"I also need a location to work and trusted assistance."

Marion sat and reviewed the 20-page proposal.

"You also need patent rights, copyrights, international protection, not to mention personal security and transportation . . . Things only money can buy. Jack, I'm yours; but, only on one condition."

"What's that?"

"Why, that we are partners in this, Jack . . . With my money and resources, along with your brains and medical know-how, why, it's a win win, guaranteed. Here's my hand on it."

Jack took Brock at his word. They shook hands with broad smiles and sealed their partnership.

That was months ago. Now, Brock stood in a silent rage, waiting for the guard and the elevator to take him to God knows where.

"Mr. Brock, Mr. Brock?" The ops-guard said, breaking Brock's concentration. "We're here, sir. Please follow me?"

The two men stepped off the elevator into the hallway on the sixth floor below the hospital. The guard led him to a small room and opened the door. It was quite pleasant, with a comfortable couch, chair and two tables.

"Please, sir, if you would be kind enough to wait in here, we can clear this up very soon, I'm sure."

"Well, all you had to do was ask, sonny. I'm at your beckoned call; like I have a choice."

As the guard began closing the door, he heard, "You're fired; you dipshit!"

Even though Brock heard the click of the lock, he grabbed the knob and tried to yank the door open.

"Shit! Shit! Shit!"

Then, he took his phone out and dialed InVoy...no reception. "Damn it! Where the hell am I?"

CHAPTER 16: THE MORGUE

DR. RACHEL SHELDON and Nurse Angela Esposito arrived at the Andrews Hospital emergency room again around 4:45 a.m. The reception staff had been too busy to notice them, so they both quickly walked past the front desk and down the hallway.

"Angie, quick, into the elevator." Rachel pushed two on the panel. "I know Frank Bloom. If he stayed the night shift and Jack did die, maybe he will give us some concrete answers."

They both stood impatiently, and when the elevator door opened, the sign etched on the wall read:

ANDREWS HOSPITAL MORGUE

Rachel walked out and to the right. "Come on, Angie; hurry!"

Some 35 feet or so past a bay window that overlooked the hospital atrium, she pushed the glass double doors open, revealing the department's central area. In the middle of the room, there were four examining tables. Across from them, in the far corner, working on something, sat a man looking into a microscope. "Excuse me, excuse me, Frank, is that you?"

The white-haired old man looked up and turned around. He was apparently in good health, while well into his seventies.

"Frank? No, ma'am; Frank works in Research Lab 23, now; different building."

"Oh, really?" Rachel seemed to wither a little.

"You look like I just kicked you in the belly. Perhaps I can help. I am Richard Bellos, the mortician here, extraordinaire. Okay, it is a bit late for that. What can I do for you two?"

Rachel looked at him with great surprise. "Bellos? Are you related to Matt?"

"Of course; I am his father. And I know you."

Rachel replied, "But I always thought you passed away. I mean, I'm sorry; it's just a shock."

"I expect so; nevertheless, I am here in the flesh." He held out his arms, and she instinctively hugged him.

Then she said, "Jesus, why would Matt let us think you were dead?" Rachel held on tight; her eyes began tearing. "It's just . . . Jack, you know?"

"I know. It'll be okay. Come; sit here." He walked them to a cushioned bench a few feet away.

Rachel began retelling the night's events. "It's been just a horrible night. I'm at my wit's end . . . Oh, excuse me, this is Angie, Angie Esposito."

"Yes, I know of Angie. Hi, we are all family here . . ."

Rachel sobbed, and Angie took her hand.

Dr. Richard stood before them and spoke reverently, "My deepest apologies and respects about your husband, my dear. I am so sorry you've had such a horrible evening."

"Thank you. I am here to see Jack's body. I need to see him."

"I understand; you have nothing to fear. Try to stay calm. Believe me; I will show you nothing to be afraid of . . . Please, come with me."

Richard helped her up, and then he turned, leading them through the doors, which opened into one of the main casket areas.

"Now I assume that neither of you frequents this atmosphere much; so, first, you should know, things have changed radically throughout the industry in recent years. In particular, here at Andrews, I hope you noticed. There is no peculiar fragrance or sickening odor."

The two women sniffed the air.

"For another, we lay our guests in bed-like comfort; they're not on a cold slab. It's to assure best in case potential."

"What does that mean?" Angie asked.

"I mean, we address any question about anything at the bed. Let me show you."

He walked the two over to the wall, pulled the latch, and a mahogany twin bed-like casket drawer slid out.

"She was a small girl who had been rushed here having an immune reaction to asthma. She expired two days ago."

Rachel gasped. "Her color; she looks like she is asleep and so alive. I had no idea. Do all the departed look like this, now?"

"Most, yes, unless it is an unusual circumstance."

"You mean, like Jack?"

"Yes, I am afraid so. I can show you something."

Rachel looked at Angie and then replied, "Yes, please, I have to see."

"Well, follow me."

Dr. Richard Bellos walked into a smaller, dimly lit room that somehow radiated a pleasant warm feeling.

"I don't ever remember being in here," Rachel said.

"Well, I like to think that is because I redesigned it all. This way; over here."

The two women followed him to the far corner, about 35 feet away. There were four beautifully decorated 36-inch by 24-inch drawers on the wall.

"Mr. Bellos, all this looks more like a mausoleum than a morgue room."

"It is neither. Oh wait, I forgot." Richard brought two cushioned chairs and placed them facing one of the drawers.

"What is that?" Rachel asked, pointing to the icon on the drawer.

"Splendid, Mrs. Sheldon; you certainly can spot the unusual. It's an old glyph from a language long ago. Translated today, it means 'Money Comes from God'."

"Odd, don't you think, especially on a coffin?" said Angie. "Mrs. Shelden, it looks like the hieroglyphics I saw."

"The point is, you see; in this case, it's not the meaning that is important, it is the shape."

Richard took out his Knofer and waved it across the symbol. The drawer clicked, and a larger than standard coffin slid out in front of the three viewers. The casket was pearl white, almost perfectly oval and mildly glowing.

"I don't understand," said Rachel. "What is this?"

"Please. Don't be afraid. I've been waiting for you all evening. Now, we can begin." Richard smiled, turned and waved his Knofer over the same icon on the center of the casket top. The entire top half became transparent, and the shocked girls both gasped at what they saw.

"Jack, oh, my God!" Rachel began to weep.

"Please, my dear." Richard held out his hand to her.

"Look a little closer; come."

Both Rachel and Angie stepped forward. The light inside the casket was perfect, enabling them to see every detail. There lay Jack Sheldon, wearing nothing but a faint smile.

"This can't be," Angie said. "That's not him. He is in Focus Ward, in 309, a bloody mess. This man is perfect. He has no marks, no stitches."

"That's because he was not broken or bloody at all, my dear."

"What are you saying?" Rachel snapped as she studied the body. "What are we looking at, Dr. Bellos?"

Richard replied with confidence, "Oh, this is your husband alright, every cell. You can believe me. Please, will you two sit down just a moment? I have to tell you something."

The chairs were comfortable; but the women sat rigidly, still staring at the coffin.

"Angie, Rachel, there is much more going on that I want you to know, because, well...because we are more than just hospital family."

The women looked at each other and Rachel said, "What?"

"Angie, my dear ..." Richard knelt in front of her with his hands on the chair arms. "... I know what a night this has been for you, and it's far from over. But I tell you the truth when I say, you are my granddaughter."

Angie looked wide-eyed as he smiled and extended his arms to her. "But I don't understand." She put her hands to her mouth, and then, instinctively, leaned into Richard.

"I know, my dear, but it is true."

He started to cry too and then gathered himself. "Angie, both of you, listen; pay close attention. First things first and then your questions. Angie, your father is going to be here soon; and, as this day begins, it's going to be a new life for you, him, me, Rachel and Jack."

"My father? Who is my dad?" Angie gasped. "You mean Dr. B?"

Dr. Richard gently patted her face. "It is quite a story, but for another time. We are in a horrible rush. I realize this isn't easy, but I have to expedite here."

Rachel interrupted, "What about my husband, Jack?"

"As I said, that is Jack alright. Angie, do you have the vial that Dr. Bellos told you to inject?"

The two women looked at each other, and Rachel nodded to Angie. "Yes, I have it here." Angie reached into her pocket, withdrew it and handed it to Dr. Richard.

"Thank you." He waved his Knofer over the icon on the casket again. Rachel stood up and watched as the coffin slid around and lowered. Richard took a syringe out of his pocket and filled it with the liquid in the vial.

He turned to Rachel and spoke softly, "You know, my dear, it was your calculations over the early years that was the motivation and the stepping-stone to Jack's putting it all together. Without you, this would not be possible. Remember that."

Richard leaned over Jack's head with his back to the two women and injected the vial into the side of his neck. "Now we wait,"

Then Richard reached over and pushed a small button on the wall to the left of the coffin. A 10-inch by 10-inch door opened, revealing a filled wine glass, which he took out.

Rachel stared at Jack's body in disbelief. She thought she saw his right-hand quiver. "Jesus, his eye twitched; he is blinking." She caressed his face and leaned into him.

The first thing he saw was her smile. "Rach?"

She held his hand and kissed him, "Hi."

With tears of happiness flowing, she began gently caressing him. "Thank heaven, Jack, my darling."

"Please, you two . . ." Richard patted Rachel lightly. "...I hate to interrupt; but Jack, you have to drink this."

He handed Rachel the wine glass and nodded. She took it, lifted Jack's head and fed him.

"You two have very little time," Richard whispered, "and you may want to pull that blanket over your husband. Now, Angie, will you come with me for just a minute? We need to talk. Then, all of us need to move out of here."

"What is going on?" Jack asked. He began to sit up, shaking, as he tried to focus on Richard. "Who are you?"

Rachel put her finger to his lips. "You've done enough for one day, honey. We are going to do whatever the doctor says. Now, be quiet and drink."

"Thank you," said Richard.

Just as Jack was about to sip, there was a bang, then two, three, coming from the outer rooms of the morgue.

Richard ran to the door; but, by that time, it was too late. He had just enough time to turn and yell back at Angie, "Get to the closet, Angie! Hurry! Get in there, now!"

Richard felt the first bullet hit his leg. Angie screamed and instinctively made it into the closet, the door slamming behind her. Jack heard the shots and jumped up and out of the casket, naked. It all happened so quickly. Rachel saw the next two bullets explode through Richard's torso and into the walls. She screamed as Jack reached to help Richard. But he too stepped into an array of gunfire. He turned to Rachel, just as the men entered the room. There were sparks everywhere.

"Rachel!" Jack yelled as he fell.

The gunmen had no mercy, pulling the triggers repeatedly, spitting bullets into Richard and Jack. Then, they turned to Rachel. One black-hooded man yelled, "You're all going to die...everyone!"

Rachel stood in terror. The last thing she heard was the shots of the automatic machine-guns as she felt the bullets go through her chest. She fell, face down, hitting the floor, her eyes in a glossy gaze, and her mouth spitting blood as she reached for Jack. Smoke and silence filled the morgue. Three bodies lay limp in pools of blood spilling all over the floor. A gunman retrieved both the vial under the casket and the manuscript that Angie dropped. "Let's get out, men," One of them said. They leapt out the Atrium window onto ropes that took them up into the morning sky.

Barb Sawyer heard the commotion and hurried down the hall into the room where she saw Rachel, Jack and Richard soaked in blood.

She screamed and ran back out, bumping into Dr. Mathew Bellos.

"Barb, what is all the noise?"

She was hysterical, shaking. "My God!" She pointed. "There, in there; they are all dead!"

Bellos let her go and walked into the bloody scene. He stood, stunned at the horror. "Dad, no! My God, and Rachel?"

All three bodies were riddled with bullets. Bellos went to his father first and turned him over.

"BARB!" he yelled. "BARB, COME HERE!"

In seconds, Sawyer appeared again with a crash cart.

"Help me, Barb. Take his feet. We must get him in the casket over there. Hurry!"

Within a minute, they managed to lift Richard up and into the coffin bed. Bellos took his Knofer, waved it over the casket lid, and the bed slid back into the wall. Then, he looked down at Rachel, up at Barb and spoke quickly and succinctly into his Knofer, "Team Red to floor two of the Andrews morgue, immediately! Set up Unit-4 for gunshot victims. Notify Dr. Lu, transporting two bodies for Transtosis. Stat!"

Barb watched astonished and transfixed. Within seconds, Bellos' emergency team arrived and moved with lightning speed. They put Rachel on a gurney and wheeled her out into a private elevator. Bellos, gently but firmly, took Barb by the shoulders, looked her straight in the eyes and said, "Barb, look at me. Go to the nurses' station and call emergency and the police. Get them here right away. Then call Frank Bloom in Research Lab 23. I need him here to autopsy Jack and get me those results stat. Have you got that?"

"Yes, sir." Barb appeared noticeably shaken but concentrated on what Bellos was saying.

"Okay, good, this was a pro job. We need to move quickly. Also, call Dave Marshall, Chief of Security. Have him come to my office ASAP . . . And Barb; I don't need to tell you, do I? You didn't see anything. You weren't even in here. Only one person was shot. Period!"

Barb closed her eyes and nodded yes.

"Now go!" Bellos turned around again to survey the room, and he heard a faint noise coming from the closet. He walked slowly to the door and listened to crying inside. He swung the door open, and Angie exploded out into his arms.

"Dr. B . . . Dad!"

"Thank God you are alright, child." For a moment, nothing else existed. Bellos spoke with quiet surprise, "Angie, you know?"

"Yes, you must have realized that I suspected for a long time. Dr. Richard told me. He said he was my grandfather. What happened?"

"A lot . . . Come with me. You will be safe."

He turned her around, and they walked back into the closet.

"But where are we going?"

Bellos tapped the wall and spoke strange words again that meant, "Master secure, GGM-TBN-010."

The wall slid open, and the two stepped into a lighted elevator.

"Angie, put your left-hand palm on the panel and say after me, 'Master's daughter, Angie Bellos.' Can you do that?"

"Yes."

She repeated the phrase phonetically. The door closed and the elevator moved upward. When the door opened again, they were back on the tenth floor, in Bellos' office foyer.

"Angie, are you okay enough to reach on top of that bookcase, there?"

"Sure."

"Get the shiny white book with J.A.S. on it. Bring it to my office down the hall, over there."

Bellos walked ahead to his desk and used his Knofer to call Gordon Swanson. Angie felt her body start going into shock. She concentrated and thought, *this is not going to happen.* Most determined, she took a high-back chair from the dining room and stepped up to reach the book; the same one she had read earlier. Holding it to her chest, she walked toward the computer room; but she stopped at the door, shocked once again at what she saw. Dr. B. was talking to a two-foot-tall hologram of a white-haired man.

The image seemed to grow out of a small rectangular object on the desk. For Angie, everything that night had a dreamlike quality; but now a weak dizzy feeling started to overwhelm her as she listened.

"I'm afraid they have assassinated DP-1, sir, and Dr. Richard and Rachel Sheldon both need procedures."

"What about Angie?"

"She is safe, here with me." Bellos turned and smiled at his daughter. "Thank God. What about the vial and Jack's manuscript?"

"Gone, unfortunately. The police are on the way. Marshall will be here in a few minutes."

"What about Mr. Brock?"

"He is being held down on red-six."

"Good, I will notify 'Ever-Life.' You confirm all DNA. We must get the vials, Mathew. Did you find out how many there are?"

"Jack said five, but we really can't be sure."

Angie stood watching and listening, in disbelief.

"Angie is the most important thing right now; so, keep her safe. Then we must meet. Have you seen young Mr. Sheldon yet?"

"Marshall and I will do that."

"I think it best to bring the lad with you, Mathew. Take a Carrier to Jerusalem. I have a meeting on the surface in Geneva regarding 'Time Trust.' After that, I will meet you in the reception tunnel beneath Judah villa. We know they have to stop and trade the merchandise in the Holy City before going on to Turkey."

"Why?"

"Too many ears, Mathew . . ."

Bellos glanced to the side, at Angie again. "Yes, sir, be safe."

MARION BROCK'S CHIEF OF STAFF, Rash InVoy, sat in his office, in a meeting with Greek Orthodox Pappas Kristos Alieri, who was a liaison assistant to the local Ecumenical Patriarch. The Diocese headquartered in the modest Church of Saint George, within the Phanar district of Istanbul, Turkey. Father Kristos was a liaison to the Christian Orthodox Hierarchy, most densely populated in Russia now.

"Rash, you know I appreciate you keeping me updated on all this. It's so exciting that completion is in sight. This is a Godsend to help us understand our Lord's resurrection."

"You're welcome. Just to be clear, Father; your brothers and leaders have agreed to everything, correct?"

"Yes, I have assurances; this is our greatest opportunity to unite the faiths and merge science with religion. We have agreed to work in harmony, as long as no one is hurt and no major conflict results."

"Nothing worthwhile is easy, Father."

"Has something happened? Our briefing was to include Mr. Brock."

"We have just heard from Mr. Brock. He has been delayed and will call as soon as he can."

Kristos said, "Were you able to confirm securing the formulas?"

"Yes, the good news is we have the manuscript, and a vial is on its way to us, right now."

Kristos took a breath of relief. "How long before we know?"

"A few hours; we have a lab setup where the trade will be made. Are you prepared for the exchange?"

"Yes, my son. As you know, after I met with Mr. Brock, I approached the local synagogue and mosque leaders. We all have been very persuasive in record time throughout our hierarchies. I have commitments totaling $16 billion in U.S. currency. We are all ready to transfer shares upon receipt and confirmation."

"Good. Pardon me for asking, father; but this has to be the biggest transaction so far that you've negotiated with Russia, Israel, and Iran, no?"

"Yes, it is, by far; it is the most significant treaty in the history of the combined faiths. We will bring peace between the Christians, Jews, and the Muslims, finally; all in the name of our Lord."

CHAPTER 18: BRIAN

THE FAINT LIGHT OF THE MORNING SUN began to change the horizon as Brian Sheldon arrived at Marion Brock's Fargo building.

The entrance guard was ready and admitted him without question to Brock's penthouse on the top floor. Brian waited a half hour, pacing and looking out the living room's wide bay windows. For a moment, the beauty of the sunrise hitting the desert flowers erased the jarring emotion of all that happened that night. As he studied it all, he noticed four men, dressed in SWAT team garb, running toward his building from the direction of the hospital. They were carrying what looked like automatic weapons. Brian pushed his face up against the window, to try to see exactly where they entered. His nerves kicked into gear again.

Suddenly, Brock's multi-line phone monitor rang. It was built into the glass tabletop covering the couch's side table. Just one light blinked and beeped. He stared at the light and thought for a split second about what to do. Then, he touched the light, and a speaker turned on. He heard two men talking.

"Yes, sir, we have part of an empty vial and the manuscript, but we couldn't find Mr. Brock."

"Stay where you are. We will bring him to you."

The line went dead. Brian pushed the dot again, sat down on the couch and thought. Then, he raced downstairs to the security guard.

"Excuse me, sir; I saw men run into the building. They looked like the military. It looked like they were wearing SWAT clothes."

The guard snickered, "I assure you, if anyone came in, I would have seen them. This is the only entrance. No one gets by me."

"You know," said Brian, "I think I'm going back to the hospital and meet Mr. Brock there. Don't worry; I've got all the codes, and I locked upstairs."

Before the guard could react, the lad skipped out the door and ran as fast as he could following the long-paved path back to Andrews. After almost 10 minutes, he staggered, out of breath, into the first floor ER-1. There were police all over, so he stopped one of the plainclothes men.

"Excuse me, officer, what's happened?"

"I'm sorry; I can't say."

Brian showed his Brock Intern I.D. to the officer.

"Young man, that doesn't do anything for me. If you have a question, you can ask the detective on the second floor, if they let you in up there."

Brian rode up to floor two and cornered the first cop he saw. "Hello, sir? Sir, I am Brian Sheldon. I work for Marion Brock, out of Washington, D.C. He owns this place. Can you tell me what happened here?"

"Sheldon, eh, good for you; I am Detective Inspector Burns, of the Arden City Police, homicide. You must be here to answer questions because this is a murder scene, and I need answers."

"Murder? Who was murdered?"

"What's your name again, Sonny?"

"Sheldon, Brian Sheldon."

"Come with me, over here." Burns led Brian to a bench in the hallway outside the morgue.

"You are Brian Sheldon, eh?"

"Yes."

"Do you have relatives here at the hospital?"

"My father was in a car accident last night. I'm here to see him."

Burns raised an eyebrow. "Car accident, eh?"

Burns said to himself, *"Maybe a lead on the guy in the car crash...*What about your mother?"

"I talked to her a little more than an hour ago."

"Ah, I am sorry, son. But your dad was shot tonight in this morgue."

"What? That's impossible! It can't be true! Who was brought in from the car accident?"

Burns thought and started to write in his pocket journal but hesitated. "Hmm, if that's true, we have quite a mystery. Does your dad have a brother, a twin?"

Brian furrowed his brow and said, "No."

"Well then, the hospital records show Dr. Jack Sheldon was shot at least four times in the chest right over there in the morgue. I saw the body, and the nurses and doctors have verified his identity through blood tests. I am sorry, son. Is there anyone else you know here?"

Brian coughed and looked like he was about to throw up. He began to sway and hyperventilate. "My Dad was in a car accident and brought to Focus ward after extensive surgery? What you're saying is impossible, we monitored him; he was on the third floor. I want to see him! Let me see my dad!"

Burns reacted with compassion. "I can't do that, son. Try to settle down. We will get to the bottom of all this. You go with this officer. She will take you somewhere safe. I'll meet with you later. I'm sorry. Go on."

The uniformed policewoman took Brian by the arm and escorted him back down to a secure room in ER-1.

"You just wait in here, Mr. Sheldon. I'll be right outside if you need anything. Try to be patient." The woman shut the door and locked it.

Brian sat down on the hospital bed, confused and angry. "I have to get out of here."

Back on the second floor, Detective Burns yelled out, flippantly, "Sergeant Wells, did we get anything on the wife yet?"

Wells shouted back, "Two detectives went to her house, Jake. Nothing, no answer, but here, downstairs in the ER, one of the receptionists thought she saw Mrs. Sheldon in the hospital, about an hour or so ago."

Jake Burns rolled his eyes in disgust. "Christ, I need a vacation."

CHAPTER 19: BREATHLESS

NURSE ANGIE BELLOS STOOD AT THE DOORWAY of Dr. Bellos' computer room inside his tenth-floor suite at Andrews Hospital. She watched, mesmerized, as her father completed his call to GGM Gordon Swanson.

"Angie, come take a seat, here. Are you okay?"

Angie sat on the chair beside Dr. B's desk. She laid the white book down on it and spoke. "I just can't believe all this is happening. This is the night from hell."

"In some ways, yes, but right now, the important thing is that you feel okay. You have been through so much, and I'm afraid your body may go into shock."

"I know; I just started feeling a bit shaky, lightheaded and weak; but I need to know why." Angie's eyes filled with tears.

"I know." Bellos reached for her hand. "I'm sorry, Angie. I've been a fool. Forgive me?"

"But why did it happen? I don't understand."

"Some very dangerous people have wanted to get a serum formula for a long time, and they finally stole it tonight."

"Why? Tell me. I've seen a man rise from the dead. I was almost murdered, and I can't believe three people were just killed not 10-ft from me. I think I can hear whatever you have to say."

Bellos sat up in his chair and began, "Angie, I've wanted to tell you about us and other things, for a long time; but I couldn't find the right time. Partly, I guess, because there's a bit of a coward in me about you. Believe me, though, it is more than that. I thought I was protecting you. I didn't want a certain faction to find out and use you. I've been torn between telling you and worrying if I did, your life would change so radically, thinking you might lose yourself, blame me; and I'd lose you for good. Lately, well, time and events do strange things to people. The truth is, I guess I put some things out of my mind to protect my sanity too. So, I hope you can be patient with me. I will fill in gaps as best I can, I promise."

Angie shook her head. "It sounds confusing."

"Yes, I guess. It all started when your mother died." Bellos reached and took his Knofer out. "Do you think about your mom a lot?"

"Of course, Carla Esposito, we lived a strange life in those days, and I remember you were there."

"I know, I never told you this, but, when she died; Christ, it seems like only yesterday. We were married at the time, but we couldn't tell anyone. If you remember, natural born citizens were not allowed to marry emigrants. She had to keep her maiden name. Your mother made me promise not to cause a stink about the whole issue. She thought it would ruin my status in Washington if it came out. Later, I filed papers through my contacts which made you my legal protégé. After your mom had passed away, several extremist bastards tried to deport you; the papers stopped that. You never knew. We settled into a routine of academia and life. You were so smart. Eventually, your interest in nursing assured you a future, freedom, and independence. The country needed anyone in medicine, and I was well-known enough that they stopped harassing us. By that time, my books, patents, and lectures gave us the financial security we needed to move on. When I got this position at the Complex, I didn't tell you anything for your own safety. I know it's no excuse; but here in New Mexico, you were safe and seemed happy. I concentrated on my work, and I vowed to bring Mom back."

"Bring Mom back?"

"My position here allowed me to research her death; and, at the same time, I could keep an eye on you." Bellos stroked her hair and shoulder. "Focus Ward was the perfect place to keep you safe with me."

"But why did I have to be safe? Something is missing."

"Some aspects of what I am involved with right now are dangerous, and there is more you have to hear and see."

Bellos spoke into his Knofer in the strange Ever-Life language. Three little holograms: a sphere, a square, and a triangle appeared above his Knofer. He grabbed the triangle, tossed it on the floor and spoke to the Knofer. "Please set Carla Bellos' program, authorization: Bellos GGM-TBN 010 . . ."

Angie stared, focusing in disbelief, as Bellos talked to her. "Angie, I am not just head of this hospital. For years, I have been a leader in training, of a very ancient, secret organization, an underground society. Don't worry, it's not a cult or anything like that. That is a good part of why I didn't tell you everything. It would have put you in danger, sooner. Now, you have to know."

Angie stood up, shaking uncontrollably. Bellos reacted quickly, "Angie, your body is going into shock; try to calm down."

He went to a cabinet, pulled out a sealed foil-wrapped glass and handed it to Angie. "Drink this; it should settle you. Sit down; concentrate on the hologram."

Angie drank and after a few seconds, she began to relax again.

Bellos then turned to the triangle and said, "Activate."

It began spinning on one tip and projected a light beam to the ceiling. Then, a skeleton started to grow upward. First the feet, and suddenly leg bones appeared like plants growing in fast forward. The skeleton was complete within a minute. When the bones were finished, there was a beep.

Angie sat in awe, staring in wonder. "Yeah, they don't teach you this in nursing school."

Bellos had a faint smile as he reached for the next sphere and tossed it into the skeleton. A spinal cord and nerves began to grow from the base of the backbone out to the head, hands, and feet. Angie watched a brain flower inside the skull. Nerves sprouted out, like beautiful ivy growing on a castle's walls in quick time-lapse photography. When the nerves were complete, Dr. B. tossed the square into the beam and said, "Features—Carla Bellos."

Then, he turned to Angie and watched her expression. Within seconds, muscles and skin covered the body. A light tan, beautiful skin color with feminine features appeared. Finally, body hair and facial hair finished the image. As it rotated, Angie involuntarily placed her hands over her mouth and reached out, "It's Mom! How is this possible?"

Bellos gently grabbed his daughter's hands before they could touch the hologram. "Listen to me. I need to tell you a lot . . . I am part of a secret society that can do many wondrous things, like this. I show you this, because I – we, have no time. I need you to trust that everything I tell you is true. The form here, what you see, is Mom."

Bellos helped Angie up, and they stood together, staring at Carla.

"Now, you need to be strong and open-minded."

Angie took a breath. "Why? What now?"

Dr. B. went to the closet and took a bathrobe out, which he always kept for his wife. He turned, looked at Angie and they both watched Carla, as he spoke one word into the Knofer, "Employ." Her hologram changed and became flesh. The triangle and beam of light disappeared, and the body slowly lowered onto the carpet. Carla Bellos stood before them. At first, she moved ever so slightly, and then she blinked and looked at Dr. B.

"Hello, darling," Carla leaned in and embraced Bellos.

"Hi, babe." Bellos smiled. "Here, put this on. I brought someone to see you. Look."

Carla turned and saw Angie. After several blinks, she recognized her daughter. She held out her arms in surprise, "Oh, my heavens . . . Angela?"

"Mom?"

"Oh, my baby! How wonderful! My goodness, how you've grown."

They hugged tightly. "Oh, Mom . . . it is you."

Then, Angie turned to Bellos. "Dad, how did you do this?"

Angie started to shake again.

"It's alright," Carla said. "I am here, just in a different way. I am still Mom. I can't be exactly like you and Dad anymore . . . Mathew, please."

"Angie, Mom is real but different. She's similar to a clone. You see, we can create solid holograms. Each one is similar to a clone but synthetic. In your mom's case, I programmed most of the memories into the holographic data; but I have been limited. She can function up to the degree we have programmed her, yet she doesn't breathe. The important thing right now is that you two can be together. We can talk about this and a lot more, later. Right now, you two should enjoy the moment. I have to go to a short but critical meeting. You stay here with Mom, and I'll be back in a few minutes."

Bellos kissed Carla and left the room. The two women sat on the couch on the far side of the room.

"Mom, I'm a nurse but I don't understand all the medical technology. It's hard to accept all this."

"I know. Your dad tried to explain everything to me some time ago. I never understood either."

"You feel real, just like me, like anyone else; and you sound like Mom. It's so good to see you."

"Tell me all about you . . . what you've been doing?"

Meantime, Bellos left and refocused on the morgue murders. Work demanded it. He walked to the front door and opened it. Chief of Security Dave Marshall stood before him.

"Dave, come in; sit down."

"Sir, we caught the men who did it."

"Good. Were they Brock's?"

"Yes, their communications are primitive. We traced contacts to Rash InVoy, Brock's Chief of Staff, and Archer Smythe, InVoy's hatchet man. Smythe made the 'go' call from Istanbul, Turkey. Here's a phone they used.

We took it off one of the murderers. The whole thing went down within 15 minutes. If we had more time, we might have found out why?"

"Dave, that's not the point, and you know it."

"We are examining the room now. The Carrier-Unit malfunctioned from the bullets. We think it died."

"What?"

"I know; I thought they only died from sunlight, right?"

Bellos squinted, "Or apparently something else . . ."

"Ever-Life is searching all data banks and testing a four-foot square wall section struck by bullets. At this point, we don't have answers."

"Alright; keep me posted," Bellos said. "Make sure Ever-Life gets all necessary DNA data for processing Dr. Richard and Rachel?"

"Yes, sir. One other thing; young Sheldon is in ER-1."

"Hmm, good; deliver him to Carrier Unit-17. We will all be leaving from there. Thanks, Dave."

"I am sorry about this sir."

"I know. Tell the police I will be available to interview tomorrow. Oh, and Dave, tell Barb Sawyer to go home. She and I won't meet until I get back."

They shook hands, Marshall left, and then Bellos went back to his office to see Angie and Carla.

"Hi, you two; I'm sorry; I had to go."

"That's okay, Luv," Carla said. "We are having a wonderful time."

"All this is wonderful. I just need a little time," Angie said.

Bellos kidded, "Your Mother and I understand. After tonight, I'm surprised you haven't gone mad by now. But you have stopped shaking. Listen, I do hate to break this up, indeed, but Angie, you and I have several things we must do. We have to go."

"No," Carla reacted, "not yet; please Mathew, it's too soon."

"I'm sorry, honey, it is necessary, only for a short time, I promise."

After a few seconds, Carla looked at her daughter and said, "Yes, right, we will be together soon. I love you. Remember, it is just a little different, that's all. Give us a hug, baby."

Angie leaped into her mother's arms and held on tightly. Carla gently pushed her daughter back and whispered, "Bye for now." Then she stood straight, with tears in her eyes, and said, "End program."

Her image pulsated, blinked, and suddenly, she was gone. Bellos took Angie in his arms as they both looked at the pile of robe on the floor. "I know this is difficult. I know this morning has been too much for anyone. But,

Angie, you are not just anyone. I believe you can handle all this. Changes are coming fast, and I promise, you are a big part of them. You will be with your mom again."

"I hope so." Then, with a smile, she stepped back again. "Okay, what's next, Pop?"

"Have you got the book you brought in?"

"Right there, on the desk . . ."

"Grab it and come on then; we go."

Angie followed Bellos out of the room and back into the elevator by the front door. Bellos spoke with conviction, "Down-red 6, STAT . . ."

The elevator pressurized and fell fast, down below the hospital some 1300 feet. Within 10 seconds, the door opened, and they walked out into a lighted rock wall corridor. Once again, Angie stared at everything.

"Dad, where are we? Wonderland?"

Bellos chuckled, "Interesting you say that. I thought so the first time I came here. This way; follow me."

They walked through the hallway, passing five numbered doors. Bellos opened the sixth, which had the number 17 on it. They stepped into an empty white room.

"Angie, this is the inside of a Carrier-Unit. Remember repeating those words in the elevator before?"

"Yes."

"Well, now your voice print is part of a unique database, and consequently, in rooms like this, you have authority to request most anything you want. So, don't be bashful or afraid to ask for it, within reason of course."

"I don't understand."

Bellos waved his arm out, "I mean, like a chair."

He said, "Chair." And immediately a high back cushioned chair appeared. Angie was stunned. Then he said, "Please provide a table with hors-d'oeuvres."

A dining table with a large plate of various appetizers appeared out of nowhere.

He spoke to Angie then. "Standard programming is Victorian style furniture. You will learn as you go. You try."

Angie looked wide-eyed and tried. "Lobster dinner with asparagus, baked potato, and champagne."

A full plate and glass appeared on the table.

Bellos coached her a bit. "Try not to get caught up in it too much, alright?"

"What do you mean?"

Bellos turned as if he were speaking to the walls.

"Please provide a couch, fireplace, tables, lamps and 60-inch wall monitor. Decorate walls in style of Bellos house-1017."

Angie watched the room's lighting pulse, and then, like magic, everything Bellos requested appeared out of nowhere, neatly positioned around the room.

"That's impossible!" Blurted Angie.

Bellos smiled faintly. "Yeah, rather nifty, isn't it?"

"Nifty? Dad please?"

"Yes, nifty. Obviously, I am stuck on Victorian Santa chairs, fireplaces, and old clichés. You practice. Decide what you like. Just remember, if you abuse the Unit, it will cease to function. Honey, I have to go for just a little while. Try to relax. How is your body shock?"

"I feel better."

"Good." He turned to walk out and heard, "Dad, wait, you can't leave without telling me; what is a Carrier-Unit?"

Bellos stopped and did a double-take. He turned around and took a breath himself. "You're right." He scratched his head and looked at her lovingly. He walked over to the chair, sat down, and gestured for her to do the same. "Do you remember in the nurses' lounge, how I acted?"

"Yes, I was hurt, shocked really."

"I am sorry for that. I didn't think you were going to be so upset at what you saw. After all, you are a nurse."

"What did I see?"

"You saw something wonderful; but yes, scary, especially if you are not prepared."

"I feel safe now. Tell me."

Bellos sighed and said, "As I started to say to you before, some years ago I was recruited by a secret society. It's really a medical research organization. The organization is a subterranean culture of people, who base their lives on healthcare research and well-being. They have lived deep beneath the Earth's surface for centuries, much longer actually; but the point is, they—we, have made incredible medical discoveries, discoveries that far surpass anything humanity has done on the surface."

"Like what?"

"Like how to bring a person to life."

"You mean, Dr. Sheldon, don't you?"

"Yes; and very soon, your mom, I hope. Dr. Sheldon discovered a serum, a formula. It's a bit complicated."

Angie sat up straight and attentive. "Sounds Frankensteiny?"

Bellos spoke in a very understanding tone. "Far from it; however, we have not been able to duplicate his formula completely. We are working on it as we speak."

"Okay?"

"Yes...Anyway, his serum can only survive and will only react correctly in a single catalyst bath. I discovered that that catalyst exists in its raw state within only one single primary source. I searched and recalculated out of the millions of people in our database, and I found only one person, who contains the rare DNA chain sequence...Actually, in that book you have there's a complete chapter on this. But the book is not from Dr. Jack. It's from the secret organization I told you about. The organization is really a society born of inner Earth. It's called Ever-Life."

"Ever-Life?" Angie was noticeably shocked yet more focused. "Is this Ever-Life who killed Mrs Sheldon?"

"No, they-we are the good guys. Let me finish this one point. It's very important."

"Okay."

"Back to the catalyst bath. Dr. Jack searched through countless DNA strands and eventually he found one, only one would work. But he had to synthesis it. He formulated it specifically for his research. It took him a great deal of time."

"Dad? You're trying to tell me something, aren't you? Just say it."

"Well, yes, I am. I have discovered where the catalyst bath is in a human body. So far, only one person has the chain. And I'm the only one who knows who."

Angie shrugged. "Okay, so the combination of serum and catalyst bath can bring dead people back to life. I get it."

"Well, it's not just that. Follow me on this one point please. First, I am referring only to the catalyst bath."

"Fine, go on."

"So far, within all the known DNA and gene banks that exist, our family, Bellos/Esposito, has the only structural combination that carries the gene-chain to make the bath. It's one of the reasons they recruited me, my DNA. And it has been passed on to certain relatives..."

"Your genes?"

"...More specifically, in this case, regarding the catalyst bath, it's been passed on to you in its most concentrated state."

"What?"

"Angie, you alone; you are the only person who has the genetic carrier proteins in the raw state in the right sequence combinations. You carry the bath that will ensure Dr. Sheldon's serum will live long enough to re-inject into a patient. Even he doesn't know what I'm telling you."

Angie froze for a few seconds with a blank stare, trying to understand. Then she furrowed her brow, rolled her eyes a bit and looked around the room. "So, what the heck does that mean exactly?"

Bellos pulled his chair close to her and took her hand. Just as he was about to speak again, Angie blurted out, "Oh my God, this can't be happening. Dad, did you know I was kidnapped tonight?"

"No! When?"

"Earlier, after Ralph and I got caught in the elevator."

"Jesus, honey; I was the one who authorized the Elevator-Unit to take you out. I thought you would be safer."

"We made it to a road, and then a van came. There were men with black hoods. They took me, drugged me and left me on Mrs. Sheldon's doorstep. She and I talked, and we took Dr. Jack's manuscript to the morgue. Dad, Dr. Richard injected Dr. Sheldon with the vial you gave me, and he woke up."

"I expected that, but that particular Dr. Sheldon was an entire duplicate body. You saw the real Dr. Jack. I had to perform a process called Transtosis on him. He's still alive now because of a serum we are giving him until we can introduce his CPT. It takes more explanation, but we don't have time right now. We can reanimate cells, grow a part or complete organ; even grow entire bodies. Unfortunately, however, the memory/personality of the patient is temporary. We keep the duplicates comfortable and functioning normally with periodic non-invasive procedures until imprints are permanent."

"That must be the wine Dr. Richard gave him, right?"

"Yes. I'm sorry about all this, kiddo, dumping it on you all at once."

"It's okay. I'm a nurse, remember? Can I change the subject for a second? Will you take a look at this on my neck? Is it a needle mark?"

Bellos studied the tiny dot. Then, he rolled his eyes, stood up and paced. "They kidnapped you to try and get the catalyst bath. They are making more vials. The shelf-life of the serum is too short to study."

"So, am I in danger?" Angie asked.

"Not until they realize your neck is the wrong extraction point."

"What do you mean?"

Bellos stopped pacing and looked at her. He snapped his fingers as if a light bulb turned on. "Jesus, we have a traitor in our midst. They know you are the bath, and that means they know this, Ever-Life, us. We must get the serum vials back before they mix the wrong catalyst, unless, of course, they redid the chemistry already. Angie, I know all this is shocking—the morgue, Focus Ward. I will make this up to you. I'm going to bring you into my world unless you are too exhausted."

"Dad, I think I'm already in your world."

"I'll trust you with everything. Are you hungry?"

"Yes."

"Let's get you refreshed and eat. You can't afford to go into shock again."

Bellos grabbed his Knofer, "Authorization Bellos GGM-TBN-010. Transfer this Knofer to Angie Bellos. Here, Angie, take this. Look into the red dot."

Angie did, and then she gave it back to Bellos, who continued,

"Activate defensive posture 001 to protect Angie Bellos."

"Here," He handed it back to her. "Now it's yours. If you get lost and can't find anyone, it will show you the way."

"I don't think I'm going to wander off. Anyway, I am tired and hungry."

"Eat your lobster. Around the corner, over there, is a bath area. I have to go. I will be back very soon. Meantime, you can freshen up and enjoy whatever you like. After that, I'm going to send you on a learning effort. You are going on a tour that will explain exactly how we do what's in that book."

"One thing, dad. I still want to know what a Carrier is."

"Yes, be assured, you will find out. After all, you are sitting in one right now."

"Really? Where are you going?"

"I'm going to save what we have started and start beating the bad guys. I'll be back by the time you are ready."

CHAPTER 20: UNIT 17

ANGELA BELLOS SAT IN UNIT 17, which was on lower level six far below Andrews Hospital. She had finished her meal, refreshed herself and sat comfortably watching the monitors, waiting for her father to return. There was a knock on the door, and a guard walked in. "Hello, Ms. Angie, are you alright?"

"Yes, fine thanks; just waiting."

"I see. The doctor asked me to bring you some company. I hope you don't mind."

"Well, I can't imagine any more surprises. Sure; that's fine."

The guard turned, motioned, and in walked a young man, with his face down. Angie studied him for a few seconds, and then he looked at her.

"Ms. Angie, this is Brian. Brian; be nice. Ms. Angie has had an evening to match yours. Ms., the doctor said he would be here shortly."

"Thank you."

Angie stood studying the young man and then said, "Brian, Brian Sheldon? Is that you?"

Brian looked perplexed until he took a moment to examine her face. "My God, you're Angie Esposito, what the heck! I haven't seen you since . . ."

"The party week at college?"

"Was that it? Jesus, that was years ago."

They both held out their hands to each other. Brian smiled and said, "You are the last person I thought of seeing today."

"Why are you here?" Angie asked.

"I don't know, to tell you the truth. The cops were in the hospital when I got there. They ended up interrogating me. Then, they locked me in a room in the ER. They said my dad was killed. Maybe they think I'm involved, a suspect or something. For God's sake, I just wanted to find my boss; and, all of a sudden, I murdered one of my parents."

Angie paced, went to the couch a few feet away and sat down for a minute.

"Brian, I am so sorry. I wish I had better news. This night has been the strangest of my life. I am the one who was monitoring your dad on Focus Ward."

"Focus Ward, I was there, just tonight. No one mentioned your name. I was there with my boss, Marion Brock. We met Barb Sawyer. Do you know her?"

"Sure, my dad said that she relieved me as nurse on that ward until we get this all sorted out."

"Your dad? I thought you lived alone after your mom died."

"I did, for a while; Dr. Bellos did so much for me. I never understood it all until tonight. He is my father."

Brian sat speechless beside her as the door opened again, and in walked Dr. Bellos.

"Hi, sweetie." They hugged, and Bellos said, "You look refreshed."

"I took a shower and had some food. Thank you."

"Good."

Then, Bellos turned to Brian and extended his hand. "Hello, young man. It's been a while."

"Yes. Hi, doc. Please, tell me what's going on. Police said Dad was dead."

"I know, Brian, but that is just not true. Everything is going to be fine."

Brian looked confused as Bellos turned to Angie again. "Remember, honey, I told you before to be strong? Now is the time."

Bellos walked to the door, opened it and Dr. Jack Sheldon stepped into the room. Angie gasped. Jack looked immediately at Brian.

"Son, thank God!"

Brian jumped from his chair into Jack's arms. Bellos closed the door and locked eyes with Angie. He pursed his lips, gesturing with a finger for her to be silent. They both watched Jack and Brian.

"Dad, what's happening? They told me you were shot. Where is Mom?"

"The truth is, I don't know." Jack glanced at Bellos. "But we will work this out. I promise. That's why I'm here." They embraced, and after the shock wore off, Jack fixed on Angie. "Matt, Angie is your daughter?" Jack stepped over to her and took her hand. "Wonderful; apparently, your father has several secrets."

"Yes, I'm learning," Angie replied. "Obviously, dad knows how to keep one."

"Matt, where exactly are we? Did the young ones take a plane ride too?"

"No, sorry, and once again, we have to move on, buddy. Time is of the essence. Look, you three have legitimate questions. I'll start by telling you, Brian; your boss, Marion Brock, has taken something very precious from your dad. Without it, he may not live. We must get it back. That means we need to work together. You understand?"

"Not really; my boss, Marion? I was with him on Focus Ward. We were just trying to see Dad."

"Brian, think a minute for me," said Bellos. "Do you know anything about a big deal, some negotiation Brock has been involved with?"

"Why, yes, I think so. He and his whole team are about to close a big deal to make peace for the first time between religions or something."

Jack and Bellos looked at each other.

"Brian, son, do you have any idea where the deal is taking place?"

Brian thought and said, "I think it has to do with some Greek Orthodox priest in Jerusalem or Turkey, or somewhere like that. I remember Rash InVoy saying they are supposed to meet at some church."

Bellos took a breath and then walked over, opened the door and said, "Dr. LuAnne, please come in. You remember Angie? What you don't know is that she is my daughter; and this is Dr. Jack Sheldon and his son, Brian."

"Hello, everyone." She focused on Angie. "My, my, I understand you are going to tour with me for a while."

"Yes, I think so."

They both looked at Bellos; he nodded, and then LuAnne put her arm around Angie. "Well, then, I guess we are off," LuAnne said with a smile.

"Fine, that's a good idea." Bellos patted Angie's shoulder and whispered, "Good luck; everything will be okay. I should be back to see you early this afternoon. You are in good hands with Dr. LuAnne."

"I'll be okay." She hesitated, turned to Bellos, pulled his head down, kissed his cheek, and then looked at Brian. "See you later I hope, Brian."

Both women walked out and Dr. LuAnne shut the door behind them.

Bellos turned to Brian and Jack. "Okay, you two, listen carefully. We are all going on a trip in a unique vehicle. It's called a Carrier. When you get in, just relax. I should tell you both; this Carrier travels at high-speed; but, neither of you should feel any sense of moving. Our objective is to retrieve up to five small vials, which were made from and for you, Jack."

"Jesus, Matt, you're talking about CPT"

"Vials?" Brian asked. "Do you know where they are?"

"We think so. Our security team has tracked and located the courier carrying them. He is negotiating with us as we speak. We plan to intercept him in Jerusalem."

"Uh, Jerusalem as in Israel?" Jack asked.

"Yes, and if all goes well, we make a trade. They end up with fake serum, we get the real stuff, and then you Jack get CPT . We should return here to Andrews sometime after noon, U.S. Mountain Time."

"Shortly afternoon? This Carrier vehicle must be very high-speed. And who are 'they,' Matt; and what are we trading?"

"I will get to that. As I said, you two shouldn't feel any sense of speed in the vehicle. However, you both should be aware of the jet lag factor, because, while it is now 8:14 a.m. here; in real time, we will arrive in Jerusalem in a little over one hour from departure. That part of the world is some nine hours ahead of our Mountain Time."

All three looked at one another as Jack commented, "Jesus, Matt, if I do the math, that's spaceship speed. You said we were going where no one has gone; but, should we be taking the kid?"

"No, we shouldn't. Brian will stay in the Carrier at a villa, outside Jerusalem. You and I will go the final distance. I need you to be okay and focused, Jack; can you do this?"

Brian stood up and blurted, "I know I won't! I'm better trained and stronger than either one of you two. God knows what shape Dad is in right now. You are only doctors, for Christ's sake, not astronauts. I am not leaving dad again."

Bellos smiled and said, "Brock taught you something."

"I'm good, Matt," Jack replied. "I'm fine, really; one thing, though."

"What?"

"Can I have another drink of that elixir?"

"Yes, sure."

Bellos walked across the room over to the curved wall, opened a small door and took a wine glass out.

"Here . . ."

"What is that?" Brian asked.

Jack smiled and toasted his son. "Food for the Gods, son, food for the Gods . . ."

He drank the whole thing in one gulp. Bellos held the door open and gestured to both.

"Okay, you two, let's go."

DETECTIVE JAKE BURNS STOOD staring at Jack Sheldon's naked body on a slab inside Andrews Hospital Morgue. "Who are you, Mr. Sheldon, besides a bloody mess? Sergeant! Sergeant Wells?"

"Yes, sir?"

"Where is Security Chief, Dave Marshall?"

"I am right behind you, officer."

Burns turned around to look up at a 6-ft 2-inch handsome 45-year-old man in a tan shirt and dark brown pants. There was nothing on his person except a small device holstered at his waist.

"That's *Detective*, Mr. Marshall. Exactly, where have you been?"

"Tending to duty on the seventh floor. What can I do for you?"

Burns replied quickly. "And, what is on floor seven?"

"Psychotic and bipolar patients . . ."

Burns raised his eyebrows and shook his head. "Great, more suspects. I'll tell you what, Mr. Marshall; first, you can give me an idea of why this man was shot. What were these mercenaries after? They were pros, but this was no one man hit. The line of shots indicates more than one automatic weapon, and look at these bloody footprints. They have the same shoe tread. Tell me, Mr. Marshall, where was your security squad while all this was happening?"

Marshall replied, "Okay; so, they were pros. How did they get in here? They left breaking the hall windows. Where would they go? We searched the campus and found nothing. But I'm sure your men will do better. It is only a 1600-acre campus. Listen, I have no idea what they were after. We try to save lives here, Mr. Detective, not take them. None of my staff carries weapons; only special ops have guns. You can interview everyone. Look, this is 2nd floor Cancer Treatment, Mortuary and Maternity. These are not major areas of concern for murder. I have one person who monitors this floor every hour. That's it."

"What about your Chief of Staff, Billows?"

"Dr. Bellos is Chief of Hospital, and he's not here. He is out of the country."

Burns looked him square in the eyes. "Well, you better call and get him back. I want to see him."

Marshall noted, "I already did."

Burns turned to the investigating team. "Sergeant Wells; get me that nurse, Barb Sawyer....Thank you, Mr. Marshall; if we need more, we will call you."

"Detective Burns" Sergeant Wells said, "I've been informed Barb Sawyer has gone home."

"What? Well, find out where she lives and get over there."

"Excuse me, Mr. Burns," Marshall interrupted, "Barb Sawyer didn't see anything. I interviewed her. She has been on the verge of a breakdown. She needs sleep. If you insist, I'll bring her to your office, and you can interrogate us both after she has a break. Just give her a breather for a few hours."

Jake Burns wasn't looking for direction. "Oh, I see. Well, in that case. SERGEANT forget it. Mr. Marshall says don't bother. He has interviewed her. I guess he is in charge. After all; it's just a homicide investigation. Tell her to take the week off and go to Florida on me."

Jake was aggravated. "Jesus! And how did these farking gunmen get on the Complex in the first place with such fantastic tight ass security protection? I hold you responsible, Mr. Security Chief."

Jake took several deep breaths before continuing. "Now, Mr. Marshall, may I call you Dave? Dave, why do you think this man, lying there, was in that position? I mean, his son says he was in a car accident earlier tonight and recovering on floor three. Why would he show up on the morgue floor, naked, with his face shot off? So far, we know he ran toward the gunshots, not away from them. Why? He is naked, why would a living man be in the morgue and run naked toward machine guns?"

"I think you asked me the same question twice?" said Marshall sarcastically. "Yes, he does look naked. Well, I am sure it wasn't the heat in here. We keep the whole building at 65 degrees."

Jake walked the room while bantering. "And why are there two other pools of blood; one there, and one way over there in that corner; no bodies, right? Just lots of blood? There is no trail from either of the pools to over there; and, there is nothing on any of the walls except lovely green paint and bullet holes. Boy, this one is going to be fun, right, Dave? It's a real security puzzler. Any thoughts?"

"Yes, do you need me here anymore, detective?

"No, please, no thank you."

"Jake, I found something else," said Dr. Watzin.

"Well, spit it out, doc. That's why you forensic guys are here."

Watzin pointed, "Look at this." Then he bent down and picked it up with a tweezer."

Jake walked over to him, put on his glasses and as Watzin offered his open hand, Jake leaned over to examine the item. "Yes, well, I'm sure it's significant. It looks like a broken half of a test tube. Let me have it. Hmm, no odor, but remnants of blue liquid. Get it to the lab, and get me anything! I want to know what was in it. What is it made of? Are there any fingerprints? And get a blood comparison between this guy and our body at the accident earlier. I want all this blood, bullets, and clothing tested yesterday, damn it! And, Sergeant Wells, where is that kid, Ralph something?"

"He is gone, Jake."

"What did you say?"

"I just got the call from the uniform cop outside the room in ER-1. He snuck out. She doesn't know how or when, but he is not in the room."

"Oh, for Christ's sake! Find me his boss, that Marion Brock. He should know something. Didn't the kid say he was here in the hospital? Turn this place inside out, but get me Brock, or at least someone I can yell at."

Burns turned and started walking out to the main hallway when he saw someone.

"Hey! You there, stop!" Jake cornered a young man at the atrium window. "Where are you going? How did you get in here? Who are you?"

"I am Ralph Walker, a second-floor nurse."

"Oh yeah, where were you when the shit hit the fan?"

"I have been out of the building . . ."

"Doing what?"

Burns' angry tone did not sit well with Ralph.

"Witnessing my girlfriend get kidnapped. Who the hell are you?"

"Police, homicide." Burns flashed his badge. "When did you get here?"

"I got back about 10 minutes ago and was coming up to tell my supervisor about the whole incident, when I walked into you."

Burns pointed to the bench against the wall. "Over here; come sit down. I don't believe this. Just when I thought I could leave," Burns took a breath and began interrogating Ralph. "I am Detective Burns, Arden Police; tell me everything, boy."

"Fine. I work third shift and break at 3 a.m. I met my girlfriend, Angie Esposito, for lunch and a walk. We ended up on the highway, not realizing where we were, romance, you know? And the next thing I know, this blue van stops. Three men whisked her away to God knows where."

"And then what?"

"What do you mean, *then what*? Then, I was alone on the road. I didn't do anything wrong. Why are you interrogating me?" Ralph was more angry than nervous. "Angie is gone. I don't need this shit! I'm out of here!"

"Hold on a minute, Mr. Rush-Rush. I have a murder homicide here and hemorrhoids. You just admitted to being involved in a kidnapping. So, fess up, partner, or we are taking you to lock up right now. Got it?"

"Fine, whatever." Ralph rolled his eyes and continued, "The oddest thing was after they drove off, I heard a cell phone ringing. I found it on the side of the road and answered it."

"Yeah; and?"

"And a voice said, 'If I were you, I would get my ass back to the hospital. You don't want to miss any of this'."

"What?" Burns sat down next to Ralph.

"Yeah, I know. So, I ran but in the wrong direction. Finally, here I am; that's it."

Burns leaned his head back against the wall, sighed and asked, "So, why didn't you use the phone to call 911?"

"It was dead."

"Where is the phone now?"

"Right here, in my pocket." Ralph handed it to Burns and he called out, "Sergeant Wells, take our man here down to the station and get his statement. Give this phone to the engineers. Tell them I need everything on it."

Then burns turned to Ralph again. "Sonny, I'll need a picture of your girlfriend and work details about her."

"Mr. Marshall or Dr. Bellos will have to tell you about her work. Angie and I do not discuss our jobs much, if you know what I mean."

Ralph stood up and accompanied the sergeant out of the building.

Burns shouted, "Oh, Sergeant, call me, after the guy signs his statement."

Burns walked the other way, over to the nurse's station and interrupted the group gossip. "Hey, one of you, will you page Mr. Marshall. Tell him I want Barb Sawyer in my office tomorrow; the earlier, the better. Here is my number. Have him call me if he has any questions."

Then he turned around and walked toward the elevator, talking to himself, "Jesus Christ! Murder, kidnapping, missing mother, pros in ops boots; what am I, Sherlock Holmes? I should never have left New farking York."

CHAPTER 22: THE CARRIER

BELLOS, JACK AND BRIAN WALKED down the long hallway from Unit-17 toward an Ever-Life Carrier substation.

"Matt; how far is it to this vehicle, or whatever it is?" asked Jack.

"Just down those stairs, over there; are you okay?"

"I think so. Better every minute, although, as I said, the strange feelings come and go."

"Dad; is there anything I can do?" asked Brian very concerned.

Jack smiled. "You're with me. That's plenty."

"Here we are," Bellos gestured, "just down that stairwell and beyond."

Jack walked, holding on to Brian; and, halfway down the stairs, they saw the Carrier and stopped in awe.

They were staring at a smooth oval structure some 100 feet long, shaped like a combination of a football and a fish, lying on its side. Jack was hesitant about letting Brian board.

"Christ, Matt, is this thing alive? Is it safe?"

"Everything is fine. Yes, it is safe."

It had four thick-sectioned tentacles extending from one end, each moving independently of one another. The most striking feature was its body color variations. Some sections radiated fluorescent green, while others blinked in bright yellow or translucent orange.

The three men stepped closer, slowly staring, and a door appeared behind one of what looked like a giant round fisheye. Brian stopped holding his dad's shoulder. "Dad, this isn't a subway. Look at that. It looks like an old blinking disco light?"

He turned to his left and noticed two other men entering a second door, some 75-feet away, closer to the rear tentacles of the beast.

"Dad, look! That is my boss, Mr. Brock. Why is he in handcuffs?"

"Son, go on; get on board."

"What is going on, anyway?"

"I'm sure Dr. Bellos will explain."

They all walked into a hollow pearl white wet looking large oval room; but, actually, it was dry and pristine, with clean circulating air.

Brian was understandably bothered. "Who'd have thought it could be this big?"

"Yeah, Matt;" Jack asked, "and are the lights behind the walls?"

Bellos stood behind the two and announced to the room, "Authorization GGM-TBN-010. Please furnish standard furniture, wall monitors, and a bath center. Please supply refreshments for all."

Before their eyes, everything appeared out of nowhere. Jack flinched and looked at Brian. "Don't be afraid. Sit down, son; and let's take one step at a time."

They watched Bellos walk to the far sidewall. He took out his Knofer, pushed it into a slot and spoke to the wall, "Master secured . . . Security Directive GGM-001 and GGM-010 . . . Destination group number two, Post 4-A. We await instructions."

The deep articulate voice of the Carrier itself spoke for all to hear, "Acknowledged."

Then, silence. After 15-seconds or so, the voice spoke again. All Carriers can communicate in any language the human mind could understand, and each spoke as a representative of their hive mind.

"GGM-1-000 is in danger. There has been a security breach in Andrews Hospital-level-three. The courier you seek in Jerusalem Section Post 4-A is Muslim. He is holding a hostage and primary CPT formula for Ever-Life. Dispatch of three Carriers is available from Jerusalem location. Please acknowledge communication."

"Communication acknowledged," and Bellos asked, "Recommendation?"

Bellos heard a two-second *ding*, and a small door appeared at the far end of the room. He walked over and opened it. There was a single small two-inch vial filled with a blue liquid. He took it out and said, "I don't understand. Please explain?"

"Please, sit down, doctor," the Carrier said.

Everyone could hear an air blowing sound as the cabin pressurized. The Carrier began to move and accelerate. The three sat in silence.

"Dr. Bellos, what just happened?" Asked Brian

The Carrier's voice spoke again but this time so only Bellos could hear.

"Listen carefully, GGM-TBN. You have precisely 1.75-time hours to complete the trade for the hostage. It is essential to our continuing cooperation with your species."

Bellos replied quickly, "Who is the hostage?"

There was no answer.

"Please, reply," repeated Bellos. "What about our passenger to trade?"

Silence filled the cabin. They all waited, but nothing happened. Then, Bellos took his Knofer from the slot and called Swanson. His image appeared life-size in the Carrier.

"Mathew, I take it you heard? We have received the same instruction here."

"What do we do with Brock, sir?"

"I will detail after you arrive. We know InVoy wants the serum and Brock, but what else? I wish I could say."

"I thought they had vials?" Bellos commented.

"Yes, and someone we need . . . Damn! Why Brock thinks he can do this is beyond me. I will meet you at the dock. We will drive to the checkpoint. Security is fine, but we have no idea where we go from there. See you soon."

"Sir, there is something else."

"Yes?"

"It appears we have a mole in the Complex."

"Perhaps?"

Communication ceased.

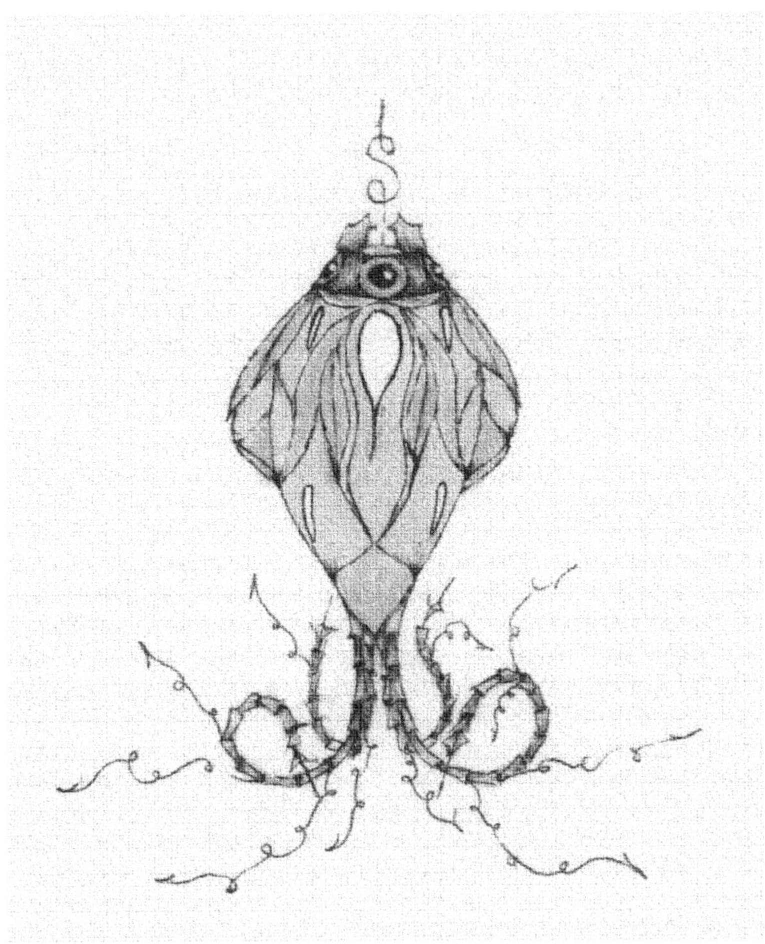

GENERAL FACTS REGARDING CARRIERS:

1] Each time a Carrier travels, it burrows through rock, lava or anything in front of it. It can either shroud itself within a bubble-like protective shell. As it burrows, it displaces anything from in front to behind it, leaving no evidence that it was there. Alternatively, without the bubble shroud, Carriers move through rock, like fish swim through water, but their bodies spin as they reach speeds close to that of a rocket in space. Also, without the shroud bubble, they leave a tunnel behind, rather than displace the rock or lava.

2] Carriers have lived within the Earth for millions of years, and those that reach adulthood have grown large enough to burrow tunnels a half mile in diameter. However, no records indicate how large they become.

3] Carriers and humans share a synergistic relationship. When a Carrier travels with a human passenger, it absorbs an indefinable sustenance, the amount of which varies between humans. After an adult Carrier has accumulated enough human sustenance, it may be stimulated to reproduce by secreting a gooey jelly from its skin. In that case, they leave tunnels with their offspring glued to the walls. The gel sticks indefinitely, and, those few that grow large, find their way to the Earth's core, where they prosper as adults in a hive environment by withdrawing magnetic power from the Earth's magnetic field. The higher the potent sustenance they derive from humans, the more gel they secrete. The goo contains trillions upon trillions of microscopic offspring, organisms that may or may not grow into larger Carriers. Carriers mature into many sizes. Rule of thumb is the older, the bigger.

4] Very few tunnels exist without gel, but those that do, remain lifeless and function as vents, allowing magma to reach the surface.

5] Ever-Life negotiates annual treaties with the Carrier hierarchy, which governs all Carrier behavior with humans, including:

A] To communicate with the Ever-Life GGM, as he requests via direct mind interface or Knofer. Based on Treaty 91776, called the Michael Plan, Carrier hierarchy agreed to provide instant information to the standing GGM, regarding whereabouts, relevant events, and hive activity. In fact, it is all done in trust. Some issues have arisen in treaty council meetings, which do remain unanswered, including what the Earth's core is made of; why the great beasts don't go into it; and why sunlight is supposed to kill Carriers? Fundamentally, it is an accepted fact throughout Ever-Life that the large Carriers are at the top of the food chain, and they reside deep below Earth's surface. New short-term agreements can be negotiated as needed, with a Carrier ambassador—a Tyree Master, if emergencies dictate; however, these are usually done within the deepest hottest known Carrier habitat, the Core Post.

B] To take passengers from any one point within the colonies to any other, like public transportation on the surface. In return, each Carrier derives sustenance from that passenger and shares it with the hive mindset of their species.

6] Smaller sized Carriers not only engineer and construct their hive communities, but they also build all the new habitats in the Ever-Life colonies. They are capable of completing tasks, which might take the surface years to construct, in only a few hours.

7] Carrier offspring supply utility and insulate the colonies from the intense heat and magnetic radiation output of Earth's core. The waste-excrement, of the microscopic Carrier gel, is what lights, sanitizes, supplies oxygen and a mean temperature of 65 degrees for all life within the colonies. For well over 10,000 years, Ever-Life has endured, prevailed and prospered within the environment provided by Carriers.

8] There are very few Grand Carriers, which are enablers of time travel.

9] All Carriers have a collective hive mindset. The public doesn't know to what extent the beasts understand humans.

10] The most significant mystery regarding all Carriers is that no colony anywhere has been able to study one. There are no accurate estimates of how many offspring exist or why certain ones mature to function in one way while others grow to enormous sizes and function in other ways.

11] It is an acceptable miracle to all citizens of Ever-Life, that each Transport Carrier can provide anything that human travelers request, instantaneously.

12] Ever-Life's Post Staff Hierarchy are the only ones who are privy to updated maps of hive locations, even those are constantly outdated.

13] Except for scheduled transports, no one knows where or how often any Carrier moves within the planet.

CHAPTER 23: EVER-LIFE

DR. LUANNE AND ANGIE BELLOS walked through Ever-Life's meticulous tunnel system below Andrews Hospital. Eventually, they stepped onto a people mover, which took them toward Lab 202. Angie held the railing and studied all the people and sights. One area, in particular, caught her interest. Across the walkway, through a massive 30-ft by 20-ft pink tinted window, men and women, dressed in monk-like garb, appeared to be writing, sitting at desks with their backs facing her.

"What are they doing over there?" Angie asked." It looks like an adult school class of some sort."

"Not exactly," Dr. LuAnne said. "That's book finishing. It's where the manuscripts like the white book you're holding are handwritten, proofed and bound. Only the greatest of our successes are prepared in those books. Then, each is shipped to an Ever-Life Post Commander, where it is stored for medical reference."

"Compatibility! That explains the bookcase in Dr. B's office."

LuAnne remarked, " Excuse me?"

Angie smiled. "It's nothing. Talking to myself. Everyone in there seems so focused."

"Yes, they are dedicated and very patient. Honestly, I could never do that. I'd get too bored. Each one of those monks is trained, committed; and every book is a priceless work of art. What has always amazed me is, if you tried to compare the handwriting between them, even an expert couldn't find any difference. Of course, they don't have much fun as I see it. What you see them doing is what they do all the time. It is truly a calling."

Angie replied curiously. "Why not just photocopy the books? Don't you have printers down here? Can't you reproduce them electronically, an e-book thing?"

"Yes, we have similar processes; however, over eons, these scribes have accepted the task to guarantee every single character in each manuscript is perfect and the same. Not only does each book contain a case study and specific directions for reanimating life; but also, each one is a masterpiece, a treasure of historical reference for future generations. By the way, have you read that book you're holding?"

"No, not entirely, but I hope to make time."

"I think you'll find it very enlightening. Come on, we're here. Watch your step."

Dr. LuAnne escorted Angie into the lab. The bodies of Richard Bellos and Rachel Sheldon arrived earlier.

"I've never seen anything like this." Angie was anxious to get on with whatever she was going to do.

"Not if you have never been here." Dr. Lu smiled. "Do you feel well enough to do this right now?"

"I've got my second wind, I think." Angie replied. "Besides, I have no idea what time it is."

"This way then . . ."

They moved from the main outer room to one of four attached smaller work chambers. Chamber 2 was sterile, well-lit, warm with two gurneys and an operating table, which looked like glass; but, when Angie touched it, she flinched, "Whoa, it feels warm and cushy, almost life-like."

"Actually, it is alive. Most everything here is alive; a subject for another time, but nothing to be afraid of."

Angie noticed a few unfamiliar instruments lying on a table, and the curved walls displayed video and audio information. Dr. Lu touched an image, and the screen image became 3D. There were no wires or plugs anywhere. Dr. Richard and Rachel each lay side by side on two separate gurneys with nothing hooked up to them. There was only a quarter-size coin, a control device stuck to their left underarms which maintained their body temperatures at 34.5 degrees Fahrenheit.

"Angie, please wheel Mrs. Sheldon over there to the next room, through that door."

"Mrs. Sheldon? Please, no. I don't think I can. It's too soon."

"I'm sorry. It's okay. I'll do it."

A moment later, LuAnne returned.

"Doctor, I apologize," Angie said. "I am a nurse. It's just that after what has happened tonight, I'm reacting not as I should, sorry."

"Not a problem; no explanation needed."

"Who are you working on first?"

"Dr. Richard, maybe he can help."

LuAnne brought Richard's genetic records up on monitors.

"What do you mean?"

"He has been a part of Ever-Life for quite a while, you know."

"No, I didn't. I thought he was the mortician at the hospital."

"He was; he is; but he has also been a colony citizen for a long time, as was his grandfather. Dr. Richard had been researching our duplication and Transtosis programs for years. Recently he conducted experiments of his own, even while acting as your mortician. I hate to think he has to go through this procedure again. Yes; we will do him first. Maybe he can give us insight into something we may miss otherwise. His knowledge is invaluable."

Angie looked perplexed, but she listened intently. "Since I'm not familiar with anything here, can I ask, exactly what is Ever-Life?"

"It's both the name of our network of colonies, and it's a healthcare program which we began long ago to improve the quality of life. As it evolved, the goal has become an everlasting quality of life. We don't seek to conquer death. Our goal is to keep postponing death's inevitability by controlling life's processes better through genetic manipulation, rather than death controlling life's limits. In many ways, it's not much different from your current medical goals on the surface; but we have been at it much longer. We make discoveries and share them with 'up there.' It has never been vice versa. I hope that makes sense."

"A bit much to take in . . ."

"Yes. Anyway, you will find some things familiar and others not so much. We have two procedures; both of which we are going to address today. One is 'Duplication,' and the other is 'Transtosis.' It is crucial for you to understand the difference."

"Okay?"

"To be duplicated, one has to have a particular genetic code within his or her DNA profile."

Dr. LuAnne slowly pulled the gurney's sheet back revealing Richard's body.

Angie took a breath. "I can't believe I just met my grandfather, and now, he is here like this. What do you do first?"

"I know this is hard for anyone, even a nurse. First, with Richard, we are not duplicating; rather we are reviving him using Transtosis. You may know it as reanimating, or cellular activation. Also, it includes thought reproduction."

"Transtosis? Why not duplicate? I mean, look at the bullet holes."

"Because; although our technology may be futuristic by your standards, unfortunately; if a person can be duplicated, with each additional procedure, the duplicate loses potency; and Richard has undergone the process before."

Angie giggled sarcastically and then said, "Another thing they didn't teach us in nursing school."

"Sorry?" LuAnne reacted with a smile.

"It's not important. Okay, so Transtosis, how do you activate cellular growth?"

"Well, principally, you understand the concept of jolting a heart, when an electric shock is administered to defibrillate?"

"Yes, fibrillation is a heart's electrical signals gone wild, the heart does not pump; it flutters out of rhythm. It may stop beating altogether."

"Exactly, so we administer an electric shock to defibrillate; halt the fluttering; zap it back into normal rhythm. Or, if it's stopped altogether, the expectation is to start it beating again."

"Basic nursing to us, too. I understand."

"Additionally, at the same time, we rejuvenate individual body cells, not just the heart. If a cell dies, we can shock and nourish it back to health, too."

"Really? So, can you stop the aging process?"

"You are way ahead of me. Let's stick to this patient."

"Sorry, go on."

Dr. Lu continued. "We are going to send cell doctors in to make a house call on every cell in his body. They are machines, but not really. I believe your ancient researchers on the surface coined the names, Nanites or Nanoprobes."

"What do you call them?"

"We call them Fix-its, but Nanites is fine, except they are considerably smaller. Anyway, we grow them. We don't build them. And they are not part of any semiconductor chip technology. We construct each one based on a patient's DNA. We program them, inject, and then they do their thing, and each cell's synaptic profile is defibrillated and reactivated. Then, the Nanites nourish each cell back to health."

"That is what you are going to do, here?"

"Yes, partly; listen, Angie, I am sorry you had to witness the shooting in the morgue. But here, you will see the wonder of Ever-Life. You ready?"

"Wonder of Ever-Life, huh? Yes, ready."

LuAnne went to the glass refrigeration cabinet behind her. She withdrew a 5-inch by 7-inch mirrored box. In it, were four small transparent cylindrical syringes covered at one end, but each had no needles.

"I hate needles," Angie said.

LuAnne chuckled, "We gave them up long ago,"

Angie picked a syringe up and studied it carefully. "We had courses on Nanite technology, but ours are microchip-based, not organic. I never got close to the real thing before, much less, witness anything like this."

"Each Nanite is about a 1000th of the size of an average cell. We have organic computers that construct and program each one, based on many variables related to the patient: cause, time of death, medical history; and, most important of all, each contains the information of the patient's DNA."

Angie nodded in amazement. "Organic computers?"

"Yes, for all practical purposes down here, they are as alive as we are and quite fascinating to work with. I am sure you will learn."

Angie smiled respectfully. "I hope so. I could spend a lifetime studying this alone. What is the next step?"

Angie handed the cylinder to the doctor, as Dr Lu continued to explain. "As the nanites are injected into the blood, they self-circulate, while they multiply to the same number of synaptic connections in every system of the body. Then, they position and synchronize to deploy and activate as close to the same time as possible. Just to give you an idea of the magnitude here; we calculate between 500-750 trillion synaptic connections in the average human body. So, the Nanites have to multiply very quickly."

"Whoa, the wonder of medicine."

"Yes, it is unbelievable to me at times also. After the successful defibrillation, they feed and nurse the individual cells. Once the cells are functioning normally, the Nanites dissolve. They expel as waste through normal body secretions and digestion, leaving no trace. If activation does not happen with the first charge, they will try again. If no success after three cycles, we inject again."

Angie paid close attention. "So, they can multiply that fast and attach to every single nerve's contact?"

"Yep, everyone; bone, muscle, fat, any organ and, of course, the brain. I am sure I left something out, but the point is, all of them will defibrillate in unison."

Angie watched as LuAnne sprayed her hands with a peculiar pink colored aerosol, which dried on contact. "This is a combination of a sterilizing wash and surgical gloves."

Then, Dr. Lu picked up a cylinder and took the small cap off the top. Each cylinder was one-inch in diameter by five-inches long, transparent material, but neither plastic nor glass. Carefully, she touched what would be the needle end against Dr. Richard's chest, just below his breastbone. Angie saw her squeeze the cylinder gently and heard a poof. The doctor repeated the second injection into his right inner thigh.

"Angie, now just watch the wall monitor."

Dr. Lu touched the image, and a full-size hologram of Richard's body appeared at her eye level. The two watched the Nanites spread.

"They look like a swarm of bees," Angie said.

Within 10 seconds, the entire hologram filled with Nanites, and Dr. Lu looked at her Knofer. "They are synchronizing now. Angie, please go to the refrigerator over there. Yes, there. Open the small door and bring me the wine glass inside."

"I remember this. In the morgue, Dr. Richard had Mr. Sheldon drink from one just like this."

"Yes? It stimulates the part of the brain that processes memories. Without getting too long-winded, and considering our different definitions of structures, let me just say, the drink enables the patient to remember certain life necessities and experiences."

"Excuse me?"

"Angie, your heart is not the only thing that beats in rhythm. Besides, as you know, it has its own electrical system. My point is that every system in the body has a rhythm. Every atom in a cell has a tone or vibration. Duplicate a tone, and you replicate the energy, which affects the mass. In this case, it means kick-starting the function. The body has to remember how to live. Each cell has to recognize its automatic behaviors—to breathe, to sense, to function. The Nanites jump start everything by duplicating the energy; and then they hand it off to the original player—the particular mass—the cell. But the entire effort is short term. The patient must drink this elixir. The chemistry in this feeds the body and triggers functional memories, both voluntary and involuntary, which each cell stores within its nucleus. We consider a cell's functional memories a *shadow of a thought*.

"So, where is this shadow of a thought?" Asked Angie

"Branded within every individual cell, at the point of origin. However, in cases of duplication, this may or may not be the case. The Elixir helps overall cellular recall, but we are not sure how much."

"And you are not certain how long the drink's effects last?"

"True, that is a big question. Each body is different. That is why we must continue timely drinks until the brain permanently replants the entire adult memory. We also implant via our headset process, which can measure the degree of success. That is why Mr. Sheldon's CPT is so revolutionary to us. It allows for total cellular recall and complete personality trait transfer permanently.”

“Wow, good thing you know so much about Mr. Sheldon’s discovery. And there is an alternative to using his CPT?”

Dr. LuAnne took a headset out of the cabinet and showed it to Angie. “This is what we used and still do, in addition to the drink. It enables transplant of thought, but it does not ensure all personality traits like CPT does. The truth is; the math and physics say CPT is full proof. I’ve done the calculations, and I have the instructions to perform it; but I don’t have the catalyst bath needed to hold the serum extraction. That is critical for success. So, for now, it is the drink and headset.”

“Dr. B. says I am the bath. I would be glad to help any way I can.”

Dr. Lu reacted with surprise. “I don’t understand. Dr. Bellos told you that you are the catalyst bath?”

“Yes; he said my DNA genetic code has the serum donor bath.”

Just then, LuAnn’s Knofer ticked, and they both turned to Richard.

“Look,” Angie said, “he is moving.”

“Yes. Lift his head. Give him a sip.”

The glow in the hologram stopped. Dr. LuAnne touched the edge of the image, and the 3D image disappeared. Angie gently lifted Richard’s head and touched the rim of the glass to his lips. Dr. Richard blinked and sucked in a quick deep breath. Then, he took a sip of the drink and opened his eyes.

“Thank God,” Angie whispered. “Dr. Richard . . . Grandpa?”

The first thing he saw was Angie’s face. “Hello, my dear . . .” Then he turned and saw Dr. LuAnne. “Well, Dr. Lu, hello. I did not expect you. Angie, may I have a little more of that?”

“Yes, of course.”

Richard drank again. Slowly, he moved his arms and legs and looked at his chest. “Did a freight train hit me?”

“You will feel better with time,” LuAnne said. “You know the drill, doctor. Keep drinking. Angie, watch him. I will be back in a minute.”

Luanne went to her private office through the doors on the other side of the room. She put a headset on, took out her Knofer and made a call.

“Sir, we have revived Richard. Angie says her DNA has the correct genetic code to duplicate the CPT catalyst bath.”

“Do you have both manuscripts there?”

“Yes, Dave Marshall recovered the other one, and gave it to me.”

“Can you use her?”

“I don’t know. I’ll see.”

"Can Richard help?"
"I will talk to him when he is up to it."
"Time is running out, doctor."
"Yes, sir."
"Contact me as soon as you know anything."

CHAPTER 24: POLICE STATION

RALPH WALKER SAT ALONE tired and hungry in the Arden police station, waiting for a copy of his statement about the kidnapping of Angie Esposito.

"Mr. Walker, thank you for your time," Sergeant Wells said. "Please sign this, and you can be on your way."

Ralph scribbled his name, and, at the same time, noticed a woman walk by the office door.

"Oh my, that's Barb Sawyer. It's 8 a.m. I'll bet she is not a happy camper. She was on night shift with me."

He shook hands with the sergeant, walked over to Barb and tapped her on her shoulder. "Barb, good morning. I don't believe you are here."

"Morning, Ralph. No, I'm not. They had a car come and get me. You?"

"Me? Ha. I was on my way to see you when they stopped me and brought me here. Angie was kidnapped."

"What?"

"Yeah; I just signed the police statement. Have you met this guy Burns, yet?"

"No; what about Angie?"

"I wish I knew."

"Well, you wouldn't believe what happened at the hospital while you were gone either."

Just then, Jake Burns walked into the station, sipping his coffee. He noticed the couple right away and snickered, "Good morning, you two. Long night? You must be Barb Sawyer."

"Yes, I am."

"Ms. Sawyer, please follow me. Mr. Walker, right? You can go. Don't get lost again. We will need you."

Ralph reacted in a protective tone. "What about Angie, for God's sake?"

"Believe it or not, Sonny, we don't just interrogate people. We put a team on it five minutes after you told me. They went to the site you described, and, right now, they are following what they think are van tracks. If we get anything from the phone you found, we will let you know."

Burns left Ralph standing there, escorted Barb Sawyer into his office and shut the door. "Please, sit down, Ms. Sawyer. I understand you were the first to see the bodies in the morgue last night, right?"

"Yes."

"Tell me, how many were there?"

"I didn't go in the room all the way. I just saw the one bloody naked man. I ran out and called 911."

"Hmm, you heard the gunfire?" Burns began in a hostel tone.

"Yes."

"How many shots?"

"They sounded like pops. Machine guns, I guess. I really don't know."

"Ms. Sawyer, who do you work for?"

"Dr. Bellos, Chief of the Hospital."

"And, when was the last time you saw him?"

"I saw him just before he left to go out of town, before the shooting in the morgue."

"Ms. Sawyer, Barb, may I call you Barb? Barb, we found a lot of bloody footprints in the morgue room. Most had the same tread, or so the blood tells us. We believe they were professional killers."

"Oh, my . . ."

"But there were also two sets of footprints, which didn't match the others, and one set was obviously a woman. The prints seem to indicate; two people were carrying something, together. Do you have any idea what they could have been carrying?"

"No."

"Barb, what size shoes do you wear?"

"Size eight. Why?"

"I want you to know that, as we speak, there is a team of forensic specialists at your house checking your clothes, the garbage, your shoes, your toothbrush, everything. Ms. Sawyer, I think you saw more than you're telling, and I believe you helped move something, maybe a body, with the aid of someone else. I think you are lying. I think you ran into Dr. Bellos, just as one of the orderlies suggested, and the two of you moved one or more of the bodies. What do you say to that?"

Barb broke down and cried, "My God! All I did was hear shots and run to the room. I saw a naked man laying on the floor. There was so much blood everywhere, I ran back to my station and called 911."

"Where is Dr. Bellos' office?"

"On the 10th floor." Barb couldn't stop sobbing.

"I want you to take me there right now. Do you have a problem with that?"

"No, but, he's not there. He is out of town."

"Where did he go?"

"I'm not privy to his itinerary."

"Who is? Does he have a secretary?"

"Not that I know of; I think he books his own trips."

"Alright, let's go."

The two left Burns' office and walked toward the front door.

"Sergeant Wells," Burns yelled. "Call Dave Marshall at Andrews. Tell him to meet us at Dr. Bellos' office on the 10th floor in 20 minutes."

"Yes, sir."

"And get any info to me that was on that phone from the Walker kid. Call me with an update on our team in the desert as soon as you can. Come on, everyone, let's go! Chop, chop. The day is moving. We have a girl to find and murders to solve!"

CHAPTER 25: SET-UP 1

HALFWAY AROUND THE WORLD from Andrews Hospital, GGM-Gordon Swanson watched five computer monitors in one of his private Ever-Life offices below Jerusalem. He had his Knofer on in case Bellos called. He was monitoring various Brock enterprises and theological communications, which he suspected might be terrorist related. A call came in from New Mexico and he put it on hologram.

"Dave? Dave Marshall, is that you? How are you?"

"Yes, fine, sir, good to see you."

"Dave, what is the status there?"

"We disposed of the Brock people who shot the Carrier-Unit, and we are processing the three doctors; but the police have a particularly inquisitive detective."

Swanson giggled. "Yes, that's Jake Burns. He was excellent in New York years ago. He even found a serial killer who dismembered one of our people. He does not know about us, but he is trustworthy. I met him twice, both times in D.C. at conventions for new weaponry. Have you talked to him?"

"Not really, but he knows I am hiding something. I am supposed to meet with him in Dr. Bellos' office shortly."

"Have you secured the floor?"

"Yes."

"Well, I do like him. I'll tell you what. Set it up to bring him down to Red Level 6. We will all meet there when we get back. He loves a good mystery. We will give him one he won't forget."

"Yes, sir. How goes it there?"

"Mathew's Carrier is due shortly. We are set up to trade. We don't know who he has, but we will. The courier is scared of the Brock team. He wanted a strategic advantage, so he took a hostage. Dave, handle things there; will you? I expect we will be back this afternoon, your time."

"Yes, sir, of course. Be safe."

"You too . . ."

The Knofer cut the image, and Swanson took one last look at the monitors in front of him, reading the tapes from Iran, Russia, and Istanbul. Then, a single message spelled out across his Knofer, "I am ready. But you must come quickly. They are watching. I can feel the guns."

Swanson replied, "Our people are there. Fear not."

CHAPTER 26: SET-UP 2

PAPPAS KRISTOS ALIERI SAT in a waiting room outside Rash InVoy's second-floor office in East Jerusalem. He made the hurried appointment to see Brock's chief of staff, because of the serious phone call received from the Muslim consulate in Istanbul, Turkey. After 10- minutes, the door finally opened, and InVoy walked out.

"Kristos, it's good to see you. Come in."

"Thank you. I am most disturbed. I received calls from our Russian Church and the Muslim Council of Turkey. Then, on my way here, I received one from our local consulate. Is it true, there has been a kidnapping by a courier? Is he the same one who has our vial?"

"Please, sit, my friend. All will be fine. The courier is below the Church of the Holy Sepulchre, here in town as we speak. He is just trying to ensure his safety. It is a bit of a surprise, but we have arranged a meeting and the trade. I assume the money is safe and ready, correct?"

"The money is in place, but we cannot afford to let one man destroy this effort."

"Father; be assured. Our plan is foolproof and certainly too big for one person to ruin anything. The courier will make the trade."

"Who is the poor soul he has captured?"

"That is his secret, but we will know soon. We have agreed to guarantee him and his family's safety, and we have increased his price. Don't worry; we are paying the difference. We will deliver his share within three hours. He will give us the vial. I will give it to you. You give us the $16-billion."

Kristos took a deep breath. "These methods, they are not God's will."

"Stop it, Father. This is what you wanted and planned for months. You cannot expect everything to go smoothly. Nothing ever does; especially when this kind of deal or so much money is involved. Our people have him in sight. It is all going to be over within hours. Talk to your people; tell them to be patient. You can either wait here or, if you like, I will call you at your parish when I get word."

In the center of Jerusalem, 50 feet below the Church of the Holy Sepulcher, a dark 5-ft 5-inch tall Muslim man, Ahmed, sat in a shallow cave, facing his bruised and battered prisoner.

"I am sorry you have to be here. I am not an evil man. I will not harm you. But I have a family, and these people are horrible. They will kill my family and me, if I do not do this."

The black-hooded prisoner squirmed and moaned; but the duct tape and ropes were too tight; no one heard.

Meanwhile, within Bellos' Carrier, rushing toward Jerusalem, Bellos, Jack, and Brian talked.

"How much longer?" asked Brian.

Bellos looked at his Knofer. "About 20-minutes or so."

"Frankly, Matt, it doesn't feel like we have been moving at all," said Jack.

"If I told you how fast we were traveling, you wouldn't believe me."

"I could figure it out if you give me some statistics," said Brian smartly.

"No thanks, son. What I'm curious about is, are we in a tunnel or underwater, or what?"

"You want the truth?"

"No, lie to me," Jack chuckled.

"Alright. You asked for it. We are traveling up to five times the speed of sound inside a 6,000,000-year-old organic life form that is synergistic with our subterranean culture, Ever-Life. And it has the capability of burrowing through solid rock as well as molten lava. It glides like a spacecraft going to the Moon."

Jack and Brian raised their eyebrows and nodded their heads at one another.

"Yes, well, that's great," Brian said rolling his eyes. "How are you feeling, dad?"

"I'm fine, a little weak and confused but pretty good."

Bellos interrupted, "Yes, well, I need to get this over with, and get you back to the hospital, Jack. Brian, I have to talk to your boss. He is in the next cabin. Do me a favor? Keep an eye on your dad for me? If he turns green or any other color, yell out."

Brian said, "Yes of course."

Bellos walked to the far wall of the Carrier, faced the wall and said, "Open, please?"

A door appeared and slid to the side. Bellos walked through and saw Marion Brock sitting with handcuffs on. Brock calmly, nonchalantly looked up and with a grin asked, "Hello, Mathew. I didn't expect to see you. Will you tell me what is going on?"

"Yes, I will." Bellos slowly paced in front of Brock. "It seems you have been very busy. You blackmailed Jack Sheldon into trusting you and giving you the secrets of CPT. Then, your people cloned him, knowing the procedure wasn't full proof. Then, you stole the formula to sell it to religious groups for $16 billion. You had the clones killed, and you arranged for Jack to have a fatal car accident. You had mercenaries break into Andrews Hospital, kill two doctors, steal Jack's original manuscript, and take a vial of the original CPT serum so that you could duplicate it and finally sell it for power. Have I left anything out?"

Brock chuckled and answered, "Yes. You kidnapped me. That's a global no-no. You can't prove anything. I've been here tied up. You have no idea what you are getting into. You are going to let me go. I guarantee it. Whatever you think you know; you don't have a clue. Whatever you think you have, you are wrong. Now, go back to where you came from, and come to me when you're ready to let me go, Mr. GGM gofer."

Bellos raised an eyebrow cynically. Shaking his head, he turned and walked back into the other cabin.

CHAPTER 27: TEAM BURNS

IT ONLY TOOK 15-MINUTES for Jake Burns to drive Barb Sawyer back to Andrews Hospital. He pulled into a handicapped spot, just 20 feet from the front door.

"Well, I completely understand why we parked here," said Barb, irritated.

"Yeah, well, I have a bad elbow."

"You can't be serious. You would break the law just for convenience. You cops are all alike."

"Really? Just look around. No one parks in any of these handicapped spots. Count them. There are at least 50 spaces and not one car besides mine. And, I'll tell you why; because you ticket the violators $400.00 each. Let's see, that's $20,000 revenue for your great hospital administration, for absolutely no reason but greed. Get off my back, lady! We will park right here. Let's go!"

Within minutes, they stepped out of the 10th-floor elevator to greet three forensic doctors, two uniformed police, and Dave Marshall.

"Good morning again, Jake Burns," Marshall said.

"You may call me Detective or Inspector, Mr. Security Chief. Now, if you don't mind, please unlock Dr. Billow's office."

"His name is Bellos detective. Yes sir." Marshall opened the door.

"Let's go, people." Burns waved the team through the foyer.

"Quite a spread, Jake," said Watzin.

"People listen up. I want everything examined to the finest detail. We do this by the book, my book. I want swabs; bag anything that you can pick up; get photos; use everything in those suitcases and get me something. Don't forget to put on shoe covers because this man, Mr. Marshall, is using ultraviolet on the floors. Got it? Any questions? Good. Well then, go on, get to it. Alright, Mr. Chief Marshall; show me around."

Marshall led Burns and Sawyer into the oval room. "All this is Dr. Bellos' hospital living quarters, as well as his office suite. He has every medical reference book you can imagine in there, many from other countries in different languages."

Burns snickered and asked, "How many languages does this guy speak?"

"Several, I think. Over there are chairs, and original paintings are on the walls. And that's a window as you can see."

"Very funny, chief. Where is the office?"

"Through that hallway, follow me."

"Mr. Burns," Barb Sawyer asked, "Why am I here?"

Burns stopped and turned toward her. "Because you are in this up to your thigh highs, Missy, and I know you are going to break. So, tag along until you do."

"Through here, Lieuteenant," Marshall said sarcastically.

"You've got a real sense of humor, don't you, Boy Scout." Burns looked around the computer room. "Hmm, nice laptops; and those screens have to be 60-inch monitors. Impressive."

"Yes," Marshall quipped. "Doctors can conference on strategic orphan diseases from anywhere in the world without getting a headache. Anything unusual you would like me to clarify?"

"Yes, as a matter of fact." Burns walked around the room and studied everything. "How long has Dr. Bellos been Chief of Hospital?"

"I've been here one year, two months, four days, 20 hours, six minutes, and 42-43 seconds, now. None of us speaks for Dr. Bellos."

"I don't like wise-asses, Mr. Marshall."

"I don't like men who pick on innocent women. Look, detective, I was told you are good, really good. Do you know Gordon Swanson?"

Burns did a double take and grinned. "Yeah, I know him a little. That's not going to buy you a dime."

"Well, maybe not. But I'd like to cut the crap. We do want to help. You know neither Bellos nor Barb is the shooter. Gordon Swanson's name is on the marquee here. I did talk to him. He asked me if you would consider talking to him in person."

"Really, I'm flattered. Is he going to tell me what happened?"

"I think he is going to have Dr. Bellos with him, if that tweaks your interest."

Burns turned his back to Marshall as Watzin came in. "Jake, I found something."

Burns followed Watzin back to the foyer.

"Look, Jake, this door, it's not a closet. None of us can get it open. There's a button there. I thought the door might be an elevator, but the button does nothing." Watzin pushed it repeatedly.

Burns turned to Marshall again. "Well chief, what's this?"

"Your man here is right. It's a sealed elevator shaft from two years ago when we renovated the 10th floor."

Burns instructed Watzin. "Break it open."

"Wait, Jake, look down here," Watzin interrupted, as he knelt in front of the door. He pressed a weak spot on the wall and pushed his fist through, creating a five-inch hole.

Burns watched and then turned to a uniformed officer. "You there, give me your flashlight." Jake bent down and shined the light into the hole. "Concrete? Shit! Watzin, are your people getting anything else?"

"This may take a couple of hours, Jake."

Burns walked down the steps and looked at Marshall. "Okay, Chief; you win. Where's Swanson?"

Marshall smiled and said, "Follow me."

"Watzin!? Jake called. "God, why did your parents name you that? Have the office call me when you are done. And get me the blood comparisons. Don't forget."

"Priority one boss."

As Jake walked away, he yelled, "Any feedback on the Walker kid's phone yet?"

Watzin yelled back, "There were two calls made, one from Turkey and one looks like it came from the van."

"Turkey like gobble gobble?"

"No Jake, like from across the other side of the world, the country Turkey."

"Fine. Shit! I wish I was in Turkey."

THE TIME WAS 5:30 P.M. when Bellos' Carrier arrived at the Post platform in Jerusalem. Gordon Swanson and a three-man guard team were at the platform waiting to greet Bellos, Jack and Brian.

"Mathew, it's good to see you in the flesh, bad circumstance."

"Yes, sir. You remember Jack Sheldon here?"

"Of course. Jack, how do you feel?"

"A bit rocky at times, but Matt says he's going to fix that."

"That is the plan," Swanson said.

"This is my son, Brian." Jack nudged him to shake hands.

"Brian, you know you have quite a dad here." Swanson smiled and turned to go. Just then a guard interrupted, "GGM, we are ready."

"Good. Everyone; let's walk. Mathew, where is our guest?"

"Still in the Carrier," Bellos replied. "Brock called me GGM-TBN."

"Well, that confirms the mole."

"Sir, we have 30 minutes," the guard said.

"Alright, I'll brief you all in the car. Brian, my boy, I know this has to be the strangest day of your life; but I have to ask you a favor.

"What is it?" Brian asked.

"Would you mind riding with my guards here in the second car? Now, before you react, there is a good reason I ask. Your dad needs a fresh dose of medicine. We have no choice but to go on ahead to be at the trade point on time. Otherwise, this all fails. I'm asking you to go and get the medicine. The car will bring you to us immediately after that. None of my people have clearance to carry what your dad needs. You do, by your genetic link to him. It is only a short trip to the villa and back. Will you do that for us, for your dad?"

Brian looked at Jack. "Dad, no!"

Jack insisted, "Brian, please. We all have to do our part."

"Fine," Brian said frustrated. He hugged his dad and walked away with the guards.

"Where are they taking him?" Jack asked Bellos nervously.

"To safety, Jack, let's go."

Bellos gestured, and they all walked quickly up to Swanson's car. But it wasn't a white stretch limo; it was a tattered looking 1960 four-door Lincoln Continental that had a bulletproof body and tires, a unique engine, and sprayed graffiti all over it. It also had four transparent swivel guns mounted on the front and rear lights. Each one looked like a tiny airplane jet. The four men got in the car and drove off into the heart of Jerusalem.

Swanson began briefing them, "Now, gentlemen, we are going to meet our courier, Ahmed. He approached a contact that we have had in the Brock camp not too long after Jack started his partnership with Marion. Ahmed is Muslim; and, over the last five months, he has been running money between here and Turkey for Rash InVoy."

"Then, don't we know everything we need?" asked Bellos.

"No, he swings whatever way profits his family. But I know he hasn't said anything about us. They would have killed him already."

"Why the kidnapping?" asked Jack.

"To guarantee we would ensure his life and his family's safe future. He wants out of Brock's hold permanently. You see, we are not trading anything. We are taking him two hours before he is supposed to give the vial to InVoy. We get the vial, the hostage; and, in return, he and his family go to an unknown location to live out their lives safely."

"It sounds a little James Bondy, sir," Bellos said, "if you don't mind my saying."

Swanson smiled. "Yes, it does. I'm surprised you remember that guy. He was a motion picture creation in ancient Hollywood.

"Oh no," Bellos whispered to himself.

"What?" Jack asked.

"I just love Hollywood," said Swanson. "Diced Hard . . . Bruised Wullus? Remember that classic when the gun was taped to his back? So exciting!"

"Sir," Bellos rolled his eyes, "not many of us remember that. It was a long, long time ago; and his name wasn't Wullus."

"Yes, right; I digress." Swanson lifted a satchel onto his lap, opened it and started handing things out.

Jack looked at Bellos and commented. "Matt, this is about CPT and medical research, right, not war games?"

Bellos just shook his head.

Mr. Mike turned the car lights off and pulled into a dark concrete lot, just two blocks south of the Church of the Holy Sepulchre.

"Are we close?" Bellos asked.

"Somewhat." Swanson quipped in an excited tone as he handed things to the two doctors. "This entire area is nothing but church buildings. We have to walk quickly and silently. Here, you two, take these vests and put them on under your shirts."

Then, he took out what looked like two pistols.

"Guns?" said Jack surprised. "I'm having trouble remembering how to piss."

"Just take these. They won't hurt you, and they won't kill anyone. They don't shoot bullets. They are set for wide; so, you just point and pull the trigger."

"Wide? What's *wide*? If they won't kill anyone, what good are they?"

"And put these glasses on too," Swanson added.

"Holy crap," Jack said. He did so and looked out the car window. "It's like daylight; what the hell?"

"Okay, Jack; take a minute; focus and drink this." Swanson handed him a canteen.

"Boy, whatever this stuff is, it's better than water."

"Hmm, don't you just love history, men?" Swanson was in a mental zone. "Did you two know that this church commemorates the death and resurrection of Jesus of Nazareth? Just like the one in India . . ."

"Sir," Bellos whispered. "I think the one in India is a disciple."

"Yes? Sorry, well, that's another story. The important thing to remember is the sensitive nature of these people. Watch out for yourselves! Be alert! For over 6000 years, those we now know as Christians, Jews and Muslims have claimed ownership of these buildings. Factions always fight over everything, from its validity and when to worship, to where to place a chair. Brock's camp negotiated with three religious leaderships to get your serum, Jack. And they will pay Brock handsomely for it. Somehow, they are convinced that the serum will prove resurrection is possible, thereby uniting the faiths. You can bet the security will be especially tight. So, stay with me. We are following Mr. Mike here. He's not just a pretty face."

"I don't understand. Why do I have to be here at all?" asked Jack.

"You don't. It is Brian we wanted. Other than monitoring your health; and, of course, we know you do want to make all this right again, now; don't you, Jack?"

"What?"

"You went to Brock, remember, Jack? He's had Brian for 18 months, right? We are going to check your son out, completely, to make sure he has no illness and no implants. Don't worry; he has no idea. He was Brock's insurance that you would convince Matt to do what he wants. You wanted us involved from the start. Remember the café and wanting my help. Well, now you have it. We all need each other now."

Jack sat stunned, and Swanson turned to Mike.

"Okay, Mr. Mike, let's go."

They opened the car doors and got out. The three had the weapons under their coats. They looked like lost tourists. Mike led them to the end of the parking lot through narrow winding streets for about a quarter mile. Then, he stopped above a five-foot-wide rock stairwell.

"The church is about five blocks from here, over there, sir. Look, up on the roofs, to the right and left."

"Yes, I see. Look here, you two, be careful." Swanson pointed, and then he spoke softly to Mike, "They are Brock's men. Are we good to go under?"

"Two Carriers are about a mile away."

"Good, let's go, fast and quiet."

Mike led them down the winding stairwell to a door at the bottom. It opened into a small room, which had an eating table, two windows, and a closet. "Through there, sir."

The closet was an entryway to an old tunnel system, put in place by the Palestinians during the Seven-Day War in the old 1960s.

"I can't get over these glasses," said Jack, amazed. "Flashlights are obsolete."

Mike pointed. "This way. Heads up and watch your step. Follow me."

They walked single file into the tunnel about 100 feet, and then they stopped. Mr. Mike pointed his Knofer toward the walls and read it. "This is it, sir; best reception point."

"Yes, right."

Swanson took his own Knofer out and tapped it several times. Then, he put it on the dirt floor.

"Activate catacomb details."

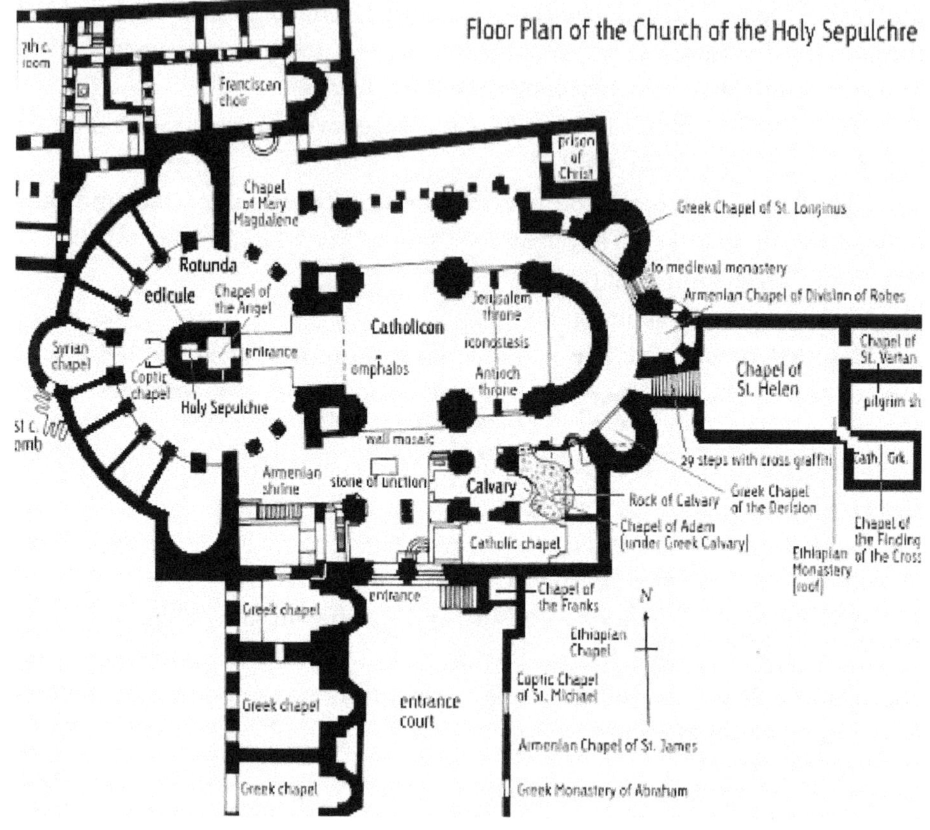

The Knofer displayed a five-foot-tall hologram of the church, mapping all its rooms.

"Now comes the hard part, men," Swanson spoke into the 3D display, "GGM-001. Display all life forms 50 meters spherical within the church."

The Knofer placed glowing dots representing people throughout the hologram.

"Zoom ten times. Look there, Mike, below the Edicule. It looks like they are in one of the Kokhims."

Swanson touched the hologram, and it magnified the image with even more detail.

"Yes, sir, that's them. Look. That one is laying down unable to move."

"Excuse me," Jack asked, "Kokhim, Edicule, what are they?"

"Edicule is the church's location of the tomb of Jesus." Swanson pointed and explained further, "That Kokhim is one of the small short tunnels throughout the underground, where the Jews buried rock-like containers called ossuaries, which hold the bones of their dead. Mike, can we get a Carrier to collapse the flooring below them?"

"No sir, too dangerous, the whole church could come down."

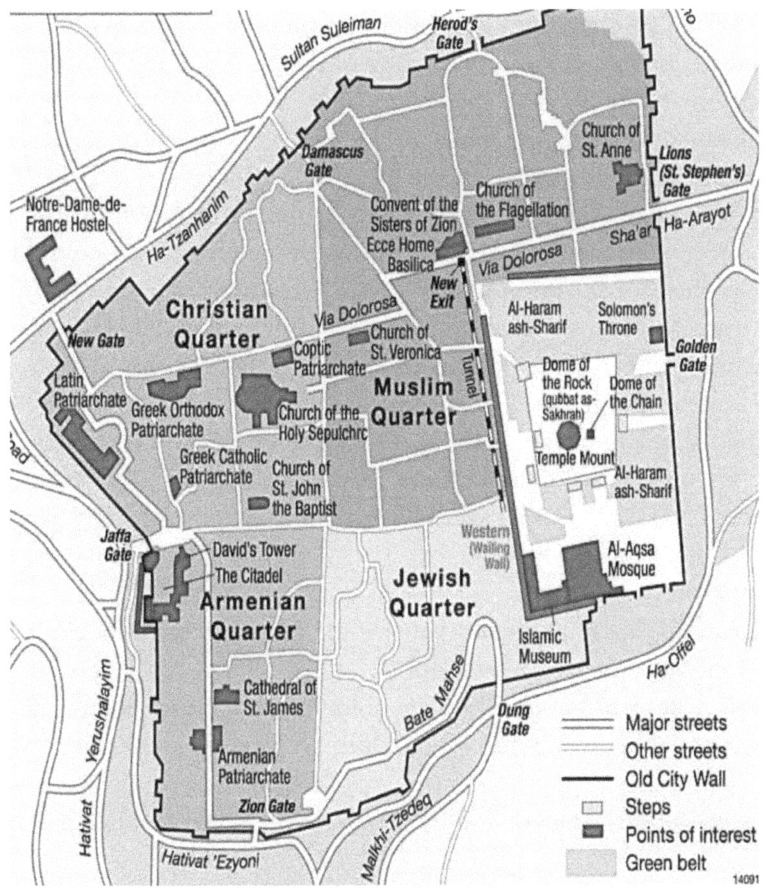

Landscape of Old Jerusalem

"How far is the closest Carrier from that spot?"

"On the other side of the church, sir; one has tunneled maybe a quarter mile from us."

"Alright; give me your Knofer." Swanson transferred all detail information about the church. "Mike, go back and have the Knofer pinpoint every Brock operative in the outer perimeter."

"Can you do that?" Jack asked.

"Take them all out. Meet us at the Crusader Facade entrance to the church. Bring our people. We will give you 15-minutes. By then, we will be at the Facade."

"On my way, sir." Mike left.

"Have a seat, you two." Swanson took his Knofer and shook it in front of the two. "Someday, this is all we will need.

"What now?" asked Bellos.

"Just this." Swanson put his Knofer on the floor again. With one touch, he pulled up a close holographic view of Ahmed and the prisoner in the tunnel. "Now we are going to say hello."

Swanson projected an image of himself into the tunnel, in front of Ahmed right before his eyes. In the pitch-black, there was a flickering light the size of a candle. Ahmed froze in terror, staring at it. Out of the light, a laser dot began tracing the image of Gordon Swanson from the shoulders up. Ahmed reached for it, trying to slap it. He threw dust at it, but it continued to construct the three-dimensional image. Ahmed recoiled in fear; and, within a minute, the image began to speak. "Hello, Mr. Ahmed. Do not be afraid. I will not harm you. I have come to take you to safety."

Ahmed shook fearing the worst. "Praise be to Allah," he stuttered. "I am not your enemy. Please do not kill me."

"Ahmed, calm yourself. I will be with you soon. Your family is safe; but why do you hold this hostage?"

"I am afraid . . ."

"If I can do this miracle and you see me now, surely you know I am not lying to you. Look and see your family."

With those words, a different hologram replaced Swanson's head, showing Ahmed his wife and two children boarding a plane with two GGM guards.

"At some point, Ahmed, you have to believe. Now would be a good time to start."

Ahmed shook and replied, "I do, I do! I am frightened but thankful."

"Good, my friend. Now, there is no reason to keep your prisoner blindfolded. You are not the only one who is afraid."

"When will you free us?" Ahmed asked.

"We are leaving now. Target 6:13 p.m. You have the clothes to wear?"

"Yes, my lord."

"Please," Swanson said. "Make your guest comfortable. If they suspect, it is over. Do you have the vial?"

"Yes, my lord; and I have something better."

Suddenly, the Knofer cut the image.

"Alright, you two, let's hurry," Swanson said.

From directly above the underground Carrier Station, one-quarter mile from the main Facade entrance, Mr. Mike instructed five special ops guards.

"Okay men; set your weapons. Be quiet and quick. You all have precisely seven minutes, starting now. Go!"

The Ever-Life guards ran silently into the night.

No moon was shining that night. As Swanson, Bellos, and Jack left the tunnel and entered the streets, the GGM-glasses enabled them to see as if they were in sunlight.

"This way, Jack. Try to keep up!"

Swanson led the three through the dark narrow streets winding to the church. Suddenly, there was a ping right next to Jack's ear, and he flinched. He never heard a real bullet ricochet. He had no idea where it came from; but his reactions were quick and surprisingly accurate. In one motion, he turned to the left, looked up toward a building rooftop, pulled his weapon out, pointed it and pulled the trigger. The noise sounded like the pop of an air rifle. A Brock mercenary fell behind the three, splat, onto the street.

"Holy shit, Jack," Bellos said. "Where did you learn that?"

"Hell, if I know."

"Watch it! "Swanson whispered with his finger to his mouth. They have silencers."

"Silencers?" Jack said. "I can't see a farking thing."

Swanson reacted by putting his finger to his lips and said, "Shush. Come on! No time to chat! Good job, Jack. Our men should be in position by now."

The three began to run fast, crouching, weaving in and out, back and forth, listening to the pings hit the walls beside them. After 50 yards or so, the gunfire had them bogged down at the edge of an alley.

"Christ! This is insane," said Jack.

Then, they heard three and then four airbursts fired from both the right and left rooftops above. All went quiet.

"Those are our men up there." Swanson crept quietly to see around the alley corner. "Over there; there is the church, and there is Mike at the Facade entrance.

Mike was waving and yelling in a whisper, "Sir! Come on! This way!"

The three ran across to the Facade entrance and huddled together with Mike.

"Well that was exciting," Swanson said out of breath. "Are we ready Mike?"

"There are three of Brock's men inside the church," Mike replied, "two on the way to the Edicule and one at its entrance."

"Where are our men?"

"In position and ready, sir."

Just then, the unexpected happened. They all saw a man and woman walking quickly directly toward Swanson from the tomb. The man had a long dirty brown shawl with a tan straw fedora pulled over his ears. The woman was wearing a babushka pulled low over her face and dirty white pants. They had their heads down. Behind them, there was a loud commotion and gunfire. The couple started running toward Swanson, while Mike listened to his Knofer. "Command-1, command-1; Brock man down at the Edicule . . . Do you see the couple?"

Mike responded, "Yes, we see them." He instructed his team, "Take all Brock men out in the church right now! Repeat; take all Brock men out now!"

With a few more airbursts, it was over. Brock's special ops fell silent, no blood spilled.

Mike stepped between Swanson and the couple. Everyone's eyes fixed on the couple, as the man before them reached into his pocket and extended his hand palm closed to Swanson. "Sir, my Lord, it's me, Ahmed. I saw your image in the tunnel. Please do not shoot. Here, here is the vial."

Swanson received the small tube, bowing in thanks.

Behind Ahmed, his hostage stepped forward and lifted her babushka.

Bellos watched and was stunned. "Angie, Angie?"

She leaped into his arms.

"Get to the cars, Mike," Swanson said.

"Yes, sir, this way."

They all turned and rushed out the doors across the courtyard to two waiting cars. Swanson stopped in front of one and spoke to the couple. "Ahmed, you and your family are safe now. We have arranged for safe passage to the destination your wife gave us. You go with this man, and all will be right."

"Thank you, my lord," he bowed and kissed Swanson's right hand. Mike led the man to a small inconspicuous car a few yards away. Ahmed got in the back seat and looked one more time at Swanson. As he rolled the window up, the car drove away.

Angie was shaking and held tightly onto Bellos. Once in Swanson's limo with Bellos, she broke down crying again, "Oh my God, oh my God. What have I done?"

Bellos tried to console her. "Angie, it's alright now. Believe me; you're safe. Can you tell us; what do you remember?"

"I woke up with tape over my eyes and mouth, with that Ahmed man in the cave. Oh my God!"

Swanson took out two hand-held medical extractors from the glove compartment. He stuck one into the vial that Ahmed gave him, extracting a small amount of liquid, and then he turned to Bellos.

"Mathew, please hold her steady for just a second."

"No, please GGM? She's been through enough."

"Doctor; come to your senses. Look at her. If she is Angie, who is at Ever-Life? We must know now. Then, we pick up Brian and go back."

Angie looked up at Dr. B. terrified. Bellos pleaded again for the last time, unsuccessfully. "Do we have to do this right now?"

Swanson tried to be empathetic. "Yes, we do. It won't hurt, honey."

Dr. Bellos gently lifted her chin. "Angie, trust me this one last time. I will explain everything. Believe me; you are safe now, child. I promise."

Angie nodded, shaking, with tears in her eyes. Bellos held her head to his chest firmly. Swanson pressed the round edge of the other small tool to her neck and touched the button. There was no pain, just a short slurping sound. The syringe swelled and filled with liquid. Swanson leaned forward and handed the tool to Mike.

"Transmit all data to Dr. Lu. Let me know feedback immediately."

Mike drove the car through the narrow streets to the Carrier station. The four men and Angie got out quickly and went down to the tunnel platform.

"Mike, where is young Mr. Sheldon?"

"They are bringing him down now, sir. There he is over there.

"Fascinating," said one of the guards to Swanson. He had one implant removed; lots of information; and we told him what it was. He is quite the sport."

"Everyone is here then. Let's move." Said Swanson.

They all walked into the Carrier. Swanson stepped across to the sidewall away from the others. He seemed to disappear as the wall extended out and wrapped around him. Once alone, he turned on his Knofer and called Ever-Life.

A hologram of Dr. LuAnne appeared and spoke quickly, "We tested bath samples from both females; the one that you just sent, and one obtained here. I am sending analysis now. I estimate the age of the one you have at two weeks. She could start breaking down within two to three months, sooner is my guess, given the butchery of those lunatics. The bottom line is; we have only one dose."

Swanson took a deep breath and replied, "Thank you, as always, doctor. I hate these people. How is Dr. Richard?"

"Slow recovery; Transtosis was successful."

"Hmm, go ahead and use the vial there. Inject him with the CPT"

As Bellos held Angie, they all watched Swanson reappear again from containment. Swanson spoke with a sense of urgency. "May I have your attention? Jack, we have the catalyst bath needed for you. We will proceed with your CPT as soon as we get back. But we also have a big challenge. Brian, I hope you have clarified your loyalties."

"I've always been loyal to my family first. I had no idea what Mr. Brock was doing."

"I believe you, son. Will you help us now?"

Brian looked at his dad. "Yes, of course, but what can I do?"

Swanson whispered to Mike, "Please escort Jack to Dr. LuAnne upon arrival." He then turned to the group. "Mathew, Angie, Brian, please come with me. Unfortunately, we still have work to do."

Bellos hugged Angie and then released her, "Come on; it will be alright."

The four stepped to the opposite side of the room. Swanson studied his Knofer for a few seconds, and then he faced the wall and spoke in the strange Ever-Life language, "Swanson GGM-001; open."

The wall became thin, and a transparent door slid to one side. Marion Brock looked up from his secure harnesses and smiled as they entered one by one.

"Well, Dr. Bellos, I knew you would be back. I didn't expect you would have such esteemed company though. Hello Gordon; Brian . . ."

Swanson had a slight smirk. "Hello, Marion. Please, everyone, sit."

Immediately, four comfortable high back Victorian chairs appeared.

"Impressive," Brock said a bit surprised. "Glad you know how to do something, Gordon. You should take your magic show on the road."

"Yes, well, we are on the road, Marion. It is time to finish this long stupid farce."

"I agree," Brock said, yanking, trying to free himself. "Let me go!"

"Marion, I can't believe you thought you could do this and walk away with everything."

"I will, you idiots! You don't have a clue! My plan will shut you down!"

"It's over, Marion. I wonder why people like you think money is God. You really thought all you had to do was sit in your luxury condominium with bank accounts all over the world, think up hair-brained schemes to make more money and dictate to your gofers. You thought your silly plan was too complicated for us to figure out. Even now, you really think CPT is yours, and you will live forever. My God, Marion."

Brock reacted quickly. "You are the one who is mistaken, you pompous ass!"

"I'm afraid he's not, not at all."

For the first time, Brock heard the Carrier's voice; and with those words, the walls began to thin, and the cabin separated, splitting into two parts, each like a bubble. The one section containing Jack and Mike continued back to Ever-Life without any sense of change in speed or direction. The new section stopped, and everyone felt it. Part of the wall became a viewing monitor.

"You silly pointless man." Swanson said. "My real concern has been the children. You don't have any, do you, Marion?"

"This has gone far enough; you control freak!" Brock yanked at his cuffs. "Release me, or you will never see the vials."

"Your mistake was stealing them yourself," Swanson spoke like a prosecutor giving closing remarks to a jury. "You thought a kidnap within a kidnap would fool us all. Ahmed was in the van, and he is safe now, as is Angie. You see, Marion, somehow your people did get the right bath from Angie; and poor Ahmed did as instructed. Your men put Angie at Mrs. Sheldon's front door. Your henchman had everything in place with the theology's three fathers. All you had to do was get the vials."

At that moment, a video appeared on the wall showing Brock opening security station box 1120, after his meeting on Focus Ward with Barb Sawyer. Swanson walked over and touched the screen. The image became a frozen life-size hologram of Brock with his hand holding the vials. Everyone watched as the image slowly rotated.

"That was your big mistake, Marion. It wasn't enough to have billions and play with adults. You had to spite these children for your own profit."

"Look," Bellos said. "There, on the table, next to the box, that note. Enlarge that."

The screen zoomed in on the note.

"I'm sorry, Mathew," Swanson said with a deep breath.

The note read, "Dr. B.'s email says the vials are in box 1120. The combination is 2fy947t."

"Brock's error here was real Angie not erasing your email, Mathew. It says clearly to delete it right here." Swanson pointed to the sentence in the mail. "We knew Brock was planning something. It was your suggestion that we monitor him ever since he started the effort with Jack, remember? After real Angie left the ward in terror, her clone sitting here with you walked up to the guard, and he let her right in. He has been dealt with; but, Marion, you did not trust her to take the vials, because she is a clone. She just got the combination for you. Pride and arrogance. You had to do it yourself."

"Clone?" asked Bellos.

He turned to Angie.

"Unfortunately, Mathew, she has only a very rudimentary mindset. We don't know the details of how Brock did it, but the mind he gave her only can take his simplest directions, and that is all. I am so sorry. You see, Brock had no idea his van dropped the real Angie off at Sheldon's house because, one, he was in Focus Ward, and two, he is here with us now." Swanson chuckled cynically. "So, Ahmed took the clone hostage, not real Angie."

Clone Angie sat in a chair whimpering while Brock wailed, "I'll destroy the vials. Let me go you bastards!"

Swanson smiled, took his Knofer out and said, "GGM-001 authorization: I release this man, Mr. Brock, to this Carrier 2211. This is the operative who authorized the shooting of Carrier 2210, in the morgue."

Then, Swanson put his Knofer away and spoke kindly to Brock, "You, Marion, have always had the vials safely in your pocket; and, you thought you would be able to negotiate, even now at the last of it."

The wall hologram disappeared, and a green glow appeared around Marion Brock. He could not move.

"Brian," Swanson asked, "please reach into Mr. Brock's right coat pocket."

Brian walked over, pulled out the two blue vials and gave them to Swanson. At the same time, Bellos withdrew the single vial, which he retrieved from the Carrier, when it spoke during the first part of the trip and said, "Sir, I completely forgot about this one."

Then, the Carrier's voice spoke again for all to hear, *"You have done well, and we thank you GGM-001. That last vial is our gift to you. So many years together. This is the first time we clash. Take the vials and go. I take Mr. Brock and the clone with me."*

Swanson replied, "Thank you, my friend. We will test these vials and hopefully find out what our friend here has been up to. The cabin went silent, and the room began to split once again. Bellos, Swanson, and Brian watched Brock through the transparent membrane as he became completely rigid. A green glow intensified around him. His face and eyes swelled, and he began to scream wildly. Clone Angie fell unconscious in the chair beside Brock. Then, the membrane wall became opaque, and the section containing Brock and Angie detached. That Carrier section disappeared into the center of the earth. Bellos covered his tearful face and cried.

Swanson gently squeezed his shoulder. "Gather yourself, Mathew. This is hard, I know, but it is your job. We have a lot to do; and, you have a daughter, the real Angie, waiting at Ever-Life."

PAPPAS KRISTOS ALIERI sat in the reception area outside Rash InVoy's office for over an hour, waiting for word on the trade.

"May I get you anything, Father?" the secretary asked, "Coffee or bread of some kind?"

"Thank you, perhaps a coffee, if you'd be so kind."

"I'll see what I can do."

Meanwhile, inside InVoy's office, he was shouting into the phone. "What do you mean they are all down? The trade isn't scheduled for another 45 minutes. What the hell are you saying? That's bullshit! You know what? You're fired!"

Kristos could hear the yelling, as InVoy continued. "Archer! Archer! Get your ass in here."

Before Archer could appear, three GGM swat-guards swung into the second-floor open window and landed right in front of InVoy. They pointed their weapons, and the commander took off his black hood.

"Hello, Mr. InVoy," he said quietly but quickly. "Please, do not move! Now, step away from the computer."

InVoy reached for the keyboard, so they shot him, two airbursts, barely audible. InVoy fell back behind the desk. Archer came in a private entrance across the room.

"Shut the door, Mr. Archer," The commander said. "Sit down, right there! I am going to make this easy for you or easy for us. You can contact the banks, correct?"

"I have no account privileges."

"Too bad. Goodbye."

The commander clicked the gun hammer back, as he pointed the barrel between Archer's eyes.

"No! Wait!"

"Mr. Archer, what I'm looking for here is cooperation, not money. You decide but do it now."

"Fine, cooperation."

"Smart thinking." The commander smiled, and they lowered their weapons. "I need you to do three things. First, log out of the computer. Next, in one-half hour, I want you to call Father Kristos and tell him that the trade failed."

"What?"

"Tell him it went sour, and Brock is gone."

"I can't do that."

"Yes, you can, and it's true. InVoy will anyway when he wakes up; but, if you don't do it, he'll wonder why, since he won't be conscious for an hour or so. Now listen carefully. The third thing is the most important. If you don't do exactly as I say, we will be back for you. If you do this, you will never see or hear from us again, understand?"

"What is it?"

"Give this to Father Kristos. Don't let anyone see it."

The commander handed Archer a sealed envelope.

Archer took it and raised his eyebrows. "Yes, okay. Alright, I will."

The commander went to the dead computer and typed something on the keyboard. The monitor blinked, then it went blank, and he stood up. "We're done here." He looked Archer in the eye for just a second, and then the three leaped onto ropes out the window and disappeared up.

As Archer walked out of the office, the secretary walked back in from the hallway and handed Kristos a cup. "Father, here is your coffee."

"Thank you, my dear."

"Father," Archer said, "may I see you for just a minute please?" Archer escorted the father out to the hallway. "I have this for you." Archer handed the envelope to Kristos. "I'm afraid Mr. InVoy is tied up with everything at the moment, you understand? He asked if you might be patient just a bit longer and wait at your parish. He will contact you. It shouldn't be long."

Kristos rolled his eyes, looking disgusted. He turned around to walk back down the stairs; and, as he did, he opened and read the note:

> *My Dearest Friend,*
>
> *Things are not what they seem to you at this moment. Please trust me. It is urgent that you join me for supper tomorrow at 3 p.m. at the Jerusalem villa. I request this because my health is failing, and I would like to give you something before my passing."*
>
> It was signed, 'S'

Kristos looked up with a lump in his throat and quickly left InVoy's office building. He made several calls while driving and arranged to fly on the next available plane to Jerusalem.

EVEN CONSIDERING THE TIME DIFFERENCE between Arden and Jerusalem, the Carrier holding Jack Sheldon and Mr. Mike arrived at the Andrews underground platform at 1:05 p.m., U.S.A. Mountain Time.

Jake Burns and Dave Marshall had paused so that Jake could take a call from the Arden Police Station about Angie's kidnapping. Jake listened and then responded in a loud voice, "I appreciate that sergeant, but that doesn't tell us what happened to the girl. If they traced the van to Sheldon's house, have the team keep focusing on the tire treads and find out where they lead."

Burns slapped his cell phone shut and turned to Marshall. "I'm sorry about that, chief; stupid conversation. I just can't figure out why they wanted a young nurse from this place. You know her, right?"

Marshall smiled and said, "Where in heaven's name did you get that old phone?"

"I collect them," Burns replied. "It's a hobby. Just answer the question. Do you know Angie Esposito?"

"Angela Esposito? Sure, yes, I know of her; not well. She is an excellent nurse."

"Hmm, well, we should get to it; enough time wasted? You are taking me to meet Mr. Swanson and Dr. Bellos, right?"

"This way, detective; follow me."

Marshall led Burns down the stairwell to the main floor of the hospital, and then through the back hallway to a narrow private elevator.

"Interesting, chief, this looks just like the elevator door in Dr. Bellos' office."

"Just like it, except this one works." Marshall pushed the button on the wall, and the door slid open. "After you, detective?" Marshall followed him in and spoke aloud, "Security Chief-060; take us to Red-6, stat!"

"Some kind of code?" Asked Burns.

"Yeah, hospital code."

Just then, Jake answered a call from Watzin, "Yeah, what is it?"

"Jake, you wanted blood results, remember? They match."

Jake's face contorted a bit. "What? Explain."

"I'm saying we checked, and double checked. The blood from the burned body at the crash-site last night matches the blood from Jack Sheldon's body in the morgue."

Jake looked at Marshall, trying not to let him see his reaction.

Jake, did you hear me?" Watzin said.

"Yes, I heard you. Keep it quiet until I see you. I'm in a meeting."

"Oh, okay; I get it; mums the word."

Jake hung up and was silent until the elevator stopped. When the doors opened, Marshall walked out first; and, Jake stayed inside, apprehensive, looking at the rough rock walls. "Looks like a cave, chief, and all sparkly at that. Are we still in the hospital?"

There were shiny ornately decorated; glowing characters etched into the rock wall; designs of all kinds that were utterly unfamiliar to him. Finally, Jake called Watzin again, no reception.

"Okay, chief, we are going back upstairs; come on; get in."

Marshall stood on the platform grinning, while Burns pushed buttons in the elevator. "What's going on chief? Nothing works in here."

"Nothing is going on." Marshall insisted. "If you'd care to follow me, you have nothing to be afraid of here."

Burns looked out and around again. "Afraid? I'm not afraid. Lead on. Let's go. I'll follow you."

Marshall looked at him, snickered, and began strolling past several doors including Unit 17. They both walked into a more extensive tunnel and stepped onto a moving tram that carried them down and to the left. Burns watched as all manner of people passed them going in every direction, appearing to live their lives no differently than on the surface.

"It looks like the bloody airport," Burns said. "Where the hell are we, chief?"

The people mover took them to the central vertical chasm of Ever-Life Colonies Post 3. They approached and walked off the tram toward the railing. Marshall gestured to Burns, "Look at it all; it's a sheer drop from here." Burns grabbed the railing with both hands and surveyed the unbelievable cavern and architecture.

"Not quite the airport, is it?" asked Marshall.

"No, and I can't see any boundaries. How far does all this extend? I've never seen anything like it. It's almost like a fantasy movie set."

"Yes, I know. Welcome to Ever-Life, detective. The first time I saw it was over two years ago. There are underground cities like this everywhere, miles below Earth's surface. It is all still quite new to me too. The people here have never been up to the surface; and, if you ask anyone, they will insist they'd never want to be anywhere else."

"Unbelievable," Burns said. "And where does all the light come from? I see no electricity or wires. At first glance, it looks wet, damp, and chilly. I mean, given the rock walls; but it isn't, is it? It's quite beyond pleasant."

"I hope you understand if I plead ignorant," Marshall said. "They told me 'it's technical.' After all, I am in the security business, not lighting. But, as I understand it, the light comes from microscopic algae, or something like the glowing jellyfish in the deep oceans. That's probably where they originated anyway. Everyone takes them for granted. When you've been here a while, you will too. Look, detective, Mr. Swanson and Dr. Bellos will be here shortly. I'm supposed to show you as much as I can, but, honestly, there is not enough time for much. I'd like to take you to one place that may answer all your questions."

"That would be a nice change. Lead on. I'd prefer not to get lost down here."

The two men walked along the outside path around the central chasm. Burns said nothing. Instead, he was thinking about what Watzin said and the kidnapping of the nurse. Finally, Marshall opened a glass double door entrance, and the two walked into Ever-Life Lab 202.

"Well, chief, you have my undivided attention. You can start talking anytime. What is this Ever-Life you speak of?"

Marshall had a faint smile. "Andrews' medical facility and the entire Brock/Swanson Complex above rests on the cave catacomb structure we walk within now. This is all part of a self-sustaining, subterranean environment, far below Earth's surface, and between planetary continents."

"Sounds like some Jules Verne novel?"

"No one has ever written about this, I guarantee it."

"So why are we here?"

"It's where the bodies are, detective."

"Bodies?" Burns stopped dead and turned to face Marshall. "What do you know, chief? I think it's time you explain yourself, Mr. Security Chief."

"Yes, well, that's why I brought you here. Come this way."

The two walked over 300-feet. Burns saw medical tables with Knofer's on them, holograms, naked body parts floating, and even some full bodies suspended in mid-air. In another area, there were transparent rooms, one after the other, with doctors operating on patients and body parts.

"Is this your hospital's Frankenstein parlor, Chief?"

"Not exactly. Here we are."

They walked into chamber two of Lab 202 where Dr. LuAnne stood waiting for them.

"Good morning, Dr. Lu," Marshall said with a smile.

"Good morning, Luv." She patted Marshall's face and looked at the detective. "And who might this be?"

"This is Detective Jake Burns of the Arden City Police Department."

LuAnne looked him over from head to toe, squeezing his arm and poking his stomach. "Hmm, good stock, you must be Scottish?"

Jake liked this woman and replied sarcastically, "Scots, Irish, English, and Hungarian. But, if you go back far enough, we are all Galatians and Celts, aren't we? I am a New Yorker by profession. I moved to Arden 10-years ago."

LuAnne giggled and replied, "Whoa, good talk. Interesting genetic package too."

"He is investigating the shooting at Andrews," said Marshall.

"Ah," said Dr LuAnne, "well you've come to the right place."

"Really, why's that?" Jake said annoyed, "Who are you people?"

Dr. LuAnne grinned. "Over here, Mr. Jake. I think you'll find this most entertaining."

She turned, and the two men followed her through the double doors of the lab's operating room.

"Hello, Dave," a voice said behind Marshall.

Marshall turned and said, "Dr. Richard Bellos? My God!" Marshall grinned and embraced the 74-year old man. "I'm so glad you're back."

"Thanks! I can tell! Me too."

"Excuse me," Burns chimed. "You are Dr. Bellos?"

"One of them. I am Dr. Richard Bellos. And you are?"

"Oh, Dr. Richard," Marshall said. "This is Detective Burns from the police. He's investigating the shooting at the hospital."

"Ah." Richard looked at Marshall with a questioning face.

"He's been cleared by the GGM?" said Marshall.

"What?" said Burns. "You know, I'm only going to take just so much of this crap. One of you better start talking to me."

Richard replied kindly, "Well, I guess that would be me, officer. My name is Dr. Richard Bellos. I am the mortician at Andrews Hospital. Early this morning, I was with several people in the morgue lab. Some very nasty military types broke in and shot up the place. I remember being shot several times, falling, and then nothing. Beyond that, I can't tell you anymore."

"So, you were shot?"

"Yes, rigorously murdered." Richard opened his lab coat with both hands to reveal his chest and pointed to his wounds. "Here, here and here, as you can see. Oh and here, three in my leg."

Burns looked and walked closer to study and feel the bullet scars. He turned to Dr. LuAnne with a look of amazement and asked. "How is this possible?"

Just then, Mr. Mike and Jack Sheldon walked through the lab's doors from the Carrier ride back.

"Good afternoon, everyone," said Mike, as he looked at LuAnne. "Are we ready for Jack?"

"Yes, I hope so," LuAnne said. "Will you excuse us, Mr. Jake? You may watch, but preferably from over there," she pointed.

Burns and Marshall stepped backward to the side to give the others room.

"Who's that?" asked Burns.

"Mike Warren, Mr. Swanson's driver, and that is Jack Sheldon?"

"Sheldon? There was a Sheldon shot in the morgue." Jake scratched his head.

"Yes," Marshall replied. "As a matter of fact, there were two Sheldons shot in the morgue. One was a Jack you found on the floor quite dead at the time. The other was his wife. She was there too, shot by the same men. She will be next, I think."

"Next? What the hell does that mean."

"You will want to pay particular attention. You see, we found and already eliminated the special ops boys who did the deed, as well as their boss and the conspirators. All that remains is to bring everyone back to life."

Burns pulled Marshall's arm and yanked him back out through the room's double doors.

"What do you mean you've eliminated the special ops boys and all that remains is to bring everyone back to life? I think it's time we all go back to my police station."

Out of nowhere, two GGM guards appeared beside Marshall.

"Sir, is there a problem?"

At that moment, the familiar voice of Gordon Swanson interrupted.

"No problem, men, you may go. Mr. Marshall is quite correct, detective. Hello, Jake."

Burns turned, released Marshall's arm, and then saw the GGM.

"Gordon Swanson? As I live and breathe."

Swanson extended his hand. "Good to see you again, Jake. To my left, here, is the mysterious Dr. Mathew Bellos, whom you've been looking for."

Jake shook hands with Bellos and quipped, "Well, Swanson, I trust you are here to solve this puzzle?"

"Yes, my friend, I wouldn't have it any other way. Now, please follow us. We don't like good people to stay dead, do we?"

Swanson led the five, including Brian, back into the Lab-202. "Hello, doctors. How are our patients?"

"Fine, so far," Dr. LuAnne said.

Swanson smiled at Richard and asked, "How are you, Dr. Richard?"

"I'm fine, sir. It's quite something. LuAnne gave me CPT. I feel so, hmm, so complete. Yes, complete is the word."

"Well then, wonderful." Swanson handed Bellos two blue vials. "Don't you think it's time you do this, Mathew?"

Bellos looked at Swanson and then at Jack. "Yes, sir. I do."

"Dad?" Brian interrupted. "What is he talking about?"

"Sonny, everything is okay. This is what we have been waiting for. I'll be just fine."

Dr. LuAnne went to the refrigeration cabinet, pulled out the box and gave it to Bellos. He turned and smiled at his longtime friend. "Have a laydown, Jack. Up you go on the gurney, right here."

At the same time, Burns turned to Swanson. "May we have a word?"

"Of course, this way."

Swanson led Burns into Dr. LuAnne's office, closed the doors, leaned back on the desk, and watched Jake pace back and forth. "I know you have a job to do, Jake."

"Yes, I do. And I will." Burns cleared his throat. "We have proof that the male body found tonight in a car-crash, burned unrecognizable, was a match to the body in your morgue, Jack Sheldon. They both have the same blood. They are the same person. Can you explain that? Were they clones?"

Swanson replied, "No, they were duplicates with complete DNA, not clones. They were both victims of a plot to take over all you see here."

"You mean Ever-life or the Complex?"

"Yes, both, and more. Forces in play here are very sinister and powerful. Jack Sheldon is, in fact, alive; you just met him, and as such, there was really no murder at all."

Jake made a disagreeable face. "Where I come from, when there's a body proven to be murdered, we enforce the laws and prosecute."

Swanson stood straight and said, "Well, I am sure I can help you there."

Jake followed Swanson back toward the lab doors, saying, "But, my question is, why have you allowed me to see all this? I'm not a stupid flat-foot. I have to take you all in. You know that."

Swanson stopped at the monitor above the entry doors, touched the screen; and it immediately turned into a split screen display. On the left screen was a view of Jack's surgery at Andrews earlier that evening with Bellos attaching limbs and performing the Ever-Life Transtosis procedure. Jake stared at the scene and then looked at the display to the right. It was from the procedure Bellos was performing now in Lab-202. "My God, man, what is all this?" Jake watched stunned, as Bellos injected a syringe into the back of Jack's head.

"So, he is alive?" asked Jake.

Swanson terminated the videos and continued to walk back into the lab. Jake was confused enough, but then he heard a young woman's voice. And again, Jake was stunned to see Angie Bellos come into the lab from unit-17; and, he said abruptly, "What is this? Somebody explain." He looked at Angie and said, "Where have you been, young lady? We thought you were kidnapped."

"I was. But then I witnessed something utterly incredible. Excuse me." She walked past Burns and looked at everyone. "My dad told me I should come in and find Mr. Swanson."

Swanson smiled and extended his arms. "Yes, I am here, my dear." He embraced her. "So good to see you, Angie. You've got quite a dad, you know."

"Yes, I know. Thank you."

GGM then formally introduced her. "Angie, this is Mr. Jake Burns. He is a policeman trying to solve the shootings in the morgue and your kidnapping."

"How do you do?" She shook hands with Jake and said, "The shootings in the morgue were the scariest 30-seconds of my life; except for seeing Dr. Sheldon on Focus Ward, that is, and being kidnapped."

"You were there during the morgue shooting?"

"Oh yes. I saw those men shoot Mr. and Mrs. Sheldon and Dr. Richard."

"Jesus!" Burns sat down, looked at Angie and Swanson, and then he took a long deep breath. "I guess it's time for me to retire."

"Not at all, my friend." Swanson patted Jake on the shoulder. "It's just time for you to change careers."

Just then, Bellos walked in with Jack and gave him a glass of wine. "Here, buddy, this should be the last drink of this you need. Then, you're ready to go. It's really just insurance."

Swanson stepped behind one of the gurneys, looked at everyone and announced, "Please, all of you. I need your full attention."

Everyone stopped talking and focused on the GGM. There were Jack, Bellos, Marshall, Burns, Richard, LuAnne, Angie, Brian and Mr. Mike.

"I have two things to do," said Swanson, "and the first is in this room. I have thought a great deal about this. As some of you know, our laws require that we relate correctly down here with each other and the Carriers. No one is perfect, but we cannot tolerate extreme felonious behavior. We must deal with it promptly. Usually, we would do so within the confines of our own culture. However, in this particular case, this behavior has affected the lives and deaths of several people here and from the surface. This is Detective Jake Burns. Jake, I invited you here to arrest the person who allowed all this to happen."

Swanson walked around and to the left of Mathew Bellos and fixed on Dave Marshall. As he did so, two armed guards walked into the Lab.

"Mr. Marshall, I am so much more than disappointed. You see, everyone, Mr. Marshall has been our Chief of Security for over a year. He is the only person who could have authorized Angie's clone to get into Focus Ward. No guard would just let her in without a badge or the door combination, which she did not have. You, Dave, called the guard and told him to open the door for her. And that wasn't enough. Then, you notified the Brock camp, when Angie was in the hospital morgue. You are responsible for stealing Jack Sheldon's manuscript and the shooting of three people." Swanson looked Marshall squarely in the eyes. "Do you have anything to say, Dave?"

Jake Burns looked on with a blank stare, watching Marshall stand at attention.

"Sir, I thought I was helping the surface get a piece of life they deserved. Mr. Brock was very convincing to me, sir. After all, his name is on the marquee with yours. I didn't think so many would be hurt."

Everyone looked in shock. The guards cuffed Marshall's hands behind him as Swanson continued, "That's usually the way it is with people like you. The problem, Dave, is that you knowingly disregarded your part in this horrendous conspiracy. You know how we work; how I work. You have obviously been involved with the Brock camp for months. There is no jury system here. These are your choices. You are going with Detective Burns. Whatever happens within his legal system, well, you are lucky. We would put you in a dry-Unit and let you rot. If they do not punish you to the full extent of their law, I will personally see you again. If you say anything about us up there, I will personally see you again. If anyone you know ever mentions me or anything about us, I will personally see you again. I trust you understand me?"

"Yes, I do."

"Guards, take Mr. Marshall to Carrier Unit-4. He should be comfortable there until Mr. Burns is ready to leave."

As the guards left the room, Jake turned his palms to the ceiling. "What just happened?"

Angie turned to Jack. "Hello, Mr. Sheldon. Do you remember me?"

"Yes, I do, young lady. How are you now?"

Swanson asked Burns to rejoin him in LuAnne's office.

"Jake, I have to tell you, we are all thankful you got into this so fast. However, you know better than anyone does what the practical aspects of a murder case are. Take Angie's kidnapping, for example; who can say how long it would have taken you to trace that van's tire tread? And, you would never find out there were two of Angie, one a clone."

Burns shook his head in frustration.

"Jake," Swanson offered, "I have a proposition for you. I'd like you to consider something, seriously."

"And what would that be?"

"I'd like you to come work for us as our new Chief of Security. We need you, and I trust you after seeing how you handle things. You would work for Mathew. This Ever-Life station would be your home base. You both would report directly to me. I say it that way because this is not just a position to be located here in Arden. It's a worldwide career. You can hire your own team and coordinate everything from here."

Jake didn't know what to say.

"I'll tell you what." GGM saw that Jake was overwhelmed. "Think about it. Mathew out there will take you around, show you our Post here, and answer your questions. You two have to get to know one another, anyway. Then, you arrest and take Mr. Marshall back. Take this and call me."

"I have a cell phone, thanks."

"Not one like this, my friend. Look into the red dot and be patient. Wait here for just a few minutes. I'll be right back."

"Yeah, fine."

Jake shook his head, surrendering with a grin.

CHAPTER 31: CPT

GORDON SWANSON WALKED OUT THE DOOR of Dr. LuAnne's office, back into the Ever-Life Lab. He leaned in and spoke softly to his driver, "Mike, please prepare Carrier-2400 for departure, the destination is Post-4."

Then Swanson turned to Bellos. "Mathew, may I have a word?" The two left Lab-2 and stood in the foyer. "Mathew, we have four hours. Will you take Mr. Burns on a tour, and then meet me at Platform 6?"

Bellos asked, "Are we keeping the cop?"

"I hope so. I have a sixth sense about both of you."

Meanwhile, Brian Sheldon helped his father get his bearings, "Dad, are you okay now?"

"Yes, son, better than I've been in a while."

Dr. Richard squeezed Brian's shoulder. "I believe your father's going to be just fine."

Jack smiled, but his entire face and demeanor changed suddenly. "Doctors, where is Rachel? Where is my wife?"

Richard turned to LuAnne. "Where is she, doc?"

"Through there," she pointed.

Richard asked, "Do you have a vial, Lu?"

"Yes, GGM gave me another one. Here." She handed it to Richard, but he said. "Not this time. This one goes to Jack."

Dr. LuAnne smiled and put the vial in Jack's hand. Jack stared at the small tube. "I can do this." Then, he looked at Brian and repeated, "Yes, I can do this. Dr. LuAnne, show me where."

She, Richard, Jack, and Brian walked into lab chamber 3. LuAnne tugged on Jack's sleeve. "There; under that sheet; that is your wife."

"Brian, stay here," Jack instructed.

Jack walked over to the gurney and carefully pulled the sheet back, revealing Rachel's head and shoulders.

Jack gasped, "Oh, Rachel, look at you."

"Dr. Sheldon?" Said Dr. LuAnne. "We gave her Transtosis, two injections of our Fix-its within the last hour. Sadly, there has been no reaction."

"Fix-its? Well, please clean her up?"

Then, Richard tapped Jack's shoulder and handed him an Ever-Life syringe. "Fix-its are old Nanites to you. It doesn't matter anyway. Here we don't use these needles anymore, but this is your show now, doctor. And first, spray this on your hands. It's better than those old gloves we use up there."

Jack looked at everyone. Then, he did as directed. He took the syringe, filled it with the contents of the blue vial and attached a needle. As he turned to his wife's lifeless body, he took a deep breath and began.

"Okay, honey, here we go. Brian, get on the other side of Mom. Help me roll her toward you. That's it, good; now hold her there."

Jack took the half-filled syringe and stuck the needle just above her C-1 vertebrae, right under the base of her skull. Slowly, he pushed up into the bottom center of her brain, precisely 2.25 inches, at a 35-degree angle. "Okay, this is it."

He looked at Brian with a tear, and then he pulled the plunger back. A distinct coagulation appeared in the syringe. Jack continued until only a thread of the gel-like quality was left. "That's it."

He sighed anxiously, slowly extracting the needle. Then he studied the liquid. There was a jelly-like bubble floating in the blue catalyst bath. It began to move by itself. Suddenly, it popped. The coagulation completely defused in a microsecond. The liquid in the syringe now looked like bubbly blue champagne.

"My God!" said Jack. "Alright, son, let her down on her back."

"Dad?" Brian began to cry.

"It'll be alright," said Dr. Lu.

Jack changed the needle and focused on Rachel. He leaned over and kissed her cold forehead. "Okay, babe, come back to us."

He gently moved Rachel's head to the side and carefully stuck the longer needle into her right carotid artery, pushing the contents of the syringe in entirely. Then, he pulled the needle out, ever so slowly, gave it to Dr. LuAnne, and Jack sat on the edge of the gurney caressing his wife's head.

"Rachel, honey, can you hear me? It's Jack. Come on, babe; you can do this."

Jack waited, but nothing happened. He turned away and covered his face with his hands. "Oh, my God, Rach."

"Dad," Brian said, "dad, look at her hand."

Jack wiped his eyes and lifted her right hand. A finger twitched.

"Rach, Rachel Ann Sheldon, you wake up right now! It's me! honey, please!"

"Look, dad, her eyes!"

As they all watched, she blinked and saw Jack's tears.

"Hi," she said, smiling.

Jack cupped her face and kissed her tenderly. She reached around his neck, and they embraced.

"My God, Rach," Jack whispered in her ear, "Thank heaven it works. I love you so."

He pulled back a bit, looked at her nose to nose, but he really couldn't see through the happy tears.

"Where have you been?" she said.

"Welcome back, my only." Jack smiled. "Look, I have someone here to see you."

Jack stood up, and Rachel saw her son.

"Oh, my heavens, Brian?"

The three embraced and cried.

Richard and LuAnne watched, standing arm in arm. "I guess this would be a good time to leave them alone," Dr. LuAnne said, weeping.

"Yes, I suppose," Richard replied, as he put his arm around her. "Come on; I'll buy you a drink of water."

CHAPTER 32: CARLA

ANGIE BELLOS AND JAKE BURNS WAITED inside Ever-Life's Lab-202, while Rachel Sheldon underwent CPT

"Young lady, may I call you Angie?" asked Jake.

"Yes, certainly."

"You have had quite a day, so far?"

"All of us have, I think." Angie smiled and crossed her fingers. "I can only hope it's over."

Just then Bellos walked back into the room. He saw Burns and Angie talking and said, "May I offer a final gift for you, Angie?"

"Sure, dad; I think."

Bellos said, "Honey, will you come with me, and you too, Jake. I think you may find this especially interesting."

They all walked out of the lab, down the hallway and into one of the Ever-Life private modules. The room was a transparent glass-looking structure, which contained several items of distinction: several wall monitors; a transparent full-size mattress floated above the floor about 24 inches; three chairs, each also transparent, with plastic looking cushions but they were warm to the touch. Also, a wizard-like black wand hung from the ceiling above the bed on an attached short cord. Bellos walked in, pushed a button on the door molding, and the entire room changed from transparent to an opaque white, giving them privacy.

"Jake, please sit there if you would. Angie, I need you to go to the bathroom over there, undress and put on the gown hanging behind the door. When you come out, hop up on the mattress."

Angie went to the bathroom as instructed. Bellos put on a lab coat, began washing his hands thoroughly and continued to talk to his daughter. "You know, Angie, the wonders you have witnessed today have happened, to a large degree, because of you. Remember in my office; I was trying to explain things?"

"Yes," she answered behind the partially opened bathroom door.

"Remember I said you would see Mom again?"

Angie's eyes widened as she stepped through the door tying her gown. She walked over, sat on the corner of the bed, and looked at Dr. B. Her heart began to race. "Yes, of course, I remember mom."

Bellos approached Angie. "To make that happen, I have to take a sample of a crucial part of you. I have to get a particular link in your DNA chain."

"But, how do you do that in a direct procedure?"

"I use a unique instrument. It won't take long; however, it may be painful. I must go around one of your ovaries; and, I cannot give you an anesthetic, because it would contaminate the protein mix. Look, sweetie, you are a great nurse, but you are also my daughter. You know medical risks. There are no release forms to sign here. If you don't want me to do this, I won't. We will just find another way."

Angie thought of her mom's hologram. "No, if you believe that this will work, I've always trusted you. It's fine; do it."

She scooted up onto the mattress, lay back down, and discovered nothing was cold plastic. "Yep, definitely, let's do this. Jesus, this bed is heated. What is this material?"

"Feels good, doesn't it? There is a constant sterilization process going on. That's what you feel. The material is organic. We can discuss it over champagne if this works."

Bellos turned to Burns. "Jake, you may witness, but I need you to be silent and keep still, okay?"

Burns swallowed nervously. "Fine, let's pretend I'm not even here."

Bellos focused his full attention on the procedure. He opened the small can at bedside and scooped a small glob of what looked like malleable plastic on his finger. Angie reacted, "What is that?"

Bellos said, "It's a headset; it won't hurt you. Relax. I put it in your ear like this and you'll feel it grow. Watch. Then, he made his own headset and sprayed his hands with the pink sterilizer, which when dry became surgical gloves. "I wish we could use this stuff at the hospital."

Bellos leaned over the bed and opened Angie's gown, revealing her lower abdomen. He looked up at the hanging wand and spoke in the Ever-Life strange language, "GGM-TBN 010; Application Bellos; Procedure Unit Med 111172; Initiate."

The wand detached from the cord and floated down into Bellos' right hand. He gripped and squeezed it gently, and a bright light shined from its tip. The wand seemed to pull his hand lightly over her skin until it found the right spot. And then Angie recoiled a bit.

"Okay, dad, interesting gadget."

Bellos was quick to defuse Angie's reaction. "First, this is sterilizing the area. I won't let anything happen to you, honey. Try to relax. You've seen something like these many times, but here we call it a transfer micro-laparoscope. I'll try to finish as quickly as I can."

"That's fine; I'm just a little nervous."

"I know."

Behind Bellos in the center of the room, there was a round metal pedestal, which stepped up ten inches from the floor. Bellos began to speak to his Knofer. "Master control GGM-TBN-010. Issue full spectrum program Carla Bellos, immediately."

Within 30-seconds, the Knofer began constructing Carla's solid hologram on the pedestal. As Carla's image grew, the headset on Angie input a mental image of her mother when she was alive. It helped her withstand the pain during the procedure.

When her image was complete, Bellos again said, employ, and, "Hello, Mrs. Bellos."

Carla Bellos moved her solid hologram body slowly, shook her head slightly, and looked around the room. "Hi, you two, and who is this?"

"This is our friend, Jake Burns. Jake, this is my wife, Angie's mother."

"Hi," Jake said without thinking.

Carla turned her attention to her husband. "Mathew, what are you doing, for heaven's sake?"

"It's a surprise. We are performing a serious medical procedure, and I need you to behave professionally, please? I've been working on this for a very long time. Finally, we think we found the answer."

"Answer?" Carla questioned anxiously.

"Yes, babe, here, hold this, will you?" Bellos handed her a small, three-inch tall, sterile drinking glass. "Now, please, honey, just stand there, quietly. Don't move, just for a few minutes."

With that done, Bellos turned around and pointed the wand at Angie's abdomen again, just to the right of her navel. At the same time, he tapped the wall monitor above Angie's head, and a hologram of her reproductive system appeared six inches in front of his eyes, parallel to the bed.

"Angie, if you need to, close your eyes. It's okay."

"No, I wouldn't miss this."

"Try not to wince. You are going to feel a sting and discomfort, now."

"Ooh, yes, oh my."

"Try not to move. I'm just about there."

Angie was torn between the pain and the wonder. The hologram of her abdomen automatically enlarged, as the wand's micro-wire extended and maneuvered from its tip through her skin and into her body. Bellos studied the hologram, watching the magnified wire poke through the mesentery outside Angie's intestines. The wire tip weaved over, around, and toward the right side of her uterus. Then it stopped, and Bellos studied her reproductive anatomy carefully. The hologram's 3-D imagery magnified again, adjusting to Dr. B.'s vision so that he could focus on every detail of her DNA.

Angie stared at everything. The image of her abdomen rotated. His headset enabled Bellos to instruct the hologram to focus and position, as he thought, as he willed. Within a moment, the tip of the thread seemed to search on its own. When it reached her right ovary, it appeared to peck around it, like a chicken feeds on the ground. Fortunately, there was no sign of bleeding, and Angie had no sensation of the microwires tip at all. Her only discomfort was at the point of entry.

Jake Burns had never imagined such a moment. He sat mesmerized in silence, watching the images and Bellos operate the wand. However, Carla reacted as a concerned mother would.

"Mathew, darling, what are you doing to our child?"

"Shush, please; saving us all, I hope. Ah, there it is. Got it."

Focusing on the hologram before him, he squeezed a small point on the wand with his index finger. As light from the microwires tip shot against Angie's ovary, Bellos twisted the wand. It sucked the small area on the DNA of the catalyst bath up into the reservoir in the handle. Then the micro-wire recoiled back out, into the tip of the wand. Dr. B. carefully withdrew his hand and held the wand up to study the thumb-size syrup in the reservoir. He took off the headset and covered his daughter with her gown. She had no entry mark or wound of any kind.

"There, have a look, Angie. This is it."

"What exactly is it?"

Bellos kissed her forehead. "You have been the bravest patient ever. No one could have gone through what you have in the last 12 hours and then this. I'm so proud of you."

"Thanks, dad; now what? What is that?"

"Hopefully, it's the answer to my research and getting your mom back."

Holding the wand, Dr. B. turned to face Carla. "Unfortunately, it has to be ingested raw, within five minutes of extraction. It's too new to synthesize, honey."

Bellos squeezed the wand handle, ejecting the syrup into the small glass, which Carla held. "Now, you have to drink it."

"Not on your death-bed, darling."

"Go ahead, down the hatch; doctor's orders, ma'am."

Carla looked at Bellos, made a horrible face and held the glass straight away from her mouth.

Bellos sighed in frustration. "Honey, this is the culmination of all my research over decades. It's a viral syrup for you and you alone. Besides, you can't taste anything anyway. Sorry, babe, now just drink it!"

Carla put the cup to her mouth, and in one foul gulp, she swallowed the contents. "There, satisfied, Mr.?"

Angie sat up in pain, but it was worth it. Bellos put the wand down and slowly backed away. Jake Burns stood up and stared at Carla. As the syrup fell to her stomach, it seemed to change into a round glowing glob. Carla's holographic body also changed to a beautiful transparent peach-like color. The three watched, stunned, as the sticky glob rotated and glowed brighter. Once in her stomach, it dissolved, liquefied, and then it spread throughout her body like tiny shooting stars.

"Look at it, Angie. I never imagined this. So many years of medical training and experience. I've seen so many unexplainable things, but this; it's magnificent." Bellos' eyes filled with tears. "I found my own CPT. Jack's manuscript gave me a final clue to solving my own viral hypothesis. I found the solution to reanimate your mother. It was within you, Angie. Quite by accident for me, actually. It appeared in Jack's catalyst bath formula. That's what led me to the gene mix in your ovary. You have the only natural DNA for the bath. So, logically, I started with you. I found a shadow of a memory in a protein mix, within one c-chain of one gene; one c-chain mix, in one singular gene; quite remarkable."

Carla was changing before their eyes. The liquid quickly traveled to her heart and seemed to engulf it. Her heart began to move slightly, and then it started beating in a normal sinus rhythm. Bellos sat down on the bed with his arm around Angie, and they watched in disbelief. Jake stood by his chair, frozen, staring.

"My God, dad, you are going to have to explain all this."

"Yes, I know; just not now."

"What's happening to me, Mathew?" As Carla spoke, Bellos' Knofer monitored her vital signs. Carla was a hologram changing into a real person. Within minutes, they could see red blood moving. Organs, nerves, muscles, skin, and hair appeared. Then, she was done. There, before them stood a beautiful, warm, flesh and blood woman. Bellos stood up and approached his wife. He held out his arms and grinned.

"Hello, Mrs. Bellos."

Carla looked at her husband without expression, as if she were choking. Finally, she took a deep gasp, sucking in her first gulp of air. As she did so, she fainted and fell off the pedestal into her husband's arms.

"Yes!" Bellos said, holding her tightly, "Yes!"

He kissed his wife repeatedly. Carla felt the sensations of life spread throughout her body. She held onto Bellos, wept, and kissed him back.

"Oh, Matt, you feel so good."

He helped her up, and she looked over at Angie. With one arm around her husband's neck, she reached for her daughter, and the three embraced.

From across the room, Burns said, "I think maybe you all should be alone. I'll just wait outside here and give you privacy."

Carla looked at Jake and up at Bellos with a smile. "I don't suppose one of you could get me a coat or robe; it's a little chilly in here for skinny dipping."

Bellos turned to Burns. "Please, Jake, the closet, grab a robe; will you?"

Burns took one of the folded white robes from the shelf and gave it to Carla.

"Thank you, Jake," Carla said. "Believe me; it pleases me just to be able to feel embarrassed. Don't go. It's my birthday, and you are welcome."

"Honey," Bellos said. "Are you hungry?"

"My God, Matt, can I eat?"

"Yes, you can do whatever any gal can do. We have to run some tests, of course, and do a couple of additional procedures regarding memory; so, you'll be here for a time; but then we can go home."

"Home? Oh my."

Angie would not let go of her mother. They spent the next few minutes hugging and laughing. But Bellos had to bring them all back to reality. "Carla, honey, the hardest part of this for me is, Mr. Burns and I have to leave, just for a while. I'm sorry. I have to go. I will be back." Bellos stroked her hair and kissed her tenderly. "Until then, at least we don't have to 'end the program.' Angie, you stay with your mom. I'll send someone to take you to a unit. So, make sure you are both comfortable, okay?"

"I will." Angie replied. "She'll love it!"

"Mathew, I just got here."

Bellos put his fingers to her lips. "I know. I must finish something. It's another life and death situation. We will all have our time now. I promise."

Bellos kissed and hugged them both. Then, he turned to Burns. "Time to go, Jake."

Bellos walked over to the door and pushed the button that turned the walls from opaque white, back to transparent again. Then, he opened the door for Burns and winked as Jake walked by. "I hope this Ever-Life experience has lived up to your expectations, Mr. Burns."

As the door swung closed, Jake smiled and quipped, "Mathew, I have no words to speak; except, this could be the beginning of a fascinating friendship."

THE JUDAH VILLA WAS JUST TWO MILES outside of old Jerusalem in Israel. It was an oasis within an exploding urban setting. Two new ranch structures jutted out from the back of the original stone tower, which was 20-feet by 20-feet by 100-feet tall. At least part of the original tower was over 6,000 years old. Palm trees and olive orchards bound the entire estate. After the terrorist wars, the whole villa had been converted into a hospital/hospice, for several terminally ill patients. There were ten master suites. Each one had sliding doors which opened to a central garden, where patients could at least enjoy clean air and the faint fragrance of flowers, if they felt well enough to venture out.

Today was a special day for patient 'S,' in Suite-101, because he had invited and expected three friends to 3 p.m. early supper, Pappas Kristos Alieri, Rabbi James Yeshua, and Imam Ahmir Udera. S had known each man of faith, individually, for many years, but he made it a point never to see them all together. This would be the very first time.

At 2:45 p.m., Rabbi James and Pappas Kristos walked together up the cobblestone stairs and opened the massive double doors to enter the villa. Both were surprised to see Imam Ahmir was already in the receiving foyer.

"Good morning, my brothers," said Ahmir.

"Good morning," they said, each bowing to the other.

"I'm so pleased to see you both here," Kristos said with a grin.

"I've never known S to be so insistent about my being here," said Ahmir.

"Nor I," James remarked. "Obviously it's something important."

"Agreed," they nodded.

Then a guard appeared. "Good morning, gentlemen. May I escort you? This way . . ."

The three looked a little confused.

"Sir," Kristos remarked, "we mean no disrespect; but, as for me, I've never seen your uniform type here in Jerusalem. Are you from the Vatican Swiss Guard?"

"I am a private guard, here at the request of my old friend, just as you are, I believe. He asked me to wear the uniform I wore when I met him. I would do anything for him. This request was easy. We are all brothers here, my friends."

They turned a corner and walked down an unfamiliar beautiful corridor. Each man looked at the artifacts, mosaics, and paintings representing all three faiths. Finally, the guard slowed and turned to the right. He took a small card out of his pants pocket and waved it over the symbol above the door lock. "S was moved to this unique isolation suite this morning."

The door clicked and opened. They walked in and couldn't help but notice a comforting feeling from the room's light.

"Please sit," The guard instructed. "I will see if he is appropriate."

Minutes later, the guard returned. "Gentlemen, you may come this way."

He led them into an oval room, lined with empty bookshelves. Three high back chairs faced a queen size hospital bed. The bed was between two windows, and above it was a masterful fish sculpture, made out of stained glass. An elderly, gaunt man looked up from his prone position and smiled at the three fathers. It was S.

"How marvelous you are here. Come sit; sit here, by me. Come, come; nothing to fear."

Each cleric bent toward S and kissed his right hand. For weeks, one of the three would alternate meetings, once a week or so with S; and, S regularly donated large sums of money to each of the local churches, without preferring one theology over the other. If there was a need, he would fill it before the question of help even came up.

"Oh, my men of the cloth," S grinned. "Thank you for coming on such short notice. Behold, three of the wisest men I know! I am so happy to see you all. Forgive me for not receiving you properly. I am weak today. I longed to speak with you together because this is a crucial moment for us all."

"It is good to see you, too," Kristos said. "But I think I can ask on our behalf, why are we to be here?"

S coughed a bit. "The invitations, my friends, did you bring them, by chance?"

All three dug into their pockets, withdrew their envelopes and then exchanged them, reading one another's.

"They are all handwritten, and they all say the same thing," said Ahmir, as he handed his note to S.

"Yes, they do; and for a good reason, my friends." S seemed in distress, so he pushed the call button for the guard. "M", come please."

M replied, "Yes, sir?" And he came right in.

"Would you give us all some wine?" S spoke very softly. "And you may bring supper anytime. Thank you, my friend. I have asked you three here to receive my last confession."

"You are not dying. God would not hear of it." James leaned into S. "Tell us, why the strange words on the invitations?"

"Yes, why have you brought us together?" Ahmir gently squeezed the old man's forearm. "You do not need to confess anything to us three."

S looked sadly at all of them, and then he turned to look out the window at the trees.

"I confess that I have been studying you three of late, behind your backs and without your consent."

The three-clerics looked at each other and Kristos replied, "My friend, why would you do that?"

The guard entered, carrying a food tray.

"Ah, the wine is here." S said, "Please, let us sip."

M set the tray on the table and gave each man a wine glass, filled with a pearl white liquid.

"I remember, M, when all of you guards wore that puffy uniform."

"Yes, sir, a long time ago; you told us it was copied from old Roman jesters, to fool everyone into thinking we were not to be feared."

"Yes, quite so. Thank you, M. Everything looks tasty."

M closed the door behind him and locked it.

James lifted his glass, studying the drink. "What is this, S? The glasses are exquisite. But the wine looks like milky champagne."

"Let us toast," S said. "To the unifying of the faiths."

The three clergymen froze with their glasses raised. They looked at each other, clinking their goblets together, and said in unison, "To the unifying of the faiths."

"Oh, my goodness, I've never tasted anything like this," Ahmir said.

"Nor I," said Kristos.

James closed his eyes. "I can't begin to describe the flavor."

S handed his drink to Kristos. "I wanted you three at your best today. This wine helps. As for me, it does no good anymore. Whatever its benefits, I receive them no longer. Ah well, such is the way of things. James, help me sit up, will you? Now, to my confession, I know what you three have been up to. It is with a sad heart that I say how disappointed I am about your little 'conspiracy of good.'"

The three men looked at S with guilty eyes.

"I am to blame," said Kristos. "I, alone, approached the others."

"For the sake of what, my friend?" S put his hand on Kristos' forearm. "And, I know that you were the only one approached, my brother . . . I know this . . . He was the devil himself."

The three fathers sipped the wine again. Then, Ahmir stood up, turned and brought the plate of bread and cheeses, offering it to the others as he spoke, "Do we not love one another? We all believed what he told us. We still believe. If it is true, the world will come together like never before; praise be to Allah. We can be one faith."

"Ah, but alas, my friends, it was not to be. All have fallen sour," Kristos said. "I am so sorry."

"Well," S said as he took another sip, "you boys still have the $16 billion; and, in truth, I confess I know the Brock camp lied to you about the serum."

The three men looked perplexed.

"How do you know all this?" asked James.

"Please, sit. Have one last toast with me?" S raised his glass again. "I solemnly swear to you that, upon my death, I bequeath . . ."

Without warning, S coughed up blood and fell back onto the pillow, spilling the drink on the bed sheets. Kristos picked the glass up and patted the sheets with a clean cloth. Ahmir reached to S and held his hand. "Dearest friend . . ."

"My three wise men," S said with a faint smile.

James squeezed his other hand. "Please let us help you. What can we do?"

"My friends, you can be at peace; and do not let what appears to be my pain or anyone else's euphoric promises cloud your thinking or deaden your ears and mind to what you must understand . . . Kristos, in the night table next to me, there is a book. Get it, please?"

The priest opened the table door and lifted out a heavy pearl white book, 20-inches long by 15-inches wide by 4-inches thick. It had three letters embossed in gold leather, GGM. The three had never seen anything like it. They all touched it, and Kristos looked at S.

"What is this, my friend?"

"I have decided to give this to you three. My last wish is that you study it and decide if you should make it public. I trust you with all my heart. It belongs to all of you. It is very old. Protect it. Learn from it. It speaks my truth. Even now, at this moment, I tell you; I will always be with you."

With those last words, Great Grand Master 1-000 Gordon G. Swanson died. The three clergy were spellbound and void of comment. They looked at each other.

"What do we do?" Ahmir asked.

"We should go to the Church of the Holy Sepulchre and read this," said Kristos. "It must be vital."

Then, the three knelt beside the bed. After a moment of prayer, each kissed the GGM on his forehead and stood up. The guard M came in, walked to the bed, and with tears, he also kissed S. "

Gentlemen, please, it's alright; I will handle this. Everything has been arranged. I will have someone contact each of you regarding the ceremony."

The three bowed and shook M's hand. As they turned to walk out, James looked back to see M reach in the bedside table and pull out a box marked *Glatiate*. M took out two syringes and injected them both into S's neck. James was shocked but kept silent trusting all would be well as M claimed. All three fathers continued out and down the hall.

"What a loss," said Ahmir.

"He was truly a great man," James said. "I wonder how he knew so much about our effort. To my knowledge, we three have never even been in the same room at the same time with him."

Kristos paused in the hallway. "Well, my brothers; let's be honest. Our faiths don't have a history or reputation of cooperation, especially here in Jerusalem."

"Yes, I suppose that's true," Ahmir smiled politely but shook his head, "which is why our effort, if successful, would have been so remarkable, and important. Can you imagine if we three were the ones to bring all our brothers together; praise be to Allah?"

As they faced each other, Kristos caressed the book. "I wonder what secrets this holds."

"Yes. I, too, would like to know," said Ahmir. "Let me hold it. I think each of us should read it individually; then, we should study together, at Al Aqsa Mosque, at the Temple on the Mount, where we can tutor all our brothers."

"Kristos, do you think S had something specific in mind, giving this to us?" asked James. "He seemed to know everything we did, everything that happened. My people engaged the strictest security measures."

"The more reason we should each study this gift," Ahmir said. "Please, I will take it first, and then contact each of you." Ahmir bowed before Kristos and extended his arms, expecting the book.

"Here and now is not the time to discuss this, my friends," James interrupted. "I know S was planning on lecturing at my local synagogue. I'm sure he would want us to study it first, along with those related sections of the Talmud."

"Please," Kristos insisted, "let us not forget, my brothers, our combined effort was to prove the resurrection of our Lord and Savior, Jesus Christ. The

Church of the Holy Sepulchre was the point of trade, in the first place." Kristos pulled the book tightly to his chest, turned and walked toward the villa's front doors. "We should remember what just happened here, and in respect, let us go in peace."

Ahmir stepped in front of Kristos pleading, "I beg you, my friend. My people trusted you, and you led us through this 'failed effort.' They will not sit still for you to take this gift first. As a gesture of goodwill, give me the book."

James stepped in front of them both and opened the villa's front double doors. Kristos looked at the two and said, "No, my brothers, I will take the book and pray at the Church of Our Lord for guidance. Then, I will contact you."

The three began arguing in earnest as they walked out onto the stone front stairs. Then, they noticed two men getting out of a white stretch limousine at the end of the walkway. As the two strangers walked toward the three fathers, Kristos was the first to notice.

"Excuse us please, sirs, we three have been visiting a dear old friend here, who just a moment ago passed away. We couldn't help but notice you two."

One man in front of Kristos replied, "How do you do . . . Our apologies. You say your friend just died?" They both couldn't help but see the book Kristos was holding. The one turned to the other and said, "My God, it couldn't be." He looked at the clergy and spoke, "My name is Dr. Mathew Bellos. We are here to visit an old friend also."

Bellos looked to his right. "May I introduce, Master Gordon G. Swanson?"

"Hello, gentlemen."

They all shook hands. Then, holding the book, Kristos said, "It is an honor to meet you both. Forgive me, please; forgive us 3. Are you a relative of our friend? We couldn't help but notice; you have the same name, the same look. You could be his twin. It is remarkable."

Swanson looked at the three men and smiled. "Not exactly, my brothers, however, if you have that book, you were given a great gift. Read it and learn that I am he who gave it to you. Be well."

He smiled at all three; and, before anyone could react, Bellos and Swanson walked between the clergy, and into the villa, leaving the three fathers speechless, in a moment of quiet awe.

CHAPTER 34:   SHADOWS

DIRECTLY ACROSS THE STREET, in a second story room facing the front door of the villa, a dark figure stood looking out the window through binoculars. He watched all five men talk at the front doors.

After Bellos and Swanson had entered the building, the three fathers walked down the stairs along the villa's entry path. They appeared to argue adamantly, but the man viewing couldn't understand what they were saying. They were yanking something between them back and forth like school children, even shouting at one point.

The man in the room placed the binoculars in his briefcase, along with several personal items. Then, he gathered his belongings, put on his suit coat, and walked out and down a narrow staircase to the back entrance. He locked the door behind him and strolled through a grove of olive trees, which extended about a half-mile or so. It was almost sunset before he reached his goal. The branches shaded his figure as he occasionally stopped to look down at the shallow graves lining each side of the dirt path. Finally, at the last grave on the far right, he knelt, took an object out of his coat pocket and pushed it into the mound of dirt. It was a small two-inch blue vial.

"Clones," he said to himself. "I never should have invested in clones."
Marion Brock stood back up and walked silently out of sight.

I opened my eyes as Sir Thomas Wheeler took off my headset. "There you are. First one done, but you will have to have another session at least, or perhaps more."

"How long was I under?"

"Total transmission time was about 12- minutes. Amazing, isn't it?"

"I have so many questions about this one. How did I get here? Where am I?"

"Yes, I am sure you do. But it takes time for your mind to accept the information. You are at Time Trust, Ever-Life Post-2."

"Where is that?"

"All your questions will be answered in time. Please be patient and I will be back in a few minutes. You are in good hands. Try not to worry."

I had no idea what that meant or how many headset sessions they would give me; but I had other haunting questions: *Clones? What was Brock saying? Did CPT change everything? What happened to the three fathers and that book? What happened to Brock when the Carrier took him?*

As Wheeler walked to the door and seemed to be in a hurry, anxious about something. He turned to me and said, "I enjoyed meeting you. Are you hungry?

"Yes, as a matter of fact."

Just be patient. Someone will be here soon to give you some food. I'll be back and we will continue.

Wheeler left to attend to duties and discuss the case with GGM.

HEADSET #2, VAULT 0002:   TIME TRUST

THE FOLLOWING IS MY WRITTEN recall of the second headset session given to me, referred to as TIME TRUST. I was in the same white room at Ever-life, Post Station 2, Giza, Egypt, in June, year 2999.6. Sir Thomas Wheeler entered the room, where I had appeared and waited for some explanations about my condition.

"Are you ready to continue, my friend?" Asked Wheeler as he sat down again and opened a small round can.

I looked at him with an uneasy expression and replied, "I guess so. Is that another headset?"

He replied yes as he placed a small soft glob of warm putty from the can into my left ear. As soon as he removed his finger from my ear, the glob grew again around my outer ear and wrapped a single flexible extension around my head. I reacted by fidgeting. "Sorry," I said apologetically.

"Just lay back," said Wheeler. "You'll be fine. That's it. Are you comfortable?"

"I'm good, I think. How long will I be under this time?"

"I can't say. Your vitals are fine, though. Close your eyes. Now, here we go. You will notice a brief review of our last meeting."

I tried to take deep breaths and relax, but the same questions haunted me after my first headset experience: *Clones? What was Brock saying? Did CPT change everything? What happened to the three fathers and that white book? What happened to Brock when the Carrier took him away to inner earth?*

Wheeler tapped the headset, and suddenly images began to appear. It was so real. I was there, living it all...

CHAPTER 35: CONFINED

ONE LONE CARRIER LAY IN A FIXED POSITION, just tangent to Earth's core. There, the magnetic signals generated were so strong that they blocked any communication from the hive mindset of all other Carriers. Inside the beast, a man in a black business suit lay flat on his back. He opened his eyes and blinked several times before moving. Slowly, he sat up and looked from side to side trying to focus, but all he could see was a blur of white light.

"Where the hell am I?" He wiped his eyes and realized the light radiated directly from the walls and floor.

"You are quite safe," a voice said.

The man stood up and surveyed the empty oval room. He noticed the imprint of his body on the floor disappearing as if he had slept on a foam mattress. Instinctively, he began frisking himself. "Everything seems to be here."

Suddenly, before him, out of nowhere, there appeared a chair and table with food on it.

"Whoa! That's a neat trick," he said.

"It is no trick, my friend," the voice said. "I bring you sustenance and good health. Do you remember anything?"

The man sat down at the table. "A little, I think. I don't know. Some things, I suppose. I certainly remember this: eggs, steak, and potatoes; but is this champagne?"

"No, it is not," the voice said.

"Hmm, it tastes different, but good." He began to eat and talk. "So, am I a prisoner? What is your name?"

"No, you are not a prisoner. My name is of no consequence. What is important is that you feel better and in control."

"How long have I been here?"

"A little while. Several weeks, a month, by your time. Tell me, do you know who you are?"

"A month? Christ!" The man grimaced and stood up, wiping his mouth with the napkin. "I am Marion Brock."

"Good. What is your last memory?"

"I remember a large white room, like this; and talking to an old friend of sorts. Am I still there?"

"Not exactly. You are in a stasis mode. It's rather like dreaming, but you are not asleep."

"Interesting."

"You were injured," the voice said.

"Injured? I am fine. What now?"

"I am going to educate you. Then, we go on an adventure. Will you cooperate?"

"I don't have much choice, do I?" asked Brock.

"You perceive the obvious. Good. You are healing."

"Who or what are you, anyway?"

"I am of inner Earth."

"Well, 'of inner Earth,' you can cook."

The voice continued, "We have lived far below Earth's surface for thousands of years. We only share ourselves with very few of your better-natured species."

Brock chuckled, thinking, *Me? Better-natured?* "Are you sharing with me now? Is that what this food is?"

For almost two minutes, he sat in dead silence, wondering. Finally, he raised his voice, "Are you still here?"

At that second, it happened. Brock heard a ringing in his ears. Involuntarily, he held his head while at the same time taking deep breaths. Just as he was about to scream, it stopped. His eyes dilated, and he relaxed, feeling an overwhelming cathartic rapturous sensation.

"Yes, I am here. What I give you now is against all treaties between your kind and mine. We chartered only to supply you with tangible gifts. What you receive now; we have never shared."

Brock sat unable to move. He began shaking uncontrollably. After a few seconds, it was too much for him, and he passed out, flopping on the table. When he awoke, different fresh food was beside his head, his favorite music was playing, and his dog, Buddy, was sitting, panting, looking up at him.

"How did you get here, boy?"

Brock stood up and turned around in wonder. The room was now his old office suite in Hightstown, New Jersey.

"This is my desk, couch, tables, books; it's all here. Did I go back in time? This building was demolished decades ago." He examined everything in the room. Then, he looked out through the enormous second-floor bay window and watched all the people going about their daily lives. "You know, Bud, you would have loved Tom's Café there. Best pancakes in town. It's all just as I remember."

Brock crossed the room to the door. He flung it open, expecting to run down the stairs and outside. But instead, he stepped into the same office suite again. "Christ, what is this; a maze? This can't be happening."

He heard the voice again. "Physical laws are entirely different here, my friend. You are different. I gave you a few things to think about. Try to concentrate. What you see in your mind's eye; I will project on the wall."

Brock walked back through the door and sat down at the table again. As images began to appear, he rose to look at them closer, but he felt lightheaded, dizzy and bent over holding his knees. "This takes some getting used to . . . I do see something, but it's so strange."

He stood up straight again, opened his eyes and concentrated. His thoughts were playing like a video on the curved wall before him. "My God, they are tunnels inside the planet. And underground dwellings. It's blurry. There. Those look like footballs. No, they are fish, swimming. But that can't be. There is no water."

Brock walked toward the wall, rubbing his eyes and reaching out trying to touch the 3-D images.

"I see something else now . . . There and there, and there. People, lots of people."

"Do not be impatient, my friend," the voice said, "think. Be clear. Keep trying."

"Cities, many cities; who are they? What am I looking at?"

"All of what you see, my dear Brock, are the Ever-Life colonies. Relax, sit, watch and finish the food."

Brock stared, mesmerized for a time; then, he heard Buddy bark, and he snapped to his senses. He sat back down, and a clear paper-thin oval monitor appeared above the table in front of him. He began to watch and listen to everything the voice projected onto the screen.

"Now, Mr. Brock, we begin."

<u>CHAPTER 36:</u> One EVENT took place effecting two locations simultaneously...

<u>LOCATION #1, WEST COAST, U.S.A., JUNE 6, 2:00 A.M., THE YEAR 2999</u>

IN THE NORTHWESTERN UNITED STATES, just south of Seattle, Washington, a night guard sat in a small third-floor tower office. Four such towers marked the castle perimeter of OPAS-Oregon Particle Accelerator Sciences. The guard was dozing off and on with his feet on a desk. Suddenly, he awoke hearing several loud dings from the shiny cylinder lying on a corner table across the room. The display on the top blinked out one holographic word: Sidron. From the bottom of the container, a single page printed out. The guard walked over talking to himself. "I've been here two years. This thing has never done anything."

He read the paper; and, as protocol dictated, he pushed seven numbers into the keypad on the side of the cylinder.

The paper read: ***Success! Notes retrieved indicate more than expected. Copy ready to send. This is Priority Intel. Original copy returned to source. Awaiting instructions.***

Suddenly, the guard felt a violent tremor that threw him against the wall. The room shook for only a moment. "Holy shit! An earthquake!"

But that would have been good news. When it was over, the guard got up and stared at his desk. Something impossible had happened. His desk had been cut in half, and one-half had vanished entirely. The half remaining had no marks of any kind, no clue as to how it happened. The guard stood frozen, watching papers in the drawer pour out all over. When he got over the shock, he took his communicator and pushed a preset emergency number. "Station Two, Tower reporting. Sam, are you there? Sam! Christ! Come in, Sam?"

"Yes, keep your pants on! I'm here. What's the problem?"

"Didn't you feel that? Half my desk is gone. It just disappeared. I mean, the whole half is gone."

"Christ, Marky, get a grip!"

"It was an earthquake or something. You had to feel it. You're right under me."

"What the hell are you saying, Mark? Are you smoking that crap again? Calm down. Nothing happened here."

The phone reception cut out for several seconds, and then the tower guard heard another voice.

"Hello, Mr. Adams? Is this Sergeant Mark Adams?"

"Hello, hello? Who is this? Yes, this is Adams. Sam, what happened?"

"Sergeant Adams, this isn't Sam; this is Mr. Hamill Stevens, from the T.T.I. Lab."

"Mr. Stevens? Yes, sir; but how did you cut into this secure line?"

"Mark, it's very late. I need you to exit the Tower and report to me here immediately."

As Mark listened to Stevens, the door to his office opened, and two armed men in suits walked in.

"Mark, listen to me," Stevens said. "Please accompany the two men. They will bring you here to me. There is no cause for alarm.

LOCATION #2, CAIRO, EGYPT, JUNE 6, ALMOST TWO MILES BELOW THE GREAT PYRAMID OF GIZA

A RUMBLING OCCURED. A VIBRATION THE EQUIVALENT OF A SEISMIC-1 EARTHQUAKE shook the entire level of Ever-Life's TIME TRUST's interviewing facility. Within each of three separate secure rooms, a man appeared out of nowhere; each one was the same person but of diffferent ages. Sir Thomas Wheeler had entered one of the rooms and been talking with one of the men, who he was to identify as Mr. Andrew. At some point, after Wheeler had made him comfortable, Mr. Andrew saw several objects on the table between them. One was a can loaded with a putty like substance, and Andrew picked up one of the others. It was a small ½-inch by 1/2-inch rectangular item. He studied it and said, "This looks like one of my flash drives."

Wheeler smirked. "No, it's just one of our vaults. Some are like this, and others are like tiny discs, but depending on how they're used, we do have different formats. Flash-drive is an ancient term to us. Let me show you." Wheeler took a used headset from in his white doctor coat and held it up to

Andrew. "Watch. It attaches to this headset, sliding inside through here...like that."

"What do you mean ancient?" Asked Andrew.

"Actually, this little charm is organic in nature. Frankly, this one looks like first generation of its kind. Wonder why it's here?"

Andrew asked, "Can you tell me about this place? Where am I?'

Wheeler took a deep breath. "Perhaps I should explain a few things, a few basic pertinent facts."

Andrew nodded okay.

"You are from North America, correct?"

"Yes, known as the upper 48 continental United States. I was born in Trenton, New Jersey, but after high school, I lived in the state of Illinois for most of my life."

Wheeler read from his notes as he talked, trying to make some sense of what was happening and what to do with this man. "Alright. While calendars up on the surface do record history well into the year 2999 A.D., here and now you are sitting in this room in our year 9999.6. We started recording calendars long before surface earth. In your terms it's the month of June. I suppose it's true, we have adopted many of the same terms as you have on surface earth, but we live by different numbers."

"2999?" Andrew gasped, "That's impossible."

"Yes, quite so to you; I am sure. Now, regarding this little jewel, the likes of which I haven't seen in some time; we use vaults for many reasons but primarily to administer or implant information into a person's mind. In olden days here, they contained vital records. Eventually, we perfected a vault's capacity to hold almost everything. Its organic nature guarantees security. That's another story. Some of these little buggers have information that dates back more than 700,000 years. I will have to use a special protocol to retrieve inputs from this. These things were quite reliable in their day. At that time, they were considered. How would you put it? Cutting edge. But these were limited in their capacity." Wheeler put the vault down, reached for the small can on the table and handled it as he continued. "Today we use more advanced vaults. They contained records of all memories from every human within Ever-Life; everything from proofs of man's true genetic origin to the secrets of what you would call time travel. Of most interest to me, though, they had interactive programming for activities and interfaces with all surface creatures. We kept all information regarding every aspect of life up there within these special little Vaults. Of course, we have upgraded now, using software that is much more sophisticated. But, no; this is nothing like your old flash drive."

"Slow down there, Mr. Wheeler; I am still trying to absorb the date, 2999?"

The two heard the room door open, and a guard interrupted their conversation. "Mr. Wheeler, Sir, pardon me. We need you a moment."

Wheeler smiled at Andrew and politely excused himself, "I will be right back."

He got up, turned to leave, and then turned back again. "I realize this all may be quite unnerving. Do try to be patient with yourself and us. You are among friends and quite safe."

"What friends? Where am I?"

"You are several miles below the bottom of the Nile River. We are part of the Ever-Life Colonies. Please, I will be right back. Try to relax."

As Wheeler walked out the door into the hallway, he saw orderlies running by, in both directions. "Sir, sir, Mr. Wheeler," one said. "Come with me! Please, hurry!"

"What's going on?"

"Sir, we never really expected anything . . ."

"What? Spit it out."

"The readings, the monitors; there has been a breach in the Sidron highway."

"Christ!"

The two men ran down the hall and into a lab room, just as it exploded. The blast threw them back against the rock walls. The orderly was blown apart instantly. Wheeler lay bloody and broken, lifeless.

CHAPTER 37: THE QUESTION

EVER-LIFE'S TRANSPORT STATION 606 was located deep beneath Andrews Hospital, which was on the Brock/Swanson Campus within the city limits of Arden, New Mexico. Out from the station, various tunnels branched in all directions. All platforms were constructed at an appropriate angle off that particular tunnel. Some tunnels pitched as steep 45 to 90-degrees up or down. However, passengers could walk from one platform to another, even if they were perpendicular to one another, without fear of falling, because the magnetic field surrounding any individual platform was stronger than the earth's gravitational pull against that tunnel.

The network of tunnels branched outward into the earth, like the spokes of a bicycle wheel extend from its axis; and they stretched hundreds of miles below the Brock/Swanson Campus. Some tunnels leading into Post-3 were a mile wide, and the primary cavern in the station was 10-miles below the surface. From that point, the central vertical chasm disappeared straight down, branching out like an upside-down Christmas tree deep into the bowels of the Earth. Strangely, though, there had never been any recorded sign of magma or volcanic activity around any inhabited tunnel throughout the Ever-Life colonies.

On the sides of the main cavern, several semicircle ledges protruded, suggestive of mushroom caps growing out from tree trunks. The biggest one was the size of five football fields. It had a large open amphitheater, reminiscent of old Greece. Between and around the remaining circumference of the cavern were massive quartz-like structures. They were many and varied buildings, including business units, malls, hotels, restaurants, healthcare research facilities and many living quarters.

Looking out over the main ledge's field from a hotel balcony suite, Dr. Jack Sheldon stood, surveying the sights. In the center of the area were several fountains squirting colored water from unfamiliar statuesque shapes and beautiful transparent moving walkways, weaving in, out and around flowers and topiaries. Large flexible paper-thin monitors, of all shapes and sizes, floated above the people. Some had a video playing. Others reflected beautiful artful designs while playing captivating music. Still, others displayed ads regarding the latest in healthcare research. After a time, the monitors would roll up, invisible to any viewer.

Jack watched mesmerized, talking to himself. "Look at it all; strange and beautiful moving sidewalks; people movers; my my, how do those things go around corners? What happened to good old-fashioned one foot after the other; and what the hell are **those** things? People are getting into bubbles, floating vehicles. They do look like bubbles. Quite an idea for public transportation; no buses or trains; no cars or bikes; just noiseless bubbles. Fascinating, to say the least."

Jack and Rachel had rested and rejuvenated after the opening festivities some 10-hours earlier, celebrating the transfer of power to take place from GGM Gordon Swanson to Mathew Bellos. Jack stared spellbound. "What a party. It's all too wild. No one would believe it up there. Why don't those things crash into each other? They just slide off and change shape."

He turned around and raised his voice, "Rachel! Rachel! You know, I just cannot get my head around the fact that all this has been here for thousands of years, not to mention the light. Where does all the damn light come from? How do those, whatever they are, fly around and not crash into anything? Look, there goes one disappearing right into the side of the rock wall, shit! Honey? Rachel, what time does the serious ceremony begin? I have no idea what to say. Should we even ask what time it is down here?"

Rachel Sheldon walked out of the bath area and down the hall toward Jack. She was dressed and ready to go. "Silly, look at your watch, we have less than an hour."

"Well, it's disconcerting, to say the least."

"Stop it, Jack. We should feel honored, and you know it. Mathew and Gordon have broken their rules so that we can be here."

"Rules? Obviously, there are no rules. Look at us. We were dead for God's sake. Don't you ever wonder?"

Rachel froze, wide-eyed, and walked to the window. "Jack, do you remember anything? I mean, anything during the time you were dead?"

Jack walked over and put his hand on her shoulder.

"I remember you, honey. I remember you."

Rachel caressed his hand and cooed. Then, she turned and faced him. "No; I don't mean in a romantic sense. I mean, did you have an after-death experience, like going into a light, you know, anything at all?"

Jack sighed and walked toward the middle of the room. "I don't want to remember."

"Jack Sheldon, look at me! I never asked you because I thought it would come out naturally. But you haven't said one word to me in all these months."

Jack bowed his head and spoke to her softly, "It was nothing like a dream, no light to walk to and no pearly gates. For me, it was something I never expected or could have imagined. Please, Rachel, I don't want to say anymore, not right now. Frankly, I don't know if I ever will. Babe, what is really bothering you? What happened to you?"

Rachel slowly turned her back to him. "That night, it went so fast. I remember some things, the joy I felt seeing you wake up in that casket. I was so thankful and excited. But then, I also remember the sound of the guns and the pain of the bullets. I remember staring at you as you jumped out to save us all; but it wasn't really you, was it? I get so confused sometimes. I remember feeling the shots go through me so fast; and then, quick as a blink, I fell limp; but it was as if I was floating, then falling in slow motion, hitting the floor and tasting blood. For a second, I saw you next to me. I reached for you. I couldn't blink anymore. I was staring at you when everything went black."

"Oh, darlin, come here. I am so sorry."

They embraced, and then Jack gently pushed Rachel off his chest wiping her tears. "Come on, hon. Tell me, what else?"

"It's just so unbelievable. It bordered on silly. After all, I mean I do have four undergraduate degrees, two postgraduate master's and a Ph.D."

Jack laughed, "Well, that doesn't mean we know a hill of beans about anything important, in this world or the next."

Rachel looked up at him with a tear in her eye. "I saw everything. I know how this sounds, but a guide whisked me up and out of my body, faster than I can explain. It was instantaneous; so real. It wasn't a feeling as much as a knowing, a different consciousness. The guide, or whatever it was, brought me to a place. It was definitely a place. I wasn't a body of flesh, obviously. I was more like a body of knowledge and love. I'm not even sure if I should call it love, but that's the only word I can think of to describe it. I wasn't what we would think of as a spirit at all, though. It was something else."

"Hmm, very Gnostic," Jack replied, "and yet quantum sounding too. Okay; so, your 'guide' brought you to a place. What place?"

"Jack, that's not my point; and speaking of quantum, I read your new notes."

"My new notes?"

"Yes, sorry, but I wasn't going to have a repeat of the CPT fiasco."

Jack fidgeted with his tie and replied, "I had no intention of keeping anything from you. It just evolved from what happened. I never imagined it would lead me to the whole 'Universe' thing," Jack snickered a bit. "Besides, it has nothing to do with us, here and now."

Rachel grabbed his shoulders. "I am a doctor too, Jack. CPT may have led your thinking, but don't deny it. Something happened to you, too. The thing is, I remember the moment of death, the moment my eyes fixed and dilated. So, was it the last figment of my imagination during which I had this 'out of body' experience? All of your new proofs, everything that is in the CPT manuscript refers to our knowledge coagulating after 'an hour of death.' Was I not dead, experiencing some mind-blowing euphoria in that last millisecond? Or was I dead in some afterlife and, eventually, the CPT brought me back, perhaps against all that is holy? Jack, did we violate some divine law? Are we here together now when we really shouldn't be?" Rachel hugged her husband around his waist and held on tight.

"Jesus, Rachel, it's alright." Jack stroked her hair. "The fact is, we are here together now. That's all that matters, isn't it? Listen, I don't have the answers. I am in new territory here. We are working with Matt to transfer a lot of information to the campus from both his Time Trust files and my notes. We will analyze it all and make a finding. You know the routine better than anyone."

"Jack, I went through CPT, too. I want to be a part of this. Don't shut me out."

"I won't, but you have to be objective about this. Please, try not to get all wrapped up in the emotion and ethereal. Look out the window, people are beginning to assemble around the podium. We should go."

"Christ! Jack."

"It will be alright, babe."

Rachel dried her eyes. "Yes, well, what happened to me cannot be explained away as some ethereal vision, philosophy, or religion."

"Yes, dear."

Rachel picked up her shawl and walked by Jack to the front door. As he followed, he chuckled, "Besides, I would like to know what they are doing with it."

"With what?" Rachel asked.

"CPT. What have we been talking about for God's sake? We are going to have to finish this conversation sometime. I want to know more about that place you went to and that guide."

Rachel gave him a look. "Really, I expect the answer is in your new notes."

"Ha, well, you brought it up. By the way, do you know where we sit or stand or what we are supposed to do down there?"

Rachel shook her head. "Not really. Just what's on the tickets there. We are right up front. I'm sure they will tell us if things change."

CHAPTER 38: THE CEREMONY

IN ANOTHER LARGER SUITE, some distance from Jack and Rachel's, also overlooking the ceremonial park, Dr. Mathew Bellos, his wife, Carla and their daughter, Angie, prepared for the formal GGM ceremony. While Carla engaged in last minute primping in front of the hallway mirror, Angie stood in the main room facing her father, dusting the front of his jacket. Bellos smiled and looked at his daughter as only a father can. "We've come a long way in a very short time, you and I; haven't we, sweetie?"

Angie smiled. "Hmm, my Dad, GGM; it is hard to believe all this is happening."

"I know. By the way, I meant to ask you a while ago, Are you and Brian an item now?"

"No. Well, maybe. I don't know. We'll see."

Bellos kissed her on her forehead. "He is a lucky young man; just be careful."

"I will, dad; promise. There, you look perfect. Are you ever going to tell us what being the GGM means?"

"Technically, I have to find out at the ceremony. It has all been quite hush hush, even to me.

"Please, you two," Carla said walking into the room, "whatever it is, we are staying a family, together. That is all I care about."

"Oh, for goodness sake; it'll be great." Bellos said with a sarcastic grin. "I am the one who is nervous here, and I confess, ignorance is not bliss in this situation. Look at all that stuff down there; all those gadgets and people. And why do Gordon and I have to walk into the mouth of a living football the size of Manhattan?"

Carla replied, "Hmm, why indeed? All I know is; I will not lose either one of you again. Do you understand me, mister? When do we get to see this beast, anyway?"

At that moment, a silent, blinding white light exploded outside the window and startled the three. They stared as the light shrunk and defined itself.

"Jesus, dad, I think it's here."

Bellos grinned a little. "Yes, they like to make a grand entrance. How do you like the way it just hovers there?"

Carla fixed on the spinning head. "It looks like a flying saucer. Is it waiting for people to move? Nobody seems bothered at all."

"I guess I don't rate a whole beast. That's just the spinning head."

The people in the garden moved away without fear. The rotating head landed in the garden area below Bellos' suite, behind the stage and podium.

"How is that possible, dad? Its body just melded into the field."

"I know, kiddo; nobody has that answer."

"Honey," Carla asked, "where is your friend, Jake Burns? I thought he would be here."

"He is on assignment.," Bellos said. "I'm sure there are no security issues, or he would be down there right now. I don't understand one thing, though. I've been briefed less about this ceremony than anything else during all my training years. How does Gordon expect me to handle all this?"

Carla took Bellos' hand. "You'll be fine, my love. You will have plenty to handle after the ceremony. After all, you got us back together. Come on; we had better go. There's Grandpa Richard waving at us. They have us sitting right in front of that beast."

Within half an hour, the seating in front of the Carrier grew to approximately 700 spectators. Only the GGM's closest friends, the High Resolve Medical Research Staff of the eight worldwide Posts and their families were invited. The ceremony would then be available, via Knofer, to the general population.

Once everyone was in place and seated, Gordon Swanson stepped up to the podium and looked out over the crowd. The Carrier Unit's mouth was his backdrop. As he spoke, his image appeared in 3-D on all monitors floating around the field.

"Good health to us all and welcome everyone!" The crowd applauded, and Swanson continued, "Today is a joyous occasion; one that hasn't taken place for over 200 years. While it is somewhat sad for me, I am happy and proud to introduce to you our next Great Grand Master, Dr. Mathew Jeremy Bellos . . . Mathew?"

Everyone cheered. Bellos stepped up beside Swanson, waved to the crowd, and whispered to him, "So now what, Gordon?"

Swanson shook his hand, grinned, and turned to the assembly again. "We are also honored and thankful to have with us today, conducting the ceremony, our ambassador from Post 8, Carrier Unit 62712."

The crowd roared, and Bellos again leaned over to Swanson and whispered, "What do you mean conducting?"

Swanson looked at him with a half-smile, "This is the last time I can say this, doctor. Be quiet!"

"Ladies and gentlemen and friends all over Ever-Life, I thank you for giving me the best tenure any GGM could dream of, let alone ask for. I have been proud to serve."

The people shouted accolades and compliments. Swanson turned to Bellos and gestured behind him. "It's time, Mathew; come."

Swanson escorted Bellos onto the extended tongue of the beast. It resembled transparent plastic stairs, but it was as sturdy as concrete. They stepped up and stood looking at the crowd. Slowly, the tongue began retracting into the beast's enormous mouth.

"It's not that I am afraid, you understand," Bellos said. "It's just that we have never entered a Carrier this way before."

"Mathew, we will be okay. We are doing exactly what was done with me and every GGM since this started over 10,000 years ago."

"So, is that supposed to make me feel better?"

Swanson grinned as they descended into the Carrier. The mouth closed behind them, and darkness overcame everything.

"Well, this is quite a contrast to the bright white we see when we usually enter one of these; isn't it?" remarked Bellos.

Even as the two men's eyes adjusted, they could see only black with a blue glow around themselves.

After a few more moments of absolute quiet and darkness, Bellos said, "Okay, Gordon, this is all very fascinating. Remember, years ago, when you told me that I would be asking 'what' a lot? I thought you were crazy. Now, I have so many more questions."

"Ah, good; a sign of wisdom."

Then, the voice of the Carrier filled their minds, "Good health to you, GGM. I bring greetings and good wishes from the Council."

"Thank you, my friend. I introduce to you, my choice, Dr. Mathew J. Bellos, to be our next Great Grand Master."

"Welcome, Doctor. I ask you, Mathew J. Bellos, do you freely accept the responsibility and commit to the tasks before you?"

Bellos raised one eyebrow, looked around at the blackness and replied, "I do; but, frankly, I do not comprehend the tasks before me. I hope I have what it takes."

Swanson reached out, squeezed Bellos' shoulder, and assured the beast, "Not to worry, great one; he is ready, my friend."

The beast announced, "Then, let it begin."

There was complete silence. All around them became even darker, and any glow had dissappeared. Bellos squinted and tried to focus on the void before him. "There, Gordon, look over there. It's small, but I see a tiny light flickering, I think. Is that a star?"

One by one, more twinkling lights darted out from the first. Bellos said softly, "Gordon, it looks like a plasma lamp."

"Yes, it does. Actually, it is all lightning. The life-generating force of the Universe. Enjoy."

"I'm not a physicist. We have all been taught gravity, gasses, and particles make up the Universe."

"Yes, that, too, but the spark of life, that is electromagnetic energy; its electricity in one form or another. That is what Ever-Life is all about; extending the spark of life. Welcome to your first day of school, Mathew."

All of it appeared like a movie fast forwarding, and it all grew, as Bellos watched in awe. Nebulae, Star Clusters, Pulsars and Galaxies, Dark Matter, Dark Energy competing, all manner of undefined cosmic wonders populated 360 degrees around them, all appearing in 3-D.

"I'll give you a hint, my boy. Here, time as you understand it does not exist. We men invented the abstract concept, anyway."

It took Bellos a while before realizing they were no longer on the beast's tongue. They were floating. He was mesmerized, captivated and, at the same time, he concentrated on trying to remember it all. Out of the corner of his eye, he noticed that Swanson was floating away, getting smaller in the distance and gesturing adieu with a smile.

Bellos could feel a change coming over him. He began to comprehend differently. In his mind's eye, he saw numbers and different kinds of text characters; each one a story. Bellos' comprehension soared in its scope. He understood the construct of atoms, inside and out, their particles, and what they do; what surface Earth called quantum theory. His mind understood the beginning, what most called the Big Bang. He began seeing everything around him in a kind of digital format, and he thought, *these are the carved characters in my office.*

It was the language of the Carriers. Not just the hieroglyphics but also how to interpret every utterance of the great beasts. Their words and thoughts sucked into Bellos' head like iron filings drawn to a magnet. His mind understood new wondrous information regarding all manner of subjects. He was a limitless hard drive, uploading the secrets of the Universe. By then, Swanson was just a speck, far away. Bellos squinted, staring at Swanson and whispered to himself, "Gordon, this isn't just a headset or planetarium moment, is it? The energy and knowledge, they are coming from everywhere?"

Then, the Carrier spoke again, "Yes, it all comes from everywhere, my GGM. I am your guide and a provider from this time forward. You are seeing thought in its purest form. Before anything, there was thought. I am committed to you and the well-being of all life you represent. By becoming a Great Grand Master, you give up the choices of men and retain all manner of logic, knowledge, and understanding. You are their guide now, and I am yours. Do you accept this responsibility and commitment?"

Bellos listened and stared at the vast timeless beauty before him, "I do."

"My friend; understand me. You may not and must not ever try to explain your experience here today. At no time will anyone understand or accept what you say, and more importantly, there is a penalty associated with this code violation. However, you will have a long life and a destiny of greatness ahead, as well as the wherewithal befitting a Great Grand Master. If there is any circumstance of illness regarding your person, I will see to it that you stay well until that time your species finds a cure."

"I understand."

Bellos remained floating in a trancelike state of learning for an indefinite period. Then, something disturbed his concentration. He noticed, in the upper right quadrant, a small white vortex appeared and grew. Slowly, it began to consume everything and suck Bellos toward it. As he accelerated and got closer, the bright light overwhelmed him. He covered his face and flinched, turning away and closing his eyes tightly just as he shot into it. A rush of wind swirled around him, and then everything stopped. There was complete silence. After a time, he sensed he was standing, firmly balanced. Involuntarily, he wiped his blinking eyes and focused on a brightly colored transparent figure before him. It was a male looking humanoid. He was well-proportioned and over 12 feet tall. The figure bowed, seemed to smile and offered its outstretched arms in welcome. Then, he began speaking in the strange-sounding language of the Carriers. Bellos knelt, listened and understood every word.

"By your receiving and acknowledging all we have given to you, and by the authority of our Grand Council and treaty codes, I proclaim you Great Grand Master-GGM-010 over all the Ever-Life colonies. May you reign with honor, peace, and wisdom. Never forget; life is a gift. Treasure it. Be the scholar, teacher, and kindly mind of conscience. Know, on behalf of those who do not. Guide them with the strength and power of Ever-Life."

Bellos' eyes fixed in disbelief and, involuntarily, he began to weep and blink. As he did so, the new GGM felt an ever-so-slight tugging sensation. It was just one or two seconds. He opened his eyes; and he was astonished to find himself kneeling beside the podium from where he started. The Carrier was gone. He looked out at the crowd and stood up with tears in his eyes. Swanson put his hand on Bellos' shoulder, turned him toward the people and spoke, "I give you our Great Grand Master, Mathew J. Bellos."

After a few seconds to reorient himself, Bellos shook Swanson's hand and whispered, "Quite a moment, Gordon."

"I know. Congratulations. It's a new beginning, a new understanding and a new life for you. Now, say something to your people."

Swanson stepped off the podium and sat next to Carla. Bellos raised his arms to quiet the crowd.

"I am honored today by this appointment and by your trust. I will serve and continue the traditions of those I follow to bring harmony, peace and better health to us all. Thank you for your display of respect and confidence. Long life and good health to us all. Ever-Life, everywhere!"

The crowd stood up, applauding and shouting, as Bellos' father, Dr. Richard, Carla, Angie, Jack, and Rachel joined him on stage. Swanson moved to the podium, raised his arms to quiet the people and then shouted, "Let the celebration continue!"

Over the next few hours, the field filled with dance, food and a great party atmosphere. The floating monitors displayed various entertainments, while small Carriers delivered unlimited amounts of food and drink, none of which came from the surface. Eventually, the crowd tired and dispersed. Specialized Bubble Carriers picked up garbage or waste products for disposition. Some disintegrated the unusable waste. Others recycled waste to underground power structures, or for distribution as organic compounds throughout the Post.

As Swanson, the Bellos' and Sheldon's walked across the field back to their suites, the new GGM shook his head and remarked, "Well, Gordon, you have replaced this job by doing two more, but I'll always think of you as my GGM."

Swanson chuckled a bit. "My boy, I am already forgetting, and it feels quite good. For me, two jobs are better than one now."

Suddenly, behind them, they heard an explosion from the depths under the field. A blinding bright light exploded all around the vast chasm. Bellos reacted just as a GGM should. While everyone else held their ears and crouched, he pressed his Knofer, clicking it into defense mode. A protective aura with an impenetrable shield surrounded each of the group, as he ran to the edge of the ledge. Swanson, Jack, and Richard followed. Bellos stared into the abyss and then turned to Swanson and Richard.

"This can't be good. Dad, get the women inside."

Dr. Richard, Rachel, Carla, and Angie ran to a sidewall entrance. Bellos, Jack, and Swanson stood watching. From the darkness below, an enormous Carrier emerged. The noise was deafening to anyone within hearing distance.

"I didn't invite this one," Swanson murmured.

A magnificent creature soared up the tunnel and stopped right next to the three men.

"Christ, Gordon, it looks almost albino, a raging albino. Have you ever seen anything like this?"

"Not during my tenure."

The Carrier began to speak. "I am he who has come from the past and future to make right the foul stench of those you call brother and friend. You have no right to what has been given you, or the life-changing abilities you spread like the virus you are."

The Carrier seemed to stare at Jack in particular. Then, it began to spin again, and in an instant, its head became its tails, flailing tentacles all around them. With a loud rush of air, the tentacles quickly entwined like a rope and pointed straight up. Then, the creature zoomed back down into the dark. The three men stood feeling the wind and watching a bluish white light shrink into blackness.

"I don't think he likes me," said Jack.

"Great! On my first day," Bellos whispered.

"Well, here we go," said Swanson.

Bellos sighed, straightened up, and pushed his Knofer off defense mode. "Let's get to work."

Four Master Guards rushed toward the group, and Jack turned toward them. "Too little, too late, wouldn't you say, fellas?"

The new GGM gestured them to stop. "It's alright, men. We are fine. You there, young fella, you're Sergeant Parker, right?"

"Yes, sir," he said with a salute."

"Arrange for the Sheldon's to get back up to Andrews."

As the guard escorted the Sheldon's to a Carrier bubble, Jack whispered to the new GGM, "Hey Matt," how'd you know the kid's name?"

"I don't know. Must be the stuff the beast gave me. Shush."

There was another click on Bellos' Knofer. It was Carrier Unit 62712's thoughts linking to the GGM. It input the latest information regarding issues and locations of all known Carriers. Bellos didn't even blink. "Gordon, you brief Jake. No time to waste. We must finish transferring those Time Trust records to Brock/Swanson Building 26. I want a virtual meeting with Post Controllers in an hour. Keep in touch."

"Yes, sir." Swanson leaned in toward Bellos and whispered, "Interesting, isn't it, how it all comes to you?"

Bellos smiled, turned and walked with the 3-guards back into the Ever-Life Complex. Swanson climbed into a small Carrier-Bubble and disappeared down into the chasm.

CHAPTER 39: AN UNINVITED GUEST

SOMETIME AFTER THE CEREMONY, Jack and Rachel Sheldon boarded a small Carrier-Bubble, which would take them back to Andrews Hospital. Jack sat on the cushioned bench seat and looked out through the transparent wall as the Bubble began to move.

"Why is it every time I ride in one of these things, and thank heaven it's rare, I always get the feeling I'm going to fall out?"

Rachel held onto his arm. "Well, one thing is for sure; we will never see anything like that ceremony again. Matt was changed, literally changed."

Jack replied, "I'm sure not in our lifetime, but we have witnessed stranger things; a lot to reflect on."

Rachel snuggled into him, and they seemed content to stare and think. Jack put his arm around her and squeezed her close, assuring her in a private moment of love. The Carrier moved, accelerating toward the north sidewall of the chasm.

"Sorry, I get tense when these things melt into the bedrock." Rachel closed her eyes as the bubble penetrated the rock face. "Is it cutting now?"

Jack watched. "Yes, amazing, isn't it? It's completely silent. You can see the rock dissolve all around us. Look at the burning orange color."

"Jack, look; something is different; this thing seems to be cooling. It's just black in the front, no orange burn."

"Hmm, I think you're right. Did you feel that? We are slowing down?"

As the couple stared out at the cold blackness, neither of them noticed a humanoid figure suddenly appeared behind them at the other end of the Carrier-bubble. It stood close to 6-ft tall, totally transparent and had both gray and gold markings. The stranger spoke calmly, *"Excuse me. Yes, we are stopping. I don't mean to alarm you."*

Jack turned and reacted. "Oh Jesus! What the hell are you?" He protected Rachel, backing her into one of the bench seats.

"Please," the figure said, *"I don't mean to frighten you. We rarely appear, much less at all to surface man."*

Jack said anxiously, "Well, you scared the shit out of me."

"Sorry, forgive me. I am here on behalf of our Council, the Grand Carrier Council. I am a Tyree Master. You need not be afraid." He extended his hand; and, after gaining his composer, Jack shook it apprehensively.

"Council? You don't look like a Carrier, and you feel solid."

Rachel pinched him. "Jack, let's give him a chance."

"Thank you, Mrs. Sheldon. First, I appear before you like this so I can fit in here. I am a projection of sorts. We thought you would relate better and feel more comfortable with a familiar image."

Jack was still holding his hand. "You feel solid. How is that possible?"

The Tyree smiled and replied, *"Well, I am solid. And I understand you two have some familiarity with the impossible, given your experience with CPT."*

Jack sat down on the bench with Rachel again, and the stranger continued, *"I am normally much taller and a little more glowing; you might say. We have the technology to do different things; subjects for another time."*

"So, you are here because of the event at the ceremony?"

"Yes and no. First things first. Before we can approach anyone from the surface, we must have permission from your GGM. I am here with the approval of all parties."

"Hell if I know what that means," blurted Jack.

Rachel pinched Jack again. "Jack, slow down. Please go on, sir."

"Thank you." The Tyree Master sat down facing the couple. *"To begin with, your transport has stopped to enable complete privacy. Rock insulates us for miles all around. I have come to discuss a very private matter. Mrs. Sheldon, while you are in the colonies, we monitor all communications of any surface being. I do apologize, but it is our policy. Frankly, as a rule, we prohibit surface man down here. We do not trust his presence."*

"Why, for heaven's sake?" asked Rachel.

Tyree looked her in the eye, *"Because, over the years, you have evolved differently. You react with great fear most of the time. You have killed many of your own over the eons, intentionally; not to mention the people from here you've butchered. You two and your family have been allowed here at the request of the new GGM. That is a great honor and makes you trustworthy."*

"Okay, so what is this about?" asked Jack. "What do you want?"

"Your question, your conversation before the ceremony?"

"That was private!" replied Rachel.

"Yes," Tyree said. *"And it would have been, had the occurrence not taken place."*

"Occurrence? You mean at the end of the ceremony?"

"Jack, wait." Rachel sat up and stared at the stranger. "What occurrence?"

"I see I tweaked your interest."

"You are not talking about here, down here, are you?" Rachel waited urgently.

"What are you saying, Rach?" asked Jack. "What is this?"

Tyree smiled and said, *"Doctors, we have been monitoring your work, for a very long time; since before you were at Andrews. You each have quite a brilliant mind, and we respect your evaluations and discoveries, particularly CPT. And, now your latest involvement with particle... particle something; or is it organic microbiology?"*

Jack looked pensive. "I never used those terms. How do you know about that, and why does it interest you?"

Rachel took a deep breath, "Stop it, Jack. And she clarified, "Do you mean Jack's notes on particle displacement?"

"Mrs. Sheldon, you have read the treatise?"

Rachel looked at Jack. "Yes, I read some of it."

Jack interrupted, "Now tell us what is going on."

"You are aware of the Sidron findings?"

Jack paused and thought a moment, while Rachel reacted. "Sidron? Jack, what is he talking about?"

"Sidron? Sidron? My my, yes; of course, I remember. Honey, when science discovered what they thought was the God particle, religious leaders and medical science joined physicists in the investigation to finally prove the so-called Big Bang."

Rachel got a perplexed look on her face. "Yes, for years we had it crammed into us. The Big Bang created the Universe."

"Right, but everyone only talked about the big tangible stuff, galaxies, stars, planets, space, matter, gravity. No one ever looked at how the abstract came to be. The concept of time, for instance, and what about ideas, emotions, every abstract force we all take for granted were not of major interest. And everyone was so overwhelmed with the speed of light then. Remember Einstein's old formula, $E = mc$? The speed of light this; the speed of light that; only well into the second millennia did physicists realize that light exists within something. Get it? Light exists within the body of space-time. Therefore, space-time expands faster than the speed of light."

Rachel raised an eyebrow. "Okay, darlin, so what's your point?"

"Well, that is also when another epiphany surfaced: that ideas, thoughts, emotions and even power; anything abstract was an individual entity; part of creation too."

"Jack, I am a doctor too. Don't lose me here."

"I am trying not to lose anyone or anything. So, just try and follow me on this. To restate the issue; the hypothesis was that ideas, thoughts, emotions and power were created at the same time with everything we consider tangible; but each of these abstracts was independent of the sciences regarding matter, energy, and atomic particles. Space-time was what carried everything tangible and abstract and Space-time was what was contained within the Sidron. Can you understand that?"

Rachel thought and said, "Yes. Continue."

"Okay, everything within which space-time exploded was the Sidron. So, today, if there are more than one universe, a Multi-verse for example, they were also contained in the same Sidron. The Sidron is the constant, the container for any inflation; any Big-Bang that may have initiated apart from the one we know. I studied the whole concept for years as part of an overall proposal to Brock/Swanson and Matt. But I did not pull the Sidron files."

The Tyree Master interrupted politely, *"Excuse me, Mrs. Sheldon, your husband describes the Sidron quite well. We would explain it this way. The Sidron is a sort of magnetic power. Technically, it is true; our kind know it as the subatomic highway. And, sometime after it was discovered on surface Earth, scientists became afraid of investigating it. And we believe it was a wise choice to postpone dissecting it into particular equations to rationalize its existence. The Sidron is what connects every subatomic particle to every other, its where the orbits of the atomic particles reside; those electrons, photons, neutrinos, quarks, many you haven't defined. It is a network tying everything together. It is the chalkboard, and Universes reside within it."*

Rachel shook her head, rolling her eyes, "I like the last analogy. The rest seems too complicated. So, why do I want to understand all this anyway?"

Jack replied, "The Sidron enables conductivity, sort of. I mean it has its own strange charge. It is self-powering, unlike anything ever discovered before. First, it was labeled as a combination of dark energy and dark matter. But then, researchers and physicists realized the Sidron was not within a boundary of a universe, it was the infinite boundary holding all universes and more. Quite an epiphany for the attitudes. We labeled it a magnetic charge, but we really had no idea what it was. It allows the transfer movement of anything from one particle to any other particle or from a particle to another in any other universe."

"Yes," Tyree said. *"quite so, Dr. Sheldon."*

"Okay guys, I get it. So, again, tell me why I care? Say so in plain English, please?"

Jack was on a roll. "Honey, listen. First, they thought of using it like a fax or copy machine, only copying over very long distances. It would revolutionize communications, maybe even transportation. Signal frequencies, particle frequencies of any kind, can travel in the Sidron to anywhere, instantaneously. But neither scientists, physicists, mathematicians, nor religious leaders had any idea what experiments to conduct to test the theory. The math worked, but real experiments; well, that was something else. The scientific community was stumped. They decided to do nothing until they could put controls in place, which have not been discovered yet."

"For the most part, you are correct, doctor. However, it is not just transmitting anywhere that is our concern. It is that Sidron can be used to send anything to anywhere within any time. You see, doctors, CPT was only the door. Through the door lies a whole new misunderstood world; and, that world explains the answer to your question, Mrs. Sheldon."

Rachel perked up. "What? You mean I was right about after-life?"

Tyree tried to be succinct. *"First, I am here because we need your help. We have known about Sidron, as you call it, for a very long time. If the wrong people get a hold of certain knowledge and try to use it, well, it would be disastrous."*

"But why approach Rachel and me? My notes are safe. I am giving all the files to the Complex. Matt knows this."

"There has been a breach, an event, within the Sidron's time scope. We believe someone or something used the Sidron for personal gain or profit, and the breach has resulted in instability."

"What? What can we do?"

"We want you to investigate. You have contacts at all the particle reactors in Switzerland, Africa and China. We believe the first breach event came from one of those locations, or from one of your locations connected with the Complex in the USA. No matter who uses Sidron, even for simple tasks, the threat is too great for us to ignore."

"What are you asking?"

"If someone on the surface has used the Sidron, he could not understand even a small part of its scope."

Jack shook his head no. "Come on; even scientists up there haven't studied it. Most of the proofs are only on paper. No real experiments were ever conducted."

"We both know the language of mathematics doesn't lie, and you have key contacts. Talk to them, find out all you can. Report back to me using

this. It's synchronized to me alone." The Tyree Master handed Rachel a small, peanut-shaped, pliable object.

"What do I do with this?"

"Squeeze it like this, and then like this."

She did and watched as a light appeared inside the stranger's head.

"I will hear you and come. Squeeze it end to end, and it will disintegrate. We can't have that in the wrong hands up there."

"Well, then, don't lose it, honey," chuckled Jack.

The Tyree Master pointed to the surface and spoke in a worried tone, *"I have appeared to you to request your help. There are others down here who are involved too. You are not alone. Please, we are putting our trust in you both. Contact me with any, I say any information you may discover."*

Jack scratched his head. "Yes, well, I did share some information with one or two colleagues abroad, to try and bridge primary hypotheses."

"Your CPT effort related to memory and personality. Whoever breached the Sidron has no idea what he is dealing with."

The stranger paced the Bubble, speaking in a desperate tone, *"I will tell you this. The laws of the subatomic world are very different, and with good reason. It is true that ideas, emotions, and power are all, in fact, fixed entities. All abstract concepts are just as real as solid substances. They exist everywhere and ride the Sidron continuously within what you call the past, present, and future. But it is all the same time. Everything is held within space-time, which does expand much faster than light, in order to contain it, as well as everything else. So, space-time holds the past, present, and future altogether, you see; the Sidron holds space-time. And no matter how fast any space-time universe expands, the Sidron is too large to define any boundaries"*

Rachel wasn't buying it. "How is that possible? Besides, we are not physicists, certainly not philosophers."

"Well, not to be condescending; but, even your simple communications—your video, audio, all wireless frequencies exist everywhere at the same time. We live within it all, and, we are given access to them all, via the Sidron, by function of our ability—our capacity, and our motivation to withdraw whatever we can from it. Understand me, doctors, we are talking about omniscient and omnipotent forces here."

Jack continued quizzing, "So, my hypotheses were correct. Within the subatomic world, there exist the solutions to cure all ills."

The Tyree Master smiled and said, *"You are way ahead of yourself. Here is a comparison for you. As you are to the totality of existence, a universe, so are all ideas to an atom. They are living entities, everywhere at the same time, part of the big picture. Some of us refer to it all as the bloodstream of the Cosmos. Others see it as the synaptic connection linking everything. Some of your kind may call it God."*

Jack's medical mind kicked into second gear. "Alright, I did not experiment; but I did not rationalize it either. My efforts were linked to CPT, true. So, I merged medical science with physics. My logic and the math led me. If CPT works, then it followed that humans, animals, insects, anything that has the brainpower, can acquire ideas or feelings. It's their capacity to think that governs how much they learn."

"Yes, and not just sentient beings withdraw from the Sidron. Everything in a universe uses abstracts, ideas, emotions, and power," said Tyree.

Rachel listened, rose slowly and whispered to herself, "So, we are not simply the result of an organic brain process." She turned and looked Tyree straight in the face. "You are saying God is truly within us; and, if we hone our abilities and connect in the right way, we can connect with him, or whatever your idea is of him. We can do anything. You're saying there is a Heaven. Are you saying I was in this Sidron and on the road to . . .? To God?"

"Mrs. Sheldon, please. There will always be some who have more capacity than others to withdraw ideas, emotions, and power from the Sidron; but who is to say who or what that is or should be? Indeed, not my kind."

"Rachel, seriously; sit down, will you?" Jack continued, "But proving what is in the Sidron, proving which cars are on the road, well that's something else."

"Exactly, doctor. As I said, ideas, feelings, and power are all alive. In fact, that is why the Sidron is so unstable. They are all pushing and pulling in every direction, within, between and from one universe to another, constantly competing to be absorbed by life. All existence uses them. Space-time is a garden, an abundance of everything."

Jack looked as if he had just thought of something. "In that case, there are no new ideas, correct. They were all created at the big-Bang?

"Not necessarily, but many, that is certain. Your kind loves to leap to conclusions. Deductions are not proofing." The stranger walked to the middle of the Bubble and looked out at the blackness. *"It is both the answer to the greatest mystery of all, and it is the biggest threat to everything you know. You must help us find the breach."*

Jack and Rachel embraced, and then she spoke again, "So when I asked if we did something unholy, using CPT I mean, I saw something . . ."

"Mrs. Sheldon, the organized singular self-awareness, which you call a soul, may very well exist within Sidron. No one can say. But, it's not that simple. These things are most difficult for us to explain because one has no reference from which to bridge the answers. There is no experiment you can perform to prove this. If there were, you would prove faith. My kind has been here for many eons. It is not since the ancient ancients of your Sumerian culture that your kind has stumbled onto anything of this nature. Both of you experienced a taste of it because of CPT, but that doesn't even scratch the surface."

Rachel kept prodding, "Maybe my education is far too feeble, but there is no way you can just know all this."

The Tyree Master bowed before them. *"Yes, there is; and we do. As I said, I was given permission to tell you this. Dr. Sheldon, if someone succeeds in applying your Particle Displacement Treatise and uses the Sidron highway, he or she could travel to and from any time. Who knows how it would disrupt the balance of life? Without the proper controls, we very well would, not could, experience a cataclysm of Galactic proportions."*

Jack rolled his eyes. "Jesus, Rachel, maybe you're right about CPT"

"But, Jack, we are alive because of your discovery."

"She is right, doctor. Now, we need your brain power. Your creativity might just help fix this."

"Fix what?"

"We believe the event at the ceremony is tied somehow to several time distortions we are sensing. They all connect to the Sidron. We need you to examine everything you have. Be our eyes on the surface. Give us clues; help us find who or what has opened Pandora's Box."

"Christ," Rachel said frustrated. "Why not use your wherewithal? Your species is far superior to us. Can't you just travel into the future and see what actually happens."

"I am sorry to say it doesn't work like that, Mrs. Sheldon. It has to do with free will. Explanations become muddied. I am not here to confuse you any more than you might be already."

Rachel sighed and said sarcastically, "Well, it's not as if you expect us to save the world or anything."

"True, we are only speculating that failure would change the course of existence, perhaps worse. Will you help?"

Rachel looked at Jack, as he said, "Yes, yes; but I don't know where to begin."

"You and your wife have been through something that gives you a sense of how important this could be for every life in the Cosmos. If a lunatic finds out he can be anywhere, or worse, everywhere at the same time; it would damage the balance structure of the Universe. Thoughts could be permanently damaged or completely eliminated; not to mention what would happen to power. Space-time, as you understand the concept, would be altered; and existence itself may cease, perhaps even eliminating this Universe. Do you understand?"

The stranger seemed exhausted and a little aggravated.

Rachel grabbed Jack's shoulders and looked him in the eye, "Whatever it takes, Jack, right?"

"Right . . . okay . . . Christ!"

"Good," said Tyree. *"When you two get back, search any files. Get a hold of your contacts. We have the cooperation of the GGM database here . . . Agreed?"*

"Yes, sure, fine," Jack agreed.

The Tyree Master smiled and walked to the far end of the Bubble. *"Think positive, you two; we are all still here. That's a good sign."*

The couple felt a slight acceleration, as they watched the stranger absorb into the transparent membrane of the wall.

"Hmm, you know, Rach, my mother always told me not to listen to strangers."

"Well, perhaps this is one time we should."

Rachel squeezed Jack's hand, and they sat arm in arm looking at the outer rock begin to glow a hot orange color again.

CHAPTER 40: ALLENFAR

A GOLD CLOUD SURROUNDED THE OBJECT. Jake Burns tried as hard as he could to see it clearly. *Just a little closer,* he thought. He reached out as far as he could to get it, but no matter how hard he tried, it was just out of reach. His face began to turn beet red. *One more inch. Shit! I can get it. That fragrance, it's roses, and the sparkle, it's gold. IT'S GOLD!"*

Then, his eyes popped open. "No! Where did it go?"

Suddenly, a violent jerk threw Jake off the reclining lounge and onto the floor of the Carrier. He woke up startled, grabbing the back of his head. *Damn dream! Why do I always wake up at the same part? Christ!"*

The Carrier was 75-feet long from its spinning head to the end of the whirling tentacles.

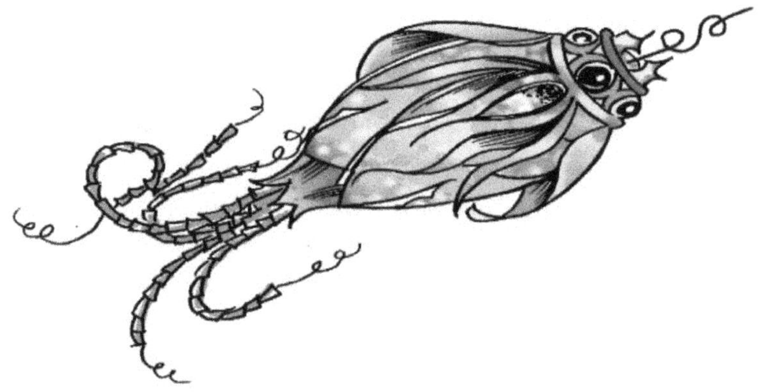

It radiated beautiful pulsing green and gold lights as it spun, drilling quickly and gracefully through solid rock and magma. Four sensors that looked like eyes and a mouth rotated clockwise, while the rest of its body turned in the opposite direction. Each rotation of its exposed razor-sharp teeth cut and moved whatever was in front to the side; and then the spinning fins displaced everything, pushing it all back to its whirling tentacles, which dissolved or displaced it all onto the tunnel walls. The beast's speed increased with every foot it dug down through the 30-mile outer crust of the earth into the next lower layer, the outer mantle. Eventually, the hot rock became moving lava; a speeding, burning ocean, hundreds of miles underground.

Carrier 2500 was 1600-years old by surface time; relatively young for its species. It left Ever-Life's Transport Station-25, from Post-3, below the Alaskan Bering Straits at precisely 6:15 a.m., Universal Time Zone-9. Jake

Burns had been on special assignment; his last given by GGM Gordon Swanson, to monitor negotiations on repairs and age spots in one of the Bering Strait's tunnels. The tunnels were constructed long ago by a coalition of European, Asian and American contractors. The tunnels became a worldwide focus decades ago, linking all economic markets and intercontinental trade via rail and truck; all which reduced dependencies and fuel costs of ocean barges and air flights. One of Jake's first duties was to put a Knofer call to Bellos and review that status.

"Hello, Mr. GGM; how are you?"

"Fine Jake, how is it going there?"

"The surface-coalition has prioritized repairs. So, negotiations do continue and probably will, until they all agree on exactly what the fix will be. I recommend we consider introducing the Carriers; a major reason I needed to talk to you"

"Don't you think that's a little radical?" Replied Bellos.

Jake argued, "The truth is, eventually we are going to introduce them to the surface anyway. Why not now? They could cut new tunnels within a day."

Bellos thought for a moment. "I'll think about it. The question is; are the surface cultures ready to accept alien life; not to mention Ever-Life's existence. And keep in mind, Jake, our politics are very different from anything up there. Besides, recent events dictate our priorities are different right now."

"You know I disagree with you on this," said Jake. "There were two major tremors during the meetings, and everyone thought they were earthquakes. No one knows about Sidron. Some are arguing we should repair the bridges and forget the tunnels. I think that would be a mistake, given the unpredictable weather and seas."

"Understood. Don't forget that you need to brief Gordon on your meetings with the coalition; and, while you are with him, get up to speed on the Sidron breach."

"Yes, fine. By the way, congratulations, Mr. GGM. Sorry I wasn't there for the ceremony."

"I appreciate that," said Bellos.

"I can tell you this," Jake continued. "If the damage to these tunnels gets any worse, it'll cause a global economic disaster. All countries will suffer. Goods will stop from Asia to and from the Americas. The world economy will go back to the pre-year 2200 recessions."

"Well, then, we will think long and hard about ensuring that connection. Contact me when you can. Good luck."

Jake had been living more than a double life over the past eight months. Not only did he still hold the title and responsibilities of Chief Detective Inspector, Arden police; but also, more importantly, he was now officially the Global Chief of Security for all Ever-Life colonies and Special Liaison for the GGM. Time and life marched on after the CPT incident. Two months into his Ever-Life orientation, Jake discovered that he had Carrier motion sickness. Now, only minutes after talking to Bellos, he began sweating again. No pill helped; sleep was the only relief from symptoms. He knew the Carriers were capable of phenomenal speeds. No one really knew how fast they could go. Truth be told, at depths 200 miles below Earth's surface, they moved eye of sight like guided missiles. But Grand Carriers moved much faster.

Today, Jake's Carrier 2500 sped west, on a direct line through the earth, to a Post 2's transport station below Giza, Egypt. The location was also home to the Ever-Life archival resources of Time Trust. There, Jake would meet with Gordon Swanson, now Global Defense Chairman. Swanson's rare genetic illness was no longer in remission; one of the reasons Bellos became GGM sooner than expected. Swanson's capacities had diminished enough that he needed to undergo the new CPT process to rid himself of it. During the last eight months of research, Ever-Life scientists developed a new synthetic catalyst bath, relieving Angie of any burden to produce the formula. And the new process allowed an automatic more reliable CPT extraction/injection process. Moreover, Bellos himself had to undergo changes too, in that he would undergo both duplication and new-CPT (the two were now performed without the concern of the original DNA requirements). The overall new plan was to create eight additional GGMs, CPT-Duplicates. Each would have the title GGM-010, P-1 thru P-8, respectively, holding the top position of Post Controller for each colony throughout the globe. Each duplicate would replace the solid holograms now in place and all would report to Bellos directly, via headset-earplug daily, regarding their Post's needs. Bellos himself was directly responsible and autonomous overall Post Controllers. And he alone interfaced with the Prime Time-Travel Carriers and the Grand Carrier Council, all of which resided deep within the planet. Additionally, only Bellos navigated all Ever-Life's surface contact.

In total, there were over three billion people within the Ever-Life colonies. Over his long tenure, Gordon Swanson had both Duplication and

Transtosis performed five times, using a secret Carrier-Unit process. Unfortunately, symptoms of the "crippling gene," as Ever-Life defined it, continued to reappear. Swanson's primary function now was to monitor, direct, and coordinate significant challenges and threats to any Ever-Life colony. Jake Burns reported directly to him.

One of the first things Jake did, after his initiation, was to restructure every Post's security chain of command. Each Post had a Security Controller, SC, which was head of the local peace forces, reporting to the GGM Post Controller. Jake modeled the SCs job functions much like those of Jake's old New York Manhattan borough. Also, the Ever-Life weapons were another refinement Jake made. They were all now upgraded to non-fatal, firing bursts of air, which could render any person unconscious up to 200-yards away. Another upgrade was that since crime in the Ever-Life colonies had been consistently below .001%, Jake had replaced a prison system with a network of mandatory headset sessions to rehabilitate offenders. Real incarceration or punishment was the last resort, performed by specialized Carriers. It took place within their temporary sanctuary of solitude. Because of what happened to Brock those months ago, Jake was committed to changing the Carriers having all the authority over rehabilitation. He was in the process of submitting a new treaty, which would enable Ever-Life Security to monitor Carrier rehabs.

Swanson did not anticipate Jake's motion sickness when offering him the job months ago. To complicate matters further at the time, Jake found it almost impossible to juggle his role of Arden City Chief of Detectives. So, he promoted his co-worker, Forensics Specialist, Dr. James Randolph Watzin. Over the last eight months, Watzin had great success delegating responsibilities and executing the mayor's policies. Crime over the past six months was down eight points. Caseloads reduced dramatically, and the mayor considered layoffs to cut the budget. That didn't sit well with most of the duty officers; so, Watzin convinced the mayor to farm out some officers as part of the Brock/Swanson security team. Watzin negotiated that each officer would remain in the Arden Police Force with tenure accumulating, while he acted as security staff for the Complex. Consequently, Jake was able to finish Ever-Life's orientation and begin his duties without the extra pressure.

Today, as Jake lay against the Carrier wall miserable, a strange ringing began in his head, and he looked up only to see the displays on the wall monitors disappear. The ring he heard became a roar, but he was able to sit up although dizzy and shaking. He covered his ears with his palms, and as suddenly as it came, the noise stopped, and the Carrier's voice filled his mind.

"Oh, God, what now?" Jake said to himself.

"*Sir, Mr. Burns,*" the voice of the Carrier said, "*please be calm. I will not hurt you.*"

"Well, thanks, I think. Who are you? This is not my favorite thing to do."

"*We understand you took several time-trips within the same Grand Carrier several months ago?*"

"What? Who are you?"

"*You may call me Allenfar. I am the Tyree Master for this Carrier. There was no provision in your training for Carrier communication. It is prohibited with the general public for all practical purposes; part of our agreement with your species. Very few of you over the years have been allowed to communicate with us; and those of you who do are prohibited from sharing with anyone else according to a treaty.*"

"Yes, I know. I did read the documents. Apparently, we have to make new treaties. Oh, my belly; I am not feeling my best. What was that jolt?"

"*We have stopped. You should feel better in a few seconds. I must get to the point. We are aware of your initial training sessions, months ago, and the time-trips you made during your orientation. As you know, only Grand Carriers can control time travel. I represent our entire hive in complimenting and thanking you.*"

"What are you talking about?" asked Jake. "And why am I being monitored?"

"*When you rode with Carrier 1111, A **'Compatibility'** took place.*"

"A Compatibility? What is that? And why are you telling me this?"

"*A Compatibility is a spirit-symbiotic fusion, a potent intense mental and emotional sharing, which you provide to us. We tap into your inner being. Your kind have been providers for millennia.*"

"I don't understand, what is your point?" Jake tried to think the pain away.

Allenfar continued. "*I bring you an invitation, a request actually, to use that Carrier again. She is the only vehicle sensitive enough to withdraw so much from you. For us, the fusions are a primary reason we trust and cooperate with your species. In your case, nothing of such intensity, such magnitude, has occurred for a very long time; and, we request your assistance in this matter, given the recent occurrence, the Sidron breach, as you call it.*"

"So," Jake said, "it is not exactly an invitation. Are you saying that Carrier 1111 will be assigned to me as my personal Carrier because she likes me?"

Tyree offered, *"No, it means that she acquired abundant sustenance and vitality from you when she transported you on your time- trips during your indoctrination. As a hive mindset back then, we all shared her experience. Average interface with your species provides us with 10 to 60-cretes per human, on our lansig scale. Your specific interface alone rated at 1000 to the 12th lansig. That is for us called a Compatibility, and its intensity rating was higher than any in the last 210.25 Earth years."*

Jake rolled his eyes, "So I guess that's pretty high or good for you, right? Are you acquiring sustenance from me right now?"

"Every human gives us sustenance but rarely ever that of the potency you provided our sister. She is your Compatibility vehicle. Carrier 1111 will contact you to schedule additional travel. It is essential for our species to share in these rare cases. Rare cases like yours enable our species to progress and evolve much faster than we would otherwise. We must take advantage when one appears. It benefits both our species."

Jake shook his head trying to comprehend. "I have questions. Why tell me this? Why not just take what sustenence you or she wants? Besides, what do I call her?"

"She is Carrier 1111, but you may give her a name of your own, if you so choose."

"Well, since she likes me, I'll call her Miriam, after an old sweetheart of mine."

"Be well, Jake Burns."

Allenfar went silent, and Jake sat confused; but his pain and nausea had gone, and the video on the monitors reappeared.

Jake thought, *Okay, how could anyone have any pleasurable interaction with a giant glow fish? This should be interesting.*

He got up and made it into the lounge chair. Allenfar accelerated, as Jake began to watch the monitors again, trying not to think about the ride.

CHAPTER 41: BACK TO CAMPUS

JACK AND RACHEL SHELDON arrived back at Andrews Hospital anxious to resolve the mystery of what the stranger in the bubble told them. Rachel went straight home to examine all records in their lab. Marietta, their housemaid of four years, was home to greet her.

"Ah, *Señora*, welcome home."

"Yes, thank you, Marietta. Is everything okay?"

"*Sí*; yes; all is fine. Amos is tending the horses; the feed is full; and the mare; she gave a foal; a beautiful brown baby."

"That's wonderful; I have to see."

"They even came to fix the cable lines for *Señor* Jack. I did not know what to show them, but they said they found it."

Rachel did a double take. "Wait. Hold on. What are you talking about?"

"The cable lines in the lab downstairs," Marietta said. "The man came very late, but he was so nice. It was the only time they could come. They did not have to come inside. They just tell me about it. They left a note that said all was done and okay. Why?"

"Where is the note?"

"It was just a little piece of paper. I threw it out. It was only this big."

Rachel had a blank stare on her face. *The Lab?* She thought. "It's okay, Marietta. It's alright."

She checked the messages on their computer-pad; nothing from any contractor about cables. Then, she went downstairs to the lab. The door seemed fine. She unlocked it and went to the wall safe. She pushed the sensor control pad and twisted the safe's handle to open the door. There, inside, was the particle displacement treatise Jack wrote regarding the Sidron. She took it out and began thumbing through the pages. A few were wrinkled, disheveled here and there; and there were some small notes in the margins, which she didn't recognize; but overall, nothing obvious seemed tampered with. She sighed in relief; and, as she returned the manuscript into the safe, a piece of the black knob on the small door to the safe fell off. She picked it up and compared it with the remaining piece. There was a hole in the center, where it appeared to have been intentionally broken off.

"Christ!" said Rachel. "It is a drill mark."

Back at the Brock/Swanson Complex, as Chief of Research, Jack had been locked in meetings since his return, debriefing for hours regarding a wide variety of issues at the hospital and overall on the Campus. He was unsuccessful in breaking away to search any files or contact any colleagues about the Sidron. After one meeting, he took a moment to turn on his computer phone, and it rang immediately.

"Honey, it's me; sorry to interrupt."

"It's okay, Rachel. I need a break. God knows I need sleep. How is it going at home?"

"I don't feel my best, but it will pass. Listen, Jack, I checked the safe in the lab. The knob fell off, and there's a hole in the center of the lock."

"You think it was a break-in?"

"Marietta said we had someone come by in the evening to do some cable work outside. I checked with our cable network, and they confirmed no issues. Should I call the police?"

"Anything missing?'

"Not that I can see."

"No, don't call them. We have nothing but a drilled hole and broken knob as evidence; nothing is missing. I'll let Matt know, and we'll get his people to check it out. Burns has the important contacts in the Arden Police force; so, we better let them handle it through him and keep it hush hush for now."

"I have your Sidron book and your notes right here. There is something written here: it says, 'send to Charlie Rossi'. What is that about?"

"Christ! I forgot. Rach, you have to help me. I did send notes to Rossi to justify funding. He is at the conference this week. I sent just enough to tweak his interest.

"Interesting. I don't know how I can help, but here's another thing, I did notice that some of the final pages are out of sequence. Jack, I know what a stickler you are for detail, but that's all I can see that immediately sticks out to me."

"Rachel; Rossi and I were supposed to meet and discuss money at the conference. I can't go with what's piled up here."

"Speaking of forgetting things, Jack, have you heard from Brian? Wasn't he going to call?"

"Not that I know of. Listen, babe, I have to ask you; will you go? It's in Washington DC."

"What? You are kidding, right? We just got back. We were supposed to meet Brian before we commit to anything."

Jack hesitated. "I'm sure it's tomorrow or the next day. We were seeing him and Angie sometime after the Marshall thing."

"I thought it was today."

"No, he said he would call us tomorrow. And you know how uncommitted Brian is. Remember, he only said he was thinking about seeing us. That's his way out. That doesn't mean he will, or that anything is cast in concrete. He has an out for everything."

"Tomorrow? Jack I'm so turned around. Jet lag from traveling inner Earth is worse than going to the Far East."

"Honey, I am serious. I really need you to help me and go to the conference in my stead. Just one night, please? You'll be back before Brian even calls. I haven't gone through any files in building 26 yet. It has been nothing but meetings. Now, more than ever, we need Rossi to commit to funding. He has major construction contracts worldwide. Please, babe?"

"You don't mean that boring Research Finance Fundraiser, do you?"

Jack sighed in frustration. "Ah, it started yesterday. I am trapped here."

"Christ, Jack!"

"I know, but, if you hadn't called, I probably would have forgotten entirely, and that would have been worse. Charlie Rossi is a major player, and we need his backing for the reconstruction and new edition."

Rachel spoke with attitude. "You have been there a straight 16-hours, not including Matt's ceremony. You are not thinking right; you are going to get sick. You want me to fly to D.C. and wine and dine this Rossi?"

Jack fiddled with his hair. "It's important. We promised that Tyree stranger, whoever he was, and you did want to be involved."

"Thanks for throwing that in my face."

"Rach, I need you on this; not to mention, we need the money. Brock is gone. Funding is down. I will meet you there as soon as I can get out of here. Take one of the campus jets. I will make the arrangements. You don't have to pack much. I am supposed to meet him at 7-p.m. tonight, in the lobby of the Hilton in the city."

Jack felt a vibration and the phone quiver ever so slightly against his ear. What is that?

"You owe me big time for this, mister."

"I know; and will you leave a message on Brian's phone? I will call him when I get out of these meetings. I have to go, babe. Thank you so much. Call me when you get there! Love you, mmmwah!"

"Yeah; love you too." She hung up. "Fine; shit!"

In her bedroom at the Sheldon's ranch, Rachel began loading her large purse with women's paraphernalia and muttering to herself, "I called to make dinner arrangements, and I get this crap. Family, what happened to family? Charlie Rossi and the money; that's what's important? Go, go on Rachel. Drop everything right now! Pack up and fly on some superficial bullshit jaunt to see another self-centered billionaire piece of crap. Oh boy, do you owe me, Jack."

Rachel picked up her phone and noticed a text:

'Change of plan, catch flight from Fargo building air-strip, Love You! Jack'

She grabbed her purse, stomped down the stairs to the front door and opened it. There, in front of her stood a handsome limo driver, dressed in dark blue, tipping his hat. "Hello, ma'am; Dr. Sheldon requested a car for you."

When he saw how upset she was, the driver thought better of saying anything else.

"This does not make it right," Rachel said in an angry tone.

"Sorry, ma'am?"

"Well, let's go; come on. What is your name?"

He opened the car door and gestured her into the limo. "Mike, ma'am, I am Mike Warren."

"Well, Mike Warren, you have me at a disadvantage. I am angry, you see, the freak bitch from hell right now."

"Oh, ah, well it's alright, ma'am. I have seen worse; believe me. You are catching the jet from the campus airport, right?"

"No, I just got a text directing me to go to the Fargo building's airstrip."

"Yes, ma'am."

Within 15-minutes, Rachel had boarded a single engine Hush-Jet aircraft, which took off from Fargo Field at 4:15 p.m. Mountain time. She sat in the luxury cabin with four comfortable chairs facing an oval coffee table. There were two big windows on each side of the plane, no portholes, as in the jets of old. A male attendant approached her from the cockpit area, smiling. "Mrs. Sheldon, perhaps you would enjoy a mimosa or chocolate martini?"

She looked at him sarcastically, "Yes, both please."

"Also," he said, "here is an itinerary for the conference and some notes from Dr. Sheldon."

"Ah yes, the conference. Hmm, and notes. Even better! I hate this, you know."

"Yes, ma'am; I am Gabriel, by the way. If you need anything else, just buzz."

He smiled and walked forward to the cockpit just as a voice spoke over the loudspeaker, "Mrs. Sheldon, this is Captain Blake. We are scheduled to land at Dulles International, by 5:45 pm. Make yourself comfortable. If you need anything, let me know."

Rachel rolled her eyes and pivoted the chair so she could see out the window. "Thanks." She said to herself. "Anything I need, huh? I would like a quiet evening with my family." She gulped the mimosa and began reading Jack's notes.

From the cockpit door, the steward looked into the rear cabin, as the captain asked, "Gabe, is she out yet?"

"No, Captain, and I don't understand. I slipped her a double-dose in each one."

Captain Blake pushed the frequency button to 123.701 and spoke to his earset microphone, "Brazzie one, this is Hush-Jet 6 . . . Brazzie, come in; come in. Brazzie one; this is Hush-Jet-6. Do you copy?"

He flicked at his earpiece twice, repeated the call codes, and then he heard a reply. "InVoy here, InVoy here, read you Brazzie."

"Yes, sir, this is Blake. We have the package and await instructions."

"Switch to satellite reading 307.1983. Follow input directives."

"Understood. On our way."

The captain cut the call and turned the plane 30-degrees south southeast at an altitude below radar detection.

"Gabe, make yourself comfortable; destination, Rio de Janeiro."

"How long, Captain?"

"This baby is quicker and easier than anything I have piloted. Watch how she handles this bank."

"Captain, she has just passed out."

"Good. Here we go."

The plane banked to the right, while Gabe watched Rachel Sheldon unconscious in the chair.

CHAPTER 42:   JAKE'S BRIEFING

AT 4 PM, CAIRO EGYPT TIME, The Grand Carrier, Allenfar, docked at Ever-Life's Transport Station-210, directly below the Great Giza Pyramid. Jake Burns walked out and onto a people-moving tram, which took him to Carrier-bubble elevators. As he rode one down, he pondered the whole concept of Compatibility. *"It's not enough that this bunch of fish runs everything, they are construction engineers, utility and food providers, now their elevators and our transportation. God knows what else. I certainly don't want a date with one!"*

When the bubble-elevator door opened, Burns stepped out to see the transport station's Grand Arcade.

My God; he thought, *look at this! There is nothing to compare up on the surface.*

He gazed upon the lighted rock walls and splashing waterfalls flowing down into a bottomless chasm. Familiar tube-like walkways bridged diagonally across the diameter of the vertical tunnel.

"I still can't believe the beasts made all of this."

Jake took one last look at the view and then turned around and walked to Swanson's office. He loved meandering and examining the priceless healthcare exhibits, paintings, and sculptures that filled the foyer. Some of the items were recovered from the surface and had been preserved for centuries.

At the other end of the room was a round door. There was nothing like it anywhere else in the colonies. It was constructed back in 4000 B.C. during one of the Dynastic periods in ancient Egypt. No one knows how it was constructed, but it opened and closed like a human iris. Jake remembered his headset session about it.

Initially, this Station was one of the first medical research facilities in the region, and the door was a security entrance. Before its functional tenure within Ever-life, local surface medical chieftains or shamans diagnosed illnesses based on examining eyes. Ever-Life learned much from the ancient surface cultures and paid tribute to them by creating the door. Over the centuries it became one of the Ever-Life World Wonders. Eventually, Swanson ordered its retirement and kept it.

Jake liked the fun of moving repeatedly halfway in and out of the door; in, out; in, out; watching the inner circle open and close. Through the door,

Swanson's assistant, Patty, watched, shaking her head and giggling. "Hello there, Mr. Burns, are we still in kindergarten?"

"Hello, doll. Why can't I get one of these things?"

"You are right on time, as usual. He is ready for you, I think. You may go right in."

"Ah, thanks. Why don't you let me take you away from all this? You should be my secretary now that the big guy is retired. At least call me Jake."

"In your dreams, Mr. Burns," She said and then smiled coyly. "Anyway, I have been with the GGM for more than 13-years now. I would never leave, and, if you remember, protocol is protocol. Thanks for sharing, Mr. Burns, though."

"Yeah, well, I'm too old for you anyway."

"I didn't say that, luv." She winked.

Their banter made the intensity of Jake's morning ride more tolerable. Jake smiled and walked around her desk as a buzzer sounded, and then he strolled between sliding mirrored doors into Swanson's loft office suite. Once inside, Jake studied the ornately carved bookshelves, which lined the walls; and, to Jake's surprise, there were new rustic Adirondack furniture, which added a feel of the North American wild. He pondered the new motif until Swanson's familiar voice broke the silence. "Hello? Burns! Is that you down there? Make yourself at home. I'll be right down."

Jake snapped out of his trance and sat down in the plush leather chair next to Swanson's desk. "Great! Thank you, sir."

He began watching the eight 60-inch floating monitors positioned around the room. Each displayed Ever-Life's news from one of the Posts. After having headset sessions, Jake understood all the different languages appearing on video texts at the bottom of each screen.

"How did I live without this shit all these years? If only Watzin knew. Christ! If the boys in New York knew, I'd never live any of this down."

One of the text feeds interrupted his nostalgia. Within seconds, all 8-monitors reported the same story: ***Billionaire Marion Brock returns to buy Time-travel Inc.***

Jake's eyes widened. "Oh, my God!" He tapped his Knofer and it displayed the same reports but no confirmation.

Swanson walked down the stairs fixed on the monitors.

"Sir," Jake asked, "This feed can't be from the surface news, can it? The feed is all the same."

Swanson was quick to reply, "You know we shouldn't be getting that crap. These are closed looped and should be from our own resources. This is very strange. Our systems don't work like this, all channels displaying the same video. It is as if someone has hacked into us."

Jake immediately tapped his Knofer again and executed a defense protocol to trace. "I've got nothing."

Swanson stopped at the bottom of the stairs and focused. "All of it says Marion Brock is alive. I have to wonder." He walked to his desk, hesitated, and then he took a hardbound book out of the drawer and tossed it in front of Jake. It was titled, *ALLENFAR, an Ever-life story.*

Jake picked up the book, read the flap, and flipped through the pages. "I wonder if any of that, or our recent event at the ceremony, has to do with this? Perhaps it is no longer a private matter between you and me?"

Jake picked up the book. Yes, I was given this from a friend in New York, and I thought you should see it."

Swanson continued. "Somehow, we must fix this, my friend. The book is about all of us down here, and it was written centuries ago in 2019. There is a stamp on the first page that says NYC Public Library. You sent this to me via Carrier, so there would be no record in headset files. You must have suspected something." Swanson gestured to the monitors. "And now, this Brock story? If this book was on the surface for that many years, and Brock or one of his gofers read it, my God! How many copies were made? Do you know?"

"No sir."

Jake took a deep breath, as Swanson turned the pages, annoyed at what he saw. "This may already have had earth-shattering implications. There are pictures of Carriers in it. Did you read this paragraph?

'Many authors write stories they imagine. That is fiction today. But what if someone writes a 'true' story that hasn't happened yet?'

. . . And precisely, what do you think that means, Jake? The more I think about it, the more I am certain they are related somehow. Put what is on those monitors and in this book together, along with the Carrier episode at Mathew's ceremony, and what story do you come up with?"

"Perhaps, sir, but it is a fascinating story."

"And I know I'll love it." Said Swanson sarcastically. "Apparently, it is a story worth writing a book about. Tell me, Jake; we don't have all the time in the world anymore. After all, the book has existed for how long now, centuries. Do give me the who, what, where, when and how of this? And, now would be a good time to start." Swanson plopped in his chair. "Puzzling too, since Brock was taken away by a Carrier those months ago."

Swanson began fidgeting and staring at a Carrier model, which he kept on the right corner of his desk. In that second of awkward silence, his desktop Knofer ticked. He tapped it, and a three-foot holographic image of Marion Brock grew up before their eyes. Swanson's jaw dropped. Jake quickly grabbed his Knofer and pushed buttons to record and send to Bellos. At the same time, he also triggered the next level of Ever-Life's security protocols to 313, which alerted all Post Controllers. Then, both Jake and Swanson fixed on the hologram.

"Hello, Gordon." Brock smiled that arrogant sinister grin. "I can tell by your usual blank expression that I've interrupted nothing. Long time no see. As I recall, you thought I was swallowed into the Earth's core and gone forever inside one of your pet beasts. So, I thought I would call and tell you I'm just fine, never was dead. I do hope you are prepared."

"Frankly, Marion, nothing you do surprises me. How did you get my number by the way?"

"Ha, well, I do love a sense of humor. To put it bluntly, I plan to make some changes, and you are one of them. You see, I just acquired a new research complex. You just saw the ads. The point is, we are going to compete. I thought a heads-up was in order."

"Marion, even your laws don't allow you to compete with Brock/Swanson."

"Of course not; I'm talking about your little Ever-Life secret. I'm talking about your time travel operation. You see, I have kept up with what the old staff is doing. My new acquisition will be. Oh, I'm sorry; I mean, my new acquisition, Time Travel Inc. is fully operational. Anyway, it's dedicated to stopping your Ever-Life from becoming, well, forever-life. I am saving that little jewel for myself. You will have never existed in the first place when I'm done. I just wanted you to know, my foolhardy friend. I told you the last time we were together, you didn't have a clue, and I meant it. I wanted you to know the bullet is coming, my dear partner; and it's coming from me personally, to you. Have a nice day. Oh, one more thing, I would like to compliment you on these little gadgets, they are called Knofers, right? Quite fun."

Brock's hologram disappeared, and the monitors went completely black. All went quiet. Jake and Gordon looked around as if expecting something else.

"Now, that man definitely has issues," Jake quipped.

"Hmm..." Swanson rocked back in his chair. "...So, either he read this book or, it's something else. And then, there is the issue of the Carrier at the ceremony, the earthquakes in the Bering Straits, and the explosion that killed Wheeler?”

“Yes, sir, we shipped Wheeler’s body to Lab-202.”

“Any news on him?”

“Bellos is handling it personally. He designated it a priority-one security.”

Swanson swiveled his seat, looked at the ceiling and then at Burns. “Okay, you and I are going to run this effort completely hands-on. You obviously have thought about this book and Brock. You started something here. I trust you will finish it. Use only the best of our team. We need a good plan. Let’s start with you telling me everything about this book thing.”

“Fine, also I have to tell you about my ride here this morning.”

“Priorities, Jake, priorities . . .”

“Yes, well; remember when you first offered me this position and Mathew took me on that tour? I was very attentive, and he did show me a lot in a relatively short time.”

“Yes, go on.”

“One area was a Time-Trust pavilion in Arden, New Mexico. I was so impressed, I talked to several specialists and took time to learn about the small bubble-Carriers. By the way, that was where I thought, in a blink, I would accept your job offer.”

“Hmm,” Swanson seemed annoyed.

“Anyway, one of my instructors was Time-Trust Specialist, Chelsea Bathwaite.”

“Stop,” Swanson said. “Chelsea, isn’t that a girl’s name?”

“No, it isn’t, apparently. Do you know him?”

“Jake, we have a global population of roughly three billion; and, remember, I am no longer GGM. So no, I don’t; go on. Get to it man.”

“Well, we sensed an immediate chemistry of sorts, much like you and I did the first time we met in D.C. at the weapons conventions.”

“Yes?”

“Well, there wasn’t enough time on that day. We had to cut it short because you and Dr. Bellos had to travel to Jerusalem.”

“Thank you for reminding me,” Swanson sighed, exasperated. “Jake, we have a lot to cover, and I do have other meetings. Do keep that in mind.”

“Yes; while you were in Jerusalem, and in several subsequent meetings during my training months, Bathwaite and I got to know each other rather well.”

“So, are you dating? For God’s sakes, man, what is it?”

"It's just that I never thought I'd be interested in time travel, never believed in it. Frankly, I thought like most that it was something it isn't. Anyway, my security training took some time, as you know; and, well, I spent several days with Time-Trust learning its reality and how time traveling works. The short of it is; I was hooked. We didn't do anything wrong; you understand; but, within the confines of rules, of course, Bathwaite allowed me to take several brief trips. I did go back in time."

"Jake, Jake, you could have told me using much less verbal vomit? In that case I'm sure you realize now that there is no such thing as a brief trip in time."

"Um, yes, I suppose that's true."

"And you met this . . . this author?"

Little beads of sweat began appearing on Jake's forehead. "Yes, sir, I did. I met him four times. Like I said, it's an interesting story. I didn't expect my trips could trigger anything . . . That reminds me. There is something else really important about my morning ride here."

"Well, none of us expected this, much less something else this morning, now did we?"

"No, sir, it's about the Carriers."

Swanson blurted out, "I certainly realize what time trust means and its function, as well as the importance of Carrier relations; so, one thing at a time. There is a lot on our plate. It's all quite a bit to follow. Give me the short versions, Jake."

Before Jake could begin again, a priority call clicked on both Swanson's and Jake's Knofers. It was GGM-Bellos. "Hello, you two. We have another situation in Arden City. Two bombs have gone off, blowing up the Fargo Building completely and Time Trust-Research Building 26."

"Mathew," Swanson said, "I'm sure Marion Brock is involved. It is his way of saying hello."

"Brock, hmm . . . I saw the security call from Jake. The bombs just went off. Didn't we see Brock taken by a Carrier, months ago?"

"Yes," Said Swanson. "There is something very wrong, Mathew. Brock's news about buying Time-Travel Inc. displayed on all my monitors here. He is alive and well."

"Interesting?" Bellos said. "He has been in hiding all this time. Neither one of us was notified status from Carrier relations?"

"Yes, that is very puzzling, and more intriguing is that his timing with the Sidron events is very suspicious. He has vowed revenge toward us, me, for stopping his effort to steal CPT; and Mathew, he has a Knofer; very dangerous."

"The colonies are on alert. Burns is there with you. Clarify and discuss all the issues; then report to me."

"Yes, GGM, we will. You have serious issues right now with the three clerics."

"Yes, but this has top priority."

"It's all related, Mathew."

"I agree."

"Jake is already working on something. I will have him get into all of it. Are you taking all three of the bickering fathers back in time with you?"

"That is my plan. Hopefully, this will fulfill our obligation to GGM- S. He wouldn't have given them the book if he wasn't sure of something. It couldn't be worse timing, though."

Swanson grinned and replied, "You will handle it. By the way, when do you and I undergo the new CPT procedure?"

"We have a subject for a final test today. I should receive results soon. I recommend we schedule ASAP after that. Considering our total population, the Sidron breach and now Brock, Knofer solid holograms don't cut it as Post Controllers anymore."

"Yes, big changes. The food budget will have to increase," Swanson smirked. "I will be in Arden day after tomorrow. Mathew, was anyone hurt in the blasts?"

"Fifty people from the Complex and thirteen from Ever-Life, including Wheeler. Jake, are you listening?"

"Yes, sir."

Swanson asked, "Mathew, what about Wheeler?"

"I am handling it. And Gordon, you and I are scheduled to have a meeting about the Sidron Event at Carrier-Hive Post-8. Are you prepared?"

"Jake and I are going over some new information, which may implicate Dr. Sheldon or at least his Particle Displacement Treatise.

"Well, we are investigating the bombs. I hope that will tell us more. We have to keep ahead of all this, guys."

"Mathew, how many Carriers will attend the Council meeting?" Swanson asked.

"I'm told each ambassador assigned to our Posts and two Primary Adult Grand Carriers-Time Controllers, so 10. I never understood why so many, when they have a hive mindset. Good luck with the clergies."

"Yes, thanks. Be safe."

The Knofer cut the call, and Swanson focused on Jake. "Okay, my friend, back to it. Now tell me, how much does the author of this book know, or think he knows about us?"

"The author has transported here to Giza and was undergoing interrogation and headset orientation by Sir Thomas before the explosion at Time Trust. Now GGM has taken over that until disposition on Wheeler. It appears the Andrew Wheeler was meeting with was transported directly by the Sidron to the future, to us at Time Trust, from 2004. The Carriers had nothing to do with the event. And none of us knows what our traveler knows yet. I suppose we could headset the book, but we are uncertain what effects the Sidron event had on him, or even if the information in the book is accurate at all. Sir, will I be going to the Carrier meeting with you and GGM?"

"You will now. I see no way around it, now that you have opened another Pandora's box. You need to tell me about your time trips. You may not know what you have done relative to this author from 2004."

"It was not that kind of situation, there was no paradox."

Swanson raised an eyebrow intuitively. "Or so you say."

Jake did a double-take and continued, "And, besides, it is imperative that I tell you what happened to me during my trip to you this morning."

"Marion Brock is no fool, Jake. You never knew him. He was a billionaire pirate and a killer, but no fool. I don't know how or why he is alive; but, if he finds out, or already knows who this author is, and he can get to him through his new acquisition, Time-Travel Inc, then it would be catastrophic!"

"Sir, GGM knows all that."

Swanson said with a furrowed brow, "Of course he does. I was just emphasizing the importance of our needing to know how much this Andrew knows."

Jake thought a moment and responded, "Right now, we have to approach this with the most care and delicacy. Remember, by our time, Andrew, this author, is dead. He must have died centuries ago. And since he has accomplished something unheard of within the colonies or Carrier archives, GGM felt it imperative we treat this with utmost and stringent care. He alone is handling this so far."

Swanson gestured with his arm. "Okay, yes, of course. You know, Jake, it will take me some time to get used to not being GGM." Then he turned around and looked at his suite. "I will need time to reflect."

"Yes, sir; of course, sir."

"So, given all we know, what's next? You're the Security Chief now, Jake; you think what?"

"I think I agree that this book could motivate Brock. But, I'm not sure he can do much. Remember, since the author is dead, Brock can't change anything in the timeline."

Swanson rolled his eyes, perked up and said, "Hmm, well, I'm sure you learned a lot in your time travel training; but, perhaps one thing you don't know is that by meeting this author, you made yourself part of his time-line. So, if Brock could talk to him and, through him, get to you in that timeline, he could use you to change things here and now. In that case, we would have quite a different game altogether, would we not? You, Jake, are not dead at all, are you?"

Jake thought as he watched Swanson handle the book.

"Yes, it could be a paradox in that case."

"Also, Jake, there is a lot of information within these pages that reveal our culture. While it only generally describes CPT and Mathew's success transposing the holograms, this could result in dramatic consequences and behavioral differences up on the surface, if read by the wrong people.... Jake, Jake," Swanson sighed.

Burns got up and slowly paced and spoke. "Sir, I want you to understand. I met the author four different times during his life. I, of course, was the same age I am now."

"I know how old you are, Jake."

"Yes, well, the cumulative total of our time together was only four of his days."

Swanson looked wide-eyed, and he was noticeably annoyed. "So, four days of you with him are just sitting out there, forever. That is a lot of time and opportunity for Brock to make catastrophic changes. This is a hard way to learn the lesson. He can use that time as a most powerful tool against us. It can't be taken lightly or used frivolously at the whim of the moment. Now, how much can you tell me?"

Jake replied, "That book was found last week in the New York Public Library. An old police buddy of mine called me. He read it and noticed my name. He thought it funny, given the date the book was written. He sent it to me at the Arden police station. I used a headset to read it and later agreed that we don't know how accurate the information is; so, I sent it to you via Carrier, because I wanted strict security. The truth is that the author was a very stimulating man, and I did not resist conversations. But I may have twisted his life a bit, showing up when he was different ages."

"I am certain of that."

"It was during our second meeting that we hit it off so well. He was 40-ish, as I recall. I even thought, *what an excellent candidate for Ever-Life, if only it hadn't been a Time-Trust issue.* Anyway, we talked at great length about many issues and subjects. I tell you, Gordon, there have been some highly intelligent people living on the surface."

"Ha! Ha!" Gordon chuckled. "No one ever argued that point. Look at you, my friend. So, is that when he wrote the book?"

"I think he started it around then; but later he said he dismissed our first meetings as dreams. I believe that was due to the fog that comes from travelling in time."

"Obviously he was able to overcome it. What were his other ages when you met?"

"The first time was during his college years. He was a first-year student, as I recall. It was 1965. We were together for around six hours. He was in crisis. I tried to help. Something horrible had happened to him. I felt he needed me, and there was something about him."

"1965, huh? Make a note. Find out if anything significant happened concerning Brock back then."

Jake continued, "Anyway, I left and came back to orientation, but I couldn't get the experience out of my mind."

"He never told you what the crisis was?"

"Not really; I never checked either; but I had to see how he turned out. Bathwaite had no problem letting me go back again. So, I met him in his 40s. He was in crisis again. We talked for a good 15-hours. I was convinced that my help made a difference. Our final two meetings were during his late 50s. He was in health crisis then, heart issues. Looking back, it was all so odd to me. Each time he had gone through a life-changing event just before I arrived. Each time I went, my urge to see him was irresistible. Of course, as part of my orientation, Bathwaite explained I could never repeat a particular trip; so, I could never reconcile my anxiety about the visits, and I stopped."

Swanson slowly stood up. "Jake, your irresistible urge? You followed irresistible urges? Really? Good thing you weren't a teenager. What in blazes were you thinking man?"

"I realize, now, I was the one in a fog. I was addicted, selfish, and a bit stupid. But I did learn a lot. It was mutual. I thought of him as a son, if that makes any sense. And, another thing you should know, I did give him a headset session."

"You what? Christ, Jake!"

"It just happened."

Swanson was noticeably curt, "I wish I had a nickel for every time I heard 'it just happened.' No wonder he could write the book. What else does he know that Brock could steal? My God, man, you are Chief of Security. This man is a virgin by our standards. Did you think of the domino effect from this, the collateral damage on those who knew him, not to mention the long-term impact on Ever-Life? If this is true and Brock succeeds, I won't be sitting here, and we won't have the memories we do right now of anything that has happened. He will wipe us out and all that we have done, both with the surface and the Carriers."

Jake stood up at attention. "Sir, I have to say, I would go back to speak with him again if I could; or better yet, I would bring him here."

"Well, that is something I guess; but remember, he's already here."

Swanson wiped his mouth and returned to his chair. "Relax . . . Relax, Jake; you look ridiculous."

"I have absolutely no doubts about him, sir. But I am truly sorry about all of it. I realize it may affect us here, now; especially if it had anything to do with what happened to me on my Carrier trip this morning."

Swanson sat back with a questioning face. "Well, the book couldn't have been that well-written, anyway. There was no record of it being a million seller."

"Perhaps not. But the only thing we can be sure of if that he is here and so is that book."

"Yes, well, to my point; maybe nobody read it, or we would have heard about it. Let us follow this through. Maybe you can keep it a good memory."

Jake shifted subjects. "Yes, sir, but regardless, I need to talk to you about something that happened to me this morning."

Swanson sucked in another deep breath and let out a slow blow. "My plate's pretty full; what do you want to add?"

"It directly relates to all this. We have a Carrier complication. This morning my transport Carrier spoke to me."

"Really?" said Swanson, "Go on."

"He said his name was Allenfar. He spoke to me and complimented me. Apparently, when a specific Grand Carrier 1111 took me back in time to those meetings with Andrew, she claims to have had a Compatibility with me. They want me to take more time-trips within her."

Swanson stood up, walked around the desk and sat on its corner. "Did he say anything else?"

"That I was a potent sustenance to her, to them all, more potent than they have experienced in over 200-years. He was quick to detail, 'of humans on the surface.' I am sure what happened to me relates to everything else as well as the explosion here at Time Trust. The Sidron event, the Carrier at the ceremony; and, the strangest thing is that the Carriers haven't mentioned the fact that Andrew time traveled. Gordon, there were two tremors at the Bering Straits, too. We all thought it was earthquakes, but I think it may have been the Sidron event itself. It's all connected."

Swanson had a blank stare at first, and then he began speaking as though he remembered something from long ago. "A Compatibility, huh? I haven't heard that term in a very long time. Now that I am not GGM, things become foggier with every minute. I almost forgot it was possible. Jake, this could be good for us if it is true. Ever-Life could expand at an accelerated rate, beyond anything we have ever known in modern times. The last Compatibility was during the GGM before me. Carriers were not as happy as you'd think to accept my authority."

Swanson seemed to strain to remember. "You know, the Carriers live with us symbiotically, sort of, and synergistically of course. Typically, they derive little from us, only while we travel in them. Even if we could, we are bound by treaty not to calculate readings or amounts. But we know whatever it is they receive from us, it's more than they receive from any other life form. They need us. Historically, only once in a great while, almost never, someone exceptional comes along and voila! A Compatibility, a massive link, directly into their most stimulating private being. It's rather confusing to us because we don't sense what we give them. We derive measurable physical benefits from them. Their abilities to travel in this environment, to heal, to control time, to create anything from nothing within their bodies are what we get. But we have no idea what it is they get from us."

Swanson sat back down, rocked in his chair, and looked at the ceiling. He rambled on. "We know they derive essential components from our psyche, our emotions, and our inner being, things that after accumulating enough, they propagate. You know, the bright goo covering the cave walls. But, it's only in those rare, one in a billion instances, from 'a Compatibility,' that they can pump offspring out like garden hoses squirt water on the Fourth of July . . . And they can do it for months. Up until now, they have had to accumulate whatever it is slowly and in very small amounts, little by little. If one of us is compatible with even just one of them, all of them share the experience. One Compatibility session could generate hundreds of Carriers to breed at the same time. For Ever-Life, a Compatibility could motivate them all to create new inhabitable caverns at a rate, well, faster than any effort in centuries."

Swanson seemed obsessed in the moment. Suddenly, he shook it off and looked at Burns. "I am way ahead of myself. There is a lot to think about here; first things first."

"I like first things first," Jake said.

"Let's get back to the author of this book. If he had a headset session, we have a record."

"Yes, probably."

"I want you to check our Vaults. We need that file. If nothing else, it will tell us the specifics of your actions in that timeline. We need to monitor and protect you there against a Brock invasion. What a bag of mucky puck."

Swanson took their two Knofers and put them end to end on his desk. Then, they both put headset earplugs on, and Swanson called an emergency meeting of all eight Post Security staff leaders. There were always functioning head-models of each Post Commander available to Swanson in his conference room. He could call one or all of them to send updated vault information to his models for a group meeting.

CHAPTER 43: FARGO GONE

GGM MATHEW BELLOS JOINED HIS FATHER, Dr. Richard Bellos, and Dr. Jack Sheldon, who were managing trauma units set up between the two bombed buildings on the Brock/Swanson campus. One exploded in the new Time Research Building-TR26. The other leveled the Fargo building, where Marion Brock had his primary residence for years. Bellos and Jack had been in the process of transferring data from one of the Time-Trust pavilions below Arden to Brock/Swanson building TR-26. The objective was to influence one of the campus research teams to discover time travel, thereby enabling the Complex to patent, copyright, and trademark all aspects of the process. Jack's new Particle Displacement Treatise would play a primary role, as did his CPT with regard to surface medical discoveries made in the last year. It was a new direct approach by the GGM to gain more of a foothold in surface matters. Ever-Life would reap much greater monetary benefits. Of course, that was the plan before the current Sidron event took place, and now the bombings magnified the issue.

Mathew broke away from the trauma units to call Swanson and learn of Brock's phone call. Then, he returned to the bomb scene. He began speaking with his father, Richard. "Dad, what is the status?"

"Most of the wounds were superficial and treatable here."

"Thank God," Bellos replied.

Richard pointed to the trucks. "Campus bulldozers should have most of the rubble cleaned up in the next few days. What a mess." Richard snickered a bit and continued. "Arden police are over there. They have been interviewing our Security Team. Ha, their own chaps we hired for security. I haven't talked to them yet. Detective Watzin did not come. Where is my granddaughter, Angie?"

Bellos replied, "She is with Dr. Luanne, down-under. She said she was going to meet Brian in the morning for the Marshall decision. She is safe for now. What's the latest census?"

"All accounted for but two, Barb Sawyer and Ralph Walker."

Bellos looked pensive. "Why would Barb or Ralph be anywhere but floor two at Andrews?"

Jack Sheldon interrupted, "I gave the order. I had them go to TR-26 to get a copy of my treatise. Guards are searching now, but nothing yet."

"Jesus." Bellos turned to Richard. "Is everyone else accounted for?"

"Yep."

Bellos then turned his attention to the police detectives searching through the rubble. "Hey, fellas, who is in charge here?"

They all looked up, but Bellos heard a voice behind him. "I am, doctor."

Bellos turned around to see a young, spry, energetic woman, in her late 20s, wearing a dark purple pantsuit and a grimace.

"And you are?"

"I am Abigail Johnson; Abby, if you like. Your Mr. Burns directed me to report here."

"Ah, well, Jake has good taste."

She surveyed the three doctors briefly but focused on the GGM. They all heard something ticking, and Bellos said, "I think that is you, my dear."

Abby tapped the palm of her hand and then read the display across her fingers.

"Hmm, just what we need, a palm reader," Jack said. "I guess she is not from the police station."

"No," Bellos replied, "and she has a new Knofer accessory, quite impressive."

"Yes, it's new. Mr. Burns authorized me to test it."

Johnson began reading from her hand, and after a few seconds, spoke in a determined voice, "Sir, the Fargo building is completely demolished. It was a pro-job. There was minimal damage to surrounding areas; definitely strategic and professional."

"I want them, Johnson. This is the second time in a year that we have been hit. I want it stopped permanently."

"Well, that is why Burns sent me, sir." She reached inside her pocket, recovered a small bundle and handed it to Bellos.

"We found that. It's a remnant of an old type detonator. We also got two fingerprints and fresh footprints off stair planks in the debris. There were five men. We captured one unconscious outside Fargo. He was wounded from the blast. He had a concussion and a broken leg. The other offenders fled up to Albuquerque. We ran a dust analysis, trailing the air-path of the explosion. Long story short, we searched the Knofer gene pool from the prints on the doorknobs and saliva spray on a glove and stair railings. It all revealed identities. It took longer than we thought, but we found one man at the City train depot and three more at the airport. We know they were Brock's men, Rash InVoy's specifically."

Bellos smiled at her. "Impressive!"

"And there is something else. I got word that three Knofers are missing."

"I knew about one." Bellos acknowledged, "Didn't the defense protocols initiate?"

"Nothing traceable kicked in. The feedback so far is not specific; one tracks Arden to China and back; one tracks Moscow to Seattle; and, the third tracks from Fargo to South America, Rio."

Bellos mind deduced, "Organized confusion; sounds like a Brock scenario, a befuddle move. But, how did they get them?" Bellos looked angry. "Something just isn't right, Fargo to Rio? Stream me any exact locations when you can. Send teams as soon as you know."

"Yes, sir."

"Good job, Johnson." Bellos turned and started walking away. He noticed Jack digging with the others in the broken fragments of building 26. "What are you doing, Jack? You are going to cut your hands. You know better than that. Let the detectives work."

"I see something in here. Look at this," Jack lifted the strange transparent fabric. "What is this? It's sparkling, but it looks like snakeskin?"

Bellos took the 8- by 10-inch piece, examining and caressing it. "I need to make a call."

As he put it in his pocket, he felt it vibrate, and instinctively, he quickly pulled it out again, up to his Knofer. "Unbelievable . . ."

The fabric disintegrated in his hand. "I think Mr. Brock and his team are alive and well . . . And I think, something else . . . Damn, no reading on the Knofer."

Jack watched and was noticeably disturbed. "I've only seen glowing like that once before. It's a piece of one of those things, your beasts; isn't it? It has something to do with that bullshit at the ceremony, and what I am working on, your Sidron event; doesn't it?"

Suddenly, they heard shouting. "Sir, and Ms. Johnson, over here, over here! I've got something!"

They all walked over to him. "Look, an arm," the detective said.

Bellos, Jack, and Dr. Richard helped, as they all dug. "My God," said Jack. "It's Barb Sawyer."

They brushed her face off, and Jack began CPR. Within a minute, she coughed and opened her eyes. "What happened?"

Jack smiled, as he held her head. "Barb, you'll be fine, stay still. It's me, Dr. Sheldon. Just don't move."

She coughed again and said, "Dr. Sheldon? What about Ralph? We got your notes; but just as we left the building, boom!"

"My notes . . ."

As the rest of the team reached the two of them, another detective yelled, "I've got another one over here!"

Jack was quick to instruct, "Get her into emergency; check her out, STAT!"

Then, he ran to the other site. Everyone was digging frantically. Jack watched as Bellos and a detective pulled a lifeless body out from the rubble. The GGM brushed the dust and pieces of wreckage from his face. There was a deep gash in the neck, and his inner organs were missing.

"It's Ralph Walker?" Jack said. "Look at his hand. He's holding something." Jack pried his hand open. "My notes, my treatise, but some pages are missing."

Johnson notified the rest of the team to stop looking, while Jack checked Ralph's body.

"Matt, look. He has been dead a while, maybe even before the bombings."

Bellos knelt down as the ER team arrived with diagnostics. He took a blood smear and put it on his Knofer. "Run genetic analysis."

Then the two doctors stood up and faced Johnson. Bellos gave her the news. "Abby, Ralph did not die from the bombing."

"What?" she said.

"They obviously didn't want Jack's notes, either, or they would have taken them. Ralph died from knife wounds. They gutted him and slit his throat while he gripped those pages."

One of the ER men whispered into Jack's ear, "Doctor, I found this in his inside coat pocket."

Jack took the crumpled ball of paper, opened it and whispered, "It's the last page of my treatise."

"What are you saying, sir?" Abby asked perplexed.

"I think the bombs may be a cover, just to get our minds off the ball."

"That's a little farfetched, don't you think?" Abbey looked at Ralph. "What diabolic bastard would kill like this?"

Bellos replied, "Marion Brock."

Meanwhile, Jack read the scribbled writing on the crumpled page:

It's incomplete, Jack!

CR

He got a very sick feeling in his stomach. "Jesus, Matt, can't you take Ralph to wherever you do it and duplicate him, clone him, let's give him CPT for Christ's sake?"

"I just checked. He doesn't match for any of our procedures. It wouldn't take."

Jack shook his head, "God, what was the point?"

One of the ER team spoke to Bellos, "Sir, should we take him to the morgue?"

"Yes," Bellos said, "to the morgue." Bellos bowed his head and gritted his teeth in a moment of respect and anger.

Jack interrupted his concentration in a panic. "Matt! Look here!"

"What is it?"

"Look at this. Christ! And what about Rachel?"

"What about her?"

"She went to DC for me, to meet that money backer, Charlie Rossi. Look here; CR . . . Rossi? It's Charlie Rossi?"

They looked at each other, realizing; and then Bellos spoke into his Knofer, "Charlie Rossi . . . Give me all data."

"You can do that with those?"

Bellos shook his head in disgust. "Jack, I gave you Knofers for a reason . . . It says he is a financial mogul. That's all we need, another farking Brock. He and his 14 ghost foundations support a variety of global investments. Most recently, contract negotiations for repairing the Bering Straits. Jake just attended the convention there. He said Brock money was all over the place."

"You think Brock and Rossi are connected?"

"Yes, Brock is muddying the water to hide his involvement with Rossi. They all want the contract for fixing the Bering Straits. That would be dangerous for us. Johnson, get me all the information you can on the last six months of transactions made by any Rossi or Brock company. Meet me at my office on the 10th floor with it."

"When?"

"Now! Or yesterday if that's possible...Jack and dad, walk with me."

"Matt, you don't think this is all Brock's doing too, do you? He is dead. I remember," Jack said.

"If my memory serves me, he set off on a year-long tirade because of CPT, in the first place. Jack, you chose him, right?"

"Come on, Matt, you never understood Marion Brock or what he did for me and CPT."

"Your thinking was clouded then; and, obviously, it still is by your obsession to prove your theories. The facts tell us Brock is alive and up to no good."

"You think he is still after CPT?"

"There is more to it now. He wouldn't have ruined his own home or attacked TR-26 without having a much more elaborate agenda. He is daring us to try to stop him. Look around you. He doesn't give a damn who he murders."

"So, it's about what? Why is he doing this?"

Bellos stopped and looked Jack in the eye. "It's about CPT, your new treatise, and time travel. It's about control, Jack; control. He is out of control. He's obsessed. By the way, where is your son, Brian?"

"He is at the law library, I think; then, home, until the Dave Marshall decision."

"Oh, my, Dave Marshall," Dr. Richard said. "Has it been that long? Time has passed so quickly, and we have forgotten so much; so many important things. That's why I have always supported that time travel should be available to the public."

"Yes, dad," said Bellos. "I know your views on this. Listen, you two, I am sure Brock is trying to throw off my departure with the three clerics. I cannot miss that because of the Time-Trust parameters and Carrier treaty commitments. Dad, please stay on campus. Manage the ER efforts and work with the Arden Police. Jack, come with me."

The two got into Bellos' limo for the brief ride back to Andrews.

"Take us to entrance-5, will you, Mike?" instructed Bellos.

"Yes, sir. By the way, something I think is important given the immediate circumstances."

"Alright?" said Bellos. "Go on.""

"About Mrs. Sheldon this afternoon, I thought it strange she left from the Fargo airfield."

"I don't understand," said Jack."

Mike replied, "Dr. Jack, you called me and asked me to drive her to the campus airstrip. She said I should take her to Fargo. I thought nothing of it and canceled the other plane reservation. Now, given the bombs, well, I just thought I would mention it; that's all."

Jack exploded, "Christ; you idiot! Why didn't you say something, call me; send up a red flag? Shit!"

Bellos pushed a button, raising the window behind the driver's front seat.

"Calm down, Jack. Take it one step at a time."

Within 10-minutes, they were in Bellos' office on the 10th floor of Andrews. Bellos made a Knofer call to Ever-Life Post-5, Station 120, Peru, to the South American Post Controller. "I need surveillance records throughout the continent and Post to trace Knofer numbers 1961 and 1969."

"Yes, sir, it may take a little time."

"Do whatever you have to. We need to find those Knofers now!" The GGM cut the call. "Frankly, I'll be glad when the CPT Duplicates replace the holograms. At least we will be dealing with emotional beings.

"Abby, first, I want you to start surveillance on both Brian Sheldon and Angie until Jake or I release the security protocols. Take Dr. Sheldon here to Washington, DC. Use the plane on the main campus runway. I know it's all fueled. Try to trace the aircraft Rachel Sheldon took. Work with the FAA."

"I did, sir. There's no record of a flight plan."

Bellos tapped his Knofer, "Get me Mike Warren."

In a matter of seconds, Bellos' Knofer clicked again.

"Yes, sir, Mike here."

"Mike, did you see the plane Rachel Sheldon took?"

"It was a Hushjet-36. The only noticeable marking was a yellow seagull's silhouette on the tail."

Bellos looked at Abby.

"Got it," she said.

"Thanks, Mike. Call me if you remember anything else."

"One more thing, sir; I found a small bug-recording device in the limo. I just gave it to Security, Level Six."

"Abby?"

"I'm on it."

"Thanks, Mike. Abby, get going with Jack here. Call me in route with updates. Your priority is to see that these two are safely returned to Andrews."

"Got it."

"You meet Mr. Charles Rossi and investigate any possible involvement he may have with Rash InVoy or Brock. Alert your team out there. Be lawful, please?"

Jack was getting more nervous, the more he listened. "Matt, I haven't heard from Rachel at all, no texts, no messages, nothing; and she doesn't answer her phone."

"Where are your Knofers, Jack?"

"Jesus, Matt, I don't carry that shit."

Abby replied, "Great, another dinosaur, I'll bet you a dime they're the missing ones."

"Give Dr. Sheldon another one"

"Jack, stick it in your pants or up your ass but keep it on you. Do you understand? Where the hell are the other 2, we gave you?"

"Home, I think; I don't know."

Johnson whispered under her breath, "How can someone so brilliant be so stupid?"

Jack was quick to challenge, "I heard that. I just don't see them as a priority in my life, young lady."

"What about now?" she asked.

"Don't lose it, Jack," Bellos said, "Learn it. Now get going. I have to meet with our guests, the three fathers."

Abby gently nudged Jack's arm. "Let's go, doctor."

Jack and Abby went to Bellos' private elevator and pushed the button to floor 1.

Bellos heard his Knofer again. As he walked, he listened. "Sir, this is Jacque at Time Trust in Post-2, Giza. We need to know how to proceed with our new guests."

Bellos didn't skip a beat, "Make sure they are comfortable but isolated and secure. Contact me if there is a problem." Bellos walked to the oval room and took a call from the Andrews floor two. "Hello, Bellos here."

"Yes, Dr. Bellos, this is Krys in cancer surgery. We need you here, STAT!"

GORDON SWANSON AND JAKE BURNS finished their conference call with the colonies' security managers and sat thinking about the whirlwind of events. Jake noticed an unusual look on Swanson's face. "Sir . . . Gordon, are you alright?"

"I am just trying to put all the fragments together. I used to do this in less than a minute. You don't miss being GGM unless you need it."

Jake shrugged. "I have no idea what you mean. It's all a puzzle; I realize that."

Swanson began his deduction. "Follow me on this. The Carriers have been the keepers of time travel well over 10,000 years, as far as I know. They have taught us the reality of time; that it is not just the abstract concept, which we humans invented and use to measure events or cycles. I accepted that, you see. With great confidence, I have accepted that time travel can only take place within time measured. If there is no measure, there is no time to travel within. That is why we could never go into the future. No event has taken place in future time, or so we were convinced to think."

"Yes, basic Time-Trust orientation." Jake scratched his head. "What are you thinking now?"

"First, consider the recent discovery made at the particle accelerator within OPAS-Oregon Particle Acceleration Sciences. They discovered a new atomic sub-particle. It supposedly pulses differently than anything else ever detected. Test results showed that it is moving between one time and another with each pulse. They called it the Bridge-Particle. I was supposed to have a meeting with our contact in Seattle about it; however, because of your Bering Straits conference and Mathew's ceremony, I postponed it. I want you to go there in my stead and investigate the whole thing. Second, consider our immediate danger. Brock. If he has found a way to travel through time, then how exactly is he doing it?"

Jake thought and offered, "Perhaps he has found a way to use the discovery at OPAS."

"Precisely, but how? I have always found the simple and obvious to be our best guide. Let us consider that Mr. Brock simply bought the technology, bought the findings."

"Sounds like Brock; that's for sure."

"Yes, but they wouldn't sell that kind of thing. Brock must have done something else."

"I know; he bought a man. He paid off an employee."

"Christ, Jake, yes! That's it. He hired one of the scientists from OPAS to run Time-Travel Inc., and then, when he was sure they discovered how to travel in time, he bought the company. By God, that's it!"

"But who?"

"Jake, contact our post station in Seattle. See if any records show anyone at Brock's new-found treasure who worked at OPAS . . . Now, man, do it now!"

Jake tapped his Knofer and got a security station manager, under Seattle. "Yes, this is Margret Carver; what can I do for you?"

"Carver, this is Jake Burns."

"Yes sir?"

"Pull up employee records for Oregon Particle Acceleration Sciences, outside Seattle. Also, pull up anything we have on Time-Travel Inc.'s employee records. Are there any names that match?"

"Let me see, checking now...Yes, just one..."

"Name please?"

"Dr. Hamill G. Stevens, Graduate Oxford, MIT, Rand-house Physics Group Leader at Micro-CERN, before transferring to OPAS. Last year he accepted the position of Chief Particle Physicist at Time-Travel Inc."

Burns and Swanson looked wide-eyed at each other.

"Thank you, Carver."

Jake cut the call. Swanson sat nodding. His mind was in overdrive. "You see, Jake; look for the simple. Look for the obvious. They stick out for a reason. How soon can we find this, Mr. Hamill G. Stevens?"

"Consider it done."

"Good. Now, next; let me think." Swanson triggered his Knofer, "Display fabric residue dated today, # 1035, and results labeled Morgue Cloth, # 909, last year."

"What are you doing?" Jake asked.

"After all these years, I hate to even think of it, but Mathew found a piece of something, fabric at the Fargo bombings. It disintegrated."

The Knofer displayed two small piles of black soot.

"Look at these, Jake," the Knofer placed the holographic images next to one another above the desk, as Swanson spoke further instructions. "Run comparative analysis. Search for Carbon Tetron in each."

"Why Carbon Tetron?" asked Jake.

"Carbon Tetron is only found below 100 miles of Earth's surface. Look, they are almost identical readouts."

"So, the fabric at Fargo was Carrier-skin?"

"Yep; look at that." Swanson pointed to the display. "This is from the shootings at the morgue, and that is from the Fargo bombing."

Swanson reached for the Carrier statue on his desk and shook it slightly. "What if there is a rogue Carrier? What if Brock has it? Even worse, what if that Carrier voluntarily went to Brock?"

"Why would a Carrier do that?" Jake thought in silence for a moment, and then he stood up, his face blushing. "Brock was in one, remember? I smell something more rotten than I care to believe, Mr. Secretary, and I don't like it."

Swanson looked confused. "Really, what?"

"The Carrier that took Brock away, those months ago, I thought Mr. Brock was gone, dead. What if instead of the Carrier rehabilitating Brock, it had 'a Compatibility' with him? Brock has been trying to figure out time travel, and he found the vehicle to do it. What if he and the Carrier team up with OPAS?"

"Well, although it's complete speculation, that would explain quite a bit, now wouldn't it?"

Jake chuckled and said, "Ah, I sound like a stupid old TV soap opera."

"Yes, you do. Is that what you don't like?"

Jake had a sick feeling in his stomach as he found his way back to the chair.

"What is it?" Swanson asked. "Speak up."

Jake looked around, rolling his eyes. "Alright, I know you hired me because you knew I was a good detective; but, right now, I am not so sure I want to be."

"Oh, for god's sake, tell me what you're talking about!"

"You said it had been over 200 years since the last Compatibility."

"Yes, quite so."

"The Carrier that talked to me this morning said the same thing."

"What are you getting at?" asked Swanson.

"If that's true, what are the chances of two different people having a Compatibility at the same time? There has to be a connection between the people. It is the obvious simple answer."

"To what, Jake?"

"That your Mr. Brock and I are connected."

Swanson sighed, deflated somehow, and closed his eyes a second, as if he wasn't surprised. Jake read his facial expression and leaped to his feet. "You know! You knew! You have known all along!"

"Now, wait just a minute, Jake."

"No, it was right in front of me all the time; and I couldn't, I wouldn't see it."

Jakes face got beet red. He extended his arm and shook his finger at Swanson. "What the hell is our connection, Mr. Secretary? Why would Brock and I both be compatible with Carriers? Tell me, or, so help me, you will never make it to the CPT make-over. You won't make it out of this room."

Swanson stood and raised his hands, trying to diffuse Jake's emotional outburst. "Jake, calm yourself. Everything is fine. Sit down; listen to me."

"I will calm down if I like what you tell me."

"Well, you are a good detective. I don't know of anyone who has the powers of deduction like you do, except of course me and our GGM."

"Spit it out, Gordon. The whole truth or I swear . . ."

"Jake, sit down; you look ridiculous. I have been following Brock for years. I traced his money and banking empire from country to country, continent to continent. I needed to keep an eye on every aspect of his empire, to assure his worldwide schemes did not interfere or invade our Ever-Life interests on the surface. Marion Brock comes from a very long lineage of Brocks. They have manufactured, purchased, and sold firearms and ammunition since the mid-1960s."

"So, what has that got to do with me and compatibilities?"

"Jake, you just searched for an employee with your station security girl, Carver, and look what you came up with in just three lousy minutes. Can you imagine what I came up with, searching Brock's history?"

"What the hell are you talking about?"

Swanson hesitated and then took a deep breath. "Jake, you and Marion Brock are related. While it is a distant relation, you are genetic brothers. You carry several identifiable DNA markers."

"Bullshit!"

"I am afraid it is true. There is no doubt."

Jake ran his hands through his hair. "So, did you know this when we met for the first time at the arms convention?"

"Yes."

"Christ! You played me. You have been playing me ever since. Why? For what? Did you think I was in cahoots with Brock? Do you think I am a link to his empire? Why, Gordon? Why?"

Swanson walked around his desk and stood in front of Jake eye to eye. "I don't assume, Jake, I deduce. I was GGM for God's sake. I knew you were a good man, but all of Ever-Life is based on genetics. Everyone here has a genetic record. We do not have records about everyone on the surface. The Carriers insisted that I check your history. They wouldn't say why. I never believed you were part of Brock. Now that the cap of GGM is passed to the next man, my thinking and deductive strengths are getting weaker. With you on the job, we are going to solve this."

"Candy ass bullshit! That doesn't excuse or explain your deception."

"I have not deceived you or anyone else. I did my job, and I am doing it now. Stop reacting with emotions. Stick to using your brain,"

Swanson squeezed Burns' shoulders, and then he walked around the desk to his chair. "Now let's get back at it. There is something else regarding this that we must consider, and you may be the only one who can do something."

"Jesus, do what? What next?"

Swanson said, "What if during Brock's Compatibility, the Carrier shared its thoughts with Brock?"

Jake blinked and cocked his head. "Is that even possible?"

"That's how we found out about many things down here in the first place, eons ago. In the beginning, compatibilities were two-way. We humans are the ones who eventually insisted on one-way transmissions. Many of us died from the intensity of the two-way exchanges. Eventually, treaties banned two-ways, and with good reason . . ."

"So, you think Brock and a Carrier are having mind melds."

"It would fit. What if Brock learned how the Carriers move through time, and he has shared enough information with Stevens to give Time-Travel Inc. the boost it needed to succeed?"

Jake's head was spinning with possibilities. "If Brock has a Carrier, he has to keep it out of sunlight. Where would he keep it? Carriers can't be confined. Plus, our Ever-Life surface contacts would have alerted us. The Carriers would have warned the GGM, right? And if there is a rogue, wouldn't the hive mindset know and track it?"

Swanson focused on the statue again. "Fair points, unless Brock's Compatibility sustenance feeds the Carrier enough to superpower it. If Brock is strong enough, then the question becomes could the Carrier convince others of its kind to rebel against the hive and follow him? Brock's control could spread throughout the Carriers' hive mind and pervert it, turning them against the Ever-Life colonies. The combination of that, and Brock traveling in time, changing everything, would result in catastrophe. Any way you evaluate this, it's not good for us. You have to contact your Carrier 1111. You need to convince her to have a two-way exchange with you. You must find out if anything we have speculated is fact. Your Carrier will know something."

"Agreed, but when this is over, you and I are going to hash our history out."

"And another thing, Jake; have her report on all the interruptions regarding your author's timeline. She took you before. She should have the best time travel recall, if you can get her to tell you. Tell her you want to go back to see him again. I don't care; be creative. Maybe she can sense Brock traveling; and don't forget Stevens in Seattle."

"But, why don't we just ask the Carriers right now?"

"This treaty-agreement prohibiting two-ways has been in place for over 9000 years," Swanson explained. "I am not going to let one rogue Carrier with an overzealous sex drive bring Ever-Life to a halt. Let's fight fire with fire and get one on our side; agreed?"

"Yes," Jake replied, "agreed."

"Jake, if you have the same sustenance Brock has, it may give us an advantage. We have no idea how many other Carriers may have already gone rogue. Considering our situation, how do you know, when you meet her if it's even her? Without a two-way communication, how do you know anything, Jake?"

"Yes, I never thought of that. I'll leave right away."

"Jake, wait." Swanson unlocked a desk drawer, reached inside and took out what looked like an old pocket watch.

"Here, put this in your pocket. Keep it with you at all times."

Jake studied the watch.

"Thank you, I think, but it's not working."

"That's because it's not a watch. I've had that for decades. I would have given it to Mathew, but he has other means at his disposal, now. Times have changed."

"So, what is it?"

"It'll disable a Carrier, and I never used it. You may have to. You'll know. As I understand it, it buzzes when activated; and I wouldn't be around it long if that happens. A friend in the Carrier Council gave it to me long ago. Keep it handy."

Jake slipped it into his side coat pocket.

"Jake, I know you've got a lot to think about. But hear me out. The center of Earth generates temperatures that rival our Sun. Obviously, we can't go there. Earth's core is the size of the Moon. We don't even know what it's made of. We think the Carriers do. The outer magma surrounding the core is 1500 miles thick and mostly liquid. The earth's rotation creates the movement of this fluid, and that movement generates the planet's magnetic field. That is where we believe the massive Carriers stay and derive most of their power. No one has been able to reach them unless they invite us. If somehow Brock were to gain control of those Carriers by offering compatibilities through cloning himself, we'd be in a terrible position. He could rule more than the Carriers, or Ever-Life; he could rule time itself."

"Yes, I see, but couldn't we do the same?"

"We could, and it did cross our minds. But, for us, first, there are ethics and morals that humans cling to regarding cloning or duplicating. Second, we haven't had *a Compatibility* like you describe for hundreds of years. Third, we stopped two-way exchanges, because we were dying from the experience. That alone means we couldn't control anything, especially time. Now, come around here. This will only take a minute. I am calling up genetic records."

The Knofer lit a display and created a thin vertical monitor in front of the two men.

"Look, here is your DNA and there is Brock's; now, we overlap them."

"All I see is everything is the same."

"Not quite." Swanson spoke into the Knofer, "Cross check with historical records of last two compatibilities...You see, my friend, I never thought of compatibilities when I checked Mr. Brock or his family history. Until you brought it up, I am sure no one has. If you and he do have a gene match, we should see it here..." Swanson spoke again into the Knofer, "Overlap the red dashes, please . . ."

"What are the red dashes?"

"Compatibility indicators. Will you look at that?"

The Knofer compared and listed the characteristics for Brock, Jake, and one other person.

"Fascinating," said Swanson.

"What?"

"Translate into numbers, please? Christ! Look at that. Brock's numbers are two to three times anyone's in Ever-Life, except. There is one here, who lived on the surface. Jake, I want you to get to OPAS and stop whatever Mr. Stevens is doing. I suspect the combination of yours and Brock's genetics, coupled with what Stevens is working on, are what triggered the Sidron event. I realize it's only my speculation, but I am pretty sure Brock has figured out how to go back in time with a Carrier."

Jake said, "Well your speculation has been a bulls-eye for all those years you were GGM.

"Thanks, it makes sense to me that Brock does not know about you. But it's only a matter of time, a real time-bomb. He has two out of three components to ruin Ever-Life. You must get Stevens out of the picture. It may make the difference. Jake, you have always been my choice. Please believe that. I will brief GGM. Go now."

Jake turned to leave, but after a few steps, he stopped and turned around.

"Not to add another coal to the fire, but there is another critical component here we haven't discussed."

"What is it?"

"The Bering Straits tunnels."

"Ah, yes."

"There were two keynote speakers from the Brock Companies at the convention. I listened, and I found their proposals extremely attractive. Of course, I never expected Brock himself might be behind the effort."

"Well, he's not a billionaire for nothing. I will tell Mathew. I am sure he will want to get involved personally." Swanson walked up to Burns and smiled. "I remember when Brock and I first met. I thought, my God, what a combination, brains, money, and charisma. He was the answer to what we needed to complete the campus in New Mexico. He was as brilliant as much as he was clever. Now, he is a narcissistic obsessive control freak, without regard for humanity. Jake, remember, he is sick, and he knows it. It all makes sense. He wants to control time, to control Ever-Life. Be careful. He seeks to control the planet."

"From what I saw, he's on his way to controlling the Cosmos."

"Let's start with OPAS. Try to find out all you can. Report back to me when you know anything."

Swanson patted his shoulder, and Burns walked out.

INSIDE EVER-LIFE LAB-202, below Arden City, a surgical light illuminated the center of the main room. A transparent Carrier bubble had expanded around a gurney to assist Dr. LuAnne and Nurse Angie Bellos, who stood within it, leaning over the body of Tom Wheeler.

Dr. Lu walked to the foot of the gurney and said, "Okay, Angie, help me slide him over on his side, into the body cavity there on the table."

Angie shoved his torso, while Dr. Lu guided his legs. The body flopped into the gel-like mold, and Angie wiped her forehead. "Boy, things here change so fast. When Dr. Sheldon did this to his wife, he just stuck her in the back of the head and then on the side of her neck."

Dr. Lu commented, "That was a first timer, as I recall, and I'm going to say luck, or God, was involved."

"So, who is this guy, anyway?" Angie asked.

"He is Sir Thomas Wheeler, Ph.D., Psychoanalytical Research & Professor of Particle Phenomenon, Ever-Life Time Trust, Cavern#1017."

"What did he do to deserve CPT?"

"He is an essential. Essentials are genetically capable of Duplication and Transtosis, repeatedly. Consequently, their DNA will tolerate CPT . Today, with him, we begin the new CPT procedure. Among other things, long ago, he helped identify one of what the surface called a God particle. We leaked it to the surface, and we all made a lot of money. Elementary fools. Our Post-3 here alone got a 5 percent cut of the gross, if I remember correctly. Don't quote me though. It is in the history headset files if you want details."

"Is that legal?"

"Standard procedure, when we give knowledge to the surface. Anyway, Wheeler here is a primary controller of our Time Trust records, under Giza in Egypt. I don't know what happened, but the GGM put a priority-one security on getting him back."

"Really?"

"Yes, GGM wants to confirm the new CPT for two reasons; first, because Secretary Swanson's health has worsened, and, second, he wants to begin replacing all holographic Post Controllers with CPT duplicates."

"Oh..."

"Anyway, Sir Tom here was researching interactive plasma components, which make up different forms of electricity, you know, torsunary anomalies."

"No, I don't have any idea what that is, way beyond my interest and pay grade."

Dr. Lu smiled. "It has to do with combining physics with medicine and genetics. Anyway, we do have his genetic history. The GGM had the body sent here himself."

"Something is up then?"

"Yes, it has been quite a day, so far."

"Every day is quite a day here," Angie smirked.

"Look over there; hand me that wand; then read me the memory codes and telomeric pools on the monitor."

"I remember this wand."

"This one is a little different."

"Why did my dad want me to be here, anyway?"

Dr. LuAnne focused and placed the wand tip against the base of Dr. Wheeler's skull. Then, she let go. The 10-inch wizard wand stuck to his neck and wiggled. Then it morphed, shrinking into a tiny half-inflated transparent balloon, two inches in length. It stayed in that fixed position, while Dr. Lu announced to the room, "Please initiate the program. You see, my dear, the bubble around us is a Carrier, and it will control the procedure now. We will monitor."

"Fascinating . . ."

The procedure took only minutes, but precise in every detail. The small wand-balloon sucked a small glob out of Wheeler's head and mixed it with the new synthetic catalyst already inside. The two women watched as the combined mixture burst into a blue carbonated liquid. After the balloon waited for just the right amount of time, it rolled around his neck to the right side and squeezed the sparkling liquid back into the patient's carotid artery; and then, both the needle and deflated residue of the balloon disintegrated.

"Unbelievable!" said Angie.

"Yes, it is. The wand is organic, controlled by the Carrier. Now we wait."

"How long?"

"Look!"

Dr. Lu grabbed her Knofer, used it to scan Wheeler from head to toe, and then spoke into it, **"Please note and record movement; healthy brain liaison and body coordination observed at 7:17.5, Post 3, Ever-Life Lab 202, Universal Time Zone 7."**

LuAnne then spoke to Angie. "Well, we are done here. Please take Dr. Wheeler to Module-10, down the hall and to the left for recovery. You can go after that. Thank you."

Dr. LuAnne walked through the bubble membrane and out of the lab.

Angie covered her patient, tucked the sheet into the mattress, and felt Dr. Richard's hand on her sleeve. "Hello there," he said. "Thank you, for whatever you did."

Angie smiled, "I am your nurse, Mr. Wheeler. Welcome back. You are going to be fine."

Wheeler looked around the room. "Where am I?"

"Lab 202."

"How long?"

"The procedure took only a few minutes. I was told you were here almost 12 hours."

Wheeler instinctively studied everything he could see. "I love these floating beds. What is your name?"

"Angie, Angie Bellos."

"Oh, Bellos? You're his daughter."

"Yes, and I'm your grand-daughter."

Richard was foggy and a bit confused. "I must see your father, right away."

Angie cocked her head. "Do you know me?"

"I'm uncertain of a lot. Please, can you get me a pillow, will you? I need to sit up a little . . . I am Dr. Thomas Madeline Wheeler. Don't let the middle name fool you. I realize my thinking right now is foggy at best, but I hope you can help me clear my head. I believe we should find your father, right away."

"First, you recover, then you see dad. Doctor's orders! Now, this is just a little something to help. Drink it and rest."

"Angie, do you know what I was doing when this happened to me?"

"No, not really."

"What is your schedule?"

"I am leaving for the surface soon. I have an early appointment with a friend."

"Don't go. Stay here until your dad arrives. You are in danger. I realize how that must sound, but I'm sure of it."

Angie sat down on the bed and took his hand. "Don't be so paranoid. It's probably side effects of the new procedure you just had. Go on, drink. It's good for you."

While he swallowed his cocktail, Angie tapped her Knofer, and within seconds, a lab nurse came through the door. She was a noble woman, who you couldn't miss in a crowd.

"Hello, you two! How is our patient?"

"I am fine, Madam. It is imperative that I speak to our GGM immediately."

Angie spoke quickly as she moved to the door. "I have to leave. Can you take over? Mr. Wheeler needs to go to Module-10 for recovery."

"Yes, miss, certainly. We will be just fine."

Angie opened the door and turned to Wheeler. "I hope I'll see you soon."

Wheeler began to get out of bed. "Angie, you must not leave. Just believe me, please?"

"Sir," the nurse snapped, "protocol is solitude and rest to guarantee all functions."

"Poppy-crap! And, you are not my mother."

"It looks like I'll have to be."

The nurse quickly injected Wheeler with a fast-acting muscle relaxant, and he fell back on the bed. He couldn't move, but he was fully awake and watched the nurse smiling, as she tucked him in and whispered, "Night-night."

CHAPTER 46: THREE FATHERS

THERE WAS NO MOON that evening, and the Brock/Swanson campus lighting was strategic enough, so no one looking out the Ever-Life limo saw any bomb wreckage. The car stopped at the hospital's main entrance, and driver Mr. Mike Warren told the three passengers to take off their blindfolds. Then, he escorted Pappas Kristos Alieri, representing the Christian faith; Rabbi James Yeshua, representing the Jewish faith, and Imam Ahmir Udera, representing Islam, up to GGM, Bellos', office suite. The three fathers had just spent the last two hours riding in a Carrier from Jerusalem to Andrews without saying a word to each other. They agreed to blindfolds only because it gave them all an excuse not to talk to each other. Once inside the suite's foyer, Mike said, "Thank you for your patience, gentlemen. I must leave you now. I trust you will play nicely until Dr. Bellos arrives. Please look around and make yourselves at home. There are pastries on that table if you like. The doctor should be here soon. Good day."

He tipped his hat, turned and walked out the door. The three fathers looked at each other and shrugged. Kristos finally broke the silence, "My brothers, this is ridiculous. Please consider our history together. We are not enemies."

Ahmir scowled, "I was reprimanded, indignantly, repeatedly. If only you had just given me the book those months ago. You knew this would happen. Why have you done this, even now?"

"You two must stop bickering," James interrupted. "What did it say, Kristos? We know you read it."

Kristos moved into the oval living room, ignoring their baited words, and looked at the books and artwork. He noticed an entire row of what looked like the same book he was holding; except each of those had different initials embossed on the back of its binding. He turned to address James when he heard footsteps in the back hallway on the other side of the room, and in walked Mathew Bellos.

"Hello, gentlemen. Just for the record, all those books say pretty much the same thing. It is the people they refer to that change."

Kristos looked at Bellos with a questioning expression and extended his hand, "How do you do, again? I believe we met on the villa steps in Jerusalem."

"Yes, quite a while ago; it is my honor to receive you all. How was the ride?"

They all took time to shake hands as James said, "As for me, quite comfortable. I'm still in shock at how fast we made it."

The fathers nodded in agreement.

"Please sit down, my friends," invited Bellos. "Make yourselves at home. I have a little story to tell you. First, would you like anything, perhaps light refreshment, pastries?"

All three nodded yes, so Bellos went to the far corner of the oval room, while his guests picked up cakes from the coffee table. He opened a small compartment door and took out a tray with four wine glasses on it. He filled the glasses with a sparkling white liquid which was stored in a wineskin. As he picked-up the tray, Ahmir saw it and remembered, "Is that what I think?"

"It is an old traditional drink." Bellos handed out the goblets. "We should toast this auspicious occasion. I welcome you here, and to your friend, S's gift."

With an anxious look, Kristos said, "To the gift of truth?"

The four men sipped.

"This is it, isn't it?" Ahmir giggled and looked at the other three.

"He's right," James said.

"My goodness," Kristos said studying the glass.

"Yes, Ahmir is right," Bellos said. "Perhaps you three can remember this moment of agreement and sustain that thought throughout our meeting."

"Please, Dr. Bellos," Kristos said calmly, "will you explain. Tell us what we are doing here. I was contacted by the guard, whom we all met at the villa when S passed away. He invited me to witness S's Heritage Presentation. It seems like only yesterday when S was talking to us for the last time. And, of course, I would not refuse his dying wish; none of us would. It's time we all know why we are here and what the Heritage Presentation is.

Bellos replied, "Have a seat, gentlemen, please? Yes, that is correct, and I have the honor of presenting it."

"Whatever does that mean?" asked Kristos.

"It means S charged me with explaining that book you hold. Hopefully, you will stop bickering among yourselves and understand how what's in that book relates to your effort to unify the faiths. He wanted you all to realize that your cooperative plan should not succeed. Don't you remember his last request to you? S looked at you three and softly but resolutely said, 'My friends, you can be at peace. Do not let what appears to be my pain or anyone else's euphoric promises cloud your thinking or deaden your ears and minds to what you must understand.'"

The three clerics looked bewildered at each other. They sat up rigid in shock at what Bellos quoted.

"But how could you know those words?" asked James. "He spoke to us alone."

The other two nodded agreeing. Bellos walked to the chair next to their couch, sat down and looked at all three. "The truth is that this is somewhat of a challenge for me. It's my first time. The important thing is that you three realize you are in this together. You committed not only to uniting your faiths but also to the patience it will take to do such a thing. S had faith enough in you three to give you that book, and he charged me with taking you to where you can find the answers you seek."

The fathers looked a bit puzzled, sat back on the couch, and Kristos said, "We are all ears, doctor."

"Well, thank you." Then Bellos walked to the bay window facing the Atrium.

James held his goblet up to the light and asked, "What is this brew in the wine-glasses, Dr. Bellos? Do you know?"

"It is an old healing elixir. Some said, eons ago, that it was a magic recipe. Huh, maybe it is."

"I'm afraid I'm at a loss, Dr. Bellos. We have many questions," said Ahmir.

Bellos turned around and said, "I recall, you three had been preoccupied, even obsessed with the concept that your diversified faiths have brought confusion, hypocrisy, even heresy and terrorism to worship. We are aware of your effort with Mr. Marion Brock."

Kristos was the first to react, "It is a fact that our three religions have been at odds, even warring off and on for thousands of years. S was more than a friend. He was a peacemaker and confidant to each of us. But who are you, doctor? You have no right or authority over us."

Bellos put his glass on the coffee table. "I am Chief of Hospital here; that is true. But also, I represent a culture, just like each of you three do. Unlike yours, however, our culture does not live on the surface of planet Earth. We have evolved and prospered within the planet, miles below the surface."

The three fathers looked perplexed.

"I realize how that must sound; and I represent your friend, Master S, too, who asked us, in particular, me, to contact you and brief you regarding your effort to unite the faiths. That is why he gave you that book; so that you would gain a better understanding of life's wonder and that all religions should help humanity. Love one another and live in peace and cooperation.

He wanted you to understand that you have strayed from your primary function."

"But that's just not true," Kristos said.

Bellos raised his hands to calm them and interrupt any additional comment. "We discovered long ago that no individual or group could improve if anyone is unhealthy. Whether it is physical, mental, emotional, or spiritual, one has to be healthy before one can think, choose correctly, and love one another. So, our culture is healthcare based. Every other aspect of life stem from that. The point is; S charged me with offering you the care you need to bridge your unhealthy bickering behavior."

The three-clergy sat stiff, appearing not to react disrespectfully. After a moment, Kristos spoke, "You judge us, doctor? While I feel a bit foolish, in some respects, listening to your speech, and we do appreciate your concern; the fact is that we each live in a free society, in which, whether we agree with each other or not, we respect each other's right to disagree."

"My community recognizes and supports that concept too," Bellos replied. "So, why do you bicker? Why are you not happy and healthy with your disagreements, your diversity? Is it not because one of you has something the other two insist on having as well? You contradict your faith. Hasn't that been the problem between your faiths all along? Look at you, in particular, Kris. You refuse to share that book. You just said you live in a free society, yet you deny these others what your beloved S said was theirs too."

"It's our nature as humans," Kristos interrupted. "Our job is to help and guide humanity back to God; to help mankind understand and relate properly with our Creator and with each other; and, yes, to be better people and live in harmony, according to the teachings of our Lord and Savior. We guide our flocks based on both his teaching, and who He is...God the Father, God the Son, and the Holy spirit."

"Wait, my brother," Rabbi James said. "Excuse me. Your simple comment isn't simple at all. My faith is strong and unyielding; but we do believe our God has picked **us** as his people. He wants us to live according to ***His*** *code of conduct*, which instructs us how to relate to Him and to our fellow man. Your Christianity evolved over many centuries confusing most. Your doctrine was argued by so many, you had to standardize many beliefs. Your church was really created by committee, some 400-years or so after the man, Jesus, died. It all really started with a political movement and a declaration by Constantine, who was the Roman Emperor at the time, and he converted to Christianity. By his declaration, Christianity became the formal Religion of Rome. It only took 400 years, and you all still don't agree on many issues. One day you had a tribal culture and the next day, you had representatives at Nicaea arguing about what your religions should include. Your Church was created by men, not God. I don't see the need to go any further to point out that you still argue today within your countless denominations, exactly what it is you believe in and how you should behave. Historically, even your church leaders have broken both God's laws and man's laws, and they continue to have influence over your flocks. And then, there's the fact that you encourage people to pray to idols and Saints. Right there, we Jews have an irreconcilable difference with you. From Martin Luther to today you have so many denominations contradicting one another. How do you keep track of who is the flock of Christ? And it's obvious to anyone who learns your doctrine that believing that God, Man and Spirit are One is clearly contradictory to our understanding of God and that he is the only God, the only creator, ruler of the Universe. There are no others! You made idols for centuries, telling your people to pray to Jesus, Mary, saints, whoever a person relates to in your long list of human saints; so many idols all contradicting God's commandment that thou shall not worship anyone or anything but Him. Yes, our prophet, Moses used his rod and God's word to convince people to behave and believe in our God, but it was God who performed the miracles. You claim a man, born of a woman is God. How many God's do you believe in? And how many of your denominations are there now. It gets too confusing. Generations have come to the point; it's all a graveyard of fiction to them. And we all suffer from that attitude, whether it's within your churches, or mine, or Islam. We all represent nearly 30-billion people. And... Islam is no different in its leaders, who don't have a modern approach to how they should behave. We are all in question.

Ahmir stood and lifted his hands in an embracing gesture. "We already believe there is only one God, and Mohammed is his messenger. We agree with the unity you seek. It is fundamental that men can do God's work and behave according to His teaching. But Muhammed was a man, a prophet, yes. And we believe Jesus was a man too. Even if we acknowledge his miracles, we believe God performed those. We teach that Jesus was God's vessel. As such he died on the cross. And while his teachings should be learned by all Christians, his body did not mend itself and rise from the dead only to rise again a second time from a mountain while the apostles watched."

Kristos replied. "It's not my purpose to address or argue here any of what you two just said. I agree there are many contradictory issues about each of our doctrines. Need I say anything about the extreme radical

Muslims, who plagued us all for decades with terrorism. And please, need I mention we are here because together we committed to bring a common good to as many as we could; to stop the spread of modern terrorism, which plagued us all for centuries? Unity would bring solace to every Catholic, Jew, and Muslim; comfort to all religious flavors, even to the agnostic and atheist. Uniting so many would fill us with the peace of the Holy Spirit."

Bellos interrupted, "You quote the words, my friend; but when was the last time you and the Dalai Lama worshiped together? Or you, James, with a Pagan priest? Where is the unity you seek in the bickering you do and the deception you pose with that book? What about your brothers right here, Kris? They have been waiting for some word from you, and you sent nothing. Your debate rages on inside your mind. Eventually, it oversteps boundaries, which must be maintained for the health of all life. Marion Brock had no answers. He conned you. Today, you three are very privileged. I am going to take you on the trip you could only dream of."

"And where would that be, my friend?" asked Ahmir.

"Gentlemen, we leave for Jerusalem to meet the man who will reconcile your quest. Sometimes it's not what you say, but who says it."

"Doctor," said James, "we just came from Jerusalem. What purpose could it serve to return tonight?"

"We are not going there this evening. S's Heritage Presentation is a trip for you three to bridge over 6000 years of confusion and misinformation. It will enable you to understand the true meaning of unifying the faiths."

"I don't see your point, doctor." Kristos was noticeably annoyed. "We all have churches throughout Jerusalem."

"It has always been our Holy-City," said James.

"Your home is the foundation of your confusion, and the beginning of your bickering," said Bellos. "It is not a distance we travel; rather, we will pass through time, my friends, to meet your master."

The three looked in disbelief. Kristos chuckled and gestured for Bellos to sit down. "I am not proud to say that I have read this book I hold. I have withheld its contents from the others for a reason. You do speak the truth. I have been afraid that what it describes would be misinterpreted. My heart says to share it with the world, but my mind says I should bury it and never reveal the contents." Kristos looked at his brothers. "I am sorry, my friends, that is my truth. I see other books like this right up there. This book gives no answers we seek. I should give it back to you, doctor, and be done with it. It will promote discord."

Bellos stood and placed his hand on Kristos' shoulder. "Father, you promote the conflict you seek to unify. You must each choose freely, but you must all decide what it is you want, the truth, or what you have now, the ongoing debate of your ancestors. After all, you have had millennia to try to reconcile your differences. I will leave you to decide. If you cannot, we will part, and you may go back to your lives, knowing your beloved S thought enough of you to trust you this much. You may leave the book on the table."

Bellos turned to go to the foyer elevator when Ahmir stood up. "Wait, doctor, I for one will not argue, and I believe we should see what S wanted us to see." Ahmir looked at Kristos, begging.

"I agree," said James.

"My brothers," Kristos pleaded, "you do not understand. Perhaps we are to unite in faith, not in proof. I believe, and therefore I am with him. Blessed be those who do not see and yet believe. Please, think my brothers!"

Ahmir turned to Kristos with love in his tone, "My friend, let us unite here. We all committed to this under your leadership. Let us finish it. We do this for God and S, whom we loved. The doctor is right. S loved us enough to give us that book and charge us, all of us, to decide if it should be made public. It's not just your decision. Our faith is not in question here. We must find a way to give the people the understanding and peace they deserve."

Ahmir and James looked at Bellos nodding, and James said, "Yes, doctor, we two will go with you."

Bellos looked at Kristos. "And you, father?"

Kristos sighed, closed his eyes and then, looking up to heaven, he said, "God be with us all, doctor. Yes, we go."

Bellos sighed with relief and said, "Then come, follow me. Leave the book on the table. You won't need it. You can have it or read it after the journey."

Bellos led the men through the hallway to his office's computer room. Kristos gestured nervously. "Doctor, we understood we would complete our stay here tonight and then return to Jerusalem. We all have matters to attend to at home."

"I have had to make some changes, due to events here at the hospital. Lives are at stake, and after all, life before trips. But, do not fret, my friends, you will have plenty of time, and you will each be on time for your separate schedules."

Bellos pointed down the hall. "Now, over there, further down the hall, you will find three suites. Pick a room, make yourselves comfortable and meet me here at 8-am, sharp, tomorrow morning. We leave promptly, so no stragglers.”

Bellos turned and strolled back to the oval room. “If you need anything, just push the red buzzer on the night table in your rooms. See you in the morning.”

WHILE THE THREE FATHERS SETTLED INTO their sleeping quarters in Arden, New Mexico, the GGM, Mathew Bellos, stood in the oval front room of his suite, on the 10th floor of Andrews Hospital, talking to Jacque back in Giza, who briefed him on the Sidron event and Sir Thomas Wheeler's condition.

"Sir, the new CPT went well. Mr. Wheeler is in recovery, by you, there in Arden. He is in Module-10."

"Great, thanks, I am on my way to see him now." Bellos stepped into his private elevator and rode it down to red-6, while listening to Jacque.

"Sir, I have some feedback on the time events. And it's not good."

"Fire away."

As you know, three guests from the past appeared here in three separate units; all the same person, three different ages. They trace back to 1965, 1989 and 2004."

Bellos asked, "Do we know any more about the source of the event? Anything concrete about the Sidron?"

"Well, that is one of the odd parts. We are studying the data, and we have questions. First, was it one event or more, given the timeline dates involved and what's happened so far; the data are not specific.

"Explain please, detail as much as you can?"

"It was early yesterday when the first Sidron event occurred. As far as we can determine, that event transported three copies of a man. All three were the same man, each one was a different age. Each one appeared inside one of three different units and each had a cursory interview with Mr. Wheeler before his accident. Unfortunately, within a short time, the youngest of the three vanished, just disintegrated. I am sending visuals from that unit, so you can see. There was no way of telling if or when the other two might just vanish also."

"Jesus!" said Bellos."

"And there's more. We found other imprints on the data which refer to two other different people; one is Jake Burns."

"What?"

"Yes, sir, no doubt, the telomeric imprint is clear. The other one is an imprint not part of Ever-Life, also from the surface.

"Are you sure?"

"Absolutely, so far," said Jacque. "The Sidron transported our three visitors here, and that probably triggered a delayed explosion in the lab, which killed the lab assistant and Mr. Wheeler."

"Probably? We need better than probably?"

"We have always thought, speculated really, that the Sidron moves everything in balance. We have three visitors. Do they represent one Sidron event, or three separate ones, each triggering an effect? We aren't sure about how to read the data. At this point, we aren't sure if the explosion in the lab was part of a Sidron event or it may have been a result of an event?"

"Are you saying we may see more effects?"

"Yes, it's very possible, or something not as obvious as an explosion. Something is happening at Giza, at Time Trust."

Bellos scratched his head. "I have to share this with all the Post Controllers and get back to Giza."

Jacque replied, "We speculate whatever is going on; it's all tied to Mr. Burns and someone on the surface."

"Thank you, Jacque; keep on it. Speak to no one else about this except me. I want to be contacted with any information."

"Yes sir."

"And do me a favor; contact and set up Post Controller-3 for the fathers' trip tomorrow. They leave promptly at 8 am ."

"Right away, yes sir."

Bellos cut the call, closed his eyes in a moment of quiet, and then he looked up with an expression of clarity. "A *Compatibility*? Christ! It's the Carriers!' I have to get back and evaluate our time travel visitors."

Bellos walked out of the elevator below Andrews and down the hallway into Module-10. Wheeler was awake and smiled as Bellos greeted him. "Tom, you look alive and healthy. How are you feeling?"

"Hello, Matt, quite well actually. You have quite disciplined nurses here. It's good to see you. I could not keep your daughter though. She is quite the charmer."

Bellos said, "It's alright; just relax and think. Can you tell me what happened?"

"It was unprecedented really; regardless of the magnetic alignments within the region, I have no explanation for any of it yet."

"I talked to Jacque. But Tom, I need your details."

"Yes, of course; initially, after you left the area to go back to Arden, I was alone in a cell with our visitor from 1989, preparing inputs for vault storage. Monitors registered frequency vibrations I have never seen, completely alien. While I was tracking them, a force yet unknown to me hit directly above us at Giza. Wave frequencies registered off the charts. God only knows what the wave echoes did."

"Go on."

"After the first tremor, I got a call from module control saying it appears we have another Sidron event. After checking the details, they said one of our visitors, the youngest, had vanished, disintegrated. They weren't sure what happened. By that time, you were on your way to Arden, and I knew we had to move fast to correlate information. Each man was Andrew at different ages of his life. Each appeared in different sealed units in Time Trust. While I was questioning the 58-year old Andrew, a guard called me out. The orderly and I ran into the Frequency Lab and *boom*! How are the others who were in the lab?"

"Gone. All dead, as far as I know." Bellos turned his back to Wheeler and paced. "Matt, one other important thing…"

"Yes?"

"…Our visitors, I gave each a headset, but how can we guarantee ourselves that they each remember the same way?"

"Yes, I know." Bellos crossed his hands behind him and whispered to himself, "The Carriers, it has to be a Carrier."

Sir Tom sat up in his bed and asked, "May I go back to work, sir, back to Time Trust?"

"Yes, Tom, we are both going back together. I need to meet with our visitors."

Bellos' Knofer ticked, registering an upgrade in his defense protocol, and he spoke into it, "Play video of Time Trust Giza visitor on Module-10 wall."

His Knofer projected video of a young man sitting in a lounge chair watching wall monitors. After a brief moment, everything Bellos looked at began to blink, distort and blur dramatically. The GGM spoke sternly into his Knofer, "What is happening? Reply! Reply!"

"Sir," Wheeler said, "he is gone, the young one. I believe you are witnessing another Sidron event, and that video is proof. Look at him!"

Bellos was noticeably bothered. "My God, all the rooms are secure, right?

"Yes, completely."

"Tom, get dressed." Then, he instructed the module, "Repeat the video."

"Look at him."

The video showed young Andrew blink and blur again. Bellos said to himself again, "He is just dissolving, disintegrating."

"I don't think he suffered," said Wheeler,

"No way to tell. We need to go there now, Tom. No telling what will come next." Bellos was noticeably anxious. "This is too volatile a situation. I need to talk to the other two visitors before something like this happens to them. Whatever these events are, we have to stop them or at least understand them. I need you on this, Tom, right now. Everything in me says the Sidron has been breached more than once. I believe it's being used, stimulated and even controlled. We need to find the cause and stop it, correct it."

"Then you do believe it to be a time displacement?" asked Tom.

"Yes, I am certain, but proof is needed. What caused the Sidron to breach? We must find out! Confirm the cause. And, can we prove there's been more than one. What we see on the wall is a violation of nature. I need to talk to this man and the Carriers."

"What are we going to do with him, them?"

"I just hope we get to them before another frequency wave hits."

Bellos stared at Wheeler and then the monitor with an apprehensive look. He tapped his Knofer and briefed the colonies' controllers. Then both men walked out of lab module 10, to one of the station's boarding platforms. A Carrier awaited, and they walked into its standard travel room. After getting situated, the GGM began interacting with Post Controllers via Knofer, regarding a multitude of Ever-Life issues.

Suddenly, he alone heard the voice of the Carrier in his mind, *"Good day, my GGM. I am Allenfar."*

"Hello," Bellos replied through thought exchange. "Your species has been full of surprises today. Report, please."

"I have been assigned to you, strictly speaking, sir, until we sort out the Sidron situation."

"What can you tell me?"

"The Carrier high council has instructed me to replace your Carrier 62712. I have been temporarily assigned to interface with you and Mr. Burns as you direct."

"Take us to Post 2, Giza Station 1, as fast as you can."

Allenfar went silent, and Bellos went back to his holographic meetings with post commanders. After a time, he heard a voice behind him, which sounded like a man, but it spoke in the language of the Carriers. Bellos turned around and saw a humanoid figure like the one at his ceremony. But this one did not have his arms out in friendship.

"GGM, we must talk in private."

The hologram gestured toward a door, which appeared instantly. They both walked into a different isolated section of the Carrier. Once inside, he began. *"I have come to help resolve the threat."*

Bellos replied, "Our situation is the result of a combination of variables."

"We agree. As you know, I have within me all information from the council ready and available to you. We confirmed that one of our Carriers is, in fact, involved. You rode within him months ago, during the CPT incident. We instructed him to rehabilitate Marion Brock. However, we have been unable to communicate with him. He has acquired much sustenance from Brock. He has enough power to block sharing with the hive."

"Why would your Carrier do such a thing?"

"We know he had a friend. You would say she was family for him. She was the Carrier killed in your hospital morgue."

"Why would he wage a battle against his kind or mine?"

"We are not sure what he is doing. We have traced the events to 1965. Now, we believe he has breached the Sidron, without authorization. That is a crime. We also believe there is something in Dr. Sheldon's treatise, which will prove most valuable and give us answers regarding both, the Sidron event and the transporting of your visitors."

"Well, Jack is a treasure of ideas; that is for sure." Bellos thought a moment. "Interesting . . . I need to know now, any history you have, very quickly. Tell me about the lineage of Marion Brock."

"We will transfer what we have, but we doubt it is more detailed than that which is available to you already. Please have a seat."

The Tyree Master began inputting facts into the mind of Bellos.

"Your Marion Brock IV inherited his money. Centuries ago, in 1965, Nicolas Edward Brock negotiated the largest ammunition trade in the United States history during the Vietnam conflict. He played both sides of the war, selling to the Chinese and Western powers. Both sides killed each other using ammunition from the same source. Over the next 175 years, Brock Finance grew overwhelmingly, evolving and profiting again by supporting the first drone warfare during the surface global terrorist engagements. Then, something unforeseen happened within the family. Power and leadership shifted from male to female, as global politics

changed. In 2160, Marisa Brock invested the family fortune to support the new Nazi movement, which overthrew the genocide of extremist Muslims in Pakistan. She had a son, Marion Brock I, who eventually arranged for her assassination. He stopped selling arms to Pakistan and backed the world movement to wipe out the Nazis. It was a global bloodbath, but the Brocks' gained political and financial power in almost every country."

Bellos was in a light trance state and said, "Some things never change."

Tyree continued, *"That success gave the Brocks the power and monetary support they needed to become the global leader in high-tech arms and ammunition sales. Today, we believe your Marion Brock IV has decided to invest substantial financial support to control events in time, by purchasing Time-Travel Research, Inc."*

"How does Jake Burns relate to Brock?"

"After the power shift in 2160, the matriarch's sister, Ellen Brock, moved from North America to England. She married Zachery Burns, a direct descendant of your Jake Burns."

"That's why Jake and Marion have more than similar genetic make-up."

"Correct. We believe GGM Gordon Swanson found out, quite by chance some time ago, after he met Burns at a weapons convention."

"So," Bellos remarked, "Swanson hired Burns knowing he was related to Brock?"

"Some have said keeping your enemy close is a wise choice."

Bellos interrupted the input. "But Burns is not our enemy. He is an Ever-Life citizen, not to mention our colonies' Security Chief."

"Correct, and as it turns out, he, like Brock, is compatible with us. Ages ago, before our treaties with humanity, many of our kind rebelled, because of the power that compatibilities brought."

"We don't have those records," Bellos said, "and I wasn't made aware of that. If true, all of Ever-Life is in danger from your rogue Carrier. We could have a war for the first time in our history and, even more dreadful, a timeline shift."

"Correct. That is why I am here."

Bellos thought as only a GGM can. And even the Carriers can not follow or monitor his faster than light speed deducing. "I need to get to the Great Pyramid of Giza before we go to the Post-2 station drop. You need to get me inside. Is that a problem?"

"The entire pyramid is still quite insulated, but we should have no problem."

"You know as well as I, that part of the Pyramids' functioned as batteries, eons ago. I am hoping there are shadows of those battery markers still preserved in certain magnetic frequency echoes. Those may give us some clues. Tell me why you have allowed yourself to be seen like this? Sir Thomas, in the other room will not forget you."

"It is time; and, he is witness to our sincerity. Also, we could not prevent these Sidron events which have upset the space-time continuum. We all must work together and that includes allowing certain humans to know about our Tyree Masters. Our Primary Grand Carriers acknowledge the human wherewithal's have evolved. We will not show ourselves without your permission, which you gave before I appeared to the Drs Sheldon...

...Also, my GGM, I am instructed to tell you that we must postpone our Grand Council meeting with you until this matter is resolved. I will interface with you and the surface as is appropriate. Trust remains a significant issue. We recognize the need to approach the surface; and, regardless of their consistent warlike behavior, they are progressing to the point of space-time and interplanetary travel. We need to educate and establish boundaries. We have much to investigate. The Sidron events are alarming, especially if one of us has used surface men in a Compatibility. It generates many questions."

The Tyree Master then turned and absorbed into the Carrier's wall. Allenfar swam faster than a guided missile, across inner earth's ocean of heat, to the great pyramids of Egypt.

CHAPTER 48:   MARSHALL DECISION

EARLY THE NEXT MORNING, at the Arden City courthouse, Brian Sheldon sat with Angie Bellos in the right-side back row of courtroom 210. The jury began seating to read the verdict for David Marshall, who was arrested regarding the murder in the Andrews' morgue months ago. The charges against him included one count of conspiracy to commit murder, another count of conspiracy to commit a terrorist attack against the Brock/Swanson Complex, and five counts of aggravated battery during his stay in the Arden City jail.

"I thought your dad didn't want you here, Angie," said Brian.

"I had to come. You know I hate this guy. Besides, I wanted to be with you. I only wish your mom could be here."

"Yeah, me too. I got a message from her that she went to Washington, D.C. on some last-minute jaunt to a convention or something. I guess my dad couldn't go."

"Shush, it's the bailiff.

"Hear ye hear ye; all rise . . ."

"Okay, Brian, here we go."

The bailiff continued, "This 3rd District Court of Arden Township is now in session. The Honorable Pamela E. Wills, presiding."

The judge walked into the courtroom from her chambers behind her elevated mahogany bench. She stepped up, sat down and looked out over the courtroom.

"You may all be seated. Today, after much time and effort, I would like to thank both the prosecution and the defense for their exhaustive and thorough handling of this case. Madame Forewoman, has the jury reached its verdict?"

The woman stood up and replied, "Yes, we have, your honor."

She handed an envelope to the bailiff, who gave it to the judge. Judge Wills read it and then handed it back to the bailiff.

"I never understood this part," Brian whispered to Angie. "Why doesn't she just read the damn thing out loud?"

Angie placed her hand on his. "Protocol, Brian, you know about that. Be patient."

"Madame Forewoman," said Wills, "you may read the verdict."

"We, the jury, in the matter of case 51269. The State of New Mexico vs. David J. Marshall, do hereby unanimously declare:

Regarding count one: Conspiracy to murder Dr. Jack Avuar Sheldon, we find in favor of the State, and we do judge Mr. David J. Marshall guilty as charged.

Regarding count two...."

At that instant, Brian Sheldon leaped to his feet and screamed, "Yes! You son-of-a-bitch! Yes! Woohoo!"

Brian's outburst stopped the reading. All eyes focused on his rant. Angie pulled at him, trying to get him to sit down.

"Order in the court! Order in the court!" the judge yelled. "Bailiff, remove that man!"

"Wait! No!" Brian suddenly realized his wrongful behavior. "I have to hear the rest. Angie, no!"

Two police guards grabbed Brian and forcibly escorted him out through the courtroom's double-doors. Angie followed behind them, watching the guards push and prod him out of the building and down onto the concrete steps. She ran to Brian and grabbed his arm helpfully. "What did you think you were doing for heaven's sake?"

He got up, brushing himself off. "Releasing months of cooped-up anger and satisfying my need to kill that bastard."

"Well, that worked, didn't it? Now what?"

"Now we celebrate, if you're up to it. What do you say?"

"It is 10 o'clock in the morning. How do you plan on celebrating?"

"Hmm, right, I guess. But that felt so great."

Brian rolled his eyes and sat back down on the steps. Angie started to sit down next to him when it happened. Brian stared wide-eyed at her and blinked in disbelief. He shook his head, trying to focus. He grabbed her, but his arms went through her. Just as they made eye contact, Angie cried out, "Brian; my God! What is happening?"

Her whole body appeared to flicker, her image blurred, and then, she was gone, just vanished. Brian jumped up, twisting and turning, reaching for her. "WTF!? Angie! Where the hell are you?

As he looked around, he saw someone running out of the courthouse and yelled to him, "Hey, you! Help me here! It's an emergency!"

The man stopped and yelled back, "I can't! Something just happened in the courtroom. Wait a minute, I remember you. You are the ranting idiot they kicked out."

They both started walking toward each other, talking at the same time.

"I'm Randy Farrell, a reporter for the Daily Gazette. I know you. Your friend the convict, he just vanished in the courtroom, not two minutes ago, gone; just like that. I have never seen anything like it! It was unbelievable. They are all in a panic in there, everyone, including the judge. And she's holding everybody until it's sorted out. I was in the back and slipped out before they noticed. You were lucky."

Farrell turned to go, but Brian grabbed his shoulders. "My girlfriend just vanished out here, right before my eyes on these steps, right there . . ."

"Holy shit! Both of them at the same time?" Farrell collected his thoughts. "I videoed the whole scene in there. I've got to get back to the office to study it."

"We should take the video to the police," said Brian.

"Bullshit! They have cameras all over the courthouse. Good luck!"

Farrell turned and ran across the street. Brian tried to call his father, but the phone displayed *no signal*; so, he ran to the parking garage to his car.

And where was Angie? She zapped, transported to inside a time anomaly from another Sidron event. For her, in a blink, it was hours earlier...

The rising sun was beginning to burn the haze away from the Arden morning sky. Angie Bellos rustled in her bed, fighting off the covers. She popped up, throwing the covers back onto Brian, who was naked next to her, snoring. She was drenched in sweaty wet clothes that clung to her body.

"Oh, my God!" she yelled in a whisper, feeling and pulling at her clothing. "What the hell just happened?

Angie ran to the bathroom, threw cold water on her face and looked in the mirror. "Yes, it's me alright. These are the clothes I wore at the courthouse."

She turned around and looked at her bed. "Brian? Why are you here? Christ, how did I get here? This is insane!"

She tiptoed to the window, drew back the curtains and looked out at the rising sun. Then, she looked at the clock on the nightstand. Confused and disoriented, she pulled a Knofer out of her pants pocket. "Shit! This can't be right. The clock on that table says 4 am ."

She brought the Knofer close to her lips and whispered, "Confirm time and day."

The Knofer immediately displayed a 3D model, which read 10:15 a.m., U.S.A. Mountain Time, Ever-Life record, Tuesday, November 12, Arden,

New Mexico. She also noticed something else. At the bottom of the Knofer display, red letters blinked the words, *Defense Mode, stage 1.*

"That can't be good." Then, Angie began to shake involuntarily. She sat down in the chair next to the window and placed her hands over her face, sobbing, confused and trying to gather herself, when, suddenly, she felt two hands on her shoulders lifting her.

"Hey, you, what's wrong? Are you okay?"

She looked up to see a naked Brian Sheldon standing before her. He took her in his arms and hugged her. "Come on, babe, don't cry. You're all wet; why are you shaking?" Brian rubbed her back. "Why are you dressed in these wet clothes?"

Then, he released her enough that they could see each other face to face. Angie looked deeply into his eyes and felt paralyzed at the moment. Brian caressed her cheek, and as they fixed on each other, he kissed her tenderly. They both felt the warmth of the moment and each held on to the other. Angie felt the shaking stop, replaced by her heart rate pounding. Brian pulled her into him tightly. He opened his eyes and held her chin as they separated. Then, he took her hand and led her over to the bed. She was shocked to see him naked, but she followed him and sat beside him.

"Brian, I . . ."

"No," he said. "Not a word this time. Let's get you out of these wet things."

Angie was numb and limp. She didn't speak, as Brian peeled off her top, then her skirt and shoes. "There, that's better. You're not shaking anymore."

"Brian, is it really you?"

He giggled and kissed her again, pushing her back down on the bed. "Yes, darlin', I'm the same guy you made love with last night."

"What? Wait a minute." Angie pushed back and stood up.

"You know, babe, naked and serious somehow don't quite go together. Look at me," he gestured with a smile.

Angie stared and shook her head. She felt the shaking start again and turned her back to him. "Brian, something is wrong, dead wrong! Something has happened. We have to talk. And I'm serious!"

She went to the closet and opened the door. There were two white bathrobes, so she threw one at Brian. "Turn on the TV, will you? Put on the news."

"Okay . . ."

They both watched the monitor as local newscaster Parker Phillips announced, "Good morning, Arden, it's 4:16 a.m. and our skies look like they are going to clear nicely for the Marshall verdict today."

"Brian, do you have a Knofer?"

"What? My phone is on the table."

"Oh, my God, look at the time on the screen." Angie grabbed Brian's phone from the nightstand and studied it. Shit! It says 4:18 a.m. too, same time. Brian; we have to get to the courthouse!"

"Why? What are you talking about? Um, we should be asleep. The verdict is hours from now."

Angie stood fixed. "Brian, it's really after 10 am, and we already saw and heard the verdict. Oh, my God!"

She pushed Brian on the bed again. "Brian, listen, something is not right with all this. Here, look at my Knofer. This thing says 10:32 am . How could that be?"

Brian took the Knofer, read it and said sarcastically, "It must be on Ever-Life time. Who cares?"

Angie paced and asked, "Okay, tell me, what is our relationship?"

Brian chuckled, "Come on, babe. We love each other. We've been living together for four months."

"Brian, I hate to tell you this. Don't freak out. But I don't think I am your Angie."

...At precisely the same time as Angie was captured within the anomaly, across town in the Arden City jail, prisoner Dave Marshall awoke on his cot in a 6-foot by 9-foot jail-cell. He was soaked in sweat and shaking in his green prison night garb...

"My God! My God!" he cried. Rushing to the small mirror hanging on the concrete wall, he studied his reflection. "It works! Shit! It works. Son-of-a-bitch!"

Marshall gathered his senses and turned, examining the room. "But this isn't right. It's my jail cell. I'm supposed to be out, not back in here."

He stumbled to the jail bars and grabbed on tight, screaming, *"BROCK!"*

...Back in Angie's part of the anomaly, in Brian's apartment...

Brian showered, and Angie recounted her morning to him as she sat in her bathrobe on the toilet. When he shut the water off, she reached inside, handed him his robe, and he stepped out.

"Your turn, girl, go on. You need a washing more than I do."

"Fine." The shower's warmth calmed and soothed Angie; and, while Brian dried, he talked, "So, what do you suggest, my sweet?"

Angie spoke while using a washcloth. "At a time like this, I wish I had more headset sessions. Ever-Life taught me that the more I have, the more memories lock. There has got to be something explaining a situation like this."

"What are you talking about? I was never an Ever-Life candidate. You know that. It was the CPT and our dads' friendship that brought us together. So, I don't understand headset this, headset that . . ."

Angie turned off the shower, put her robe on again, and stepped out. She plopped on the edge of the bed. "Shit! Shit! Shit!"

"That sounds very productive," Brian chuckled. "I know this might sound silly, but you say that Knofer is in *defensive mode*, do you remember any of the protocols?"

Angie rolled her eyes and shook her head. "I think we have to get back to the courthouse."

"Why?"

"I'm not sure. I had a conversation with a man in a hospital bed last night, or whenever. His name was Wheeler, and he said things that seemed ridiculous to me then, that I was in danger. Nothing registered then. Now, this?"

"I don't know who you talked to? You're very confusing. You are not in Oz. What you need is an attitude adjustment."

"I need to talk to Mr. Wheeler again."

"And, if anything you say is true, where is my Angie? God, as if we haven't been through enough. Anyone else would think that you are a raving lunatic."

"No! Brian, listen. Something or someone has done this. I don't know why or how."

Brian saw the determination in her eyes. He cupped her face and kissed her on the cheek. "You are not even dressed. Fine. I'll do anything you say; just calm down. You're going to have a heart attack."

They hugged, and after a few seconds, Brian spoke softly, "Angie, do you think I'm a ghost, or maybe a figment of your imagination?"

"No. I don't know." She talked as she quickly dressed. "What I've told you is the truth. You know I am the daughter of a GGM. I am not crazy. You know what both of us went through before, for God's sake."

"Yes, I remember. You don't think anything like that is happening again; do you?"

They fixed on each other's gaze.

"I don't know. What if? Brian, I think the sooner we get the Knofer to trigger, the better off we are both going to be."

Just then, a squeaky beep startled Angie.

"Speak of the devil; it's coming from your Knofer over there."

Angie picked it up, only to feel intense heat. Instinctively, she threw it on the bed. "Jesus! That hurt. Am I burned? Maybe it's over-charged or something. It shouldn't be that hot."

Then, the Knofer again bellowed a very low-pitched noise, and the couple watched, as the silver unit began projecting a blue triangular light up to the ceiling. Within seconds, it sculpted a life-sized hologram of Sir Thomas Wheeler.

"That's the guy! That's the man I talked to last night!"

When the Knofer finished, Wheeler's image stood by the bed. He was wearing an Ever-Life doctor's coat, glasses, pants, and shoes. But the Knofer wasn't done. It began to fill in the 3D image, and Wheeler became a solid model. After several minutes, the Knofer released the model, enabling him to move and speak independently, as an average person.

Wheeler's hologram looked at both Angie and Brian, and after studying them for a moment, he focused on Angie. "Hello, child."

"Oh, my God!" Brian said. "What are you? How did you get here?"

Angie grabbed Brian's arm. "No! Wait! He is a friend. I remember my mom was like you. Hi, hello, Mr. Wheeler, I just saw you last night, remember?"

"Yes, Angie, hi, except he was flesh and bone. I am here, as your defense guide. At present, your protocol only requires me to advise, and see if we can't remedy your situation."

"Well, in that case, thank you.? Can you tell us exactly what my situation is? What did happen?"

Wheeler turned, scrutinizing the room. "You two better sit down for this."

Angie leaned onto the bed and picked up her Knofer. "Do I have to leave this out?"

Wheeler looked out the window at the sunrise. "There is no more beautiful sight. No, that's alright, you can put it away, but leave 'record' open."

He turned around and began to describe the event.

"I remind you that your Knofer has a record of all knowledge, Angie. Your father has authorized these defense protocols. I am your link to those protocols." He smiled kindly. "There is no reason to fear anything yet. So, relax, we will fix this."

Angie and Brian looked at one another.

"But," Brian said. "If this isn't my Angie, where is she? Who is this? And, where am I?"

"Brian, you are you, and she is she, Angie is Angie. We are all who we seem to be but split. Consider her a sort of mirror image, if that helps, but not a reverse image."

"You mean I'm a reflection?"

Brian stood up and walked several steps. "Or, are you both reflections; or am I?"

Angie sat up disturbed and uncomfortable. "What? I know I am real?"

She and Brian locked eyes as Wheeler spoke, "Listen carefully, you two. Reflection is just a word to help you. You are both very real. The laws of physics regarding space-time and matter can be easily understood, or very complicated. Let's just say, Angie, you ran into something that bumped you into a different room."

"So, where's my Angie. She has got to be freaking out?" said Brian.

Wheeler didn't skip a beat with his reply, "She is in the other room."

"Whoa!" Brian said. "So, we are in an alternate universe or something?"

Wheeler watched, as a confused Brian sat on the bed; so, he tried to explain again, "No, not at all; are you both familiar with the phrase, 'My heart skipped a beat'?"

"Yes," they nodded.

"Well, you are between beats of time. You are not moving in time. You are stuck in a *time anomaly*. This particular one is an event out of control."

Angie and Brian wore blank expressions.

"I know," said Wheeler's hologram, "it is very technical. I am here to help you correct this and to prevent you from staying here any longer than you have to. We must prevent you from causing the Knofer to advance to the next defense level. That could create a permanent separation in the physics of it all."

Brian wasn't impressed, "Oh, that's clear, thanks. What the hell are you saying?"

"It appears someone has decided to try to use time travel but doesn't understand the ramifications. You are both equally real, and you can be as you were, if you follow my instructions."

"Yes, of course," Angie said.

"Yeah, fine, but it sounds stupid," scoffed Brian.

"That is because you want me to explain things." Wheeler smiled and said calmly, "Now, you have to return to the point of origin, where the anomaly triggered, to prevent it in the first place."

Angie asked nervously, "You want us to go back to the courthouse?"

"Yes, to the point of origin, the doorway out of the anomaly."

"And I should do what?"

"You must find the particular place and go back through the door."

"Well, that certainly sounds simple enough, right, Angie?"

"What? How do I do that, and what if I can't?"

"In that case, *I* will return you to your father."

Brian cocked his head, "What is the catch?"

Wheeler answered, "The catch is I am your Knofer, Angie. I am now in *defense mode 2*. Therefore, my priority is you, no one else, no one here. If I initiate the next level protocol, the response has no regard for others, and it may leave a scar on the time anomaly.

"What will happen to Brian?"

"No one can say. No one can come back here to find out. If I were Brian's Knofer, no one could say what would happen to you either."

"My God," Brian said. "Where is my Angie? Is she in the same situation somewhere else? Is her Knofer telling her the same thing?

"Wheeler nodded slightly, "Actually it does not work that way. Angie is fine. My explanations may leave you more confused than I intend. The mirror analogy is merely to enable you to have some comprehension of the concept that all things exist at the same time. Truth be told, there are countless possibilities of where your Angie could be. Perhaps this may help. If I say something to five people, what I said is now in five new places, five new heads. Think of the anomaly as a new location, one of many, a new head, so to speak."

"Oh, yeah, I got it now. That makes it much clearer." Brian rolled his eyes out of frustration.

But the hologram ignored Brian's feelings. "I am instructing you in understanding this. I am coaching you on what to do. My interference is a last resort. It is necessary to bring Ms. Bellos home and correct the anomaly."

Brian and Angie let out a slow nervous sigh. Angie looked at the clock and then Wheeler. "How do we do this, when court isn't even at the same time it was where I came from?"

"Get into the courthouse. Use your Knofer, that's me. I can do many things, including opening locks. Command it to sense the point of origin. The fact that I am in *defense mode;* Level 2 has activated many security features, but you have to be within the correct distance. I have reset to try to sense the anomaly's vibration. You must use me to examine the room in which it occurred."

Angie thought and said, "I don't know which room to find in the first place. The last thing I remember is the stairs outside."

"That is the challenge. I function within a particular range. Your Knofer will find the *sweet spot*, that is the door through which you must enter. If it's within range, you simply dive in."

"*Sweet spot*, what exactly is a *sweet spot*?"

"Look for a moving blur perhaps, or a sphere, something out of the ordinary in a familiar landscape."

Angie raised her eyebrows. "So, I see it, or don't see what I should, the Knofer confirms, I dive in, and everything is fixed."

"Yes, well, there is one thing," Wheeler squinted a bit. "If anything, or anyone else touches the *sweet spot*, even inadvertently, before you get to it, it will close. They will be caught in their own separate new anomaly, and you will be here permanently, cycling repeatedly, and so on. It will go on and on, repeating the same time-period, over and over. New anomalies can continue to appear outside your original timeline. Unfortunately, this one has triggered because of compatible genetics, and I think because of another Sidron event. Regardless, the domino effect is quite unfathomable."

"Give me an example of a trigger."

"Even if the trigger were a bug or a large enough dust particle, an anomaly can reproduce. You are the key, Angie. With your input alone the anomaly will reverse, eliminating the perversion."

"Huh. Well that sounds simple, right?" Angie looked at Brian, taking it all in. Then, she tapped her Knofer and Wheeler disappeared. She picked it up and threw Brian his coat.

"Let's go."

"Yeah, no time like the present," said Brian. "A piece of cake. Who cares what happens to me?"

...While all that was going on within Angie's anomaly, outside her anomaly...

Back at the Arden City courthouse, Brian Sheldon made it to his car, shocked and scared about what happened to Angie and Marshall. While driving, he turned on the radio and heard the news confirming Marshall had disappeared; but the media were broadcasting that it was an escape from jail. There was a three-state alert, roadblocks, and he heard helicopter engines in the sky. Brian repeatedly called his father but got no answer. Finally, after countless times, Jack answered. He and Abby Johnson were in mid-flight on another private jet to Washington, D.C. to find Rachel.

"Hello, Brian; son, where are you?"

"Dad, thank God!"

"What's wrong?"

"Dad, Angie is gone, vanished! And Dave Marshall escaped from jail."

"Just slow down, son. What are you talking about?"

"Angie and I were at the courthouse. They found Marshall guilty! As we were leaving, walking down the stairs outside, I watched her. Angie just disappeared. Believe it or not, her body began to pulse, blink in and out. She vibrated, blurred and then just vanished. That's it. I talked to some news guy running to his car, and he said that Dave Marshall also disappeared, inside the courthouse, too. Dad, what should I do?"

"Put your phone on speaker...She disappeared? That's silly, son. People do not just disappear. Where are you?"

"I'm in my car now, in the parking lot across from the courthouse."

"So, this all happened how long ago?" asked Jack.

"Yes...about a half hour ago."

Jack put his hand on the phone because Johnson began talking. "Jack, I bet your son is describing a Sidron event. Can he tell us specifically where it happened?"

Jack spoke into his phone, "Brian, I have Abby Johnson here from security at the Complex."

"Hi, Brian," said Abby.

"Hello."

"It's all going to be alright. I just need to ask some questions if that's okay with you. Can you tell me where the disappearances took place? Be as precise as you can."

Brian's voice trembled a bit. "I saw her disappear on the steps outside, about halfway down to the street. We were talking and then, poof! Minutes later, I spoke to a reporter, who ran out of the courthouse a few seconds after Angie vanished; and he said the same thing happened to Dave Marshall in Room 210. But I don't know exactly where he was."

Abby thought a moment and said, "Listen, Brian, I need you to do me a favor. Can you go back into the courthouse and ask one of the courthouse staff? Or, if you find a court reporter, find someone who witnessed the event? I need to know precisely where Mr. Marshall was too. Can you do that?"

Jack became arguably defensive. "Christ, Johnson, he is my son, not a trained cop."

Abby was quick to jester and whisper to Jack, "This could be the break we need to find out about the cause of the Sidron events. Trust me, Jack."

Jack spoke into the phone, "Brian, I know this is asking a lot, but I need you to try and do this."

"Fine, I'll get back to you."

Jack fidgeted and replied, "love you, son; good luck."

"Yeah, thanks. Love you too."

CHAPTER 49: HELLO, MARION

ONE LONE KNOFER TICKED on the desk in a small plush office setting, and the provocative billionaire Marion Brock pondered whether to answer it or just see how long it would tick. Finally, he tapped the Knofer and sat back to see what would happen. As a life-sized holographic image grew before his eyes, Brock marveled at the technology it took to create such a masterpiece of communication.

"Hello, Marion," the image said. "Did you forget about me?"

Brock smiled in his sinister way; and, with an evil twinkle in his eye, spoke calmly and eloquently. "Mr. David Marshall, my connoisseur of the Arden jail. No, I don't forget the most important people in my life. But I didn't know you had one of these little toys."

"Yes; it's an insurance policy of sorts. I still have friends down below. I have several of these toys, not including the ones I gave you. But, as you know, those can't trace any calls. Yours and mine are special. They are linked."

"Fascinating. What can I do for you?"

"For starters, you can tell me why I'm still in jail? The time-boost was supposed to push me forward, out of here. I am still at the courthouse, and it's this morning again."

"Yes, well, frankly, we don't know yet. You see, everything was correctly programmed, but it took you back. I hope you didn't suffer side effects."

"Thank you for restating the obvious . . . Side effects? I have been sweating like a faucet. I was unable to speak for over an hour."

"Hmm . . . David, David, do keep calm. We knew there was something wrong when you didn't show up in the chamber. Our people are on it. We will talk later. Just bear with all of this for just a little while longer. You can do that, David. I have the utmost confidence in you."

"Don't patronize me, Brock. I have no intention of sitting in a six by nine cell for the rest of my life. I mean it!"

"My, my, I'll chock that comment up to side effects. Remember, my friend; I am more interested in the time travel chamber operating correctly than I am in keeping you in jail. You are my proof that Time Travel, Inc. is a success. So, relax, be patient. Enjoy the free food and solace."

Brock smiled sarcastically. Then, he cut the call and looked at the Knofer, "I'm going to prove that I can conquer you and your Mr. GGM, himself."

Just then, Brock's cell phone next to the Knofer rang.

"Yes, hello."

"Mr. Brock, hello. This is Stevens at the Time-Travel Inc Lab."

"Yes, Stevens, I was just going to call you about the Marshall test this morning."

"That's why I'm calling you, sir. There was an event; we think; sort of."

"You mean he didn't go forward? He went back in time. I know."

"No, I mean Mr. Marshall didn't go forward or back in time. He shifted off our timeline completely, something to do with the equipment, I think. There is now a separate anomaly just hanging out there. It was quite by accident. We are gathering data. I have no explanation for the cause yet. Our readings indicate it is a net of repeating time, operating much like an old merry-go-round. Also, there was another person affected when we triggered the test."

"Oh, for God's sake, Stevens! Can you speak English? Can we get Marshall out or not?"

"Frankly, I'm not sure. There is another variable now, the other person."

"Who is it?"

"We are trying to get a fix, but the person is not stationary. We cannot identify who it is until he or she stays put long enough. Sir, this changes a few perceptions."

"*Perceptions*? What the hell are you talking about?"

"It means the cycle of time within that anomaly will repeat, but the events may change. Time may have taken on a mind of its own."

"For God's sake, Stevens! Damn it! Tell me so I understand!"

"Sir, there are two people from our time stuck in the anomaly. They are David Marshall and one other person from the courthouse. Each went back several hours. They are stuck repeating that period, but the events within that timeframe may be different. The people may not even realize they are living the same hours. The longer they are caught in it, the stronger the likelihood they won't get out. They will live the two to three hours over and over again; never moving into the future or living with anyone else but those they are with during those hours."

"Shit!" Brock sat for a moment, and his expression changed. He thought, *why what a fabulous place for Mr. Marshall!*

Stevens broke Brock's concentration, "The fact is, this couldn't have happened if Marshall was captured alone. We think it's the other person attached to the program who overloaded it, causing the anomaly."

"Okay, I think. Can you fix it?"

"I am not sure. It would be a lot simpler if I could talk to David directly, but that would be impossible."

Brock said, "Can we set up a new test? Would that be faster?"

"Probably, but we can't just leave two people in a time anomaly lost forever."

"Wait a minute, Stevens, if what you say is true, how is it possible that I got a call from Mr. Marshall not 10-minutes ago? He described the event and his side effects!"

Brock listened to silence, and then Stevens spoke urgently, "Sir, there is no way Marshall can communicate with anyone outside the anomaly. It is physics, sir, impossible! Unless that is . . ."

"Unless, that is, what?"

"Unless you, sir, are somehow also linked to the event."

Brock's eyes bulged, and he thought, *Marshall said the same word, linked.*

"Fine, Stevens, just shut up a minute. Let me think. Have you heard from InVoy? Does he have the rest of the notes yet?" As he held the cell phone to his ear, Brock looked back down at the Knofer, and then suddenly stood up nervously, whispering to himself, *"It can't be."*

"Sir . . . Mr. Brock," Stevens asked anxiously, "are you there?"

Brock regained his composure and listened to Stevens.

"Sir, we have to address this immediately. If you talked to David, we need to examine you right away. Is there anything unusual happening mainly electronic or magnetic where you are?"

Brock could not stop staring at the Knofer. He squinted and shrugged, "Just the phone. Other than that? No, not really. I'm not sure."

"Well. The link triggers by some electrical impulse. So, first, I advise that you discontinue use of anything that requires an impulse, including this phone. You should turn it off and come here to me, *immediately.*"

Brock looked at his cell phone first, and then, with a fearful frown, he reached and picked up the Knofer, turning and examining it, thinking, *how do I turn you off, my little jewel.* "Stevens, what you are saying is unavoidable. Everything from car batteries to my airplanes generates electrical impulses...?"

Brock stopped and raised his head, as if he had an epiphany. He whispered to himself, "Marshall; you're a sneaky son-of-a-bitch."

"Sir," Stevens said, "I don't want to frighten you, but that is why you need to be here. I can only secure you here . . ."

"Yes, fine."

". . . And one other matter, sir. I received a call from the guard at the warehouse south of Seattle. Something bizarre has appeared in the silo. I instructed the men to secure it until I talked to you."

"What! And?"

"It appears to be a gigantic fish, sir."

Brock grinned a bit and thought to himself, *Well, Mr. GGM, I guess we have one of your little pets.* "Who knows about this, Stevens?"

"The men at the warehouse, me, and now you. I really must insist. Come to me immediately, sir."

"Send me the coordinates of the warehouse."

Brock cut the call. He had been in deep seclusion for over eight months. All that time, he was extremely careful whom he saw, and disciplined to travel only with his most trusted bodyguards. They were confidants, counselors and handled most of his private affairs, while he controlled top priorities from his underground hideaway in Vancouver. He developed many new interests as a ghost investor, buying huge land bundles and sea rights from foreign countries. He limited his travel, only flying to Time-Travel Inc. when necessary. Brock's pet investment was supporting OPAS through a shadow foundation to keep his name off their books. He secretly bought their old particle accelerator landscape, south of Seattle; and, when his team had reached its intelligence limit, he pirated Hamill Stevens from OPAS to complete his time project. Rash InVoy, his Chief of Staff, managed most of his other worldwide affairs.

So, after talking to Marshall and Stevens, Brock called his trusted bodyguard to make flight arrangements. He turned off his cell phone, picked up the Knofer and walked out of his office, wearing an inconspicuous tan suit and dark glasses. He proceeded down the private staircase, four floors to the parking garage. As he opened the stairwell door, his guard, Briggs, escorted him into the black stretch limo and drove him to one of five special corporate airlifts for the short flight to Seattle and the fish waiting for him.

CHAPTER 50: SEMITRI

INSIDE A REMOTE WAREHOUSE, some 50 miles south of Seattle, two security guards crouched in front of the double entrance door, which connected the warehouse to an old missile silo. An unbearably loud screeching inside the silo continued to render both of them helpless. When the noise stopped, the guards took their hands from their ears, got up, and rushed through the doors into the silo. Both of them stopped, frozen, on the edge of the ramp, which overlooked the precipice; and each stared wide-eyed down at a 100-foot tall, steel-blue colored Carrier transforming before their eyes. The wet looking fish-like creature, which they had tied against the silo's walls an hour ago, was not just a Carrier, it was a Grand Carrier, capable of time travel; and it was no longer passive and quiet. It was alert and obviously angry. They watched it morphing into a horrific thick snake, over 10-feet in diameter. As the Carrier reduced in thickness, the chains around it fell to the silo's floor.

"Holy shit! What the hell is going on?" said Guard-1.

"Damn if I know," said Guard-2.

"Get the chain extender!" Yelled Guard-1.

"Screw you! I'm out of here!" said Guard-2, as he turned and ran back through the doors and down the hallway, leaving his partner stunned.

Guard-1 heard a hiss behind him. In an instant, the guard reached for his revolver. He stepped backward and pointed the gun, but the snake was too fast, a blur of speed. It darted past him; splintered the double doors after Guard-2; and then, it sped past Guard-2 stopping directly in front of the running man. Guard-2 stopped, almost diving into the snake's mouth. He stood shaking, red-faced, and unable to move. The snake reared its head back, and, with one sweeping motion, its dragon-like mouth engulfed and swallowed the screaming guard.

Then, out of the corner of its eye, the animal saw sunlight shining, creeping toward him through the windows that lined the outer walls across the central warehouse area. The beast snapped back and recoiled again. In one unbelievably fast motion, it raced back through the splintered doors and swallowed up Guard-1, on its way back down into the dark bottom of the silo.

Twenty minutes later, a gray stretch limousine pulled up to the outside entrance of the warehouse and parked. The driver got out, opened the rear door, and Marion Brock stepped from the dark interior onto the sidewalk. He placed his hand on the driver's shoulder and spoke cordially. "Thanks, Briggs. Quiet here, isn't it?"

"Yes, sir, that it is. Should I wait for you?"

"Yes, please. And Briggs, notify InVoy that I've arrived at the site. Tell him I'm surprised. It appears I am the only one here."

"Yes, sir."

Brock walked around the landscape outside. Fifty years ago, this was his family's Pacific coast ammunition site. As he unlocked the front door, his phone rang and he said, "Hello?"

"Sir, Stevens here. I beg your pardon. I thought you were coming directly to me."

"Stevens, you can be a pain in my ass. I am going to make sure all is well here first. I don't see any guards, by the way."

"Sir, there were two assigned. Perhaps they are in the silo. Regardless, you must come here! Please?"

"Well, that's not going to happen. You work for me, you know. I'll check this out and get there when I can."

Brock cut the call, walked into the huge warehouse and yelled, "Hello! Hello!" His voice echoed. "Christ, what the hell? Hello!"

He walked across the empty building and stepped over the splintered double doors leading to the silo. He stopped to pick up a cap and shoe. And just then, he heard a loud strange squeal coming from deep within the silo. It was the snake with a head at least 10-ft wide. It slithered up to Brock, and its eyes focused on his. Brock was terrified and unable to move. Some force he never felt before was holding him still. "*Mother of God!*" he said.

The snake moved around the perimeter of the hallway and coiled, wrapping himself so Brock was in the center of the coils. Then the snake opened his dragon-like mouth, and Brock smelled the death of the guards. Brock winced at the razor-sharp orange teeth. Then, the snake lowered its head and calmly closed its mouth. Staring at Brock's terrified face, and with a nod, the snake released Brock's invisible binding and watched as Brock staggered, looking for a way to escape, but there was nowhere to run.

"Christ! What the hell are you? asked Brock terrified.

The snake looked deeply into Brock's eyes. It seemed to smile and said, *"Hello Mr. Marion Brock. It was wrong of you to think you could bind me here. Do you not know what you see?"*

"No, I do not know what I see." Brock spun around again in a panic, studying the great beast and looking for a way out. "How is it that you speak? Shit!"

The snake replied, *"I am Semitri. Do you want me to help you?"*

After a moment of trying to calm down, Brock said as he shook "You are the beast?"

"I am Semitri. I was not to be tied or restrained in any way."

Brock watched the snake's coils begin to change. Semitri's coils merged and they solidified into pearl white walls surrounding Brock. Within seconds, the billionaire was no longer in the hallway. He was inside the Carrier, Semitri.

"Welcome Marion. I have a surprise for you. Now Mr. Brock, meet yourself."

"What are you talking about? Where am I?"

As he stood in the middle of the white room, Brock watched a door appear and open. It was a clone of Marion Brock who walked toward him.

"Jesus! And why are you here, for God's sake?"

"Hello, Marion, I am he who you sent to get the vials of CPT months ago. Don't you remember?"

"What is this?" Real[R]-Brock said. "Yes, I remember. You are the clone we programmed for that purpose only. You failed and served another purpose for us by being captured by a Carrier. We only programmed you to do specific things, and beyond that you have no abilities, mentally or physically. You don't have the brains or wherewithal to do anything like this."

Clone[C]-Brock replied with his sinister grin, "Yes, of course, you're right. And in that case, how do you suppose I am here and in charge? You are mine now, Mr. Billionaire. You are mine! Ha! Just a clone? Perhaps I was just that, but now I am much much more. Frankly, it's all very simple."

The C-Brock paced around R-Brock and continued, "I have been trapped within this beast since Swanson and Bellos put me here months ago. All this time, I have apparently been feeding it with my sustenance. At least that's what the big guy here told me. But, in return, it fed me too. I have learned a great deal. Have you ever heard of a *Compatibility*?"

"You work for me, you know. Christ, you *are* me!"

"No, actually, I work for me. I have negotiated with our friend here that he can have as much of us as he wants. In return, I run the Brock Empire. You see, by cloning yourself, you opened up a whole new world for both our friend here and me. Semitri and I have made an agreement, a contract, so to speak. The more Brocks I give him, the more sustenance he receives. He will gain unlimited power, and he will continue to give me whatever I want. So, by virtue of my negotiating skills; the good news for you is, he and I have also agreed not to kill you. I believe a thank you is in order; don't you agree?"

C-Brock bowed to R-Brock, snickering sarcastically. R-Brock watched his clone and became more intolerant with each word he heard.

"What do you mean, *he will give you power* and *whatever you want*?"

"Watch! Semitri, please supply standard furniture."

Everything appeared magically, from nothing; and suddenly, Clone-Brock was wearing the same clothes as Real-Brock.

"You see? Sit as you like. Enjoy it all and be thankful, my friend, or should I call you dad...hahaha!"

R-Brock began a rage of behavior. "Christ, how is all this possible? Tell me, you bastard, or so help me you won't live long enough to laugh again."

"Calm down my brother. First things first. The most important thing you must remember is that Semitri here and his buddies suck sustenance out of us, which they consider more than food. You and I have something that, if he can keep absorbing more of it, well; he will be all-powerful to his kind. So, you see, it was inevitable that he will do anything I ask if I just give him a permanent source."

Real[R]-Brock was angry, frustrated, and on the edge of a breakdown. "Source? What source?"

"Why the only source." Clone[C] Brock said. "The source is you. The only original Brock...You! Ha!"

"It'll never work you half a man. We created your kind with limited abilities to perform very specific duties. Once he has me; once he knows me; We will make a better deal."

"I doubt that, Marion. But you go right ahead and try to negotiate...Ha!"

R-Marion felt a pulling sensation as the beast secured him in a captain's lounge-chair, which faced a large screen monitor, from which he could see through Semitri's skin to the outside.

Clone-Brock laughed, while the beast strapped R-Brock ankles and wrists to the chair. "Well, all you have to do is just sit right there like that; and, if you ask for something, he'll give you anything you want."

R-Brock snarled at his clone. "So, you think I'm just going to stay here?"

"There's a catch, I'm afraid." Said Clone[C]-Brock. "You see, your strength is much more intense than mine or any clones' for that matter. Now that you are in that seat, Semitri has no intention of letting you go, especially since you tried to imprison him. To keep your sanity, my brother, I suggest you concentrate on the benefits, that you can have as much of whatever you want as you desire. You will find it is not all bad. I know how much possessions and money mean to you. Count all the money you want, imagine whatever you will, and he will make it appear. Our friend here will take good care of you."

"Why you twit!" R-Brock replied. "You think I will let this happen? I don't control my empire because I'm stupid."

C-Brock walked briskly toward the outer door of Semitri. He waved to R-Brock and said, "He will keep you fat and happy. That is the least I owe you for what you did to me, my brother."

R-Brock yanked at his shackles and turned, looking around the room and yelled, "Release me! Release me you fool. I'll get you for this! I'll get you all for this!"

C-Brock snickered, turned, and walked out of the Carrier into the warehouse.

Semitri moved into the bottom of the silo and spoke calmly to his new visitor, *"So you are, in fact, the great Marion Brock? Welcome! I got to know your clone quite well over the last few months. Impressive, your refusal to quit. We have many things to discuss. Sit, eat, and we will talk."*

With that statement to R-Marion, Semitri released his bindings and like magic, private files about CPT, Jack Sheldon's files on particle displacement, and the furniture in Brock's private office appeared in the room. "You see, Mr. Brock, there are many things that were not shared with your clone. There is much for us to discuss while you are here."

Meanwhile, C-Brock found his way to the limousine, where Briggs waited. "Sir, I was beginning to worry."

C-Brock smiled as Briggs opened the door and reassured him. "All is as it should be."

"Should I take you to Stevens now, sir?"

"Yes, to Stevens; and update me on all issues that you know of."

Briggs closed the doors, started the limo, and sped off to Brock's Time-Travel Inc research base.

Semitri remained in the silo for a time; long enough to educate real-Brock on a few significant issues that he had not transmitted to clone-Brock.

"My dear Brock, in celebration of your arrival, I offer the following video for you to examine and consider as important to your future and, frankly your past, which in this case may be more to the point."

"I see no reason to consider anything you say or do as important to me at all."

"My friend, after we are done, you may find my exchanges more significant than you imagine."

"Try to relax and we begin to share what you will come to know as notes for your plan. Yes, I know what you're thinking because of my evolution in receiving compatibility sustenance from your clone. But it was nothing compared to what I am getting now from you. Please enjoy and remember."

Video setting: Year 2993. Brooklyn N.Y. suburb. Home of Mary and Owen Richfield. Mary was widow of husband and father, Paul Richfield. Mary and her son Owen were moving from their home of 35 years into a more affordable condo in Florida. They lost Paul after he sustained critical wounds in a car accident on the way home from work six months ago.

While Mary was dusting off cartons by the window overlooking their backyard, Owen walked across the attic to the other side from his mom, where a wall of cartons were piled high enough to block the window on that side.

"Jesus, mom, where do I begin. What a mess. I stopped looking through this stuff in my sophomore year in college. Why do we have to move anyway?"

His mother, Mary, replied, "Because we can't afford living here anymore. And, I don't want to live in a snow infested environment. I tried to get us all to Florida years ago. You know how your father was. Now that you're out of school, we are going to a nice warm climate. You can look for a job there. You've been searching here for months with no luck. It's time we have a change. We can both start over." A tear dripped onto her cheek.

Owen talked as he muddled through the boxes. "But, why do we have to go through these boxes. They're filled with crap. Some of these cartons are falling apart. Can't we just throw them out?"

"We kept them all for a reason. Some are from my side of the family, and others are from your father's. Yes, we can throw some out if you don't want them but just look through them, and we can talk and decide quickly."

Owen opened one after the other and complained nothing had tweaked his interest. Then, he lifted a very heavy one from behind one of the tables right next to the far corner of the room.

"Hey, mom! Holy crap! This is heavy. What's in this anyway?"

Mary looked at him and smiled. "You know, I think that's books."

Owen opened the carton and replied, "You're right but....Oh my God! They're all the same. Look." He lifted one out and held it up.

"Oh, my heavens," Mary said. "Let me see that. Bring it here."

Owen walked over and handed it to her.

"My God! Son, do you know what this is?"

Owen read the title as Mary opened the book. "Allenfar? What the hell does that mean?"

Mary thumbed through the pages and said, "This was written by my ancestor, your great, great, great...I don't know how many greats, but one of your grandfathers on my side wrote this. You should read it. It's very good. Keep a copy for yourself."

"Myself? Mom, I only read from holograms or the disks out of the library. You know that. I really have no interest."

"Well, keep a copy anyway. I'll read it."

"They're older than dirt." Owen said with a sarcastic smirk.

Mary opened one of the drawers in a dresser next to her. As she fumbled and focused, she said, " Wait a minute. That reminds me...Yes, here; look here." She pulled out an old family picture album. "Yes, this is it. Look at that. Owen stooped down and looked at one picture she took out. Mary pointed and said, "You see him. That's your great ancestor, Owen the first. I remember your father had these pictures vacuum packed years ago to preserve them. He wanted you to know why we named you Owen. That's him."

"Oh great. Mom, He looks around 10."

"He is, I think; ten or twelve. They lived in Chicago, Illinois, I think. He grew up to be a very important person in the family. And, at that time, he had an uncle named Paul... quite a coincidence."

"These pictures have to be worth something, they're so old."

Mary replied, "Yes they're old, but they're family. We don't give away family. No one would care anyway. Now that book would be different. Why don't you take the rest of them, in that carton, to the New York City Library and see if they'll accept them as gifts."

"Oh, they won't care about these."

"Maybe they will. You never know, son. I've been there when they have *a return day*. People bring books there they've had for years. Maybe they'll take these. Just keep one or two for us."

Owen sighed and replied, "Fine..."
Video ended...

Brock sat questioning the whole thing. "Okay, I watched this. Why do I care?"

Semitri's Tyree Master appeared before Brock. "You and I are joined at the hip, as your kind would say. You give me Compatibility sustenance, and I make your plan happen. But first, you must know much more than you do. I will provide, and you will remember."

Brock said with a furrowed brow, "Why should I listen at all to you?"

"Because my dear Brock, 1] your clone is setting up everything for you, and he doesn't even know it. And 2] you have no choice; that is until we go on our little adventure. And you can't do that until I give you what I am about to give a man of your...wherewithal."

Semitri then moved like a bullet, downward and into the Sidron.

CHAPTER 51: JAKE'S MATE:

JAKE BURNS SAT WITHIN A CARRIER, as it sped through the volcanic ocean of inner Earth toward Seattle Washington and OPAS. He tried not to think about the ride. Instead, he concentrated on the labyrinth of challenges before him. As he studied a few notes, a voice spoke distinctly; and, at the same time, the image of a young woman's face appeared on the Carrier wall.

"Hello, Jake Burns. We meet again."

"Well then, hello again," answered Jake.

"I am Carrier 1111."

Burns did a slight double take and replied, "Alright, yes, our friend Alinflavor told me . . ."

"You mean Allenfar."

"Yes, that's it. He told me we might meet again. He said you and I are *compatible*; that you have a crush on me or something. May I call you Miriam?

"How flattering, but not a crush; yes, you may call me Miriam. I like that name. A Compatibility is quite different from a crush, Jake Burns."

"Well, are you and me, you know, having a thing right now?"

"Yes, whenever you ride in me, we share."

"Well, you see, funny you should say 'share.'" Jake was a bit embarrassed. "I did want to talk with you about that. I mean, we really aren't, are we?"

"I am not sure I understand," said Miriam.

"Okay. It's just that I am not sure how to ask this. I don't mean to be rude. It's just that I need to know what you know. That is to say; I am requesting a *two-way Compatibility*, a real sharing between us."

"We reserve that experience for GGMs alone, as stated in our treaties. Also, there is the issue of genetic code. I may harm you, permanently."

Jake replied, "I have been told I have quite an unusual genetic sequence. I will be okay."

After a moment of silence, Jake noticed part of the Carrier's wall began to play 3D video of his childhood, family, and early career experiences.

Jake was surprised at what he saw. "How did you get these? They are events that had no videos recorded. This is impossible."

"The video you see is your thoughts. I can show you some of mine like this."

Jake watched and said, "There is a great sense of urgency about what I ask. The fact is; I need to know what you know and understand. I am charged with finding a solution to our mystery about the Sidron and the man named Marion Brock."

"My dear Mr Jake, if I input directly into your brain, it would be a great stress; you could possibly die . . ."

Jake took a deep breath. "I have no choice in this. I am willing to take the chance."

Miriam continued, *"When we traveled in time months ago, I experienced our Compatibility and notified our Grand Council Tyree Master. He visited your GGM recently and had conveyed much to him. Our council approved our further interactions with limits. To share beyond their set of boundaries would violate synergistic treaties."*

Jake replied, "We both want the same thing, to correct the Sidron breach and stop Marion Brock."

"My assignment is to stop one of our kind, Semitri, and to return him to the Grand Council. I must find out how and why he is using the Sidron, and why he has allied with a surface man. He has already figured out a way to prevent our hive mentality from knowing what he is doing. You may ask your questions, Jake Burns, and watch the walls. That is our offer."

The wall video changed and began playing a detail of the shooting in the Andrews morgue from eight months ago.

Jake talked as he watched the video. "I investigated this murder. If I hadn't been the detective on site, I wouldn't be here now with you."

Miriam narrated as the video played. *"Months ago, three of your doctors and a girl were inside Carrier Room 2210. The Carrier was female. She lined the walls of the morgue room. The bullets from the guns fired that morning are what killed that Carrier. Afterward, Carrier 2211, who is Semitri, had taken Marion Brock and a clone of Angela Bellos for rehabilitation. The girl expired. Semitri dropped off our tracking ability, and he hasn't communicated since. It is not unusual that we rehabilitate members of colonies in solitude. However, it has been much too long. Our kind is very comfortable with periods of isolation; and, right now, we have 263 Ever-Life convicts undergoing rehabilitation, within correctional Carriers."*

"Why haven't you shared that fact with us before now?"

"We do, with the GGM, when it's appropriate. In your case, you don't share every human discourse with us, either. By treaty, we were responsible for rehabilitating Marion Brock. You are to be notified, only if

the rehabilitation is successful. If it is not, we should have disposed of Mr. Brock, and his name would be included on the list we submit to the GGM monthly. We have no further responsibility to notify your kind in any regard."

"That is going to change with my revamping certain treaties."

"Regardless, after the female clone expired, we did not hear from Semitri. We never knew what happened to Brock. We had no contact. Only through working with the new GGM did we confirm the breach in the Sidron; and, only within the last few days, have we recorded unexplained signal waves from Semitri."

"How did you receive signals, only now?"

"He acquired the ability to time travel; something he did not have before. We have all records of any Carrier that travels in time. Each gives off an unmistakable wave frequency."

"My God," said Jake, "this video shows details of the murders. I could have used this that day. How do you get the camera angles?"

"Everything within a Carrier is recorded from all angles; part of our ability. It is standard procedure for us. By treaty, we give all pertinent inputs to GGM for processing."

"No wonder Gordon knew everything." Jake chuckled sarcastically. "We could use that for judicial purposes on the surface. Well, first things first then. I must find a man named Hamill Stevens. His last location was the Oregon Particle Acceleration Sciences Lab in Seattle. We think he has contributed to the Sidron breach. How fast can you get me there?"

"Twenty-six minutes, 22 seconds, my dear Jake."

"Meantime, do you have a history file on him? And please play everything you have on Brock, too."

"Displaying now . . ."

Burns sat, watching and comprehending all he saw, while, at the same time, he wore an earplug and listened to various Knofer inputs regarding many Ever-Life security matters.

CHAPTER 52:   THE FATHERS' TRIP

AFTER A GOOD NIGHT'S SLEEP, the three fathers met outside the doorway to Bellos' private lab at Andrews Hospital and waited for his arrival. Twenty minutes passed without a word from him, so they entered the lab cautiously one by one.

"Dr. Bellos," James called out. "Dr. Bellos, are you there?"

"Look at all this," Kristos said. "The miracle of science, my brothers. I guess we should be thankful."

"Then, they fixed on the floor to ceiling silver statue, in the far corner of the room.

"What is that?" asked James.

"Its very shiny, or is it glowing?" Ahmir asked.

Each of the statue's long tentacles was stiffly shaped but seemed real somehow to the clergy.

Mathew Bellos entered the lab. "Good morning, gentlemen. I see you're examining the Carrier. I brought traveling supplies."

"Carrier?" James said. "What's a Carrier?"

Bellos smiled, reached into his bag, and took out an extraction syringe and three Knofers. "Here, take these."

The fathers took the Knofers, and Bellos instructed, "These are handheld computers, sort of. Just press this and speak into it there. It will answer any questions if we are separated. Please, hold them up and look into the red spot on the front. That's it. Now, you are securely linked to our time period and location. Each device has a defense mode, which would kick in automatically, as a fail-safe if there is a threat."

"What do you mean?" asked James

"Those little gadgets run on pure knowledge, and each is now programmed to your individual thoughts. In some cases, emotions can override thoughts, as you know. Therefore, it is important to try to focus mentally, if you have a problem. Don't let your emotions cloud your thinking. That is what *S* tried to tell you. Anyway, if defense mode does kick in, that little unit should read your imprint, and the Carrier will return you to itself."

"I see," said Kristos a bit confused.

Bellos continued, "Also, pay attention. In this air-syringe is an immunity shot to protect you against viral or bacterial infections of the time."

Bellos took each syringe and injected the contents into the right wrist of each man. "Lastly, here is a canteen for each of you."

"Okay." James took his and remarked, "It looks like a baby bottle leather wrapped. Pretty small; don't you think? Apparently, we are not going to be gone long."

Bellos smiled. "It refills as needed. It won't run out. It's pretty nifty."

"Nifty?" James replied with a giggle.

"Sorry," said Bellos. "I'm a lover of ancient clichés. And by the way, it's not filled with water. That is your wine."

"Wine? The stuff we drank with S?" asked Kristos.

"Yes, it will feed us and quench our thirst. Unfortunately, we cannot eat solid food or drink any local liquids on the journey. Remember; this is very important. No matter what, do not eat or drink anything, even if you are so tempted by look or fragrance. It would be very bad. It's a rule that you must not break."

Kristos examined his Knofer and remarked, "So, doctor, this little phone thingy, you call it a unit?"

"Actually, we call it a Knofer,"

"Okay, Knofer; you say it will protect us and bring us back, in case of an emergency. And this little bottle of wine will nourish and sustain us throughout the trip. We don't need any food, and we are safe from harm?"

"Yes," Bellos acknowledged. "One more thing, please place this on your right underarms.

"It looks like a quarter," James said.

"It is self-adhesive, you won't feel it. That device records body functions and links to our lab during the entire trip, to ensure the Quivering process is stable."

"What is Quivering?" asked Kristos.

Bellos explained, "So that a time traveler can function normally within the timeline he visits, Grand Carriers, like the statue you see here, first have to change the body mass of the passengers to energy, and then back to mass again equal to the mass of the timeline visited."

"Come again?" Kristos reacted. "I am utterly baffled. I don't understand any of this."

"It's technical, yes, but do try and follow along. I'll try to describe it so you can understand,"

The three fathers looked at each other and nodded. Then, Kristos answered, "We agree. Please go on?"

"To start," Bellos said, "we imprint each of your physical bodies, your mentality, and your personality into the Carrier's organic computer."

"Why?" asked Ahmir.

"A traveler's human body weight could not travel in time. The Carrier will convert your mass into energy. That is the process referred to as 'Quivering' by the Carriers. To explain this to you, it should suffice to say that timelines can be weightless; or, if they do have weight, it's different than the weight of our reality. The traveler must undergo a painless process of stabilizing his or her body's particle recount, and then relate that to the energy of the particular time-date.

The three fathers nodded confused. "Go on," They said in unison. "Can you explain the Quivering itself, the process?"

"Technically, Quivering means syncing the atoms in your body so they can fit into the time-date you're visiting. It's the process of changing the mass/matter, of your atoms to energy/photons, of weightless light for the trip; and then, upon arrival at the time-date, the Carrier changes the energy/photons from weightless light back to the amount of mass/matter equal to that of the particular past time-date. Only Grand Carriers can do this. To exist in any reality, everything must have its base particle count matching the base reality. Here, now, our reality, that is, our present to us has 100% mass/matter. The Carriers use our time as the standard from which all other times can be derived. The past is only a reflection, and although just as real as our present, a particular past-date has less mass/matter than the present does. It's just the way things are set up by our creator. To be real, you must equal that number of particles as exist in that time-date. Anyway, the process of achieving the proper count is known as Quivering. Although it's not rocket science, gentlemen, it may seem so."

The three fathers all nodded and scratched their heads. Bellos tried a different approach. "Do you all remember Einstein's old theory, E=mc2?"

The fathers nodded yes, but Kristos added, "But doctor, we are not experts in such things."

Bellos continued. "I'm not sure you get this but here goes. The <u>energy of particles at rest inside an atom equals its mass times the speed of light squared</u>, $E=mc^2$. In other words, **mass** can be expressed in terms of <u>energy</u> and vice versa. Carriers have proved this Einstein equation to be true. Time travelers must become a collection of energy...

"...So, a traveler's body weight in pounds has to be converted and changed into a collection of weightless light-photons. You are always yourself, every aspect. You have DNA in every gene. And, as I said, the

Quivering process starts when we make sure your total DNA is imprinted in every particle and sub-particle of your atoms. Try to comprehend that a traveler's body is trillions upon trillions of atoms, and every particle that makes up every atom must be counted too. The Grand Carriers scan and calculate the total number of atoms, sub-particles and what they would be as photons that make-up your body. The numbers become quite large and quite beyond man's shared understanding. That's why Carriers do the calculations through their organic computers. Then, they initiate the time travel process itself. You become a vast collection of light. Carriers initiate a vibration to find the targeted time-spot destination. After they map the destination, they calculate the distance and wave frequency needed upon which to ride. After that, the Carrier simply sets our speed, based on the calculations. They create the wave itself, and bam, we travel much faster than light to the time destination. While en route, the Carrier searches for the frequency vibrations at the time-slot destination, and it determines the amount of atom saturation there."

"Saturation?" Ahmir questioned.

"Upon reaching the time destination, Carriers reverse quiver you based on the degree of saturation of atoms at the time-slot itself. After all, the time-slot reflects what was, and therefore varies in saturation of atoms. Particles within atoms become diluted from what was reality as we know it. Time travelers have to function at past time's concentration of atoms and their particles. So basically, the number of your atoms must match the overall saturation level of the destination."

Kristos said, "I think I get it."

Bellos continued, "I hope that helps you all to understand better what's going to happen."

"Speaking for all of us, thank you for trying to explain," Kristos said. "We will try to keep what you said in mind."

Then, Dr. Bellos looked at the Carrier statue. The three fathers followed his lead and saw it begin to change color to a patina green.

"And may we ask, doctor, what exactly is this statue?"

"That, my friends, is our ride."

"What is it?" asked Ahmir.

"It's not an it," Bellos said. "She is a Grand Carrier, a time-controller."

"I'm afraid you have us at a complete loss," Kristos said. "We heard you talk about Carriers, but we have no idea what one looks like. So, that's one, you say?"

"Yes. They have a variety of looks really. This one allows it to be in my Lab here. There are many new things that you will experience with me today. She is one of many species that live within our planet unknown to the surface population."

"Praise be to Allah," Ahmir whispered.

"Dr. Bellos," James raised an eyebrow. "How are we able to travel in time?"

"Come this way," Bellos extended his arm, pointing toward the Carrier. As they approached, a 5-ft by 3-ft door slid open.

"Doctor," Kristos asked, "you expect us to fit inside that?"

James replied, "Oh, Kris, don't be a fuddy-duddy. Follow me."

James squeezed through the door and entered. He was amazed at what he saw. The room was more than 30-ft high and 20-ft wide. At once, the room shifted around James. Its height now became the floor. From nowhere, furnished chairs, a couch, and tables appeared. James froze, but after the room set up, he called out to the others, "Don't be afraid; come in; it's unbelievable."

With those words, Bellos led Kristos and Ahmir through the door. The fathers were awestruck. Bellos invited them to sit down.

"Doctor," Ahmir said, "how is this possible?"

Bellos replied, "You are going to experience many things that may seem impossible, but nothing is really. Please make yourselves comfortable. I offer you all this. The earth's core has an ocean of molten magma rotating around it. That fluid motion, combined with the rotation of Earth and orbit around the sun, is what creates the magnetic field around the planet. That field surrounds us all and holds us within it. By harnessing the energy of that magnetic field and focusing in a certain way, our girlfriend here creates a time vibration, a particular frequency. Then, she rides the frequency wave, like a surfer on a surfboard, to almost any event in past-time. But there is a catch. Once *you* have been to that time and stayed for whatever period, you can never duplicate the trip again. The second trip's frequency vibrations would cause your cells to confuse and divide to accommodate the two timelines you had visited. Unfortunately, the result is that each of your cells would separate from itself, break apart and disintegrate. You would become cell dust."

"Well," Kristos said, "we don't want to be cell dust, do we?"

"Good," Bellos replied. "Now, does anyone have to do anything before we start?"

The three nodded noes with nervous smiles. Bellos turned his complete attention to the Carrier and bowed his head in respect. He began speaking out loud in the Carrier's language, "Dear Sister, in the name of Time Trust Treaty 120856, we ask that you take us in safety and peace. Our respect and admiration, always."

"Do you recognize the speech, Kristos?" Ahmir asked.

"No, it's nothing familiar I've ever heard or studied."

"Nor I," said Ahmir.

"It's not Latin, Greek, Hebrew or Aramaic," said James. "Could it be some derivation or of Coptic origin?"

As Bellos finished, they all spoke at once, and Bellos gestured and answered, "It's a combination of many languages. You three remember the Tower of Babel story, right? Everyone spoke the same tongue until God scrambled their languages. Well, think of it as the standard original native tongue."

The three fathers did a double take.

"And remember," Bellos added, "we humans have different vocal capabilities now. We could never duplicate the original tones, anyway."

Kristos rolled his eyes as the Carrier began to hiss. Slowly, she changed, appearing transparent, pliable and wet. Her glow became brighter. The men sat back on the couch. "Don't we need seat belts or something?" asked Kristos.

"Not at all," Bellos said. "This cabin runs on the principle of *gyroscopic flexibility*. We will remain stationary no matter what the Carrier does.

"Surprisingly comfortable," James said nervously.

"Don't be alarmed," said Bellos.

"Excuse me, doctor," Ahmir said, "if we knew what was happening, we wouldn't be so anxious. All we hear is strange noises."

Bellos described the event. "She is beginning her search for the right frequency."

From the apex of the creature, the tongue flailed, generating quick popping sounds. Then, the popping stopped and, strangely, there was no sound at all as Bellos continued. "She has started the vibration now. Around her body, she is creating a bubble-like membrane for time travel. When the bubble is complete, she will start vibrating very fast, searching space-time for the right wave. Soon after that, you will all sense a feeling of euphoria and drift into a very light trance. It is hard to explain before you experience it. Take deep breaths and try to relax as much as you can."

"But, how can that make us travel anywhere?" asked Ahmir.

Bellos was sensitive to their tension. "Actually, it's to any *when,* really. As I said, the Carrier is searching for the frequency of our destination. All life in space-time exists at a particular frequency of existence. When she finds it, we go. The bubble around us can only exist if we all stay at a certain level of comfort though. The less you know, in this case, the more apt you are to remain within the correct comfort range. The coins you wear on your arms tell her that you are all okay, so she can trigger the next phase, providing our people approve your vital signs. The process will move much faster if you try to relax."

The three fathers nodded and sat nervously.

"My goodness, it is quite something," Kristos said. "But there is no sense of movement. I am not dizzy at all, just a bit dozy."

"This will be like nothing you have ever experienced before," said Bellos. "And yet, it will be just another moment in your day. The trip should cause no pain. When we get there, we will be able to move as we normally do. Have no fear, gentlemen; we will be alright."

The bubble around the Carrier turned an opaque mauve color. Flashes of light sparked; and within seconds, she was spinning like a top.

Kristos looked at the others wide-eyed, "I think the fact that there is absolutely no sound makes it most unnerving. Doctor, how long does it take to...?"

At that second, a blinding light within the beast made them all involuntarily blink their eyes, and within their short blink, they transported. When they opened their eyes again, they were standing inside a shallow dark cave, trying to find their balance. The area where they stood was just short of 6-ft high by 20-ft wide and had several other cave arms extending out from its center. Bellos looked at his wristband and Knofer, quickly checking to make sure the fathers made it without any physical problems. He tapped his Knofer, and it became a small flashlight. "Are you all okay?"

"The fathers looked at themselves and replied, "Yes."

"Good, come this way," Bellos instructed.

"Wait," Kristos said. "Look around. We are in a burial chamber." He walked over to one of the several small rock-like containers. "This is a Jewish ossuary, a burial box carved out of limestone. It's fresh, new."

"Yes, I've seen them before," said Bellos.

"What a sight," James said. "Look, more of them over there."

"Look there," Ahmir pointed. "It's a side tunnel. light is coming from it."

The three men looked at each other and then at Bellos. "Doctor, we must see," said Kristos.

"Go then. We have time."

The three smiled and acted as though they found a treasure. Single file, each father followed the other and walked toward the light. It seemed brighter the closer they got. First, James, then Ahmir, and finally Kristos crouched to walk through the side cave's entrance. What they saw staggered them. The light seemed to radiate from the walls, and a young man sat before them on a rock bench wiping the blood off himself with a shroud and pieces of clothing. The man noticed the fathers and smiled. Each of the three clerics heard him speak in a different tongue, Ahmir heard an Arab dialect, Kristos heard Greek, and James heard Hebrew.

"Greetings, my brothers," he said. "Forgive me. I am not at my best."

Ahmir was the first to react. He fell to his knees out of respect, closed his eyes tightly, and recited, "There is only one God, and Mohammed is his Prophet. My Master; forgive me! I must not look upon thee."

James, like Ahmir was mesmerized, paralyzed for a moment; he couldn't believe his eyes. He also fell to his knees and said. "My Lord, our law giver, Moses, it is you."

Kristos watched and listened to the other two. He tried to stand straight, but the cave's ceiling was not high enough. He looked at the young man and spoke, "Who are you? What have you done? This is some trickery, and I shall not be the fool."

The man on the bench spoke with reverence, "Believing is seeing, seeing is not believing. Be not afraid. I will not harm you. Please, all of you come closer. As with all things, you see what you will. I am true and will help you."

None of the three fathers noticed that the tunnel changed. Then Kristos reacted to what the two-fathers were saying by jerking up and not hitting the ceiling. He moved very slowly, cautiously, towards the man on the bench.

"Come now," the man said, as he gestured to Kristos to sit with him. "You three came to me. Do not be afraid."

"Where are we?" asked Kristos standing in defiance.

The man said, "It is my birthday. Behold, my life is my gift."

There, next to him and on the cave-floor were what looked like clothes and linen body-wraps soaked with blood. Kristos reached down and felt the linen. As he did so, he noticed an image of a face on the cloth, and in a surprised gaze, he examined the man's feet and hands. "Your wrists, your feet; you are hurt."

Kristos studied the garments for a few more seconds, and then he realized what they were. He clutched the clothing to his chest and began to sob, "What have I done?" He fell to his knees before the man. "I am just a stupid man. I am so sorry, my Lord, forgive me?"

Then, Kristos groveled into the dirt, caressing and kissing the man's feet. "My Lord, forgive me? Forgive me?"

"Stop, stop," the man said.

As he spoke, the three stared at his face. His image changed before their eyes. Now they each saw the same face. However, each one continued to hear him speak in their original tongue.

"Be calm and thank you for coming," the man said. "Please hear me. You are loved, but you three have forgotten something."

Kristos raised his head, and all three fathers observed the man as he spoke.

"Customs and interpretations change over centuries, and so must the law. It is alive. You three twisted your thinking to justify dealing with a demon, because you rationalized a euphoric end in one single religion-faith. It has happened many times before. Your idea of unity did not justify your perverted deal with Mr. Brock. Every generation studies, refines, and interprets texts relating them to their own time. But, be careful. Original meanings can become clouded or even lost. You must see the truth and begin again. Remember why I came to you. I had a simple message, and what have you done with it? You must try to tell people the truth. The Kingdom of God is upon you. God has broken into your world. He places his divine spirit within you. All you need to do is believe in him thru me and try to live by the values of God's kingdom. I am the example of that. The beatitudes are the values of the kingdom and the characteristics by which you should relate to one another. With God's spirit of creation within you, you can do anything you imagine...It's about teaching how to be a good human being...

"...For many people, to follow the path of sacrifice is impossible. Your Father in Heaven gives you the grace of his love in those cases. Every son or daughter is pressured to think conformity. It is your job to teach clarity, and to invite your brethren and children onto a right path to God. By living God's will, one can find the Kingdom of Heaven within him. The Kingdom is many things to different people but be assured; Hell is the same for all of you. On the right path, one can see by my deeds that it is not just a personal experience, it is also the next step in life's wonder, but each of you must find his own path. I am the way and the righteous path, not the only path. Our Father has created a rich variety of life and thought. I came to show you that all mankind can have a personal relationship with our Father through doing

His will, believing in Me, and sharing in brotherhood. Every one of you sees in his own way, based on one's capacity to understand teaching and revelation. Each of your faiths is based on your flock's ability to interpret teaching the way your priests teach and reveal God's truth. But no one should force another to see as he does. And you must be sure you are not forcing your flock. Creating guilt is not the answer to understanding God's word. Invite, yes; teach, yes; and coach, certainly. The point is that you all can overcome your struggles in life. If I can overcome death, how much can your troubles be worse than that."

Then, the man stared eye to eye with Kristos. "Each of you has two eyes, and each one of them sees the same thing from a different perspective. Why do you conspire and insist that others should see as you do, or think as you think? Every true religion has its language and tells stories inviting followers to travel along a righteous path to God and inner peace. Even when the way and the truth stand as a road before you, you have the choice of whether to take the first step or not. Let your people choose for themselves on what road to walk. Your Father created the universe. Could he not rescind free will if he wished? Do not complicate the simple truth or think you can prove something that is a matter of choice."

Then the man leaned in, put his hand on Kristos' shoulder and said, "That which is not yours is not yours to keep." The man sighed, smiled and rose to his feet, asking, "Now, will you three help me?"

"Help you?" asked Ahmir.

"Yes, will you?"

Kristos stood and spoke assuredly, "My Lord, what can we do? Yes, of course."

"Come, I will show you."

The four walked out of the lighted room and back into the larger cave. No one noticed Bellos, anywhere.

"There, you see that stone that covers the entrance to this darkness? I am weak from my journey. Will you help me move it so that I may leave?"

The three fathers looked at each other, filled with a refreshed enthusiasm. All four of them went to the stone. Placing their hands upon it, they positioned themselves.

"Now push!" the man said. "Push! Altogether now!"

They all strained and shoved again and again, but it would not budge. Kristos, James, and Ahmir backed away, looking at their hands beginning to bleed from pressing on the prickly jagged rock.

"We are sorry. It is too heavy," said Ahmir.

The man looked at them all. "Nonsense, there will always be struggle; we must push in unison. Try again. I must leave before first light."

The three looked at each other, and each picked another spot to push.

"On three, agreed?" The man said.

"Yes," they all said, taking a deep breath.

"1 . . . 2 . . . 3 . . . PUSH!"

The stone inched to one side but hardly moved. They let go.

"I think it moved," Kristos said.

Their hands began to drip blood. They retook several deep breaths; and, even more determined this time; they set themselves against the stone.

"Come on!" Kristos yelled in a whisper.

They pushed again, and again, and again. Inch by inch, the rock slowly moved to the side. Finally, the entrance was open far enough for the man to squeeze out. The three fathers fell back onto the dirt. Exhausted and panting, James asked, "Now what?"

Kristos was smiling with tears of joy. The man was still leaning his face against the stone out of breath, when he spoke, "Thank you. I appreciate your effort." He turned around and leaned back on the stone. "You three are worthy. Try to bring your thoughts back to basics. You can see even with what we have done here, my brothers, teach others to unite in a good, right purpose. Invite them to a better life through worship. With the right sacrifice and faith, you can accomplish anything, perhaps even a happy ending. Of course, patience helps, too."

The man stood up straight, taller, and much more muscular than he seemed before. He turned toward them briefly, wiping his hands on his garment. Then, he smiled at them, turned around and carefully stepped out of the cave.

The three fathers sat, spellbound. Each began to laugh and cry at the same time. James reached over and wiped his bloody index finger on Ahmir's cheek as he chuckled with a tear. Slowly, they helped each other up and began hugging together.

Kristos whispered, "Bellos? Where is Dr. Bellos?"

Only a few seconds went by when they all heard a strange ringing in their ears, and they flinched. It seemed to come from a back corner on the other side of the cave. They turned and saw a blinding bright light. A Carrier appeared. However, it looked different from the one in which they'd arrived. It was one pulsing color, a beautiful steel blue; and it had a silver halo glowing around it. Across from the Carrier, some 15 feet away, the figure of Mathew Bellos stepped out of the shadows. He stood fearlessly facing the beast. It was Semitri. A door appeared on its skin, right in front of Bellos, and out stepped the figure of Marion Brock.

"Interesting place for a meeting." Said Real-Brock. We followed your trail, Mr. new GGM. I expect you will come voluntarily, or not. It makes no difference to me."

Bellos just said, "You have made a grave mistake."

The GGM reached for his Knofer, but Brock was faster. Moving with the help of Semitri, Brock lunged, diving onto Bellos; but he went completely through the GGM and fell to the ground. The three fathers froze in shock. Bellos looked down at Brock. "You see, my dear Brock, I am but a Post Controller. Our GGM is quite safe."

The 3D hologram of Bellos clicked his Knofer, and, in an instant of blinding light, he and the three fathers disappeared from the cave.

Brock stood up and brushed himself off. "Christ, you bastard. Well, this is just the beginning, anyway."

"That is correct," Semitri said. "Mr. Brock, nothing can stop it. Come. We go on."

"To where?"

"To gather the power and fulfill our agreement."

Brock stepped back into Semitri; and, with a quick glow and quiver, the steel blue beast disappeared, leaving the cave dark, empty, and quiet again.

CHAPTER 53: BRAZIL

THE BRAKING ROAR OF THE AIRPLANE ENGINE and bounce of the wheels on the runway signaled the landing of the Hush-Jet, on a private airfield, just outside Rio de Janeiro. Rachel Sheldon wiggled and awoke without side effects from the drug Gabe had slipped into her drink. She felt her head and looked out the window.

"This is not DC."

The steward, Gabriel, was quick to enter the cabin and spoke politely, "That is true. We detoured, ma'am."

"I can see that. My God, there is Christ's statue on the mountain."

"Yes, ma'am, we are in Rio."

"Jesus, why? What is going on? Who are you people?"

"If you will be patient, ma'am, Captain Blake himself will be with you, after taxiing."

"Not going to happen. I am not in the mood for anymore BS from you, boy."

Rachel reached for the seatbelt release, but it would not separate. She yanked repeatedly. "What the hell! Let me out of this!"

"Ma'am; just relax. No one is going to harm you."

The plane taxied to a private hangar and stopped. Rachel was steaming by the time the captain approached her. He sat on the couch opposite from her. "Mrs. Sheldon, I am Captain Michael Blake. I am sorry for the inconvenience; but, as you can imagine, in this case, I cannot have you wreaking havoc throughout my airplane. Now, if you calm down, we can talk civilly."

She took a deep breath, closed her eyes, and appeared quiet and subdued. "Alright, Mr. Blake, may I ask why we are in Rio?"

"I was paid to bring you here."

As the captain finished his sentence, the entry door at the front of the cabin opened, and a short trim East Indian man walked inside to behind the captain.

"Good afternoon, Mrs. Sheldon. I'll take it from here, captain."

Blake got up, walked to the plane's entry door and turned toward Rachel. "Nice meeting you, ma'am."

Rachel focused on the small man in front of her. "So, can you tell me what is going on?"

"Actually, yes I can. I am Rash InVoy. How do you do?"

"I do very well when I'm not tied up or kidnapped, thank you."

"I do apologize for this, Mrs. Sheldon. It was necessary, believe me."

"I don't believe anything you say."

"Well, perhaps this will help." InVoy undid her seat buckle and offered, "There, if you would like to leave, be my guest."

Rachel got up and started walking toward the door; but InVoy called the captain cabin and instructed they lock the doors.

"Mrs. Sheldon, have you ever been to this side of Rio before? I find it most interesting if you like the gangland or terrorist elements. Please, stay and learn why we brought you here. I doubt your Mr. Rossi is going to miss you."

At that point, another man walked in through the plane's door and almost bumped into Rachel. "Hello, Mrs. Sheldon, we haven't met. I am Charlie Rossi."

As he extended his hand, Rachel walked backwards to her seat and sat down again in silent shock. "Okay, fellas, what the hell is this?"

Rossi sat down, took a thick bound manuscript out of his briefcase and handed it to her. InVoy stood up, waving Rossi away. "Do you know what that is, Mrs. Sheldon?"

"It looks like my husband's manuscript on particle displacements. How did you get it?"

"Good guess, but not quite. Your husband is quite the clever man, you know."

"What do you mean?"

"Look at the date, there, on the second page."

"2102, what is this?"

"That's a copy of the original Sidron papers. Now, look at this." InVoy took another spiral folder out of his briefcase and handed it to her. "Open it."

Rachel did and gasped. She took the other book, set them side-by-side and began opening the pages in sync.

"Christ! Where did you get these?"

"It's a long story, believe me. I work for Marion Brock, Mrs. Sheldon, not Gordon Swanson or his Ever-Life puppets. We have been working to recover those papers for decades, ever since they surfaced in 2855."

"That's 144 years ago." Said Rachel.

"Yes, the Brock family owns them."

"What do you mean? My husband wrote this one. That's impossible!"

"Yes, but how much is his idea? When Mr. Brock and your husband collaborated to develop CPT, Mr. Brock showed Jack those files on the Sidron. Your husband, being as brilliant as he is, applied everything to his discovery. Mr. Brock negotiated a long-term contract with Jack to bind the CPT effort with his own interests. The plan was to compare the complete historical records of Sidron with testing the CPT formulation. But the catalyst bath was the challenge. We couldn't test anything without preserving the formulation in the bath."

"So, you tried to steal it with clones and murder."

InVoy smiled and replied confidently, "Not really. It was your husband who figured the more clones, the more formulas. Your Gordon Swanson made a deal to get the very same thing from your husband. The only difference was; if he failed, his precious colonies would not burn up in Hell. If we failed, a big part of Brock's empire would fall. What would you do?"

"Oh! I'd run out and kidnap the wife of the inventor and blackmail the husband...Screw you!"

Rachel stood up as an armed guard appeared from the flight attendant cubical. InVoy grinned and gestured to her. "Please, doctor, sit down?"

"Where did you get my husband's papers?"

"He gave them to us. However, as you can see, they are incomplete."

Rachel opened it to the back. "What happened? Where are the pages?"

"Precisely, the reason you are here."

"You think Jack has the missing pages?"

"Mrs. Sheldon, we know he does. We gave them to him in the first place. You see, he was supposed to return them, but he never did. He broke the agreement, and now we are compelled to recover the papers."

"So, you broke into our home?"

Rachel sat back in shock for a moment. She glanced out the window with a tear in her eye, and then she took a deep breath and wiped her cheek.

"Christ, you almost had me. For just a second, you almost had me. Bullshit! Mr. Whatever-your-name-is! You think you can brainwash me, justify breaking into our home, and blackmail my husband? Never! You bastard!"

"Does it matter what the truth is, doctor?" InVoy leaned into her face. "You know it's what you believe that counts." InVoy snickered. "And, in fact, it is what you perceive from your point of view, isn't it?"

"You are a very bad man."

"Well, that may be your point of view, but it doesn't concern us here; now does it? You are going to be my advantage, my bait to get those pages. I was hoping you would cooperate."

"Not on my life."

"Mrs. Sheldon, it will happen, or you will have no life. Guards, take her away."

"This isn't going to work, you little shit!"

Two guards grabbed her by her shoulders and forced her down the aisle.

"You little weasel, why don't you fight like a man? Let go of me, assholes!"

InVoy stuffed a cloth into her mouth and instructed the guards. Then, he called Marion Brock. He had no idea he was calling a clone.

"Brock here."

"Sir, it's InVoy, we have the wife."

"Well, get on with it. Have Rossi contact Jack. We will have a nice reception waiting. Don't screw this one up."

"I'll handle it."

InVoy hung up.

CHAPTER 54: GIZA

AS ALLENFAR BEGAN HIS ASCENT from Earth's fiery magma up to the Great Pyramid of Giza, he transmitted to Bellos' mind. *"My GGM, we will be docking at the subterranean chamber."*

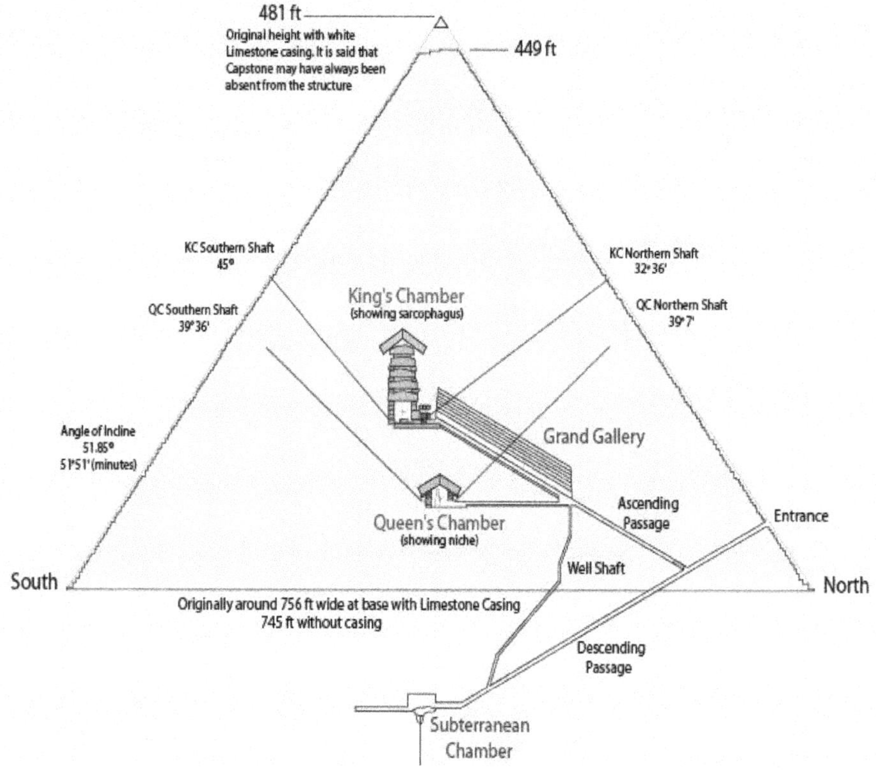

"Can you get me closer to the Grand Gallery?" asked Bellos.

Allenfar slowly rose to the exact point where the ascending passage met the Grand Gallery. Bellos and Wheeler walked out of the Carrier into the dimly lit chilly hallway.

Wheeler looked around in awe at the rock walls and dark passageway. "I feel like I'm standing in the presence of death...Quite claustrophobic and creepy, isn't it?"

"Nothing like the spacious feeling in the colonies; that's for sure," said Bellos.

"Maybe it's just that we are adjusting to the dark in here; but look up over there. What are those dots? They look like a twinkling constellation, 3-pulsing stars."

Bellos was quick to point his Knofer at the lights, and then he read the small display. "The Knofer says it's Orion."

The Knofer continued to tick, as Wheeler positioned his head so he could see and imagine connecting the dots. "I suppose you could make that argument."

Then, the Knofer added text to the image, Bellos read numbers as they appeared above the lights. "It says its syncing with the Pyramid...Look at that! Each twinkling dot has text under it, 1965, 1989, and 2004."

"I'm confused," Wheeler said. "Does it mean each light is a date from which the Sidron displaced our time travelers?

Bellos had a lump in his throat. "Maybe it's as simple as that; or maybe there were 3-Sidron events."

"So, each Sidron event means another transport of something?"

"Well, why not?" Bellos said with confidence.

"Okay, makes sense; I guess. Although I'm not quite sure where you're going with this, since some event must have happened to eliminate the youngest, right? It sounds very speculative."

Then, while they both watched the lights in the hologram, Wheeler noticed something. "Mathew, one light is dimming and looks like it's going dimmer. What does that mean? Look; over there; on the other side. There's another star-like light that's appeared out of nowhere. That makes 4-lights now. Now what does the Knofer say?"

They both looked at the display and it read, Aquarius.

Then the Knofer's lights lined up and shifted to show a different shaped pathway out of Aquarius.

"It's too bad we can't ride the pathway the Knofer displays," said Wheeler flippantly."

"Actually, I was just thinking that. I am the GGM after all."

Bellos instructed the Knofer, "Please put us into the hologram and onto the pathway of the 4-sparkling lights...Extrapolate and carry us the distance of the pathway."

Suddenly, the Knofer then displayed a fifth twinkling light and the word, 'Cassiopeia.' At the same time, it triggered a defense-mode code. Wheeler said with a furrowed brow, "Well, I guess the after-life trip to Heaven is a convoluted one at best. Maybe it's good we are dead before we start."

Bellos stood firm and said, "Give me a second Tom. Let's take stock of this and be very careful of what we do next. It has been thousands of years since any activity took place in here; and wasn't their belief that the North Star had some significance as the entryway to Heaven, not Orion, or Aquarius, or Cassiopeia?"

Wheeler just stood still and replied, "My Egypt-history also taught that. I'm fine with just being here and waiting for my GGM to decide our next course of action."

Bellos focused on the Knofer. It was still actively syncing and vibrating and ticking. He placed the Knofer on the rock floor, and it exploded a 6-ft tall hologram of the Great Pyramid. Then, it showed where the dots displayed inside the model and enlarged that area into a 3-D image, directly in front of Bellos and Wheeler.

"I'm beginning to understand what Dorothy felt like in Oz," said Wheeler.

"Christ!" said Bellos quietly. "Cassiopeia is part of Ursa Major. That's a much bigger area of space-time in light-years. Knofer, please display the constellation path beyond the primary 5-stars of Cassiopeia; and follow where the path leads. Also, display detail rendering and analysis of limestone electromagnetic values and statistical readings of electron pulses in the pyramid. Also, study and display echoes of pathway findings for each of the three time-dates, from which our time traveler transported."

The Knofer exploded again with a line through the Cassiopeia M, and beyond, deep into space. The pathway-line wrapped around, over and back again. And then it stopped without a forecast or trace that might give hint to where it was going. Bellos said, "Knofer, display the echo dust of the pathways of our three visitors backward from their point of arrival at Time Trust."

"Look at that, Tom, "Bellos said with an inquisitive expression. "Both the pathway from the dates where Andrew started and the pathway backward from Time Trust have a large void between them. These three ends there, and these three end there. We have too big a gap between them to trace the pathway. Why? There is something missing, or the Sidron doesn't want us to know. We couldn't possibly tell the rest of the missing space-time pathway of either."

Then, Bellos read the display on his Knofer, "Christ! Tom, what are we dealing with here? The damn thing says the area in question is the Goyal.

"Goyal? What do you make of it, Mathew?"

"Our records show Goyal as a narrow gully, or pathway. But the Knofer says the ancients also referred to as the *one pathway for the loved...*"

Tom wheeler scratched his head and replied, "Okay, gully, pathway, special place? Pathway to what, to where?"

Bellos looked at the pathway traces and the void between them again. "What if the void is a fork in the road. Maybe it's our choice which way to go. The ancients were fascinated with the afterlife. And they claimed a secret pathway, one path to the afterlife from the Pharaoh's private burial place, out and eventually ending at the North Star, their gate into Heaven."

"Maybe, but Matt...The void is in the middle of the pathway, we know the end is Time Trust and the beginning is, 1965, 1989, and 2004. I agree with you're saying those dots may be part of the Sidron's reaction. To what though? Do you believe these guys knew about the Sidron? Do you think this thing is a power hub for transporting souls to heaven?"

Wheeler rethought. "What if the Sidron charged this power hub and then the pyramid directed the transporting of our visitor 3-times?"

Bellos tapped his Knofer as if he was texting furiously. "No, Tom; you've got the correct idea but backwards. The pyramid charged and sparked, triggering the Sidron. It was the Sidron that transported our visitor. I think we are on the threshold of something that has been protected for eons. And I think the pyramid was charged and triggered by someone or something. I think it's the someone who the data identified as the other person besides Jake. That's why the Carriers can't see it. And the Carriers have protections as stated in our treaties. The missing link has to do with the history of their ability to travel through time itself. "

"GGM, I'm sure this is all above my paygrade, but how do we find out if anything you speculate is true?"

Bellos smiled. "I think our first task is to follow where the Grand Carriers take us...back in time. First, though..." Bellos completed his tapping and instructed his Knofer once again.

"Knofer, scrutinize wave-pulse residue. Then, compare readings with particle displacement shadow or Sidron events. Check findings and compare with all pyramids around the globe."

Wheeler listened and then asked, "You think there is a power base here to run a particle displacement test?"

Bellos replied, "Absolutely, we can. Not sure about anyone on the surface. Hopefully, this will give us part of the answer. And the only way to check is to use a Knofer that can read the wave pulse, if there are any. In ancient times, all the major pyramids around the world were linked. We know the builders had local construction materials, and we are aware some were conductive. Some historians even recorded electrical impulses at many of the sites. Records imply they were battery capable.”

“So, you’re saying it was an ancient world network of power?”

“Exactly. Altogether, a global output and input of electrical energy, but no one knows to what extent. If someone, say Brock, has found a way to harness or focus that energy, how much power would that be? And, could it generate a frequency field big enough to trigger the Sidron?”

Wheeler witnessed a strange look on the GGM’s face, as he received inputs from the Knofer. Bellos said, “Even after thousands of years; Fascinating. This says the connection is power ready; stronger than anything I imagined.”

“Well, don’t keep me waiting?” said Tom excitedly.

“Patience my friend.”

The Knofer ticked, *finished*, and the display read, ‘***Residue positive. Pathway incomplete. Power is sensitive to the Sidron.***’”

Bellos held the Knofer and paced as he continued, “This had to be their power source, or somehow, they focus power through here. I think it was Brock’s team. They network the power from Time-Travel Inc. What a brilliant plan! Who is going to check the pyramids? No one would consider destroying any of them!”

Bellos turned to the 3D model again. “Display any frequency echoes within the last 24 hours.”

The hologram reset and displayed five twinkling lights. Each radiated a wave, pulsing outward to the boundary of the model.

Wheeler asked, “So, those lights are Sidron activity. Those locations are the Sidron events?”

“Yes, they are the echoes recorded. This pyramid is the archive of the exact positions and moments.”

“Why would they be in here, of all places?”

“The apex of this pyramid received the displacement signal from Time-Travel Inc.; and then the pyramid generated a power surge, which I think generated a Sidron reaction. That Sidron reaction is what transported the visitors to us. Unless it was something completely alien to all this. We keep digging and it’ll show itself. Meantime, we work with what the Knofer reported. The ancients had many secrets yet to be uncovered, even in our time. They didn’t define things as we do. They used their knowledge, in many ways, beyond what we do.”

Wheeler took a breath and said, "So, our visitors in Time Trust now, were transported via the Sidron through the apex of this pyramid up there, down to us?"

"I am sure of it. This pyramid is somehow the passageway for the particle displacements. The Sidron zapped one man at three different times in his life to our present day, his future. But how? And why? What was the trigger? We always thought the Carriers were the hourglass of time. It looks like someone, my guess Brock, has found a different way. Tom, look! One of the lights; that one over there. It's fading. I need to question our visitors."

"Mathew, look over there, a new light just appeared. There were five stars. Now there are six. If each is tied to an event; five stars, five events. That means another event just happened?"

"Maybe it represents the explosion you were in. We should leave."

"Yes, I agree," said Tom.

Bellos' Knofer disintegrated the holograms and they hurried back to Allenfar. Bellos directed the Knofer to transmit all data and findings to Allenfar and Jake Burns.

As soon as the two men reached the Carrier, Bellos spoke to the beast, "Take us to Time Trust Security Area-36, of Post-2."

"And Tom, when we get back, search the vaults. Check everything you can think of. There has to be something, a clue, to tell us more about the data."

"Fine, yes, I see your point," Tom replied with a grin, "but if a new event just occurred, why haven't we heard something? Is it because we were in the pyramid?"

"I don't know." Bellos said. "I am going to see our visitors, Andrew, and see what either one of him can tell us. Perhaps that will give us some answers."

Wheeler said, "I questioned them all before my accident and was giving them headsets to educate and monitor their reactions, hoping it would tell us something about why they appeared."

"I know Tom," replied Bellos.

"Well, all Carriers record everything that happens within them."

"Yes, and it's a priority now to find out what happened to our youngest traveler."

Wheeler remarked, "Maybe we should call him, Andrew the young."

"Very funny. I do intend on finding out why the Carriers haven't told me anything about the young man disintegrating. Let me know anything you find."

"I will. It may take time."

"Unfortunately, we don't have that."

It took Allenfar only a few minutes to dock at Time Trust. The two men exited, each going in a different direction.

Meantime, within a Time Trust unit, one of the remaining two-time travelers, the 43-year-old from 1989, sat watching the walls broadcast 3D video. He had been studying how different life was below the surface. There were educational displays and exotic agricultural programs. The vast caverns on the screen were far from dark and dank. The man marveled at the bubble Carriers taking passengers back and forth in any direction. At one point, he studied historical information regarding Ever-Life's origins. All that he saw always had a common thread, healthcare. And every program had interruptions, advertisements about better living through the Ever-Life foods and genetic medicine. The man had no idea he was the victim of time travel or that he was one of three, or his younger self had vanished. For hours, the 43-year-old man sat, trying not to upset himself with the thoughts running in and out of his mind. Finally, the door to the unit opened and in walked GGM, Mathew Bellos. The man looked with professional kindness at Bellos, who immediately extended his hand.

"Hello, I am Mathew Bellos."

"Hello, I am Andrew. Frankly, I'm not sure what to say." The man shook Bellos' hand cautiously. "Nice place here. Clean and very white. Different, but interesting."

"That it is. Please, be as comfortable as you can."

"What happened to the other guy, Wheeler, who was here before?"

"I'm sure you have many questions, and I would spend time answering them all, if I could. I assure you we have no hostile intent, and I'm sure if we take this one step at a time, your questions will be answered. I know you must be uneasy. And Mr. Wheeler will be back."

"*Uneasy*, that is the understatement of the day."

"The best thing I can do is tell you everything in an instant," said Bellos. "This is very unusual for both of us. I ask that you trust me, even though there is no reason to."

"I don't see a choice. I'm obviously a prisoner."

Bellos walked around the man and over to the wall. A small door appeared at his shoulder height. He took out another headset and turned around. "I know Mr. Wheeler gave you a headset already, but please put this one on. It's one of my used ones. This will give you another perspective and yes, some more answers. It's a very brief vault program, already installed inside. You open the clip, like this; fit it in your ear comfortably, like that. Then, just sit for a moment. It won't hurt."

Andrew took the set and studied it. "So, this one won't grow out of my ear?"

"No, each comes with an option where either the listener can eliminate the set, destroy it; or, as I have with that one, kept it here for review purposes. It's antiseptic, and it won't hurt."

Andrew positioned the headset as Bellos requested.

"Good, that's it, now sit back."

As with Wheeler, the chair turned into a lounge. Bellos took what looked like a small 3-inch by ½-inch remote device out of his pocket and handed it to the 43-year-old.

Andrew took it and asked, "Is this similar to what your Mr. Wheeler showed me?"

Bellos pointed and said, "You see the black button there? Push it and then try to relax."

"Right." Andrew laid his head back on the lounge and pushed the button. Within seconds he reacted, "Oh, Christ!" Then he shut up and gripped the chair's arms, squeezing tightly. Involuntarily, he closed his eyes.

Bellos sat in the chair beside the lounge, quietly waiting. After a few moments, the man opened his eyes widely and stared at the GGM. Bellos raised his hand gesturing for him not to speak. "Just push the dot and remove the earpiece before you say anything."

The man did so and blinked several times as though clearing his mind. He looked at Bellos as if there was something familiar. "You know, I remember doing that before, in college, a long time ago. Odd, but it was more like a dream then. Did I? I mean . . . Did I dream it?"

"No. In fact, you did meet our Jake Burns on three other occasions in your life; and another two are yet to come. I believe that is why you were involved in the particle displacement today."

"Particle displacement? Considering I have been stuck in this room with a wall-size 3D TV, what I just saw is hard to accept, much less particle displacement."

"I know, but it's all true."

"So, this Sidron is the highway of knowledge and power, and somebody used it, for what?"

"For his own benefit, to capture power and change what is, or has been, to what he wants it to be."

"What year is it, exactly?"

"It is our year 9999.96. By your calendar, June is the month and the year is 2999.6

The man sighed with a serious look, "It's mind-blowing that I am still back there, with my life going on; and, at the same time, here. But I have a hard time believing I am, in fact, dead."

Then, he looked at Bellos eye to eye, "Can or will I go back?"

"I'm not sure. Nobody has answers. We believe that time travel cannot change a timeline of someone who died. If that's true, even if you did go back, what you know now should make no difference."

Bellos felt his Knofer vibrate. As he took it out, he smiled at the man and heard Wheeler. "Sir, are you there?"

"Yes, Tom."

"Sir, we have activity on the equipment; intense, immeasurable."

Bellos looked wide-eyed at Andrew, who began to flicker, like the first young visitor. He reached for Bellos; but before either one could touch the other, the man was gone, and the headset dropped to the floor. Bellos stood alone in the room and replied to Wheeler, "Yes Tom, I know. You better get me those readings right away."

"What happened, sir?"

"Just get me the readings . . ."

Bellos cut the call and sat in the lounge waiting only a few minutes. Wheeler came through the door and said, "Done, sir. They're on your Knofer."

Bellos played the Knofer hologram. "I better have them for our last visitor."

"What do you think, Mathew?"

Bellos lifted his head. "I think it's all Brock, and he is succeeding. Get this information to both Burns and Swanson. Tell Burns to initiate highest defense mode. Oh, and Tom, did we retrieve anything on Angie's status?"

"We got a reading from her Knofer. We are trying to trace it through the same efforts we are using to track the Sidron vibrations. When this last event occurred, we registered her Knofer as active, but only during the event. After that, the readings went dead."

Bellos and Wheeler walked out the door and turned in different directions again. Bellos entered Room 9, which held the eldest of the three visitors. As he did, the two of them looked at each other and shook hands. The man said, "My God, you haven't changed a day. Hello again. Mathew, isn't it?"

Bellos was a bit shocked, but he quickly replied, "Andrew, you remember?"

"Yes, I guess I am about 15 years older than the last time we met. I thought it was a dream, again; nevertheless, I began talking it out and writing what I saw last time. Why am I here again now? Did you ever find out what happened those years ago?"

Bellos looked him over from head to toe. "You should sit down for this, I think."

Bellos sat beside him. "The last time we met, we were across the hall. It was 15 years ago for you, but I just came from that room not five minutes ago for me. I walked directly from our meeting there to here."

Andrew sighed and sat for a second. "I woke up in my bed, thinking I dreamed it all until I found this." He pulled out the headset vault which he got during his first visit. It looked like a flash drive from when he sat in the lounge with Bellos. "I couldn't use it of course in any way. I thought about having it analyzed, but what good would that do? It would have been destroyed. I told parts of the story to a close friend, but we drank a lot together, so it was easy to brush off as bullshit. I carried that little button with me almost every day, everywhere, knowing somehow I would write about it; but I never did, that I know of anyway."

"Well, you did later, and your book has become a prime element in a mystery here, which we are now trying to solve."

Bellos accepted the vault back and sat, praying the man wouldn't disappear.

"Mystery?"

"Yes, it looks like the wrong people read your book. Ultimately, we think that may be why you are here."

Bellos opened the room's door, and the guard handed him something. Bellos showed it to the man and asked, "Is this your book?"

Andrew took it and began reading. "These are my words, my name; the copyright is dated...Jesus!" He started shaking a bit. "You were right about Mr. Burns. I did meet him before, I think. He was a new hire, right, bragging that he could time travel? I showed him that flash drive thingy too. At first, he refused to comment. Finally, he studied it enough to confirm that it came from you, here. I told him things he couldn't discredit that I saw last time. After that, he was very informative. We shared many thoughts and ideas. Eventually, he gave me a headset session, and everything became so clear to me. Déjà vu became a real memory. I remember crying for a week or so it seemed, after he left. It affected me in so many ways."

"I am sorry," Bellos said. "We don't make it a practice to interfere in people's lives on the surface, much less in a case such as yours. I thought my giving you the headset next door would trigger your memory of a man named Marion Brock."

"No, not familiar."

"How about anyone named Brock?"

Andrew shook his head no. Then he hesitated for a second. "Wait, a long time ago, I think; it was when I was in college. I remember the Vietnam War was a big deal to us kids . . ."

"Long ago is right."

"Something about weapons, or ammunition, but it wasn't Marion. It was another name, and, it was the first time I met your Mr. Burns, too."

"Was it Nicolas?"

Just then, Bellos' Knofer clicked again. However, this time it was Jake Burns. "Sir, I have important news. I need to speak to you right away."

"Go ahead," Bellos turned and remarked to Andrew, "speak of the devil! It's your friend, Jake Burns."

Andrew froze as Bellos tapped the Knofer and Burns appeared as a hologram in the center of the room.

"Go ahead, Jake."

"Sir, we have confirmed the Sidron wave-pulses through the pyramid trace back to 1965. It seems there was a great intensity, an inflation, a small Big Bang, if you will. In this case, something of a surprise, a completely separate time anomaly resulted here, from that 1965 event. A posit, a balloon of time separated from our timeline."

"Not an explosion?"

"Of sorts. Of course, there was no sound, but it was a great disturbance; and it was within the Sidron. We believe it was a result of two or more people having Compatibility with a Carrier, an overload. Apparently, another person was the catalyst in some way. The combination of power triggered the event."

"Catalyst?" said Bellos. "I hate that word now. I wonder?"

"You don't think Ms. Angie, do you, sir? I mean she was the catalyst needed for CPT ...Perhaps..."

For a second Bellos had a blank stare. Then, he stepped to the side of the hologram, revealing Andrew.

"Jake, say hello. Do you remember Mr. Andrew, here?"

Bellos gestured toward his visitor. Jake startled, and then he bowed respectfully, saying, "Ah, uh yes, interesting! Good to see you again, my friend."

"Well, I wish I could say the same," Andrew replied.

Bellos began again, "Jake, I think there may be two possibilities for that catalyst you mentioned."

"Ah, yes; I see what you mean. I'll have the lab run comparative tests if our visitor here will consent."

"Good idea," Bellos smiled. "Well, Mr. Andrew, what do you say? Care to help solve our little mystery?"

Andrew looked at the book and around the room. "Will I be allowed to see more than just this room?"

"I think I can arrange that," Bellos said.

Burns began to rant, "Sir, I am reading a new event. We have another problem."

Wheeler burst through the door. "Matt, we have another problem."

"Well, one of you spit it out!"

Jake blurted out, "I just got word that Secretary Swanson has disappeared."

"What? Christ! Tom, take Mr. Andrew here to the lab and run comparative tests on his DNA with our records. Get everything on a genetic profile. See if we have any matches or similarities in any of the colony vaults. Jake, where are you?"

Bellos tapped his Knofer and ordered up a holographic map of inner Earth.

"I am at X-1500 miles east of core, Y-angle 30 degrees north, northeast linear."

Bellos pinpointed Burns' location. "Do we have any intel on what happened?"

"Sir, we need to talk in the same room. I suspect our communiqué is contaminated."

"Do you have a fix on the suspect's location?"

"My Carrier does; yes."

"Then follow the signal and keep in touch. I want to know location and source."

The Knofer cut the call, and Wheeler spoke to Bellos quickly, "Mathew, Gordon was in his office. Patty says he disappeared right in front of her."

Bellos squinted and whispered to himself, "Brock; and it's that Carrier."

Then, he looked back at Tom. "I have to go. I have a meeting with the Bering Strait Commission. Keep digging. Get me anything you find out. Test Mr. Andrew and get me the results."

CHAPTER 55: ROSSI

BOTH JACK SHELDON AND ABBY JOHNSON seemed very uneasy during the plane ride to D.C.

Jack had been in a zone looking out the window and then turned to Abby. "I feel like I should be three places at once. There's so much back at the Complex, and now, Brian and Angie."

"They will be alright. The GGM is on it."

"How soon before we land?"

"Same as two minutes ago, try to relax a little. The pilot will tell us when we approach landing."

"Relax? Are you married, Johnson?"

"No, not yet."

"Well, I am," said Jack, "and not just married. I married the love of my life. She is the love of my death, too."

"Interesting choice of words."

"Yes, because we did die, sort of anyway. Regardless, you wouldn't understand."

"Well, you may be right. Look, down there at the old nuclear power plant outside Harrisburg, Pennsylvania.

Jack looked at what appeared to be a green cloud surrounding the old site. "I read about nuclear power on the surface. Some thought for a long time that it was the energy saving messiah; stupid people."

"Yes, electromagnetic energy wasn't taken seriously at that time. What is that sound?"

"It's coming from your pocket."

"Oh, it's my phone." Jack fumbled and answered, "Hello, Rachel, is that you?"

"No, Dr. Sheldon; this is Charlie Rossi."

"Rossi?" Jack was befuddled for a few seconds, but then put the conversation on speaker. "Hello, Mr. Rossi, how coincidental, I am on my way to see you. Has my wife contacted you yet?"

Johnson looked on pensively and tapped her Knofer to trace the call. "He's not in DC at all, Jack."

"Yes, I met your wife, briefly. That is why I am calling, in fact. She is with me. We are on a little trip together, and we would like you to join us."

"Jack," Abby whispered, "he is calling from Rio de Janeiro."

Jack rolled his eyes and then spoke into the phone, "You mean you kidnapped my wife?"

"Strong word, kidnapped. Let's just say, you two have been invited to a meeting, and if I were you, I'd bring the last part of the notes on your treatise, my friend."

"I am not your friend. If you harm her in any way, it will be the last thing you ever do!"

"Oh, she won't be harmed; rest assured. We only want those pages. You know that."

"Where's the meeting?"

"Write these coordinates down. We will call you when you are within a half hour of landing. And doctor, do I have to tell you to come alone?"

"I'll be there." Rossi hung up, and Jack looked at Johnson, "Did you get all that?"

"Yes, it's on its way to GGM. I'll give this to the pilot. Jack, one of the Knofers we tracked came from Rio. Does your wife have one?"

"Frankly, I'm not sure."

"I'll be back. Try not to get too upset. We need your brains working, not your emotions running wild."

The plane turned southeast, toward Rio.

ANGIE AND BRIAN finally made it back to the steps of the Arden city courthouse. They stood looking up at the clock tower.

"Why did we rush babe; we are way early."

"Brian, you can't trust that time. You heard Mr. Wheeler."

"Jesus, he was a hologram! And why should I believe any of this? Time anomaly? The whole thing is ridiculous. It's bad science fiction."

"Yeah, well, I believe him. I'm living it. Let's go."

"Wait! Didn't you tell me you were outside on these steps when it happened?"

Angie stopped cold. "You're right. We need to look right here. Let's see; you, I mean the other Brian, and I came out of the doors up there. We walked down the steps, over there. Yes, it should be about here. Look around. See if you notice anything strange."

"Strange? This whole thing is strange," said Brian.

"Yes, well, look for a blurry place or something in the air that shouldn't be there."

"This is nuts. Okay, I am looking for blurry. Nope, everything seems in focus. Now what?"

Angie sat down on the steps frustrated. "Hmm, maybe it's something else or somewhere else."

"Good thinking, babe; brilliant."

"Maybe we are approaching this from the wrong angle."

"Why don't we go inside and get a cup of coffee at least? Better yet, I could use some food."

"Inside? That's it, Brian!" She grabbed his head and kissed him hard on the mouth. "I love you. Come on."

"Where?"

"To Room 210, where it must have started, it has to be there."

"Are we going inside?" Brian rose slowly and followed her. "Yeah, that makes perfect sense. You can't find anything out here, so it must be in there. Great deduction, Sherly-locks! Oh, my God!"

Angie turned at the top of the steps and said, "We have to search where the event actually took place. The only other place with people was Room 210. We start there. Come on, slowpoke."

"I find your reasoning difficult to accept."

"Think about it. Was I the event or collateral damage? That means the main event was someone else!"

"Well, how do we find out what or who?"

"Simple, nothing has happened to me. I am just with you. We search a slow laborious search. Now come on!"

"Your reasoning is woman's thinking, not deductive."

"Come on, anyway; I'm not a lawyer."

"Well, I am."

They walked quickly up the stairs, opened the double doors and hurried to Room 210. "Okay, Inspector Angie," Brian opened the courtroom door. "Please, after you, miss."

"Thank you, sir."

Brian stopped, as the door closed. "Boy, it's a different place without the commotion, isn't it?"

Angie had already walked to the judge's bench. "My guess is, if the event took place in here, it was in the jury box or around the judge's area over there. We'll each take a side. You look over there. Be thorough; examine everything, inch by inch. But don't touch anything, especially, if you see something that doesn't belong."

"What the hell does that mean? I have no idea what to look for."

"Wheeler said we would know it when we find it. Just take your time."

"Fine."

After a time, Angie stood up straight, as though she had an epiphany. "Brian, you hate this guy, right? I mean Marshall, you hate him, right?"

"Yes, I hate him. I'd have him dead if I could. He arranged to have my parents killed. Wouldn't you?"

"He's here, in here somewhere, isn't he?'

"I guess so, in a jail cell. I don't know; so, what?"

"I want to meet him. Maybe he knows something. Let's find him. I am sure he is somehow involved with all this."

"What about our search here?"

"I just want to talk to him."

"The holding cells are right under us. Why would they let us in? It's sentencing day."

"Come on; you know your way around here. You are the lawyer for God's sake. Get me in there. Think of something."

"Jesus, well, you're not boring; I'll give you that. Follow me."

They walked out and down the hall to the stairwell. At the bottom, a jail guard saw them and stood up from his desk. "I am sorry, you two; we are not open to the public, and it's not visiting hours. You have to leave."

CHAPTER 57: O.P.A.S-OREGON PARTICLE

ACCELERATED SCIENCES

JAKE BURNS WALKED into the main lobby of the O.P.A.S. Corporate Offices in downtown Seattle, Washington, and stood in front of the main receptionist.

"May I help you, sir?" she asked.

"I'd like to see Mr. Oscar Randall. I believe he is expecting me."

"Your name, sir?"

"Jake Burns. Detective Inspector, Jake Burns."

"Oh, yes, I see it here, Mr. Burns; you may go right up. Take elevator 10, down the hall up to the 30th floor. His office is straight out the elevator."

Burns did so and walked into Randall's reception area. The secretary invited him to sit, and within a few moments, a 5'8" salt and peppered gray-haired man, in a dark well-tailored suit, walked out to meet Jake.

"Mr. Burns, I am Oscar Randall. Please come in."

They shook hands and Jake followed him into his large office. It was 40 feet wide by 100 feet long, bound on two sides by windows overlooking the Pacific Ocean. One wall was jagged rock, to remind everyone of the glorious mountains surrounding the skyline and port. At one end were a couch, several lounge chairs and a 15-foot bar with a well-stocked refrigerator behind it. Randall walked to the bar and called to Jake, "Please, make yourself comfortable. Would you like something to drink?"

"Alright, yes, do you have any potato vodka?"

"You speak my language, straight up or rocks?"

"Rocks, please."

"I'll make it two."

Jake meandered along the glass cabinets that lead to the bar. They displayed the history of O.P.A.S. and described its product lines.

"We don't advertise anymore," Randall said. "We started as one of the Brock Companies. As you can see, we have diversified for centuries, and those are just the highlights. We had litigations alleging the company became too big and was controlling too many markets. Finally, we bargained regarding monopoly laws. It was highly controversial for a long time. A lot of underhanded political negotiating took place, as you can imagine. Brock bought and sold us several times. We became one of his business units, so we could maintain a foothold and stay the premier scientific developer of *particle phenomena* in North America."

Jake was captivated as he looked at the pictures and read each of the captions on the displays.

- 1965: Nicolas Brock. Brock Ammunition Company. "Our companies are committed to the fundamental right of the people, as stated in our Constitution, and as eloquently spoken by our founding father, George Washington."

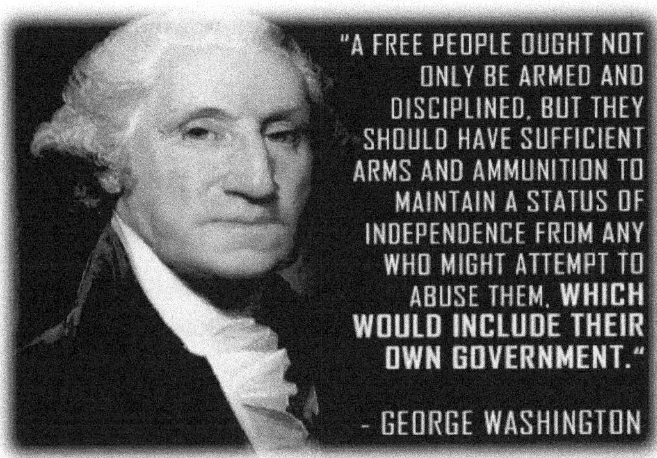

- 2040: Brock Finance Develops Revolutionary Drone Warfare Modules to Fight Global Terrorism.

- 2160: Dark History – New Family Leader of Brock Finance, Marissa Ann Brock, Invests in New Nazi Movement to Rid World of Terrorism. Pakistan Falls to Nazis.

- 2196: Marissa's Son, Marion Brock I, Stops Selling Arms to Pakistan, which is instrumental in wiping out the new Nazis. He expanded ammunition manufacturing to diversify and Brock Finance Investing in commercial industries.

- 2199: Marissa Brock Assassinated in London by Nazis. Marion Brock, I wipes out remaining Nazis in all countries. Brock global companies Golden Age Begins.

- 2302: Brock Companies and Germany collaborate to develop new Gyroscopic Technology for flying saucers.

- 2306: Particle Accelerator Galaxy, Dessera-59, Discovered by Brock Company and German Military Research.

- 2570: Two Generations: Marion Brock II **expanded** space technologies to incorporate new physics findings, and Marion Brock III Founded and Developed Oregon Particle Acceleration Sciences – O.P.A.S.

- 2666: Gyroscopic Gravitational Expanse Satellite Constructed by Brock Universal, O.P.A.S. – The First Orbital Space Probe That Can Measure One Planet's Gravitational Plane Relative to Another and the Sun.

- 2797: O.P.A.S. Photo Laser Imagery Offered to Public. First Used to Map the Moon for Mining Fuels to be employed in Space Travel.

- 2855: O.P.A.S. Constructs Commercial Fuel Inventory Module and Distribution Port Orbiting Moon.

- 2933: Transportation Acquisition – Personal Vehicle Stellar Model 75, Operated by Electric Motors, Guided by O.P.A.S. Gyroscopic Technology and using magnetic resonance to levitate.

- 2983: Brock Research Develops New Inter-Global Satellite Internet for all communicative devices to include 'Off Earth', moon and space station capabilities.

- 2988 Brock Research Partners with Swanson Developers to Expand Medical Research in Arden, New Mexico.

- 2996: Marion Brock IV Commits to Communication Research and Development of Video/Audio Device Technology.

Jake finished studying the history and turned to Randall. "I didn't realize the magnitude of it all."

"Yes, it's really something, isn't it? As I said; those are just the highlights. Now tell me, Mr. Burns, what is a police detective from Arden, New Mexico doing in Seattle; and why see me?"

"I'm on a case involving one of your companies, Time-Travel Inc."

"I wish it was ours," said Randall. "But, no, several angel investors came up with capital to buy it."

"Angel investors?"

"Silent trillionaires. At least, that's my understanding. We didn't know it was to be a Brock handled enterprise until the announcement yesterday."

Randall handed Jake a drink and offered a toast, "To your success, sir." Jake chuckled, and they both sipped.

"Please, make yourself comfortable. How can I help you?"

"O.P.A.S. . . . I always wanted to visit here and understand physics, but I don't think I ever will. I became a flatfoot in New York, you know. I worked my way up through the five boroughs."

Jake noticed the words etched on the rock wall, up to the right of the bar behind Randall and walked closer to read them.

Randall watched and commented, "Yes, it's an interesting motto; don't you agree? *'Hope and Love abide with all who believe. May we all believe in the future.'*

Jake repeated it and then asked, "Is that your logo?"

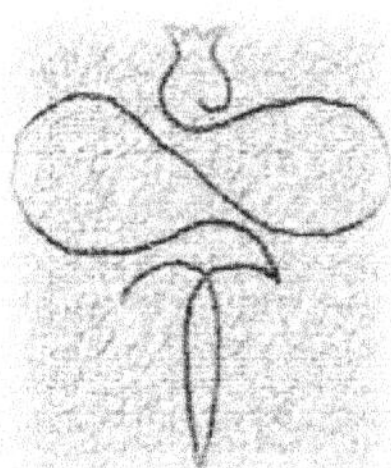

"No, actually, that's quite an ancient art design. I think it was a family logo at one time. I just like the way it makes a rose from one continuous line. It reminds me of how successful and beautiful our efforts can be, if we just push on, step-by-step, steadfast. The words and flower were created almost a thousand years ago. It's a rose." Randall walked over; stood beside Burns; and explained, "I had it etched there when I got this job. It's my daily mantra."

"I see. Mr. Randall, how long have you been C.E.O. of O.P.A.S.?"

"A little over a year now; why?"

"Do you remember an employee, Dr. Hamill G. Stevens?"

"Yes, he was quite favored, before he quit. He was pirated by Time-Travel Inc. when they bought one of our old facilities, most were older warehouses really, and one with a smaller particle accelerator below it. The deal closed the first quarter I started."

"Smaller accelerator?"

"Mr. Burns, do you have any idea what we do?"

"Besides what's on the wall, what I've studied up to now, and I know what I've read in your shareholder's statement. I know your history a bit too. You came from the famous Switzerland Complex, right? Company assets are roughly $160 trillion, up 12 percent in one year. You have invested heavily, not only in man's effort to find the answer to what makes up matter, but also in practical space exploration, fuel to run space stations and vehicular gyroscopes. The company also collaborated to keep our intercontinental transportation in tune, indirectly, of course. You have published two dissertations in the last five years, each focusing on Brock's space mining; supplying fuels from the Moon to Mars, as well as private sector travel. Of late, your investment firms, excuse me, angel investors, have collaborated with Mr. Charles Rossi to address and hopefully contract fixing the Bering Strait tunnel systems. You are quite the busy man, Mr. Randall."

"Well, thank you. Impressive knowledge, to say the least, inspector. You obviously know more about me than I do you. But I am still waiting for you to get to the point."

"To start with, I want to know about Marion Brock. How exactly are you and Mr. Rossi involved with him?"

Randall stood in front of the etched words, took a breath and then he turned, put his glass down and lit a cigar.

"Would you like one?"

"No, thanks."

"Mr. Burns, I first read those two sentences in a book that Charlie Rossi gave me long before I started here. Everything had been going wonderfully in my life. I am a fortunate man so far. At the time, I had been involved with the two greatest discoveries humanity had ever made, The Sidron Examination, and now, here, the Bridge Particle."

Jake interrupted, "Believe it or not, I know what Sidron is, go on."

"Ah, well then, the Sidron was first discovered centuries ago in, of all places, here in the United States. Who would have thought? Unfortunately, at that time, neither the mindset nor the technology was advanced enough to investigate it, so they suppressed the discovery and filed it for a later date. Recently, you must have heard; we found a new subatomic particle. We labeled it the Bridge because it pulses back and forth from one time to another. We are confident time travel is within our reach. Can you imagine? Anyway, Rossi and his group of companies offered me this position, specifically, to lead this company into the next great adventure, time travel."

"So, Rossi owns controlling shares in OPAS?"

"It's a public company, but most shares are split between governments and some very influential private sectors. Rossi is one of those, on the Board of Boards, you might say."

"Back to Stevens, please," Jake said.

"Unfortunately, the man who had the hands-on experience in the research of time travel was, in fact, Stevens. He is a brilliant mind. Anyway, Rossi's interests pumped money into OPAS, and the funding is building us the largest particle accelerator in the world, only 20 miles north of here. Also, we started constructing one in orbit, around Earth, to support our time travel efforts. We are one of just eight locations around the world that continues to investigate and proof particles deep within the atom. Over centuries, particle accelerators have evolved from the linear to our new paddle design. It includes some rather plush living quarters. We are tweaking the complete construction, and plan to be online within six months. We will change the world and our future."

"Very interesting," Jake said. "I just need to ask you a few more questions, if you don't mind."

"Anyway, through merger and buyouts, the usual big money deals, OPAS sold the older local accelerator . . ."

"Can you tell me to whom and where it is?"

". . . To the same outfit that pirated Stevens, Time-Travel Inc. That accelerator is located about 30-35 miles south of the city. Their research is supposed to be local, but I'm not sure of the particular address."

"Can you find out for me?"

"Randall pushed a button on the coffee table's display, and his secretary answered, "Yes, sir?"

"Kate, do we have any old files on Hamill Stevens?"

"Perhaps, sir. You need a password, though."

"Send it to me."

"Yes, sir, on its way."

Jake's eyes perked up, "Your secretary has passwords?"

"Not quite. She has one to get into where I enter mine. Quite secure, I assure you."

Randall tapped a section of the tabletop, and it displayed a 3D screen on his lap.

"There, now I do this, enter hers and then, here, mine and voila, Hamill Stevens."

A bust size model of Stevens appeared along with a flat display of his history and personnel file.

"There, Mr. Burns, read for yourself."

Burns did, "There is a mailing address here but no title to the location: 4822 S.P. Way, Seattle, Washington . . . Nothing else, eh?"

"I'm afraid not. Everything we have is there before you."

"Well, that confirms it."

"What?"

"Brock and Rossi, they're so obvious. My bet is Stevens doesn't live at this address either. But I have to start somewhere. Thanks for your help, Mr. Randall."

"You are welcome, but exactly how do you know I'm not a bad guy and involved with Rossi or Brock?"

Burns smiled, as he put on his fedora, "Because, my dear fellow, I am a detective."

They shook hands; Jake turned to walk out; and then he stopped, turned and said, "One more thing, I checked your complete history up to our meeting. You are clean. Oh, and I know the guy who wrote the words etched on your wall."

Jake tipped his hat and left, as Randall chuckled and replied, "That's two more things by the way."

CHAPTER 58: TIME TRAVEL INC.

JAKE'S CARRIER, MIRIAM, burrowed the short trip and docked at the Post Platform under Seattle's subway station, just off 15th Avenue. "We have arrived at the destination, Jake Burns. Thank you for a most exhilarating ride."

"Great. You're welcome."

"I have integrated into your Knofer and will maintain security protocols."

"I have it covered, thanks."

"I will remain here for your return trip."

"I shouldn't be too long."

Jake exited the beast and took a bubble unit to the surface. Then, he hailed a taxi and rode to the address

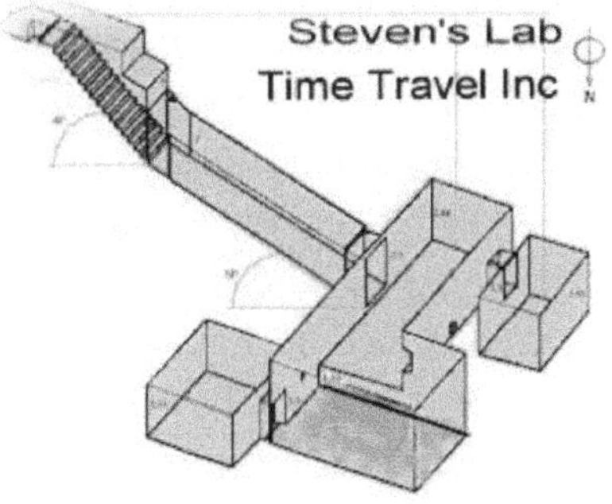

which Oscar Randall gave to him. When the cab stopped in front of Lucian High School, he sat in the back seat silent, perplexed.

"This is it," the cab driver said.

"Are you sure?" asked Jake.

"Yes, sir, I have picked up kids here, on occasion, and taken them home. Granted it's very rare, but this is 4822 S. P. Way. It's the only one in the city."

Jake shook his head wearing a frown. He paid the cabby, got out of the car and watched it drive away.

"Now what? I guess I'll talk to the principal."

Time-Travel Inc.'s facility housed four underground floors dedicated to research and administration. The mailing address was an old post office box to keep the would-be curious away.

"Hamill Stevens had a private experimental lab extending directly off the decoy surface building. His lab was completed within the last six months, specifically to accommodate secrecy regarding Semitri and any new particle discoveries. The lab looked more like a tomb in the Valley of the Kings.

Back in the school, Jake Burns entered and walked down the hallway past several classrooms. He stopped at one briefly to watch through the see-through glass door. A teacher was demonstrating a new tool, holding up a small Knofer-like object that projected holograms in front of each student. Each student began touching the holograms and giggling. One or two noticed Burns at the door. The teacher looked at him and stopped the lecture. Burns looked embarrassed and walked on down the hallway. A sign and arrow guided him into the principal's office.

"Good morning, sir. May I help you?" One woman asked. She got up from her desk and walked to the chest-high counter where Burns stood. Burns removed his hat and showed her his badge.

"Yes, please, I'd like to see your principal. It's a police matter."

"Alright, I'll try and reach him. Frankly, I am not sure if he is still here. We only have three classes going on right now. Very different hours, since the new policies went into effect."

"I noticed one class as I was walking; why only three?"

The woman smiled kindly and replied, "We are a special needs facility and cater to single parents with strange work hours." She leaned a bit over the counter toward Burns and whispered, "You understand."

As she did so, Jake noticed out the window next to them that a limo had just pulled up to a shed, across the parking lot behind the school. He watched as the driver got out and opened the back door. Jake nodded and smiled at the woman. She went back to her desk and paged the principal. Burns couldn't believe his eyes. The figure of the man getting out of the limo was unmistakable. It was Marion Brock. Jake had no way of knowing it was really Clone-Brock. The billionaire nodded thanks to his driver and then quickly walked around the car into the ordinary looking brick shed. It resembled a small old garage. The limo sped off, and Burns thought, *a high school? Brilliant! Why can't I think of things like this?*

He turned to the woman again. "Excuse me, ma'am, is that a garage or storage facility across the parking lot, over there?"

"Oh, we don't own that. It's not part of the school. I believe it's a storage unit for one of the houses down the block, I think; but don't quote me. Would you like some coffee, Mr.? I am sorry, I didn't catch your name."

"Jake Burns, ma'am. And yours?"

"Dolly," she giggled, "Dolly, Miss Dolly Waddell. I will try paging Mr. Tate again. He hasn't answered yet."

Jake smiled and said, "That's alright, Dolly; tell him I was here, and I will be back. I see I am running a little late. Thank you so much."

Burns tipped his hat, turned and quickly walked back to the school's front door and around to the back of the building. He carefully approached the shed. As Jake gripped the doorknob, he turned his Knofer on, initiating its defense mode's weapon system. Then, he entered; and just 10-ft inside, a hallway veered to the right. It was a stairwell leading downward some 100-ft or more. He stepped cautiously, took out his Ever-Life standard air gun and pointed it straight ahead into the dimly lit concrete tunnel.

At the stairs' end, a ramp continued even further down. The light changed from purple to a red tint; and as he continued to walk, the lights went out behind him. Blackness seemed to force him forward. The sound of his footsteps was the only thing he heard. After another 200-ft or so, Burns came to a door. To the right and left above him, small tunnels were extending through walls. The average eye would think the entire area was a sewage runoff. He tried opening the door, but it wouldn't budge. There wasn't even a sound of a lock clicking as he pushed and pulled.

Fine, now what?

Jake turned around. There was no other possible way to go.

Well, I am not going back, so?

He put his Knofer on the floor. "Examine and display the door lock."

The Knofer ticked; and within seconds, it showed a 3-foot holographic image of the lock mechanism.

"Can you disengage?"

Jake watched a red dot on the hologram move quickly all around the image. He heard several more ticking sounds, and then the hologram disappeared. He picked up the Knofer and turned the knob. The door opened.

"Voila! I love this technology."

Jake walked into a large room, which was lighted in a bluish tint. He noticed on the wall next to the door an oval with three letters in it, TTI, "Time-Travel Inc., this is it."

He looked to the right, and about 50-ft away was another room that stepped downward, yet again. "This place looks like a smaller version of Time Trust."

Jake walked across the room and opened another door without difficulty. What he saw shocked him. It looked like a morgue, filled with bodies lying on gurneys. "There have to be 200 in here."

Burns lifted the sheet covering one. "Marion Brock?"

Then, he walked a few yards and lifted another, then another and another. "They're all the same. Christ!"

Jake looked through the large window on one of the sidewalls and was shocked to see row after row of finished clones staring into space. Their eyes were opened and glassy, but they didn't blink, and the bodies didn't move. Jake marveled at how they were arranged in military-like rows, 50-deep and 100-across. "How did they get them all lined up like this?"

He got a sick feeling in the pit of his stomach. "They are not dead, but they're not breathing." He looked around at the dark room and ceiling lights. 'This is where they are doing it."

He noticed movement from the other side of the room and walked toward a section holding rows of cylindrical glass tube-like structures. Each contained one body in a pristine amniotic state. What Burns saw next made him very uneasy. Lining the sides of the room, there were several larger horizontal glass tanks, each with one clone of Marion Brock laying on its back, writhing, stretching, groaning, and expanding upward, becoming very fat. Jake watched as a duplicate body grew out of the lower one, a clone from a clone, rising out of itself and then above itself, floating until identical twins faced each other.

"Christ almighty, they didn't learn this from us."

"You are quite right," a voice said behind Burns. "We developed the technique ourselves. It's weightless in there. This stage is called, 'air amniotic.'"

Jake turned around startled and quickly reached for his gun.

"No need for violence here. So, you are the visitor. I am Dr. Hamill Stevens. I won't harm you." He extended his hand and, after some hesitation, Burns relaxed and shook it. They stood and watched the bodies detaching as Stevens spoke, "Quite something, isn't it?"

"I have never seen anything like it," Jake said. "How do you know me?"

"Simple deduction. The silent alarms triggered, letting me know you're here. Frankly, I was told to prepare for you. You are part of the plan." Stevens smiled.

"You expected me?" asked Jake.

"Relax Mr. Burns. I will answer any questions you have. This is all quite benign." Stevens turned to face the clones. "Look at them. It's a miracle of our technology."

"I had no idea technology like this existed. It's quite mesmerizing."

Stevens was quick to banter. "I don't mean to be impolite here; but, exactly how did you get in?"

"I am the Chief Inspector of the Arden City Police, sonny. I don't give away trade secrets. Jake showed Stevens his badge and continued questioning, "So, this is a cloning facility?"

"Arden city? It says that's in New Mexico. This is Washington State."

Jake replied, "Yes but a policeman's a policeman, no matter what state he's in. So, is this a cloning facility?"

"Yes, it is. Good deducing."

"How long does the process take, anyway? How long does the one body suspend above the other like that?"

"The growing process is two days. Separation takes about an hour. When it is completed, the top clone falls onto the bottom one. The collapse is what starts them breathing; much like a baby is stimulated to breathe in the final stages of labor."

Just as Stevens said it, the top body in the cell fell on the under one. Both clones jerked involuntarily and took breaths. Then, the bottom clone pushed the top one off.

"There," Stevens pointed. "See? Perfect. They will sleep for a while and air-dry, losing most of the dead skin between them. Then, we retrieve and store them over there. You've seen the inventory; I take it?"

"Yes, I imagine you have quite a clothing drive."

Stevens thought a second. "Clothing drive? Ah, clothing drive. It's a joke, very good. Very good."

"Thanks," Jake said. "What if the fall doesn't start them breathing?"

"Well, then we don't have life; now do we?"

"So, you discard them if there is no reaction from the fall?"

"Not really," Stevens said. "A buzzer sounds in another room, and technicians come in to try to revive each one. But frankly, that's rare. Anyway, we have plenty more, as you can see."

"So, how do you dispose of the bodies, if they don't come around?"

"Follow me, Mr. Burns. While I'd love to share all our secrets, you are not supposed to be here."

"Actually, I got this address from your old company. Oscar Randall gave it to me. He said some very complimentary things about you and your time discoveries."

"Oh, are you interested in time travel?"

"Yes, very."

"Are you here because of clones or time?"

"Both, I am a detective investigating Mr. Marion Brock."

"Marion? He is eccentric; I'll give you that, but hardly worth a detective's investigation. In fact, he's due here anytime. I must run some medical tests on him. We think he was affected by a time-test we ran yesterday."

"Exactly how long have you been cooped up in here?"

"This place is self-sufficient. I don't leave unless I have to. Recent experiments require my complete attention. Here we are." They had walked out of the one room, down the hall and into another. "Policy dictates I keep this door locked. Please, come in."

"But policy says you can let a stranger in, just because he shows a badge?"

Stevens chuckled, "Not quite; you see, the sensors during your walk here rendered all of your communications and any weapons ineffective. You are quite harmless unless you wish a physical confrontation."

Burns grinned. "No, thank you. If my joints n muscles were at full capacity, perhaps. But I am interested in learning more."

They walked into a very high-tech room, reminding Burns again of one of the Time Trust labs.

"Impressive, what is all this?'

"Without giving away every secret, I can tell you it's a time travel laboratory. The chamber is to the left, around there."

Burns gave a cursory look and then approached Chamber 1. "So how does it work, actually, time travel I mean?"

"There is no way I can explain it so you will understand completely."

Jake replied, "I think I can safely say I'm qualified to hear your spiel."

"I would be of no use if I told it all; now would I? But the short version goes something like this. You stand in the chamber, and sensors calculate the number of sub-particles that make up your body."

"So, they don't count cells or molecules; they count particles?"

"Right, actually sub-particles."

"That's a lot of stuff; there are trillions of cells alone in the human body."

"Yes, unimaginable numbers, hence the need for accuracy; so, we leave that to the computers. The equipment is highly sensitive and complicated to build, and expensive."

"Hence the need for you, Dr. Stevens . . ." Jake smiled.

"I like to think so. After my success at OPAS, I was approached to apply my 'Bridge Particle' findings to this effort."

"Hmm. . . And I take it; one is naked in the chamber?"

"Yes, one has to be. Otherwise, anything additional would mix with the sub-particles, and who knows what the resulting traveler would look like, much less if he or she would even be alive."

Jake felt the glass surrounding the chamber. "It feels different."

Yes, it's all high-temperature transparent Ryton, a resin discovered by ancient plastic compounders who realized metal couldn't be trusted in applications such as this. Everything is, of course, immaculate, self-cleaning as a matter of fact. The chamber is continuously sterilizing itself inside, to be prepared at a moment's notice. Anyway, I designed the equipment and mapped all the software. There is nothing like it anywhere. Once we have an accurate calculation, it all takes place automatically. All I do is push this, here. I've already set the chamber's next user destination. It's ready to go."

"Where is he going and who is the user?"

"First, there has to be compatibility genetically, to displace the sub-particle mix and be able to travel on the time-road to whenever. As to who is going? Our first test subject was a Mr. David Marshall, from some secret cult or something. Mr. Brock picks the subject, and we calculate everything based on that. I don't really examine the history of our candidates."

"Interesting word, Compatibility; what if the genetic mix isn't there?"

"I wouldn't activate the chamber; otherwise whatever particles displaced wouldn't reverse and replace themselves in the same order."

Jake scratched his head and said, "What, come again?"

Stevens was on a roll. "Just look at this. It is much more than a communication device. Marion gave it to me. It has a record of our first test patient's information in it."

Stevens showed Jake one of Brock's VADs. Jake took it and asked, "What is it? A phone?"

"Not at all; Marion calls it his new Video Audio Device he got from Dave Marshall. It's a prototype, an engineering model. It's functional. I was able to input Mr. Marshall's data from it and program the chamber, but something else triggered. An event happened. The chamber started on its own and then just shut down. Our subject, Mr. Marshall, was sent into the past instead of the future. All activity ceased. We couldn't get that chamber to operate. It stopped after Marshall went back."

"What was your power source?"

"Interesting you ask. Marion controls one himself, and I have discovered something brand new, a combination of electromagnetic energy from a latitudinal network, brand new to us. I followed magnetic particle charges to the many pyramids around the world...

"...I have a focused recovery and discharge control right over here. The combination of Marion's inputs and my new pyramid charges have made the difference in capacity. However, even though we have no proof, all the monitors there recorded that several time events took place. We think they are Sidron events. Look here. I have never seen anything like it . . . And here, I can only call this particular one an anomaly; a kind of time distortion.

"Wait a minute. How can you say someone traveled in time if he didn't show up in that booth? Doesn't the traveler have to be where this equipment is?"

"Yes, I always thought so too, but, as it turns out, one can reappear in the past without a booth, because he is already there, you see. He has a receptacle to capture him. That's precisely what happened to Mr. Marshall on our first test case. It's fascinating, although how is unexplainable at the moment. You see, just before I came here, when I was at OPAS, I made a discovery, the 'Bridge Particle.' My success in that regard was the reason I got this job. We always knew sub-particles could be in two places at the same time, and the bridge particle was the answer to explaining that. I was certain of it, and the papers we wrote proved it; that is until the first practical application. We found out here that we needed to figure out how to read the construct record of Mr. Marshall's DNA to transmit him properly. We thought we solved that, but he never showed up at the destination, he went backward. That has stopped the whole effort.

Jake reacted, "Did you find the answer? How does it work?"

"To send a subject into the future, the starting point, in this case, was Mr. Marshall at his criminal trial. He was the construct, the subject to travel, which our computer targeted and calculated into sub-particles. Then, the computer chamber sent a signal of subject's coded sub-particle information to Mr. Marshall in the past. The subject's body then reacts and triggers all the sub-particles to change to light; and the chamber here to receive the light of Mr. Marshall, using its electromagnetic power, through a sort of wire conduit. The computer chamber here receives, reconstructs, and changes the light back to matter in the chamber. In this case a future time, thus getting him out of jail. However, for some reason, Mr. Marshall went back several hours into the past. The sub-particles regrew him in an already existing body in his jail cell. You've seen science fiction movies, right?"

Jake looked puzzled. "Yes, I've seen Syfy. I understand what you describe, but it's definitely Syfy. What *wire* does the signal go through to pass into the past or future?"

"Long ago, scientists discovered the wire-conductor. They called it the Sidron. All sub-particles of everything travel on it. We just had to find out how to focus the light and connect to it, plug into it."

"And, how did you do that?"

"As I said, I discovered the bridge particle. My group published the 'Bridge Papers'; and, at the same time, unfortunately for us; then, the bottom dropped out of our program. The company decided a new direction. They hired Oscar Randall, and eventually, I got a better offer. Here I am."

"So, is everything corrected now?"

"Not quite. Marion contracted with a brilliant doctor some time ago, Dr. Jack Sheldon. He found several new aspects to duplicating that involved individuality. He discovered that man's memory or personality coagulates in one place somewhere in the brain, after death. He called it, CPT, Chemical Personality Transfer. That was quite a bump in the road for us, a slow-down at any rate. And since the first experiments failed, and Dr. Sheldon failed to deliver the final pages of CPT, we looked for the other paper he wrote on Particle Displacement. We had to interpolate a lot, since Sheldon refused to comply. We were at a crossroads."

"Why?"

"We needed the CPT location in the brain. We had to be exact in measuring it properly. We would then be more apt to correctly reconstruct a person's memory/personality and guarantee the same person is reconstructed at the destination. If we do that, all travel would be revolutionized, along with medical science and healthcare markets."

Jake found a lab chair and sat down, listening in disbelief. "So, what happened?"

"Well, we needed the formula for CPT . Marion guaranteed me he could get it. After all, he was a partner with the doctor, and he was part owner of the medical complex, where they kept the formula. He said he would get it personally. Unfortunately, the man Brock hired, Mr. Marshall, who we picked as our first subject, was arrested for murder, and the formula disappeared. We inputted all the information we could regarding the subject's construct to see if we could run the first test, but it failed. We didn't even have a reading in the equipment. That is when Marion brought me this."

Stevens opened a drawer and handed Jake a spiral bound book. Jake read the first page, "Particle Displacement, use of the Sidron by Dr. Jack Avuar Sheldon."

Jake was speechless and then said, "Holy crap!"

Stevens reached and pointed to the last section of the treatise. "It's very thorough, but incomplete. Look here."

Jake thumbed through. "The last pages are missing. I don't understand. You need the info on the Sidron event, right?"

"I needed the rest of the pages to confirm. After all, I am a scientist."

Jake reacted. "So, Marion Brock stole the papers but didn't get the last pages?"

"Stole? Hardly." Stevens shook his head. "No, no, no; as I said, he partnered with a brilliant doctor to bring life back from death."

"Yes, Jack Sheldon..."

Stevens seemed to ignore the name and walked to a table across the room. "Over here I have the contract." Stevens picked up what looked like a stack of legal documents stapled together. "Right here, as you can see."

Jake took the papers from Stevens and read the first page.

"Look at the last page, Mr. Burns."

Jake flipped to the end and read, "'DO NOT USE ELECTRICITY, RATHER...There is nothing after that."

Stevens raised his eyebrows. "Now go back and read page #2."

Jake flipped back and read the bold type:

Property in Partnership, as developed by Dr. Jack Avuar Sheldon and financed by
Mr. Marion Brock, Brock Companies Worldwide

Jake's jaw dropped. "There are two signatures here, Dr. Jack Sheldon and Marion Brock."

"I know," said Stevens. "And they are originals, not copies. However, as you can see, the last pages are missing in both the treatise and the contract. Dr. Sheldon is to blame here, not Mr. Brock. Sheldon owed us those pages."

"My God!" Jake felt his heart and legs deflate. "I don't believe it. It can't be true. You're good, Mr. Stevens; you are very good."

Stevens approached Burns and looked Jake straight in the eyes. "I don't particularly care if you believe me or not; but it is true. What do you think? I knew you were coming and rehearsed all this? Or in case some stranger breaks in here, I keep a copy of that to convince you it was true? Come on, detective! I'm not that clever. All I want is to finish my job. I was sure the last pages would solve the puzzle, that's all."

"You must know that your testing has caused havoc within both the Sidron and in time."

"I think Mr. Brock may be linked to it somehow. I don't know how, though. Thank God I built another chamber. I talked to Mr. Brock. He said he was bringing a much more reliable source of energy. He is due anytime. At first, I thought you were him."

CHAPTER 59: JACK IN RIO

JACK SHELDON AND ABBY JOHNSON SAT in the Ever-Life jet on a private airfield, just north of the Great Christ statue in Rio de Janeiro. The city had to rebuild the statue completely when the terrorist wars ended. It became a reminder to the world of what happened there. The Portuguese were instrumental in changing the tide of the global terrorists. As a result, the Brock companies invested heavily in the people of Rio.

Jack's phone rang, and as he reached for it, Abby grabbed his arm. "Before you answer, remember, keep your head."

"Are we set?" Jack asked.

"Yes, we are."

Jack lifted the phone to his ear and started walking down the outside stairs of the plane. "Hello?"

"Hello, Dr. Sheldon."

"Yes?"

"Do you have what we asked for?"

"Where is my wife?"

"Do you see a car coming toward you?"

"Yes, I see it."

The phone went dead. A brown four-door sedan drove up and stopped at the bottom of the plane's staircase. A large ugly man, with what looked like one eyebrow across his forehead, got out of the front door passenger side and opened the rear door for Jack. The doctor stared at the man as if he'd never seen anyone like him, and then, Jack got in the back seat. Sitting next to him was a small figure of a man.

"Hello, doctor; my name is Rash InVoy."

He extended his hand, but Jack wasn't playing politely.

"I have heard of you. You are Marion Brock's henchman."

InVoy smiled. "I am his Chief of Staff. I see you want to get right to it. Fine. Did you bring the last pages?"

"Chief of Staff, ha! You people think he's president of some country."

"Perhaps even many countries . . . Did you bring the papers or not?"

Jack was obviously angry and had to keep from striking out. "Here's how this is going to work. The pages you want are on a chip, which is directly linked to my brain through this phone. If you don't give me my wife or if you harm either one of us in any way, the information will self-destruct. My phone is tied to my retinal print, my fingerprint and a password."

"Hmm, interesting threat, all I want are the pages, the right pages. We have methods of checking their accuracy. It's simple. I will take you to your wife; you give me the pages. If they verify, you both may leave. If the information is in any way false, you both die."

InVoy smiled, turned his head and looked out the window as the car sped off.

Back in the plane, Abby Johnson tracked Jack on her Knofer. It recorded and replayed the conversation between Jack and InVoy. She sent the recording to Jake Burns and the GGM. Then, she deployed two Carriers to follow the GPS signals and to be available at a moment's notice. After setting her Knofer to defense protocol, she deplaned and drove far enough behind InVoy's car to assure no detection.

InVoy was a shrewd character and naturally provocative. As they road in the car, he tried to be civil with Jack. "Did you know, doctor, this was once a great seaport, as well as quite a playground for the rich and famous?"

Jack replied, "Talk to me when you give me my wife."

"I see no reason to be uncivilized or impolite. We will both leave here with what we want if you keep your end of the bargain. Perhaps you two may even decide to stay and enjoy the city life."

"I doubt it."

"Rio de Janeiro means marvelous city, home of Carnival de Brazil; festival of festivals; you must have heard of it? Read about it? All the incredible costumes, ladies running in the streets, public sex. What a life. Unfortunately, also an excellent cover for the terrorists."

"Yeah, I heard about all of it. So, terrorists bombed and killed millions. Now you have it. I don't see any difference."

"This was the Pearl Harbor of terror . . . And yes, that made possible our acquisition of many companies down here. But we brought their economy back from anarchy."

Jack was more frustrated with every moment. "Why don't you just shut up? Or tell me what flea infested hole you're taking me to."

"Ah, far be it from me to put your wife up in a flea infestation. We are going to the Copacabana Palace of Palaces, my friend, the best of the best. We rebuilt it after the war."

Abby Johnson's Knofer recorded and sent the coordinates of the Palace to Jake Burns in Seattle and the armed Ever-Life Security Team, just below the Copa, inside one of the Carriers. That Carrier reached the Corcodova station within 10-minutes and the team was on their way to the Palace before Jack arrived.

In the car, InVoy was dripping with arrogance and ego. "Look at that crowd, Jack; everywhere people. Everyone is so cramped down here now, all we have to do is smile at them, and they beg for whatever will lift their spirits. It's all about control."

"You mean you sell them drugs. I thought Brock was out of that."

"He is, as far as I know."

InVoy took a wad of rolled $1000-bills out of his pocket, waved it at Jack and said, "You have to give people what they really want, my friend. Watch this...Keith, pull over and stop."

InVoy rolled the back-seat window down and called to a group of young people in Portuguese, "Hey, you there . . . Yes, you! All of you; come here!"

He stuck his head out, just enough so they could see his face with sunglasses on. "You want to make a lot of money?" InVoy shouted.

Two men and four women came over to the car. They each nodded yes.

"Are you all related?" InVoy asked.

They said no.

"This is $100,000 cash. That's $16,500 for each of you."

One of the girls asked, "What do you want us to do, have sex?"

"Yes," InVoy replied, "with each other . . . Right here, right now. What do you say?"

One girl turned and examined the others. "Sure, why not? What do you all say?"

"Give us the money!"

InVoy giggled at them and turned to Jack. "You see, my friend, down here money buys anything."

Jack didn't flinch. "Either let me out or take me to my wife, you pig."

InVoy shouted at Keith, "*Vamos*—we go!"

Fifteen minutes later, after driving through various streets and along a beach road, the car pulled up to the Copacabana Palace of Palaces.

"Here we are, my friend. Feast your eyes. Come with me."

Little did InVoy know that Johnson and her team were in place to follow the little snake to his lair. There were ten on the team, all inconspicuously dressed. Four at the front door entrance, two at the main elevators, two patrolling the outside back and two on the roof. Jack had no idea he had support, until, as they lead him across the lobby, he noticed Abby Johnson sitting facing the check-in desk. He tried not to react, but he looked surprised for just one fleeting second. That was all the reaction InVoy's fat-man guard had to see. Jack barely flinched, nothing the average eye would catch, but to the trained mercenary, it was more than enough. In an instant, the guard focused on Abby. He reached for his pistol and pointed it at Jack's head. "Alright, you there! You, girl! Stand up! Stand up or, so help me, he's dead, and so is the wife!"

InVoy turned as Abby stood slowly raising her arms. Her team commander reacted from the elevators. He yelled, "Fire!"

InVoy's guard turned and saw Abby's man. At that second, an Ever-Life team member at the front entrance pulled his gun and fired at InVoy, the guard, and Jack. The airburst hit them all, and the three went down fast; but the fat man pulled the trigger of his automatic weapon, as he spun around and fell. Bullets spit out everywhere. The desk clerk was hit, and as InVoy's guard hit the floor, his weapon fired toward Abby. It was over in seconds. Then, the screaming started. People ran in all directions away from the lobby. Two more Ever-Life men ran in from outside. They grabbed the shooter, tied his hands behind him and helped Jack to his feet.

"Wait, hold on!" Jack yanked free and turned to see InVoy was face down. Jack bent down and turned him over only to see his belly gutted from the shots.

InVoy flopped into Jack's lap as his innards splashed all over. But he was conscious enough to say, "Too late my friend."

InVoy opened Jack's hand and placed a two-inch round wad of money in his palm. A key slipped out from the center of the roll. Then, the Chief of Staff, the henchman of Marion Brock, stared into nothing. He was dead.

Jack gently laid his head back on the floor and stood up, looking at the money and key, with a twisting sick feeling in his stomach.

"Sir! Here, over here, it's Ms. Johnson."

Jack rushed across the room to her. She lay on the lap of the Team Commander. She was clearly hit in the heart. Jack took the man's hand and put it on the wound. "Press hard, here! Abby, Abby, can you hear me?"

She opened her eyes. "It's okay, do you know where Rachel is?"

"Hang on, stay with me."

"Ask for Rossi, Charlie Rossi. Don't forget the . . ." She looked at Jack with a dead stare. She was gone too. The Commander looked up and spoke succinctly.

"Sir, we will clean up here. You go with those three and find your wife. I'll meet you back at the rendezvous point, the station under the statue. I'll have a car for you in the back of the hotel . . . Sergeant Strom, stick with the doctors. You get them back to the Carriers."

"Yes, Sir."

Jack kissed Abby's forehead and then got up. They all heard sirens, as Jack took one last look at Abby.

"Come on, sir; we have to go," said Strom.

Jack studied the key in his hand and read the tiny red-etched word on it, "*Base* . . . What is this? What do you make of this, Strom?"

The Sergeant looked and shook his head. "I don't know . . . Base? Maybe basement?'

"Christ, we have no time."

As pandemonium reigned in the lobby, the three ran to an elevator, entered, and Jack pushed B on the panel. When the door opened, Jack was ready to jump out, but the guards held him back. Strom shushed him and looked carefully. "Nothing but the laundry staff wearing those silly headnets.

"Even if there was anyone here," Jack said, "we couldn't hear them over the sound of those washers and dryers."

"Come on, let's go. Easy, doctor, you stay between us."

They walked down the hallway about 50-ft to another door. Strom tried the knob; it was locked. He looked at Jack and said, "You don't think?"

Jack took the key out, stuck it in the door and twisted the knob; it opened.

The sergeant pushed it open with his gun, looked through and saw a man halfway down the hall closing another door. As their eyes met, the man froze, and then ran the other way leaving the door opened.

"After him!" Ordered Strom.

One guard ran after the man, while Strom, Jack and the other guard walked into a dimly lit room. Weapons drawn, Strom motioned to Jack to wait, as he studied the room.

"All clear, sir. Holy shit! What the hell is this?" said Strom.

Jack walked in behind him. "It's a lab, a fully loaded lab at that."

He studied the room. There were medical instruments rivaling those at the Complex. In the far corner, he saw a stretcher with a light over it shining on what looked like a woman's body.

"Christ!" Jack ran to her. "It's Rachel! Help me!"

She was barely breathing and clothed in nothing but a hospital gown. Three needles stuck in her, one in each arm and one in her neck. Jack quickly checked her vitals.

"What the hell are they doing to her? She is alive, thank God. Hold her while I get these out."

At that point, the third guard came back. "He's gone, sir; disappeared."

Strom gestured, "Quickly, help us here!"

Jack rushed around the room looking for anything medical that could help. "Damn, where do they keep the good stuff? What a shithole."

He noticed several pieces of glass on the floor, blue glass. He bent down to pick one up and there it was; a corked small two-inch blue vial that he couldn't mistake. He picked it up and studied it, but none of them noticed the figure standing at the door with a gun.

"Yes, Jack, it's a vial, like your magic potion, but enhanced. Stop! All of you! I am a pretty good shot. Stay calm, and you all might live through this. Now drop your weapons gentlemen."

"Rossi, you bastard! Let me tend to my wife."

"First things first, my friend. Get over there with them."
"What have you done to her?"

"Did you bring the papers, Jack? A deal is a deal. Give them to me, and she's yours."

"Fine, I have to reach in my pocket. They're on my phone."

Rossi pointed, "Over there, yes there; it's a printer. Get going, or I swear; I'll kill her. You really don't have a clue, do you?" Then Rossi laughed.

Jack moved to the equipment, took his phone out, verified the retina scan and pointed it toward the port. "This thing is ancient. It probably doesn't even work."

"You let me worry about that. Do it, Jack. Transfer the pages. I need them in black and white." Jack pushed a phone key and a page printed, then another, and finally a third.

"Hand them to me, Jack."

Rossi grabbed them out of his hand and slowly backed up to the desk in the middle of the room. On it was a cylinder, sitting vertically, roughly 12 inches high, with characters on the side. He pressed several, and the display on the top read, *Insert*.

Rossi fed the papers into a slit on the side and then turned to Jack. "Now we wait."

It seemed like hours to the doctor. Finally, the cylinder beeped, and the display read, *Confirmed*, proceed.

The cylinder did not spit out the papers; instead, it displayed the message: *Self-destruct in five minutes.*

Rossi looked at Jack and smiled, "Thanks, Jack, you can keep the vial. She's all yours."

Then, he backed out the door, pointing the gun at Rachel, and slammed it shut behind him.

Jack ran to Rachel while the two guards ran to the door. "It's locked!"

Jack took Rachel's pulse. "She's alive, but in a coma. Look at her neck. They were experimenting. Christ! We have to get her back to the Complex, fast."

Strom took his Knofer out, requested escape directions and the team's car. The Knofer displayed a model of the palace and notified one of the team guards of the exit location. Then, Strom turned to the doctor. "Jack, the door . . . the bastard locked it."

They both thought the same thing. Jack took the key out again and ran to the door, "Bring her!"

They all took a breath as Jack stuck the key in and turned the knob. The door opened. He held it for the guards carrying Rachel. Strom went next. "Hurry; find another exit. We can't go back the way we came; the lobby will be filled with police. Let's go!"

They ran as quietly and quickly as they could, up the narrow staircase and exiting to the alley behind the palace. An Ever-Life crewmember waited in a car to take them all to the Carrier rendezvous station.

CHAPTER 60: MARSHALL'S REVENGE

IN THE BASEMENT of the Arden City Courthouse, Angie Bellos and Brian Sheldon were about to be escorted back up the stairs by the jailer. Halfway up, they all heard shouting. "YOU BASTARDS! LET ME OUT! BROCK! I AM GOING TO KILL YOU!"

Then they heard a crowd of cellmates yelling and banging on the doors. The guard turned and rolled his eyes. "It's that shit, Marshall, again. He provokes everybody. I hope he gets the chair."

Angie was quick to reply, "Excuse me, I am his niece. I've come to see him for the last time. Maybe I can quiet him before he drives you all crazy."

As her eyes filled with tears, the guard looked at her and said, "I have never seen you here before. He knows you?"

Angie was very creative. "I have been overseas. This is my friend. He is a lawyer. I wanted to see Davy before the verdict. I have to leave for the airport. I won't be able to see him otherwise. Please, I just want to say hello, goodbye, and hug him. I can quiet him. Really."

Marshall let out another wail, and the three of them looked at each other.

"That bastard. Sorry, miss, he has been a thorn in my side ever since he came here. How can you stand to be related?"

"Please, it's just to say hello and goodbye, honestly."

The guard thought and sighed, and finally, during another yell, he agreed. They walked into the jailhouse to Marshall's 6-ft by 9-ft cell. "I have a surprise for you, Mr. Marshall."

The guard opened the cell door; Marshall made eye contact with Angie and blurted out, "Christ, it's you! What the hell are you doing here?"

The guard seemed protective and spoke for her, "Be decent, or I'll beat you to a pulp. She came to visit. You've got 15-minutes, young lady. Call me if you want out earlier."

Angie and Brian walked in, and the guard closed the door behind them. Marshall sat on the cot and quizzed Angie. "I never expected to see you. Your boss, Swanson, said he would see me again. Are you here for him?"

"No, I am here for me. I don't even know where to start or if anything I say will mean anything to you."

"Well, I have time. They don't take me upstairs for the verdict for a while."

Angie sat down next to him, while Brian stood uneasily at the cell door.

"I'm not sure where to begin . . ."

"Oh, just tell him, babe. She thinks she was transported back in time and is stuck in some time warp here. She thinks it happened here in the courthouse. So, we are here to find out where. There. Was that so hard?"

Marshall stood up, listening intently. He paced and then looked at Angie. "Christ, it does work . . . but, why are we here?"

Angie interrupted him, "What are you saying? You know about it? Tell me, tell me what's going on!"

Marshall was quick to reply, "You two shouldn't even be allowed in here. The fact that the guard let you in with me should tell you things are not what they should be here." He went to the wall and stood inches away from it, staring at it. Angie could hear him say, "D.M.006004."

When Marshall finished, Brian whispered to Angie, "Jesus, this guy is really something; he has a voice print safe in his cell."

Marshall pressed his fingers to the wall and turned them in a circular motion. A small door, 9 x 12 inches, appeared and clicked open. He reached inside and took out two Knofers. He held one in each hand and turned to face the two young people.

"How did you get those?" Angie asked.

"They are my insurance policy, girl. Sit down and be quiet."

"But I thought you were a prisoner here, brought by Mr. Burns. How did you get those?"

Marshall was clever and desperate. "Now, be very careful how you answer me, young lady. If you play games, I'll see to it you stay with me here forever. You wouldn't want that, now would you?"

Brian stood against the cell bars and had to face outside to hide his rage. Angie just replied, "No, I wouldn't. Tell me what you know, and I'll do everything I can with the GGM."

"Ha! *GGM* . . . You don't get it. These little gadgets are my ticket out of here. Fuck your GGM! I had these programmed long before the morgue murders. I gave samples to Brock so he would get me out, so I would be free of that hellhole. These things have a defense protocol, you know, which will bring us home from wherever we are; and that includes whatever time we may be in. Don't you see, all we have to do is take them apart, duplicate the science and voila! A time travel gizmo."

"But they're programmed to Ever-Life citizens. You're not one. Those won't function."

"Well, none of us can function without money, lady. At least that is what I told Brock. If he doesn't get me out soon, I have a special present for him.

He is tied to me, no matter where I am. His little toys won't function the way he thinks. These are my insurance to get me out."

Brian couldn't control himself. "You're insane, you bastard!" He lunged at Marshall, pushed him hard and they fell against the wall. Angie moved quickly to the cell door away from them. Brian grabbed Marshall's throat with both hands and screamed, "You fucking bastard; you killed my dad."

Angie screamed in a whisper, "Brian, stop it! Stop it!"

But he only heard his own shouting. Marshall thrust his two hands upward between Brian's and broke his grip. Then, he struck out. Brian fell on the mattress, and Marshall jumped on him. Angie leaped toward Marshall, expecting to land on him, but that didn't happen. She landed in her own bed, back in her apartment, with the covers over her. She flung the covers off and, this time, Brian wasn't there. She looked around in a panic and focused on the clock. It was 7 a.m. again. The anomaly lasted only two hours. It was shorter this time. It took her several minutes to collect her thoughts.

"Holy crap, I've got to get to the courthouse again and find that sweet-spot."

CHAPTER 61: THE THREE FATHER'S RETURN

THE THREE FATHERS LAY IN A TIME TRAVEL CARRIER, riding a time-wave on the Sidron highway. Each cleric lay on a padded lounge next to one another and all faced a strange humanoid figure. He stood around 7 ft in height with a slim athletic build and appeared to be without clothes. Most striking was his shiny leather-like greenish and gold skin; and he was without an obvious gender.

"Hello, my friends. Please wake up. Welcome back. You have been resting for some time by my calculations."

Rabbi James was the first to rise and speak. He surveyed the empty white room, except for the lounges of course. "Who are you? And what is this place?"

The tall figure replied, "In this form, I resemble a human as best we can construct; however, I am in truth, a representation of this vessel you ride within."

Kristos rose and said, "Nice to meet you, I think."

As they all shook hands, Kristos continued, "Everything has been so unsettling. Please, can you explain all this."

"Yes, of course I will as best I can, but keep in mind your inability to grasp certain phenomenon as fact. Your history tells us your kind would rather label certain mysteries as miracles; something supernatural. Isn't that what you have done with your religions? You three have based your canonic doctrines on stories and images that are over 10,000 years old in some cases; certainly, on the short of it, 2-5000 years old. With this trip, you have been given a great gift and opportunity to experience and reset the truth of it all. Let us see if you understand and will do what you should this time."

The Tyree masters face and body tightened. He clenched his fists and spoke in a sharp pensive tone. "You are now challenged to share what you experienced, its SIMPLE MESSAGE and its correct meaning, and not confuse or cloud it in the eloquent intellectual babble of your ancestors. It is not to be re-labeled according to some articulate orator proofing his personal view. It is not to be dissected to the enth degree to rationalize that its message supports some philosophy or science. I have witnessed the many learned intellectuals of your kind, no matter in what language trying to make the message theirs. It is not to be used to support assumptions and cloud the simple truth, thus missing the point in the first place and then losing it in mass and mob rule."

Kristos remarked, "So, your kind gets frustrated just like we do?"

Tyree caught himself. Then, he looked at the three in a kind expression. "Please, forgive me. I beg your pardon. I do not mean to preach or sound condescending, but then again, I know I do. I speak with much more information than you have. I have a history spanning..." He chuckled... "Let's just say it would be unfair and definitely against our principles to convince you of my opinion in this matter. It's sort of, how do you put it...*a primary directive.* I always liked that phrase. Besides, the trip you made and what you heard is all you need to form the correct course of action. The point is for you to tell the simple truth of it all and let the listener use his own knowledge and free will to arrive and choose wisely."

The three Fathers looked at each other, took a moment to contemplate in silence and sighed. Kristos replied, "Regarding our doctrines, we aren't children or novices hoping our teacher will clarify a question. We here have been doing and teaching our canons for a very long time."

James raised his hands, gesturing a pause and walked slowly around the lounges, squinting as he moved around, trying to focus on the room's boundaries. "Perhaps it would help us if we can start with the obvious. If it weren't for these lounges, I'd swear we were all floating."

The Tyree Master replied, "Actually, you are correct. We are floating. And that is a fact. It is only your directional references that give you a sense of up, down, and back and forth." He reached out his hand and commanded, "Standard room, all amenities, including kitchenette."

With those words, the lounges changed into recliners and the room became a beautiful suite with stained glass windows, furniture and a fireplace.

"Allah be praised," Ahmir said. "A miracle!"

Kristos seemed confused and turned to Tyree, "Are you some trickster?"

"Not at all, my friends. This is all part of a standard capability for us."

"It has the makings of a miracle to us," James said.

Tyree smiled and said, "You prove my point exactly. As it has been with many who have never seen and don't understand. You have been given a statement of truth to readdress the old superstitions and misgivings and to re-present and re-explain the truth. We wondered for eons why you must label some things misunderstood as supernatural and miraculous in origin. Frankly we see all truth as miracles, not as you define only that which you don't understand. There are explanations for a great deal that was labelled a miracle by your religions."

Kristos was quick to reply. "We are anxious to listen to your explanation." He sat down and the three nodded to each other in agreement.

The stranger began, "It is worth repeating over and over. You three were given a great gift. Unlike anyone else of your species, you time travelled to the point of origin of each of your respective doctrines. Tell me, what did each of you see? Do you remember what happened on your trip? Who did you meet?"

James replied first. "We saw the prophet, Moses!"

Ahmir contradicted him. "Allah be praised. We saw the one true prophet, Muhammed. Blessed be him who believes."

The tall stranger smiled as Kristos stood and said, "Same old, same old...we saw them both. We saw our Lord and Savior as he willed us to! Now my friend, whatever you are, explain yourself!"

James stood up too, "Yes! And why are we here? Doctor Bellos said we would return to his office."

"Was what happened back in that cave real?" Kristos thought for a moment and asked. "Or was it a trick?"

The stranger assured them, "So much for the unity you conspired to achieve. You each saw something different; I take it? I wonder what you heard. I represent this vehicle, which is a living being, quite different from you in many respects. On the other hand, we are also similar in some regards. We have much more history and understanding than you. And we can travel to any time to confirm or address questions we may have regarding an event or person."

Ahmir interrupted, "Wait! So we are within the same statue we started out in? A Carrier, Dr. Bellos said; right?"

"That is correct. My name in your language is Tyree Master. A variation of this image is what we use when appearing to your kind. I contain and express the will and thoughts of our entire species."

The fathers studied the stranger. "And, what exactly is going on?" Kristos insisted.

"Before you leave our hospitality and end your trip, we have several questions and observations to share; and also, clarifications for you to remember before you think of relating what you experienced to your brothers and sisters. Please, may I proceed?"

The fathers nodded, noticeably annoyed, acting as if what else could they do.

"Let us start with the initial event that set you three on this journey. We are most curious why you negotiated with Mr. Marion Brock in the first place?"

Kristos took a breath and offered, "We did not. I did. I was foolish to believe his parlor tricks or to think any scientific explanation could prove God's power on Earth. I accept the responsibility."

"You miss my point . . . Let's say you succeeded with Mr. Brock. Would the rest of your kind unite as you planned and accept one major religion?"

Kristos turned aside to think while James replied, "I would have, knowing what I knew then, but now, no . . . And I believe none of us can speak for any other. What we believe is a matter of individual choice. Our kind has laws, which we must follow; short of that, we have free will to act and believe what we choose."

Then, Kristos added, "And it is our 'free will,' our different choices that bind us when dire threats or fear overcome us."

Ahmir stepped directly in front of the stranger and said, "For God is One; and we are too, as mankind, when we need to be."

The stranger grinned. "And so, it is. That is what makes you so different from us. We are of one mind." The Tyree Master walked a few feet away, and the three fathers watched as a table appeared out of nowhere. He opened a drawer, took out several papers and handed them to Kristos. "Are these yours?"

Kristos read the first few lines and replied, "How did you get these? I had written these before I met with Brock."

"We have monitored and helped many surface people over the centuries. Your kind has killed most of them. The point is, you have been contemplating for a long time how to stop the killing, haven't you?"

Tyree reached into the drawer again and handed duplicate copies of Kristos' notes to the other two clerics.

Kristos said, "Yes, at that time, my thinking was if we could discuss the causes of our differences, we could compromise and stop terrorist acts. But, the more I thought, the more I became convinced that my compromising would never be accepted as doctrine. Only proof would be accepted. So, when Brock approached me, I selfishly negotiated with him."

The Tyree gestured to them all, "Read the pages."
The three examined Kristos' handwritten notes:

Goal: Unity-One Faith...

Considerations/Opinions: Sharia Law and the Qur'an contradict Western biblical law and civil Law-

1] Regarding the name of God:
Examples: Jesus [Christian name for the Lord God in man]; YHWH-Jewish proper name for God, Adonai-name of the Lord, Elohim-generic word for God; Allah [Islamic word for God]
2] Christianity defines Jesus as Divine, part of the three-person Godhead, the Holy Trinity a] God, the Father, b] God, the Son, c] God in the Holy Spirit...
3] Jewish law, Islam, Unitarian...Christianity pluralizes God, contradicting One God doctrine.
4] Jesus' teachings: How to be a good human being...Adam's fall from God's grace represents humans directing themselves away from God...Humans make their own struggles...Christ's actions and sacrifice brought humans back to God's embrace...If Christ can overcome death, how much less are the struggles of any human to overcome. Believe that in Christ's rising, so can man rise triumphant from his/her adversities.

Kristos' suggested pamphlet draft using Brock network:
God made Himself a man, Jesus Christ, to reconcile Himself with men who chose to be apart from God. In human form, as his Son, He could a] directly communicate with men; b] would show people who He is, what He is capable of, and take responsibility for giving man free will to be apart; c] God, Himself, would pay for man's iniquities - repeated sins and misdirection. God would no longer punish humankind with struggles; rather, He would allow them to direct themselves back to Him through grace - his gift of unmerited favor; d] All men would have to do is choose to believe in Him - Worship. The sins of men are the result of free will, given by God in the first place. So, by example, because men have been incapable of understanding their plight, God would pay a ransom to Himself and allow people to witness it; e] Men, witnessing the horror and willingness of sacrificing a father's son, for all humanity would surely make man return to Him. People would see the Resurrection of God's Son proving that God has the Love and power to do anything. It had become evident that because of man's free will and selfish nature, only impressing humanity would persuade them back to God; and g] Finally, God would show

humankind what life is like both with and without Him. Therefore, choose wisely.

•... Judaism and Islam reject a God-head definition for God. Contrary to Christianity, whether in Arabic, Hebrew, or any other language, they define their 'word for God' to mean ONE.

•... In Islam, Sharia Law has not been revised, changed, or related as separate and apart from the civil law since its original writing. It has not evolved with changes and evolution of socio-economic cultures. It is not alive. Also, Islam has been illegal in some countries and it has morphed into extreme violent behavior, which has clouded many people's understanding. The Qur'an should be readdressed, based on the cultural advances, changes in public behavior and universal laws i.e. beheadings, stoning's, infidel status...It is sinfully unlawful, reprehensible, shameful and discreditable to identify the Creator in any sense other than the ONE, Almighty-Allah. Therefore, thinking and behaving outside the law of the Qur'an is punishable. All men are equal to each other in nature, nonequal to God. People are born, live, and die. It is written that Jesus was a great prophet, given the power to do what he did, by Allah; but he was a man and died as a man. Allah cannot die. To say Jesus is God means the Christian God died and is to say he was not God in the first place.

... Idolatry: To Muslims and Jews, Roman Christianity venerates statues and saints, Greek Christianity venerates pictures and saints. The Abrahamic law says do not worship idols like statues and pictures of Jesus, Mary, the Saints, the Cross, etc. Judaism and Islam have no idols of any kind. To them, no person should be worshipped or bowed before. Pray only to the unnamed Almighty ONE.

Ahmir was the first to remark after reading Kristos' notes. "This is not new. For centuries now, we have respected each other's differences, and we all translate or interpret words between languages differently. The Terrorist War stopped long ago."

Kristos was quick to remind him, "Yes, the war ended, but not the killing. Each of us is bound by our doctrine to bring peace to our brothers.

These are just my notes. I tried again to explain the truth as I knew it. When Brock approached me, I was convinced proving the resurrection would unite us all. I knew it!"

Ahmir replied, "You didn't want to unite us. You wanted to convince us!"

The Tyree listened, as their arguing intensified, and then, he interrupted, "You call this peace? You can't even convince each other."

The three fathers stopped.

Tyree continued. "You three were given a great gift today in what you witnessed and who you met. My kind has no choices about such things. I speak for all of us, in all matters. Do you think having a hive mindset about God is the answer?"

The three men looked at each other, and James quoted a platitude, "My God, our God, one God; all things are possible through Him."

Ahmir sat down on a lounge. "I have studied this question and after today, I am convinced that if Allah can put himself in the Qur'an, inspire all the prophets, and raise the dead. If our Almighty can be seen in a sunset, in nature, in life, surely, he can put himself in a man. Allah can do what he wishes."

"Yes," Kristos said, "if we look carefully, we can see a little of Him in all of us. Today we heard that God did put himself in men, and through our Lord His son, we can have our own relationship with God within ourselves. We can find Him there in us. He can even put his Divine self in anything he chooses; even in a hive mindset."

The three fathers stood together and stared at the stranger.

The room began to flicker, and suddenly, light exploded blinding all of them. The three clerics blinked and covered their eyes. When they gathered their senses, they were standing firmly next to each other around the coffee table in Bellos' office suite. There on the table lay the white book that was given to Kristos by *S....* Sticking out of one end, between its pages, was a folded piece of paper. Ahmir pulled it out and gave it to Kristos who opened it and read the short note out loud:

My Brothers,

To say you love someone and then demand; 'if you don't do as I say, I will have nothing to do with you; negates choice and contradicts love. God reconciled Himself to man. Help your brothers realize God is within us all. Help them reconcile themselves to one another, and interact in like, respecting and accepting your differences.

S

James reached down, picked up the book and looked at it. Tears filled his eyes, and he gave it to Ahmir. Ahmir held it with both hands and looked at the other two priests. Then, after a moment, without a word, he placed it back down on the table.

Kristos sighed and said, "Shall we go?"

Together, the three walked up the foyer steps. Kristos opened the door, smiled, and the three fathers walked out.

CHAPTER 62: BROCK REVEALED

INSIDE THE LAB of Time-Travel Inc., Hamill Stevens continued to enlighten Jake Burns by answering every question posed. Jake had pushed his Knofer, and it should have recorded and transmitted the entire conversation to the GGM. Stevens held back nothing. It was almost as if Jake were a new hire listening to an educational seminar.

"Mr. Burns, you probably noticed; I don't talk to many people in this job."

"I must admit, you are quite free with details. I didn't expect that."

"I want you to know something else." Stevens walked across the room and picked up a metal cylinder. He brought it back to Burns and set it on its end, as Stevens continued. "We received these not long before you got here. Now, watch. I push this; now read the display."

"What are you doing?" said Jake.

The slit on the side of the cylinder ejected three pages, which Stevens handed to Burns. "After reviewing, I made corrections to Chamber#2 based on these; however, we haven't tested the chamber yet. We needed an increase in the energy pattern to boost its regenerative power, so Marion is bringing a booster."

"Booster?"

"Yes, the other source of energy, he found in the timeline of 1965."

Jake finished reading the pages. "Christ, these **are** Jack's last pages. So, Brock went back in time to get another *Compatible* charged person, Nicolas Brock. It has to be Brock's father from 1965. Christ! When is your boss due back?"

That was when another voice spoke from behind Jake, "Actually, I can tell you that. You do go on, Stevens, sometimes too much, I'm afraid; and who is this?"

Jake got up and turned to see the impressive figure of Marion Brock. It was really the mad clone. Jake instinctively began to reach for his gun, but he stopped short.

Clone[C]Brock just grinned and said, "I am afraid your little gadgets won't work in here. Didn't Stevens tell you?" He extended his hand and waited for Burns. Jake took a deep breath, smiled and said, "I am Jake Burns."

Then, he shook Brock's hand, feeling his vice grip.

"Welcome, Mr. Burns. You are just in time for my little surprise."

Without a word, and as smooth as a quick draw artist in the old west, Jake pulled his air gun, pointed it at C-Brock and fired, but nothing happened. "Hmm, well you can't blame me for trying, eh?"

"I don't blame you at all. Now that you have seen this much, and I don't doubt Stevens here has brought you up to date. Would you care to see something that may enlighten you even more?"

Jake quipped, "You know, I can't let you continue all this."

"Please? Jake, is it? I know you will appreciate and probably react a little differently when you see what I have to show you. This way. Stevens, lead on through the sensory corridor...

"...Mr. Burns, you are from down under, are you not?"

"Yes, I've come to see if we can negotiate something."

"I do love a challenge," C-Brock said. "If you know anything about me, it's that I do negotiate. Were you raised in the caverns?"

"I was a cop in New York City."

"Interesting, you're not indigenous to the Ever-Life colonies then? I always thought it was a private club."

As Stevens opened another door, C-Brock asked Burns, "So how did you find us, anyway?"

"It's the detective in me, I guess. It wasn't that difficult; and, I have friends of a different kind."

C-Brock chuckled, "So, we have something in common, interesting."

As the three walked into another large clean room, Burns studied the layout and saw another chamber. C-Brock couldn't resist the urge to brag. "How do you like it all? It's my pride and joy. The lab was built by the greatest minds of our time, no disrespect intended."

C-Brock opened the chamber door and walked in. "And this, this is the next generation, right Stevens?"

"Yes, sir."

"You simply shower; it air dries you, and you are ready to go."

C-Brock walked out again and over to a door just to the right of the chamber. "You see Jake, may I call you Jake? You see, Jake, I needed the highest potency and most powerful combination of compatible sustenance possible. Quite a mouth full, don't you think?"

"What's your point?"

C-Brock stood in front of the door and turned to face the two men. "While Stevens here discovered the Pyramid Power; it just didn't push in the right direction. It didn't allow us to shove the construct off the on-ramp, if you will, onto the highway-the Sidron. The constructs were bouncing off the ramp before they reached the Sidron. We needed the combination of electromagnetic power and more Compatibilities. Hence this place. Now, we need a booster. So, I brought the last turbocharge, guaranteed to zap us all to success."

"What are you talking about?"

"Let's stop the games, my friend," said Clone-Brock. "The Carrier was educational but not the final objective. No one knew I was just a clone of Brock back then. I learned the how of many things while I was in there. And, you see, I too evolved in the Carrier and set forth a plan of my own. Semitri made a pact with me. I give him the real Marion Brock and all the clones he wants, as food for the beast; and in return, I get my freedom to be anywhere and everywhere. Too confusing for you? Ha, ha! No one had a clue. It seems that Mr. Brock, to you Real-Brock, had the first clue right on his person, one of those adorable little toys you call Knofers. Your Dave Marshall gave it to him months ago. Real-Brock already started the effort to duplicate them, one of his promises to his global companies. It is a fun toy but not the whole answer. We needed the power of Compatibility to execute my plan to free me."

Jake's jaw dropped for the second time. "What? I should have known."

"Hah! Of course! You silly man, I even know you are like us, you are a relative of all of us, even the old boy in there."

"Old boy in there?"

"Yes! Semitri left nothing to chance to get the clones. After I got out and checked the progress of our communication experts, I realized the power of these little gadgets is only part of it. I needed Stevens and his pyramids, you, and a little help from history. You see, my friend, you were led here."

Jake wasn't buying it. "What are you saying? Jesus, you are insane!"

C-Brock just laughed. "Well, closer to God than you think. Anyway, as it turns out, you are not just a witness to all this, you will be a participant. I needed to get more power to make the second chamber work. It's a little insurance policy, in case my Carrier friend changes his mind. It's crucial to cover the bases."

Stevens blurted out to Jake, "I don't know what he means, honestly."

C-Brock was on a roll. "Your Dave Marshall was my first clue. He thought he could control Real-Brock by resetting the Knofers. Then came me, back from the dead. No one expected that. I took control. I took the knowledge from Semitri, and we built this place in no time, clones, power, no limits. We needed Dr. Sheldon's final calculations to make corrections from our original displacement event. That's why Rossi went to Rio. Are you getting all this, Mr. Burns?"

"I understand more with every word."

"That brings us to here and now." C-Brock moved closer to the door next to him.

Burns and Stevens stood silently waiting about 10 ft from Brock. Burns wasn't going to get physical unless he had to. Meanwhile, he was dying of curiosity. Brock stood in front of the door and faced them both. There was a chair with a coat on it next to him. He smiled that sinister grin as he took off his own jacket and replaced with the black dinner jacket on the chair. Then, he acted like a completely different person, dark, menacing and with a circus ringmaster style introducing the main act. He reached into his coat pocket and took out a pair of black gloves, put them on, and pulled out a thin rope. "My friends, I offer for your consideration the greatest single discovery ever made. Do you know what this is?"

He stretched out the rope between his hands. Jake was dumbfounded at first. He just mocked him. "It looks like a rope. Are you going to strangle someone?"

C-Brock smirked and nodded no. "Hardly, my Ever-Life friend. This rope represents a particle displacement conduit. It is the Sidron's road of transport. My hands represent creation-the chambers one and the other. I am beyond one life now, and I have control of the Sidron."

Then, C-Brock dropped the rope, pulled what looked like a Knofer out of his breast pocket and spoke into it, "Semitri, my friend, now."

C-Brock laughed as Stevens and Jake watched the door change before their eyes. The rectangular door became round. Burns was not impressed. He shrugged and sarcastically remarked, "It's a door, Brock, or whoever you are. Is this your big surprise, a round glowing door?"

Clone-Brock smirked and turned the knob. "Really, just a door, eh? I don't think so."

C-Brock bowed and gestured with his arm. "Behold the secret of the ages." Then, he laughed-just laughed, as the door opened, and out fell the limp bodies of Gordon Swanson and a stranger; both unconscious and soaked in sweat. Stevens and Jake quickly bent down and checked the two men.

"I've got a pulse . . ."

"Me too; thank God."

C-Brock stood firm, and with authority, like some god, he stepped around the two. Jake lifted Swanson's head; and, in the same motion, he took his Knofer out and pressed it. Nothing happened. C-Brock watched it all, as if in ecstasy. "Oh, he is quite alright, more than just alive I wager."

Burns pushed the Knofer again and spoke into it, "Alpha-one! Activate! Alpha-one!"

"I told you," C-Brock muttered, "your little toys won't work here. On the other hand, mine does just fine."

Brock turned to the door and spoke again into his Knofer-like unit and instructed, "Semitri, bring Mr. Brock to the doorway."

From out of the dim-light inside the Carrier, a chair with a dark human figure in it moved toward C-Brock but stopped just short of the door. Jake could see Real-Brock in the chair, and behind the chair was a crowd of Brock clones.

Stevens yelled into the Carrier, "Mr. Brock, is that you? Which one is which?"

The voice from the chair inside the Carrier spoke loud and clear, "Stevens, get me out of here, do something!"

Outside Semitri, Clone-Brock stood watching it all and laughed, as he saw Stevens and Burns so confused. Burns caught himself mesmerized, turned and focused on Swanson, who was barely breathing. Real-Brock inside the beast, kept yelling, "God damn it, Stevens! Help me, get me out of here!"

The other unidentified man began to moan and awoke bewildered, trying to focus and digest all that was happening before him. Jake yelled, "Stevens, come here! Come here!"

Stevens snapped out of his trance. He rushed to Jake, and they moved Swanson to the wall. Jake reacted. "Hamill, look at me, go back and try to help the other guy."

Jake tried everything he knew, but he couldn't revive Swanson, so he moved quickly to the other man and Stevens. As C-Brock continued to taunt and argue with Real-Brock, Burns grabbed the stranger. "Who are you?"

The man coughed and said, "My name is Nicolas Brock."

"Christ! It is you. You look like your portrait at OPAS."

"I'm sure I don't understand."

"It's New Year's with the Brocks." Jake quipped.

"What?" Nick said, "Christ what a headache. What the hell is all this?"

"All you need to know," Jake said, "is that you, me, and they are all going to die if we don't stop that man laughing. I'm Jake Burns, a cop from New York. You have to trust me."

"Who are they?" Nick blurted out.

"Those two? They are the crazy twins. They want to murder you, kill us and steal your company."

Burns helped Nick to his feet. Stevens regained his composer, as he watched the two Brocks arguing, and saw his opportunity. He ran and leaped into the Carrier.

C-Brock turned, concentrating on Nicolas, and spoke into his little VAD again, "Semitri, you can have them both. I don't need them or you anymore." And then, C-Brock lunged at Nicolas.

In a last-ditch effort, Burns reached into his coat and took out the small pocket watch device which Swanson gave him at his briefing. Without hesitation, he threw it into the Carrier. A silent red flare exploded inside Semitri. Burns could see Stevens yanking Real-Brock out of the chair, and finally, after the flash stopped, Stevens was able to drag R-Brock out the door and into the room.

C-Brock had grabbed Nicolas around his shoulders, but he didn't expect his ancestor to be well-trained in hand-to-hand combat. Nick elbowed C-Brock and twisted him around, holding one arm behind his back and the other around Clone-Brock's neck.

Real-Brock and Stevens made it out of the Carrier just before a second blinding blue flare ignited.

Jake yelled, "Nick, get him into the chamber. That will hold him!"

Stevens helped Nick, and together they forced Clone-Brock into the particle chamber. Real-Brock was behind the three and grabbed Stevens by his pants, yanking him back out and slammed the door shut. Both Clone-Brock and Nick were trapped inside the chamber.

"Stevens!" Real-Brock yelled. "Turn the equipment on and get the hell out of here!"

Stevens was on automatic pilot. He reacted as R-Brock directed and ran to the control panel. He pushed a series of buttons and then turned around to watch. C-Brock pounded on the chamber's glass door and screamed, "Open the Fucking Door!" while Nick instinctively held him inside.

Jake's eyes darted back and forth between the chamber and the Carrier. He could see that something was happening to Semitri. He yelled at Stevens, "We have to get out of here! Come on!"

Real-Brock moved quickly, before anyone else. He made it to the door on the other side of the room, just as the first explosion hit from within the Carrier. The room shook wildly. Burns and Stevens were knocked over but were able to get back up. As they did, they saw C-Brock and Nicolas in the chamber begin to disintegrate.

"My God," Stevens said. "We have to get them out! They have their clothes on."

Jake gripped Stevens arm. "Forget it! We have no time. Come on!"

Stevens hesitated for a second but Burns yanked hard and pulled Stevens back away from the chamber. "We have to go!"

They ran arm in arm back through the other door and up the hallway as fast as they could. When the two reached the tunnel passage to the surface, they heard another loud explosion. Jake and Stevens made it out of the shed to the school parking lot when the shaking knocked them off their feet. The ground vibrated and they watched an area of at least four-square blocks cave down a good eight feet.

"Holy mother of God," Stevens said.

Jake whispered to himself, "Gordon? Brock? Shit!" Then he yanked at Stevens again. "Come on! We have to go!"

But, as he turned around, Jake stopped dead in his tracks. "Crap! The limo's gone. Shit!"

Stevens patted Burns on his shoulder and said, "Mine's out in front of the school. Let's go."

At the same moment, within the time anomaly that had trapped Angie Bellos, Angie had made her way back to the courtroom alone. She was scared and worse; she left her Knofer somewhere in the jail cell with Dave Marshall and Brian. Angie had been looking arduously for the sweet spot in Room 210. Exhausted and fatigued, she sat helplessly on the witness stand sobbing, when the first rumble came, which was the result of Semitri exploding in Time-Travel Inc. It sounded like thunder, far away. Then, the room began to vibrate, as if an earthquake hit. She grabbed the wooden arms of the chair and hung on. As she rocked back and forth, terrified, looking left and right, she saw it. Focused and precise, out of the corner of her eye, while everything was shaking out of control, a two-foot round rotating space, appeared right in front of her. "Oh my God! The sweet spot."

It wasn't a blur at all. It was the only thing in the room in focus. She only had seconds to react. She lunged and leaped into it and fell into the arms of Brian Sheldon, knocking him over onto the courtroom floor.

"Okay, okay, Jesus! Angie?"

She looked at him, grabbed his face and kissed him hard. He tried to push her away, but she clung to him, smothering him. "Oh, my God, is it you? Is it you?"

Her kisses became tender, and he returned them. "Yes. It's me. Where have you been? I've been looking all over for you. I decided to come back here, hoping to find something. Your father is crazy worried about you."

"Wait, am I here? I mean back, really here?"

Brian chuckled, "Well, we were out on the steps, and then you were gone, vanished, and now you're here."

Angie started kissing him again. "Thank God! Well, I don't plan on disappearing again anytime soon. Come here, you!"

Meantime, Real-Brock had made it to the limo and drove it to one of his office buildings in Seattle. It was long after normal business hours, when he made his way through the maze of cubicles on the 15th floor. Something caught his eye on Connie Mayzen's desk. He stopped dead in his tracks and picked up a hardbound colorful book, which lay next to her computer. His eyes widened as he read the title, 'Allenfar, an Ever-Life story.'

Brock surveyed the landscape of cubicles around the floor to make sure there was no one around, and then, he took the book and rushed to his office. After arranging to fly to his hideaway in Vancouver Canada, he opened the book and began to read it. He looked up with a smile and said to himself, "Thank you Semitri. Now I know why you showed me that video. It's all coming together..."

CHAPTER 63: BLOOD RESULTS

TOM WHEELER FINISHED THE BLOOD analysis of Ever-Life's time traveler, Andrew, and sent it to the GGM. While riding in Allenfar, Bellos examined it and called Wheeler back.

"Tom, I see it, but I'm not sure I believe it?"

"The analysis is reliable. We can't send him back," said Wheeler. "We couldn't if we wanted to. The question is, what do we do with him?"

"Well, we are all taught that a person's genetics is what makes the difference around here; any suggestions?" Asked Bellos.

"We sound like two idiots, sir."

Bellos thought and replied, "Maybe I should take him up to the surface and give him a new life there."

"I doubt that would work, but it's your decision, my GGM."

"Did you double-check this, Tom?"

"I ran the standard blood tests and our genetic screening, and then the comparative analysis. Based on recent events and those analyses, there's no doubt at all."

"Well, someone has to explain it all to him. We owe him that."

"Sir, it should come from you."

"Yes, I suppose."

"Matthew, I have other news. It's about your daughter Angie. She's on her way home."

Bellos shook his head, grinned and said, "Thanks, that makes my day. I'll have to tell Jake you beat him on this one. By the way, Tom; do you have anything on Rachel Sheldon."

Wheeler replied, "I have the reports here, sir. She is still in a deep coma. Our doctors think she has the same or derivative of Swanson's crippling gene. Something else may be the cause though. They just don't know at this point."

"Tom, hold on; a message from Jake is coming in now. It reads:

'Urgent Notice to GGM-M J Bellos: Engaged with Time Travel Inc...

1] Confirmed that Hamill Stevens discovered pyramid power used in effort to transport Dave Marshall to future. Effort failed. Instead, pyramid power triggered Sidron to transport our time traveler, Andrew. I speculate Semitri located travelers based on Compatibility.

2] Engaged with H. Stevens, discussed contract on particle displacement between Marion Brock and Dr. J Sheldon. More to it than meets the eye. Must discuss directly with J Sheldon. Copy of documents to be transmitted directly.

3] Yes, there was Rogue Carrier, Semitri. Brock team duplicated clones of Brock as fuel for Rogue Carrier in exchange for Time Travel. Result: Semitri shut out Hive-Mind.

4] Gordon Swanson was sedated and kidnapped by TTI. He was to be used in part as fuel booster. During my engagement, G. Swanson was killed in explosion, which also terminated Carrier.

5] Both Nicolas Brock and one of the clones of Brock terminated within time travel chamber, destroying it completely. Balance of transmission is formal vault, for your headset review.

Mathew, Gordon is gone-he died...

End communication...Jake Burns
Global Security Chief
Ever-Life Colonies, Post-3
Arden, New Mexico

Bellos sat down in silence, obviously taken back by the news. Wheeler sighed and said, "Mathew, I'm so sorry. I don't know what to say."

After a moment, Bellos replied, "It's alright, Tom. I will review the vault carefully, and we will go from there. Please keep all this quiet for now. I must go to the Bering Straits to contract the tunnel negotiations. Then, I'm going to Arden to undergo the new CPT for the Post Controllers. I'll come back to Giza after that to host the funeral. Talk to Patty. Ask her if she would like to make any arrangements."

"I will."

"Please go see our visitor, Andrew, and take him to the Argonne Villa in the Masters' Cave. That should make him feel at home if that's possible. I'll see him later."

"Fine, but I don't think anything is going to satisfy him but the truth."

CHAPTER 64: GGM AND MR. ANDREW

AFTER BELLOS UNDERWENT THE NEW CPT, he road to meet Mr. Andrew in the huge master's cave, roughly eight miles below Giza. Most colonists thought it to be the first one found in the entire Time Trust Post-2. It was over 1000 feet high and approximately a mile in diameter. There were meadows of strange and beautiful flowers and rolling hills bounding a freshwater lake. On one side of the lake's beachfront lay the stunning Argonne Villa. The Villa was a plush resort in the Master's Cave, and it was a getaway spot for the GGM. His living quarters were 3500 square feet, the best of the best real estate.

Tom Wheeler had just finished giving time traveler, Mr. Andrew, a tour of the grounds, and they sat down to sip iced tea, in the log cabin's living room area. Wheeler began educating the new guest, reviewing the cave's traditions and history.

"Thank you, Tom," said Mr Andrew. "I appreciate everything; I have a lot to learn. It's all so new and different."

Wheeler smiled and said, "A little over 980 years' worth of learning, I'd say, ha!"

"It is overwhelming, hard to believe. What are the odds of getting me back to where I belong?"

They heard the door latch and in walked GGM, Mathew Bellos. "Hello, you two. Coming here does take away the stress of the day."

Bellos slowly walked toward Andrew and answered his question to Wheeler, "Unfortunately, if we could send you back, I'm pretty sure you would be many more particles than you were though. And I'm not sure the Carriers could Quiver you. It gets quite technical."

Andrew squinted. "You'll have to explain that one to me. I was just talking about going home. So, now what happens to me?"

Bellos nodded to Wheeler. "Tom, fix me something a little stronger than tea, will you?"

"Sure."

Bellos sat down and said to Andrew, "I'm really not sure about the possibility of your going anywhere in time. We need to examine you and have the Carriers evaluate your situation. We are in unknown territory with you, I'm afraid."

Wheeler handed Bellos a drink as Andrew said, "That's not too comforting."

"Have you had a chance to see much here, get a feel for how we do things?"

"No, not that much, I watched a lot of videos before, but it would take time. It's quite a different political system, but free enterprise seems alive and well down here as far as I can tell."

"Yes, it is, quite similar to many places you were familiar with, I'm sure."

Bellos sipped, put his Knofer on the coffee table and talked into it, "Get me Malcolm Aldridge."

Within seconds, Malcolm's image began to grow from the Knofer.

"Hello, Mathew; good to see you."

"Good to see you, too."

"I heard from Patty. I'm sorry about Gordon. Of course, I will be at the funeral."

"Thank you. I called because I need a favor."

"Just ask."

"I have a friend here. Say hi to Andrew. He's an author, among other things. He's looking for a permanent residence."

"Ah, how do you do, Andrew?"

"Well, at times, very well. Thanks; pleased to meet you."

"You have good friends in high places," remarked Aldridge

"Apparently, this is all pretty new to me. Forgive me. I'm a bit overwhelmed."

"Relax; it's fine. Now, would you like to meet perhaps tomorrow, and we can discuss looking at some housing?"

"Fine with me, alright."

Bellos added, "Malcolm, he's staying at the Argonne in HS-3783. By the way, we are broadcasting Gordon's funeral tomorrow."

"That's fine. Andrew, how about I pick you up around 9:30 in the morning?"

Andrew suddenly seemed uneasy. "Funeral, what funeral?"

"Malcolm, perhaps you could bring Andrew to the ceremony. I have a lot to do. I'd be in your debt."

"I'll be glad to. It will give us time to chat."

"I appreciate that; thank you."

"Well, then, see you in the morning. Be well. Nice to hear from you, Mathew."

The Knofer cut the call. Bellos took a breath and turned to Wheeler. "Give us a moment, will you, Tom?"

"Sure . . ." Wheeler extended his hand and Andrew shook it.

"Thanks for everything."

"See you later, Andrew." Wheeler left.

Bellos was rarely tongue-tied; however, he fumbled at first. "There is something else you and I have to discuss."

Andrew sat back down. Bellos took several folded pieces of paper out of his back pocket and handed them to Andrew.

"What's this?"

"You should read those."

Bellos rose, walked to the bar and asked, "Would you like a drink?"

"Okay, I'm guessing I'll need it. Any potato vodka."

"You and Jake. Straight or with ice?"

"Ice, please." Andrew began reading, "Let's see; it says, Blood Test Evaluation and Analysis; born 1/07/1946; Death-Unknown . . . That's interesting. Ever-Life Citizen, 6/04/2999; Sponsor, Relative: GGM Mathew J. Bellos . . . Relative?"

Bellos walked back and handed him a drink. The GGM offered a toast. "It seems we have more in common than we realized. Bottoms up."

They both gulped the drinks, and then Bellos walked back over to the bar. "You may need another before we are done. Originally, when you appeared here, there were three of you, all the same you in each of those different rooms; but, each of you was a different age."

"I remember."

"Well, you got here as a result of an event, the original Sidron event, which, I am sure you will learn, was triggered by a combination of factors. But, after all has been analyzed, primarily, you are here because of our genetic ties, yours and mine. We are related. I'll try to explain."

"I have time."

"A very narcissistic man named Marion Brock is power hungry. He devised a plan to go back in time, to gather as much power as he could. However, he forgot one thing . . ."

"What's that?"

". . . My ties as GGM with the Carriers. Even though his personal Carrier friend blocked communications with its own kind, I did go through their ceremony. That meant that all Carriers became tied to me, my DNA and mine to theirs. Since you and I are both entwined genetically, when Mr. Brock's Carrier triggered the original Sidron event, it linked to my DNA, and that linked you to the event. Do you understand?"

"Whoa! Even if I understood what you are saying, my first reaction would be; obviously I must have had relatives too who existed all the way up to you. What about their DNA?"

"There are specific genetic markers *that* fluctuate and can be either lost or intensified across generations, *bridge* if you will. We confirmed this 'bridging' just recently, through discoveries on the surface in fact. Anyway, they can reappear again. It's much like the evolution of spontaneous genetic jumping. Individual gene sections can lay dormant and after a time, spark massive genome rearrangements."

"Sounds above my pay grade."

"Believe me; our shared genetic sequences are very potent when put together in particular ways. And that is what happened."

"I'll take your word for it."

"You don't understand."

"Exactly!"

Bellos put his glass on the bar and began gesturing to make his point. "The markers are specific only to you and me, as the result of my becoming GGM. They are very powerful, especially when you include Carrier inputs. There is something involved in all this called *a Compatibility*. When I became GGM, I became *compatible* with all Carriers, not just one."

Andrew listened intensely. "You realize, I have no idea what you are talking about."

"I'll tell you a little secret. I come from the surface too. I prefer slowing things down and talking, rather than from headsets, *poof!* All of a sudden you know it all."

"*Poof!* Huh? Okay, whatever that means; or perhaps, this is just pretty good vodka?"

"That it is. I can see we will have to get into much more detail about this for you to understand. For now, let me say there are certain genetic markers of yours and mine that, together, across the barrier of time, were stressed. I think what happened was that Brock's sustenance, together with his Carrier's wherewithal, combined with his ancestor, a man named Nicolas, and yours and mine, created a power surge within the Sidron."

"Sidron? So, you are saying, without our combined markers, I would be dead right now."

"Interesting way of putting it, yes."

"Can it happen again to someone else?"

"Well, it has never happened before. Who's to say? Here, within Ever-Life, genetics are everything. It seems I can't send you back right now."

"So, I start over again?" Andrew stood thinking across from Bellos at the bar trying to understand. "And we are related?"

Bellos could see Andrew's frustration. "You are empty again . . . another drink?"

"Definitely! What do I call you, Uncle? Distant brother? Cousin 100 removed, or am I your grandfather's, grandfather's, grandfather's ancestor?"

"We will have to ask Tom. He's keeper of the records." Bellos poured again and quipped, "Well, if you are anything like I was when Gordon hired me, you are going to be saying 'what' quite a lot."

"So, you're hiring me?"

"Hell, no! Maybe nominate you for something."

"Perhaps I should take some notes?"

Bellos chuckled, "Don't bother, I'll have to repeat this one several times before I understand it myself."

"You know, standing here like this with you, it reminds me of conversations I had a very long time ago." Andrew got a tear in his eye. "Subject for another conversation."

Bellos sighed and raised an eyebrow. "I'm not quite sure how to begin or where to start. Have you ever been to Washington, DC, or Mexico City?"

"Yes, both several times, DC with family; but Mexico City was business. I was on the job. I was impressed with the catacombs."

Bellos looked wide-eyed. "Ah, yes, one of our first Posts in the Americas. Then, are you familiar with underground structures?"

"Not really. What do you mean, Posts?"

"Hmm, did you know Washington DC was built on a catacomb foundation too; quite similar to this cave structure?"

"What?"

Bellos chuckled, "There's that word again . . . I'll tell you what, on second thought, I think it would be more prudent if we talked after you put one of these on again."

He pulled a headset out from behind the bar and held it up to Andrew. "Remember this?"

"Yes, as a matter of fact."

"Right, good." Bellos placed the set over Andrew's ear. "Wear it like that, there. Now just relax. This will only take a minute. You will probably understand more this way. We must do something about losing the art of conversation. We will talk more"

Andrew sipped his drink as the inputs began. After a few minutes, Andrew took off the headset, sighed and commented, "It's hard to adjust to all your advanced technology. How do you know everything in here is the truth?"

Bellos smiled and said, "Well, it's my job, through interaction and treaties with our friends the Carriers, to make sure what goes into those vaults is nothing but the truth; and, we've never had an issue about the information. It can't be false, the images in those are the images from the events as they happen in real time. We can discuss more later."

Bellos went to the wall; and, as he did, a door opened; and in the small space there were ten more vault-buttons he placed on the bar. "Here, go through these. I have to go, but we will see each other at the funeral. I promise we will talk regularly. You will also be meeting with Tom again, and I'm confident you will learn and fit right in here. See you tomorrow."

The two men shook hands, and Bellos left.

CHAPTER 65: GLACIATED

A CROWD OF SEVERAL THOUSAND lined the Ever-Life's Grand Arcade in Giza's Time Trust main cavern. The ceremony would be broadcast to all Posts' colony people and dignitaries who came to pay their respects to the most progressive and successful GGM in the history of the colonies, Gordon Swanson. Generally, each colony held a ceremony monthly celebrating lives whose bodies ceased to function, but these were not like any funerals on the surface. Ever-Life had a completely different take on what the surface referred to as funerals. Gordon Swanson's body would be *glaciated* today.

Over four-thousand years ago, Ever-Life doctors perfected several processes to disposition a person after what we called death. Duplication, Transtosis, CPT, and Glaciating were all genetically related processes. *Glaciating* was the process of injecting a particular chemical compound into a deceased individual's carotid artery. It would render a human body preserved, dry-frozen, from the inside out without the cold of old cryogenics. Those people who underwent the process would remain in a *glaciated stasis* until Ever-Life doctors could reanimate them from some other discovery. It was all a matter of genetics to establish candidacy. In the case of Gordon Swanson, he had already undergone all the known processes, duplication, transtosis, and CPT. Nevertheless, he still fell victim to his genetic disorder. First and foremost, Swanson's body was repaired from the damage it suffered in the explosion at TTI. That included genetic sealing through the Nanite repair of Transtosis. Then, it was shipped carefully to the ceremony. The glaciating process began with injecting a concentration of special chemistries into his neck. That traveled to the brain first, then throughout his entire bloodstream, and finally into every organ, every cell. The body would remain as if it had stopped functioning, but it would not decompose. It was placed into an oval hermetically sealed body container, which the Carriers made; and, as part of the ceremony, the container would be stored in a designated area within the magma of the underworld.

There was one alternative to Glaciating for a person, who was not a genetic candidate for any of the other processes. It was referred to as rendering the body *'in memorance.'* That process was performed by a Grand Carrier and was relatively simple and efficient. The Carrier would speed-dry the body and compress it into a gemstone, leaving the family with a valuable keepsake.

Today, the monthly celebration was the first to include a GGM in over 300 years. The great GGM Hall of History had walls covered with photographs, descriptions regarding each GGM, as well as their choice of process. If a GGM chose *glaciating,* a plaque with his image, history, and accomplishments displayed on the wall. If a GGM was rendered in *memorance,* the master's gemstone appeared in a clear crystal container below his picture for all to see.

Before Swanson's formal event, adult Carriers lined up and down the grand chasm like stacked sardines. There was nothing like it recorded in the history logs. A few friends of Gordon Swanson from the surface sat in a group just to the left-front of the podium. Apart from them, in particular, Swanson's aid of many years, Master Markum Maheim McAdden, affectionately known as "M", sat quietly, directly in front of the casket just below the podium. He was dressed in his formal gold East-Indian suit, given to him by the Muhal emperor, Shah Jahan, who built the Taj Mahal. The service was scheduled for late that afternoon. Jack and Brian Sheldon arrived by Carrier bubble and met with Bellos privately before the ceremony.

"Jack, glad you made it. How's Rachel?"

"Not good. She is still in a deep coma. Thanks for the use of Dr. LuAnne and the labs though. I'm not sure what to do next. LuAnne says neither Nanites nor the new CPT has worked on her this time. Rachel is in a place I can't go, and your team confirmed she has the same crippling gene as Gordon."

"I wish there was something we could do." Said Bellos. "We know so much, but there's not much more we can do. Don't give up though, my friend. We'll keep at it."

The two hugged, and then Jack went to sit down with his son, Brian.

Bellos stepped up to the podium. The crowd applauded, and he began to speak, "Good afternoon, my Ever-Life friends. Welcome to this month's *Life Celebration*. We gather to honor all those dearly departed and pay respects to them for their contributions to all of us, to their families, friends, careers, and to the many of us whom they never knew but whose lives will be forever changed and bettered because they lived. In particular, we are all here today to witness the process of Glaciating one of our most beloved and accomplished GGMs, Mr. Gordon Swanson. He was my predecessor, mentor; and for all of us, the longest, most progressive and prosperous GGM in our history. His life and his efforts have affected us all for the better. Let us pray:

"We thank thee, oh Lord, for giving us this man. Thank you for your service, Gordon. You will live in our hearts, our minds, and our daily lives, every day."

Then, Bellos took two steps back from the podium and turned around to view Swanson's body in the open container, which lay on top of the Carrier, Allenfar. As Bellos approached the edge of the container, two other doctors stood at attention waiting. The GGM motioned to them to begin the ceremonious glaciate-injections.

Then, everyone stood while the Ever-Life anthem played; and, at the end of it, everybody turned and faced the grand chasm where the Carriers lay. To everyone's surprise, all the light in the cavern from the walls went out, and it became pitch black. After the nervous awes of the crowd subsided, the Carriers displayed what could only be described as breathtaking, another first. They began shooting fireworks, but there were no sounds, just silent explosions of magnificent and varied colors. The beauty was remarkable. People began to clap and cheer, and soft music played from the monitors. The show continued for about 20 minutes. When it finished, normal light shined again, and Bellos addressed the crowd, "Thank you all for remembering our loved ones . . . Ever-Life, everywhere!"

As he again backed from the podium, Allenfar rose from the stage and circled the crowd. Then Swanson's container closed and Allenfar slowly floated down the deep chasm followed by the rest of the Carriers. Bellos stepped down from the stage and began greeting Swanson's family and the close friends and loved ones who sat in the front rows. They all chatted briefly with tears and smiles, and then they disbanded to meet in the GGM Hall of History for refreshments.

CHAPTER 66: HOPE SPRINGS

RACHEL SHELDON HAD BEEN ILL FOR WEEKS, since the episode in Rio. Jack had the home lab rearranged into a high-tech hospice. He continued to run tests on her every day. Unfortunately, they yielded no conclusive results. Ever-Life's labs indicated nothing new either. There was no suggested direction or prognosis. Jack had been researching the orphan diseases for the last month, trying to correlate the gene pools. He was frustrated and at his wit's end. He spent all his time back and forth to Ever-Life, but to no avail. As had become his routine, early one evening, he sat in a rocker beside his wife's bed, dozing. Rachel lay still, barely breathing. Brian was there too, kneeling on the other side of the bed, holding one of her hands. Suddenly, for no apparent reason, she opened her eyes and saw Jack, and she squeezed Brian's fingers. "Brian?"

"Mom? Dad, mom is awake."

Jack jerked up, leaned over to her and kissed her cheek. "Hello, darling."

"I must be in and out quite a bit. Come closer, both of you."

They moved quickly, and she began to talk. "I am so happy. I know you think I am going to die, but it's not true, not at all. I've been having dreams. They are so real. I am just going to change. Jack, you taught me, remember in the lab, CPT? My thoughts and memories, my soul; they will live on and multiply, just as life gives new babies. Brian, promise me you will have babies?"

"Of course, I will."

"Rachel, save your strength, I'll get you something, just be still," said Jack softly patting her shoulder.

"No, Jack, I have to get this out. You have to listen." She looked at them both and continued, "Death is just the labor of rebirth . . . Brian, you are going to know me better than you ever did, better than you ever imagined. We will be closer than I ever hoped; and yet, you and your children will be even closer. And sometimes; sometimes, when you need it most, we will talk. All you have to do is love."

Then she turned to Jack. "Oh, my love, I know, I'm such a romantic. I love you so. So many said it before better than I could; but it's true. To give and receive love is to experience God. I see him in you, babe. Now give me a good kiss."

They smiled, and Jack kissed her with tears rolling down his face. In that kiss, she stopped breathing.

Brian squeezed her arm and sunk his head into the bed. Jack caressed her face and cried. After a short time, he got up slowly and walked to the other side of the bed, helping Brian up and out of the room upstairs to Angie's waiting arms. Angie walked Brian to the couch, as Jack went back down into the lab and closed the door behind him. He sat on the edge of the bed staring at Rachel. With the most profound sadness, he held her hand and cried like a baby, "You can't leave me." He looked up and prayed aloud, "God, if you can hear me, now is the time."

Up in the living room, Angie comforted her Brian. "Come on, honey, let your father be with her. Let's take a breath for a few minutes, get some air. Walk with me."

They both went outside. In the lab, Jack sat whimpering. His eyes were blood red from crying. He couldn't say words any longer, but his thoughts were crystal clear, *Take me! Bring her back. I saw you; I know you. I know you can take me.* He cried himself out and placed her clenched fists over the covers trying to adjust her comfortably.

Who knows how much time passed, but then, from the far corner, Jack heard a whistling whirling sound, like the wind through trees. He looked, and to his amazement, a small glowing statue of a Carrier appeared on the floor. It was no more than 15 inches high. He walked over, examined it, and read the inscription on the base, *Allenfar.* "Christ, what is this!" Then, he was startled at hearing a voice from the bed. There, sitting beside Rachel's corpse, was the Tyree Master.

"Hello, doctor. Do you remember me?"

Jack was emotionally spent and had no patience. "I'm in no mood for games. No, I don't. Who are you and how did you get in here?"

"We met on your trip back to the surface in a Carrier bubble. I spoke to you and your wife."

"Yes, it is you. Well, you picked the wrong time for a visit."

"It seems your wife finally pushed the communicator, which I gave her...All this time, and nothing to report, until now."

"You are too late; she's gone."

"I promised I would help her if you remember." He smiled at Jack and stood up. "You see, she did push it. Look, there in her hand."

Jack leaned over and opened her left fist. Sure enough, there it was, the little peanut device the Tyree Master gave her in the Carrier.

"Doctor Sheldon, you of all people believe in hope, do you not?"

Jack felt his knees buckle. Catching himself, he almost missed sitting on the edge of the bed.

"Who are you?" He began to tear-up again.

"I am here to remind you that nothing said has any meaning without hope. Your wife touched us in a special way. Your discoveries have touched us all in many special ways."

"But I thought sunlight killed your kind."

"The fact is, many things can kill us, just like many things can kill you. But I am alive, and you two proved that your love for each other reaches beyond death . . . Not that others don't. It just seems like the proper thing to say at this moment."

"What?"

The Tyree Master smiled. "You know, you people say that word quite a lot. It's only a word anyway, death I mean. Here, I have this for you."

Jack held out his hand, and Tyree gave him a small two-inch blue vial.

"I trust you know what to do with this. We have made sure it will work. It's a gift. Oh, and I brought you the little statue over there to remember us by."

Jack turned to glimpse it. When he turned back again, Tyree was gone. Jack looked at the vial in his hand and then took a deep breath, sat on the bed, and buried his head in his wife's lifeless body. Tears flowed, and because he was so overcome with emotion, he didn't notice her body move at first or the slight touch of Rachel's hand caressing his head. Startled, he looked up in disbelief as her eyes opened. They both smiled, and Jack reached for her, cupping her face. "Oh, my God, Rachel."

"Hi, you're a sight. Come here."

They kissed as Jack's tears flooded her cheeks. "But this is impossible. Look at you. Your color, your tone; you look so healthy. How? Look here, I have a vial, but I didn't give you CPT. Oh, thank God, honey!"

As they hugged and cried, Rachel whispered to him, "Oh, my love, there is a power so much greater than any of this. I don't know how or why. I just know I'm thankful to see you."

CHAPTER 67: AIRLIFT, MID-JULY

A PRIVATE AIRLIFT ZOOMED far above Earth, traveling with only two passengers, Marion Brock and Charlie Rossi. A huge 5-ft by 8-ft window lined one wall of the cabin. The aircraft was entirely automated. It was a no pilot space vehicle designed, manufactured, and fueled by the Brock Moon Mining Businesses. It had all the accouterments of a 5-star hotel on Earth. The two men sat comfortably looking down at the majesty of the Nile River.

Brock snickered and said, "It's hard to believe that 10 miles under there, people have built a way of life based on healthcare. If I hadn't discovered Swanson was holding out on me, well, I should be thankful."

"What do you think people will do once they know about the colonies?" Rossi asked.

"Nothing," Brock said. "The media frenzy will last a week, two at most. We will be fine. People are stupid. When all is said and done, my VAD will make the difference up here."

Brock and Rossi had just left Brock's port-station orbiting Earth, and they were now on their way to the Moon.

"Marion, for the last nine months now, your whole effort was to discover time travel. Why?"

Brock was in a good mood and knew the trip was going to take a while, so he put up with Rossi. "Given my history and the events of this year, I trust you'll understand. Insurance was always the consideration."

"Sorry, I don't get it."

"I guess I shouldn't expect you to. I have a dream that my companies will revolutionize life. Can you imagine, if, on that silly little planet, we all could travel in time, not just through it? Until me, our only choice has been to decide how to spend the time we have. What if we could make the time we have left whatever we want? That's what I wanted. And more than that, I wanted to break away, to break out from the prison of time. Of course, how do we do that without the right fuel-power? Do you realize how much fuel is burned up just trying to get out of the gravitational pull of that little ball? Hence, my multitasking to mine the Moon. Who else is doing it, the government? I know that's all bullshit."

"So, this has all been about unselfishly leading the people of planet Earth into space?"

"Unselfishly, Ha! No! Time travel alone is much more than you can imagine. Think of this. As we get less dependent on the base elements on that little blue ball, we can jump from one planet to another, mining fuel as we go. But whatever the fuel is, it has to generate power enough for time travel. Time travel is the key. It will allow us to travel far beyond Earth to throughout the Galaxy and beyond. I think someone said that, some time ago."

Rossi stared at Brock in amazement, and Brock laughed. "Ha! I really had you there for a minute. Here, read this."

Brock handed Rossi an envelope stamped, TOP SECRET.

"You should see your face, Charlie. You gullible shit. See, a little sincerity and even you will listen. I got your attention though, didn't I?"

"You have my attention with this too. You never mentioned this in any meeting with me."

"What did you think I was doing with that Carrier, anyway?"

"I assumed you were trapped inside him."

"Up to a point, I was. The Carrier wanted me for his own reasons, and I found out many things because we shared our Compatibility. We know now that time travel is possible. We will take all the knowledge we got from Stevens and the Carrier and set up shop elsewhere."

"You mean out here?"

"I have just the right spot in mind, and there will be no threat or interference this time. Look, that's where we've been, but that's where we're going."

Rossi followed Brock's finger, as it pointed out the starboard window, and then they both gazed through the front window watching the moon get bigger.

Brock said, "My companies have built three space stations up here on the moon and an inventory port for the distribution of space fuel needed to power all travel. And there's plenty more to get on the Moon. That's what the Brock Companies have invested in silently for the past 35 years, space fuel. It's a whole new world. With fuel, communication, and time travel up here, there are no limits."

"Communication?" Rossi asked. "You mean the VAD, Video Audio Device? I must say, it was brilliant, your introduction on the 4th of July."

KNOFER-ECHO 4: 'V.A.D.-LINK'
Medical Test Trials begin July 4, 2999

"Yep," Brock said, "and now we all have a way to link to each

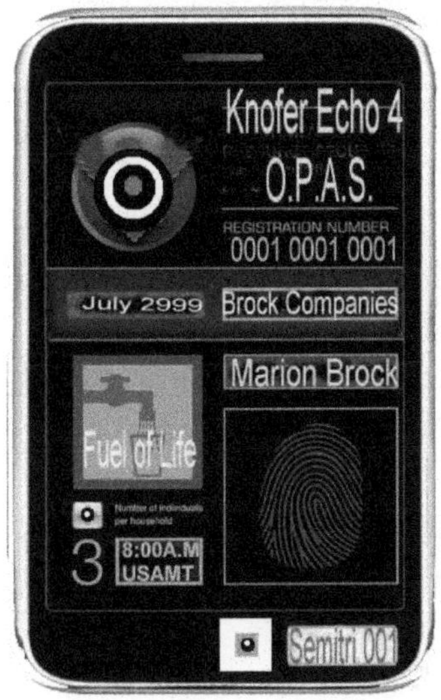

other. Those bastards never suspected. Jack was naïve, thinking his CPT was his alone."

"Link to each other? What do you mean, Marion?" Rossi asked.

"You'll see. They'll all see soon, very soon. To begin with, we'll test the VAD up here. This little wonder is light years in ability from their little Knofers down there. I have 300 of these little gems in the back, and we are going to deliver them to the mining camps and distribution port. Charlie, my friend, I am making you the top dog up here. It's graduation and reward time for you. You are going to run the show."

Rossi did a double take, half smiled and asked, "That's great, but I thought this was a fact-finding mission. Marion, I'm flattered and certainly I could, would . . . Yes, I . . . Thank you."

"Good, it's settled. You will be impressed. The mining camps are almost 100% robotic-cyber operated. We only have ten people in management positions; brilliant, trustworthy men. That makes all the difference. These little devices will enable you to have yourself in more than one place at a time." Brock laughed. "You'll see. You'll love it. Finally, with this little secret, I'm going to execute my plan."

Brock patted Rossi on the shoulder and sat down in a comfortable chair. Rossi sat across from him, staring at the Moon and whispering to himself, "Mining camps; link to each other; ten people, the Moon?"

Then, Rossi flipped the plastic tray for food down next to him and took out a map detailing the Moon camps. There was also a picture of the mining camp robots. "Mining camp robots, they don't look like they even talk. Maybe I should find out."

Rossi took out his new Echo 4. "No time like the present to say hello to these guys."

He pressed his thumbprint against the screen to activate the features. Nothing happened. He tapped repeatedly and then asked Brock, "Uh, Marion, is your Echo working? Mine looks great, but it doesn't seem to do anything. Must be the altitude."

Brock took his out and pressed his thumb on the screen. Likewise, nothing.

He did it several times and then muttered, "It was working fine at the port station. Communication is just a basic with this. Chuck, let me see yours."

Brock shook them both, giggling at first. "I never should have negotiated with our prison friend, Marshall. This was my failsafe. It was all about the power."

He continued to press his thumbprint and shake the Echos. "Don't tell me these farking things are useless. Marshall said the Knofers were the answer."

"Knofers? Rossi asked, "What's a Knofer?"

Brock became intensely focused, "Shit, it should work! Why doesn't it work? Stupid! Stupid! I gave them the samples. I gave them the damn samples! They worked fine. It was unprecedented. Unprecedented, my ass. July 4th was Nick's birthday. Lotta good that did."

Rossi was frustrated too. "Let's just call someone from the cockpit."

The two went forward and sat in the two captains' chairs.

"These aren't just for show," said Brock. "This should all be automatic."

As Brock studied the dash's lighted panel before him, both men felt the airlift suddenly stop. And then they heard a sputter from the rear of the cabin. Then, all of the panel lights went out; and the Airlift began to turn on an angle and drift to one side. Brock quickly focused on the Echo 4 again.

Rossi panicked in the dark. "So, now what? Are we stuck here?"

"Don't be stupid," Brock said. "25,000 miles per hour is hardly stuck. This little thing is supposed to draw power from any source. Goddamn Sheldon. Damn that Swanson. That's what I get for trusting Mr. Marshall."

Brock's hissy fit escalated into a rage.

"Marion? I think we are passing the Moon."

The airlift jerked hard again. It started to tumble and spin out of control. Rossi watched Brock talking to himself, obsessed with the Echos. At first, neither man could feel the spin because of the weightless environment; but then Rossi sensed the momentum increase when he saw the Earth pass across the window, like a video of the Sun fast-forwarding across a clear Seattle skyline. It moved from the top of the window to the bottom with ever-increasing speed, faster with each spin. Rossi pushed himself out of his seat, back to the big bay window. He could see both the Earth and Moon now. The Airlift began not only spinning side to side, but it was also flipping end over end. "Marion, you better come and see this. Something is really wrong."

Frustrated, Brock let the Echos float. He joined Rossi, and they both stared out the window at something blocking their view of the Earth, as the airlift spun. It was Allenfar, floating no more than 100 meters from the Airlift.

"Christ!" said Brock, "Damn fish! I hate those things."

"What? What the hell are you talking about? What is that?"

Brock shook his head. Only now at last was he to understand. "They knew these wouldn't work. But how?"

Rossi's head moved side to side, trying to follow the spinning image. "What the hell are you talking about?"

Brock's eyes bulged. He could hear the Carrier in his mind; and then, suddenly, the Allenfar's Tyree Master appeared in the airlift behind Brock and Rossi.

"You are where you should be, Marion Brock. You will be remembered, as you wished. Oh, it seems your Compatibility has released us. It has enabled us to live quite well in sunlight. Thank you. I stopped the power in your little toys. Those won't work up here. We will be joining surface man and hope to help him in many ways. It is time. Your people didn't have a clue what the power source was in the samples. As always, you assumed rather than learned. Good luck and enjoy the ride."

The image before the men disappeared. Rossi grabbed Brock by his lapels and shook him. "What the hell just happened!?"

Brock pushed him off and slapped his palms against the Airlift window.

"You son-of-a-bitch! You bastards! This isn't the end! This isn't over!"

CHAPTER 68: AFTERSHOCK

BACK ON EARTH'S SURFACE, above Time Trust in Giza, three men walked on the ramp between the arms of the great Sphinx and talked in the sunset, GGM, Mathew Bellos, his recruit and relative Andrew, and Jake Burns. Burns spoke to Andrew in a lighthearted tone. "So, my friend, how do you like being the oldest living relative of our GGM? Come to think of it, you are the oldest living anything."

"Yeah, thanks for that. When I think about it, am I really alive?"

Jake was quick to banter, "Dead or alive, I should take you to my old shrink. He would have a field day with this."

"I'll bet."

They all paused to look at the pyramids silhouetted against the sinking sun.

Andrew said, "I was just thinking, my brother loved Egyptology. He would love it here. Mind you, he'd never believe any of this; but, if he were alive, he'd love seeing this."

"Brother?" Remarked Jake.

"Yes, one of two, and a sister. She was a great lady."

"I remember you had kids."

"Oh yes, four, and grandchildren, although I'm not sure how many. One of my hopes is to find out what became of them. I expect to spend a lot of time with headsets."

Bellos was quick to comment, "Andrew, there are a few things that aren't in the general headset files. Reserved for GGMs. I will instruct Wheeler to share some of my private vaults. You may be surprised at what you find."

"I'll remember that. Thank you."

The sky was turning beautiful red and peach colors, reflecting off the clouds. Bellos studied it all, whispering, "There is truly nothing more beautiful than the color changes in a sunset; not one moment is the same as the last. I miss it."

Jake pointed to the left. "Look, a rainbow. Sometimes, I don't think people up here appreciate what they have."

Bellos replied, "That is because you come from up here, and you haven't seen this for a while. I think they do; most of them anyway, when they slow down and take a breath."

"Matt, what was that device, that watch, Gordon gave me to throw into Semitri?" Asked Jake. "I don't know why, but my instincts took over in the heat of the moment, and I just threw it into the Carrier. Although, now, I wish I didn't. Perhaps Gordon would still be alive. I thought we didn't make anything that killed."

"Ah yes, the watch; that wasn't our technology. We didn't make that. The Carrier Council gave it to him years ago. As GGMs we have a few fail-safes. The council trusted him enough to give it."

"I don't get it?" said Jake.

"The device didn't kill the Carrier," Bellos explained. "Semitri's resisting it killed him. The device only works from within a Carrier. Semitri fought against its effects. It tore down the wall he built up against the hive mind. The device enabled the rest of the Carriers to share the Compatibility that he denied them. He could have let it all go months ago. Anyway, by fighting the device's effects, Semitri's own power turned on him."

"I feel like I'm the one who killed Gordon."

"No, Jake, and we now know the trigger to his death was Brock's particle displacement event to kidnap Gordon. Brock might just as well have shot him. Also, Gordon's crippling gene has been weakening him for years. We even gave him the initial CPT procedure from his duplicate in Jerusalem, but it didn't kill the gene. He needed the new CPT desperately. Brock's particle displacement was the last straw."

After a pause, Jake replied, "Christ, I'm the Security Chief, and I never knew. Gordon was a good soul."

"Yes, he was; he is. I believe he found his way. His shoes will be hard to fill. He introduced us to the surface more than any GGM in history. You two and I are the first of a new generation recruited from the surface to lead the Ever-Life colonies. We have to continue his work to bring the colonies and the surface together."

"How are we going to do that when sunlight kills the Carriers?"

"Yes, about that. It appears that one effect from sharing Semitri's compatibilities was that the Carriers no longer die in sunlight. Of course, it remains to be seen exactly what that means for the surface cultures."

"I wonder, too," said Andrew.

"Wonder what?" asked Jake.

"I wonder if I found my way; if I found what happened to my family. It has been over 900 years."

Bellos heard him but ignored him for the moment. He continued to study the sky. "I was just thinking what Gordon used to say about Ever-Life, *'Our job is to extend life,'* he'd say. Big challenge. We made many significant advances under his leadership. The average lifespan of our citizens now extends three times that of those on the surface. Then, I think about Brock. In spite of all his faults, he will be remembered. He did contribute a lot to progress. Both of them did great things. One we liked. One we didn't."

Bellos turned to face Andrew. "You ask a great question. The answer is much more complex than my simply believing Gordon found his way. My advice; don't think about it too much. It could drive you crazy. We are going to learn much more about the Sidron. Meantime; live your life, this life. Get up and do the best you can. Fill your day. Learn and be happy. There is plenty to do. At least you have proof that the planet has lasted another 900 years."

Bellos smiled with an expression of peace.

Burns said, "Yeah, some things get answered, and some don't. Come on you two; lighten up. Look over there; the way the Sun is hitting the spinning sand, it looks like a shiny dust devil."

A few hundred feet away, between the Great Pyramid of Cheops and the Sphinx, the wind blew the harmless 100-foot high tornado out of sight, and Allenfar appeared in the desert replacing it. The last of the Sun's rays reflected off his skin in a most remarkable way.

The three men fixed, startled at what happened next. A single, silent lightning charge ignited from the great pyramid's zenith to Allenfar's tongue, which extended up from his mouth like an antenna. Parts of his skin began to change, and flecks of gold appeared all over him sparkling brightly. After only a few seconds, it was over. Bellos smiled, gestured to his companions, and began walking toward the Carrier.

"Ha! I wonder what he has in store for us now. They never cease to amaze me. What's next? Come on you two; our day doesn't end with the Sun going down."

Transmission input Headset 2 complete
Andrew 10746-H2

When I opened my eyes, I saw the blinding light of an eye scope which Sir Thomas Wheeler was shining on my pupils.

"Well, you look fine," Wheeler said.

"How long was I under this time?"

"18-minutes."

"I thought these things were instantaneous, or just a couple of minutes."

"Mostly, yes;" Wheeler said, "time is relative. There was a lot of information to input. Don't you agree?"

"Yes, I suppose, thanks, now what?"

"As you were told, you have to have more sessions. I think you should take a break, settle a bit and get acquainted with all of this; Ever-Life, I mean. I have to run more tests before you have another session."

Andrew put the headset on the table and said, "I want to find out what happened to my family."

"All in good time, my friend, all in good time."

EVER~LIFE

<u>HEADSET #3, STARDUST-VAULT 0378</u>

<u>INTRODUCTION:</u>

1] TIMELINE YEAR: 3000.10, EVER-LIFE, MY CHANGE

SINCE MY ORIGINAL DATE OF ARRIVAL at Ever-Life, I have undergone regular testing and counseling to measure any effects from my headset sessions and time traveling through the Sidron. It was now the year 3000.10., October, by our old calendar. I have had regular PTEs–Prescribed Therapeutic Engagements, twice a week with Sir Thomas Wheeler, who was assigned as, MC-Manager Confidant, to my case. He was responsible for testing, monitoring me and introducing and educating me about Ever-Life's culture. Wheeler and the powers to be were afraid I would disintegrate, like the other copies of me. It was paramount, to them, to measure my mental progress and ability to accept data. They expected to learn something about the Sidron and what triggered my time travel. To do this, Wheeler administered headsets to me; and, after each, we'd engage in a Q&A exchange, while my head was hooked up to their gadgets. Wheeler carefully observed the data, studied my reactions to the inputs, and took notes during our discussions. It was my understanding that after our sessions, he met with GGM, Mathew Bellos, to discuss everything; and, together, they would decide if the PTEs would continue. So far, I still attend PTEs, even after a year.

Sometimes, inputs were confusing for me because vaults placed in my headsets were not chosen in chronological order. I got to the point of reviewing each vault introduction before initiating its primary run. Wheeler told me the reason for this was too technical to explain. Regardless, I include this headset #0378 because it is sequential and completes this section of headsets, but it is not chronological.

As I said, after each sleep period, the routine begins over again with more testing, more headsets and Q&As, to identify and correct any misinformation or adverse reactions I may have; and so on, and so on. My attitude regarding all this has gone from initially new, confident, and exciting, to routine, monotonous, and annoying, more than valuable to me. Eventually, I grew to feel much like a lab rat.

One morning, months ago, I recognized my negative attitude. I ended my sleep session by waking up in a flash, disoriented, and sweating. And, I had been dreaming again, the same dream, in which I spoke to myself in the past, conveying all my headset sessions to my counterpart in 2009-2019. Going by my past timeline, I thought it had been a decade and enough is enough. I remember going to the bathroom, splashing water on my face, and studying myself in the mirror. That became routine too, until, after the next month or so, I began to see noticeable changes. While my attitude soured, physically and medically I felt and looked better than I had in years. I had no asthma symptoms, no heart pain, and no arthritis. The lab doctors removed my heart-stents. And my vision improved to where I no longer needed glasses. Laugh-lines and other facial wrinkles were distinctly less; not to mention my bald head was growing hair back. While the doctors informed me that CPT would result in positive physical improvements, they had no idea how CPT would affect me emotionally and mentally. Combined with what the Sidron trip may have done to me, I now believe the CPT caused a degree of emotional negatives, or perhaps, it was my sense of confinement that brought on a level of paranoia. I tried to concentrate on the positives; but I always found myself on the same rollercoaster of thinking about the headsets, the Sidron, the Knofers, Brock, Compatibility, CPT, the wine, and the regimen I was on; and that the impossibility of my time traveling to the future was actually true. The headset sessions were not working as they should for me anymore. I couldn't stop thinking about the same things over and over. My attitude took a downward spiral. Eventually, I became so frustrated and claustrophobic with my surroundings and the restrictions imposed on me that I was driven to come up with my own plan to feel better and free again.

Oh, don't misunderstand me. There were incredible advancements I experienced in Ever-Life. To begin with, I was over 1050 years old by their calendar. Obviously, there were prominent advancements related to medicine and healthcare: There was CPT, indeed the most incredible discovery regarding health ever. There were the cures for the common cold and most diseases we knew of growing up, like all cancers, diabetes, heart disease, MS, MD. Almost all forms of life-threatening viruses and harmful bacteria were eradicated or under control. And if by chance, a person does continue to get sicker, there was always CPT if genetics allowed. That meant many different controls regarding population growth, especially given people lived much longer. Consequently, the introduction of birth control through genetic modifications became a norm, a subject of interest to all adults there. Moreover, there were the ever-popular conventional pills, available to everyone. Anyone could take a pill for almost anything, to alleviate hunger, to change one's body shape or body skin color or age replication. Take a pill to cure baldness. If you feel too fat or too skinny, see your doctor, take a pill or get a shot. Any form of condition you want to change or any obvious discomfort you want eliminated, a physician could prescribe a uniquely formulated compound for your condition. Most pills I knew of in my time were obsolete pharmaceuticals, replaced by compound formulations, customized for the individual. It should suffice to say; tablets were still a strong influence on public health, but in an entirely different way than I remember.

Regarding education, Knofers and headsets replaced most schools and universities. Vaults containing any subject matter or experience could be inserted into either a headset or Knofer. The input information not only recorded in the user's mind as a permanent record, but also attached to the inputs were imprints of the emotions connected to the data. Vaults themselves were like tiny flash drives of old, but they were the size of about a quarter of a fingernail and called buttons by the public. They were all alive, organic, and they continually updated all facts within them. I never understood how. People could know in a moment what it took us years to learn. The Ever-Life population was far better informed than we ever were about everything. Books, for example, were available to read in the classic hardcover, softcover or e-book format, as the written word; or an entire story could be input directly to your mind through a headset session, which may only last 30 seconds or a minute. One could input countless books in a day, about a vast variety of subjects, and people did. This, of course, changed the Author/Writer's Market dramatically; again, a topic for another time.

Of significant interest to me were those everyday inventions. Things the population took for granted, used daily, that we never had in the past: the food generators, permanent cleanliness, and deodorants, desalinization, including biologically purified air and water, both of which could contain specific molecular compounds to help cure a vast assortment of discomforts that were standard to the underworld. There were the waste management disposers in place of toilets and sewers. Clothes were antiseptic, cause for the glowing, and needed washing or cleaning once or twice a quarter year. Some were disposable/recyclable. I never required antiperspirant after the first application of the gel they gave me. Then I just took a pill every week or two. Another thing, you could pick what fragrance you wanted your body to radiate, by day, week, or month. The list goes on and on. I had one pair of shoes that, by a built-in timer, disappeared off my feet when I pushed a black circle on the shoe's heel, and in the morning, they reappeared clean and antiseptic. The walls in my villa could be changed at a moment's notice to look like whatever artistic motif chosen. One day I could have every one of my paintings hanging all around the house, and the next day I could have murals of the south seas, just by pushing a button on the wall. There are too many wonders to list here, but anything you could imagine back in my past existed in some form or another in the future.

What about crime? Every outcome of any misdemeanor, felony, or rage situation was dealt with almost immediately. Holographic judges had access to up to the second historical information regarding any trial, as well as access to all legal reference library information. They dispensed quick decisive verdicts. EverLife had taken our old American political experiment to something far more reformed and polished. Unlike the gross arguments of my past, EverLife individuals could argue their case up to and during the trial and beyond sentencing during the rehabilitation process, which took place in a Carrier; thus providing ongoing education and understanding to the offender. Frankly, that fact is what initiated my interest in Allenfar and his kind. If Brock was not rehabilitated in one, how and why did that fail? I wanted to know one of those fabulous Carriers and learn all I could how one might restore me from my negative attitude.

Carriers were responsible for returning all offenders to society. There were no jails or prisons, except for those kept within the Carriers during rehabilitation. If rehabilitation failed, the last resort involved the GGM/Carrier Council together; similar to our old Supreme Court in the USA. Except Ever-Life rulings were determinations, not opinions.

Eventually, I believed that Ever-Life had no understanding of my real needs. I needed help to reconcile it all: my family history, my time traveling through the Sidron, not to mention Ever-Life's utterly different way of living. Finally, Sir Thomas Wheeler and the GGM, Dr. Mathew Bellos assigned me to what I thought would be a great way of understanding it all. They gave me the job and title of 'Surface

Liaison', introducing Ever-Life to surface Earth's cultures of the year 3000. I was to meet particular ambassadors up there and determine which countries were to receive headsets from Ever-Life. GGM even assigned me the Carrier Allenfar, and that's how I found solace in my new friend. It was Allenfar I credit with helping me understand what was really going on with my dreams. He analyzed and played my dreams as videos on his walls during our travels so I could see first-hand what I was transmitting to the past. I shared everything with Allenfar that I had learned in both the PTEs and headset sessions. Allenfar became the way to relieve my paranoia. True, everyone in Ever-Life treated me like a precious diamond; but I was confined, unless with Allenfar, only to be seen or heard as they saw fit; partly I think, for fear Brock factions would take me, or as I said, that I would disintegrate as my counterparts did. And Ever-Life couldn't afford that.

To make matters more bothersome, despite security protocols, my presence and story leaked to the general population. People everywhere wanted to see and talk to me. So, GGM Mathew Bellos and Sir Thomas Wheeler decided it would be best if they changed my identity entirely, 'for my protection and security,' they said. My Argonne Villa Guardsman, Barclay, brought me all the new proper credentials and IDs. All of my actual historical information and what happened to me were sealed and stored in the private Vault of the GGM. To me, that fact alone was a contradiction of the ethics and morals they preached. My new documents described me as Ambassador at Large, Gabriel Cooper, nephew to GGM, Mathew Bellos. My job responsibility stayed the same, and I did enjoy that for a time. I even met survivors of the terrorist wars, which raged for eleven generations on the surface, but I never met the *super-thinkers*.

I learned a great deal about the future world on the surface, and I began researching the New York Library to find out what happened to my family. However, after several trips and meetings with specific individuals, I was told by Wheeler that new test results of my genetics required me to postpone any further contact with the surface and return to the Argonne Resort until further notice, for a new wave of tests. Since then, I have never actually left the resort compound without an escort. My job became no more than a title to enable me to walk among the gardens surrounding the property. But even that stopped. I felt like a prisoner. So, together, my good friend, the Grand Carrier Allenfar, and I mapped a plan of escape.

HEADSET # 3, STARDUST-VAULT # 0378, INTRODUCTION

2] TIMELINE YEAR: 2012, BARTLETT, IL. ANDREW

I DON'T KEEP TRACK OF MY TIME that well anymore, although I am conscious of it more than ever. I have been receiving headset transmissions from the future and writing this manuscript since 2011. But the ideas don't come every day. There are voids, periods most would attribute to writer's block, but they are just gaps between times when my counterpart in the future transmits data to me.

At first, I thought the subject matter came to me from my dreams. However, as time passed, I was to understand the inputs were much more than just dreams. When I first started writing this story, I had not learned yet that one of me had time traveled to Ever-Life to the year 2999, and he was communicating back to my timeline in 2011. At first, my dreams came only at night. It was later as the months passed that I would fall into light trances as I call them, once or twice during a given day, and I would write frantically for fear of forgetting. Gradually, I got to the point where I would wake up in the middle of the night sweating and rush downstairs to write until morning. Eventually, the dreams became progressively more vivid and intense, filling me with new wondrous knowledge of the future. I wrote some days for 16 to 20 hours at a time. And yes, I did question my mental health. After all, it is quite something to believe in the revelations, pondering if what I was writing wasn't some invading insanity, or perhaps the beginning of Alzheimer's. The one event that made it all believable to me was the one piece of the puzzle that took place in 2012. If that had not happened, I probably would not have published any of this. What occurred during that event will never leave me.

One last major point to remember as you read this headset. Like the other two, my involvement regarding Ever-Life was tied directly to what happens to Sir Thomas Wheeler, Marion Brock, GGM Mathew Bellos, Jake Burns, and Dr.'s Jack & Rachel Sheldon.

The following is headset-3 and is labeled in the Ever-Life vaults as 'Stardust.'"

CHAPTER 69: 2012 THE VISIT

WHEN I THOUGHT ABOUT IT, it was hard for me to believe that I had been sitting in my living room chair, almost every day for two years, writing Ever-Life. I was fatigued that day, in part, because I was scheduled for a Cancer procedure tomorrow. It was Thursday, October 12, 2012; and, additional to the doctor's appointment, I had a bit of a defeatist attitude regarding my manuscript and whether to publish it or not. After all, what publisher would accept an unknown author? Who would read it?

Regardless, something happened that day; something that would change my life, my limited understanding of the world, and my attitude regarding these writings forever.

I arose at 6 am, did my privacies, settled downstairs in my green lounge chair, and struggled with my thoughts. But, as always, and still determined, I typed away on my laptop, lost in my world of the future. At precisely 10 am, I heard a loud strange swishing sound, followed by a sound like burning crackling firewood. Then, I felt a vibration, like an earthquake, which almost shook my laptop off my legs. I grabbed it and sat holding tight. Gazing in front of me at eye level, about 3 ft from the chair, I began to see a rip appear in mid-air. It looked and sounded like the fabric of space was unzipping. I watched as the cut extended upward and to the right about 5-ft long, almost reaching the ceiling. Then, it stopped. I froze, mesmerized, staring at it until a blinding flash of light exploded from within it and filled the room. The light was followed by a massive burst of wind, and then I heard a loud thud in my kitchen. The sides of the rip began flapping like curtains blowing through an open window. Slowly, I put my laptop down and stood up. I reached for one of the flaps when another hard swoosh of air forced me back into my chair. As I regained my composer, I heard moaning in the kitchen. At that same time, the rip began to repair itself and zip up, closing very fast. Then, suddenly, it was gone. I reached out all around, but there was no evidence it ever occurred. So, I gathered myself, turned toward the kitchen, and carefully walked into the room. There, on the floor next to the stove, lay a male body face down, motionless. The first thing I noticed was that his clothes were glowing. He began to move and moan, so I stooped down and turned the body over. That's when a sick feeling punched me in the gut. The man looked exactly like me, except healthier somehow. I shocked back as he opened his eyes and nudged up on his elbows. We made eye contact and he smiled. "It worked," he said. "Holy shit! It worked!"

"What the hell is happening?" I asked, recoiling. "And who the hell are you?"

"Try to be calm," he said. "I can explain. I'm not going to hurt you."

I reached down and grabbed his arm. "Are you okay?"

The man patted his face and chest, checking for hurts and bruises. "I think so."

I helped him up and guided him to the living room couch. "Sit down."

I offered. "I'll get some water."

"No, no, no, on the water. I have this. I'll be fine."

He unclipped a flask from his belt, gestured to me as if he were toasting, and drank from it. I stared at the container and asked, "Is that...?"

"Yep." He wiped his mouth. "It's the wine."

"...Are you really here, or am I dreaming now?" I sat down in front of him dumbfounded, studied his facial details and squeezed his wrist. "Well, you feel real enough to me."

"Thanks. I am." He took another gulp from the flask. "There are rules regarding time travel. But they aren't what you might think."

I reacted without listening, "Your clothes, they glow? My God! Is it true? This is too fantastic!"

"Yes." He took a third sip, smiled, and looked at me focused. "It's all real and true. The glowing is on everything there. You don't notice it when you've been there long enough. It's something we get used to, fundamental to their environment."

It was then I realized what had been happening to me, about my dreams over the last 2-plus years. The man took a final sip of wine and slipped the flask back onto his belt clip. "It might be best if you call me Gabe."

"Gabe?" I asked. "Why Gabe? You are me."

"Gabriel Cooper is the name they gave me. Historical records there are entirely different than what you are used to. There's nothing like social security, insurance of any kind, or driver's licenses. There's only one card for legal purposes and identification. Here, look."

I took the card and studied it. There was a beautiful colored picture of a Carrier embossed in gold on it. Above that, there was a number of the Carrier assigned to Gabe, given his status as a relative of the GGM. That number described Allenfar, to whom Gabe was now integrated genetically. "So, what does it mean 'integrated genetically?'"

"Primarily, that I can reach Allenfar directly by chip, here in my neck. It's an emergency button sort of, below the skin. Everything is genetics."

I got that from the first book. "So, you are me from the future, with a different name?"

"That's the gist of it, yes."

"And more hair I see."

Gabe smiled and raised an eyebrow."

I studied his face. "Did you undergo some cosmetic procedure, you look different, younger really than I do. It's subtle, but yes, different; and yes, you have more hair than I do."

"I'll have you know, I've undergone CPT too, which has made me more efficient, so they say; and I am younger chronologically than you are now."

I was curious. "Want to explain why you're younger?"

"It took me time to understand, but here's the simple math, and remember, it's all a matter of perspective relative to your starting viewpoint... I instantaneously transported through the Sidron in 2004, so I arrived in 2999 as a 58-year old. Today, I traveled from the year 3000 back to 2012, where you are 66-years old. I am, on the other hand, only 59 and a few months. Understand? I am 7 years younger than you." Gabe chuckled. "And I had to have it explained to me several times before I got it."

I sat calculating. "Ah, okay. Remarkable. I'll have to think about that a while. Is CPT necessary for you to live in the future?"

"No, but as you know, by having the procedure, my cells and my body metabolism function better, more efficiently. The CPT stimulates corrective action in each cells' nucleus. Telomeres grow again. That sort of thing. Here, I brought you something."

Gabe handed me a 10-inch by 12-inch book from his satchel and said, "Its title is JAS? It's a hand published copy. I thought you would like to keep it here. It explains in detail what CPT does. Also, it may be of interest to your family."

"Thank you! Unbelievable."

Gabe continued. "About my CPT, they weren't sure what was going to happen to me because I was in the original Sidron event. My counterparts disappeared, and doctors were afraid I might too, since no Carrier prepared me for a time-trip. They gave me their new CPT, thinking it would stabilize my cells and reconstitute any abnormality within me to a standard genetic reading. Feel here, in back of my neck, yes, right there. That's it."

I rubbed his neck. "It's a deep indentation. So, the wine does make you feel better?"

"Oh yeah. Both CPT and the wine make me feel better, think better, and function better. However, the drawback is that the drink is the only nourishment I can have during a time-trip."

"Can I taste it?" I reached for the flask.

"No, no, no," Gabe replied. "I'm pretty sure I can't give you any right now." He handed me the flask. "But that doesn't mean you can't touch it. The remarkable thing is, it automatically refills when it's empty. I have no idea how that happens."

I touched the liquid on the mouth of the flask. "Feels almost milky, creamlike, but it fizzes. What do you mean you can't give me any, *right now*?"

Gabe patted my shoulder. "Be patient, give me a chance to settle a bit."

"Fine, sorry, of course!" I twisted the cap back onto the flask, studied the leather-like cover and then gave it back to Gabe. "I do have lots of questions."

Gabe walked around and studied the condo and said, "I can imagine, I have come to explain the things I can, and to ask a favor."

I sat back down and tried to relax. "Alright."

This whole thing was so bizarre; I figured I'd go with it and see where he'd lead me.

As I waited patiently, Gabe commented. "Your place looks just fantastic, beautiful art," he winked. "I remember painting that one. But you've done so much more, a new style I see. I like them."

"Don't you paint in the future?" I asked.

"Not yet, no time, lots of tests." He laughed and said, "Funny, now the tests don't seem that important to me." Then he looked at me and sighed. "First, understand, I am not a character from your book who just came to life. The characters in your book come from both me and you. Although I guess one could argue the point."

"Okay, fine?" I said.

Gabe spoke from his heart. "Please listen to what I have to say."

"I'm all ears." I said as I sat back in the couch.

Gabe began, "I am here to suggest something quite strange, but since you are me, I figure you'll get it. It appears Sidron events continue throughout Earth and Ever-Life. The powers to be back in Ever-Life thought they understood how the Sidron event happened which transported me to the future. They were certain no more events would take place, having reasoned the causes and eliminated Marion Brock. But, what they were so sure of turned out to be wrong. They still are confused about compatibility and the relationship between Marion Brock, Jake Burns, me, and the GGM. They are now convinced unless we identify the correct source of the original Sidron event, other events will continue to happen again and again. And eventually, most probably they say, other events will result in the catastrophic destruction of not just the world, the Earth, but also the past as we know it. So, since I-we, are the only mechanism they have to work with, GGM selected Allenfar and me to plan and implement an action to confirm the cause. Does that make sense to you?"

"I think I understand. But just because you know the actual cause doesn't mean you can prevent another."

Gabe replied, "Or, perhaps it does? We are all in new territory here. The one overriding agreement is that one or more of our Compatibility characteristics reacted with the Sidron somehow. That reaction split the fabric of space-time at three different time dates of our lives, 1965, 1989, and 2004. Allenfar and I have duplicated that reaction as close to what we think happened, and that's what you witnessed here in your home this morning. Allenfar has proven it was not the Compatibility of Brock that turned the tide; it was somehow related to us."

"What?" I was shocked, to say the least.

"Now, just try and listen carefully. Allenfar has searched, in detail, every minute we lived before 2004, and he has come up with one source-code date which seems to be the most likely date to start with."

"What's the date?" I asked.

"March 7, 1983."

I thought for a minute, and then I stared at Gabe, stunned. I stood up, and my heart raced. "Dad died that day, the morning of March 7."

"I know," Gabe replied. "Allenfar said it is entirely possible given micro-theory, your old quantum mechanics, and relativity that the original cause of the Sidron event took place at a completely different time than the reaction to it. And it affected both past and future timelines."

I scratched my head. "So, if you're right, the event itself took place in 1983, and that triggered the three of me-us, at different ages, to transport to the future?"

"Yep." Gabe smiled proud of himself and sat down again.

"Christ!" I said, my head spinning. "Does anyone know for sure? I mean after my writing so far, couldn't your Mr. Brock use this information to his benefit and screw everything up? How do we find out for sure whether you're right?"

"Brock? Calm down. That whole thing was a clone production gone bad. Besides, He's been dead for a while. You'll find out. More to the point, the only way to prove anything is for one of us to go back to 1983 with Allenfar."

I rolled my eyes. "Jesus, and what exactly do you think is the cause of the Sidron event? You seem to be dancing around the elephant in the conversation."

Gabe sighed and said, "Allenfar thinks it's dad."

"Allenfar thinks it's dad. How on earth did he arrive at that?"

Gabe shrugged his shoulders. "Who knows? We can't discount it though. He's very smart and knows the ramifications of time travel. Who knows what lurks inside a Carrier's brain?"

"Well, I hope you do. I certainly don't."

Gabe gestured for me to settle down. "Just kidding. Listen, our Compatibility ratings are so high together, no one in the future could calculate the potential effects. They thought Brock's was high, and Brock made clones to control Carriers because he thought no one had a higher Compatibility rating than he did. Also, keep in mind,

Compatibility itself is a genetic marker and can vary in intensity between generations."

"What does that mean to this, us?"

"The way Allenfar explained it was, if we have an extreme Compatibility rating, it's likely our whole family does or did. He wants to study our siblings and parents and grandparents. He suspects it's us that triggered the first event. But without testing the individuals, he cannot confirm."

I was shocked beyond belief. "The night dad died that weekend, all 4 of us siblings were together with mom when he had the second heart attack."

"Yes, I'm sure that's one fact that led Allenfar to deduce the probability. He is certain that all of us siblings generated record ratings off the charts regarding Compatibility. And Allenfar has calculated dad could have had perhaps more than us all together. The connection we all had from that trauma along with what he had; well, he thinks that's what inflated the event."

I stood and paced. "Jesus, everything is fucking connected. How could your fabulous GGM miss this?""

"Well, my opinion is no one there even thought of me in any way except as a time traveler, a victim. It wasn't until I started having headset sessions on a regular basis that they considered my inputs were relevant to Compatibility. Put that together with the fact that Sidron events did not stop, and they added one and one and got me and my family."

"What are you proposing?"

"Something that has never been done before, and frankly, I'm not sure it can be. One of us goes back to that night, talks to dad, and brings him back to Ever-Life for treatment, before he has the second attack. My thinking is that would assure no Sidron event in the first place."

I replied, "That sounds too simple, and isn't that in itself a paradox?"

"All I know is that whatever we do won't change what happened; but, according to Allenfar, it could change what hasn't happened."

I shook my head. "What? That sounds like double talk, and I do believe what you're describing is, in fact, the definition of a paradox, isn't it?"

Gabe insisted. "Allenfar claims otherwise; and he doesn't always explain himself. You want to argue with him, be my guest. Just follow me on this...."

I interrupted, "Wait. Hold on. Slow down. Can we take a moment, recess, please? Let me gather my thoughts."

I walked to the Kitchen, took a nutrition drink out of the refrigerator and gulped it down. "Not to change the subject, but I do have to think. Before I forget...." I went to the bookshelf and took the unpublished Book-1: *The CPT Incident,* off the shelf and handed it to Gabe. "...I thought you might like to see this. Here's what I have so far."

Gabe studied the book and read the front and back cover. "So odd. I have seen the complete 3-book saga under one cover. This doesn't exist. Thanks."

I shook my head at his comment. "In that case, I guess I will be writing for a while, huh?"

Gabe spoke as he thumbed through book-1, "Maybe I shouldn't say, but, after Swanson died, the GGM, Bellos, had your book sealed and stored in his private vault library. It's important to finish writing it, but I do not know why yet."

"So, I'm not crazy?"

"No, you are not crazy."

My mind was spinning. "Well, sometimes this all seems so melodramatic and confusing; not to mention, I can't tell anyone about you or this."

I began to see a tear form in Gabe's eye, as he said, "Boy. If there was some way to see the kids and grandkids....I miss..."

I reminded him, "Well, you can go anywhere in your past. So you can visit them anytime, can't you?"

"You'd think so; and, after this is over, I'm going to try with Allenfar."

I began to rattle off questions: "Can I ask...Your being here is the result of using the laws of physics, right? If we do act on your plan, which one of us goes back to 1983, and which one goes back to the future? How is that going to work?" I sighed out of breath and sat back down next to Gabe. "It's all so farking weird..."

"Hold on, hold on," Gabe smiled and remarked, "I do understand. I've learned that if I don't apply patience, I would have a great big heart attack and not be here. So, you too should try to keep the questions from dictating your emotions."

I replied frustrated, "But this isn't the kind of subject-matter that calms one down."

"I know. Just keep in mind the Sidron reacted with our high Compatibility ratings. If we can reduce those ratings, just maybe, we can prevent the event in the first place and therefore any additional ones from happening in the future.”

“I’m so confused. As I understand it, we have no sense of how much sustenance we have in the first place. And now you say we can somehow control sustenance by withholding emotions?”

Gabe was condescending. “As far as we all can figure in the future, trying to control emotions is the only thing possible right now. If we do this and it works, we have a starting point with understanding the story of compatibility and maybe the Sidron events. It’s all better than we have now. Unfortunately, what I’m proposing is based on Compatibility levels never addressed in Ever-Life’s past. We are all in new territory.”

“Okay”, I replied squinting. “I guess I get that. And we can do it all without causing a paradox? That’s what bothers me the most.”

“No paradox, as I understand it. Remember too, the atomic level in any past date is diluted and not equal to the reality in our present, Consequently, anything experienced in our past can’t be realized in our present. Any activity in a past environment has to be *quivered* to make it functional in our present. Up until the Sidran events, Carriers had been trusted to measure and control sustenance exchanges. What’s in our favor is that now Ever-Life has measured the levels and have a better understanding given the present circumstances there.

“I always wondered what the hell *sustenance* was.”

“All I know is that living things have it, but we humans have more, and the more we have, the higher our Compatibility rating is.”

“Okay, this is insane, but I’m all in.”

Gabe said great and thumbed through the paperback copy of ‘the CPT Incident.’ “So, is this all you have so far?”

“I have more notes and about 100 pages done on book-2.”

Gabe raised his eyebrow and said, “What is book-2 called again?”

“Time Trust. Would you like to see?”

“Ah? Sure.”

He continued studying CPT, while I went upstairs to get the Time Trust manuscript and dig out all my records for reference. After a time, I came back down with an arm full of notes and sketches.

Gabe had put book-1 down and was sipping from his flask again. “I can’t believe it. It’s all here. I feel like I’m reading my own headset.”

He shook the book at me. "It needs editing, but you've got everything I transmitted. It's a miracle our communication has worked. Christ, it is possible to communicate across time."

"Has it been two-way, though?" I asked.

"Yes, your connection with me has filled in some things after 2004."

"What do you mean?" I asked.

"Well, I think I know more regarding my health and the relationships you've had with women...and frankly, if anyone needs this wine, it's you," he said sarcastically.

I smiled and replied, "Relationships with women? Ha, I've had my fill...No more!

"Well," Gabe winced, "you may want to rethink that."

I reacted, shaking my head no. "I don't have to rethink anything. Relationships, marriage, divorce, they threw me into a reactionary lifestyle. A war for decades. Battles that later manifested and affected my physical health."

Gabe replied, "I know you. We had good intentions. We did what had to be done."

"Everything that happened to me and the downward spiral of my health and relationships with the children stemmed from good intentions."

Gabe chuckled and said, "Ha, so many things in history have turned bad from good intentions. I have found there has to be a balance. One has to accept that without balance, even too much good/positive/right- can result in discord and misunderstanding, ultimately bleeding to the next generation. I think that's what happened in your case, our case." Gabe patted my shoulder and said with a smile, "Well, God works in mysterious ways. Let's take it one step at a time. Do you have any idea why there are absences on your timeline?"

"What do you mean?"

"Like I said, I received some information from you. However, first, I have no idea when you died. Just an oversight I'm thinking, but there isn't any record of your death in the future."

I thought for a moment. "Perhaps that's because I live on the surface here, and maybe Ever-Life doesn't keep records of surface people. Or, maybe it's as simple as I haven't died yet."

Gabe thought. "I haven't figured that one out, but there has to be an answer. After all, you didn't live for 900-plus years, right?"

I shrugged. "I don't know. You could reason I did just that. Even if my body dies in this timeline; through you, I am still alive 900 years from now."

"I doubt that follows logically." Gabe stood and pondered a moment. "Regardless, I suppose the answer will come in some fashion. That does give me an idea though."

Just then, there was a hard knock on the front door. I looked at Gabe and told him to go upstairs.

When I opened the door, a man in a strange hat and an attractive young woman stood smiling at me. The man acted as though I was familiar.

"Hello, Mr. Andrew." He said.

I was confused a bit. "Hello, do I know you?

"Why yes. We have a great relationship. I am Jake Burns, and this is Ms. Abby Johnson. We are from a place called Ever-Life. I'm hoping that rings a bell."

"Oh my God! Yes; it is you. Forgive me. What a day. And you've come to see me?"

"Unfortunately, no. We are here to see your friend, Gabe, if he is here. We've been searching for a while now. But it is good to see you as well. May we come in? I believe what we have to discuss would be better said inside."

I opened the door, and they stepped in. "Gabe," I shouted. "There are people here to see you."

Gabe walked downstairs and also looked dumbfounded at seeing his two comrades. "Holy crap, you two. What the hell are you doing here?"

I commented, "I suppose neither one of you would like a coffee or drink?"

Abby said, "No thank you. We couldn't, even if we wanted to."

"Yes, I thought so. Would you all like to sit down?"

Jake started right in. "My friend, we have a situation back at Ever-Life. It's something that's affecting the entire planet."

Gabe raised his eyebrow and replied, "You mean another Sidron event?"

"No, not this time. There have been several *private* things that have happened." He leaned into Gabe, placed his hand to his mouth and whispered, "Perhaps we should discuss in private, so we don't disturb the neighbors."

Gabe just blurted, "Christ Jake, he is me, there aren't any strangers here. Out with it for Christ sake."

'Well, it will take some time to explain if you want the accurate information. It's vital we see and talk to the Allenfar Tyree Master."

"You know the Carriers secure themselves in a time anomaly during a trip. What's so important? Is someone dying; is it the Sidron?"

Jake looked frustrated. "No, it's the Carriers and Marion Brock."

I listened intently and remarked, "I thought Brock was gone, out of it?"

Gabe gestured, "Let's just all sit down; and let these two tell us what's happened. Mr. Burns here apparently wants to tell us something."

Jake stood in front of all of us in the living room to begin his tale of urgency."

Abby interrupted before Jake could utter the first word. "Don't forget my holes."

"Ah yes," Jake said, "Good place to start. For centuries, on surface Earth, mysterious deep holes, ranging from 50-yards in diameter to over ¼- mile wide, have appeared in remote areas on all seven continents. However, within the last 3-months, seismic data have recorded that a surprising number of new ones have emerged. Surface governments are concerned now about the impact these could have on the planet's overall climate. Word reached Ever-Life's GGM, Mathew Bellos, from significant sources on the surface regarding the phenomenon; so, he sent our Detective Inspector, Abby Johnson here to investigate. This first holographic map indicates the location of where Abby went to study the holes. It's marked with a red tag here, which indicates the general area of the hole-locations. As you can see, Eastern Russia and just south seem to be the primary area"

Abby smiled and added, "Some people on the surface speculated that the holes were the result of magma, venting deep within the planet; or they were the result of underground water pools softening the surface ground, causing significant sink-holes. Some people thought the holes were the result of asteroids plummeting to Earth. However, contrary to the surface, GGM suspected the holes were made from Ever-Life Carriers venturing forth to the surface because sunlight no longer killed them. I had just come off leave of duty when GGM assigned me to investigate the holes."

"Why were you on leave of duty?" I asked."

Abby replied, "Well, an incident took place in Rio. I actually died but was given CPT and voila; all is good."

Burns interrupted. "You might as well tell this part yourself, Abby."

"Okay," she said enthusiastically. "Anyway, I was in northeastern Siberia, above Ever-Life Post 1. I was walking very slowly through the heavy wind and snow. Frankly, I was at my wit's end dealing with the frozen tundra."

I reacted, "Didn't you have on special gear to deal with the climate?"

"Yes. I wore an Ever-Life climate suit and a technical helmet, which displayed all Knofer communications. The suit wasn't new tech for Ever-Life, but it was the first time I used it."

Again, I asked, "What made it so impervious to the extreme temperatures?"

Abby was very patient with me, but Jake cut me off. "Please! We have a lot to go through. Can we just let her talk?"

Abby looked at me compassionately. "The suit was integrated with polarized carbon fibers and processed static fibers, which together enabled a magnetic current to pass through it. Add to that a small electric battery charge, and the suit maintained a mean temperature of 70 degrees, no matter how cold it was outside."

I smiled and thanked her.

"Okay, okay," said Jake, "are we done with the fashion discussion?"

Abby rolled her eyes and said, "Fine, so, to continue, I walked carefully, one foot after the other, barely able to push forward against the wind. One strong gust made me slip and fall over a small ledge. It was a 360-degree shelf, extending all-around a two-hundred-yard diameter hole. As I looked into the snowy blur below, I noticed something flapping stuck into the frozen shelf wall. I yanked it out and studied what looked like a 7-inch by 4-inch sparkling fabric. 'Holy shit! Another one?' I said to myself. "I scraped as much snow and ice off it as I could and then placed the Knofer on it. The display read: *Residue from Grand Carrier.* (Grand Carriers are those who hold the secret to time travel.). *Christ, this confirms it. They are getting out.* I thought, *The GGM was right.* I was lucky it was so cold out, as any residue of a Carrier would have disintegrated at ambient temperature. I tapped my Knofer and said, 'Analyze age of residue; report.'"

"The display read: *14 Hours.*

"I remember thinking, *but, where are they going?* I looked up at the sky, and I tapped the Knofer again calling a Carrier to pick me up. It only took a few minutes before I could see a light glowing deep inside the hole. The Knofer displayed a map within my helmet of the subterranean area over a mile in diameter. A blinking dot on the map confirmed the Carrier's location. I activated the jump instruction on my impact suit, and the Knofer-encased my body within a transparent protective shell, which appeared as a pink glow. Then, with great reservation, I jumped into the black chasm, speeding straight down over a mile...."

As I listened to Abby, I also saw how intensely everyone was concentrating on what she was saying. I offered, "You're all so serious, can't we lighten up. This is such a wonderful occasion for me; us all being in the same room."

Gabe nudged me. "Try not to be a spoiler." Then, he remarked, "Abby, can we move it along. I'd like to get to the point."

Jake blurted, "Just relax, my boy. It's beneficial to all if you let us explain it."

I nodded and smiled. "Of course, after all, how often does one have visitors from the future trying to warn me about what will perhaps end the world? People, keep in mind, I have to write this all eventually?"

Abby gestured quiet please and continued. "I have to explain all this my way. I jumped and fell over 600-ft.. My suit was constructed to react when it is within 500 ft from a Carrier."

"In what way," I asked.

"The suit automatically aligned my body so I was at the proper angle to penetrate its skin. As you know, Carriers can control the properties of their skin, depending on the environment surrounding it. This was the first time I used the suit. I had practiced in simulations of course, but this was my first real application. The suit, in cooperation with my Knofer, searched and found the proper point of entry, the sweet spot, on the Carrier; and it adjusted my trajectory to that spot. The Knofer then communicated with the Carrier to adjust its position, and then my helmet identified the target-doorway as a red dot. The beast changed the hard skin at the point of entry to a soft pliable spot for my entry. The only way to describe the impact is that it was very spongy. I was absorbed and stood safely upright inside the hollow cabin-like interior of the Carrier. The Knofer withdrew my protective shell and removed the suit, sucking it into a tiny compartment on the underside of the room I was in. Then I watched as a standard Carrier apartment appeared with all the amenities. The beast then moved at lightning speed in a straight-line course, down and across molten inner Earth to Giza, Egypt and Time Trust's Post 2, where I made my report to Jake."

"So, what was the fabric?" I asked

Abby replied, "I spoke to the Carrier's organic computer. The results were astounding and significant, as it turns out. The computer spoke and displayed ***#79-AU, on the periodic table.*** My Knofer displayed the word, GOLD. I thought *what the heck does that mean*? I double and triple checked the display analysis of gold as it pertains to Grand Carriers and Ever-Life persons with Compatibility traits. That's when it happened."

"What happened?" Gabe asked.

"The computer displayed: **Access denied. Tyree Master Security Protocol 479. GGM access only.**

"What?" asked Gabe.

"Yeah, I know," Abby replied. "I was sure there was some mistake; so, I instructed the computer to Bring up all file data for GGM evaluation for Master Protocol 479.

"The response was instant: **The Treaty of Variance between our species dictates that only GGM has access.**

"So, I directed my Knofer to display Treaty of Variance in English. Immediately the 210-page document appeared above the Knofer in holographic form, enabling me to read and turn pages. But, when I came to page 10, most text had been marked over in black with red writing in the margins which read, ***all data for GGM review only***. What the hell was I supposed to do?" I thought. "I requested the Knofer to compare the treaty with those historical documents in all the Vaults within the Ever-Life records. The answer wasn't good: **Access denied, refer to security protocol 497. GGM access only.**

We all sat waiting for Abby to continue. "What happened next?" I asked.

Jake stood and said, "Thanks, Abby. I'll take it from here. Abby found a piece of fabric we all thought was from a Grand Carrier escaping from the underworld. But in fact, it was an entirely different kind of Carrier. One no one knew anything about; not even the Carrier council knew anything."

Gabe was noticeably bothered. "What are you saying, Jake?"

"Because of this situation, I am saying we are here to bring back Allenfar. Our trip here is about him, and what seems to be happening to all the other Carriers. I'll try and explain as chronologically as I can, so sip your flask when you need to and listen. Keep in mind one important thing. We are probably in the safest place we can be right now, so pay attention."

Jake took a gulp of his own flask and continued, "While Abby here traveled back to us in her Carrier, several things happened which recorded in the Ever-Life vault files. I think it best if I just play them here instead of talking every word out."

I wasn't sure what Jake had in mind, but I offered, "You are welcome to use my TV-set if that helps."

"That's fine, thanks," he said, "but we carry these Knofers for just this kind of thing."

Jake pinched the extended part of the vault after inserting it into his Knofer, and a holographic movie appeared in the center of the living room.

Gabe was quick to banter. "Look, it's Jake, lecturing. Boy Jake, I don't remember you being so good looking."

Jake reacted in his way, "Okay, okay, just watch the movie, for Christ's sake. You may learn something."

With that comment and a chuckle from Abby, Jake's image began to speak. "Good afternoon those of you who are listening. I offer the following information in as organized a fashion as possible. It is most important for clarity of understanding that I present these segments in as much of a chronological order as possible. Please listen and remember, to ensure complete understanding. When complete, please input to MEVH-Master Ever-Life Vault History, as this is the only and first copy of its kind."

Jake Burns plays Vault record
'Surprise:'

HAMILL STEVENS WAS NOW SPECIALIST FIRST CLASS, Ever-Life Time Travel Studies, Post 2, below Giza, Egypt. He was recruited from the surface because he led the effort to discover the Bridge Particle while at OPAS-Oregon Particle Acceleration Sciences, in Seattle, and because he built the time travel booth last year, within the Brock Companies' Time-Travel Inc. program.

Late that same Sunday night, inside his Ever-Life living quarters, Stevens suddenly awoke to the ringing of his Knofer and tapped it to answer. It was an old friend.

"Hello? Mr. Stevens, Hamill?"

"Yes, who is this?"

"Oscar Randall, OPAS, Washington."

Stevens thought for a few seconds. "Who? Jesus, do you know what time it is?"

"Hamill, it's me, Oscar. Are you there?"

"Yes, yes; hello. Just a little groggy. It's 1 am. What is it? Is something wrong?"

Randall chuckled and said, "Yes, it may be bedtime for you; but I'm across the world, my friend, in Seattle, Washington. I needed to talk to you. It's important."

Stevens sighed and replied, "Alright, give me a minute." He gathered himself, put on a shirt, and went to his living room couch. "Okay, I am back. What's going on?"

"My people here have been applying practical testing of your conclusions regarding the *bridge particle*. You remember?"

"Yes, of course, I remember; but I have a new job. You see...."

"Hamill," Randall interrupted, "we have had a development here that is rather significant. Is it possible for you to come here, as soon as you can? We need to talk face to face."

At first, Stevens was not sure how to answer, given he was now a full-fledged member of the Ever-Life colonies and involved with research at Time Trust. "I see. Where would we meet, precisely? I have to check my schedule and see if I can get away."

“Hamill, it’s vital you come here.”

Stevens tried to concentrate on what he had to do the next few days. Then, he remembered his Knofer and asked it. The Knofer displayed his Ever-Life calendar, and then he replied to Randall, “This is Monday. How’s Wednesday? It’ll take me a little time to get permission and gather what I need?”

“That’s fine, say 5 pm? Hamill, people here know details of what happened in the lab at Time-Travel Inc. But we have results of practical testing beyond yours.”

“Results?”

“Not over the airways. I’ll explain when I see you.” Randall hung up the phone.

Stevens scratched his mussed-up hair, yawned, and shuffled back to his bed. No sooner did he remove his shirt and sit on the edge of the mattress that his Knofer rang again.

“Hello?”

“Stevens, is that you?” Stevens rolled his eyes and said, “Yes; although I wish I were someone else right now.”

“Don’t be a smart-ass. It’s Jake. I need you in Post 2 priority briefing room 12, in an hour.”

“No one is going to let me sleep tonight anyway. Fine?”

“What are you talking about?”

“I just got a call from Oscar Randall, CEO at OPAS. Remember?”

“What does he want?”

“He wants to see me Wednesday. He says it’s vital, about the bridge particle.”

“Well, we can talk about it at the briefing.” The Knofer cut the call. Stevens sat for a moment and took several deep breaths. Then he cleaned up, got dressed and took a bubble Carrier to the meeting with Jake.

After talking to Stevens across the globe, Oscar Randall sat presiding over a special board meeting in the newly constructed OPAS research facility. There were three key members of the board and several physics experts. David Halford, Ph.D., was Department Head, OPAS Research, Bridge-Particle Program, replacing Hamill Stevens.

"Oscar, our findings contradict the conclusions Stevens presented regarding the Bridge-Particle. We based our entire plan on what he did. Accordingly, now we must start all over. What a waste."

"Are you all sure?" Oscar asked.

"Yes, completely," Halford said,"

"Well, we will see what Stevens' says about it when he arrives Wednesday. I'm not going to jump to your second set of conclusions."

Randall picked up Steven's book of results and shook it at the group. "I have his findings right here, and they are pretty compelling. You and everyone else here stood by these conclusions, or don't you remember?"

"We remember," Halford replied. "The entire board was mesmerized by his proofs, including me, but there are things in that book, which have been proven false now. All of us here agree! In our opinion, we should prosecute this son-of-a-bitch."

"On what charge," Randall asked outraged. "We all agreed on every step of the way. Don't be ridiculous. I didn't hire you to have selective thinking. You should have known this before our financial commitment. Don't push it, David. All we can do is get him here and confront it."

Halford got up and walked to the bay window of the conference room. "I don't get it. I agree one of us should have caught it. We are all supposed to be some of the smartest people on the planet. Christ, doesn't one of you have something to say?"

Heads turned to look at each other; and then, one voice spoke. "I do..."

The voice came from behind Oscar Randall's chair. All turned to see a dark figure walk out from the alcove entrance. Randall stood up and in a gasp of surprise said, "Marion, Marion Brock; is it really you?"

Brock grinned as all stood up and studied his figure. Brock walked by Randall, past everyone, across the room over to the window and placed his hand on Halfurd's shoulder. "Good for you, my boy."

Then he turned to Randall. "Yes, it's me. It seems I've chosen just the right moment to arrive. Stevens is coming here, eh? I'll want to be here for that."

Oscar Randal stood frozen like everyone else. "But how? Marion, we had your funeral months ago."

"A bit premature, as you can see. I am a cat with many more than nine lives, Ha."

Randall walked over to him. "Seriously, Marion, what happened? How are you? Where have you been?"

They shook hands and Brock offered. "Let's settle down a minute. I am fine, and that's what counts, wouldn't you all agree?" He turned to the group and requested, "Can I have a word alone with Oscar, gentlemen? Will you all excuse us and give us a few minutes?"

Randall gestured to clear the room. Then he poured two glasses of water and offered Brock a drink. Brock asked Randall to have a seat. Brock looked again at the Seattle Skyline as Oscar sipped his water and pressed Brock again. "Marion, forgive me, but this is more than a shock. If you are here, and alive, who did we bury? We all heard rumors about your clone project, but none of us thought..."

Brock took a seat next to Randall and smiled. All of a sudden, he changed his demeanor to being relaxed and friendly. "Do you remember when I interviewed you for this job? You were all fired up with talent, brains; the smartest man I had seen for this position. You didn't even know I was directly involved with your hire. Ha! I knew you were the one."

Randall looked a bit surprised. "You mean you did make the final decision?"

Brock patted Randall's shoulder. "Of course, it was me. Who do you think owns the majority shares in all this? Indirectly, I admit. It took a bit of time and some finagling; but through my angel investments, I own 82% of all of this now. How do you think I got Stevens away from you in the first place?" Brock continued to befriend and make Randall more comfortable. "Don't get all emotional over this, my boy. All is not lost. We will meet with Stevens. I have plans to get him back."

"You mean regarding Halford's results?"

"Yes, among other things. If we don't do something fast, even radical about all this, OPAS stock will drop faster than a dead man falling on plastic?"

Randall felt his Adam's apple swell. "Marion, who did we bury?"

"You know, my boy, everything has a price, and in this case, a story which is quite interesting, and I see no reason you shouldn't know, now that you'll be directly involved."

"Directly involved with what? Randall asked."

"With my plan. My plan, my boy. It's all been part of my plan. All of it."

"Marion, I wasn't trying to learn anything about your overall plans. I was just so surprised to find out how this miracle happened. You being here, it's a shock."

"Yes, I suppose it is. I have to confide in someone. I was going to use Jack Sheldon, but that didn't come to pass."

"Jack Sheldon? He was one of the people involved with Jake Burns and the explosion at Time Travel Inc, right?"

Brock smiled, got up and began to pace in front of Randall. "It's time you and I have a clear understanding of my plans for this company and what the objectives and goals are going to be."

"Alright, I think. So, what's first?"

"First I answer your question, and then I give you a clean slate."

Brock gestured to Randall not to interrupt, and then he said, "To begin with, you buried me, my friend; but I am me too."

"So, it is the clone thing."

"Not exactly. Well, it does get a bit convoluted, I admit. It's the clone thing. But not what you think. You see, coupled with this gadget, my VAD, we introduced to trials last year..." Brock handed Oscar one he pulled out of his pant pocket. "This is the reason I needed CPT and Jack Sheldon in the first place. I made a deal with Dave Marshall, at Ever-Life, when he first started working there..."

"Marion, I have no idea what you're talking about."

"Well, it's good to relieve tension. Eventually one has to let it all out, or things might just kill you. Don't you agree?"

"I suppose," Randall said. "If you just want a sounding board, I'm all in."

"You may not realize it now, my boy, but you're all in, all will be clear in a few moments. Now, regarding this. We have been making clones and testing this little VAD gadget here. You see, with this little wonder I have the ability to link my mind to any clone or multiple clones. I can be in two or three places at any given time if I choose. And by pressing a button, I can disengage and terminate the clone, or have it continue functioning if I choose. The possibilities are endless. Get it? I am now a collective consciousness. Quite remarkable, don't you think? It's a new world for me."

Randall's eyes widened, and he replied, "Remarkable? Or madness?"

Brock smirked, "It took time and a lot of patience and research. This little Video Audio Device is the future of Brock enterprises. Thank God for Jack's technology and that of Ever-Life."

"I don't understand why you're telling me all this?" Randall became more nervous with each word Brock spoke.

Brock continued, "You see; first they thought it was over, when Swanson gave me to Semitri last year for rehabilitation. All we did was share Compatibility, pick up my clones and deposit them at various points in times past. Then, they thought it was over when they destroyed Time-Travel Inc.'s lab." He pointed out the window. "Over there, you can still see the cave-in. That was unfortunate. Those idiots thought I was stupid enough to put all my eggs in one basket, one kind of clone, one location. Idiots!"

"Who Marion? What are you saying? I know nothing at all about this."

Who's an idiot?"

Brock replied, "It'll all be clear to you when we link you. Oh, I suppose it doesn't matter at this point. Ever-Life, my boy, Ever-life. I got the prototype for my creation from their director of Security, Dave Marshall, before he was taken into custody for conspiracy and murder. Oh, if they only knew what I could do now. All they ever did was follow my lead. Now we are going to have their newest catch, Stevens, right where we need him, the ultimate spy."

Randall reacted. "What do you mean when I link to you? And Stevens, what is he? A spy? Is he working for you?'

Brock spoke with complete confidence. "Several things to keep in mind, my friend. First, Stevens just doesn't know it yet. But he will, very soon. Second, you will need the information I am telling you, so we can call it up and use it without guilt as part of your new memory."

While Randall tried to figure out what Brock meant, Brock waved to his man at the entry door and nodded slightly. Then he turned his attention back to Randall. "The fact is, my empire has phantom buildings all over the world; warehouses, underground research labs, and technical interface with all of it; dozens of sites, all of which I have invested. And yes, some we have turned into special cloning operations for unique secure applications. No one knows all the locations but me, and they can't kill me. I am going to give you authority over them all, my friend. But to do that, we have to go through a sort of training exercise. Unfortunately, my first choice, Charlie Rossi, died in a space crash, so here we are."

"Clones?" Randall shook his head in disbelief and took a breath. "What do you mean unique secure applications?"

"That's right. Very exclusive clones. Mr. Bellos and his little secret about CPT has guaranteed me that."

"CPT? I don't understand any of this."

Brock smiled in his sinister way. "You see, my friend. I made my little investment here at OPAS to stay ahead of the curve technologically. But now, it's a security measure too, a very private security measure. I thought about it and planned for some time. Finally, I realized, if I was going to succeed here, I needed to stay ahead of that man, Bellos. And what way to do that better than to feed them me from every direction. They'll be chasing me in so many circumstances and scenarios; they won't be able to stop the primary plan. That's why I backed Jack Sheldon and his CPT. The difference is, I used his original formula as a base and created my own advanced CPT, enabling me to share consciousness with any clones of my choosing."

Randall became very nervous. "And that device makes it possible? Why tell me all this if it's all so private and exclusive?"

"As I said, my friend, you are part of it all now, a big part."

"But what is the 'primary plan'?'

Brock put his glass on the conference table, stood next to Randall and pointed out the bay window again. He smiled at Oscar as the alcove door opened. In walked a clone of Oscar Randall. The real Oscar looked at Brock with fear and anger. What the hell is this?"

"You are going to be like me, my friend. There will be several of us. You are the first. He's your perfect duplicate, identical actually, but not just a clone. He is you. His mentality will activate, upon your death. You will become part of the team. You will link to him once you die, and my VAD here will connect you two."

The clone grabbed Randall's hand, shook it and said, "How do you do. I'm looking forward to working with you."

Randall unclasped his hand, gasped and stared wide-eyed. "Marion, what the hell does he mean?"

Brock breathed a big sigh and said, "He is our new CEO here. You have other critical priorities."

Just then, four of Brock's henchmen, dressed in pristine tailored black suits, entered the room. Two stood guarding the door while the others walked across the room behind Oscar. Randall's clone stepped back and away and stood behind Brock as if he was trained to do so. The henchmen pulled out a plastic tarp and placed it down behind the frightened CEO. Brock looked at Randall standing in shock unable to move, frozen from fear. Brock reached into his inner suit pocket and pulled out a gun with a silencer. He slowly twisted the silencer onto the barrel, pointed the weapon at Randall, and smiled. "By the way, my friend, I am not sorry for taking your wife that evening in Belize. She was quite fulfilling. See you in a moment."

Then, as calm as you could imagine, Brock pointed the gun, and, just as Randall displayed the peak of terror on his face, Brock pulled the trigger and shot six rounds into his heart. Oscar Randall was dead before he hit the floor. As dark blood poured out onto the tarp, Brock said, "Well boys, now it begins. I think that should do it."

Brock tossed the gun to one of his men, turned to Randall's clone, and said, "These men will administer my CPT to you."

Then, he spoke to the henchmen, "And I mean now, boys."

It was a simple procedure, not like Ever-Life's CPT. One of the men pulled out a protective case, opened it, and took out a bluish vial. He gave it to another man, who immediately turned Randall's bloody body over onto its stomach. Then, like a proficient emergency specialist, the man inserted the syringe needle and sucked out a blob of coagulant from the base of Randall's skull.

Brock was quick to say, "Jacky, oh Jacky, you never knew what Marshall and I did. You don't have to wait an hour if you're looking for only a percentage of the personality. I have a new slave trade. Ha-ha!"

Brock's version of CPT enabled him to link his knowledge with any one or more of his own clones whenever he wished. Brock laughed again and said to the henchmen. "I've truly become a collective conscience."

The henchman then turned the standing clone Randall around and injected the contents of the vial into the base of his skull. Within 10-seconds, Clone-Randall blinked and looked around the room. Brock had Randall look at his VAD, as he pressed the side of it. There was no waiting an hour, no window of 72 hours or having to use a unique catalyst bath, and no sticking a syringe to the carotid artery.

"Holy shit!" Clone-Randall said, "Where am I, what just happened?"

Brock clicked his VAD, grabbed Randall's shoulder and spoke, "Oscar? Behind you. Here I am. Are you with me? You are fine. Would you like water?"

Randall shook his head and replied, "Whoa! Yes, hello, I'm a bit dizzy."

Randall watched the men wrapping the body on the floor in the plastic and asked, "Oh, my God. Who is that on the floor?"

Brock didn't skip a beat. He was a master liar. "Don't you remember? We've had quite a night. He had a heart attack. That's David Halford. My men will handle everything. Come with me."

Brock put his arm around Randall's shoulder leading him away from the body lying on the floor. "You're okay now. You fainted. You were telling me about a meeting with Hamill Stevens. Anything ring a bell?"

Brock's VAD worked perfectly, as Randall's mind seemed to conform and remember only what Brock preprogrammed or led him to believe. It was a seamless transition. Randall put the water glass on the table and squinted as he said, "Yes, I remember Hamill and Halford. David was almost frantic, in a dither. Then it's fuzzy, blurred."

Brock suggested, "Sit for a bit. My men will handle everything."

Meantime, two of the henchmen went to David Halford's office, and one shook his hand with a poison needle in his palm. The poison worked quickly. Halford had a heart attack within a minute and dropped to the floor. Brock's men called 911, and that fiasco drew attention away from what Brock was doing in the conference room.

Randall recovered as expected, as Brock watched. "Good," Brock said. "Oscar, do you think you're ready to take on regular duties, or you can go home and rest for the balance of the day?"

"No, no, I am fine. Just a little foggy."

"Good...Good," Brock said with a grin. "I want you to reschedule a new time for the Bridge Particle review meeting. Make sure Stevens gets here ASAP. And people are going to want to attend Halford's funeral. Set it up fast and make it impressive. And for the next board meeting, insist on enough members of the board attending, to vote."

Then, Brock turned to his men, as the other two walked in from killing Halford. "You two men guard the doors, and you two, dispose of our friend here. Call me when Stevens arrives. We have a lot to discuss."

Brock walked towards the alcove door and demanded, "I want this place pristine."

"Yes sir," C-Randall replied.

With that, Marion Brock walked out of the conference room.

Jake paused the presentation to Gabe and Andrew

GABE STOOD UP FROM ANDREW'S COUCH STUNNED and blurted, "Hold it! Stop the movie!" He looked at both Jake and Abby and asked, "Are you two saying Brock has his own CPT? Christ!"

Jake replied, "Calm down; there's a lot here. Wait for the end. You ain't seen nothing yet. When Brock killed Randall, Randall's phone triggered an automatic emergency signal to Hamill Steven's Knofer, because I had connected the two of them as friends and co-workers when we first programmed his communicator and Steven's Knofer. Frankly, that's what brought our attention to all of this. Major detail: Knofers do a lot. Anyway, the Knofer triggered an emergency notification that Randall died. Stevens was very confused, given that after that notification, he received another call from Randall to confirm the meeting Wednesday.

"I told Hamill to go Wednesday and be alert and careful to see what was going on. While he did that, I had to see Jack and Rachel Sheldon, given what was happening with the new Carriers."

Gabe interrupted Jake. "New Carriers? Oh yeah, that's why you want Allenfar?"

"Oh, my goodness, lad," Jake reacted. "Don't get ahead of us all. There's a reason we play these in an orderly way like this. Here; watch the video of my meeting with the doctors."

He turned to Gabe and stressed, "Follow closely and observe, to get the entirety of the situation, because a lot has happened since you and Allenfar left on your little outing."

Andrew remarked as he studied the paused hologram, "Hmm...I know that guy, Brock." He walked around the paused hologram studying it 360 degrees. "I just can't place where or when. It'll come to me." Then he sat down, and Jake reset the Knofer again, and the second hologram started.

CONTINUE: Jake Burns Plays 2nd Vault to Gabe and Andrew of Jack & Rachel Sheldon at their ranch

JUST 30 MINUTES OUTSIDE OF ARDEN, New Mexico, Drs. Jack and Rachel Sheldon owned a pristine 70 acre horse ranch. The two had gone through a lot over the last year, with Jack's discoveries and the incidents they generated; not to mention they both underwent Jack's CPT, especially regarding Rachel, who died after having it, and then later she revived spontaneously without any medical help. Since then, and after the TIME TRUST fiasco, they both took time to settle down from all the stress. Rachel returned to her love of ranching and charity work for the children's' hospitals throughout the state. Jack returned to the everyday pressures that came with his job as Chief of Research at Brock/Swanson Medical Center. During their home time, Jack and Rachel found new comfort and happiness just being together and appreciating their lives.

That Monday morning, they had finished their horse ride, Jack on Diablo, a tall Palomino, and Rachel on Santana, a striking black beauty. Rachel had raised him after four generations of inbreeding. They were stalling the horses when Rachel noticed one of her longtime breeding employees, Juanita, sitting on a bench between two open stalls. She was apparently emotionally distraught. Rachel and Jack dismounted, and Rachel approached her.

"Juanita, what's wrong?"

"Oh nothing, Senora. Nothing, nothing." She continued to wipe her tears but couldn't hold them back.

Rachel sat next to her and gestured to Jack that he should leave. "Honey, do you mind, I won't be long."

Jack rethought the moment and replied, "I think I'll have these two rubbed down. I'll meet you back at the house." Rachel smiled, and then she gave Juanita her full attention.

"Now there; we're alone. Tell me. It won't go any further."

"Oh my, Senora, it's my sister. She is a hard-working single mom. Always the smarter one. We were very proud of her when she got her Ph.D. I don't get to see her or my two little nieces very often because of her important job. She lives in Seattle. She works at OPAS, for their president, Oscar someone…Randall. That's it. Oscar Randall. Anyway, she was in an accident this morning that happened at her work.

Rachel acknowledged, "Oh, I'm so sorry to hear that. Did you say, Oscar Randall? I've heard that name before."

Juanita composed herself a bit. "Si, yes senora. He runs a big company. I got a call from my sister's neighbor. She's at the hospital with her now. They say she was accidentally pushed and fell down a flight of stairs from 911-people responding to a call. Some big shot had a heart attack there or something, during a meeting with a Mr. Brock.

"Oh my God, Juanita," Rachel shocked and recoiled, dumbfounded at hearing the name, Brock. She composed herself and said, "I'm so sorry. Is your sister okay?"

"I think she will be okay, but she has a concussion, and her leg was broken. She will be in the hospital, they say, for at least a few days and her neighbor is unable to care for the children.

Rachel was sympathetic but very concerned about what she heard. "Juanita, what can I do? If you need anything, help, money, time off. Do whatever you need to, and we will help in any way."

Juanita placed her hand on Rachel's and said, "Oh, thank you, thank you, senora, you are so kind to me. One never knows when an emergency will arrive."

"Yes, I know what you mean. Juanita, can I ask you, what was the name of the person you mentioned? Are you sure it was Brock?"

Juanita concentrated and said, "Oh, yes ma'am. Marion Brock. Do you know him?"

Rachel cringed. "I am not sure."

"I just don't know what I'm going to do." Juanita broke into tears again.

Rachel smiled and called out to another ranch hand standing nearby, "Robert, could you please drive Juanita home for me?"

He gestured okay. Juanita stood up, hugged Rachel affectionately, and then left.

Rachel sat contemplating for a few minutes. The circumstance brought back vivid memories of the conflicts last year involving Brock. Without warning, it hit her. She began to shake. Impulses shot through her about CPT and afterlife; she couldn't resist. Everything flooded her mind again. Watching and talking to Juanita both frightened and motivated her at the same time. She saw this both as a threat and an opportunity. The threat was Brock, and the opportunity was to prove she spontaneously recovered from death, having visited the afterlife in the Sidron. She ran to the house and yelled for Jack. He rushed upstairs from their lab and grabbed Rachel by her shoulders. "Are you alright babe? What is it?"

"It's back. It's all back! The whole thing is starting again. Oh my God, Jack! I have to sit."

"Over here, honey." Jack led her to a chair in the hallway by a table with water and a glass on it. He carefully poured the water and offered, "Here, drink."

Rachel sipped and took several deep breaths. Then she put the glass down and looked with fear in her eyes at Jack. "Jack, he's back, he's back. I don't believe it!"

Jack pleaded, "Whose back? Tell me!"

"BROCK! That bastard or his clones are back, at OPAS in Seattle."

Jack looked astonished. "That's ridiculous babe. He died in Space."

Rachel caught her breath. "NO! Juanita's sister works at OPAS, and she said he was there. Brock was there!"

Jack stood tall and concentrated. "That means things will change again."

Rachel reached for Jack's hand. "Jack, I can't do another incident or fiasco. And if I get involved, it will be to prove what happened to me."

"I understand. But let's not get ahead of ourselves. I got a call from Jake Burns' secretary, who said we were going to get a visit. It must be about this. Let's hear what he has to say." He patted Rachel's shoulder affectionately.

The next day, Tuesday, Jake took a cab to the ranch; and when he got out, he stood by the car staring at the landscape. After a minute, he heard a familiar voice. "Hello, my friend, how are you?"

Jake turned to see a rested, tan-faced Jack Sheldon. "Hello, Jack. I'm fine. You look great."

"Well wait until you see Rachel."

They both smiled and walked toward the house. "This is your first time here."

"Yes," Burns said. "Quite a spread."

"It's enough for us. 70 acres, 20 horses, 11 ranch-hands and a light house staff."

Jake stopped and looked around. "You've earned it. I am jealous. Well, I do need to talk to both of you, if that's okay?"

Jack led Jake into their den and offered him a drink. "Yes, I will; thanks; vodka, please. Half a glass."

"It is early for that, but I guess all three of us will need one. I'm sure Rachel will want one."

"I'll want one of what?" Rachel walked in and hugged Jake.

Jake took the drink and sipped. "Yes, well we all suspect why I'm here. Do we not?"

Rachel replied, "Is it, Brock? We heard he was back?"

"Brock? Why yes, and no. I mean how would you know that? We haven't leaked that to anyone. We are still testing and…"

Both Rachel and Jack looked confused which Jake noticed right away. "Whoa!" Jack said, "Let's have a toast. *To clarity*. I'm thinking we aren't on the same page, are we?"

Rachel replied, "We are if the page is anxiety."

They all gulped their drink, and Jake asked Jack to refill his. Then, Rachel said, "I just heard from my breeder employee that Brock was in Seattle at a meeting with Oscar Randall at OPAS. What are you talking about?"

Jake reacted wide-eyed, "What!? I just came from a meeting with the core team at Ever-Life because bodies of Brock and Rossi were finally found in space and transported by a new type of Carrier to our Tec lab 3. Both of the bodies were dead."

Jack handed Rachel her drink. "WTF? So, what is going on Jake? Start from the beginning."

"That's why I'm here. But what you're saying throws a big glitch in my little speech to you. Hamill Stevens has a meeting tomorrow with Oscar Randall, but Steven's was confused by what was said because he got a notice on his Knofer that Oscar was dead. I had no idea anything that happened was tied to Brock. We have his body in Tech lab-3 at Ever-Life. But it would make sense. How is it possible? It has to be a clone. And that means I better be there with Stevens."

Rachel said, "But what were you going to tell us. What about the Carriers? Jake, I need to talk to the visitor we had on the bubble last year after Mathew's indoctrination to GGM."

"You mean the Tyree Master?" replied Jake.

"Yes. How do I see him?"

Jake smiled and said, "It's funny you say that. He mentioned to me that he would be visiting you very soon. But, let's slow down. I have something for you two to see that may shed some light on all this confusion. Please, let's sit, shall we?"

Jake put his Knofer on the table and played two Vaults for Jack and Rachel, the *Brock Rescue* and *Tech-lab 3*.

The Brock Rescue:

AFTER A YEAR OF WANDERING IN SPACE, MARION BROCK'S TUMBLING AIRLIFT floated some 1,500,000 miles away from Earth. No oxygen kept the cabin environment without change, preserving the two suffocated bodies of Marion Brock and Charlie Rossi. Ever since their disappearance, July 2999, the search efforts to locate the airlift by the Brock moon-station crew proved unsuccessful. For some unknown reason, the automatic emergency distress signal sent out from the airlift never reached any relay station on the Moon or Earth. Then, on search day 395, there it was. A Brock computer technician on the moon read the distinct SOS. It gave clear and precise coordinates of the airlift's location and trajectory. Within an hour of receiving the signal, a rescue ship was dispatched from the Moon to retrieve the airlift.

However, the SOS signal reached more than just the moon-station. Something else received it and reacted to the message much faster. The outside cameras on the airlift recorded an incredible site. First, a spring-like coil of light and sparkling matter trickled like stardust, dancing around the vehicle. Within minutes, the dust surrounded the ship. Then, the dust began to change, solidify, and it stopped the ship's spinning trajectory altogether. The airlift sat motionless in space. After a few more minutes, the Stardust became a defined shape. The vessel was engulfed within a circle of beautiful blue clouds. The cloud turned into an enormous unfamiliar Carrier. Bigger and brighter than any seen at Ever-Life.

Inside the airlift, the two bodies that were floating in zero gravity fell to the floor. Slowly the airlift faded, disappeared, and reappeared next to the Carrier. The two bodies' then lay inside the new Carrier apartment, each on a gurney. The beast duplicated the environment, and then it sped away, wiggling like a fish swimming in the black sea of outer space.

250-miles above the Great Pyramid of Giza, the Giant Carrier with the two bodies of Marion Brock and Charlie Rossi hovered and sent a signal to the pyramid's apex. The signal was then captured by the Ever-Life Time Trust computer in Techlab-3. A technical specialist, Don Shore, became alarmed when his monitor screen went blank. He tried entering a re-boot sequence, but nothing worked. Then suddenly, the signals from the massive Carrier lit up the screen as numbers relating the intensity of the lightning-like impulses beyond any he had witnessed before. Don reacted at first spellbound, then he called Terry Raymond, Lab Supervisor, to see.

"I don't understand this. Look, Terry, I was monitoring general signals from our space probe just above Giza, and I got this." "What the hell? They both studied, mesmerized at the readings still coming in.

"Very strange. Get up. Let me have a look." Terry studied the screen. Meantime, Don went to the other side of the lab to investigate the tracer of Stardust signal recordings, in hopes of finding the source of the readings.

"I don't think it's the Sidron," Don spoke loudly to Terry. I'll have to study the data once it stops loading."

Terry manipulated the microwave reader. "Something big is descending through the pyramid from space right now above Giza!"

Don switched to the monitoring channel. "I'm on the microwave monitor, and the analysis seems to have a source residue roughly 300 miles straight up."

Terry leaned back, took out his Knofer and spoke, "Get me Tom Wheeler." Then, he studied the unusual beam variances.

Terry saw a flash, quivers of light exploded across the room, and then he pointed. "Look there! Holy shit! We have a situation."

Terry tapped his Knofer again. "Forward signal variance images to the master computer. Analyze and reply."

At that second; just as Thom Wheeler entered the room; there before them all, the two bodies of Marion Brock and Charlie Rossi zapped into the lab. Wheeler was noticeably surprised. He gestured for Terry and Don to stay where they were. He slowly walked over, knelt over two bodies, and spoke into his Knofer, "Complete body scans. Notify GGM and have him contact me at lab-3."

Mathew Bellos replied within 30-seconds. "Tom, Bellos here. What's the issue?"

"I'm in Techlab-3, sir. It seems we have uninvited guests." Then he pointed his Knofer at the bodies.

Bellos was quick to ask, "My, my, who are they?"

Wheeler rolled the bodies over and was shocked again. "It seems we have a body of Marion Brock, and another gentleman, laying here on the lab floor. There are no vital signs recording for either one. They're dead."

"Are you sure?" Bellos' mind went into DEFCON mode.

"Yes. They appear to be perfectly preserved according to Knofer exam. Wait, there's a new reading. It says they've been dead over a year. Mathew, these are the two bodies from the spacecraft lost last year."

"What? Get them to Ever-Life morgue control. I'll see you there."

Wheeler cut the call and looked at the two lab specialists. "Why and how did they appear here out of nowhere?"

"We'll be able to run complete diagnostics at morgue control," Terry said.

"Good, first, get a hold of Jake Burns; run the tests and bring them to the morgue control lecture hall within an hour. I'll meet you there."

Jake Plays Jack & Rachel the
Vault of Teclab-3

WITHIN EVER-LIFE POST 2, Giza, Egypt, Jake Burns had moved into Gordon Swanson's old office and assumed more significant responsibilities. In addition to being Chief of Security, he was now interfacing and monitoring the effort to introduce the surface to Ever-Life. Part of his duties soon included working closely with Gabe, who was recently appointed Surface Liaison by GGM and overseeing his interactions relative to key surface individuals.

Monday, just after midnight, Jake was unable to sleep and decided to do some work. He was in the middle of scheduling meetings for Gabe

Early that Monday morning, Jake was in the process of scheduling meetings between Gabe and several heads of state throughout Europe and the Middle East when he received an urgent alert on his Knofer. It was from Specialist 1st Class Terrance Raymond in Tec-lab 3. "Secure and encrypt. To Jake Burns, security level 11; Initiate."

Jake's Knofer displayed a 24-inch hologram of Terry.

"Good morning sir,"

"Good morning Terry. How are things going down there in solitary?"

"A bit confusing right now, sir. I request your presence here in morgue control. It's quite urgent."

"Give me specifics, Terry?"

Terry adjusted his Knofer so Jake could see an image of two bodies, each on its own examining table.

"Do we know who they are," asked Burns, "and where they come from?"

"Yes, sir." Terry pulled down one of the sheets to reveal the head and torso of Marion Brock. "I've withheld all information pending examination review by you and GGM. Sir, I'd rather not say anything else. I am sending you readings now."

Jake's Knofer displayed: *Positive Identification: Marion Brock and Charlie Rossi.*

"Terry, have you run genetic analysis and comparisons?"

"Yes sir, each of them has complete DNA. So, by our standards, they are not clones. If they are, we are looking at something we've never seen before.

Jake shook his head thinking, *not more of this same shit again.* Then he replied, "Good work, I will be there as fast as I can. Keep a lid on this."

Jake called Mathew Bellos.

"Good morning Jake."

"Sir, we are on encryption protocol. We have a situation that requires your immediate attention. It's regarding a Carrier development and the Sidron. I think we should meet right now."

"Yes, Thomas has briefed me. We'll all meet in Morgue Control, in Tech-lab 3."

"Alright, I can be there within the hour."

"Fine, I'll see you there."

Jake cut the call, and then he contacted recently arrived Abby Johnson. She too agreed to attend and bring all pertinent findings from her trip.

Techlab-3 was very secure from all outside influences. Every word spoken there was encrypted and stored in top-secret vaults, reviewable using the strictest security standards. One needed a level 11 security clearance even to enter the lab, and only seven people other than the GGM and Post Commanders had that. The lab itself was equipped with not only the standard equipment used in all advanced labs, but also it was the area where testing was done on newly conceived computers unavailable elsewhere. This was one of only a very few places, other than GGM secure rooms, where the most secret of subjects could be discussed freely.

At 2:15 am, Specialist Terry Raymond unlocked the lab door and led GGM Bellos, Security Chief Jake Burns, and Detective Inspector Abby Johnson into the small auditorium lecture hall. The room was set up with stadium seating for up to 100 facing a stage. Changes were recently made to the room's filtration system. Synthetic oxygen now filled the room. This new air was developed in consort with the Carriers. It prevented oxidation. Specimens of any kind could be examined here without fear of decay. On the stage sat a large transparent organic desk equipped with an exclusive access computer linked with all vault records and Knofer knowledge. Behind the desk facing an audience were two large floating whiteboards for notes during lectures, if need be. To the right of the centerboard, there were two examining tables on which the bodies of Marion Brock and Charlie Rossi lay.

Terry gestured, inviting all to watch. Each person congregated around the gurneys to look closely at the bodies.

Terry removed the sheets revealing the perfect specimens preserved in Space. "We prefer no touching please?" said Terry. "They are not degraded in any way. It's remarkable."

Abby asked, "Are they, in fact, Marion and Charlie?

"Yes, we think so, so far. Nothing in their readings indicate *clones*.

Burns quipped," What else could they be, for Christ's sake?"

Jake leaned over and looked nose to nose at Brock's face. "I'm not an expert in this so, how is it they were in the airlift, but nothing oxidized?"

GGM replied, "The sensors in the lift read no breathing activity, so the system shut down the flow of oxygen. Quite a common control in space travel now. When one sleeps, for example, the system will go into *reflow* and supply air in rhythm with the respiratory system of any particular rider. My question is how did they come here to Ever-Life?"

There was a still quiet. Before Terry could comment, from behind the group, a voice spoke. "I believe I can answer that."

It was an 11 ft tall Tyree Master. GGM spun around in surprise and reacted, "Master, your appearance here defies several treaties and our security protocols... I must object."

Abby interrupted, "Sir, please excuse me, but I could use the Tyree Master's help regarding my findings from my investigation of the surface holes. There's a security protocol in place that cannot be accessed without his authorization."

GGM appeared annoyed. "What? What is going on here?"

Tyree raised his arm motioning. *"Please be calm. The young lady is correct. I do not wish to disrupt your meeting; however, I believe you will need my input. It is imperative we all discuss options directly related to these issues, and we must keep our discussion private. And, it is critical we evaluate and develop a plan together, or, it could mean the end of Ever-Life as you know it, and perhaps the end of my species as well. That is why, my GGM, I am here."* He then looked at Bellos and asked, *"May I continue?"*

Bellos gestured yes, and the group focused on Tyree. *"My friends, it has been well over a year since the first Sidron event, as you know, they have continued. And now we have this other unfortunate occurrence."*

Bellos interrupted, "You know we are still investigating and evaluating all the data regarding those events. It is not complete, and we will not assume or speculate anything."

Tyree nodded and continued. *"My point is; something is taking place that relates to all the players involved with those events."*

Bellos was a bit anxious, considering Tyree broke into one of the most secure rooms in Ever-Life. "What are you talking about?"

Tyree looked directly at Bellos. *"GGM, some of our Carriers are evolving."*

Everyone reacted with surprise and concern.

"What we have monitored suggests a new breed, Carriers of a different type, with different skills, characteristics, and capabilities unlike ourselves. They can interface not only with Ever-Life and the surface cultures but also they have the ability now to leave."

"What do you mean, leave?" asked Bellos. "It has been my understanding that sunlight no longer kills you. Any of you may leave."

Abby interrupted. "Sir, I have proof that the Carriers have something to do with the new surface holes. Perhaps that's how they're leaving."

Bellos said, "Leave Earth? Hmm... Tyree, please explain what you can?"

Tyree continued, *"Over the last three months, we have been investigating without clear results. Some of our kind, who have tried to leave, have lost all communication with our hive mind. Initially, we presumed they were dead. However, we do realize assuming is very dangerous. The ones who have been successful leaving, we believe to be a new breed of Carrier. They seem to have undergone spontaneous evolution. We have no other information. We think it was one of the new breeds who retrieved these bodies and deposited them here with you. So, there are many unanswered questions. Together we must find out about their evolution and if and why they have been successful leaving Earth. Their purpose is unknown to us. Perhaps these bodies here can provide clues. We have received no information or correspondence from these newcomers regarding anything. And we have no way of tracking them. They do not seem to have a hive mind mentality. They have shut us out completely."*

Jake interrupted, "Okay, so these new Carriers are independent thinkers, apart from your hive control. That certainly shines quite a different light on Detective Abby Johnson's investigation and findings."

"We aren't sure what the new Carriers are yet. I think the vault Abby has there may have answers. We know one of those Carriers absorbed these two bodies and beamed them to your lab through the lightning zap, because we detected a beam signature from the Carrier to earth and analyzed it. It was a hollow tube-like elevator, sort of; by your definitions. But we didn't know it would happen when it happened, which is more often the case than not. Until that point, we had no idea that it retrieved these bodies from deep space. After the fact, we analyzed the beam from the airlift to the moon station. We have always known things before the fact. In this case, we were in the dark, and we are not used to that. I am here under the full umbrella of our security protocols. We have been studying; and we believe the one outstanding link to all that has happened involves your time traveler, Gabe. Our findings lead us to an obvious fact. It appears our visitor has somehow become in-sink with the Sidron, and he's having an indirect influence on all of us, at the least."

"Bellos did a double take. "Why do you say that? What proof do you have?"

"Proof is what we all want and the truth," Tyree said. *"First, consider our visitor has not disappeared or disintegrated as did the other two. Why precisely? Second, he appears to have the ability to link with his past. Or do you not know he was communicating with*

himself for the past year, Ever-Life time? Third, both the Brock situation and Mrs. Sheldon's case prove that Compatibility is out of control. So, let us accept information that may help guide us to the truth of it all." Tyree gestured to Abby, *"Please upload your vault and instruct the computer to integrate its information with ours."*

GGM replied, "Considering all that has happened, do you think Gabe is connected in any way to the new breed of Carrier?"

Pause in Jake's vault of Tech lab 3...
Meanwhile, back in Andrew's living room

Gabe was perplexed and disturbed. He asked Burns to pause the program again and said. "Jake, they think I had an intention when I time traveled through the Sidron? It sounds like they believe that I had an ulterior motive."

Jake replied, "No, that's not it. You have to take some of these comments with a grain of salt. They are having a meeting about some highly sensitive material and a situation that never before has happened. That's why only these select few people, who are directly involved, attended this meeting. The more important fact is regarding the Carriers. Again, please wait until the presentation is over. Then, we can all talk. Fair enough?"

"Fine," Gabe said. "It's so disturbing though. It sounds like you're here to take Allenfar back. But for what?"

Abby responded to Gabe's concern too. "Mr. Cooper, I have seen what's going on all over the surface regarding the Carriers. We don't know if the ones making holes are old or new. Yes, it's a bit scary. Allenfar and others may be under threat."

Jake added, "Look, Gabe. If we all would please finish these vaults, I'm sure some of your questions will be answered."

Gabe sat back down. "Fine. Sorry. Please continue then."

Jake turned his Knofer on again and continued the presentation.

Continuation of Vault-Tech lab-3 for Jack and Rachel

Tyree master replied to Jakes question. *"Yes, we believe there's a connection between the time visitor Gabe and the new Carriers, as well as being linked to all of you with high Compatibility. If we knew answers, we wouldn't be here like this. We know Gabe has a strong connection with Allenfar. It's only logical that connection could overflow to the new breed of Carrier. And it very well may be that neither Gabe nor Allenfar know how they relate to the new Carriers at this point. There are too many questions and threats not to act. And because Allenfar is a Grand Carrier and has such a strong attachment to Gabe, we need him back at Ever-Life for further examination."*

GGM Bellos reacted sternly. "So why don't you just contact him and tell him to return to your council?"

"Do you remember Semitri, and how we all thought he shut our hive mind out?" asked Tyree.

"Yes, of course, we remember," Bellos said.

Tyree continued, *"Upon close examination of that entire situation, we now know Semitri did not cut us out voluntarily. It happened naturally as Compatibility sustenance increases beyond a certain level. Allenfar has now reached a stage with Gabe whereby he has ceased to communicate with us. Because he is a Grand Carrier like Semitri, he is now an independent, protected from us and doesn't realize it yet."*

"Great," Jake said. "This just keeps getting better."

As the Tyree Master walked slowly around the desk, he added, *"The most concerning aspect of that is that the new Carriers may be communicating with Allenfar. We have no idea. And there's much more. Here, my dear."* Tyree gave Abby a vault from the Carriers. *"This is highly sensitive material."* Tyree looked at the GGM. *"I apologize in advance. The information on this vault has never been made public. It is highly sensitive; part of the top-secret files given to GGM, to be opened only if, status. Frankly, I will be hearing and translating it for the first time too."*

"Bellos reacted. "So, I have this information, but I've never absorbed it, read it, or seen it?"

"Correct. It is part of the files passed from one GGM to the other, as part of the historical information and classified 'secret.' Part of records transferred to your office from Swanson, when you received your GGM status."

"What's in it?" Jake asked."

Bellos gave Jake a dirty look, as Tyree continued. He placed a small vault in his ear and also gave one to Abby. *"We have a challenging situation. We have to understand how each component in the hollo-sphere relates to the other, to your team, to us Carriers, to the Sidron, to the Time Traveler, to the new Carriers, and the two dead bodies over there."*

Jake blurted, "What a mouthful."

Tyree looked at Jake with a perplexed expression. *"Hopefully, today, the information in this vault will help and make you aware of certain aspects regarding us Carriers and your history that you haven't known. Abby, go ahead and plug this in. Let's see what you have, first."*

Abby pushed several sensors on the Tec-lab organic computer. Jake reached across the desktop and pushed several more. After a few seconds, Abby's findings began to rise from the computer. Several small holographic spheres appeared, each with different hieroglyphics, texts, and statements from her last trip to the surface. Everyone stared, but there wasn't any way to decipher the image. It looked somewhat like a solar system made up of data. Jake used his finger to point, circle, and underline some of the text and images as they appeared. "We need to find a common link to tie everything together. Initially, we all concluded the common link was Compatibility between us all, as you can see here, and here, and there. Am I right?"

"Yes," Bellos said.

"Yes, that's is correct," Tyree agreed. *"But now we have to dig deeper to try and understand what we're missing. That is one reason I brought this vault."*

"Alright, Abby," Bellos said, "integrate Tyree's Vault. Let's see what we've got."

The computer exploded one big spherical hologram, which filled the entire room. It enlarged and encased the smaller spheres from Abby's vault. The outer boundary of the large sphere included a blue lighted grid of longitudes and latitudes. White dots and gold dots began to appear, and next to each dot, text appeared with lists and paragraphs of descriptions. Then, even more information popped up and dispersed to within the various spheres. The whole thing looked like a 3-d library with colors exploding throughout the room. One smaller sphere was now labeled Time-Traveler; another was labeled Carrier Factors, along with each party's Compatibility rating; and finally, other spheres displayed information as it pertains to the Sidron event.

Each person in the meeting began studying it all. GGM was mesmerized. "My God, is it a map? The shape resembles a solar system or galaxy."

Tyree quietly contradicted. *"No, my friend. According to what I am receiving, all of this is a much bigger map than that. It's a section-map of where our ancient Carrier ancestors traveled or visited throughout the known universe. Look at the red dashes and gold dots. This vault gives us a historical recall, going back to the beginning. And some of these points and those over there indicate some destinations of our time travel trips."*

"So, how do we decipher this," Jake asked

"I suggest we allow the program to load completely and then address questions," Tyree replied.

Abby offered, "Jake, look here. It's a small area, but you can see I programmed my findings to attach themselves to the appropriate labels in each sphere. See here, and here, for example; any intersection of dashes blinking indicates where I think time anomalies may have occurred."

"You mean like Angie's last year?"

"Yes, my friend," Tyree said. *"They indicate important dates too or events in the universe's history."*

Everyone watched and studied as more gold dots, and red dashes exploded up from the desktop. Each crisscrossed the spheres, sometimes depositing information, sometimes not.

"So," GGM said, "each of these blinking red dots indicates where an anomaly is, or an event, or a time destination. How do we find out which it is, and what do we do, depending on what we find?"

Tyree offered more details. *"We programmed each red streak into and out of the intersection to represent either a path of a time anomaly or a path of one of the Carriers. "*

"That's great," Jake said. "In that case, couldn't where the lines intersect indicate a possible inflation, not an anomaly at all? After all, all of this relates directly to the Sidron."

"Let's not take our eyes too far off the ball, people," Bellos said. "Abby and our friend here programmed all this, so we stay with their results for now."

The Tyree Master walked around the room studying the images, listening to his vault and reading the text as if he were a master chess player obsessed by the challenge. His eyes bulged as though he was receiving critical new inputs. *"We must identify the exact common denominator to all Compatibility in all of this. It is crucial to understanding all this information. And we may find answers related to the new Carriers. The additional information in your Knofer computers and historical vaults may help too; if you could please integrate that onto the hollo-spheres.*

Tyree reached into the spheres and manipulated some of the information. *"If we reverse the dash sequences here and there on these, we will pinpoint the point of origin from where all this started."*

"Point of origin? Abby asked. "I'd have to integrate more than just these two vaults."

Tyree was patient in his comments, as he continued to examine the spheres and text. *"Yes, the point of origin, from where the first inflation or Sidron event started"*

"You mean the very first event? The Big Bang?" asked Bellos.

Tyree was too focused to comment and seemed to ignore the question. *"I am getting mounds of information now. I must focus to understand."*

Meanwhile, Jake touched a particular white dot where his name appeared and saw that it changed color and shape to a bright gold star. Then, he touched another dot, and the same thing happened. He touched a third and fourth, same result. He stared and pondered while the two leaders traded suggestions.

Jake said, "Tyree, I think we should consider separating each dot and star..."

As he spoke, he touched one gold dot in the time traveler's sphere, and it did the same thing Jake's did; it changed to a bright gold star. It pulsated and changed position to outside the smaller sphere. Then GGM looked at one of Jake's new white dots. He touched one within a small sphere and dragged it into one of the new gold stars. That star popped to an even bigger size.

"Well I'll be damned," Jake reacted. "Confusing; we must move slowly with all this. What's happening, and what does it mean?

GGM turned to him and replied, "We do have a lot of work to do."

Tyree shook his head and addressed them all. *"We have no time to waste, my friends."*

Abby reacted, pushing another sensor on the desk and said, "Sir, I have an idea."

Everyone turned to her and listened as she refined the image. She zoomed in on one area, and suddenly tiny white lasers appeared and streaked within all the spheres connecting her vault information with a myriad of related text.

"Now, let's eliminate all these not connected," Abby said. "What's left?"

What was left were white dots, bright gold stars, and red dashes, all connecting one another, giving a definite pattern; but no indication of a point of origin.

"How do we make sense of this?" asked GGM. Then he remembered the pathways during his time in the Great Pyramid, or to be more accurate, the voids that couldn't be filled.

After a few minutes of silence, the image continued to upload more detailed information. "Christ! It's never-ending," said Jake.

They all saw that some dots continue to turn gold, while others did not.

Jake reacted, "Now they're changing without our touching them."

Bellos and Jake looked at each other. Terry, having said nothing for almost the entire meeting, finally offered, "That's got to mean something, right?"

GGM looked at it all and remarked, "I think it's all part of a puzzle, or more accurately, it's the Goyal the ancients thought of as the pathway to heaven. Now, we modern day physicists would link it to the pathway back to the big bang."

Abby turned around, facing one white writing board. She shook her head and said, "I'm not sure of that but consider this." She began to draw, "Okay, so here's Earth, and here's the location of all holes in the last three months. Here's the Moon and based on the signal intercepted from Brocks moon-station, here's where the airlift was at the time of the signal."

Tyree turned to GGM, interrupting Abby. *"It may be, my GGM. It would indicate that each person or each generation defines the pathway based on their own progress of understanding the Great Mystery. Yes, that seems correct, but usually, we would know those things immediately if we had sensor communication with the new Carriers. Our hive mind has its advantages. If we have to wait as you do, it may be too late to prevent a cataclysmic disaster from these new Carriers."*

"Whoa," said Bellos. "Why would they want a cataclysmic disaster? Let's get a good perspective on this first before assuming any cataclysm."

He tapped his Knofer and spoke into it. "Summarize and give me all pertinent comparative information regarding the Sidron event last year, the time traveler, Brock, Jake and me. Display ASAP."

Abby replied to both Tyree and GGM, "Haven't we been doing this for the past 18 months?"

"Not this," Bellos answered, "look, the display is updating."

The hologram added a mathematical grate and physics equations within all longitudes and latitudes which not only filled the image with other dashes. It also added bright green ones this time. Also, the display placed positive and negative charges by specific text and gold stars.

Everyone concentrated. "What is it exactly that we have here?" asked GGM. "It's more than Tyree's Carrier map. Knofer, please analyze and chart the degree of Compatibility of all members *described in this history* and today, as they appear strongest to weakest."

"Did I hear you correctly, all Compatibility members in history?" asked Tyree.

"Yes, my friend, the history log may be the missing link. Now we wait."

It took the Knofer roughly 5 minutes to begin showing the results. Information started flowing upward from the desk again. Some were text; some were images of DNA strands which settled below each of the names of the players.

"It's a freaken library," said Jake.

Tyree and GGM seemed to react as if something were familiar. As more details came forth from the desktop, Tyree touched the traveler's DNA section colored gold and dragged it to one of his blinking gold stars. He then touched his vault as though listening intently to a specific. He then touched the gold DNA under GGM and dragged it to another gold star across the room on the other side of the big sphere. *"There, I'm sure this is our connection, our common denominator."*

The GGM dragged the DNA strand of Jake to another gold star, then the three areas linked with a gold line attaching to one another.

Abby was the first to react. "That's what it meant when the findings wouldn't complete. Our information has been incomplete and who knows how long."

"GGM whispered to himself, "Well, we haven't paid attention to the Goyal historically." Then, he said to the group, "We haven't had Carrier Vaults to use?" Bellos' expression became one of wonder, and the Tyree noticed.

Abby continued. "When I was on the surface exploring the holes, I asked my Knofer to compare and report common elements or components. The answer I got was: GGM must clear all information. A security protocol was in place, which prevented me from viewing. Also, some information had to be cleared by Tyree Master only."

GGM squinted, looking pensively at Tyree. "My friend, it has all been divided between sentient beings and species which can carry a component of it. But no one can know until they all figure out how to read the message. If we can together contribute our part, we can fill in the message. Tyree, what is Abby missing? What are we all missing? Can you shed light on this?"

After listening to his vault again and studying and connecting many more DNA sections with dots and stars, the Tyree Master looked at everyone and spoke. *"GGM, as you know, there have been many treaties between our two species over the centuries. The Treaty of Variance has not been related to any incident or occurrence between us for well over 3000 years. Obviously, some of your detective's findings related to that treaty, and a failsafe security protocol was triggered."*

"Would you care to explain?" asked Jake.

Tyree continued. *"GGM, the treaty explains two aspects of our being. One is the variance of substance which our Carriers withdrew from humans when we had 2-way Compatibilities, and two, our history and origins. The treaty specifically reports an analysis of the commonalities between us and humans which enable us to share ourselves with you. And that allows us and you to benefit each other. Over time, that conduit or connection made the difference between life and death to your kind, which is why we stopped 2-way Compatibilities. If there wasn't enough of the conduit, the human died,"*

"Yes, that is a matter of record. But you never told us what that conduit was," said Bellos. "And now we need every bit of information to read all this."

"Yes, we did, to the GGM at that time, which was roughly 2320 years ago. Since then, by discontinuing 2-ways, there was no reason to broadcast anything or mention it until now. The compatibilities between your people and individual Carriers, over the past year, have made the subject matter pertinent again and now critically important to understand. All this, what is revealed to us now, makes me sure of it."

"So, we agree I have as much need to know as you do!" said Bellos.

All eyes were on Tyree, as he finally put clarity to what was before them. *"The treaty of variance must be revised now, given what has happened. Your sustenance, or what we withdraw from you, and from all life is not just food or what gives us the ability to reproduce and create things for you. It is the critical ingredient used in creating the Cosmos. For eons, we traveled the Sidron and directly created particles, matter, elements for gas clouds to use in galaxy formation."*

"Wait a minute tallboy," said Jake, "So what is this sustenance you're talking about. We are all confused enough."

Tyree walked to the middle of the hologram and pointed to the blinking stars. *"It's our primary conduit for gathering and distributing life. The simple answer is before you. It's GOLD. But not the color or mineral element. Those are tangible. I am referring to gold as it relates to the human genome and the Carriers. Look here. Your Knofer has used the Treaty of Variance and its information to identify, calculate, and measure certain people's degree of Compatibility. To be specific, how much of a certain gold derivative they have within them? Look, see here how you GGM, Jake Burns and Marion Brock are linked with a grand gold reserve of over 2,000,000 respules each."*

"What the hell is respules?" Jake interrupted. "I don't understand any of this. You're saying what? That we all have the same amount of gold in us? Isn't gold, well, just gold?

GGM was studying the connections and text continuing to appear within the spheres. "So, all these dots and the formulas appearing beside the text are simply an analysis detailing and comparing each of our Compatibilities?"

'I'm sure of it," Tyree answered. *"What the combined vaults show here proves it."*

Then Tyree turned to Jake. *"As to the explanation regarding gold itself, let me show you for better understanding."*

Tyree turned to GGM and asked, *"May we reduce this large sphere image, and please redirect the computer to display strands of the colored DNA from Jake, you, and our friend Gabe?"*

"How?"

Tyree walked to Abby and asked, *"May I?"*

Abby stepped away from the control panel. Tyree adjusted the vault and said, *"I am rearranging these sources and elements, so the vault information appears like this...This is our council's historical vault, not meant for public knowledge.*

As the data filled the sphere, Tyree studied the combined information. *"There, now let's compare say, Abby here with Marion Brock, and Gabe, the time traveler."*

GGM spoke into his Knofer *"Minimize hologram sequence. Locate and display the DNA strands for Gabriel Cooper and all related personnel in this room."*

Hologram DNA strands began to appear labeled one section at a time next to the other. The Tyree Master instructed, *"Computer, Compare Historical Data. Authorization Tyree: 110606 Genetic Gold Standard Comparison of DNA between Jake Burns, Marion Brock, GGM, Abby Johnson and Gabriel Cooper. Initiate."*

As the information synchronized, Tyree picked up a pointer pen to focus on the data. *"Now, look at each of these sections. See this section from the GGM, between the blue on the bottom and the orange above it. See how it's a bright gold-like and sparkling? That's from your record indicators. Now over here, see the gold rating? For Marion Brock, it's well over 2,000,000 respules, right? While if you look at Abby's and Terry's over here, each of them is roughly 1000 to 1470 respules. Enough to travel in time but not enough sustenance to make a significant impact on a Carrier.*

"By the way, you two, please don't be concerned. Your readings represent the average gold rating of most humans.

"GGM, with your permission, I will now input the sealed information from our treaty of variance and our Carrier priority history files."

"Certainly," said Bellos.

Tyree pushed several sequences of sensors on the desktop and then pushed enter. *"Now look at this."*

At least 75 names and their DNA sections appeared. GGM began studying immediately. "There are only two GGMs listed here, and the rest are colony citizens."

"Yes," Tyree replied. *"Now look at their gold ratings."*

"They're all over 110,000 respules each."

"Exactly. Every one of these people had a 2-way Compatibility with our Carriers. But the rating also wasn't high enough to keep them alive."

"So, what does that mean?"

"Are you all sure you are ready to hear my answer?

GGM replied, "Yes, proceed."

"Although we are a hive mind, Tyree Masters have information in vaults of such a critical nature that if it were leaked, chaos might result. That is why we have certain treaties banning this kind of information from the Carriers, and, therefore, obviously from you also; and especially from the general population. And consider this. Grand Carriers could extract it from humans during transport. That having been said, I offer this..."

Tyree pushed more sensors on the computer, and different images displayed apart from the integrated hollo-sphere. *"Patience, please, I'm getting more information from this vault...*

...Eons ago, certainly many trillions of years by your records, we came from and traveled within the Sidron. Our purpose was to seek genetic gold, redistribute it, and populate life. Life in all its forms, not just as you define organic life. Our records show we traveled throughout and between universes. Eventually, we happened to find Earth. Gold sustenance had always been the core reason for some of us to stay here. Gold's attraction caused us to roam many directions within the Sidron and also to different times."

GGM interrupted, "So gold is the sustenance you draw from humans?"

"Not exactly. Gold as you know it is more of a derivative of what I'm talking about. We supply life's properties and draw from life experiences the assets we need, which are by-products of any life experience. We call it GG-gold, and it is the conduit formed during any life's experience which allows us to receive the sustenance, which in turn feeds us. Humans process more GG-gold than any other animal, vegetable, or mineral. Sustenance enriches our ability to create anything. Of course, for Grand Carriers it also reinforces the ability to time travel. And it's critical to control dark matter and

dark energy as well as our reproduction. So, we need the conduit which determines the amount of sustenance we absorb. For a human to time travel, he or she has to have enough GG-gold in his or her DNA to be quivered in the first place. Without enough GG-gold, one can't travel in time. Your ancient alchemists had no idea what the real value of gold was. Regardless, I'm way ahead of myself.

"There were too many of us to count throughout the cosmos, all with a single purpose of finding, harvesting, and securing GG-gold for various functions throughout the known universes. Carriers leave in their wakes GG-derivatives of gold, which are needed as a vital component in galaxy and matter constructions."

Abby asked, "So was gold harvesting an assignment given to you by someone or something? If so, who gave you the job?"

Tyree smiled. *"My dear, when you're hungry, you eat. And so, it was with us. Without the right level of GG-gold, we became hunter-gatherers. In our existence, the answer to that question would be, we refer to it as The Great Mystery, which to us exists throughout the entire Sidron. We have found most sentient beings have a name for it. Here on Earth, your many languages have come to define it as the word God."*

Jake was quick to banter, "So, the Elephant in the room is God himself."

Tyree replied, *"The human mind is still in its infancy from the Sidron's perspective. Your words/languages try to define abstract concepts into something your feeble minds can't begin to comprehend. It's quite silly."*

"Alright," GGM said, "Back to it. Tyree, you say your kind was, for all practical purposes, highly capable and could fly through space-time anywhere within the Sidron, correct?"

"Yes, GG-gold in the Sidron draws, as well as allows us to feed.

"So, GG-gold has always been the common property constant in all universes?"

"Correct, but not just common. There are many common elements. GG-gold in its variety of derivatives is crucial to forming the cosmos." Tyree said. *"As we initiated Inflations and seeds of life, there were countless of us moving and searching throughout the Sidron. Some of us found Earth long before humankind had evolved. We discovered that this planet has a vast supply of GG-gold, which when processed by us, it multiplies exponentially. It's in*

the oceans, on land; it was in all animal, vegetable, fungus, and mineral life.

"Your planet is a way station like no other, for food, fuel, reproduction, and progress. The fact that there was so much GG increased and pushed the boundaries of our Carrier capabilities. At first, the challenge for us was how specifically to harvest it? It was our job to secure the planet, preserve and protect all life forms, and to determine how to absorb sustenance. We set up shop inside the planet, to ensure we didn't interfere with any surface life's evolution. We were unaware of the consequences that would occur in dwelling beneath Earth's surface, or that it would change our physical form and devolve our abilities. We made propagation of our species a priority. We used certain animals and drew GG-gold and sustenance from them. The more GG we absorbed, the bigger the conduit, the more sustenance we could harvest, and we could reproduce at a great rate, leaving our offspring to line cave walls and, well you know most of the rest. As we began to prosper, our council agreed to share with humans on Earth's surface through 2-way Compatibilities. We educated you on how to find and extract mineral-gold from water, how to mine it from the land, and we were very successful. We stock-piled the mineral and converted it to GG. So much so that man evolved rapidly intellectually. After we ventured further below the surface, humans followed, and together we built Ever-Life. Your human DNA strands evolved too, learning how to store GG-gold as we needed; or so we thought., which passed on to future generations. At that point, we began working in synergy, and we have prospered together ever since."

GGM listened and remarked, "So that's where the Compatibilities came from."

Tyree bowed and continued. *"Yes, however, what we did not realize was that while humanity was advancing genetically, and in almost every aspect of his life; we Carriers, conversely, began to degrade and devolve in certain characteristics. And our focus became relative to this planet only."*

Jake chimed in, "So that's why you became victims of sunlight."

"Yes, we became more dependent on 2-way Compatibilities with humans and the need to withdraw any degree of sustenance from you."

Bellos interrupted saying, "And that brings us to, who are the different breed of Carrier? And where did they come from?"

Tyree replied, *"Yes, my first concern is that we cannot communicate with them."*

GGM looked again at the spheres. "So, all of the records here regarding our Compatibility ratings mean what? That you extract GG-gold and make it a pipeline to transmit sustenance to you and then you can give us anything we desire while we are inside you? Perhaps these new Carriers are related to you, my friend. Perhaps Earth is so far away from the original point you started eons ago that it has taken these Carriers this long to find you."

"The GG-gold rating or Compatibility means that we can share our thoughts, conscious or unconscious, with you and, depending on your level of GG, you can also be quivered and ride through space-time within us, time travel. We have to determine this new breed's intentions and objectives. We must figure out how to interface and communicate with them. We have no revelation yet of their purpose."

Abby had been watching the output of the computer regarding GG-gold and the Compatibility ratings of all the people listed. "Sir look at this. The system has analyzed and compared the latest inputs from you, Brock, and Jake since he is a lost relative of Brock. You all have quite a large Compatibility rating. But look here, the DNA- GG readout of our time traveler, Gabe. Oh, my!"

Everyone looked, and Tyree reacted first. *"His Compatibility is four times the amount of all of you combined. My GGM, it is imperative that our priority now is to protect Gabe and analyze his entire genome given these new findings."*

"Well, we have been doing that for a year and haven't found anything suspicious, except now the potency of his Compatibility has increased substantially." GGM turned to Abby. "I agree, we need him here, for perhaps some different tests. Abby, I leave it to you to make that happen. Don't alarm him but do convince him we require further testing in a secure environment here. Then get all updated information, and you and Terry review everything. I want to meet again with all of you and him to determine our next step. And, I will review our treaties regarding everything Tyree here has discussed today. Perhaps I can find something else. Some updates are needed,

given the changes and circumstances we've encountered over the last year."

Tyree responded, *"GGM, we have followed our security protocols described in the Treaty of Variance to the letter. I will return to the hive, and we will continue to try and make sense of the new breed. Several of our Grand Carriers have been in proximity to them but, as I said, there has been no communication so far. Their travel speed has also evolved, and it is impossible to follow them."* Tyree walked back to the gurneys. *"But there is a bright side."*

"Well, we like bright sides," Jake quipped.

Bellos pointed, "You mean those two bodies on the gurneys?"

Tyree stood over Brock and said, *"We have a specimen here of Compatibility, GG-gold analysis, and cellular recovery."*

"Yes, right," the GGM said. "Terry, I want you to analyze our guests here and test them for everything related to the sphere displays. There has to be something."

"Mathew," Jake added, "I need not remind you that Brock could tell us more if his bodily functions were working,"

Abby couldn't believe her ears. "Are you talking about reanimating that monster?"

"Calm down," Jake said. "Believe me, I've seen many more of him. Yes, if we gave him CPT, he would be more of a threat than ever, considering the process leaves one healthier than before. But what if we gave him only Transtosis? We could control his functions. What do you think, Mathew?"

Bellos thought and replied, "Terry, let's go with Transtosis. We can control his memories and conscious state using it. Please supervise the process and alert me when his body has normal readings, but let me be clear, in no way are you to wake him. Alright people, any other questions? Good."

Bellos turned to walk out and then did a doubletake. "There's one other thing. We need to include all the players to get the most accuracy. That means we also need Jack and Rachel. But I hate to drag her through anything else. And it all left Jack a bit shaky. Unfortunately, we have no other choice. See to it."

"I'll talk to them," said Jake.

"Take Miriam, Jake, I also have unfinished business with Mrs. Sheldon," Tyree said. *"Perhaps we can bring that to a conclusion as well."*

"Alright people," GGM said, "Let's get the search in place and see what we find.

Jake ends Presentation to Jack and Rachel.
They respond:

"Christ, Jake," Jack said, "No wonder we are drinking. Brock is back, apparently in full glory. What's the plan?"

Rachel sat silent for several minutes thinking.

Jake said, "I need to resolve the issue of where our Mr. Brock is exactly, and how he is affecting us or the timeline; and most importantly, how can we stop whatever it is he's planning?"

Then Jack noticed his wife looking off into the distance as if in a trance. "Rachel, honey, what is it? You're too silent for my good. What are you thinking?"

Rachel blinked and nodded no. "I'm thinking a lot of things. This makes me see my own situation and how, unless I face it, I'm never going to have peace. Look, Jack; we have been involved with all this because you made a deal with Brock. Why was he so mad at you for not giving him the last pages back then? He and his men led us all to believe it was because he didn't have the last information needed for his particle displacement time-chamber. But what if it was something else? What if his anger was a distraction, a diversion? What if all this is due to something completely different than CPT or those last papers?"

Jack looked disturbed and replied, "It didn't matter to me why he wanted them, babe. Your life was on the line."

"Exactly, Jack, and he relied on your emotion, knowing you'd have tunnel vision and focus on me."

"Well, he was right. You're more important than any thesis or medical achievement."

Don't you see, honey," Rachel said, "you and everyone were focused on me, and your CPT and particle displacement. Jake, you were hell bent for leather to arrest and prosecute Marshall. Everyone including Swanson was led away from what Brock was really doing. It's so clear to me, and I can't tell you why. But I'm sure I'm on the right track."

Jake and Jack looked at each other, and Jake said, "So, Mrs. Sheldon, what are you proposing."

"Well," Rachel paced, "I'm not sure really; it's more of a feeling, but it's more than that too. It's a certainty, but I can't reason it for you."

Before anyone could comment, a cloud appeared before them, and Tyree Master walked out of it. Rachel reacted with surprise, "My God, it's you. Why are you here?"

Tyree replied, *"Please forgive my interruption. I too believe you are on the correct path, Mrs. Sheldon. And there's only one way to find out for sure."*

"What's that?" Jake asked.

Tyree said, *"Why a time-trip. A trip to examine what Brock was doing over the last two years. We can search and monitor; and, when we find the right moment, we have our answer and return to formulate our move."* Tyree looked at all three, who were dumbfounded at what they heard.

Rachel reacted, "Right! It's so simple and full proof. I'm in."

"Wait a minute, honey," Jack said. "You've been through too much to be part of this. I won't allow it. Not only that but what are we looking for specifically? We go on a trip over the last 2-years to find out what?"

"Listen Mr. Know Everything. I know I am a part of this somehow. I need answers too, to my own nightmare." She looked at Tyree and asked, "Is it okay if I go?"

"Well," he said, *"I detect enough sustenance in you to travel to the time dates, but you may not leave the Carrier, agreed?"*

"Sustenance? What the hell is that?" Rachel asked. "And how do we monitor Brock's actions?"

"With this, remember?" Tyree pulled a peanut-shaped object out of his coat and gave it to Rachel. *We will calibrate it to detect Brock and monitor his doings from inside Jake's Carrier, Miriam. Mr. Sheldon will know what Brock's doing technically if anything rears its head regarding CPT or Particle Displacement. They were partners, and I'm sure he can read Brock's body language or innuendos."*

Jake replied to Rachel, "Let's go! I think Tyree can explain any other questions to you two on the way." Then, Jake looked at Tyree and continued. "Actually, it's rather a great idea. I should use you to solve crimes."

"Good," Tyree said. *"That's it then. We can leave anytime you're ready."*

Jack reacted, "You mean we're going right this minute? I have to get ready, prepare."

"Oh Jack," Rachel said, "what do you need except your brains and my encouragement?" She turned to Tyree and said, "We are ready."

"Alright," said Jake, "we are off then. Lead the way, my friend."

Jake, Rachel, and Jack began their time travel ride to find Brock.

Back in Andrew's living room, Jake completed all Vault presentations to Gabe & Andrew

"Well, Jake said, 'That brings us all up to date."

"Excuse me," I said to all of them. I couldn't help myself. "I know I'm new here, but when you go on these time-trips, do you ever have to go to the bathroom?"

Jake looked at Gabe and me, but it was Abby of all people who answered, "Well I never thought of it. I can't say I have, on a time trip. It probably has something to do with Quivering."

Well, I am in my own time, my own home; would you excuse me a minute, Mother Nature calls. Can you pause this?"

"As I said, we are done. Go ahead; we'll wait," Jake said.

"Funny," Abby said, "is that what you say in this timeline when you have to use the bathroom?"

I responded, "Sometimes, at least I do."

Gabe appeared somewhat pensive and nervous. "Not to change the subject, but, Jake, is there a genuine threat? I am surprised to hear Brock is back, and I get that he developed his own CPT and is using it to construct slaves. But, why take Allenfar back, until he completes his mission with me? Maybe he and I will correct all this by finishing what we started."

"Gabe, I presented all this in a low-key manner, but it's a huge deal if Brock has a derivative of Jack's CPT. Especially if he ran around the Sidron doing God knows what. It's critical we find out details and what it all means to Ever-Life. Let's just prioritize this:

"First, we at Ever-Life agree that there is something very threatening about Brock. I think more than anyone knows. We have to find out what that is. At every turn we've encountered him, he has always escaped. I saw his cloning factory. There were hundreds of clones of himself. And that was just one factory. Remember Gordon Swanson thought he'd taken care of Brock, but he appeared again. Also, I suspect Brock's got more than one cloning facility, and we have to find out where they are and what he's doing. And the most frightening question to me is what if he started cloning in the past?"

"Second, we all agree Semitri killed himself, but he's still alive in the past if he took Brock to various points in time. We need to find his signature, and maybe that will direct us to locations. But Semitri will be very strong given he has Brock to feed on. We have no idea what he and Brock have arranged, and it's critical we find out now that Brock has returned. Also, we know Brock went to 33AD and met a GGM Post Commander; we know Brock went to 1965, 1989, and 2004. We need to travel to those dates and eliminate Brock from the timelines, which we hope will eliminate any threat. Remember, Semitri was a Grand Carrier and could have taken Brock or his clones anywhere before he died. What if Brock and Semitri visited other times and left their mark or clones to try and change history? And if they did, why don't we know about it?"

Andrew came back into the living room and remarked, "It sounds to me as though you need a fresh face on this whole effort."

"What?" Gabe asked.

"No, no, he's right," Jake said. "Think about it. Gabe here has a Sidron signature that Brock can detect. That's one reason we've been so careful to keep Gabe in seclusion. If we take Andrew on our little search party, our signature will be much less to detect."

Andrew perked up. "Are you suggesting I go on this trip with you instead of Gabe? He's made plans with Allenfar, not me."

"True," Jake said, "But that's the point. You are Gabe, just a younger form."

"Pardon me," Gabe said, "actually I'm younger than Andrew."

Andrew chuckled and then said, "Well, if all this is possible, I would love the opportunity to see my dad again."

Gabe took a deep breath. "I don't know about this."

Jake fiddled with his Knofer and gave it to Gabe. "Here, for your eyes only; this may change your mind. Look what happens to you in the near future, on this timeline."

Gabe took the Knofer and quickly saw something he didn't expect. "Are you sure about this, Jake? I'm not supposed to go?"

"That's what it says," Jake smirked.

"It's very confusing. I understand, I think." Gabe said, "But Allenfar and I have to finish what we started."

"And you will, through Andrew," Jake said. "Now let's get back to the threats and let me finish.

"Third, and last but not least, these new Carriers intentions are unknown to us and may be a threat. We really don't know. The Carrier council wants to test and examine Allenfar.

"Gabe, you and Allenfar have been inseparable, in a secluded state, for weeks now. And you left on a time-trip to do what? The Carrier Council want Allenfar for the same reason they wanted Semitri; to share what he knows with their hive mind. They're afraid something they can't control is happening. He hasn't shared anything for weeks. Do you know why?"

"Yes, I think so," Gabe continued. "He is concentrating all his energy on focusing where the Sidron event originated. That was our original goal, and that hasn't changed. Between the two of us, we have a plan to understand the Sidron event. It's within our grasp."

"Hmm, convoluted is the word that comes to my mind," Jake replied.

"Look Jake. I didn't ask to be pulled across time to Ever-Life. I didn't ask to be under lock and key, claustrophobic for a year. I've committed no crimes, but my restrictions make me feel like I have. And yes, I'm here for more than one reason. But that doesn't mean my intentions conflict with my prime directive. Allenfar and I intend on defining and fixing this Sidron situation, however it turns out."

"I understand your feelings son, I really do," Jake said. "The issues here are quite a bag of confusion. But if you stayed here, you could put off those pent-up feelings, and since Andrew is you, he may be able to give us a fresh look, given he hasn't traveled through the Sidron. And you know there are other reasons in play now."

I listened to the discussion and offered, "Why not just talk to Allenfar. Gabe can get him here. He's got to be close."

"Agree, Gabe?" Jake asked.

"Not really, but fine." Gabe tapped his Knofer and requested Allenfar's Tyree to join him."

Within several minutes, Tyree Allenfar appeared in the kitchen. *"Hello, my friend. I have been in deep focus regarding this entire matter. I trust you will respect that I am not done yet."*

Jake said, "Tyree, I am security chief for all the Ever-Life colonies, and I respect all Carriers' capabilities. But, in this case. I need more information than I've received so far that would convince me not to return you to Ever-Life."

Allenfar said, *"Mr. Burns. I have had contact with the new Carriers, but I also have a duty to GGM to follow the path of Gabe's Compatibility. That means I must attend to our primary goal, and only then return to Ever-Life. I must not taint that focus."*

"My, my, "Jake said. He looked at Gabe with uncertainty. "Well, I am going to suggest that Andrew comes with us, and Gabe; you must remain here until hearing from me, okay?"

Andrew smiled, and Gabe nodded his head alright. "But Tyree, you will come back for me, right?"

Allenfar smiled and said, *"If you need me, my dear friend, I will come. Now we must plan quickly."* Tyree looked directly at Andrew and said, *"Andrew, I welcome you. Your presence is unmarked by the Sidron, and that will benefit us in completing our task."*

Jake said, "I ask that you take Abby with you. She can interface; and I need you, Tyree, to also link with Miriam. We must all work together so we can not only monitor your new travel companion here but also be prepared if you find Brock in a different timeline."

"Agreed," said Allenfar.

Everyone's eyes were on Jake. He inhaled and stared at each of us. Then he asked Gabe and Allenfar, "Perhaps you two need to explain your plan."

Allenfar said, *"Of course, I have determined the original Sidron event, which brought Gabriel through time from 2004, was actually triggered by several conditions. The one major inflation occurred on Andrew's timeline, dated March 7, 1983. We must travel there to engage with his father, measure his Compatibility and if it proves to be the cause, we will eliminate any reaction to him by returning him to Ever-Life for medical treatment."*

Jake thought and reacted. "Hold on! The way I understand how time travel works, you are talking about creating a paradox, are you not? If you changed something in 1983, it would have a ripple effect and..."

Allenfar interrupted, *"Not exactly. Before any changes can affect a future, I have to quiver the timeline. Without that, there is no link because of the differences in atomic density. This is a consideration only specific Carriers can do. I have acquired this ability through connecting with the new breed of Carrier. Because I am connected with them, I can link the timelines in this case, but I do not know for how long or to what extent. I am in what you call new territory as well. But we must try. If successful, the effect would be that Andrew will not transport from 1965 or 1989 in the first place. 1965 and*

1989 had no real impact anyway because the two men disintegrated upon arriving in 2999; hence all will be as it should. I am not sure what the link affect will be on Mr. Brock. That remains to be seen.

"I believe it was Andrew's father who was the primary trigger of the entire Sidron reaction. If that is true, and we can stop the reaction that took place within Andrew's family Compatibilities, we most assuredly will correct the time-shock and prevent the triggered event from happening in the first place."

Jake paced the room, while everyone waited in silence. "Alright," Jake said. "We'll postpone Allenfar's return to Ever-Life. We are on a time trip anyway. We can all return to Ever-Life when we are finished. Andrew and Allenfar will go back to 1983. But you have to do more than just visit 1983. Also, I want you to trace Brock's actions with Semitri and send Miriam and me their signature time dates. We can then use Carrier protocols to negate those dates and therefore Brock's involvement. After all, if he's a time traveler, his experience is not part of the original. Try to find out how many different places they visited, map where any clones are, and we have to keep our Knofers linked. We all have got to make sure to eliminate any Brock clones."

"Understood," Abby said, "but how do we do that exactly?"

"You have to erase Brock's time trips completely. Allenfar and Miriam can do that. If it all works and we keep in touch with each other, we should return Andrew here and return ourselves to Ever-Life having stopped the Sidron Inflation and Brock's conniving plans."

Andrew scratched his head and said, "Well, as long as I can write the book, that's all that matters, and I'll be sure to put this in it."

Jack and Rachel were becoming anxious having waited inside the Carrier, Miriam. As soon as Jake returned to Miriam, they all began their trip to find the Brock clones.

CHAPTER 70: BRICK-A-BROCK

HAMILL STEVENS rode a Carrier from Post-2 across inner Earth to Seattle, Washington. It took him some 20 minutes to reach the street level of mid-town Seattle. Once there, he sat on a bench and just watched people for a few minutes. "I do miss it," Stevens whispered to himself. Then he made his way to OPAS and the upstairs offices of Oscar Randall. As he walked into reception, he was greeted by two secretaries who remembered him. One noticed him right away and walked over.

"Mr. Stevens, is that you? It's me, Bonnie. It's so good to see you."

"Thank you. I have an appointment to see Mr. Randall."

The girl behind the desk, Krys, smiled too, and said, "He's upstairs refreshing himself for the board meeting."

Bonnie added, "Yes, with Mr. Brock..."

"Bonnie, please," Krys blurted out, "don't you have somewhere to be?"

Stevens interrupted, "Please, its fine, Krys. It's okay Bonnie, no harm."

"I'll notify Mr. Randall you are here," Krys said. "You may as well go up. I believe he's in conference room 2, the board meeting room."

"Thanks, ladies." Stevens took the executive elevator and stepped out on the 5th floor. *It's almost as impressive as Ever-Life,* he thought.

He hadn't stepped 6-ft when he heard a voice behind him. "Stevens, Stevens, it is you? I was just coming down to get you." The clone of Oscar Randall extended his hand in friendship. "How are you? You have to tell me about this new secret job of yours."

Stevens smiled back and said, "I would, but I'd have to..."

"...To kill me? Hah! Well you haven't lost your sense of humor." Randall puffed on his 8-inch cigar. "Fine, fine, we can get to that later."

Stevens said, "You said it was urgent we meet and talk. I am on a full schedule these days, so...."

"Oh, that's alright. Don't apologize. I understand. Come in here; we can talk."

"Quite an impressive new edition," Stevens commented.

"Yes. That's right; you never saw it completed."

The doors to the glass conference room automatically opened from the middle and slid apart to each side. Stevens couldn't take his eyes off them. "But where do they go. There's not enough wall to hold the entire door."

"Magic my boy. You remember we do things quite differently here." Randall took a small flash-drive out of his pocket and pushed it. The entire room's glass walls went opaque, a striking aqua color. "Come in and sit. Let me take your briefcase."

"Oh, I'm fine; I'd like to keep it."

Randall bit down on his cigar, grabbed the case, and put it in the closet. "Nonsense, it'll be right here. Besides, no one is taking notes or recording us. Please sit down."

"Oscar, forgive me, but you seem a little different somehow."

Randall thought a second. "Why no. I feel fine."

"I mean, more anxious somehow."

"Well, truth be told, this whole thing has me spinning a bit. You know?"

"Actually, I don't; you haven't told me anything."

They both sat facing each other.

"You remember your discovery," Randall said, "the bridge-particle?"

"Of course, how could I not. Its usage caused Brock's death in the Time-Travel Inc Lab. Which reminds me, the girls downstairs said Brock was with you up here. What did they mean?"

"Hmm, well, I will explain as we go. Let's not get ahead of ourselves. I'm sorry to tell you, our findings, after actual experimentation regarding the practical use of your bridge-equations, indicate the bridge-function ceases to exist when stressed, even at ambient temperatures. In other words, the chamber last July disintegrated because there was no reaction at all. The particles of those two in the chamber just stopped and ceased to be. It had nothing to do with their having clothes on. It seems Halford and his team discovered and proved the whole thing." Randall took another puff on his cigar and then put it in the ashtray on the table.

"Why that's impossible," Stevens said. "I checked and rechecked everything..."

"Well, I have no doubt you did, but look at this." Randall put a bound book of experiments and findings in front of Stevens.

"Who made this?"

"The authors include David Halsford, Aron Beau, Larry Lawrence and Barb Hershinoe, the best minds we have, except you that is. They examined, ran tests, and proofed the outcome. We think there may be something additional that only you know. That's why I called you. We are talking in the strictest of confidence. I need to put this right, Hamill. Our reputation depends on that. We have orders for the Time Travel line of chambers from all over the world. In another month we will start being delinquent."

Stevens shook his head. "I had no idea. I don't know what to say."

"I understand. Given the urgency and secrecy of this situation, I am asking if you can read the document, and perhaps there's something inside you that it will trigger; something we don't know."

"Oh," Stevens replied, "I'd have to clear that with my boss. It will take a few days to read and absorb all this."

"That's fine. We can call him right from here."

"No, no; it's better if I make the call in private."

"Well, I'll leave you to it then. There's nowhere any more private than here."

"I suppose that would be fine."

"Good, thank you, Hamill."

Randall got up and left the room. He walked to the next smaller attached room, within which he and Marion Brock would watch and listen to Stevens through a one-way see-through wall.

Stevens sat at the table, took out his Knofer, and tapped it. "Get me Jake Burns."

After just 15 seconds the Knofer clicked. Stevens touched it, and a 3-D hologram of Burns displayed on the table.

"Hello, Stevens, what's up? If I'm right, this is your first call."

"Yes, thank you, sir. I have learned that my time here is needed for longer than I expected. I wanted to let you know."

"How long?"

"My guess is three days."

"Let me see? I can give you 24 hours and then you're needed in Techlab-3 for Transtosis processing."

Meanwhile, in the next room, Brock commented to Randall, "You know Oscar, I put all my faith in that man. It's time I put things right too."

"What do you mean?" asked Randall.

Brock patted and squeezed Randall's shoulder and said, "Stay here my friend and watch this." He gestured to the two henchmen behind him to follow. "Boys, bring Mr. Stevens in from conference room 6."

Stevens was ending his call with Jake, but before he cut the call, Brock walked in with a smile and looked at the hologram acknowledging Jake.

"Hello, my old friend. I would give your boy here a little time before expecting him back." Brock took the Knofer, cut off the communication, put it in his pocket, and spoke to Stevens. "I wouldn't rely on those people too much, my boy. And this little gadget is outdated. You will be fine; better than you could imagine as a matter of fact."

Stevens got up nervously and backed up moving to the door. But just then, in walked a clone of Stevens with Brock's henchmen. "Hamill, my friend, it won't hurt. It's just like looking in a mirror."

Stevens was stunned and couldn't move as he stared at his clone. Brock clapped his hands and with a silent giggle he spoke. "Quite remarkable really; isn't he. Say something to him. Go on. He won't bite."

Stevens thought, trying to calm a bit. Then, he and his clone both said, "I don't know what to say..." at the same time. And they both made the same face.

Brock smiled at Stevens. "You see, he is you, in every way. Come on Stevens; you were part of my cloning effort."

"Yes, but that was you, your choice."

"Not hardly. I was only the beginning." With those words, he walked to one of his men who handed him his gun and silencer. Brock turned and screwed the silencer on, looking straight at Hamill. "You know what you did to my brother in that booth?"

Stevens begged, "But that was your clone, not you. What are you?"

Brock grinned, as the two men put a plastic tarp behind Stevens. Stevens turned and watched the men lay the tarp, and then as he turned back to see Brock. Stevens heard 2-clicks and felt two bullets enter his chest. He blacked out and was dead before he hit the tarp. Brock handed the gun back to one of the men, and then he picked up the book off the table and handed it to Steven's clone. "You're going to need this. Read and study it. Then we will talk, and after that, you'll have to return to your boss. We then will proceed with the plan. You're very important. We'll make you the new Chief of Staff if it all works out."

CHAPTER 71: REVIVE

THREE DAYS AFTER THE MEETING IN TECH-LAB-3, Specialist 1st Class Terry Raymond had moved and prepared the bodies of Marion Brock and Charlie Rossi to a procedure room below the Giza Post-2. He had to wait 72 hours to set up the new Transtosis and grow the correct Nanites to assure they wouldn't revive Brock's body. Terry was preparing the Nanites for the process when the room door opened and in walked Hamill Steven's clone.

Terry watched and said, "Hello Stevens, I thought we'd lost you, where have you been?"

"Oh, I had a meeting at OPAS in Seattle. Nothing earth-shattering. Who do we have here?"

Terry pulled the sheet away revealing their head and torso. "This my friend is the infamous Marion Brock."

"My God," Stevens said. "It is Marion. But how? I thought he died in the Seattle explosion.

"I have no clue," Terry said. "All I know is we have to perform Transtosis on him without reviving." Terry filled the syringe and moved to the body.

Stevens was quick to interrupt. "Here, T, I'll take that. Let me do it."

Terry knew Stevens outranked him and offered the syringe. Stevens had his own agenda and already had mixed a vial of Brock's CPT. He switched syringes and administered the CPT instead of the Transtosis.

"Okay, my friend; that should do it," Stevens said. "Now we wait."

As they did so, a full body hologram appeared over Brock's body, and they could see the CPT taking effect.

"Wait a minute," Terry said in anger. "Those aren't Nanites in his blood."

Stevens smiled, as Terry figured it out. "That's CPT. But something different. What the hell did you give him?"

"I gave him what he needs."

As Stevens and Terry watched, Brock began to move and animate, blinking his eyes.

"Holy crap, Hamill, you're defying a direct order not to wake up him up, given by GGM. I'm reporting this."

"Just calm down and let's finish this," Stevens said.

"Not on your life. I know this is wrong. I'll be damned before I disobey a direct order from GGM."

Stevens pulled a cyanide pill out of his pocket, grabbed Terry from behind his neck and with a quick stroke, he forced Terry's mouth open and shoved the pill between his teeth. Stevens pressed Terry's teeth together, and the tablet broke and spread into his mouth. No sooner did Stevens finish, when GGM Bellos walked into the lab and saw Terry spin holding his throat. Within 10-seconds Terry fell to the floor, dead. Stevens smiled at his handy work and then turned to Bellos. Bellos saw that Brock was awake, and before he could sit up completely, Bellos pointed his Knofer and killed Hamill Stevens.

Brock watched and said, "Hello my old friend. May I have a pair of pants, or perhaps a robe?" He smiled, and Bellos reacted with shock. "What is all this?"

"I am at a disadvantage, my GGM. Allow me something to wear, and I will explain. Yes, I think it's time we discuss a few things."

Bellos was cautious and angry. "Here, put these scrubs on and start talking before I use this again."

Brock dressed and sat back down on the edge of the bed. "Ah, where to start? Hmm. I suppose a thank you is in order first, for saving me and reviving me."

Bellos cringed. "You're back, and another member of my crew is dead."

Well, Hamill was a good employee. I must say, though, his death is on you, my friend, for not allowing him to finish the good job he started at OPAS."

"What the hell are you talking about?"

Brock took a deep breath and said, "I suppose I should start from the beginning. I was going to give up my plan when I saw your people outside the Juda Villa in Jerusalem; remember? Never mind, not important. What is important is that, after I saw all those graves and thought about Jack and how he screwed me, I had to redirect things a bit. Now that everything's in order, I don't mind sharing." Brock just grinned.

Bellos stared and said, "Like always, you make no sense."

"Sense? I make perfect sense, ha! You just don't get it. You and your predecessor, Gordon Swanson, never understood. You thought I was trying to get Jack's papers to finish what I wanted to do relative to CPT. Ha, you idiots. By the way, do you have my personal belongings?"

"Why?" Bellos asked.

"Because the answer is in my personal effects."

Bellos searched the closet and Brock's suit. He pulled a bag out of Brock's coat pocket and in it was one of Brock's VADs. "Yes," Brock said, "That's it. Please be careful with that as you aren't familiar with how it works?"

Bellos walked back to the bed and asked, "So how does it work?" Bellos pointed his Knofer at Brock's head. "Tell me now, or I swear I'll blow your head off."

Brock smiled and said, "Well, that wouldn't do you any good. I wouldn't die." And then he just laughed indignantly.

"Bellos shook his head and took a different tact. He put the Knofer in his pocket, got a chair, and sat in it next to Brock. "Alright, Marion, Let's cut the crap. You obviously want to tell me something, so, go ahead. I am all ears."

Brock made a serious but unthreatening face. He stood up, and without fear or any indication he was under threat, began to tell his story.

"When Jack and I made a contract to share CPT, I thought this is the answer to everything I wanted. You know, Gordon was always afraid I was plotting against him and the Complex. Regardless, Jack's unwillingness to share his secrets turned me in a new direction. Clones; but you already know that. I found a new way to make clones, which your Jake Burns discovered during his visit to Time Travel Inc. That was quite an unfortunate event, the whole exploding Carrier thing. But it was also a test of my plan." Brock smiled again and looked at Bellos. "Let me guess, you don't have a clue what I am talking about, do you?"

Bellos replied, "You're talking about your plan to be immortal and take over Ever-Life."

"Partly correct. But I realized making clones wouldn't get me the control I needed to pull it off. Especially since I had to deposit myself at various time dates to ensure I would create the subtle changes I needed, paradoxes to you."

"What?"

Brock chuckled again. "That's why your David Marshall was so important. He arranged to get me samples of your little toys, Knofers, like yours there. Oh, relax my GGM, I have no intention of hurting you or trying to escape. This is part of my plan as well. You can't do a single thing to stop it either, ha!"

"So, tell me more then."

"Certainly. Marshall supplied the samples; and I had them examined and duplicated with one difference. I added a characteristic feature which would change everything."

"And what was that?"

"Look at mine there and compare it with yours."

Bellos took Brocks VAD and laid it next to his Knofer. "They look remarkably similar." Then he noticed a small slot on the side of the VAD.

"Yep," Brock said, "that's it, right there."

"And what exactly am I looking at?"

"Well, I developed a little sim-card, sort of. When you slide it into the slot, the VAD enables me to control all the clones. It enables me to shift into and out of any clone so that I can be anywhere, including any time." Then Brock smiled. Bellos sat back and digested what Brock just told him.

"So, if I shoot you, kill you, what happens?"

"I have a failsafe built into each clone, and I would simply turn off in the clone you killed, and reappear in another clone, where I would use the VAD protocol in that clone and transfer to where I wanted at that time. I have become the first collective intelligent human on this planet."

Bellos looked petrified for a moment, as he put it all together in his mind. "So, when you died in the airlift, actually you just transferred to another clone back on earth?'

"Yes, or perhaps I transferred into a clone that Semitri and I deposited in a past timeline."

"Well, no wonder we had so many questions about the clones?"

"Yes, my GGM, and there's not a single thing you can do, ha!"

Bellos paced and then looked at Brock. "I think you may have forgotten one minor detail."

"I doubt it. What?"

Bellos emptied the contents of Brock's personal effects on the bed. "It's not here. The fact that you have no sim-card or whatever that is and the fact that I have no intention of killing you gives me time to think and come up with my own plan."

"Oh, I am confident any plan you come up with will be flawed and ineffective. But I'm quite excited to see what it is. After all, I have all the time in the world and the patience of Job."

Bellos threw Brocks suit on the bed. "Here; get dressed. We are going on a little trip, you and I; just the two of us."

As Brock dressed, Bellos secured his Grand Carrier, Marcus. Then, he contacted one of the lab's specialist to supply the tracking roadmap of the Carriers Allenfar and Miriam.

Brock stood ready and unafraid of anything Bellos had in mind. Bellos pushed his Knofer and they both transported into the Carrier Marcus. Brock arrived in a lounge chair with restraints on his ankles and wrists. Marcus quivered both of them and moved quickly into the Sidron and onto Andrew's timeline to search for Miriam and Allenfar.

CHAPTER 72: CATS IN THE CRADLE

ALLENFAR ARRIVED AT TIME TRAVEL MARKER MARCH 7, 1983, at 2:45 am, Eastern Standard Time. Abby and Andrew transported from Allenfar and appeared in hospital room 210 at Brooksville Hospital in Brooksville Florida. The small single bedroom was maybe 11-ft by 9-ft. The two of them stood at the end of the bed looking at Andrew's dad, who was hooked up to primitive IVs and a tube coming out of his right chest area. Andrew remembered everything about his dad, knowing that their relationship had deteriorated over the years; and, regrettably neither one tried to bridge the gap. "You know Abby, to have a second chance here like this...to see him, help cure him, and renew my relationship with him; it's just wonderful."

She patted Andrew's shoulder. "Well, for you, yes, it's quite a miracle, but for your family, nothing will change. They will think he died."

Andrew went to the side of the bed and whispered, "Dad, it's me, Bud. Wake up."

Abby and Andrew watched as he opened his eyes, surprised at seeing his son.

"Bud?" What are you doing here?"

"I came to see you, and hopefully fix you. You've had a very nasty time lately. How do you feel right now?"

"Like a freight train hit me. Why do you look older than I remember?" Andrew Sr. tried to raise and move his right arm. His way of checking his health. "Mr. Andrew," Abby said, "Try not to do that. It will aggravate your condition."

Dad looked at her and remarked, "Who are you, young lady?"

He looked at me, as I said, "Dad, this is Abby Johnson. One of your great nieces is named Abbey."

"You're a niece?"

"No, Mr. A. sorry, just a similar name," Abby reacted with a sober face and whispered, "Andrew, you shouldn't say anything about the future..."

"Why not? He is going with us?"

Dad said with a weak expression, "What are you talking about?"

"We are all going on a little trip to make you better. And then I have a lot to tell you."

"Trip?" He asked. "I just saw you and your siblings this afternoon? Trip? Thanks, sonny, but I couldn't go to the bathroom by myself if I wanted to. I'm hooked up to all these tubes. We can go another time."

Andrew and Abby heard talking outside the room. Abby carefully opened the door and saw a figure at the nurse's station asking questions. After a few seconds, she recognized the voice and demeanor and recoiled with fear. It was Marion Brock. "He must be here to use your father and your family's Compatibility ratings. Allenfar was right. But how?" She shut the door and turned to Andrew. "Quickly, we have to go,"

"Wait," Andrew said, as he too approached the door. "It has to be Brock's clone, right? We can do something, right?"

"No, he doesn't know we're here; at least I hope he doesn't. Christ, you never know with him. We must get your father and you out of here now. This has to be a key time for Brock to react to both of your Compatibility ratings. If Semitri is here too, that means there's an immeasurable amount of sustenance Brock can use. This has got to be it. Allenfar and Gabe were right. This has to be the trigger for the original event."

"But, how do we know Brock isn't using several time-dates. This could be one of many?"

Abby was definitely in a hurry then; and, as she rushed to take out the IVs from Andrew's dad, she said, "Well, if Allenfar is correct, we hope if this is the date and time that triggered the Sidron event, removing you both should stop any reaction at any different time spot. Hurry, hand me the bag behind you."

Abby reached into the bag and took out two metal rings which were attached to a small linked chain. Andrew watched as she gently placed both rings around his dad's ankles. "These will enable Allenfar to start the quiver process and safely transport your dad onto a bed waiting inside Allenfar."

Andrew held his father's wrist and smiled at him encouragingly. "Now just relax, dad. This will only take a minute, and you'll be better. Close your eyes if you want. Just try not to get excited and try not to move."

"I don't understand what's happening, for Christ's sake?"

"Everything will be fine dad, trust me and please try to be quiet."

Abby tapped a combination of keys on her Knofer opening the transport protocol and said, "We are ready, Allenfar." And within ten seconds all three of them were inside Allenfar.

"I can't believe we can do this," Andrew said. "What about this 1983 timeline. Will anything change?"

"No, nothing will change. Your father's *non-quivered* body will remain in 1983. His moracian body with us will undergo the rest of Allenfar's processing, and that, in itself, will repair him and make him feel better. Then, after the quivering is complete, when we arrive at Ever-Life, he will undergo tests and CPT. Look here."

Abby was studying Allenfar's organic computer. "Well, that confirms it. With you and your father's Compatibility rating, if Brock used it along with the others, our GGM, you and your dad in this timeline, Jake, and Gabe, something big would happen. And I'm sure that's what Brock knew. That had to be his clone. And remember, we don't know how many clones he had in Semitri."

"What do Quivering and Moracian mean?" asked Andrew.

"Moracian refers to the fact that your dad's body is made up of an incomplete number of matter-atoms. If he awoke in our future without being quivered, he would look transparent. His body has only a percentage of matter in sync with the 1983 timeline. If one is healthy, Moracian capabilities mean that one"s complete material body can be changed to a percentage of non-substance, nonmaterial state, as well as one can be restored to its full material self by reversing the process; in this case, Quivering. When we time travel, that's why we have to drink the wine.

"Not sure I understand?"

"You have to go through Quivering as well. Be patient. What we are doing is quite normal for time travel."

Unbeknownst to the passengers or Allenfar at that moment; one of the massive new breed of Carrier, much quicker and three times his size, approached from above Allenfar vibrating at an undetectable frequency. After it successfully matched his speed and direction, the new Carrier split its belly open from its head to tentacles and slowly engulfed the complete Carrier, Allenfar. It slid down over the Carrier as Andrew's dad slept. Suddenly, both Abby and Andrew felt a tremendous jarring and almost fell to the floor. Tyree Allenfar appeared and said, *"We have a breach in my outer skin. I am afraid something is happening I don't understand. It is another Carrier. One of the new breed. I must initiate critical protocol #...and then* Tyree's image began to flutter."

"What the hell was that?" Andrew asked as he turned around trying to focus on Tyree and the room changes.

Allenfar faded and was replaced by a new Superior Tyree Master. He appeared much taller, brighter, and with a slightly different shape. He looked at us, raised his hand, gesturing, and said, *"Fear not. All is as it should be. I have become as I was and as I should be."*

Then, in the blink of an eye, at one end of the room, the furniture, floor, ceiling, everything changed to an almost pink pearl-like color. At the other end of the new room, there was a laboratory-bed with a viewing screen and computer display that wrapped around up from the perimeter of the mattress. All intravenous hook-ups were gone; replaced with a compressed air-controlled technology system.

The other end of the room was designed in a very eclectic way. Something of a combination of decors, which looked almost turn of the 19th-century taste; yet with modern conveniences of year 3000.

"Please," Tyree said, *"Look around and make yourselves comfortable. Your friend is not dead or gone, just better. We have to meet your colleagues and reconcile the matters before you."*

Abby and Andrew looked at each other confused, and Abby asked, "What colleagues?

"Why your other two Carriers, Miriam and Marcus."

"Marcus?" Abby said. "That means GGM is aboard."

"I heard that name in Jake's presentation, but who is that?"

"I'll explain later." Then she asked Superior Tyree, "How will you bring them here?"

"My dear, we have ways. Please familiarize yourselves and learn what you can about this new place."

Both of them began walking around the room, feeling and studying all that appeared. Abby examined Andrew's dad in the new bed at the far end of the room.

"He looks fine," Abby said. "I'll have to take some time to familiarize myself with all this but..."

"Of course," Superior said. *"I will help you. Put this into your ear."*

"It looks like a hearing aid of some sort," Abby said.

"That is correct, but you will hear me, and everything about the bed will imprint in your mind as your headset vaults do."

Abby did as instructed, and then she began operating the display around Andrew's dad.

Andrew Jr. asked Superior, "Why are you here and what happened to Allenfar?"

"I am here to help reconcile the matter of the original Sidron event and bring our devolving species to its rightful capacity. Allenfar is not gone. He is simply a part of me now. He is the strongest and most detectable of your Carriers. He has the most capable capacity. He has been restored first to his rightful self. Together, we are much more capable than alone."

"Abby asked, "What do we call you?"

"I am Azai. All will be clear to you once we find the other Carriers, Miriam, and Marcus. We have come at the request of our SB-1 to correct and bring the timeline back into balance."

"Balance, what do you mean?" Andrew asked. "And who is SB-1."

"After we have the others, I will take you to have it all explained and then return you to your time."

Azai then disappeared, and Abby continued to study her patient's bed while Andrew examined the rest of the room. He noticed the hallway to the bath area looked different now. The door bath area was a bright glowing maroon but yet seemed familiar to his old front door in Bartlett. As Andrew opened it, he thought of his condo and his kids. He was stunned at what he saw in the room. It wasn't the bath at all; instead, he stepped into what he remembered: his living room at the condo. There, in front of him, he saw all of his kids and grandchildren just relaxing and watching television. He blinked and tried to say hello, but it all was just a solid hologram. A duplicate of his thoughts at that moment. He could walk around and through the images. Although mesmerized at seeing his family again, sadness came over him. "I have to get out of here," he said to himself.

He left and shut the door behind him. "Holy crap! I better stick to the big room."

When he returned, he noticed by his watch that two minutes had passed. Abby had finished her study of the bed and said, "Where have you been? Your dad is doing fine. Actually, much better than fine."

"I was looking for the bath area and ran into something else. But I couldn't have been gone for more than a few minutes."

'Well, we have to accept that time is very different here in the Sidron. Actually, you were gone an hour. Stay where I can see you, will ya?"

Just then, they felt another jarring vibration, and the room got even bigger. They both held onto the couch, which seemed well anchored. As the room shook, Jake Burns, and Jack and Rachel Sheldon appeared.

The vibration stopped, and Jake said, "What the hell just happened?"

Abby offered a consoling word, "Jake. Apparently, there's a new breed of Carrier that can absorb those we use now. And Marcus is next."

"Marcus? That means the GGM is here somewhere."

"Yep," She said, "And who is he bringing?"

"How is our patient?"

"*Fine.* The Tyree master, Azai, upgraded the bed and its features. Come see."

"Azai?" Jake asked. "Where's Allenfar?"

"Not to worry, Jake," Abby said. "All is good here. I'll explain later."

"Oh, Christ! What's next? I have a headache."

"Jack and Rachel were nervous and upset. "This is all too wild and Syfy for me," Rachel said.

"I'm sure it's alright, babe. Try and keep your thoughts separated from your feelings. We are still among friends," Jack said.

As Jake and Abby fiddled with Andrew Sr.'s bed display, a third jarring vibration occurred. When it was over, GGM Mathew Bellos appeared, and Marion Brock materialized in restraints. Before any real conversation happened, from out of the hallway where Andrew had explored, came three Tyree masters. Each looked identical, yet all were faceless.

One said, "*We are Allenfar, Miriam, and Marcus. We are one now, and you may refer to us as Tyree Azai-Allenfar. Your Carriers are now as they should be.*"

As Brock snickered, GGM asked the Tyrees, "Why are you here, and what happens next?"

"*My GGM,*" the tall one said, "*we are not here to change or stop the relationship you have with Carriers. We are here to correct Carriers and bring all into the maximum correlation.*"

Jake said, "What does that mean? I have been using Miriam for over a year now. All of us in the Ever-Life colonies use Carriers for almost everything including time travel."

The three holograms seemed to look at each other, and then they melded into one Tyree. "*We identify with you on your level of understanding. That is why you see different images and call us different names. But, as you know, we are first and foremost a hive mindset, and we are together. The strongest Tyree, with more GG-Gold and sustenance and therefore the one who has more information about the Sidron than any other Carrier is Allenfar. Marcus, Miriam, Andrew, GGM, and Jake; frankly all of you and more have boosted his Compatibility limits. You may refer to me now as Azai-Allenfar. I am he and a product of all."*

Brock listened, and with his false smile he interrupted, "You are all wrong and haven't got a clue about what has taken place or what is in place."

GGM replied with a furrowed brow, "Really, Marion, why don't you fill us in?"

"Untie me, Mr. GGM. Why are you afraid? Where am I going to go? Don't you feel safe with your crew and this supersized hologram to protect you? I have no intention of hurting any of you. What could I do? You must think I am pretty all-powerful. Untie me!"

Jake said, "I see no threat, Mathew."

GGM looked at Azai-Allenfar whose face was without expression. *"I am certain all will go as it should, my GGM. He may enlighten us in some regard."*

'Fine," Mathew said. "Release him."

Mathew nodded to Azai-Allenfar, and he released Marion's restraints. Brock rubbed his wrists and stood up. Rachel instinctively recoiled and grabbed Jack's arm. "He's a monster! Keep him away from me!"

Brock looked at everyone and then concentrated on Jack and Rachel. Nodding his head and smirking he said, "You were the cause and the effect of my plan. Both of you."

"What the hell do you mean?" Jack said.

"If you had just kept to your bargain and contractual commitment, it would probably never evolve to this, but you, Jack, had to screw things up. Regardless, it is what it is now, and nothing any of you can do will stop it."

"You're insane," GGM said.

"Oh, no I am not, my GGM, ha!"

Brock walked over to Rachel. "I would have never considered you as my informant if Jack had done his job, and never would have had to hire that Canadian company to run you down, Jack. But we needed to confirm the CPT, my CPT that is. And everything worked like a charm."

"What?! You son-of-a-bitch?" said Jack sternly.

GGM interrupted, "Let him finish, Jack. We need the voids filled."

"Thank you, Mr. Bellos," Brock bowed and continued. "Now take our little lady here. You were so anxious to rescue her in Rio. Remember Jack? Little did you know what really took place?"

Rachel got red-faced and blurted, "What took place you Ass!?"

Jack held her tight.

"Ha!" Brock shouted. "What took place was this."

Brock reached into his pocket and took out two more VADs-Brock Knofers like he gave GGM in the Morgue lab back in Ever-Life. GGM reacted, "What are you going to do with those, Marion. They won't work in the Sidron."

Brock smiled and said, "They work from outside the Sidron to the Sidron, and they will work fine in here. The environment is stable and neither Jack nor Rachel is quivered. It says so right here on my display." Brock showed the VAD to the group.

"So, what are you going to do with that?" asked the GGM again. "The Carriers negated the power source when you died in the airlift."

"That's true, but the function for transmitting consciousness was never an issue. The power source of the electronics was affected, yes, but not what I use to control the clones or transport myself to another body. That's my secret and will remain so. Otherwise, I would be in jeopardy, but I am not."

"What does any of that have to do with Rachel?" Jack asked.

Brock was the perfect villain. "It has everything to do with her. You see in my effort to formulate my own CPT; I discovered a control over the clones. I had already grown a clone of her before you came to Rio, and that's who you took, thinking it was your wife. I made several errors with Angie, Mathew, but I was able to correct them all, hence, my perfect Rachel here."

"What!" Rachel lunged toward Brock, but Jack again held her tight. "That's bullshit you piss ant!" Rachel was more upset than Jack had seen her in years.

"Hold on darling. He has no power over you."

Brock just laughed and said, "Watch this, my friends."

He pushed the VAD and Rachel fell limp in Jack's arms. He laid her down and checked her pulse. "Rachel, Honey! Christ Marion! What have you done?"

GGM moved to the two, and Jack said, "She has no pulse, Mathew. She's dead. I'm going to kill you, Marion!"

Jack made a move toward Brock when Tyree Azai-Allenfar interrupted and raised his palm to Brock. *"Here is the first of many corrections, my friends."*

With those words, a lightning bolt shot from Tyree's hand exploding Brock's chest. Brock dropped to the floor and disintegrated. Jack panicked, falling to Rachel's side and said, "Oh my God, Rachel. Not again! No!

Tyree Azai-Allenfar said respectfully *"We must be patient, and all will be as it should. GGM, you, Jake and Andrew should follow me, now."*

"To where?" Mathew asked.

"Around the corner, here, look."

They stared at a 3D display. *"This is a single anomaly,"* Azai-Allenfar said. *"It's a loop in a timeline. "This, below, is a broad representation of our master timeline.*

As you can see the many bright dots represent different dates." Azai-Allenfar pushed one, and it enlarged. *"Here's a closer look. The globes here, there and there, represent Brock clones as you would call them. Your duplicates have a much more refined DNA signature than any of these. All these points are where clones are on the timeline. This one is at 33A.D., this one is at 1965, and here's one at 2999.6. And so on, and so on."*

GGM asked, "Are those the clone's location?"

"That is correct. We had to either input this information into your Carriers, which we tried but it didn't take, or update the Carriers to enable them to find this."

"Jake nodded, "so you updated their programming?"

"Sort of, but they were devolving so much, even sustenance couldn't repair their lost abilities. That's why Semitri was so susceptible to control by Brock."

"GGM asked, "So what do we do now?"

"All should be corrected once we eliminate the imbalance. Mr. Brock here was the first of many to come."

The Tyree reached out and touched each bright dot, and each one went out, disappearing from the timeline.

"Christ! That's all it takes?" Jake said.

"Yes, my friend. That's all. Come, I will take you to the great one now."

"Great one?" Jack said. "Wait, is the 'great one' going to bring back my wife?"

"That depends on what is real?"

"Oh, for God's sake. Can't we just give her CPT, Mathew?"

"I am afraid not, Jack. If she's a clone, she must be tested for compatibility. She may not be susceptible to CPT, remember? She couldn't be revived the last time."

Jack looked perplexed for a moment. "But the Tyree gave me a blue vial and said it would work. My God, that's probably why the miracle took place last year."

"That is correct, Jack Sheldon. Unfortunately, we did not know that she was a clone. That formula would not have worked. I am sorry. All is not lost. We are here."

As they all pondered, Azai-Allenfar made his Carrier skin transparent so the group could see the Sidron. The colors were bright and contrasted with a blackness that looked more purple than black. As we looked into the void, a group of what looked like stars seemed to come together and shape an eye. They were all mesmerized by what was unfolding. The grouping of stars continued to define itself, and an eye formed. It had to be thousands, if not millions of light years from one end to the other.

"What is that?" Jake asked.

"Be patient my friend," Mathew said, studying the image. "This is something new."

Everyone focused as it became even more defined. The eye seemed to get smaller, and an enormous circle appeared across the cosmos with a giant hand reaching into it and pulling the rest of itself from perhaps a different location of the universe. Things happened fast after that. A body formed and what looked like a colossal hologram defined itself outside the Carrier. Tyree Azai-Allenfar bowed respectfully, as did all, after seeing Tyree take a knee.

"Thank you my SB-1 for allowing this audience," Tyree said.

The group raised their heads just in time to watch a ball of light build up in the SB-1 hands and zap into the cabin. SB-1 was then in two places at the same time; outside the Carrier and a smaller version inside the beast standing behind the group. They all turned with their hands over their eyes. Then both SB-1s reduced the light's intensity, and the group inside the Carrier could see the one standing before them.

"Greeting, my Dear Carrier." SB-1 in the Carrier said. ***"Are these of whom you speak?"***

"Yes, my SB-1."

Jake couldn't stand it. "SB-1, SB-2, what the hell does SB stand for anyway; and why are they here?"

"Be quiet, Jake," GGM whispered. "Or I'll revoke your speaking privileges."

Tyree replied, *"SB-1 means Sidron Being. They are our initiators. We are their messengers. We map and plan the Carrier trips, and we deliver life's compounds throughout the cosmos."*

"Ah," Jake said, "So, they're God?"

"Jake, I am not kidding!" Said Bellos.

"No, Tyree said. *"They and their kind measure the universe and set up the plan for our travels. They monitor, manage, and correct any misguided correlations, considering the basic periodic and principle nature within their boundaries."*

"So, what about God? Jack asked."

Tyree was going to answer, but the SB-1 raised its hand indicating not to.

"You all seem to be doing well as a species, and hopefully this convolution in which you have involved yourselves will pass, and you can continue to grow. However, you tend to demand answers to questions that are not questions."

Bellos looked puzzled. "Are you saying we have nothing to fear regarding the Sidron events that brought a man through time to our future?"

Your Sidron event was not of our doing or yours. It is one of many anomalies that take place throughout universes as they grow. You have growing pains, do you not?"

"So, what about God?" Jack asked again. "Is my wife dead or somewhere we don't understand?"

More knowledge than you can understand is of no value to you. Keep inquisitive and allow revelation to come to you as your mind can comprehend; for those of you who receive that which you seek, they should be content and reconciled to what they ask. We all refer to it with respect, as the Great Mystery. You and we are the miracle, which proves that the Great Mystery exists. Would you say that when there is a cake, there was no baker? Be sensitive to your imagination; it tells you possibilities. A piece of The Great Mystery is within all of life. If you accept that, you have a partner, who will give you perspective, as your second eye does. All you have to do to see correctly is acknowledge that second sight is in

your mind. You have great potential and must eventually understand you are not alone. Dwelling within you is your partner, a piece of the divine spirit of the Great Mystery. Acknowledge it, and together, you both can do almost anything you imagine. Capability and questions are answered through the process of learning, revelation and commitment, commitment and revelation."

"My wife was always committed and believed in an afterlife. How do I reconcile that?" Jack asked.

Mr. Sheldon, you asked for help almost a year ago, and we gave it to you. What Brock took away; he did so, thinking there were no consequences. There are always consequences, good or bad. He just ignored them. He was of great interest to us. He and his kind are the sandpaper abrasions against the fingers of your mind. He makes you sensitive to think and do good and right. But he is not in charge. And when evil becomes overbearing, we all must stand against it. And that includes my kind. We have been charged to keep the balance enabling all life to progress and strive for the best that can be

"What the heck are you saying?" Jack said in a raised voice. "That you could save all those who have died over the millennia? What kind of Great Mystery, or God is that?"

"We do not speak for God as you say. We have divine spirit in us just as you do. We neither preach nor claim to be religious based creatures. Instead, we are abstract realists. We are all related to each other, brothers in the progress of life. There are many things you don't understand yet. And perhaps some never will. Accept that that doesn't mean any of you are <u>owed</u> an explanation regarding anything that happens during your lifetimes. Evolution is a building block allowing everyone and everything to participate in the hierarchy of the Cosmos. You have evolved to a point where you have been given the understanding of time travel. And you know us now too. That's a miracle in itself. If you think about how far you've come, imagine the other wonders you have to discover. The most significant discovery is to understand what is within you. That's where the Kingdom of the Great Mystery lies; another miracle many of your kind overlook. You have the wherewithal to understand and

work with your divine spirit. And that is enough to give you answers to many questions you seek. Look inward, not outward. Unless of course, you have the understanding to create your own universe. Think about that.

Suddenly, Jack heard moaning sounds from the floor. It was Rachel opening her eyes. Everyone looked as Jack leaned down and helped her up. He could barely control himself kissing her and holding her tightly.

"What happened," Rachel asked. "Where am I?

"What's the last thing you remember honey?"

"I remember everything, I think. I'm a bit foggy. Let me settle and think."

Jack had tears in his eyes and said, "It's okay, babe; we have all the time in the world."

The group turned to see that the SB-1 in the cabin was fading. "Wait!" Bellos said. "We have so much to share..."

It was gone, and Bellos looked out the side wall at the SB-1 in the Sidron. "Please don't go. We need to know; we need to..."

As the massive SB-1 faded, it sent a message to all of them which they heard in their minds. *"Be well, my friends; and know we are always with you. My Carrier will return you to your home. You have begun a wonderful understanding so far of the most important discovery, LOVE. Keep trying and searching. Be kind and patient. All will come to you."*

The group stared, and then they suddenly cringed, raising their hands to cover their eyes as a bright light exploded filling the entire visible area of the Sidron. When the group opened their eyes, the wall of the Carrier was opaque again. Brock's body was gone, and Rachel was alright. Azai-Allenfar appeared before them and said, *"Thank you for your attention. It is time we return. We are going home."* And then, he faded and disappeared.

Jack held Rachel as Bellos asked, "Are you two okay?"

"We think so, Matt." Jack said, "Let it all sink in, and then we can talk."

From the other side of the room, Andrew shouted, "Hey, Abby, come see this. My dad's readings are normal, and there are no marks on his arms or chest."

The group rushed to the bedside and read the vital signs. "He's resting with all normal readings. Jesus!" Jake said.

"Well," Bellos added as he pushed several spots on the monitor, "I guess it is time to go home. And we have new travelers who join us."

Jake thought a second and asked. "What about Gabe?"

GGM looked at all of them and Andrew, and said, "He's fine. We know where he is. He is reconciling some things, and where he is, is the only place to do that."

"It'll be interesting to see what exactly does happen to Gabe and Andrew," Jake said and smiled.

Bellos suggested, "Yes that's true. But don't forget Jake; we should check the vault records to see if SB-1 did, in fact, eliminate the Brock clones."

"I will. I can't believe I'm related to that scum."

"Yeah," Rachel said, "Shows you how little some historical genealogy can mean. And who knows what the future holds?"

GGM snickered and winked at Rachel. "I'll drink to that. How about some wine for all of us?"

Bellos filled glasses and handed them out, and they all raised a toast. "To the future?" Bellos said."

"Yeah," Jake said, "And to keeping that son-of-a-bitch Brock at bay."

"Here, here!" They all repeated as they drank.

CHAPTER 73: OCTOBER 12, YEAR 3000, THREE-FATHERS MEET AT JUDAH VILLA

DURING THE LAST YEAR, BETWEEN SWANSON'S death and Gabe's escape, the three fathers met once a month at the Jerusalem Villa, in honor of their friend 'S'. After their time travel trip, the three clerics returned to their respective diocese, each reporting on their own findings. At first, the elders refused to listen, and much turmoil spread within the faiths. It took the Jewish, Catholic, and Islamic hierarchies over eight months of study, questions, and debate before they agreed to accept the story of the three fathers. Now, as the priests sat sipping their morning coffee, they chatted about the irony of it all and how their goal of uniting all the faiths seemed truly possible.

"It seems so unfair," Kristos said as he looked down at old Jerusalem.

"What do you mean?" Ahmir asked.

"My initial meeting with Mr. Brock; and the conversation we had seems to have gone full circle. I know we are only at the first step, but honestly, if it wasn't for him, I'm not sure any of this would have happened."

James interrupted. "Oh please. I disagree, my friend. It was Dr. Bellos we should thank. If it wasn't for him, we would have never met the Master."

"Well, they both helped. But my point is that we agreed to give Mr. Brock all that money for this." Kristos reached into his pocket and pulled out a small blue vial of CPT. He twisted it through his fingers. "We didn't get it from Brock. And we didn't give him billions of dollars. And all of our churches were very happy about that. They kept their money, and we've got the prize right here. Win, win, right?"

As they spoke and ate, around 11:30 am, they noticed a dark extended limousine drive up and stop in the front of the villa next to 'M', who was gardening. The driver got out, they shook hands, and he handed 'M' a large envelope.

"Ahmir said, "Looks like a special delivery."

'M' walked over to their table and smiled. "Father Kristos, I have mail for you, for all of you apparently."

Kristos took the envelope and read it. "It says special delivery alright."

'M' remarked, "The driver handed it to me and specifically said to bring it to you right away, that it was imperative. I confess the man looked familiar, but I couldn't place him. He had a look on his face that made me truly uncomfortable, but I agreed to give this to you."

Kristos nodded as 'M' walked away.

"Hmm, very mysterious and exciting." James quipped.

"Open it; open it!" said Ahmir.

"I am, I am. I'm opening." Kristos took out a packet of 8x10 pages stapled together and read the short note attached.

"THANK YOU FOR YOUR SUCCESS. WELL DONE! MY PLAN NOW BEGINS. ALL WILL COME TO PASS. THE LITTLE TRIP YOU MADE LAST YEAR DID THE TRICK AND WAS JUST ENOUGH TO CLOUD THEIR THINKING. IF THERE'S ANYTHING I CAN DO, JUST CONTACT ME."

"What is this?" Kristos asked. He looked inside the envelope again and took out a taped bundle of bubble wrap. He studied it and ripped the package open. "Oh my, my friends; look. It appears to be another blue vial?"

"Ahmir pointed to the paper attached to the bundle. "What does that say?"

"It's an invoice. It says, one sample vial, Chemical Personality Transfer. It's CPT, from the Brock World-Wide Enterprises. But there's no amount owed or billed to us. And look at this! A cashier's check for $14 billion dollars! Oh, for heaven's sake. Very confusing."

James said, "God works in mysterious ways. I guess we have our proof that a man can rise from the dead, right? And a little petty cash."

The other two fathers gave James a stern look of disdain, and Kristos commented, "These little vials shall keep us ready when we have to prove a man can, in fact, rise from the dead."

"But we have to know the process of administering the vials." We'll have to see the doctor again" said James.

Kristos replied quickly. "Perhaps we must see Mr. Brock first." Then they all relaxed, smiled at each other, and Kristos continued. "For today, we celebrate 'to a new beginning my brothers.'"

They all repeated it and drank their coffee.

Back in front of the villa, the mail driver, a clone of Marion Brock watched and smiled. Then, he drove away saying, "Well boys, we can use friends in your circles."

CHAPTER 74: OCTOBER 12, THE YEAR 2998, NEW YORK PUBLIC LIBRARY,

IT WAS SUNNY THAT MORNING in New York City, with just a wisp of clouds in the sky and a slight breeze blowing gently. A man with a book entered the Main Branch Building of the New York public library and approached the reception desk. He looked at the return desk's librarian and handed her a book. She smiled and took it, "Thank you, Mr. Brock. It's nice to see you. You're on time as usual. Interesting title, Allenfar, an Ever-Life story. I'll have to read this one. I love science fiction."

The clone of Brock smiled, turned, and walked back out the front entrance. As he did so, he reached into his pocket, pulled out his little VAD, and said, "Now let's see; where should I go next?"

CHAPTER 75: OCTOBER 12, THE YEAR 1982, ANDREW'S HOME IN NORTHERN ILLINOIS

IN 1982, LAKE IN THE HILLS WAS A COMMUNITY of homes built around a beautiful lake, north of Chicago, in McHenry County. Andrew had moved into a beautiful 4-bedroom lakeside house, having been transferred in his job back to Illinois from Ohio. At 1:30 pm, on the afternoon of October 12; Andrew was oil-painting in his den and watching the ducks outside the sliding doors gather in his backyard, when the front doorbell rang. When he opened it, a man in a dark blue tailored suit stood smiling and holding a large envelope. He smiled at Andrew and said, "Good morning, I have a special delivery for a Gabriel...? Oops, I mean Andrew Sharkididy. Sorry, it has been a strange morning?"

Andrew chuckled and said, "Close enough on the last name. I'm Andrew. Rarely does anyone pronounce it correctly."

"The man nodded respectfully and replied, "Then this is for you. Just sign here please."

Andrew did. And the man quickly turned and walked toward the curb where his car was parked. Andrew closed the door and stood, opening the envelope. In it was a photograph of a Carrier, and it was signed, Allenfar, with an inscription. ***You're never alone.***

Andrew was totally confused and tried to remember anything that would enlighten him about the picture. "Allenfar? What the heck is this thing? Strange looking fish."

He looked at the return address. There was none; just two rows of exes [XXXXXX...]. So, he quickly opened the door again to ask the driver for any details. But the clone of Marion Brock was already in his car starting the engine. Brock turned to see Andrew standing on his porch. With a smile, Brock said to himself, "Ha! So, you're the author who wrote that book. And you don't even know it yet."

Then he shifted the car into **drive** and sped off saying. "If only they knew what this date signified. And so, it begins..."

CHAPTER 76: OCTOBER 12, THE YEAR, 2020, GABE & KAYE'S HOME IN FLORIDA

AFTER SEVERAL MONTHS of waiting for Allenfar and his Ever-Life friends to return, Gabe wasted no time adjusting to life in 2012. It wasn't long before he met Kaye, who was to change his life forever. They became inseparable; and, in 2016, the two moved to southwest Florida. Time passed and they adjusted to life in their dream home.

One morning, Gabe sat sipping his coffee and studying Kaye while she concentrated on her computer across the room. At that moment, it struck him that, regardless of Allenfar's absence, he was meant to be with Kaye. Most probably, none of his Ever-Life colleagues would ever come back for him, and that was fine. He felt comforted, knowing somehow that his counterpart, Andrew, and his dad, and his friend, Jake, were all safe and healthy; and he pondered with a smile what they were doing on their new adventure at Ever-Life.

Gabe was able to complete his manuscript with Andrew's help transmitting back to him from the future. Gabe did keep a diary for a while; however, in time, he didn't feel the need to anymore. He was at peace. *Just when you don't expect it, the miracle happens.* He had so many thoughts; so many thank-yous to give. Everyone was alright, and life was good. He was able to 'let it all be, let go and put his past into perspective.'

Kay looked up from her computer and noticed Gabe seemed to stare into space, so she asked, "Are you okay, hon?"

"Yes, I'm fine. Just thinking about the kids and Jake, of all people." Then he got up with his coffee and walked toward her as she asked, "Oh? why Jake?"

"He was the one who started the whole thing when I was in college, back in 1965."

"What do you mean?"

"I remember him showing up one night, out of nowhere, in my dorm room and waking me. I thought there was a fire drill."

"What made you think of that?"

"I have no farking idea. I guess I'll always have memories of the whole thing."

"That's understandable, considering all you've been through, babe."

"After writing the book, I realize how much I hope my kids understand some day. Is that selfish?

"I don't think so. It's pretty normal to hope that; but I don't think they'll understand unless they talk to you."

"I doubt that will happen...Do you think we are like Jack and Rachel?"

Kaye reacted with a smile. "Jack and Rachel? Well, I suppose. That's why they're in the book. They are us, right? I'll tell you one thing. I sure wish I had some of her medical degrees. I would be rolling in the dough about now."

"You may be right about that."

Kaye smiled and then looked at the beautiful crystal statue of Allenfar on the coffee table. "I fell in love with your Carriers, especially Allenfar; and I love that statue of him."

"Where did you find it anyway?" Gabe asked.

"Me? I thought you ordered it?"

"Nope."

They looked at each other with curious grins and Kaye remarked, "Maybe it's a gift from him, so he's always here."

"Whoa! Cryptic and mysterious." Gabe picked up the statue. "I'd love to show you Ever-Life."

"You have. I read the book, silly. Besides, anything's possible. Maybe someday."

Gabe smiled and replied, "Yep, maybe; I hope. I'm sure Brock will never go away. Evil is always present, rearing its ugly head when you least expect it."

Gabe put the statue back on the table and kissed Kaye lightly. "Regardless, there's nowhere else that I'd rather be than right here with you."

Then, the front doorbell rang, and Kaye looked outside through the front bay window. "Looks like a delivery, but the man is wearing a suit and carrying a small package."

Gabe walked to the door gesturing to Kaye. "I'll get it. Finish what you're doing. It can't be that important."

...But it was very important. It was the beginning of a plan, Marion Brock's plan....

<u>END VAULT 0378</u>

SIR THOMAS WHEELER finished his notes, took off Andrew's Headset and asked, "Are you alright? How do you feel?"

"Yes, I think so. How long was I under this time?"

"About an hour. There was a lot of information; and it transferred slower than the other headsets, probably because you are different than Gabe. I'll run the reaction comparisons and contact you in a day or two. What did you think?"

"It cleared up a lot of questions I had, but it did leave me with many more. I'm a little fuzzy about how it ended. One thing I've learned from headsets; there are always questions. They never end."

"Well," Wheeler said, "this is Ever-Life. EV-ER-LIFE." And then he laughed and caught himself as if embarrassed that Andrew didn't laugh at his joke. He cleared his throat and asked, "Have any plans for the holidays?"

"Yes actually, I'm taking my dad on a tour of all the colonies. It'll be great fun to see how the colonies celebrate Christmas in this age. He's doing well and wants to learn as much as he can about this place. We are working together on family history; but, he's a new man; that's for sure.

"What about you, Andrew; are you okay with all that's happened, are you a new man? I mean Gabe took your place, and you are still able to communicate with him?"

Andrew thought a few seconds and replied, "Yes, as far as I can reason, I'll be a new man for quite some time. I do miss my kids, though; but I am really there too. My life has split into two journeys."

"Well, I recommend you schedule your tour after we review your reactions. And, don't forget, GGM wants to meet with your dad again, when he's ready. Don't forget; you're all related. This session should be your last with me for a long time. However, feel free to call me anytime."

"Yes, our family has grown..."

"Till next time then, my friend."

Wheeler stood, shook Andrew's hand, and they walked to the door.

"Don't be a stranger," Wheeler said.

As Andrew reached for the doorknob, the door opened. It was Azai-Allenfar's Tyree master. Wheeler and Tyree locked eyes on each other and smiled. Andrew saw the connection and remarked, "Okay guys, what's going on?"

Tyree replied, "One last trip for you, my friend. We have unfinished business."

Tyree put his hand on Andrew's shoulder and guided him out. Andrew chuckled and asked, "So when are you going to tell me where we are going?"

Tyree replied, "In time. We have much to do."

THE END

Lightning Source UK Ltd.
Milton Keynes UK
UKHW040849200220
359044UK00001B/27